CRUSADE'S END

'Warmaster,' came a voice from the centre of the yurt.

The word was spoken softly, and the audience let out a collective gasp at such a flagrant breach of etiquette.

Karkasy saw the Warmaster's expression turn thunderous, understanding that he was obviously unused to being interrupted, before switching his scrutiny back to the speaker.

The crowd drew back from Erebus, as though afraid that mere proximity to him might somehow taint them with his temerity.

'Erebus,' said Maloghurst. 'You have something to say.'

'Merely a correction, equerry,' explained the Word Bearer.

Karkasy saw Maloghurst give the Warmaster a wary sidelong glance. 'A correction you say. What would you have corrected?'

'The Warmaster said that this world is compliant,' said Erebus.

'Davin is compliant,' growled Horus.

Erebus shook his head sadly and, for the briefest instant, Karkasy detected a trace of dark amusement in his next pronouncement.

'No,' said Erebus. 'It is not.'

THE HORUS HERESY®

Many of these titles are also available as abridged and unabridged audiobooks. Order the full range of Horus Heresy novels and audiobooks from
blacklibrary.com

THE HORUS HERESY®

CRUSADE'S END

The rise and fall of Horus

BLACK LIBRARY

A BLACK LIBRARY PUBLICATION

The Wolf of Ash and Fire was first published in 2014.
Death of a Silversmith was first published in 2011.
Horus Rising was first published in 2006.
False Gods was first published in 2006.
Galaxy in Flames was first published in 2006.
Lord of the Red Sands was first published in 2013.
This edition published in Great Britain in 2016 by
Black Library,
Games Workshop Ltd.,
Willow Road,
Nottingham, NG7 2WS, UK.

10 9 8 7 6 5 4 3 2 1

Produced by Games Workshop in Nottingham.

A CIP record for this book is available from the British Library.

UK ISBN 13: 978 1 78496 157 2
US ISBN 13: 978-1-78496-158-9

See Black Library on the internet at

blacklibrary.com

Find out more about Games Workshop
and the world of Warhammer 40,000 at

games-workshop.com

Printed and bound by CPI Group (UK) Ltd, Croydon, CR0 4YY

THE HORUS HERESY®
It is a time of legend.

Mighty heroes battle for the right to rule the galaxy.

The vast armies of the Emperor of Earth have conquered the galaxy in a Great Crusade – the myriad alien races have been smashed by the Emperor's elite warriors and wiped from the face of history.

The dawn of a new age of supremacy for humanity beckons.

Gleaming citadels of marble and gold celebrate the many victories of the Emperor. Triumphs are raised on a million worlds to record the epic deeds of his most powerful and deadly warriors.

First and foremost amongst these are the primarchs, superheroic beings who have led the Emperor's armies of Space Marines in victory after victory. They are unstoppable and magnificent, the pinnacle of the Emperor's genetic experimentation. The Space Marines are the mightiest human warriors the galaxy has ever known, each capable of besting a hundred normal men or more in combat.

Organised into vast armies of tens of thousands called Legions, the Space Marines and their primarch leaders conquer the galaxy in the name of the Emperor.

Chief amongst the primarchs is Horus, called the Glorious, the Brightest Star, favourite of the Emperor, and like a son unto him. He is the Warmaster, the commander-in-chief of the Emperor's military might, subjugator of a thousand thousand worlds and conqueror of the galaxy. He is a warrior without peer, a diplomat supreme.

Horus is a star ascendant, but how much further can a star rise before it falls?

CONTENTS

THE WOLF OF ASH AND FIRE

Graham McNeill

"A son can bear with equanimity the loss of his father, but the loss of his inheritance may drive him to despair."

– The Black Tacitus of Firenze

ONE

The hand of the ship
Oaths of Censure
Speartip

'I was there,' he would say, right up until the day he died, after which he spoke only infrequently. 'I was there the day Horus saved the Emperor.' It had been a singular moment, the Emperor and Horus shoulder to shoulder in the fiery, ash-choked depths of the scrapworld. Blood-lit in the broil of combat for almost the last time, though only one of them knew that.

Father and son, back to back.

Swords drawn and their foe all around.

As perfect an encapsulation of the Crusade as any later immortalised in paint or ink.

Before remembrance of such times became a thing to be feared.

The scrapworld of Gorro; that was where it had happened, deep in junkyard space of the Telon Reach. The greenskin empire that once claimed dominion over its stars was in flames, assailed on all sides by the inexhaustible armies of the Imperium. The aliens' empire was being overturned, their muddy fortress-worlds burning, but not quickly enough.

Gorro was the key.

Adrift in the distant light of a bloated red sun, where no planet had ever been wrought by inexorable time and gravity, it drifted on an erratic path. Not a wanderer, an intruder.

Its destruction was made the Crusade's highest priority.

The command came from the hand of the Emperor himself, and his most favoured and brightest son answered this call to arms.

Horus Lupercal, primarch of the Luna Wolves.

Gorro wasn't dying easy.

Any expectation that this would be a swift strike to the heart was dashed the moment the Sixty-Third expedition surged towards the system boundary and saw the scale of the scrap-fleet protecting it.

Hundreds of vessels, pulled back from the fighting at the core of the Reach to defend its warlord's planetoid citadel. Vast corpse-ships brought to hellish life with flaring plasma reactors at their heart. Warhulks welded together from rusted wreckage scavenged from celestial graveyards and returned to life by hideous mechanical necromancy.

Anchoring the fleet was a colossal, hollowed-out asteroid fortress, a mountainous rock encrusted with pig-iron and ice. Kilometres-wide engine cowlings were bolted deep into its bedrock and its craggy surface was thick with immense batteries of orbital-howitzers and mine-lobbers. It lumbered towards the Luna Wolves as rabid scrapship packs raced ahead like feral, club-wielding barbarians. The vox howled with baying static, a million tusked throats giving voice to the primal instinct of the ork.

The engagement volume became a swirling free-fire zone, an impossibly tangled mass of entwined warships, collimated laser fire, parabolic torpedo contrails and explosive debris fields. Void-war engagements normally fought at ranges of tens of thousands of kilometres now began so close that ork marauders with crude rocket-packs were launching boarding actions.

Atomic detonations fouled the space between the fleets with electromagnetic distortion and phantom echoes, making it almost impossible to separate what was real and what was a sensor ghost.

The *Vengeful Spirit* was in the heart of the fiercest fighting, its flanks ablaze with broadsides. A hulk tumbled away, bludgeoned into molten submission by multiple decks of concentrated explosive ordnance. It trailed scads of burning fuels and arcing jets of plasma. Thousands of bodies spilled from its ruptured innards like spores from a fungal mass.

There could be nothing subtle in such a fight. This wasn't a battle of manoeuvre and counter-manoeuvre, it was a brawl. It would be won by the fleet that punched hardest and most often.

And right now, that was the orks.

The *Vengeful Spirit's* superstructure groaned like a living thing as it manoeuvred far faster than anything as massive should ever be asked. Its ancient hull shuddered under thunderous impacts, and the deck vibrated with the recoil of multiple broadside decks firing in unison.

Space between the brawling fleets was thick with debris storms, atomic vortices, duelling attack squadrons and flash-burning vapour clouds, but within Lupercal's flagship, discipline held firm.

Cascading data-slates and shimmering wire-frame holos bathed the vaulted strategium in a rippling, undersea light. Hundreds of mortal voices conveyed the shipmaster's orders, while chattering machine tickers recited damage reports, void strengths and ordnance firing schedules over the binary cant of Mechanicum priests.

A well-drilled bridge crew in battle was a thing of beauty, and were it not for the caged-wolf pacing of Ezekyle Abaddon, Sejanus might have been properly able to appreciate it.

The First Captain slammed a fist on the brass rim of a hol-olithic table displaying the engagement sphere. The scratchy, flickering threat vectors burped with angry static, but the grim picture of battle surrounding the *Vengeful Spirit* didn't alter.

Greenskin warships still vastly outnumbered those of the Luna Wolves, outgunning them and appearing – in defiance of all reason and sense – to be outmanoeuvring the commander.

It was most vexing, and Ezekyle's choler wasn't helping.

Nearby mortal crew, their faces limned by data-light, turned at the sudden sound, but looked away as the First Captain glared at them.

'Really, Ezekyle?' said Sejanus. '*That's* your solution?'

Ezekyle shrugged, making the plates of his armour grate together and the gleaming black of his topknot shake like a shaman's fetish switch. Ezekyle loomed, it was his *thing*, and he tried to loom over Sejanus as though he actually thought he could intimidate him. Ridiculous, as it was only the topknot that made him taller.

'I suppose you have a better idea of how to turn this disaster around, Hastur?' said Ezekyle, glancing over his shoulder and careful to keep his voice low.

The pale ivory of Ezekyle's armour gleamed in the light of

the strategium. Faded gang markings survived on those plates that hadn't been replaced by the armourers, faded gold and tarnished silver. Sejanus sighed. Almost two hundred years since leaving Cthonia, and Ezekyle still held onto a heritage best left in the past.

He gave Abaddon his best grin. 'I do, as it turns out.'

That got the attention of his other Mournival brothers.

Horus Aximand, so like the commander with his high, aquiline features and sardonic curl of the lip that they called him the truest of the *true sons*. Or, if Aximand was in one of his rare, lighter moods, *Little Horus*.

Tarik Torgaddon, the idiot joker whose dark, saturnine features had avoided the transhuman flattening common among the Emperor's legionaries. Where Aximand would puncture the humour of any given moment, Torgaddon would seize upon it like a hound with a bone.

Brothers all. The confraternity of four. Counsellors, war-brothers, naysayers and confidantes. So close to Horus, they were likened unto his sons.

Tarik gave a mock bow, as though to the Emperor himself, and said, 'Then please enlighten us poor, foolish mortals who are grateful merely to bask in the radiance of your genius.'

'At least Tarik knows his place,' grinned Sejanus, his finely sculpted features robbing the comment of malice.

'So what *is* your better idea?' said Aximand, cutting to the heart of the matter.

'Simple,' said Sejanus, turning to the command station behind them on a raised dais. 'We trust in Horus.'

The commander saw them coming and raised a gauntlet in welcome. His perfect face was all finely chiselled lines, piercing ocean-green eyes flecked with amber and freighted with aquiline intelligence.

He towered over them all, the broad sweep of his shoulder guards swathed in the pelt of a giant beast slain on Davin's plains many decades ago. His armour, white-gold even in the battle light of the strategium, was a thing wrought from wonder and beauty, with a single staring eye fashioned across the breastplate. Graven across its vambraces and pauldrons were armourers' marks, the eagle and lightning bolt of Lupercal's father, esoteric symbolism that Sejanus didn't recognise and, almost hidden in the shadows of overlapping plates, hand-scratched gang markings from Cthonia.

Sejanus hadn't noticed them before, but that was the

commander for you. Each time you stood in his presence you saw something fresh to delight the eye, some new reason to love him more.

'So how do you think it's going so far?' asked Horus.

'I have to be honest, sir,' replied Tarik. 'I feel the hand of the ship on me.'

Lupercal smiled. 'You don't have faith in me? I'd be hurt if I didn't know you were joking.'

'I am?' said Tarik.

Horus turned his gaze away as the strategium shook with a pounding series of percussive impacts on the hull. Shells from the many guns of the asteroid fortress, judged Sejanus.

'And you, Ezekyle?' said Horus. 'I know I can rely on you to give me a straight answer and not fall back on superstition.'

'I have to agree with Torgaddon,' said Ezekyle, and Sejanus suppressed a grin, knowing that admission would have cost Ezekyle dearly. Tarik and Ezekyle were so alike in war, but polar opposites when the killing was done. 'We're going to lose this fight.'

'Have you ever known me to lose a fight?' the commander asked of his namesake. Sejanus saw the imperceptible tilt at the corner of Lupercal's lips and knew the commander had engineered the First Captain's answer.

Horus Aximand shook his head. 'Never, and you never will.'

'A flattering answer, but a wrong one. I am as capable of losing a fight as any other,' said Horus, putting up a hand to forestall their inevitable denials. 'But I'm not going to lose this one.'

Lupercal ushered them to his command station, where what looked like a skeletal armature of gold and steel with embedded portions of pale meat stood plugged into the main battle hololith.

'Adept Regulus,' said Horus. 'Illuminate my sons.'

The emissary of the Mechanicum nodded and the hololith bloomed to life. The commander's station gave a clearer rendition of the battle, but, if anything, that only made his current orders more confounding.

The hololith's low light shadowed the commander's eye sockets while sheening the rest of his face in deep red. The impression was of an ancient chieftain squatting at a low-burning hearthfire in his wartent, gathering his generals on the eve of battle.

'Hastur, you always had the best grip on void tactics,' said Horus. 'Take a look and tell me what you see.'

Sejanus leaned over the hololithic plotter, his heart swelling in pride at Lupercal's words. It took an effort of will not to puff his chest out like one of the III Legion peacocks. He took a deep breath and stared at the grainy, slowly-updating schemata of battle.

The greenskins made war without subtlety, no matter in what arena the battle was fought. On land they came at you in a berserk horde, braying, foaming and smeared with faecal warpaint. In space their rad-spewing reaverhulks stormed into the fray with every gun-deck throwing out shells and atomic warheads with abandon.

'Standard greenskin tactics, though I baulk at dignifying this mess with the term,' said Sejanus, swaying as sequentially enacted orders from the commander's station threw the *Vengeful Spirit* into a savage turn. Echoes of crashing detonations travelled through the flagship's structure. Whether they were impacts or outgoing fire was impossible to tell.

'Their sheer force and numbers is bending our line back on itself,' he continued, as Regulus shifted the focus of the hololith to highlight the fiercest fighting. 'The centre is retreating from that asteroid fortress, we just don't have the guns to hurt it.'

'What else?' said Horus.

Sejanus pointed to the slowly rotating image. 'Our right and upper quadrants are being pushed out too far. The left and lower quadrants are the only ones holding firm.'

'What I wouldn't give for another fleet,' said Tarik, nodding at an empty region of space in an upper quadrant of the volume. 'Then we'd have them on two flanks.'

'No use wishing for what we don't have,' said Little Horus.

Something wasn't right, and it took a moment for the suspicion to crystallise fully in Sejanus's mind.

'Adept, bring up the tally of enemy launch-to-impact ratios,' he ordered. Instantly, a glowing pane of data light appeared in the air before Sejanus. He ran his eyes down the statistics and saw his suspicion confirmed.

'Their damage capability assessment is far above average,' he said. 'They're on-target with over seventy-five per cent of their launches.'

'That's got to be a mistake,' said Ezekyle.

'The Mechanicum do not make *mistakes*, First Captain,' said Regulus, his voice like steel wool on rust and pronouncing *mistakes* like the vilest of curses. 'The data is accurate within tolerances of local parameters.'

'Greenskins are as likely to hit their own ships as any other,' said Sejanus. 'How are they doing this?'

Horus pointed towards the crackling outline of Gorro and

said, 'Because these greenskins are atypical in that I suspect they are ruled, not by warriors, but by some form of tech caste. It's why I petitioned Adept Regulus to join the Sixteenth Legion in this prosecution.'

Sejanus looked back at the display and said, 'If you suspected that, then it makes all this doubly confusing. If I may be candid, my lord, our fleet tactics make no sense.'

'What *would* make them more tactically sound?'

Sejanus considered this. 'Tarik's right. If we had another fleet element *here*, our current strategy would be sound. We'd have them between hammer and anvil.'

'Another fleet?' said Horus. 'And I am supposed to simply conjure one from thin air?'

'Could you?' asked Tarik. 'Because that would be really useful right now.'

Horus grinned and Sejanus saw he was savouring this moment, though he couldn't imagine why. The commander looked up to one of the tiered galleries rising up behind the command deck. As if on cue, a solitary figure stepped to the ironwork rail, bathed in the lambent glow of a spotlight whose arc of illumination was too providential to be accidental.

Slender and spectral in her white gown, the *Vengeful Spirit*'s Mistress of Astropathy, Ing Mae Sing, pulled back her hood. Gaunt-cheeked and with sunken, hollowed-out eye sockets, Mistress Sing was blind to one world, while being open to another secret world Sejanus knew little about.

'Mistress Sing?' called out Horus. 'How long now?'

Her voice was faint. Thin, yet with an authority that carried effortlessly to the main deck.

'Imminent, Primarch Horus,' she said with a faintly scolding tone. 'As well you know.'

Horus laughed and raised his voice for the entire strategium to hear, 'You're quite right, Mistress Sing, and I hope you will all forgive me this little moment of theatre. You see, something magnificent is about to happen.'

Horus turned to Adept Regulus and said, 'Send the manoeuvre order.'

The adept bent to the task, and Sejanus asked, 'Sir?'

'You wanted another fleet,' said Horus. 'I give you one.'

Space parted as though cut open by the sharpest edge.

Amber light spilled out, brighter than a thousand suns and simultaneously existing in many realms of perception. The blade that cut the void open slid through the passage it had made.

But this was no blade, this was a void-born colossus of gold and marble, a warship of inhuman proportions. Its prow was eagle-winged and magnificent, its length studded with vast cities of statuary and palaces of war.

It was a starship, but a starship unlike any other.

Built for the most peerless individual the galaxy had ever known.

This was the flagship of the Emperor himself.

The *Imperator Somnium*.

Flocks of battleships attended the Master of Mankind. Each was a titanic engine of void-war, but the immensity of their master's vessel rendered them ordinary.

Still crackling with shield ignition, the Imperial warships surged into battle. Molten spears of lance fire stabbed into the exposed rear and flanks of the greenskin hulks. A thousand torpedoes slashed through space, followed by a thousand more. A glittering flurry of booster contrails painted the void in a web of glittering vapour-wakes.

Ork ships began exploding, gutted by timed warheads or cut in half by precision-aimed lances. Secondary explosions rippled through the hamstrung xenos fleet as raucous plasma reactors achieved critical mass and engines running insanely hot spiralled into explosive death throes.

The ork attack paused, turning to face this new threat.

Which was just what Horus Lupercal had been waiting for.

The XVI Legion fleet – which had been on the verge of being overwhelmed – halted its dispersal, its vessels turning about with astonishing speed and banding together in mutually-supporting wolf packs.

And what was once a fleet in apparent disarray transformed in minutes to a fleet on the attack. Individual greenskin vessels were overwhelmed and bombarded out of existence. Larger groups banded together, but they were no match for two coordinated war fleets led by the galaxy's greatest warriors.

The greenskins drew together around their monstrous asteroid fortress as the *Vengeful Spirit* and the *Imperator Somnium* bore down upon it. Escorting warships blasted a path through the stricken reaverhulks, clearing the way for Horus and the Emperor to deliver the killing blow.

Coming in at oblique angles, both ships raked the asteroid with unending broadsides. Void flare and electromagnetic bursts from the cataclysmic volume of ordnance wreathed the hulking fortress in flaring detonations. This was planet-killing levels of fire, the power to crack open worlds and hollow them out as thoroughly as ceaseless industry had done to Cthonia.

At some unseen signal, the Imperial vessels pulled away as hell-ish firestorms engulfed the asteroid. The nightmare machinery at its heart, which empowered the guns and engines, exploded and split the rock apart.

Geysers of green-white plasma energy, thousands of kilometres long, arced around its corpse in crackling whips of sun-hot lightning. Like attracted like, and the lightning sought out the plasma cores of the greenskin vessels and ripped them apart in coruscating storms that burned everything it touched to ash.

Barely a handful escaped the tempest of destructive energies, and those that did were savaged by the prowling wolf pack squadrons.

Within the hour of the Emperor's arrival, the ork fleet had been reduced to a vast cloud of cooling debris.

An incoming vox-hail echoed through the *Vengeful Spirit*'s strategium. The storms of plasma boiling in the greenskins' graveyard made inter-ship vox choppy and unreliable, but this transmission was so clear the speaker could have been stand-ing next to Lupercal.

'*Permission to come aboard, my son?*' said the Emperor.

The moment was so sublime, so unexpected and so awe-inspiring that Sejanus knew he would remember it for the rest of his life. It had been a long time since Sejanus had found himself awed by someone other than his primarch.

The Emperor went without a helm, his noble countenance bearing a wreath of golden laurels about his brow. Even from a distance it was the face of a being worthy of eternal fealty, con-ceivable only as an impression of wonder and light. No god ever demanded respect and honour more. No earthly ruler had ever been so beloved by all.

Sejanus found himself weeping tears of unbridled joy.

Father and son met on the main embarkation deck of the *Vengeful Spirit*, and every legionary aboard had mustered to honour the Master of Mankind.

Ten thousand warriors. So many that every Stormbird and Thunderhawk in the deck had been flown out into the void to make room.

No order had been given. None had been needed.

This was their sire, the ruler who had decreed the galaxy to be humanity's domain and wrought the Legions into being to turn that dream into reality. No force in the universe could have kept them from this reunion. As one, the Luna Wolves threw back their heads and loosed a howling cheer of welcome, a pound-ing, deafening roar of martial pride.

Nor were the legionaries the only ones who came. Mortals came too – waifs and strays the Luna Wolves had swept up in the course of the Great Crusade. Itinerant poets, would-be chroniclers and promulgators of Imperial Truth. To see the Master of Mankind in the flesh was an opportunity that would never come again, and what mortal would miss the chance to see the man who was reshaping the galaxy?

He came aboard with three hundred members of the Legio Custodes, god-like warriors cast in the mould of the Emperor himself. Armoured in gold plate with crimson horsehair plumes streaming from their peaked helms, they carried shields and long polearms topped with armed photonic blades. Warriors whose sole purpose was to give their lives in order to protect his.

The Mournival followed Horus at the head of the entire First Company, marching in a long column alongside the warriors of the Legio Custodes.

As all warriors do, Sejanus measured them against his own strength, but could form no clear impression of their power.

Perhaps that was the point.

'Jaghatai taught it to me,' said Horus in answer to a question of the Emperor's. 'He called it "the *zao*". I can't pull it off anything like as fast as the Warhawk, but I make a passable fist of it.'

Sejanus saw Horus was being modest. Not enough to keep pride from his voice, but just on the right side of arrogant.

'You and Jaghatai were always close,' said the Emperor as they marched between the proud lines of Luna Wolves. 'Of all of us, even me, I think you know him best.'

'And I hardly know him at all,' admitted Horus.

'It is how he was made,' said the Emperor, and Sejanus thought he detected a note of profound regret.

They marched between the thousands of cheering legionaries, leaving the embarkation deck and moving up through the grandest processionals of the *Vengeful Spirit*. Companies of Luna Wolves peeled off the higher they went, until only Ezekyle's Justaerin elite and the Mournival remained.

They marched down the Avenue of Glory and Lament, the soaring antechamber with embossed columns of dark wood that bore the weight of a shimmering crystalline roof, through which the roiling, plasmic death throes of the greenskin fleet could be relished. Coffered panels running fully half the length of the avenue bore hand-painted lists of names and numbers, and the march to the bridge only stopped when the Emperor paused to kneel by the newest panel.

'The dead?' asked the Emperor, and Sejanus heard the weight of uncounted years in that simple question.

'All those where the *Spirit* was present,' said Horus.

'So many, and so many more yet to come,' said the Emperor. 'We must make it all worthwhile, you and I. We must build a galaxy fit for heroes.'

'We could fill this hall a hundred times over and it would still be a price worth paying to see the Crusade triumphant.'

'I hope it will not come to that,' said the Emperor.

'The stars are our birthright,' said Horus. 'Wasn't that what you said? Make no mistakes and they will be ours.'

'I said that?'

'You did. On Cthonia, when I was but a foundling.'

The Emperor stood and put a mailed gauntlet upon Lupercal's shoulder, the gesture of a proud father.

'Then I must prove worthy of your trust,' said the Emperor.

They met later, when the order for war had rung out all across the *Vengeful Spirit*. There was much yet to be done, battle group formations to be decided upon, assault preparations to be run through and a thousand other tasks to be completed before the attack on Gorro could begin.

But first *this*.

'I don't have time for your pointless little ritual, Hastur,' declared Ezekyle. 'I've a company to ready for war.'

'We all do,' said Sejanus. 'But you're doing this.'

Ezekyle sighed, but nodded in acquiescence. 'Fine, then let's get on with it.'

Sejanus had chosen a seldom-visited observation deck in the rear quarters of the ship for their meeting. A vivid screed of plasma storms blazed beyond the crystalflex dome, and forking traceries of lightning danced on the polished terrazzo floor. The walls were bare of ornamentation, though scratched with Cthonian murder-hexes, bad poetry and gruesome images of murdered aliens.

A deep pool of fresh water filled the heart of the chamber, glittering with starlight and made bloody with light from the system's bloated red star.

'It's not even a proper moon,' said Ezekyle, staring at the pallid reflection of Gorro in the mirror flat waters.

'No, but it will have to do,' answered Sejanus.

'The Justaerin are going to be fighting alongside the Emperor,' said Ezekyle, mustering one last objection to a ceremony he'd never liked being party to. 'And I'll not have us shown up by those golden martinets.'

'We've been doing this since Ordoni,' said Tarik, kneeling to set the gleaming silver of his gibbous moon token next to Aximand's half-moon medal at the edge of the pool. 'It's what keeps us honest. Remembering Terentius.'

'I don't *need* keeping honest,' snapped Ezekyle, but he too knelt to place his lodge medal. 'Terentius was a traitor. We're nothing like him.'

'And only by constant vigilance will that remain so,' said Sejanus, and the matter was settled. He set his crescent-moon token next to those of his brothers and said, 'The Legion looks to us. Where we lead, they follow. We're doing this.'

Sejanus drew his sword and his Mournival brothers drew theirs. The XIII Legion favoured the short, stabbing gladius, but Lupercal's sons bore long-handled war blades, capable of being wielded one-handed or as brutal double-handers.

'Who are we?' asked Sejanus.

'We are the Luna Wolves,' said the others.

'Beyond that,' said Sejanus, almost growling the words.

'We are Mournival.'

'Bound together by the light of a moon,' roared Sejanus. 'Sworn to a bond that only death will break.'

'We kill for the living,' shouted Ezekyle.

'We kill for the dead!' they cried in unison.

Their swords lowered, each warrior resting the tip of his blade on the gorget of the man to his left.

Sejanus felt Ezekyle's sword at his neck as he held his own on Aximand, who in turn placed his at Tarik's neck. Lastly, Tarik placed his sword on Ezekyle, grinning at the faintly treasonous action of baring a blade to the First Captain.

'You have your Censures?'

Each warrior held out a folded square of oath paper that would normally be used to record an objective to be achieved in battle. Such oaths would be affixed to a warrior's armour, a visible declaration of martial intent.

Each Mournival brother had written upon their paper, but instead of a deed of honour, they had chosen a punishment for failure. These were Oaths of Censure, something Sejanus had instituted in the wake of the war in the Ordoni star cluster against the traitor Vatale Gerron Terentius.

His brothers had resisted the idea, claiming that to threaten punishment was to impugn their honour, but Sejanus had insisted, saying, 'We hold to the essential, unchanging goodness of the Legions, in their rational appraisal and rejection of evil. We invest our primarchs with divine qualities, with moral and rational faculties that make them both just and wise. We simplify the complexity of the galaxy by believing there is an unbreakable wall between good and evil. The lesson of Terentius is that the line between good and evil is all too permeable. Anyone can cross it in exceptional circumstances, even us. Believing that we *cannot* fall to evil makes us more vulnerable to the very things that might make it so.'

And so they had reluctantly agreed.

Sejanus held out his helmet, its transverse crest pointed to the deck. His censure paper was already in the helmet, and the other three dropped their punishment in with it. Then, each warrior reached inside and selected a paper at random. Aximand and Ezekyle tucked theirs into their belts. Tarik placed his into a leather loop on his scabbard.

Sejanus had read of the tradition from the ancient texts of Unity, where the ochre-painted warriors of Sarapion each crafted censures and cast them into a vast iron cauldron on the eve of battle. Each man would file past and draw a punishment should they fail their king. None knew which punishment they had chosen, thus no warrior could devise a lighter punishment and expect to receive it himself.

By the time the drop pods launched, each of the Mournival would have an Oath of Censure wax-sealed onto a secret place upon his armour.

In the years since the first censure had been written, not one had ever been read.

And none ever will, thought Sejanus.

The Oaths of Moment had been sworn, the straining Stormbirds let fly. The Luna Wolves were en route to Gorro. Drop pods and gunships in the tens of thousands raced to the surface, ready to hollow the scrapworld from the inside out.

Gorro's death was to be won the hard way.

Field technology unknown to the Mechanicum bound the layered depths of Gorro together, and those same technologies made it virtually invulnerable to bombardment.

Macro cannons capable of levelling entire cities barely scratched its rust-crusted surface. Magma bombs and mass drivers with the power to crack continents detonated in its atmosphere. The lethal radiation of destroyer warheads dissipated into the void, half-lives of tens of thousands of years degraded in hours.

Lupercal watched his warriors race to battle from the golden bridge of his father's vessel. He wished he was part of the initial wave, the first to set foot on Gorro's alien surface. A wolf of ash and fire, bestriding the world as an avenging destroyer god.

Destroyer? No, never that.

'You wish you were with them, don't you?' asked the Emperor.

Horus nodded, but didn't turn from the viewing bay.

'I don't understand,' said Horus, feeling the might of his father's presence behind him.

'What don't you understand?'

'Why you wouldn't let me go with my sons,' said Horus.

'You always want to be first, don't you?'

'Is that so bad?'

'Of course not, but I need you elsewhere.'

'Here?' said Horus, unable to mask his disappointment. 'What good will I do from here?'

The Emperor laughed. 'You think we're going to watch this abomination die from here?'

Horus turned to face the Emperor, now seeing his father was girt for battle, towering and majestic in his gold-chased warplate of eagle wings and a bronze mantle of woven mail. A bluesteel sword was unsheathed, rippling with potent psychic energies. Custodians attended him, weapons at the ready.

Upon the largest teleporter array Horus had ever seen.

'I believe you call it a speartip, yes?' said the Emperor.

"The mind is its own place, and in itself can make a heaven of hell, a hell of heaven."

– The Blind Poet of Kaerlundein

TWO

Cthonia in iron
Brothers divided
Into the abyss

A blaze of light, a vertiginous sense of dislocation and a world out of joint with itself. No sense of movement, but a powerful sense of time. Phosphor bright light faded from Horus's eyes, replaced by a furnace coal glow of seething workshops and volcanic fissures.

The bridge of the Emperor's flagship was gone.

In its place was a vision conjured straight from his youth.

Cthonia rendered in iron and mud.

Horus had explored the very depths of his adoptive home world, beyond the deepest ore-delvings, where the insane and the crippled waited to die. He'd even ventured beneath the dripping cadaver pits, avoiding the screeching murder-haruspex with their disembowelling knives and organ cloaks.

Cthonia was a warren of nightmarish rookeries filled with unimaginable horrors at every turn, its claustrophobic tunnels lit with pulsating light from magma fissures. Thick with ash, a toxic miasma clogged the lungs, fouled the eyes and stained the soul.

This was just like that. Bowing ceilings laced with knotworks of rusted reinforcement, caged bulbs that sputtered with fitful light and a fug of sulphurous fumes.

The scrapworld stank of hot iron and flames, of oil and sweat and waste matter left to rot. The chamber was rank with the stench of beasts, as though the herds of livestock were kept here and never mucked out. This was the fetor of the ork, ammoniac and strangely redolent of spoiled vegetable matter.

A thousand or more greenskins roared to see several hundred armoured warriors appear without warning in the midst of the wide chamber. Every ork was encased in rusted plates of hissing iron, strapped and bolted to their swollen bodies. Horus's suspicion of a ruling tech class was all but confirmed at the sight of the wheezing pneumatics, cracking power generators and hissing, lightning-edged weapons.

'At them!' bellowed the Emperor.

Much to Horus's chagrin, the Custodians moved first, bracing their spears and letting fly with an explosive volley of mass-reactives from their guardian spears. The Justaerin opened fire a heartbeat later and the ork line bloomed with fiery detonations.

Then the Emperor was amongst them.

His sword was a bluesteel shimmer, too fast to follow with the naked eye. He moved through the orks without seeming to move at all, simply existing at one point to kill before appearing elsewhere to reap greenskin lives by the score. Each blow struck with the force of an artillery impact, and shattered bodies flew from his sword as though hurled aside by a bomb blast.

Nor was his sword the Emperor's only weapon.

His outstretched gauntlet blazed with white-gold fire, and whatever the flames touched disappeared in explosions of red cinders and ash. He battered orks to bonelessness with bludgeoning blows, he crushed them with invisible coils of force and he repelled their gunfire with thoughts that turned their rounds to smoke.

They came at him in their hundreds, like iron filings to the most powerful magnet, knowing they would never find another foe so deserving of their rage. The Emperor killed them all, unstoppable in his purity of purpose.

A crusade of billions distilled in one numinous being.

Horus had fought alongside the Emperor for well over a century, but the sight of his father in battle still had the power to awe him. This was war perfected. Fulgrim could live a thousand lifetimes and never achieve anything so wondrous.

Horus fired his storm bolter, decapitating a monster with twin rotating hooks for hands. It spun around and gutted another greenskin that stared stupidly at its unspooling entrails for a moment before collapsing. Horus followed his father into the mass of alien flesh and steel. His sword slashed low, taking the leg from a towering ork of absurdly oversized machine-musculature. He crushed its skull beneath his boot as he pushed over its thrashing body.

The Justaerin fought to his left and right, a solid wedge of black-armoured terminators battering their way through an ocean of iron-hard green flesh. Ezekyle led them with characteristic bullishness: shoulders squared against the foe, fist sawing back and forth like a relentless piston as his twin-bolter spat explosive death.

Horus had waged every form of warfare imaginable, but never relished it more than in a bloody broil with the greenskin. Hundreds of greasy bestial bodies surrounded him, howling, yelling, screaming and braying. Fangs snapped on his vambrace. Roaring cleavers shattered on his shoulder guards. He shrugged off every impact, rolled with every blow, killing his attackers with pure economy of force.

Stinking alien viscera coated him, hissing from the blade of his sword and the barrels of his storm bolter. Next to him, Ezekyle slew with furious urgency, pushing himself to the limit to stay by his primarch's side.

The Custodians hewed the orks with precisely aimed blows of their guardian spears. They could wield them in lethally inventive ways, but this was not the place for elaborate fighting styles. Here it was kill or be killed. Strikes that would end any other life form thrice over had to be repeated again and again just to put a single beast down.

The orks fought back with all the primal, animalistic fury that made them so dangerous. Even terminator armour could be breached, legionaries killed.

The orks were doing both.

At least a dozen Custodians were dead. Perhaps the same again in Justaerin. Horus saw Ezekyle go down, a colossal spiked mace, twice the height of a mortal, buried in his shoulder. An ork war-captain, ogryn-huge, wrenched the mace clear and swung the weapon around its immense body to deliver the death blow.

A shimmering sword sliced in to block the descending mace.

Bluesteel, two handed and wreathed in fire.

The Emperor rolled his wrist and the monstrous weight of the spiked head fell from its wire-wound haft. The Master of Mankind spun on his heel and the fire-edged sword licked out in a shimmering figure of eight.

The towering greenskin collapsed in four keenly-sliced segments. Its iron-helmed head still bellowed defiance as the Emperor bent to retrieve it from the deck. He waded into the orks, the roaring war-captain's truncated torso in one fist, sword in the other.

Horus dragged Ezekyle to his feet.

'Can you fight?' demanded Horus.

'Aye,' snapped Ezekyle. 'It's just a scratch.'

'Your shoulder is broken and the bone shield on your left side is fractured. As is your pelvis.'

'They'd need to break every bone in my body keep me from your side,' said Ezekyle. 'As it is for you and the Emperor, beloved by all.'

Horus nodded.

To say more would be to shame Ezekyle. 'No force in the galaxy will keep me from his side.'

As if Ezekyle's words were a dare to the galaxy, Gorro convulsed in the grip of a violent quake that ripped up from far below.

'What was that?' asked Ezekyle.

There could be only one answer.

'The gravitational fields keeping Gorro coherent are spinning out of control,' said Horus. 'The scrapworld is tearing itself apart.'

No sooner had Horus spoken than the deck plates buckled throughout the chamber. Metres-thick sheets of steel ripped like paper as geysers of oily steam belched from the depths. Bulging walls collapsed inwards and debris rained from the splintering ceiling. Cracking fissures spread across the bloody ground, tearing wider with every second as Custodians, Justaerin and orks fell into the scrapworld's fiery depths.

Horus fought for balance, pushing to where he saw the golden light of the Emperor surrounded by greenskin marauders.

'Father!' yelled Horus.

The Emperor turned, one hand outstretched to Horus.

Another quake struck.

And the scrapworld swallowed the Emperor whole.

Sejanus had no idea where they were. Everything was smoke and ash and blood. Three of his squad were dead already, and they hadn't even laid eyes on the enemy. Red light painted the interior of the smoke-filled drop pod, dripping wet where Argeddan and Kadonnen's bodies had been explosively gutted by spikes of penetrating debris. Feskan's head rolled at his feet, leaving spirals of blood on the floor.

The drop pod's boosters had failed and what should have been a controlled landing with the rest of the Fourth Company instead became a violent descent through hundreds of layers of honeycombed scrap towards Gorro's core.

According to the squalling, static-filled sensorium on his visor, his company was around two hundred kilometres above him. The reek of scorched metal and rotten food poured in through tears in the side of the drop pod.

Sejanus heard the booming, clanking, screeching sound that was the hallmark of greenskin technology. And behind that, the guttural bark-language of orks. The sound had a grating metallic quality to it, but he didn't have time to dwell on that now.

'Up!' he shouted. 'Up now! Get out!'

His restraint harness endlessly ratcheted as the deformed metal tried to unlock. He wrenched it away and pushed himself upright, turning to rip his bolt pistol and sword from the stowage rack above. For good measure, he took a bandolier of grenades as well. The rest of his squad followed suit, freeing and arming themselves with complete calm.

The base of the pod was canted at a forty-five degree angle, the drop-hatch angled towards the ground. Sejanus kicked the emergency release. Once, twice, three times.

It gave, but only a little.

Two more kicks finally freed it, and the panel fell out with a heavy clang. He dropped through the hatch and spun out from underneath its groaning remains. One by one, the survivors of his squad joined him on the scorched ruin of the deck. They followed him out from under the drop pod, bolters ready.

The ground was rumbling, the after-effects of a quake or something more serious? Powerful forces travelled through the ironwork lattice of Gorro. Metal and crushed rock lay in dust-wreathed heaps.

Sejanus looked up to see a rain of debris tumbling from the high ceiling, a wire-tangled hole marking their drop pod's entry to the crackling, lightning-filled vault.

Smashed machinery surrounded the crashed pod. Spars of metal and bodies had been pulverised by their impact and the quake. Arriving this deep had caught the half-dozen ork survivors here by surprise, but the clanking, smoke-belching things closing in on them weren't greenskins.

At least not of the flesh and blood variety.

'Throne, what are they?' said Sejanus.

Heavily armoured in what appeared to be all-enclosing suits of crudely-beaten iron, he'd taken them for ork chieftains, brutish war-leaders able to demand the heaviest armour, the biggest, loudest weapons.

But that wasn't what they were at all.

Their skulls were metal, as were their bodies. No part of them was organic, they were entirely formed of rusted iron, perforated vent chimneys hulking buzz saws and enormous cannons with flanged barrels.

Hundreds of tiny, shrieking, green skinned menial *things* surrounded them. Cackling, mean-looking serviles by the look of them, though even they were augmented with primitive bionics. Some carried smoking ad-hoc pistols, others held what looked like miniature blowtorches or tools more surgical than mechanical. Sejanus dismissed them as irrelevant.

The clanking, hissing metal greenskins stomped towards them and a hail of wild fire blasted from their guns. Sejanus skidded into cover. The gunfire was hopelessly inaccurate, but there was a *lot* of it. Grating speech that sounded like a machine badly in need of oiling ripped from the ironclad orks.

It always surprised Sejanus that the greenskin had mastered language. He supposed it was to be expected, given the incongruent levels of technology they possessed, but that so bestial a race *communicated* offended him on a gut level.

Shells exploded overhead, tearing through the heavy machine sheltering him. Almost immediately after, the snapping, cackling servile creatures swarmed over the top. They were tiny, virtually inconsequential. Until one started blowtorching the side of his helmet.

Sejanus pulverised it with a sharp headbutt. It exploded like a green blister over his helm. He rolled and wiped the stinking mess of its demise from his visor. They were all over him, cutting, stabbing and shooting with their tiny pistols.

He scraped them off. He stamped on them like insects.

He had dismissed them as irrelevant, and individually they were. But throw a hundred of them into a fight, and even a legionary had to take them seriously.

Because while he was killing them by the score, the ork ironclads were still coming. The swarm kept attacking, fouling the joints of his armour with their ridiculous little tools, screeching with glee as they sawed serrated blades into seams between plates. The rest of his squad fared little better, fouled like prey beasts in a net.

'I don't have time for this,' he snarled, snapping off the string of frags from his belt. He snapped the arming pins and lobbed them into the air.

'Brace for impact!' shouted Sejanus, dropping to a crouch with his arms over his head.

The frags blew out with a rippling thunderclap of sequential detonations. Red-hot shrapnel scythed out in all directions.

Fire engulfed Sejanus, and the overpressure threw him forward against the hulking machine. His armour registered a few penetrations where the creatures had managed to weaken the flexible joints at his knees and hip, but nothing serious.

The serviles were gone, shredded to bloody scraps on nearby machinery, like leavings from an explosion in a doll manufactory. Only a few remained alive, but even those were no threat. He rose to his feet, slathered in alien blood, and aimed his pistol at the oncoming ironclads.

'Take them,' ordered Sejanus.

The Glory Squad, that's what they called the warriors Sejanus commanded. Dymos, Malsandar, Gorthoi and the rest. Favoured by Horus and beloved by all, they had more than earned the name. Some thought the name vainglorious, but those who had seen them fight knew better.

Malsandar killed a beast with twin blasts from his plasma carbine, the ironwork effigy going up like a volcano as the searing beam set off a secondary detonation within it. Gorthoi put another down with a slamming right hook from his power fist, going on to tear it limb from limb as though he were back in the kill-pits of Cthonia.

Dymos and Ulsaar kept another at bay with concentrated bursts of bolter fire while Enkanus circled behind it with a melta charge. Faskandar was on his knees, his armour aflame and ceramite plates running like melting wax. Sejanus could hear his pain over the vox.

Sejanus picked his target, an ironclad with enormous bronze tusks welded into a serrated metal jaw. Its eyes were mismatched discs of red and green, its body a barrel-like construction with grinding pneumatics and beaten-metal weapon limbs. He put his bolt-round through the centre of its throat. The mass-reactive detonated and blew its head onto its shoulder in a shower of flame and squirting bio-organic oils.

The thing kept coming, raising a heavy, blunderbuss-like weapon with a flared muzzle. Sejanus didn't give it time to shoot and vaulted from cover. His boots thundered into its chest. The ironclad didn't fall. It was like slamming into a structural column.

A claw with monstrously oversized piston-driven motors snapped at his head. Sejanus ducked and thumbed the activation stud on his chainsword's hilt. The saw-toothed blade roared to life and he hacked through the last remnants of spurting oils and whirring chains holding the ironclad's head in place.

Its horned skull fell to the deck, and Sejanus stamped down

on it. Metal splintered, and viscous fluid, like that cocooning the mortal remains of a mortis brother within his dreadnought, spilled out alongside a twitching root-like spinal cord. Sejanus felt his gorge rise as he saw what lay within the iron skull.

A spongy, grey green mass of tissue, like a fungal cyst of knotted roots filled the skull. Two piggish, red eyeballs hung limp on stalks from the broken metal, both staring madly up at him from the ruin of the metallic skull.

His horror almost cost him his life.

The headless ironclad's snapping claw fastened on his chest and lifted him from the deck. Black smoke jetted from the exhausts on its back as its pincer claw drew together. The plates of his armour buckled under the crushing pressure. Sejanus fought to free himself, but its grip was unbreakable.

Mars-forged plate cracked. Warning icons blinked to life on his sensorium. Sejanus cried out as his bones ground together and blood began filling the interior of his armour.

He braced his feet against the ironclad's chest and twisted to bring his pistol to bear. The red eyes within the slowly draining helm were looking up at him, relishing his agony. The bolt-round exploded and the brain matter of the ironclad and its body convulsed with its destruction. The claw spasmed, dropping Sejanus to the deck.

He landed badly, his spine partially crushed. White light smeared his vision as palliatives flooded his body to shut the pain gate at the nape of his neck. He'd pay for that later, but this was the only way to ensure there *was* a later.

Sejanus took a moment to restore his equilibrium.

The other ironclads were dead.

So too was Faskandar, his body reduced to a gelatinous mass by the fire of the unknown greenskin weapon. Dymos knelt beside their fallen brother.

'He's gone,' he said. 'Not enough even for an Apothecary.'

'He will be avenged,' promised Sejanus.

'How?' demanded Gorthoi, belligerent to the point of requiring admonishment.

'In blood. In death,' said Sejanus. 'Our mission is unchanged. We move out and kill anything we find. Does anyone have a problem with that plan?'

None of them did.

Dymos looked up at the ragged hole their drop pod had torn.

'The rest of the company's got to be hundreds of kilometres above us,' he said. 'We're on our own down here.'

'No,' said Sejanus, 'we're not.'

His armour's systems were picking up an Imperial presence. 'Who else is this deep?' asked Malsandar.

Sejanus had never seen this kind of signature, but whoever it was, not even the electromagnetic junk fouling the air and the hostile emissions from the ork machinery at scrapworld's core could obscure his presence.

Only one person would be visible this deep in Gorro.

Sejanus grinned. 'It's the Emperor.'

Horus dropped down through the scrapworld's interior, a pearl-white angel trailing wings of fire as he fell. He'd jumped without a second's hesitation, blind to any thought other than following his father.

The quake had ripped the structure of Gorro apart. Its sedimentary levels of agglomerated junk were coming undone. Layers were separating and compacted debris was crumbling as its structural integrity collapsed at an exponential rate.

That meant two things.

Firstly, Horus was able to follow roughly the same route his father had fallen.

And secondly, the spaces opening up below him were getting wider, meaning his descent was getting faster. He smashed down through warrens of dwelling caves, stinking feeding pits and labyrinthine workshops that blazed with emerald fire.

Horus endured impacts that would have killed even a legionary as the scrapworld's death throes tossed him around like a leaf in a hurricane. He looked up, seeing tiny figures in black and gold falling after him.

Justaerin and Legio Custodes.

They'd followed him down, heroic and selfless.

But, ultimately, doomed.

They weren't primarchs. They could not endure what he could.

He saw Justaerin incinerated by a gout of plasmic fire billowing from a ruptured conduit. Custodians who dropped in arcing dives were smashed by falling debris or deforming structural elements. Their limp, lifeless bodies followed him down into the depths.

Eruptions flared up from the depths in kilometres-long forks of lightning. Ork war-machines exploded and swirling contrails of wildly corkscrewing ammunition ricocheted from every surface. Some of it struck him, scorching his armour and blistering his flesh.

Horus dropped through cavernous spaces filled with towering engines that no adept of Mars would ever dare build, let alone get to function. The world spun around him as Gorro's structure twisted and screamed with its imminent destruction. Cliff-like walls slammed together, giant girders wrought from the keels of wrecked starships bent like wire, and gouts of molten metal poured from collapsing foundries.

Horus slammed into a wall that might once have been a deck plate. Angled enough to slow his descent, but only just. The ground below was a nightmarish mass of cascading debris and fire. Horus punched his fist through the metal, ripping a jagged furrow in his wake to slow his descent.

Even with his speed reduced, Horus still slammed into the ground too hard. He bent his knees and rolled through the flames, feeling the heat of them scorch his armour and reach through to his flesh.

The deck plate shuddered and tore free of its moorings.

It tipped him over a yawning abyss limned in blue-white radiance from below. For a second, Horus was held aloft in an incandescently bright void of competing gravitational forces, wrenched in a thousand directions at once. Then one force, stronger than all the others combined, took hold of him and drew him down.

Horus fell and only at the last instant managed to right himself. He slammed down, bending his knee and punching a crater into the ground with the force of his impact.

For an instant he couldn't believe his senses.

The space in which he'd landed was a vast, spherical chamber where endlessly reconfiguring gravimetric forces were at play. There was no up or down, no cardinal direction in which gravity would act. Lightning leapt from enormous brass orbs spaced at random intervals around its inner surfaces, and a dizzyingly complex series of impossibly inverted walkways and gantries surrounded a colossal vortex of energy. At least a thousand metres wide, it seethed like a caged beast of plasma fire. Lashing silver fire forked from its expanding mass, tearing at Gorro's structure and breaking it apart.

As blinding and mesmerising as the runaway plasma reaction was at the scrapworld's heart, it was to a beleaguered golden light that Horus's eye was drawn.

The Emperor was fighting his way through a howling mob of the largest greenskins Horus had ever seen. Most were the equal of a primarch in stature. One even dwarfed the Emperor himself.

His father fought to reach a fragmenting ring of iron surrounding the blinding plasma core, but the greenskins had him surrounded.

This was a fight not even the Emperor could win alone.

But he was not alone.

✠ ✠ ✠

Sejanus and his Glory Squad fought through the disintegrating ruins of the scrapworld in the old way. No subtlety, no finesse. Like a raid on a rival warlord's territory back in the day, when all that mattered was brute force and shocking violence. Where you stabbed and bludgeoned and shot until you either killed everyone in front of you or were dragged down in blood.

His armour was pearl-white no more, but slathered in viscera. He'd been forced to discard his pistol when a mechanised slug creature had latched onto it and tried to detonate the ammunition. His sword broke on the armoured skull of another ironclad, spilling its disembodied, fungal brain to the deck.

None of that mattered.

His fists were weapons.

His mass was a weapon.

Enkanus and Ulsaar were gone, murdered with motorised cleavers and energised hooks.

All that mattered was that they reach the Emperor.

Sejanus had settled into a rhythm of battle, that cold void within a warrior where his world shrinks to a sphere of engagement. Where the truly great are separated from the merely skilled by virtue of their ability to be aware of everything around them.

Dymos fought on his left, Gorthoi his right.

They pushed ever onwards, wading knee deep in greenskin blood and flesh. The stench of the abattoir and offal pit was overpowering, but Sejanus blocked it out. The raging tide of orks was a mass of green flesh clad in beaten armour. They saw more of the ironclads, and many other technological abominations that made them seem almost comprehensible.

In the course of the Great Crusade, Sejanus had seen many examples of the crudely effective greenskin technology, but what lay beneath the surface of the scrapworld were orders of magnitude more advanced and abhorrent.

The Emperor's signal never once wavered in his visor, though every other return fizzed and screamed with distortion.

Ahead, Sejanus saw a ragged archway through which spilled blazing white light. The Emperor lay beyond it.

'We're here,' he gasped, even his phenomenal transhuman physique pushed to the limits of endurance by this fight.

He stormed through the archway and into a vast, spherical chamber with the brightest sun at its heart.

'Lupercal...' breathed Sejanus.

Horus's sword was broken, his twin bolters empty of shells. The sword had snapped halfway along its length, the edge dulled

from hewing countless greenskin bodies. He'd fought his way
onto a stepped bridge, killing scores of monstrously swollen
orks to reach a crumbling ledge just below the Emperor.

Blood drenched him, his own and that of the orks.

His helmet was long gone, torn away in a grappling, gouging
duel with an iron-tusked giant with motorised crusher claws for
arms and a fire-belching maw. He'd broken the beast over his
knee and hurled its corpse from the bridge. Rogue gravity vortices hurled it up and away.

More of the greenskins followed him onto the bridge, grunt-
ing and laughing as they stalked him. Their grim amusement
was a mystery to Horus. They were going to die, whether he
killed them or they were burned to ash by the colossal plasma
reactor's inevitable destruction.

Who would laugh in the face of their death?

The Emperor fought an armoured giant twice his height and
breadth. Its skull was a vast, iron-helmed boulder with elephan-
tine tusks and chisel-like teeth that gleamed dully. Its eyes were
coal-red slits of such vicious intelligence that it stole Horus's breath.

Horus had never seen its equal. No bestiary would include its
description for fear of being ridiculed, no magos of the Mechanicum would accept such a specimen could exist.

Six clanking, mechanised limbs bolted through its flesh bore
grinding, crackling, sawing, snapping, flame-belching weapons of murder. The Emperor's armour was burning, the golden
wreath now ashes around his neck.

Chugging rotor cannons battered the Emperor's armour even
as claws of lightning tore portions of it away. It was taking every
screed of the Emperor's warrior skill and psychic might to keep
the mech-warlord's weaponry from killing him.

'Father!' shouted Horus.

The greenskin turned and saw Horus. It saw the desperation
in his face and laughed. A fist like a Reductor siege hammer
smashed the Emperor's sword aside and a fist of green flesh
lifted him into the air. It crushed the life from him with its
inhuman power.

'No!' yelled Horus, battering his way through the last of the
greenskins to reach his father's side. The mech-warlord turned
his spinal weapons on Horus, and a blistering series of lightning strikes hammered the walkway.

Horus dodged them all, a wolf on the hunt amid the ash and
fire of the world's ending. He had no weapon, and where that
wasn't normally a handicap to a warrior of the Legions, against
this foe it was a definite disadvantage.

No weapon of his would hurt this beast anyway.

But one of its own...

Horus gripped one of the warlord's mechanised arms, one bearing the spinning brass spheres and crackling tines of its lightning weapon. The arm's strength was prodigious, but centimetre by centimetre Horus forced it around.

Lightning blasted from the weapon, burning Horus's hands black. Bone gleamed through the ruin of his flesh, but what was that pain when set against the loss of a father?

With one last herculean effort, Horus wrenched the arm up as a sawing blast of white-edged lightning erupted from the weapon. A searing burst of fire impacted on the mech-warlord's forearm and the limb exploded from the elbow down in a welter of blackened bone and boiling blood. The beast grunted in surprise, dropping the Emperor and staring in dumb fascination at the ruin of its arm.

Seizing the chance he had been given, the Emperor bent low and surged upwards with his bluesteel sword extended. The tip ripped into the mech-warlord's belly and burst from its back in a shower of sparks.

'Now you die,' said the Emperor, and ripped his blade up.

It was an awful, agonising, mortal wound. Electrical fire vented from hideous metal organs within the wreckage of the greenskin's body. It was a murderous wound that not even a beast of such unimaginable proportions could take and live.

Yet that was not the worst of it.

Horus felt the build up of colossal psychic energies and shielded his eyes as a furious light built within the Emperor. Power like nothing he had ever seen his father wield, or even suspected he possessed. All consuming, all powerful, it was the power to extinguish life in every sphere of its existence. Physical flesh turned to ash before it and what ancient faiths had once called a soul was burned out of existence, never to cohere again.

Nothing would ever remain of he who suffered such a fate.

Their body and soul would pass from the finite energy of the universe, to fade into memory and have all that they were wiped from the canvas of existence.

This was as complete a death as it was possible to suffer.

That power blazed along the Emperor's sword, filling the greenskin with killing light. It erupted in a bellowing golden explosion, and lightning blazed from the coruscating afterimage of its death, arcing from ork to ork as it sought out all those who were kin to the master of Gorro. Unimaginable energies poured from the Emperor, reaching throughout the entirety of the chamber and burning every last shred of alien flesh to a mist of drifting golden ash.

Horus watched as the power of life and death coursed through the Emperor, saw him swell in stature until he was like unto a god. Wreathed in pellucid amber flames, towering and majestic.

His father never claimed to be a god, and refuted such notions with a vengeance. He had even castigated a son for believing what Horus now saw before him with his very own eyes…

Horus dropped to his knees, overcome with the wonder of what he was witnessing.

'Lupercal!'

He turned at the sound of his name.

And there he was, his wolf on the hunt.

Sprinting along the bridge was Hastur, howling his name over and over while pumping a fist in the air. He had fought beyond the limits of endurance and sanity to stand at the side of his primarch and his Emperor.

The wondrous light behind him was eclipsed by blue-white plasma, and Horus turned to see the Emperor silhouetted in the cold fire of Gorro's seething core.

His back was to Horus, sword sheathed at his hip and arms raised high. The same golden fire that had so comprehensively destroyed the greenskin warlord dripped from his spread fingertips like immaterial fire.

Horus had no knowledge of the insane mechanics behind the greenskin power core, but any fool could see that it was spiralling to destruction. The powerful tremors shaking Gorro apart was evidence enough of that, but to see the bound starfire straining against its bonds was to know it for certain. Had the death of the Mech-Warlord been the final straw in breaking whatever bonds of belief held its monstrous power in check?

How long would it be before it exploded? Horus had no idea, but suspected it would be long before any of them could escape the depths of the scrapworld.

'This can't be how it ends,' whispered Horus.

'No, my son,' said his father, gathering the golden light within him once again. 'It is not.'

The Emperor clenched his fists and the air around the seething plasma ball *folded*. It turned sickeningly inwards, as though reality was merely a backdrop against which the dramas of the galaxy were played out.

And where it folded, the spaces behind were horribly revealed, great abysses of crawling chaos and unlimited potential. Howling voids where the combined lives of this galaxy were but motes reflected in the cosmic dust storm. An empyrean realm of the never-born, where nightmares were birthed in the foetid womb of mortal lust. Things of void-cold form writhed in the darkness, like a million snakes of ebon glass coiled in endless, slithering knots.

Horus stared deep into the abyss, repulsed and fascinated by the secret workings of the universe. Even as he watched, the Emperor drew the fabric of the world together, sealing them around the greenskin plasma core. The effort was costing him dear, the golden light at his heart waning with every passing second.

And then it was done.

A thunderous bang of air rushed to fill the void left by the plasma fire, and the backwash blew back into the chamber in a gale of sulphurous wind.

The Emperor fell to one knee, his head bowed.

Horus was at his side a heartbeat later.

'What did you do?' said Horus, helping his father to his feet. The Emperor looked up, colour already returning to his wondrous features.

'Sent the plasma core into the aether,' said the Emperor, 'but it will not last long. We must withdraw before the warp fold implodes and takes everything with it. The entire mass of this scrapworld will be soon crushed as surely as if it had fallen into the grip of a black hole.'

'Then let's get off this damn thing,' said Horus.

They watched the final death agonies of Gorro from the bridge of the *Vengeful Spirit*. With the Mournival before them, the Emperor and Horus stood at the ouslite disc from which he had planned the void war against the scraphulk fleet.

'The greenskins will never recover from this,' said Horus. 'Their power is broken. It will be thousands of years before the beast arises again.'

The Emperor shook his head, drawing a shimmering orrery of light from the disc. Gently glowing points of light rotated around the edge of the disc, scores of systems, hundreds of worlds.

'Would that you were right, my son,' said the Emperor. 'But the greenskin is a cancer upon this galaxy. For every one of their ramshackle empires we burn to the ground, another arises, even greater and ever more deeply entrenched. Such is the nature of the ork – and this is why their race is so hard to destroy. They must be eradicated wholesale or they will return all the stronger, time and time again, until they come at us in numbers too great to defeat.'

'Then we are to be cursed by the greenskin for all time?'

'Not if we act swiftly and without mercy.'

'I am your sword,' said Horus. 'Show me where to strike.'

The Emperor smiled, and Horus felt his heart swell in pride.

'The Telon Reach was but a satrapy of the largest empire we have ever encountered, one that must fall before the Crusade can continue,' said the Emperor. 'It will be magnificent, the war we will wage to destroy this empire. You will earn much honour in its prosecution, and men will speak of it until the stars themselves go out.'

'And this is it?' asked Horus, leaning over the glowing hololith. First one, then dozens, and finally hundreds of worlds were outlined in green.

'Yes,' said the Emperor. 'This is Ullanor.'

DEATH OF A SILVERSMITH

Graham McNeill

I am dying, that much I know. What I do not know is why. My throat has been crushed, and what little breath I can manage will not keep my brain functioning for long. He did not kill me outright, though he could have easily. I remember him looking down on me as my feet scrabbled at the floor of my workshop, gasping for air like a fish tossed onto a riverbank. He watched me as though fascinated by the transition of my body from life into death. But I am stronger than I look, and I was not going to die quickly.

But now that I think about it, perhaps that is what he wanted.

He did not even stay to watch me die, as though he had no interest in how long it took, only that it would be a drawn-out event. In fact, I think he used the precise amount of pressure needed to crush my larynx just enough to make my death slow. If I were not dying, I would almost admire the exacting attention to detail and controlled strength that such an act requires.

He wanted me dead, slowly, but did not care to watch the outcome.

What sort of a mind thinks like that?

I have no gods to pray to, no one does. The Emperor has shown us the folly of worshipping invisible deities whose existence is falsehood. The fanes and temples have all been torn down, even the last one across the silver bridge. The heavens are empty of supernatural agencies that might hear my dying thoughts, but right now I wish they were not.

Any witness to my death would be better than none. Otherwise it will be just a statistic, a report filed by the armsmen of this mighty vessel. Only if someone were to hear my last words or understand my last thoughts will they matter. I suspect that you would not forget a man dying in front of you.

Even though he killed me, I wish he had stayed to the end. At least then I would have had something to look at instead of the blackened ceiling of my workshop. The lumen globes maintain a steady glow, though I think they are fading.

Or is that me?

I wish he had stayed to watch me die.

He was so much bigger and stronger than me. Engineered, of course, but still, even before his genetic enhancements, I am sure he would have been more than a match for me. I have never been a violent man, the physical and martial pursuits never having interested me. From an early age, I was a tinkerer, a dismantler of working parts, and I possessed a fastidious mind that moved like the most intricate clockwork. My father wanted to apprentice me to the Mechanicum of Mars, but my grandfather would not hear of it. The priests of the red planet had been the enemies of Terra two generations ago, and my grandfather, a lapidary with exquisitely long fingers who fashioned incredible bracelets and neck ornamentation in the style of Ascalon's Repoussé and chasing, still held grudges from that chaotic time.

Making weapons and war machines for the Imperium of Man was a waste of time for someone with the skills I possessed. My grandfather was an artisan in the true sense of the word, a craftsman worthy of the name, and the raw talent evident in his work had skipped my father and passed straight to me. Not that my father was ever jealous; far from it. He lauded my triumphs and proudly displayed my work, even from an early age when the brooches, earrings and glittering chokers I produced were, at first, amateurish and derivative. I worked for many years, learning my trade and developing my talent until it became clear that my ability now outstripped that of my grandfather. Crystallisation of his joints had turned his hands to claws, and it was a day of tears when at last he hung up his pliers and draw plate.

Work was never hard to come by, even though the last death spasms of the war still jerked and spat in the far reaches of Terra. The ethnarchs and despots had fallen one by one yet, even during times of strife, always there was a general's mistress who desired a fashionable necklace, a tetrarch in need of a more impressive sword hilt or a bureaucrat seeking to impress his peers with a filigreed quill.

As the wars drew to a close, and stability of a sort was restored to Terra, money began to flow around the globe in glittering golden rivers. And with it came the desire to spend copious sums commemorating Unity, lamenting the fallen or immortalising the future. I had never been so busy, and the frenetic demand drove my creativity to new heights of wonder.

I remember a particular piece I fashioned for the Lord General of the Anatolian Theatre. His soldiers had been lucky enough to fight alongside the warriors of the X Legion in one of their last battles on Terra. A rebellious branch of the Terawatt clans had thought to retain control of their Urals forges instead of turning them over to the Iron Hands, and had fought their mortal representatives.

Vengeance was swift in coming, and the forge complex fell after a month of heavy fighting, in which the Anatolian brigades bore the brunt of the strange and deadly weapons wielded by the blind clan-warriors. But, so the Lord General told me, the primarch of the X Legion had been so impressed by the courage of his soldiers that he snapped the iron gauntlet from one of his Chapter's banners and presented it to the Noyan in command of the first brigade to breach the gates to the inner furnaces.

Needless to say, that particular commander never got to keep the finial, but dutifully passed it to his superior, and so on, until it reached the hands of the Lord General. Who in turn brought it to me, instructing me to create a worthy reliquary – though he laughed at the antiquated term – for the gift.

To work on so incredible a piece was an honour, and I lavished all my skill upon this particular commission. The gauntlet itself was clearly a trifling piece for the Iron Hands, but as I studied the intricacy and precision of the workmanship, I appreciated the incredible skill that had gone into its creation. I had heard of the miraculous hands of the great Ferrus Manus, but to think that I worked on a piece touched by a primarch himself, one of the Emperor's sons, gave me purpose and inspiration beyond my wildest dreams.

Day and night I worked, eschewing all human contact and turning away many wealthy patrons in the process. The brilliance of the gauntlet drove my passion and skill to new heights of invention and within the month I had created a wonder, a golden reliquary of such exquisite detail, delicate filigree and precious gems that it might have sat next to any ancient repository for the bones of one regarded as a saint, and not looked out of place.

Though the Emperor had forbidden the worship of false gods
and unclean spirits, I had a number of old, mildewed books
rescued from the ruins of a toppled fane by a friend in the Con-
servatory who knew of my interest in such things. Though their
talk of gods and spirits and magic was clearly nonsense and
lurid hyperbole, the artwork and symbolism inspired by such
belief was extraordinary. Swirling lines, interconnecting weaves
and spirals of such breathtaking complexity and perfect geo-
metries that I could stare for hours at their beguiling patterns
without losing interest.

In those books I found the perfect inspiration, and the finished piece was a thing of beauty.

The Lord General wept when he saw it, and I knew from our
many meetings that he was not a man given to expressing his
emotions. He embraced me and paid me twice the cost of the
commission, and it took all my self-control not to hand the
money back. Simply being allowed to work on such a piece
was payment enough.

Word of the reliquary spread, and my talents became more in
demand than ever, but nothing ever moved me to such creative
heights as had my work on the reliquary. Even so, my work was
astonishing, and it was not long before it came to the attention
of those who were shaping the future of this world and those
beyond the star-sprayed heavens. On a wintry day, as I worked
upon an onyx pommel stone wound in a globe of silver, the
course of my life was changed forever.

A man, noble in bearing but unassuming in mien, entered
my workshop in the foothills of the Sahyadri Mountains and
politely awaited my attention. He spoke with a cultured voice
in an accent I could not place, and told me that I was being
offered a place within an unofficial artel he wished to establish. I smiled at his use of the old word, for none here now
used it – too redolent of a long-dead tyrant. When I enquired
who would form this artel, the man spoke of craftsmen, poets,
dramatists and historians, men and women who would travel
the stars with one of the Emperor's crusade fleets and bear witness to the greatest endeavour our species had ever known.

We were to show that such an organisation was necessary, to
add weight to the growing chorus of voices urging a more formal and authoritative celebration of mankind's reunification.
We would show what such an organisation could achieve. Our
task would be no less vital than that of the warriors of the Expedition Fleet!

He saw my amusement, and smiled as I declined his offer.

I was happy on Terra, and had no wish to venture into the unknown reaches of space. Pulling back his hood, he allowed long white hair to spill around his shoulders and told me that the very highest authority had requested my cooperation. I wanted to laugh in his face, but dared not as I saw a depth of understanding and a world of memory in his eyes. This man, this ordinary man with the weight of the world in his eyes, simply placed a cream envelope upon my workbench and told me to think carefully before I refused this offer.

He left without another word, leaving me alone with the envelope. It was many hours before I dared lift it, turning it over in my long fingers as though I might understand what lay within without opening it. To open it would indicate a tacit acceptance of his offer, and I had no wish to leave the comfort of my workshop. The flap was sealed with a blob of crimson wax, and my heart skipped a beat as I recognised the crossed lightning bolts and double-headed eagle.

But, as are all men of a creative bent, I was cursed with insatiable curiosity. I eventually opened the envelope, as my visitor had known I would, and read its contents. Though worded as a request, the words were so eloquent, so passionate and so full of hope and power that I immediately knew who had written them. The stranger, whose identity I now knew, had not lied when he had told me the importance of the individual who requested my presence.

Within the day I had packed my meagre possessions and was on my way north to the mountains of the Himalazia to join the rest of my hastily assembled companions. I will not attempt to describe the immense majesty of the Palace, for words alone can do it no justice. It is landmass rendered in geological architecture, a wonder of the world that will never be surpassed. The artisan guilds strove to outdo one another in their efforts to glorify the Emperor's deeds, creating a monument worthy of the only being who could ever bear such an honorific without need of a true name.

Those early days are a blur to me now, though that may be because my brain is beginning to die from lack of oxygen. Suffice to say, I was soon travelling into the darkness of space, where shoal after shoal of starships thronged the heavens and greedily sucked fuel and supplies from the enormous continental plates locked in geostationary orbit.

At last I saw the vessel that would be my home for nearly two hundred years, a leviathan that shone in the reflected glow of the moon. It gleamed whitely as it spun gracefully to receive the flotilla of cutters and shuttles rising from the planet below. This was the *Vengeful Spirit*, flagship of Horus Lupercal and his Luna Wolves.

I quickly established myself on board, and though my possessions were meagre, my wealth was substantial, and my vanity only scarcely less so. All of which allowed me to extend my span and retain the appearance of youth with superlative juvenat treatments.

As I lie here on the floor of my workshop in the artisan decks of the *Vengeful Spirit*, I wish I had not bothered. What difference do a few less lines around the eyes and smoother skin make when every breath might be the last and a pleasing bliss enters my mind as portions of my brain begin to fade out?

I prospered on the flagship of the 63rd Expedition, creating many fine works and obtaining many commissions for embellished scabbards, honour markings, oaths of moment and the like. I made friends among the rest of my fellow remembrancers (as we came to be known after Ullanor): some good, some ill-chosen, but all interesting enough to make my time aboard ship extremely pleasurable. One fellow, Ignace Karkasy, wrote such hilariously irreverent poetry concerning the Legions that I fear he may one day wear out his welcome.

The work of the Expeditionary Fleet continued, and though many worlds were made compliant by the work of warriors and iterators, I saw little of them save in the words and images of my fellows. I created a lapis lazuli recreation of the world map found in the depths of one uninhabited planet, and embossed many helmets with icons of fallen brothers after the war on Keylek.

Yet my greatest commission was to come in the wake of the Ullanor campaign.

From the accounts of those who had fought on that muddy, flame-lit world, it was a grand war, a towering victory that could have been won by no other warrior than Horus Lupercal. Ullanor marked a turning point in the crusade, and many were the war-leaders who came to my workshop, looking to celebrate their presence on that historic battlefield with an ornamented sword or cane.

The Emperor was returning to Terra, and a great Triumph was held in the ruins of the greenskin world to forever stamp that moment on the malleable alloy of history.

In the Emperor's absence, Horus Lupercal would lead the final stages of the crusade, and such a weighty duty required an equally weighty title.

Warmaster.

Even I, who had little taste for war or the tales of its waging, savoured the sound of that word in my mouth. It promised great things, glorious things, and my mind was awhirl with the magnificent works I might fashion to commemorate the honour the Emperor had bestowed upon Horus Lupercal.

As the Warmaster was anointed, so too were we accorded an honour. The founding of the Remembrancer Order is one of my proudest memories, one that made me weep when I heard of its ratification by the Council of Terra. I remembered the white-haired man who came to my workshop and raised many a glass to him in the liquor halls of the ship.

The day after the Triumph, a warrior came to me, a beautiful man encased in battle plate that gleamed white with lapping powder and smelled of scented oils. His name was Hastur Sejanus, and never have I been so captivated as I was by his countenance. He showed me his helm, cut with a crude marking just above the right eye. Without asking, I knew it was the crescent image of the new moon.

Sejanus bade me fashion four rings, each in silver, each set with a polished moonstone. One stone would bear the crescent moon of his own helmet, another the half moon, a third the gibbous and the fourth the full. For this work, I was to be paid handsomely, but I declined any remuneration, for I knew to whom these rings would be presented.

The Mournival.

Abaddon would bear the full moon, Aximand, called Little Horus by some, the half moon, and Torgaddon the gibbous. Sejanus would bear the final ring of the new moon.

It was honour enough to craft these things for warriors of such pedigree.

For weeks I laboured, shaping each ring with all the skill I possessed. I knew such warriors would despise frippery and over-ornamentation, so I kept my more elaborate design flourishes to a minimum until I was sure I had created rings worthy of the Warmaster's closest lieutenants.

With my work on the rings complete, I awaited the return of Hastur Sejanus, but the demands of war kept him from my workshop, and other commissions came across my workbench in due course. One such commission, simple enough in its conception, proved to be my undoing, coming also from a warrior of the Luna Wolves.

I never knew his name, for he never volunteered it, and I never dared ask. He was a blunt-faced man with a deep scar across

his brow and a belligerent demeanour. He spoke with words
accented with that particular harshness of Cthonia, so typical
of the older warriors of the Luna Wolves.

What he wanted was simple, so simple it was almost beneath
me.

From a pouch at his waist the warrior produced a silver disc,
like the blank die of a coin, and placed it upon my workbench.
He slid it towards me and told me that he wanted medals made,
each bearing the image of a wolf's head and a crescent moon.
Rarely do I take such specific commissions. I prefer to bring my
own design sensibilities to each project, and told him so. The
warrior was insistent to the point where I felt it would be dangerous to refuse. A wolf's head and a crescent moon. No more,
no less. I was to craft the mould for such a medal, which he
would then take to the engineering decks to have produced in
greater numbers in a hydraulic press.

So banal a task did not interest me, but I nodded and told
him a mould would be ready within the day for him. I did not
miss the similarity in motif to that required by Hastur Sejanus,
but said nothing. Words could only antagonise this warrior,
for he had the air of one to whom casual, shocking violence
was no stranger. To fear the Legiones Astartes was natural; they
were, after all, bred to be killers, but this was something else,
something more immediate than simply the recognition of his
purpose in existing.

He left, and I immediately felt the air of my workshop become
lighter, as though it had been pressing down on my skull. The
animal part of me knew I had been in terrible danger, and
screamed at me to flee, but my higher self could find no reason for that fear. If only I had listened to my instinctual heart
and fled, but where could I hide aboard this starship that one
of the Warmaster's chosen would not find me?

I turned my attention to the silver, pushing aside all thoughts
save those of working the metal. Such a simple task should have
taken only a few hours, but I found I could not free myself from
thoughts of the warrior and his threatening presence. Each carv-
ing lacked life and any spark of inspiration, so I turned to the
same dusty books I had consulted when crafting the reliquary
for the Lord General.

Within their pages, I found plentiful references to wolves
and the moon: the Neuroi of ancient Scythia transforming into
wolves once a year; the fear that the eyes of a she-wolf could
bedazzle the senses of men. Some saw wolves as omens of victory, while others saw them as heralds of the world's last days.

In the end, I found a fragmented tale of a chained wolf that broke its bonds and swallowed the sun before being slain by a one-eyed god. Given that my carven wolf was to be set against the moon, it seemed an apt choice.

With the design set in my mind's eye, I quickly sculpted the piece, rendering the wolf with simplicity and elegance. A noble creature, set proudly against a crescent moon, head tilted back as though about to loose a wild howl. Though the work was not difficult, and the design plain, I was, nevertheless, proud of it. I felt sure my nameless patron would be pleased with the final piece, and my fear of the violence that lurked at his core receded.

As promised, he returned the next day as the ship's bells sounded the beginning of the evening cycle. He demanded to see what I had created and smiled as I placed the silver carving on his absurdly huge palm. He turned it this way and that, letting the light catch the embossed image. At last he nodded to me and complimented my work.

I bowed my head, pleased my creation had met with his approval, but no sooner had I raised my gaze than his hand fastened upon my neck. Fingers like iron cables closed around my throat and I was lifted from my feet, kicking the air as I felt the inexorable pressure of his grip. I looked into his eyes, struggling to understand why he was doing this, but I could see nothing to explain his murderous attack.

I could not cry out, for his hand prevented anything other than a strangled wheeze escaping my mouth. Something cracked and I felt a tearing pressure inside me. Then I was falling, landing hard on the floor of the workshop and scrabbling my feet as I struggled for breath. Only tiny wisps of oxygen made it through my ruined throat to my lungs, and I watched as he knelt beside me, with a sardonic expression on his blunt features.

Words struggled to reach my cyanotic lips, a thousand questions, but I had breath for only one.

'Why?'

The warrior leaned down and whispered in my ear.

An answer of sorts, but one that made no sense.

I was dying. He could see that. Within minutes I would be dead, and without waiting to watch my last moments, the warrior turned and left my workshop.

I am stronger than I look, and though I cannot know for certain, I do not believe I am dying as swiftly as my killer might have imagined. I draw the thinnest of breaths, enough to sustain me for moments longer, but not enough to live. My sight grows dim, and I feel my body dying.

This silversmith is no more, and I fear no one will ever know why.

Yet, what is this?

Is that a draught of wind across my skin, the sound of a shutter door opening?

It is! I hear a cry of alarm, and heavy footsteps. Something huge and pale looms above me. Beautiful features swim before me, like the face of a rescuer viewed from beneath the waters of a still lake.

I know this warrior.

No finer figure in Mark IV plate.

Hastur Sejanus.

Even as he lifts me from the floor, I know he will not be able to save me. I will not survive, no matter how swiftly he brings me to the medicae, but I am sanguine. I will not die alone, someone will watch as I shuffle off this mortal coil. I will be remembered.

As he lays me upon my workbench, he is not careful of my possessions, and sweeps a tray of completed commissions aside. My head lolls to the side and I see four rings fall onto the floor. I watch him accidentally tread on one of them, flattening it completely beneath his bulk.

It is the ring I made for him.

He leans over me, his words urgent, and his grief at my passing is genuine.

Sejanus barks questions at me, but I can make little sense of them.

Life is slipping away. My eyes close, but before I am gone, I hear Sejanus ask his last questions.

'Who did this? What did he say?'

With my last spark of life, I dredge the dying memories left to me and force my killer's last words up through my ruined larynx.

'*I can't say.*'

Dan Abnett

HORUS RISING

The seeds of heresy are sown

~ DRAMATIS PERSONAE ~

The Primarchs

HORUS
: First Primarch and Warmaster, Commander-in-Chief of the Luna Wolves

ROGAL DORN
: Primarch of the Imperial Fists

SANGUINIUS
: Primarch of the Blood Angels

The XVI Legion 'Luna Wolves'

EZEKYLE ABADDON
: First Captain

TARIK TORGADDON
: Captain, Second Company

IACTON QRUZE
: 'The Half-heard', captain, Third Company

HASTUR SEJANUS
: Captain, Fourth Company

HORUS AXIMAND
: 'Little Horus', captain, Fifth Company

SERGHAR TARGOST
: Captain, Seventh Company, Lodge Master

GARVIEL LOKEN
: Captain, Tenth Company

LUC SEDIRAE
: Captain, 13th Company

TYBALT MARR
: 'The Either', captain, 18th Company

VERULAM MOY
: 'The Or', captain, 19th Company

LEV GOSHEN
: Captain, 25th Company

KALUS EKADDON
: Captain, Catulan Reaver Squad

FALKUS KIBRE
: 'Widowmaker', captain, Justaerin Terminator Squad

NERO VIPUS	Sergeant, Locasta Tactical Squad
XAVYER JUBAL	Sergeant, Hellebore Tactical Squad
MALOGHURST	'The Twisted', equerry to the Warmaster

The XVII Legion 'Word Bearers'

EREBUS	First Chaplain

The VII Legion 'Imperial Fists'

SIGISMUND	First Captain

The III Legion 'Emperor's Children'

EIDOLON	Lord Commander
LUCIUS	Captain
SAUL TARVITZ	Captain

The IX Legion 'Blood Angels'

RALDORON	Chapter Master

The 63rd Imperial Expedition Fleet

BOAS COMNENUS	Master of the Fleet
HEKTOR VARVARAS	Lord Commander of the Army
ING MAE SING	Mistress of Astropaths
ERFA HINE	
SWEQ CHOROGUS	High Senior of the Navis Nobilite
REGULUS	Adept, envoy of the Martian Mechanicum

The 140th Imperial Expedition Fleet

MATHANUAL AUGUST   Master of the Fleet

Imperial Personae

KYRIL SINDERMANN	Primary Iterator
IGNACE KARKASY	Official remembrancer, poet
MERSADIE OLITON	Official remembrancer, documentarist
EUPHRATI KEELER	Official remembrancer, imagist
PEETER EGON MOMUS	Architect designate
AENID RATHBONE	High Administratrix

Non Imperial Personae

JEPHTA NAUD	General Commander, the armies of the interex
DIATH SHEHN	Abbrocarius
ASHEROT	Indentured kinebrach, Keeper of Devices
MITHRAS TULL	Subordinate Commander, the armies of the interex

PART ONE
THE DECEIVED

I was there, the day Horus slew the Emperor...

'Myths grow like crystals, according to their own recurrent pattern; but there must be a suitable core to start their growth.'

– attributed to the remembrancer Koestler (fl. M2)

'The difference between gods and daemons largely depends upon where one is standing at the time.'

– the Primarch Lorgar

'The new light of science shines more brightly than the old light of sorcery. Why, then, do we not seem to see as far?'

– the Sumaturan philosopher Sahlonum (fl. M29)

ONE

Blood from misunderstanding
Our brethren in ignorance
The Emperor dies

'I was there,' he would say afterwards, until afterwards became a time quite devoid of laughter. 'I was there, the day Horus slew the Emperor.' It was a delicious conceit, and his comrades would chuckle at the sheer treason of it.

The story was a good one. Torgaddon would usually be the one to cajole him into telling it, for Torgaddon was the joker, a man of mighty laughter and idiot tricks. And Loken would tell it again, a tale rehearsed through so many retellings, it almost told itself.

Loken was always careful to make sure his audience properly understood the irony in his story. It was likely that he felt some shame about his complicity in the matter itself, for it was a case of blood spilled from misunderstanding. There was a great tragedy implicit in the tale of the Emperor's murder, a tragedy that Loken always wanted his listeners to appreciate. But the death of Sejanus was usually all that fixed their attentions.

That, and the punchline.

It had been, as far as the warp-dilated horologs could attest, the two hundred and third year of the Great Crusade. Loken always set his story in its proper time and place. The commander had been Warmaster for about a year, since the triumphant conclusion of the Ullanor campaign, and he was anxious to prove his new-found status, particularly in the eyes of his brothers.

Warmaster. Such a title. The fit was still new and unnatural, not yet worn in.

It was a strange time to be abroad amongst stars. They had been doing what they had been doing for two centuries, but now it felt unfamiliar. It was a start of things. And an ending too.

The ships of the 63rd Expedition came upon the Imperium by chance. A sudden etheric storm, later declared providential by Maloghurst, forced a route alteration, and they translated into the edges of a system comprising nine worlds.

Nine worlds, circling a yellow sun.

Detecting the shoal of rugged expedition warships on station at the out-system edges, the Emperor first demanded to know their occupation and agenda. Then he painstakingly corrected what he saw as the multifarious errors in their response.

Then he demanded fealty.

He was, he explained, the Emperor of Mankind. He had stoically shepherded his people through the miserable epoch of warp storms, through the Age of Strife, staunchly maintaining the rule and law of man. This had been expected of him, he declared. He had kept the flame of human culture alight through the aching isolation of Old Night. He had sustained this precious, vital fragment, and kept it intact, until such time as the scattered diaspora of humanity re-established contact. He rejoiced that such a time was now at hand. His soul leapt to see the orphan ships returning to the heart of the Imperium. Everything was ready and waiting. Everything had been preserved. The orphans would be embraced to his bosom, and then the Great Scheme of rebuilding would begin, and the Imperium of Mankind would stretch itself out again across the stars, as was its birthright.

As soon as they showed him proper fealty. As Emperor. Of mankind.

The commander, quite entertained by all accounts, sent Hastur Sejanus to meet with the Emperor and deliver greeting.

Sejanus was the commander's favourite. Not as proud or irascible as Abaddon, nor as ruthless as Sedirae, nor even as solid and venerable as Iacton Qruze, Sejanus was the perfect captain, tempered evenly in all respects. A warrior and a diplomat in equal measure, Sejanus's martial record, second only to Abaddon's, was easily forgotten when in company with the man himself. A beautiful man, Loken would say, building his tale, a beautiful man adored by all. 'No finer figure in Mark IV plate than Hastur Sejanus. That he is remembered, and his deeds celebrated, even here amongst us, speaks of Sejanus's qualities. The noblest hero of the Great Crusade.' That was how Loken would describe him to the eager listeners. 'In future times, he will be recalled with such fondness that men will name their sons after him.'

Sejanus, with a squad of his finest warriors from the Fourth Company, travelled in-system in a gilded barge, and was received for audience by the Emperor at his palace on the third planet.

And killed.

Murdered. Hacked down on the onyx floor of the palace even as he stood before the Emperor's golden throne. Sejanus and his Glory Squad – Dymos, Malsandar, Gorthoi and the rest – all slaughtered by the Emperor's elite guard, the so-called Invisibles.

Apparently, Sejanus had not offered the correct fealty. Indelicately, he had suggested there might actually be *another* Emperor.

The commander's grief was absolute. He had loved Sejanus like a son. They had warred side by side to affect compliance on a hundred worlds. But the commander, always sanguine and wise in such matters, told his signal men to offer the Emperor another chance. The commander detested resorting to war, and always sought alternative paths away from violence, where such were workable. This was a mistake, he reasoned, a terrible, terrible mistake. Peace could be salvaged. This 'Emperor' could be made to understand.

It was about then, Loken liked to add, that a suggestion of quote marks began to appear around the 'Emperor's' name.

It was determined that a second embassy would be despatched. Maloghurst volunteered at once. The commander agreed, but ordered the speartip forwards into assault range. The intent was clear: one hand extended open, in peace, the other held ready as a fist. If the second embassy failed, or was similarly met with violence, then the fist would already be in position to strike. That sombre day, Loken said, the honour of the speartip had fallen, by the customary drawing of lots, to the strengths of Abaddon, Torgaddon, 'Little Horus' Aximand. And Loken himself.

At the order, battle musters began. The ships of the speartip slipped forward, running under obscurement. On board, Stormbirds were hauled onto their launch carriages. Weapons were issued and certified. Oaths of moment were sworn and witnessed. Armour was machined into place around the anointed bodies of the chosen.

In silence, tensed and ready to be unleashed, the speartip watched as the shuttle convoy bearing Maloghurst and his envoys arced down towards the third planet. Surface batteries smashed them out of the heavens. As the burning scads of debris from Maloghurst's flotilla billowed away into the atmosphere, the 'Emperor's' fleet elements rose up out of the oceans, out of the high cloud, out of the gravity wells of nearby moons. Six hundred warships, revealed and armed for war.

Abaddon broke obscurement and made a final, personal plea to the 'Emperor', beseeching him to see sense. The warships began to fire on Abaddon's speartip.

'My commander,' Abaddon relayed to the heart of the waiting fleet, 'there is no dealing here. This fool imposter will not listen.'

And the commander replied, 'Illuminate him, my son, but spare all you can. That order not withstanding, avenge the blood of my noble Sejanus. Decimate this "Emperor's" elite murderers, and bring the imposter to me.'

'And so,' Loken would sigh, 'we made war upon our brethren, so lost in ignorance.'

It was late evening, but the sky was saturated with light. The phototropic towers of the High City, built to turn and follow the sun with their windows during the day, shifted uneasily at the pulsating radiance in the heavens. Spectral shapes swam high in the upper atmosphere: ships engaging in a swirling mass, charting brief, nonsensical zodiacs with the beams of their battery weapons.

At ground level, around the wide, basalt platforms that formed the skirts of the palace, gunfire streamed through the air like horizontal rain, hosing coils of tracer fire that dipped and slithered heavily like snakes, die-straight zips of energy that vanished as fast as they appeared, and flurries of bolt shells like blizzarding hail. Downed Stormbirds, many of them crippled and burning, littered twenty square kilometres of the landscape.

Black, humanoid figures paced slowly in across the limits of the palace sprawl. They were shaped like armoured men, and they trudged like men, but they were giants, each one hundred and forty metres tall. The Mechanicum had deployed a half-dozen of its Titan war engines. Around the Titans' soot-black ankles, troops flooded forward in a breaking wave three kilometres wide.

The Luna Wolves surged like the surf of the wave, thousands of gleaming white figures bobbing and running forward across the skirt platforms, detonations bursting amongst them, lifting rippling fireballs and trees of dark brown smoke. Each blast juddered the ground with a gritty thump, and showered down dirt as an after-curse. Assault craft swept in over their heads, low, between the shambling frames of the wide-spaced Titans, fanning the slowly lifting smoke clouds into sudden, energetic vortices.

Every Astartes helmet was filled with vox-chatter: snapping voices, chopping back and forth, their tonal edges roughened by the transmission quality.

It was Loken's first taste of mass war since Ullanor. Tenth Company's first taste too. There had been skirmishes and scraps, but nothing testing. Loken was glad to see that his cohort hadn't grown rusty. The unapologetic regimen of live drills and punishing exercises he'd maintained had kept them whetted as sharp and serious as the terms of the oaths of moment they had taken just hours before.

Ullanor had been glorious; a hard, unstinting slog to dislodge and overthrow a bestial empire. The greenskin had been a pernicious and resilient foe, but they had broken his back and kicked over the embers of his revel fires. The commander had won the field through the employment of his favourite, practiced strategy: the speartip thrust to tear out the throat. Ignoring the greenskin masses, which had outnumbered the crusaders five to one, the commander had struck directly at the Overlord and his command coterie, leaving the enemy headless and without direction.

The same philosophy operated here. Tear out the throat and let the body spasm and die. Loken and his men, and the war engines that supported them, were the edge of the blade unsheathed for that purpose.

But this was not like Ullanor at all. No thickets of mud and clay-built ramparts, no ramshackle fortresses of bare metal and wire, no black powder air bursts or howling ogre-foes. This was not a barbaric brawl determined by blades and upper body strength.

This was modern warfare in a civilised place. This was man against man, inside the monolithic precincts of a cultured people. The enemy possessed ordnance and firearms every bit the technological match of the Legion forces, and the skill and training to use them. Through the green imaging of his visor, Loken saw armoured men with energy weapons ranged against them in the lower courses of the palace. He saw tracked weapon carriages, automated artillery; nests of four or even eight automatic cannons shackled together on cart platforms that lumbered forward on hydraulic legs.

Not like Ullanor at all. That had been an ordeal. This would be a test. Equal against equal. Like against like.

Except that for all its martial technologies, the enemy lacked one essential quality, and that quality was locked within each and every case of Mark IV power armour: the genetically enhanced flesh and blood of the Imperial Astartes. Modified, refined, post-human, the Astartes were superior to anything they had met or would ever meet. No fighting force in the galaxy could ever hope to match the Legions, unless the stars went out, and madness ruled, and lawful sense turned upside down. For, as Sedirae had once said, 'The only thing that can beat an Astartes is another Astartes', and they had all laughed at that. The impossible was nothing to be scared of.

The enemy – their armour a polished magenta trimmed in silver, as Loken later discovered when he viewed them with his helmet off – firmly held the induction gates into the inner palace. They were big men, tall, thick through the chest and shoulders, and at the peak of fitness. Not one of them, not even the tallest, came up to the chin of one of the Luna Wolves. It was like fighting children.

Well-armed children, it had to be said.

Through the billowing smoke and the jarring detonations, Loken led the veteran First Squad up the steps at a run, the plasteel soles of their boots grating on the stone: First Squad, Tenth Company, Hellebore Tactical Squad, gleaming giants in pearl-white armour, the wolf head insignia stark black on their auto-responsive shoulder plates. Crossfire zigzagged around them from the defended gates ahead. The night air shimmered with the heat distortion of weapons discharge. Some kind of upright, automated mortar was casting a sluggish, flaccid stream of fat munition charges over their heads.

'Kill it!' Loken heard Brother-Sergeant Jubal instruct over the link. Jubal's order was given in the curt argot of Cthonia, their derivation world, a language that the Luna Wolves had preserved as their battle-tongue.

The battle-brother carrying the squad's plasma cannon obeyed without hesitation. For a dazzling half-second, a twenty-metre ribbon of light linked the muzzle of his weapon to the auto-mortar, and then the device engulfed the facade of the palace in a roasting wash of yellow flame.

Dozens of enemy soldiers were cast down by the blast. Several were thrown up into the air, landing crumpled and boneless on the flight of steps.

'Into them!' Jubal barked.

Wildfire chipped and pattered off their armour. Loken felt the distant sting of it. Brother Calends stumbled and fell, but righted himself again, almost at once.

Loken saw the enemy scatter away from their charge. He

swung his bolter up. His weapon had a gash in the metal of the foregrip, the legacy of a greenskin's axe during Ullanor, a cosmetic mark Loken had told the armourers not to finish out. He began to fire, not on burst, but on single shot, feeling the weapon buck and kick against his palms. Bolter rounds were explosive penetrators. The men he hit popped like blisters, or shredded like bursting fruit. Pink mist fumed off every ruptured figure as it fell.

'Tenth Company!' Loken shouted. 'For the Warmaster!'

The war cry was still unfamiliar, just another aspect of the newness. It was the first time Loken had declaimed it in war, the first chance he'd had since the honour had been bestowed by the Emperor after Ullanor.

By the Emperor. The true Emperor.

'Lupercal! Lupercal!' the Wolves yelled back as they streamed in, choosing to answer with the old cry, the Legion's pet-name for their beloved commander. The warhorns of the Titans boomed.

They stormed the palace. Loken paused by one of the induction gates, urging his front-runners in, carefully reviewing the advance of his company main force. Hellish fire continued to rake them from the upper balconies and towers. In the far distance, a brilliant dome of light suddenly lifted into the sky, astonishingly bright and vivid. Loken's visor automatically dimmed. The ground trembled and a noise like a thunderclap reached him. A capital ship of some size, stricken and ablaze, had fallen out of the sky and impacted in the outskirts of the High City. Drawn by the flash, the phototropic towers above him fidgeted and rotated.

Reports flooded in. Aximand's force, Fifth Company, had secured the Regency and the pavilions on the ornamental lakes to the west of the High City. Torgaddon's men were driving up through the lower town, slaying the armour sent to block them.

Loken looked east. Three kilometres away, across the flat plain of the basalt platforms, across the tide of charging men and striding Titans and stitching fire, Abaddon's company, First Company, was crossing the bulwarks into the far flank of the palace. Loken magnified his view, resolving hundreds of white-armoured figures pouring through the smoke and chop-fire. At the front of them, the dark figures of First Company's foremost Terminator squad, the Justaerin. They wore polished black armour, dark as night, as if they belonged to some other Legion.

'Loken to First,' he sent. 'Tenth has entry.'

There was a pause, a brief distort, then Abaddon's voice

answered. 'Loken, Loken… are you trying to shame me with your diligence?'

'Not for a moment, First Captain,' Loken replied. There was a strict hierarchy of respect within the Legion, and though he was a senior officer, Loken regarded the peerless First Captain with awe. All of the Mournival, in fact, though Torgaddon had always favoured Loken with genuine shows of friendship.

Now Sejanus was gone, Loken thought. The aspect of the Mournival would soon change.

'I'm playing with you, Loken,' Abaddon sent, his voice so deep that some vowel sounds were blurred by the vox. 'I'll meet you at the feet of this false Emperor. First one there gets to illuminate him.'

Loken fought back a smile. Ezekyle Abaddon had seldom sported with him before. He felt blessed, elevated. To be a chosen man was enough, but to be in with the favoured elite, that was every captain's dream.

Reloading, Loken entered the palace through the induction gate, stepping over the tangled corpses of the enemy dead. The plaster facings of the inner walls had been cracked and blown down, and loose crumbs, like dry sand, crunched under his feet. The air was full of smoke, and his visor display kept jumping from one register to another as it attempted to compensate and get a clean reading.

He moved down the inner hall, hearing the echo of gunfire from deeper in the palace compound. The body of a brother lay slumped in a doorway to his left, the large, white-armoured corpse odd and out of place amongst the smaller enemy bodies. Marjex, one of the Legion's Apothecaries, was bending over him. He glanced up as Loken approached, and shook his head.

'Who is it?' Loken asked.

'Tibor, of Second Squad,' Marjex replied. Loken frowned as he saw the devastating head wound that had stopped Tibor.

'The Emperor knows his name,' Loken said.

Marjex nodded, and reached into his narthecium to get the reductor tool. He was about to remove Tibor's precious gene-seed, so that it might be returned to the Legion banks.

Loken left the Apothecary to his work, and pushed on down the hall. In a wide colonnade ahead, the towering walls were decorated with frescoes, showing familiar scenes of a haloed Emperor upon a golden throne. How blind these people are, Loken thought, how sad this is. One day, one single day with the iterators, and they would understand. We are not the enemy. We are the same, and we bring with us a glorious message of redemption. Old Night is done. Man walks the stars again, and the might of the Astartes walks at his side to keep him safe.

In a broad, sloping tunnel of etched silver, Loken caught up with elements of Third Squad. Of all the units in his company, Third Squad – Locasta Tactical Squad – was his favourite and his favoured. Its commander, Brother-Sergeant Nero Vipus, was his oldest and truest friend.

'How's your humour, captain?' Vipus asked. His pearl-white plate was smudged with soot and streaked with blood.

'Phlegmatic, Nero. You?'

'Choleric. Red-raged, in fact. I've just lost a man, and two more of mine are injured. There's something covering the junction ahead. Something heavy. Rate of fire like you wouldn't believe.'

'Tried fragging it?'

'Two or three grenades. No effect. And there's nothing to see. Garvi, we've all heard about these so-called Invisibles. The ones that butchered Sejanus. I was wondering–'

'Leave the wondering to me,' Loken said. 'Who's down?'

Vipus shrugged. He was a little taller than Loken, and his shrug made the heavy ribbing and plates of his armour clunk together. 'Zakias.'

'Zakias? No…'

'Torn into shreds before my very eyes. Oh, I feel the hand of the ship on me, Garvi.'

The hand of the ship. An old saying. The commander's flagship was called the *Vengeful Spirit*, and in times of duress or loss, the Wolves liked to draw upon all that implied as a charm, a totem of retribution.

'In Zakias's name,' Vipus growled, 'I'll find this bastard Invisible and–'

'Sooth your choler, brother. I've no use for it,' Loken said. 'See to your wounded while I take a look.'

Vipus nodded and redirected his men. Loken pushed up past them to the disputed junction.

It was a vault-roofed crossways where four hallways met. The area read cold and still to his imaging. Fading smoke wisped up into the rafters. The ouslite floor had been chewed and peppered with thousands of impact craters. Brother Zakias, his body as yet unretrieved, lay in pieces at the centre of the crossway, a steaming pile of shattered white plasteel and bloody meat.

Vipus had been right. There was no sign of an enemy present. No heat-trace, not even a flicker of movement. But studying the area, Loken saw a heap of empty shell cases, glittering brass, that had spilled out from behind a bulkhead across from him. Was that where the killer was hiding?

Loken bent down and picked up a chunk of fallen plaster-work. He lobbed it into the open. There was a click, and then a hammering deluge of autofire raked across the junction. It lasted five seconds, and in that time over a thousand rounds were expended. Loken saw the fuming shell cases spitting out from behind the bulkhead as they were ejected.

The firing stopped. Fycelene vapour fogged the junction. The gunfire had scored a mottled gouge across the stone floor, pum-melling Zakias's corpse in the process. Spots of blood and scraps of tissue had been spattered out.

Loken waited. He heard a whine and the metallic clunk of an autoloader system. He read weapon heat, fading, but no body warmth.

'Won a medal yet?' Vipus asked, approaching.

'It's just an automatic sentry gun,' Loken replied.

'Well, that's a small relief at least,' Vipus said. 'After the gre-nades we've pitched in that direction, I was beginning to wonder if these vaunted Invisibles might be "Invulnerables" too. I'll call up Devastator support to–'

'Just give me a light flare,' Loken said.

Vipus stripped one off his leg plate and handed it to his cap-tain. Loken ignited it with a twist of his hand, and threw it down the hallway opposite. It bounced, fizzling, glaring white hot, past the hidden killer.

There was a grind of servos. The implacable gunfire began to roar down the corridor at the flare, kicking it and bouncing it, ripping into the floor.

'Garvi–' Vipus began.

Loken was running. He crossed the junction, thumped his back against the bulkhead. The gun was still blazing. He wheeled round the bulkhead and saw the sentry gun, built into an alcove. A squat machine, set on four pad feet and heavily plated, it had turned its short, fat, pumping cannons away from him to fire on the distant, flickering flare.

Loken reached over and tore out a handful of its servo flexes. The guns stuttered and died.

'We're clear!' Loken called out. Locasta moved up.

'That's generally called showing off,' Vipus remarked.

Loken led Locasta up the corridor, and they entered a fine state apartment. Other apartment chambers, similarly regal, beckoned beyond. It was oddly still and quiet.

'Which way now?' Vipus asked.

'We go find this "Emperor",' Loken said.

Vipus snorted. 'Just like that?'

'The First Captain bet me I couldn't reach him first.'

'The First Captain, eh? Since when was Garviel Loken on pally terms with him?'

'Since Tenth breached the palace ahead of First. Don't worry, Nero, I'll remember you little people when I'm famous.'

Nero Vipus laughed, the sound snuffling out of his helmet mask like the cough of a consumptive bull.

What happened next didn't make either of them laugh at all.

TWO

Meeting the Invisibles
At the foot of a Golden Throne
Lupercal

'Captain Loken?'

He looked up from his work. 'That's me.'

'Forgive me for interrupting,' she said. 'You're busy.'

Loken set aside the segment of armour he had been polishing and rose to his feet. He was almost a metre taller than her, and naked but for a loin cloth. She sighed inwardly at the splendour of his physique. The knotted muscles, the old ridge-scars. He was handsome too, this one, fair hair almost silver, cut short, his pale skin slightly freckled, his eyes grey like rain. What a waste, she thought.

Though there was no disguising his inhumanity, especially in this bared form. Apart from the sheer mass of him, there was the overgrown gigantism of the face, that particular characteristic of the Astartes, almost equine, plus the hard, taut shell of his rib-less torso, like stretched canvas.

'I don't know who you are,' he said, dropping a nub of polishing fibre into a little pot, and wiping his fingers.

She held out her hand. 'Mersadie Oliton, official remembrancer,' she said. He looked at her tiny hand and then shook it, making it seem even more tiny in comparison with his own giant fist.

'I'm sorry,' she said, laughing, 'I keep forgetting you don't do that out here. Shaking hands, I mean. Such a parochial, Terran custom.'

'I don't mind it. Have you come from Terra?'

'I left there a year ago, despatched to the crusade by permit of the Council.'

'You're a remembrancer?'

'You know what that means?'

'I'm not stupid,' Loken said.

'Of course not,' she said, hurriedly. 'I meant no offence.'

'None taken.' He eyed her. Small and frail, though possibly beautiful. Loken had very little experience of women. Perhaps they were all frail and beautiful. He knew enough to know that few were as black as her. Her skin was like burnished coal. He wondered if it were some kind of dye.

He wondered too about her skull. Her head was bald, but not shaved. It seemed polished and smooth as if it had never known hair. The cranium was enhanced somehow, extending back in a streamlined sweep that formed a broad ovoid behind her nape. It was like she had been crowned, as if her simple humanity had been made more regal.

'How can I help you?' he asked.

'I understand you have a story, a particularly entertaining one. I'd like to remember it, for posterity.'

'Which story?'

'Horus killing the Emperor.'

He stiffened. He didn't like it when non-Astartes humans called the Warmaster by his true name.

'That happened months ago,' he said dismissively. 'I'm sure I won't remember the details particularly well.'

'Actually,' she said, 'I have it on good authority you can be persuaded to tell the tale quite expertly. I've been told it's very popular amongst your battle-brothers.'

Loken frowned. Annoyingly, the woman was correct. Since the taking of the High City, he'd been required – forced would not be too strong a word – to retell his first-hand account of the events in the palace tower on dozens of occasions. He presumed it was because of Sejanus's death. The Luna Wolves needed catharsis. They needed to hear how Sejanus had been so singularly avenged.

'Someone put you up to this, Mistress Oliton?' he asked.

She shrugged. 'Captain Torgaddon, actually.'

Loken nodded. It was usually him. 'What do you want to know?'

'I understand the general situation, for I have heard it from others, but I'd love to have your personal observations. What was it like? When you got inside the palace itself, what did you find?'

Loken sighed, and looked round at the rack where his power armour was displayed. He'd only just started cleaning it. His private arming chamber was a small, shadowy vault adjoining the off-limits embarkation deck, the metal walls lacquered pale green. A cluster of glow-globes lit the room, and an Imperial eagle had been stencilled on one wall plate, beneath which copies of Loken's various oaths of moment had been pinned. The close air smelled of oils and lapping powder. It was a tranquil, introspective place, and she had invaded that tranquility.

Becoming aware of her trespass, she suggested, 'I could come back later, at a better time.'

'No, now's fine.' He sat back down on the metal stool where he had been perching when she'd entered. 'Let me see... When we got inside the palace, what we found was the Invisibles.'

'Why were they called that?' she asked.

'Because we couldn't see them,' he replied.

The Invisibles were waiting for them, and they well deserved their sobriquet.

Just ten paces into the splendid apartments, the first brother died. There was an odd, hard bang, so hard it was painful to feel and hear, and Brother Edrius fell to his knees, then folded onto his side. He had been struck in the face by some form of energy weapon. The white plasteel/ceramite alloy of his visor and breastplate had actually deformed into a rippled crater, like heated wax that had flowed and then set again. A second bang, a quick concussive vibration of air, obliterated an ornamental table beside Nero Vipus. A third bang dropped Brother Muriad, his left leg shattered and snapped off like a reed stalk.

The science adepts of the false Imperium had mastered and harnessed some rare and wonderful form of field technology, and armed their elite guard with it. They cloaked their bodies with a passive application, twisting light to render themselves invisible. And they were able to project it in a merciless, active form that struck with mutilating force.

Despite the fact that they had been advancing combat-ready and wary, Loken and the others were taken completely off guard. The Invisibles were even hidden to their visor arrays. Several had simply been standing in the chamber, waiting to strike.

Loken began to fire, and Vipus's men did likewise. Raking the area ahead of him, splintering furniture, Loken hit something. He saw pink mist kiss the air, and something fell down with enough force to overturn a chair. Vipus scored a hit too, but not before Brother Tarregus had been struck with such power that his head was punched clean off his shoulders.

The cloak technology evidently hid its users best if they remained still. As they moved, they became semi-visible, heat-haze suggestions of men surging to attack. Loken adapted quickly, firing at each blemish of air. He adjusted his visor gain to full contrast, almost black and white, and saw them better: hard outlines against the fuzzy background. He killed three more. In death, several lost their cloaks. Loken saw the Invisibles revealed as bloody corpses. Their armour was silver, ornately composed and machined with a remarkable detail of patterning and symbols. Tall, swathed in mantles of red silk, the Invisibles reminded Loken of the mighty Custodian Guard that warded the Imperial Palace on Terra. This was the bodyguard corps which had executed Sejanus and his glory squad at a mere nod from their master.

Nero Vipus was raging, offended by the cost to his squad. The hand of the ship was truly upon him.

He led the way, cutting a path into a towering room beyond the scene of the ambush. His fury gave Locasta the opening it needed, but it cost him his right hand, crushed by an Invisible's blast. Loken felt choler too. Like Nero, the men of Locasta were his friends. Rituals of mourning awaited him. Even in the darkness of Ullanor, victory had not been so dearly bought.

Charging past Vipus, who was down on his knees, groaning in pain as he tried to pluck the mangled gauntlet off his ruined hand, Loken entered a side chamber, shooting at the air blemishes that attempted to block him. A jolt of force tore his bolter from his hands, so he reached over his hip and drew his chainsword from its scabbard. It whined as it kicked into life. He hacked at the faint outlines jostling around him and felt the toothed blade meet resistance. There was a shrill scream. Gore drizzled out of nowhere and plastered the chamber walls and the front of Loken's suit.

'Lupercal!' he grunted, and put the full force of both arms behind his strokes. Servos and mimetic polymers, layered between his skin and his suit's outer plating to form the musculature of his power armour, bunched and flexed. He landed a trio of two-handed blows. More blood showered into view. There was a warbled shriek as loops of pink, wet viscera suddenly became visible. A moment later, the field screening the soldier flickered and failed, and revealed his disembowelled form, stumbling away down the length of the chamber, trying to hold his guts in with both hands.

Invisible force stabbed at Loken again, scrunching the edge of his left shoulder guard and almost knocking him off his feet. He rounded and swung the chainsword. The blade struck something, and shards of metal flew out. The shape of a human figure, just out of joint with the space it occupied, as if it had been cut out of the air and nudged slightly to the left, suddenly filled in. One of the Invisibles, his charged field sparking and crackling around him as it died, became visible and swung his long, bladed lance at Loken.

The blade rebounded off Loken's helm. Loken struck low with his chainsword, ripping the lance out of the Invisible's silver gauntlets and buckling its haft. At the same time, Loken lunged, shoulder barging the warrior against the chamber wall so hard that the friable plaster of the ancient frescoes crackled and fell out.

Loken stepped back. Winded, his lungs and ribcage almost crushed flat, the Invisible made a gagging, sucking noise and fell down on his knees, his head lolling forward. Loken sawed his chainsword down and sharply up again in one fluid, practiced mercy stroke, and the Invisible's detached head bounced away.

Loken circled slowly, the humming blade raised ready in his right hand. The chamber floor was slick with blood and black scraps of meat. Shots rang out from nearby rooms. Loken walked across the chamber and retrieved his bolter, hoisting it in his left fist with a clatter.

Two Luna Wolves entered the chamber behind him, and Loken briskly pointed them off into the left-hand colonnade with a gesture of his sword.

'Form up and advance,' he snapped into his link. Voices answered him.

'Nero?'

'I'm behind you, twenty metres.'

'How's the hand?'

'I left it behind. It was getting in the way.'

Loken prowled forward. At the end of the chamber, past the crumpled, leaking body of the Invisible he had disembowelled, sixteen broad marble steps led up to a stone doorway. The splendid stone frame was carved with complex linenfold motifs.

Loken ascended the steps slowly. Mottled washes of light cast spastic flickers through the open doorway. There was a remarkable stillness. Even the din of the fight engulfing the palace all around seemed to recede. Loken could hear the tiny taps made by the blood dripping off his outstretched chainsword onto the steps, a trail of red beads up the white marble.

He stepped through the doorway.

The inner walls of the tower rose up around him. He had evidently stepped through into one of the tallest and most massive of the palace's spires. A hundred metres in diameter, a kilometre tall.

No, more than that. He'd come out on a wide, onyx platform that encircled the tower, one of several ring platforms arranged at intervals up the height of the structure, but there were more below. Peering over, Loken saw as much tower drop away into the depths of the earth as stood proud above him.

He circled slowly, gazing around. Great windows of glass or some other transparent substance glazed the tower from top to bottom between the ring platforms, and through them the light and fury of the war outside flared and flashed. No noise, just the flickering glow, the sudden bursts of radiance.

He followed the platform round until he found a sweep of curved stairs, flush with the tower wall, that led up to the next level. He began to ascend, platform to platform, scanning for any blurs of light that might betray the presence of more Invisibles.

Nothing. No sound, no life, no movement except the shimmer of light from outside the windows as he passed them. Five floors now, six.

Loken suddenly felt foolish. The tower was probably empty. This search and purge should have been left to others while he marshalled Tenth Company's main force.

Except... its ground-level approach had been so furiously protected. He looked up, pushing his sensors hard. A third of a kilometre above him, he fancied he caught a brief sign of movement, a partial heat-lock.

'Nero?'

A pause. 'Captain.'

'Where are you?'

'Base of a tower. Heavy fighting. We–' There was a jumble of noises, the distorted sounds of gunfire and shouting. 'Captain? Are you still there?'

'Report!'

'Heavy resistance. We're locked here! Where are–'

The link broke. Loken hadn't been about to give away his position anyway. There was something in this tower with him. At the very top, something was waiting.

The penultimate deck. From above came a soft creaking and grinding, like the sails of a giant windmill. Loken paused. At this height, through the wide panes of glass, he was afforded a view out across the palace and the High City. A sea of luminous smoke, underlit by widespread firestorms. Some buildings glowed pink, reflecting the light of the inferno. Weapons flashed, and energy beams danced and jumped in the dark. Overhead, the sky was full of fire too, a mirror of the ground. The speartip had visited murderous destruction upon the city of the 'Emperor'.

But had it found the throat?

He mounted the last flight of steps, his grip on the weapons tight.

The uppermost ring platform formed the base of the tower's top section, a vast cupola of crystal-glass petals, ribbed together with steel spars that curved up to form a finial mast at the apex high above. The entire structure creaked and slid, turning slightly one way then another as it responded phototropically to the blooms of light outside in the night. On one side of the platform, its back to the great windows, sat a golden throne. It was a massive object, a heavy plinth of three golden steps rising to a vast gilt chair with a high back and coiled arm rests.

The throne was empty.

Loken lowered his weapons. He saw that the tower top turned so that the throne was always facing the light. Disappointed, Loken took a step towards the throne, and then halted when he realised he wasn't alone after all.

A solitary figure stood away to his left, hands clasped behind its back, staring out at the spectacle of war.

The figure turned. It was an elderly man, dressed in a floor-length mauve robe. His hair was thin and white, his face thinner still. He stared at Loken with glittering, miserable eyes.

'I defy you,' he said, his accent thick and antique. 'I defy you, invader.'

'Your defiance is noted,' Loken replied, 'but this fight is over. I can see you've been watching its progress from up here. You must know that.'

'The Imperium of Man will triumph over all its enemies,' the man replied.

'Yes,' said Loken. 'Absolutely, it will. You have my promise.'

The man faltered, as if he did not quite understand.

'Am I addressing the so-called "Emperor"?' Loken asked. He had switched off and sheathed his sword, but he kept his bolter up to cover the robed figure.

'So-called?' the man echoed. 'So-called? You cheerfully blaspheme in this royal place. The Emperor is the Emperor Undisputed, saviour and protector of the race of man. You are some imposter, some evil daemon–'

'I am a man like you.'

The other scoffed. 'You are an imposter. Made like a giant, malformed and ugly. No man would wage war upon his fellow man like this.' He gestured disparagingly at the scene outside.

'Your hostility started this,' Loken said calmly. 'You would not listen to us or believe us. You murdered our ambassadors. You brought this upon yourself. We are charged with the reunification of mankind, throughout the stars, in the name of the Emperor. We seek to establish compliance amongst all the fragmentary and disparate strands. Most greet us like the lost brothers we are. You resisted.'

'You came to us with lies!'

'We came with the truth.'

'Your truth is obscenity!'

'Sir, the truth itself is amoral. It saddens me that we believe the same words, the very same ones, but value them so differently. That difference has led directly to this bloodshed.'

The elderly man sagged, deflated. 'You could have left us alone.'

'What?' Loken asked.

'If our philosophies are so much at odds, you could have passed us by and left us to our lives, unviolated. Yet you did not. Why? Why did you insist on bringing us to ruin? Are we such a threat to you?'

'Because the truth–' Loken began.

'–is amoral. So you said, but in serving your fine truth, invader, you make yourself immoral.'

Loken was surprised to find he didn't know quite how to answer. He took a step forward and said, 'I request you surrender to me, sir.'

'You are the commander, I take it?' the elderly man asked.

'I command Tenth Company.'

'You are not the overall commander, then? I assumed you were, as you entered this place ahead of your troops. I was waiting for the overall commander. I will submit to him, and to him alone.'

'The terms of your surrender are not negotiable.'

'Will you not even do that for me? Will you not even do me that honour? I would stay here, until your lord and master comes in person to accept my submission. Fetch him.'

Before Loken could reply, a dull wail echoed up into the tower top, gradually increasing in volume. The elderly man took a step or two backwards, fear upon his face.

The black figures rose up out of the tower's depths, ascending

slowly, vertically, up through the open centre of the ring platform. Ten Astartes warriors, the blue heat of their whining jump
pack burners shimmering the air behind them. Their power
armour was black, trimmed with white. Catulan Reaver Squad,
First Company's veteran assault pack. First in, last out.

One by one, they came in to land on the edge of the ring
platform, deactivating their jump packs.

Kalus Ekaddon, Catulan's captain, glanced sidelong at Loken.

'The First Captain's compliments, Captain Loken. You beat
us to it after all.'

'Where is the First Captain?' Loken asked.

'Below, mopping up,' Ekaddon replied. He set his vox to
transmit. 'This is Ekaddon, Catulan. We have secured the false
emperor–'

'No,' said Loken firmly.

Ekaddon looked at him again. His visor lenses were stern and
unreflective jet glass set in the black metal of his helmet mask.
He bowed slightly. 'My apologies, captain,' he said, archly. 'The
prisoner and the honour are yours, of course.'

'That's not what I meant,' Loken replied. 'This man demands
the right to surrender in person to our commander-in-chief.'

Ekaddon snorted, and several of his men laughed. 'This bastard can demand all he likes, captain,' Ekaddon said, 'but he's
going to be cruelly disappointed.'

'We are dismantling an ancient empire, Captain Ekaddon,'
Loken said firmly. 'Might we not display some measure of
gracious respect in the execution of that act? Or are we just
barbarians?'

'He murdered Sejanus!' spat one of Ekaddon's men.

'He did,' Loken agreed. 'So should we just murder him in
response? Didn't the Emperor, praise be his name, teach us
always to be magnanimous in victory?'

'The Emperor, praise be his name, is not with us,' Ekaddon
replied.

'If he's not with us in spirit, captain,' Loken replied, 'then I
pity the future of this crusade.'

Ekaddon stared at Loken for a moment, then ordered his
second to transmit a signal to the fleet. Loken was quite sure
Ekaddon had not backed down because he'd been convinced
by any argument or fine principle. Though Ekaddon, as Captain of First Company's assault elite, had glory and favour on
his side, Loken, a company captain, had superiority of rank.

'A signal has been sent to the Warmaster,' Loken told the
elderly man.

'Is he coming here? Now?' the man asked eagerly.

'Arrangements will be made for you to meet him,' Ekaddon snapped.

They waited for a minute or two for a signal response. Astartes attack ships, their engines glowing, streaked past the windows. The light from huge detonations sheeted the southern skies and slowly died away. Loken watched the criss-cross shadows play across the ring platform in the dying light.

He started. He suddenly realised why the elderly man had insisted so furiously that the commander should come in person to this place. He clamped his bolter to his side and began to stride towards the empty throne.

'What are you doing?' the elderly man asked.

'Where is he?' Loken cried. 'Where is he really? Is he invisible too?'

'Get back!' the elderly man cried out, leaping forward to grapple with Loken.

There was a loud bang. The elderly man's ribcage blew out, spattering blood, tufts of burned silk and shreds of meat in all directions. He swayed, his robes shredded and on fire, and pitched over the edge of the platform.

Limbs limp, his torn garments flapping, he fell away like a stone down the open drop of the palace tower.

Ekaddon lowered his bolt pistol. 'I've never killed an emperor before,' he laughed.

'That wasn't the Emperor,' Loken yelled. 'You moron! The Emperor's been here all the time.' He was close to the empty throne now, reaching out a hand to grab at one of the golden armrests. A blemish of light, almost perfect, but not so perfect that shadows behaved correctly around it, recoiled in the seat.

This is a trap. Those four words were the next that Loken was going to utter. He never got the chance.

The golden throne trembled and broadcast a shockwave of invisible force. It was a power like that which the elite guard had wielded, but a hundred times more potent. It slammed out in all directions, casting Loken and all the Catulan off their feet like corn sheaves in a hurricane. The windows of the tower top shattered outwards in a multicoloured blizzard of glass fragments.

Most of Catulan Reaver Squad simply vanished, blown out of the tower, arms flailing, on the bow-wave of energy. One struck a steel spar on his way out. Back snapped, his body tumbled away into the night like a broken doll. Ekaddon managed to grab hold of another spar as he was launched backwards. He clung on, plasteel digits sinking into the metal for purchase, legs trailing out behind him horizontally as air and glass and gravitic energy assaulted him.

Loken, too close to the foot of the throne to be caught by the full force of the shockwave, was knocked flat. He slid across the ring platform towards the open fall, his white armour shrieking as it left deep grooves in the onyx surface. He went over the edge, over the sheer drop, but the wall of force carried him on like a leaf across the hole and slammed him hard against the far lip of the ring. He grabbed on, his arms over the lip, his legs dangling, held in place as much by the shock pressure as by the strength of his own, desperate arms.

Almost blacking out from the relentless force, he fought to hold on.

Inchoate light, green and dazzling, sputtered into being on the platform in front of his clawing hands. The teleport flare became too bright to behold, and then died, revealing a god standing on the edge of the platform.

The god was a true giant, as large again to any Astartes warrior as an Astartes was to a normal man. His armour was white gold, like the sunlight at dawn, the work of master artificers. Many symbols covered its surfaces, the chief of which was the motif of a single, staring eye fashioned across the breastplate. Robes of white cloth fluttered out behind the terrible, haloed figure.

Above the breastplate, the face was bare, grimacing, perfect in every dimension and detail, suffused in radiance. So beautiful. So very beautiful.

For a moment, the god stood there, unflinching, beset by the gale of force, but unmoving, facing it down. Then he raised the storm bolter in his right hand and fired into the tumult.

One shot.

The echo of the detonation rolled around the tower. There was a choking scream, half lost in the uproar, and then the uproar itself stilled abruptly.

The wall of force died away. The hurricane faded. Splinters of glass tinkled as they rained back down onto the platform.

No longer impelled, Ekaddon crashed back down against the blown-out sill of the window frame. His grip was secure. He clawed his way back inside and got to his feet.

'My lord!' he exclaimed, and dropped to one knee, his head bowed.

With the pressure lapsed, Loken found he could no longer support himself. Hands grappling, he began to slide back over the lip where he had been hanging. He couldn't get any purchase on the gleaming onyx.

He slipped off the edge. A strong hand grabbed him around the wrist and hauled him up onto the platform.

Loken rolled over, shaking. He looked back across the ring at the golden throne. It was a smoking ruin, its secret mechanisms exploded from within. Amidst the twisted, ruptured plates and broken workings, a smouldering corpse sat upright, teeth grinning from a blackened skull, charred, skeletal arms still braced along the throne's coiled rests.

'So will I deal with all tyrants and deceivers,' rumbled a deep voice.

Loken looked up at the god standing over him. 'Lupercal...' he murmured.

The god smiled. 'Not so formal, please, captain,' whispered Horus.

'May I ask you a question?' Mersadie Oliton said.

Loken had taken a robe down from a wall peg and was putting it on. 'Of course.'

'Could we not have just left them alone?'

'No. Ask a better question.'

'Very well. What is he like?'

'What is who like, lady?' he asked.

'Horus.'

'If you have to ask, you've not met him,' he said.

'No, I haven't yet, captain. I've been waiting for an audience. Still, I would like to know what you think of Horus–'

'I think he is Warmaster,' Loken said. His tone was stone hard. 'I think he is the master of the Luna Wolves and the chosen proxy of the Emperor, praise be his name, in all our undertakings. He is the first and foremost of all primarchs. And I think I take offence when a mortal voices his name without respect or title.'

'Oh!' she said. 'I'm sorry, captain, I meant no–'

'I'm sure you didn't, but he is *Warmaster* Horus. You're a remembrancer. Remember that.'

THREE

Replevin
Amongst the remembrancers
Raised to the four

Three months after the battle for the High City, the first of the remembrancers had joined the expedition fleet, brought directly from Terra by mass conveyance. Various chroniclers and recorders had, of course, been accompanying Imperial forces since the commencement of the Great Crusade, two hundred sidereal years earlier. But they had been individuals, mostly volunteers or accidental witnesses, gathered up like road dust on the advancing wheels of the crusader hosts, and the records they had made had been piecemeal and irregular. They had commemorated events by happenstance, sometimes inspired by their own artistic appetites, sometimes encouraged by the patronage of a particular primarch or lord commander, who thought it fit to have his deeds immortalised in verse or text or image or composition.

Returning to Terra after the victory of Ullanor, the Emperor had decided it was time a more formal and authoritative celebration of mankind's reunification be undertaken. The fledgling Council of Terra evidently agreed wholeheartedly, for the bill inaugurating the foundation and sponsorship of the remembrancer order had been countersigned by no less a person than Malcador the Sigillite, First Lord of the Council. Recruited from all levels of Terran society – and from the societies of other key Imperial worlds – simply on the merit of their creative gifts, the remembrancers were quickly accredited and assigned, and despatched to join all the key expedition fleets active in the expanding Imperium.

At that time, according to War Council logs, there were four thousand two hundred and eighty-seven primary expedition fleets engaged upon the business of the crusade, as well as sixty thousand odd secondary deployment groups involved in compliance or occupation endeavours, with a further three hundred and seventy-two primary expeditions in regroup and refit, or resupplying as they awaited new tasking orders. Almost four point three million remembrancers were sent abroad in the first months following the ratification of the bill. 'Arm the bastards,' Primarch Russ had been reported as saying, 'and they might win a few bloody worlds for us in between verses.'

Russ's sour attitude reflected well the demeanor of the martial class. From primarch down to common army soldier, there was a general unease about the Emperor's decision to quit the crusade campaign and retire to the solitude of his palace on Terra. No one had questioned the choice of First Primarch Horus as Warmaster to act in his stead. They simply questioned the need for a proxy at all.

The formation of the Council of Terra had come as more unpleasant news. Since the inception of the Great Crusade, the War Council, formed principally of the Emperor and the primarchs, had been the epicentre of Imperial authority. Now, this new body supplanted it, taking up the reins of Imperial governance, a body composed of civilians instead of warriors. The War Council, left under Horus's leadership, effectively became relegated to a satellite status, its responsibilities focused on the campaign and the campaign alone.

For no crime of their own, the remembrancers, most of them eager and excited at the prospect of the work ahead, found themselves the focus of that discontent everywhere they went. They were not welcomed, and they found their commission hard to fulfil. Only later, when the eaxector tributi administrators began to visit expedition fleets, did the discontent find a better, truer target to exercise itself upon.

So, three months after the battle of the High City, the remembrancers arrived to a cold welcome. None of them had known what to expect. Most had never been off-world before. They were virgin and innocent, over-eager and gauche. It didn't take long for them to become hardened and cynical at their reception.

When they arrived, the fleet of the 63rd Expedition still encircled the capital world. The process of replevin had begun, as the Imperial forces sectioned the 'Imperium', dismantled its mechanisms, and bestowed its various properties upon the Imperial commanders chosen to oversee its dispersal.

Aid ships were flocking down from the fleet to the surface, and hosts of the Imperial Army had been deployed to effect police actions. Central resistance had collapsed almost overnight following the 'Emperor's' death, but fighting continued to spasm amongst some of the western cities, as well as on three of the other worlds in the system. Lord Commander Varvaras, an honourable, 'old school' veteran, was the commander of the army forces attached to the expedition fleet, and not for the first time he found himself organising an effort to pick up the pieces behind an Astartes speartip. 'A body often twitches as it dies,' he remarked philosophically to the Master of the Fleet. 'We're just making sure it's dead.'

The Warmaster had agreed to a state funeral for the 'Emperor'. He declared it only right and proper, and sympathetic to the desires of a people they wished to bring to compliance rather than crush wholesale. Voices were raised in objection, particularly as the ceremonial interment of Hastur Sejanus had only just taken place, along with the formal burials of the battle-brothers lost at the High City. Several Legion officers, including Abaddon himself, refused point blank to allow his forces to attend any funeral rites for the killer of Sejanus. The Warmaster understood this, but fortunately there were other Astartes amongst the expedition who could take their place.

Primarch Dorn, escorted by two companies of his Imperial Fists, the VII Legion, had been travelling with the 63rd Expedition for eight months, while Dorn conducted talks with the Warmaster about future War Council policies.

Because the Imperial Fists had taken no part in the annexation of the planet, Rogal Dorn agreed to have his companies stand tribute at the 'Emperor's' funeral. He did this so that the Luna Wolves would not have to tarnish their honour. Gleaming in their yellow plate, the Imperial Fists silently lined the route of the 'Emperor's' cortege as it wound its way through the battered avenues of the High City to the necropolis.

By order of the Warmaster, bending to the will of the chief captains and, most especially, the Mournival, no remembrancers were permitted to attend.

Ignace Karkasy wandered into the retiring room and sniffed at a decanter of wine. He made a face.

'It's fresh opened,' Keeler told him sourly.

'Yes, but local vintage,' Karkasy replied. 'This petty little empire.

No wonder it fell so easily. Any culture founded upon a wine so tragic shouldn't survive long.'

'It lasted five thousand years, through the limits of Old Night,' Keeler said. 'I doubt the quality of its wine influenced its survival.'

Karkasy poured himself a glass, sipped it and frowned. 'All I can say is that Old Night must have seemed much longer here than it actually was.'

Euphrati Keeler shook her head and turned back to her work, cleaning and refitting a hand-held picter unit of very high quality.

'And then there's the matter of sweat,' Karkasy said. He sat down on a lounger and put his feet up, settling the glass on his wide chest. He sipped again, grimacing, and rested his head back. Karkasy was a tall man, generously upholstered in flesh. His garments were expensive and well-tailored to suit his bulk. His round face was framed by a shock of black hair.

Keeler sighed and looked up from her work. 'The what?'

'The sweat, dear Euphrati, the sweat! I have been observing the Astartes. Very big, aren't they? I mean to say, very big in every measurement by which one might quantify a man.'

'They're Astartes, Ignace. What did you expect?'

'Not sweat, that's what. Not such a rank, pervasive reek. They are our immortal champions, after all. I expected them to smell rather better. Fragrant, like young gods.'

'Ignace, I have no clue how you got certified.'

Karkasy grinned. 'Because of the beauty of my lyric, my dear, because of my mastery of words. Although that might be found wanting here. How may I begin…?

The Astartes save us from the brink, the brink,
But oh my life how they stink, they stink.'

Karkasy sniggered, pleased with himself. He waited for a response, but Keeler was too occupied with her work.

'Dammit!' Keeler complained, throwing down her delicate tools. 'Servitor? Come here.'

One of the waiting servitors stalked up to her on thin, piston legs. She held out her picter. 'This mechanism is jammed. Take it for repair. And fetch me my spare units.'

'Yes, mistress,' the servitor croaked, taking the device. It plodded away. Keeler poured herself a glass of wine from the decanter and went to lean at the rail. Below, on the sub-deck, most of the expedition's other remembrancers were assembling for luncheon. Three hundred and fifty men and women gathered around formally laid tables, servitors moving amongst them, offering drinks. A gong was sounding.

'Is that lunch already?' Karkasy asked from the lounger.

'Yes,' she said.

'And is it going to be one of the damned iterators hosting again?' he queried.

'Yes. Sindermann yet again. The topic is promulgation of the living truth.'

Karkasy settled back and tapped his glass. 'I think I'll take luncheon here,' he said.

'You're a bad man, Ignace,' Keeler laughed. 'But I think I'll join you.'

Keeler sat down on the chaise facing him, and settled back. She was tall, lean-limbed and blonde, her face pale and slender. She wore chunky army boots and fatigue breeches, with a black combat jacket open to show a white vest, like a cadet officer, but the very masculinity of her chosen garb made her feminine beauty all the more apparent.

'I could write a whole epic about you,' Karkasy said, gazing.

Keeler snorted. It had become a daily routine for him to make a pass at her.

'I've told you, I'm not interested in your wretched, pawing approaches.'

'Don't you like men?' he asked, tilting his reclined head on one side.

'Why?'

'You dress like one.'

'So do you. Do you like men?'

Karkasy made a pained expression and sat back again, fiddling with the glass on his chest. He stared up at the heroic figures painted on the roof of the mezzanine. He had no idea what they were supposed to represent. Some great act of triumph that clearly had involved a great deal of standing on the bodies of the slain with arms thrust into the sky whilst shouting.

'Is this how you expected it to be?' he asked quietly.

'What?'

'When you were selected,' he said. 'When they contacted me, I felt so...'

'So what?'

'So... proud, I suppose. I imagined so much. I thought I would set foot amongst the stars and become a part of mankind's finest moment. I thought I would be uplifted, and thus produce my finest works.'

'And you're not?' Keeler asked.

'The beloved warriors we've been sent here to glorify couldn't be less helpful if they tried.'

'I've had some success,' Keeler said. 'I was down on the assembly deck earlier, and captured some fine images. I've put in a request to be allowed transit to the surface. I want to see the war zone first-hand.'

'Good luck. They'll probably deny you. Every request for access I've made has been turned down.'

'They're warriors, Ig. They've been warriors for a long time. They resent the likes of us. We're just passengers, along for the ride, uninvited.'

'You got your shots,' he said.

Keeler nodded. 'They don't seem to mind me.'

'That's because you dress like a man,' he smiled.

The hatch slid open and a figure joined them in the quiet mezzanine chamber. Mersadie Oliton went directly to the table where the decanter sat, poured herself a drink, and knocked it back. Then she stood, silently, gazing out at the drifting stars beyond the barge's vast window ports.

'What's up with her now?' Karkasy ventured.

'Sadie?' Keeler asked, getting to her feet and setting her glass down. 'What happened?'

'Apparently, I just offended someone,' Oliton said quickly, pouring another drink.

'Offended? Who?' Keeler asked.

'Some haughty Space Marine bastard called Loken. Bastard!'

'You got time with Loken?' Karkasy asked, sitting up rapidly and swinging his feet to the deck. 'Loken? *Tenth Company Captain* Loken?'

'Yes,' Oliton said. 'Why?'

'I've been trying to get near him for a month now,' Karkasy said. 'Of all the captains, they say, he is the most steadfast, and he's to take Sejanus's place, according to the rumour mill. How did you get authorisation?'

'I didn't,' Oliton said. 'I was finally given credentials for a brief interview with Captain Torgaddon, which I counted as no small success in itself, given the days I've spent petitioning to meet him, but I don't think he was in the mood to talk to me. When I went to see him at the appointed time, his equerry turned up instead and told me Torgaddon was busy. Torgaddon had sent the equerry to take me to see Loken. "Loken's got a good story," he said.'

'Was it a good story?' Keeler asked.

Mersadie nodded. 'Best I've heard, but I said something he didn't like, and he turned on me. Made me feel this small.' She gestured with her hand, and then took another swig.

'Did he smell of sweat?' Karkasy asked.

'No. No, not at all. He smelled of oils. Very sweet and clean.'

'Can you get me an introduction?' asked Ignace Karkasy.

He heard footsteps, then a voice called his name. 'Garvi?'

Loken looked around from his sword drill and saw, through the bars of the cage, Nero Vipus framed in the doorway of the blade-school. Vipus was dressed in black breeches, boots and a loose vest, and his truncated arm was very evident. The missing hand had been bagged in sterile jelly, and nanotic serums injected to reform the wrist so it would accept an augmetic implant in a week or so. Loken could still see the scars where Vipus had used his chainsword to amputate his own hand.

'What?'

'Someone to see you,' Vipus said.

'If it's another damn remembrancer–' Loken began.

Vipus shook his head. 'It's not. It's Captain Torgaddon.'

Loken lowered his blade and deactivated the practice cage as Vipus drew aside. The target dummies and armature blades went dead around him, and the upper hemisphere of the cage slid into the roof space as the lower hemisphere retracted into the deck beneath the mat. Tarik Torgaddon entered the blade-school chamber, dressed in fatigues and a long coat of silver mail. His features were saturnine, his hair black. He grinned at Vipus as the latter slipped out past him. Torgaddon's grin was full of perfect white teeth.

'Thanks, Vipus. How's the hand?'

'Mending, captain. Fit to be rebonded.'

'That's good,' said Torgaddon. 'Wipe your arse with the other one for a while, all right? Carry on.'

Vipus laughed and disappeared.

Torgaddon chuckled at his own quip and climbed the short steps to face Loken in the middle of the canvas mat. He paused at a blade rack outside the opened cage, selected a long-handled axe, and drew it out, hacking the air with it as he advanced.

'Hello, Garviel,' he said. 'You've heard the rumour, I suppose?'

'I've heard all sorts of rumours, sir.'

'I mean the one about you. Take a guard.'

Loken tossed his practice blade onto the deck and quickly drew a tabar from the nearest rack. It was all-steel, blade and handle both, and the cutting edge of the axe head had a pronounced curve. He raised it in a hunting stance and took up position facing Torgaddon.

Torgaddon feinted, then smote in with two furious chops.

Loken deflected Torgaddon's axe head with the haft of his tabar, and the blade-school rang with chiming echoes. The smile had not left Torgaddon's face.

'So, this rumour...' he continued, circling.

'This rumour,' Loken nodded. 'Is it true?'

'No,' said Torgaddon. Then he grinned impishly. 'Of course it bloody is! Or maybe it's not... No, it is.' He laughed loudly at the mischief.

'That's funny,' said Loken.

'Oh, belt up and smile,' Torgaddon hissed, and scythed in again, striking at Loken with two very non-standard cross-swings that Loken had trouble dodging. He was forced to spin his body out of the way and land with his feet wide-braced.

'Interesting work,' Loken said, circling again, his tabar low and loose. 'Are you, may I ask, just making these moves up?'

Torgaddon grinned. 'Taught to me by the Warmaster himself,' he said, pacing around and allowing the long axe to spin in his fingers. The blade flashed in the glow of the downlighters aimed on the canvas.

He halted suddenly, and aimed the head of the axe at Loken. 'Don't you want this, Garviel? Terra, I put you up for this myself.'

'I'm honoured, sir. I thank you for that.'

'And it was seconded by Ekaddon.'

Loken raised his eyebrows.

'All right, no it wasn't. Ekaddon hates your guts, my friend.'

'The feeling is mutual.'

'That's the boy,' Torgaddon roared, and lunged at Loken. Loken smashed the hack away, and counter-chopped, forcing Torgaddon to leap back onto the edges of the mat. 'Ekaddon's an arse,' Torgaddon said, 'and he feels cheated you got there first.'

'I only–' Loken began.

Torgaddon raised a finger for silence. 'You got there first,' he said quietly, not joking any more, 'and you saw the truth of it. Ekaddon can go hang, he's just smarting. Abaddon seconded you for this.'

'The First Captain?'

Torgaddon nodded. 'He was impressed. You beat him to the punch. Glory to the Tenth. And the vote was decided by the Warmaster.'

Loken lowered his guard completely. 'The Warmaster?'

'He wants you in. Told me to tell you that himself. He appreciated your work. He admired your sense of honour. "Tarik," he said to me, "if anyone's going to take Sejanus's place, it should be Loken." That's what he said.'

'Did he?'

'No.'

Loken looked up. Torgaddon was coming at him with his axe high and whirling. Loken ducked, side-stepped, and thumped the butt of his tabar's haft into Torgaddon's side, causing Torgaddon to mis-step and stumble.

Torgaddon exploded in laughter. 'Yes! Yes, he did. Terra, you're too easy, Garvi. Too easy. The look on your face!'

Loken smiled thinly. Torgaddon looked at the axe in his hand, and then tossed it aside, as if suddenly bored with the whole thing. It landed with a clatter in the shadows off the mat.

'So what do you say?' Torgaddon asked. 'What do I tell them? Are you in?'

'Sir, it would be the finest honour of my life,' Loken said.

Torgaddon nodded and smiled. 'Yes, it would,' he said, 'and here's your first lesson. You call me Tarik.'

It was said that the iterators were selected via a process even more rigorous and scrupulous than the induction mechanisms of the Astartes. 'One man in a thousand might become a Legion warrior,' so the sentiment went, 'but only one in a hundred thousand is fit to be an iterator.'

Loken could believe that. A prospective Astartes had to be sturdy, fit, genetically receptive, and ripe for enhancement. A chassis of meat and bone upon which a warrior could be built.

But to be an iterator, a person had to have certain rare gifts that belied enhancement. Insight, articulacy, political genius, keen intelligence. The latter could be boosted, either digitally or pharmaceutically, of course, and a mind could be tutored in history, ethic-politics and rhetoric. A person could be taught what to think, and how to express that line of thought, but he couldn't be taught *how* to think.

Loken loved to watch the iterators at work. On occasions, he had delayed the withdrawal of his company so that he could follow their functionaries around conquered cities and watch as they addressed the crowds. It was like watching the sun come out across a field of wheat.

Kyril Sindermann was the finest iterator Loken had ever seen. Sindermann held the post of Primary Iterator in the 63rd Expedition, and was responsible for the shaping of the message. He had, it was well known, a deep and intimate friendship with the Warmaster, as well as the expedition master and the senior equerries. And his name was known by the Emperor himself.

Sindermann was finishing a briefing in the School of Iterators when Loken strayed into the audience hall, a long vault set deep in the belly of the *Vengeful Spirit*. Two thousand men and women, each dressed in the simple, beige robes of their office, sat in the banks of tiered seating, rapt by his every word.

'To sum up, for I've been speaking far too long,' Sindermann was saying, 'this recent episode allows us to observe genuine blood and sinew beneath the wordy skin of our philosophy. The truth we convey is the truth, because we say it is the truth. Is that enough?'

He shrugged.

'I don't believe so. "My truth is better than your truth" is a school-yard squabble, not the basis of a culture. "I am right, so you are wrong" is a syllogism that collapses as soon as one applies any of a number of fundamental ethical tools. I am right, ergo, you are wrong. We can't construct a constitution on that, and we cannot, should not, will not be persuaded to iterate on its basis. It would make us what?'

He looked out across his audience. A number of hands were raised.

'There?'

'Liars.'

Sindermann smiled. His words were being amplified by the array of vox-mics set around his podium, and his face magnified by picter onto the hololithic wall behind him. On the wall, his smile was three metres wide.

'I was thinking bullies, or demagogues, Memed, but "liars" is apt. In fact, it cuts deeper than my suggestions. Well done. *Liars*. That is the one thing we iterators can never allow ourselves to become.'

Sindermann took a sip of water before continuing. Loken, at the back of the hall, sat down in an empty seat. Sindermann was a tall man, tall for a non-Astartes at any rate, proudly upright, spare, his patrician head crowned by fine white hair. His eyebrows were black, like the chevron markings on a Luna Wolf shoulder plate. He had a commanding presence, but it was his voice that really mattered. Pitched deep, rounded, mellow, compassionate, it was the vocal tone that got every iterator candidate selected. A soft, delicious, clean voice that communicated reason and sincerity and trust. It was a voice worth searching through one hundred thousand people to find.

'Truth and lies,' Sindermann continued. 'Truth and lies. I'm on my hobby-horse now, you realise? Your supper will be delayed.'

A ripple of amusement washed across the hall.

'Great actions have shaped our society,' Sindermann said. 'The greatest of these, physically, has been the Emperor's formal and complete unification of Terra, the outward sequel to which, this Great Crusade, we are now engaged upon. But the greatest, intellectually, has been our casting off of that heavy mantle called religion. Religion damned our species for thousands of years, from the lowest superstition to the highest conclaves of spiritual faith. It drove us to madness, to war, to murder, it hung upon us like a disease, like a shackle ball. I'll tell you what religion was... No, you tell me. You, there?'

'Ignorance, sir.'

'Thank you, Khanna. Ignorance. Since the earliest times, our species has striven to understand the workings of the cosmos, and where that understanding has failed, or fallen short, we have filled in the gaps, plastered over the discrepancies, with blind faith. Why does the sun go round the sky? I don't know, so I will attribute it to the efforts of a sun god with a golden chariot. Why do people die? I can't say, but I will choose to believe it is the murky business of a reaper who carries souls to some afterworld.'

His audience laughed. Sindermann got down off his podium and walked to the front steps of the stage, beyond the range of the vox-mics. Though he dropped his voice low, its trained pitch, that practiced tool of all iterators, carried his words with perfect clarity, unenhanced, throughout the chamber.

'Religious faith. Belief in daemons, belief in spirits, belief in an afterlife and all the other trappings of a preternatural existence, simply existed to make us all more comfortable and content in the face of a measureless cosmos. They were sops, bolsters for the soul, crutches for the intellect, prayers and lucky charms to help us through the darkness. But we have witnessed the cosmos now, my friends. We have passed amongst it. We have learned and understood the fabric of reality. We have seen the stars from behind, and found they have no clockwork mechanisms, no golden chariots carrying them abroad. We have realised there is no need for god, or any gods, and by extension no use any longer for daemons or devils or spirits. The greatest thing mankind ever did was to reinvent itself as a secular culture.'

His audience applauded this wholeheartedly. There were a few cheers of approval. Iterators were not simply schooled in the art of public speaking. They were trained in both sides of the business. Seeded amongst a crowd, iterators could whip it into enthusiasm with a few well-timed responses, or equally turn a rabble against the speaker. Iterators often mingled with audiences to bolster the effectiveness of the colleague actually speaking.

Sindermann turned away, as if finished, and then swung back again as the clapping petered out, his voice even softer and even more penetrating. 'But what of faith? Faith has a quality, even when religion has gone. We still need to believe in something, don't we? Here it is. The true purpose of mankind is to bear the torch of truth aloft and shine it, even into the darkest places. To share our forensic, unforgiving, liberating understanding with the dimmest reaches of the cosmos. To emancipate those shackled in ignorance. To free ourselves and others from false gods, and take our place at the apex of sentient life. That... *that* is what we may pour faith into. *That* is what we can harness our boundless faith to.'

More cheers and clapping. He wandered back to the podium. He rested his hands on the wooden rails of the lectern. 'These last months, we have quashed an entire culture. Make no mistake... we haven't brought them to heel or rendered them compliant. We have *quashed* them. Broken their backs. Set them to flame. I know this, because I know the Warmaster unleashed his Astartes in this action. Don't be coy about what they do. They are killers, but sanctioned. I see one now, one noble warrior, seated at the back of the hall.'

Faces turned back to crane at Loken. There was a flutter of applause.

Sindermann started clapping furiously. 'Better than that. He deserves better than that!' A huge, growing peal of clapping rose to the roof of the hall. Loken stood, and took it with an embarrassed bow.

The applause died away. 'The souls we have lately conquered believed in an Imperium, a rule of man,' Sindermann said as soon as the last flutter had faded. 'Nevertheless, we killed their Emperor and forced them into submission. We burned their cities and scuppered their warships. Is all we have to say in response to their "why?" a feeble "I am right, so you are wrong"?'

He looked down, as if in thought. 'Yet we are. We *are* right. They *are* wrong. This simple, clean faith we must undertake to teach them. We *are* right. They *are* wrong. Why? Not because we say so. Because we *know* so! We will not say "I am right and you are wrong" because we have bested them in combat. We must proclaim it because we know it is the responsible truth. We cannot, should not, *will* not promulgate that idea for any other reason than we know, without hesitation, without doubt, without prejudice, that it is the truth, and upon that truth we bestow our faith. They are *wrong*. Their culture was constructed upon lies. We have brought them the keen edge of truth and enlightened them. On that basis, and that basis alone, go from here and iterate our message.'

He had to wait, smiling, until the uproar subsided. 'Your supper's getting cold. Dismissed.'

The student iterators began to file slowly out of the hall. Sindermann took another sip of water from the glass set upon his lectern and walked up the steps from the stage to where Loken was seated.

'Did you hear anything you liked?' he asked, sitting down beside Loken and smoothing the skirts of his robes.

'You sound like a showman,' Loken said, 'or a carnival peddler, advertising his wares.'

Sindermann crooked one black, black eyebrow. 'Sometimes, Garviel, that's precisely how I feel.'

Loken frowned. 'That you don't believe what you're selling?'

'Do you?'

'What am I selling?'

'Faith, through murder. Truth, through combat.'

'It's just combat. It has no meaning other than combat. The meaning has been decided long before I'm instructed to deliver it.'

'So as a warrior, you are without conscience?'

Loken shook his head. 'As a warrior, I am a man of conscience, and that conscience is directed by my faith in the Emperor. My faith in our cause, as you were just describing to the school, but as a weapon, I am without conscience. When activated for war, I set aside my personal considerations, and simply act. The value of my action has already been weighed by the greater conscience of our commander. I kill until I am told to stop, and in that period, I do not question the killing. To do so would be nonsense, and inappropriate. The commander has already made a determination for war, and all he expects of me is to prosecute it to the best of my abilities. A weapon doesn't question who it kills, or why. That isn't the point of weapons.'

Sindermann smiled. 'No it's not, and that's how it should be. I'm curious, though. I didn't think we had a tutorial scheduled for today.'

Beyond their duties as iterators, senior counsellors like Sindermann were expected to conduct programmes of education for the Astartes. This had been ordered by the Warmaster himself. The men of the Legion spent long periods in transit between wars, and the Warmaster insisted they use the time to develop their minds and expand their knowledge. 'Even the mightiest warriors should be schooled in areas beyond warfare,' he had ordained. 'There will come a time when war is over, and fighting done, and my warriors should prepare themselves for a life of peace. They must know of other things besides martial matters, or else find themselves obsolete.'

'There's no tutorial scheduled,' Loken said, 'but I wanted to talk with you, informally.'

'Indeed? What's on your mind?'

'A troubling thing…'

'You have been asked to join the Mournival,' Sindermann said. Loken blinked.

'How did you know? Does everyone know?'

Sindermann grinned. 'Sejanus is gone, bless his bones. The Mournival lacks. Are you surprised they came to you?'

'I am.'

'I'm not. You chase Abaddon and Sedirae with your glories, Loken. The Warmaster has his eye on you. So does Dorn.'

'Primarch Dorn? Are you sure?'

'I have been told he admires your phlegmatic humour, Garviel. That's something, coming from a person like him.'

'I'm flattered.'

'You should be. Now what's the problem?'

'Am I fit? Should I agree?'

Sindermann laughed. 'Have faith,' he said.

'There's something else,' Loken said.

'Go on.'

'A remembrancer came to me today. Annoyed me deeply, to be truthful, but there was something she said. She said, "could we not have just left them alone?"'

'Who?'

'These people. This Emperor.'

'Garviel, you know the answer to that.'

'When I was in the tower, facing that man–'

Sindermann frowned. 'The one who pretended to be the "Emperor"?'

'Yes. He said much the same thing. Quartes, from his *Quantifications*, teaches us that the galaxy is a broad space, and that much I have seen. If we encounter a person, a society in this cosmos that disagrees with us, but is sound of itself, what right do we have to destroy it? I mean… could we not just leave them be and ignore them? The galaxy is, after all, such a broad space.'

'What I've always liked about you, Garviel,' Sindermann said, 'is your humanity. This has clearly played on your mind. Why haven't you spoken to me about it before?'

'I thought it would fade,' Loken admitted.

Sindermann rose to his feet, and beckoned Loken to follow him. They walked out of the audience chamber and along one of the great spinal hallways of the flagship, an arch-roofed, buttressed canyon three decks high, like the nave of an ancient cathedral fane elongated to a length of five kilometres. It was gloomy, and the glorious banners of Legions and companies and campaigns, some faded, or damaged by old battles, hung down from the roof at intervals. Tides of personnel streamed along the hallway, their voices lifting an odd susurration into the vault, and Loken could see other flows of foot traffic in the illuminated galleries above, where the upper decks overlooked the main space.

'The first thing,' Sinderman said as they strolled along, 'is a simple bandage for your worries. You heard me essay this at length to the class and, in a way, you ventured a version of it just a moment ago when you spoke on the subject of conscience. You are a weapon, Garviel, an example of the finest instrument of destruction mankind has ever wrought. There must be no place inside you for doubt or question. You're right. Weapons should not think, they should only allow themselves to be employed, for the decision to use them is not theirs to make. That decision must be made – with great and terrible care, and ethical consideration beyond our capacity to judge – by the primarchs and the commanders. The Warmaster, like the beloved Emperor before him, does not employ you lightly. Only with a heavy heart and a certain determination does he unleash the Astartes. The Adeptus Astartes is the last resort, and is only ever used that way.'

Loken nodded.

'This is what you must remember. Just because the Imperium has the Astartes, and thus the ability to defeat and, if necessary, annihilate any foe, that's not the reason it happens. We have developed the means to annihilate... We have developed warriors like you, Garviel... because it is necessary.'

'A necessary evil?'

'A necessary instrument. Right does not follow might. Mankind has a great, empirical truth to convey, a message to bring, for the good of all. Sometimes that message falls on unwilling ears. Sometimes that message is spurned and denied, as here. Then, and only then, thank the stars that we own the might to enforce it. We are mighty because we are right, Garviel. We are not right because we are mighty. Vile the hour when that reversal becomes our credo.'

They had turned off the spinal hallway and were walking

along a lateral promenade now, towards the archive annex. Servitors waddled past, their upper limbs laden with books and data-slates.

'Whether our truth is right or not, must we always enforce it upon the unwilling? As the woman said, could we not just leave them to their own destinies, unmolested?'

'You are walking along the shores of a lake,' Sindermann said. 'A boy is drowning. Do you let him drown because he was foolish enough to fall into the water before he had learned to swim? Or do you fish him out, and teach him how to swim?'

Loken shrugged. 'The latter.'

'What if he fights you off as you attempt to save him, because he is afraid of you? Because he doesn't want to learn how to swim?'

'I save him anyway.'

They had stopped walking. Sindermann pressed his hand to the key plate set into the brass frame of a huge door, and allowed his palm to be read by the scrolling light. The door opened, exhaling like a mouth, gusting out climate-controlled air and a background hint of dust.

They stepped into the vault of Archive Chamber Three. Scholars, sphragists and metaphrasts worked in silence at the reading desks, summoning servitors to select volumes from the sealed stacks.

'What interests me about your concerns,' Sindermann said, keeping his voice precisely low so that only Loken's enhanced hearing could follow it, 'is what they say about you. We have established you are a weapon, and that you don't need to think about what you do because the thinking is done for you. Yet you allow the human spark in you to worry, to fret and empathise. You retain the ability to consider the cosmos as a man would, not as an instrument might.'

'I see,' Loken replied. 'You're saying I have forgotten my place. That I have overstepped the bounds of my function.'

'Oh no,' Sindermann smiled. 'I'm saying you have *found* your place.'

'How so?' Loken asked.

Sindermann gestured to the stacks of books that rose, like towers, into the misty altitudes of the archive. High above, hovering servitors searched and retrieved ancient texts sealed in plastek carriers, swarming across the cliff-faces of the library like honey bees.

'Regard the books,' Sindermann said.

'Are there some I should read? Will you prepare a list for me?'

'Read them all. Read them again. Swallow the learning and ideas of our predecessors whole, for it can only improve you as a man, but if you do, you'll find that none of them holds an answer to still your doubts.'

Loken laughed, puzzled. Some of the metaphrasts nearby looked up from their study, annoyed at the interruption. They quickly looked down again when they saw the noise had issued from an Astartes.

'What is the Mournival, Garviel?' Sindermann whispered.

'You know very well...'

'Humour me. Is it an official body? An organ of governance, formally ratified, a Legio rank?'

'Of course not. It is an informal honour. It has no official weight. Since the earliest era of our Legion there has been a Mournival. Four captains, those regarded by their peers to be...'

He paused.

'The best?' Sindermann asked.

'My modesty is ashamed to use that word. The most appropriate. At any time, the Legion, in an unofficial manner quite separate from the chain of command, composes a Mournival. A confraternity of four captains, preferably ones of markedly different aspects and humours, who act as the soul of the Legion.'

'And their job is to watch over the moral health of the Legion, isn't that so? To guide and shape its philosophy? And, most important of all, to stand beside the commander and be the voices he listens to before any others. To be the comrades and friends he can turn to privately, and talk out his concerns and troubles with freely, before they ever become matters of state or Council.'

'That is what the Mournival is supposed to do,' Loken agreed.

'Then it occurs to me, Garviel, that only a weapon which questions its use could be of any value in that role. To be a member of the Mournival, you need to have concerns. You need to have wit, and most certainly you need to have doubts. Do you know what a naysmith is?'

'No.'

'In early Terran history, during the dominance of the Sumaturan dynasts, naysmiths were employed by the ruling classes. Their job was to disagree. To question everything. To consider any argument or policy and find fault with it, or articulate the counter position. They were highly valued.'

'You want me to become a naysmith?' Loken asked.

Sindermann shook his head. 'I want you to be you, Garviel. The Mournival needs your common sense and clarity. Sejanus was always the voice of reason, the measured balance between Abaddon's choler and Aximand's melancholic disdain. The balance is gone, and the Warmaster needs that balance now more than ever. You came to me this morning because you wanted my blessing. You wanted to know if you should accept the honour. By your own admission, Garviel, by the merit of your own doubts, you have answered your own question.'

FOUR

Summoned
Ezekyle by name
A winning hand

She had asked what the planet was called, and the crew of the shuttle had answered her 'Terra', which was hardly useful. Mersadie Oliton had spent the first twenty-eight years of her twenty-nine-year life on Terra, and this wasn't it.

The iterator sent to accompany her was of little better use. A modest, olive-skinned man in his late teens, the iterator's name was Memed, and he was possessed of a fearsome intellect and precocious genius. But the violent sub-orbital passage of the shuttle disagreed with his constitution, and he spent most of the trip unable to answer her questions because he was too occupied retching into a plastek bag.

The shuttle set down on a stretch of formal lawn between rows of spayed and pollarded trees, eight kilometres west of the High City. It was early evening, and stars already glimmered in the violet smudge at the sky's edges. At high altitude, ships passed over, their lights blinking. Mersadie stepped down the shuttle's ramp onto the grass, breathing in the odd scents and slightly variant atmosphere of the world.

She stopped short. The air, oxygen rich, she imagined, was making her giddy, and that giddiness was further agitated by the thought of where she was. For the first time in her life she was standing on another soil, another world. It seemed to her quite momentous, as if a ceremonial band ought to be playing. She

was, as far as she knew, one of the very first of the remembrancers to be granted access to the surface of the conquered world.

She turned to look at the distant city, taking in the panorama
and committing it to her memory coils. She blink-clicked her
eyes to store certain views digitally, noting that smoke still rose
from the cityscape, though the fight had been over months ago.

'We are calling it Sixty-Three Nineteen,' the iterator said,
coming down the ramp behind her. Apparently, his queasy constitution had been stabilised by planetfall. She recoiled delicately
from the stink of sick on his breath.

'Sixty-Three Nineteen?' she asked.

'It being the ninteenth world the 63rd Expedition has brought
to compliance,' Memed said, 'though, of course, full compliance is not yet established here. The charter is yet to be ratified.
Lord Governor Elect Rakris is having trouble forming a con-
senting coalition parliament, but Sixty-Three Nineteen will do.
The locals call this world Terra, and we can't be having two of
those, can we? As far as I see it, that was the root of the problem in the first place...'

'I see,' said Mersadie, moving away. She touched her hand
against the bark of one of the pollarded trees. It felt... real.
She smiled to herself and blink-clicked it. Already, the basis of
her account, with visual keys, was formulating in her enhanced
mind. A personal angle, that's what she'd take. She'd use the
novelty and unfamiliarity of her first planetfall as a theme
around which her remembrance would hang.

'It's a beautiful evening,' the iterator announced, coming to
stand beside her. He'd left his sloshing bags of vomit at the
foot of the ramp, as if he expected someone to dispose of them
for him.

The four army troopers delegated to her protection certainly
weren't about to do it. Perspiring in their heavy velvet over-
coats and shakos, their rifles slung over their shoulders, they
closed up around her.

'Mistress Oliton?' the officer said. 'He's waiting.'

Mersadie nodded and followed them. Her heart was beating
hard. This was going to be quite an occasion. A week before,
her friend and fellow remembrancer Euphrati Keeler, who had
emphatically achieved more than any of the remembrancers so
far, had been on hand in the eastern city of Kaentz, observing
crusader operations, when Maloghurst had been found alive.

The Warmaster's equerry, believed lost when the ships of his
embassy had been burned out of orbit, had survived, escaping
via drop pod. Badly injured, he had been nursed and protected

by the family of a farmer in the territories outside Kaentz. Keeler had been right there, by chance, to pict record the equerry's recovery from the farmstead. It had been a coup. Her picts, so beautifully composed, had been flashed around the expedition fleet, and savoured by the Imperial retinues. Suddenly, Euphrati Keeler was being talked about. Suddenly, remembrancers weren't such a bad thing after all. With a few, brilliant clicks of her picter, Euphrati had advanced the cause of the remembrancers enormously.

Now Mersadie hoped she could do the same. She had been summoned. She still couldn't quite get over that. She had been summoned to the surface. That fact alone would have been enough, but it was *who* had summoned her that really mattered. He had personally authorised her transit permit, and seen to the appointment of a bodyguard and one of Sindermann's best iterators.

She couldn't understand why. Last time they'd met, he'd been so brutal that she'd considered resigning and taking the first conveyance home.

He was standing on a gravel pathway between the tree rows, waiting for her. As she came up, the soldiers around her, she registered simple awe at the sight of him in his full plate. Gleaming white, with a trace of black around the edges. His helm, with its lateral horse-brush crest, was off, hung at his waist. He was a giant, two and a half metres tall.

She sensed the soldiers around her hesitating.

'Wait here,' she told them, and they dropped back, relieved. A soldier of the Imperial army could be as tough as old boots, but he didn't want to tangle with an Astartes. Especially not one of the Luna Wolves, the mightiest of the mighty, the deadliest of all Legions.

'You too,' she said to the iterator.

'Oh, right,' Memed said, coming to a halt.

'The summons was personal.'

'I understand,' he said.

Mersadie walked up to the Luna Wolves captain. He towered over her, so much she had to shield her eyes with her hand against the setting sun to look up at him.

'Remembrancer,' he said, his voice as deep as an oak-root.

'Captain. Before we start, I'd like to apologise for any offence I may have caused the last time we–'

'If I'd taken offence, mistress, would I have summoned you here?'

'I suppose not.'

'You suppose right. You raised my hackles with your questions last time, but I admit I was too hard on you.'

'I spoke with unnecessary temerity–'

'It was that temerity that caused me to think of you,' Loken replied. 'I can't explain further. I won't, but you should know that it was your very speaking out of turn that brought me here. Which is why I decided to have you brought here too. If that's what remembrancers do, you've done your job well.'

Mersadie wasn't sure what to say. She lowered her hand. The last rays of sunlight were in her eyes. 'Do you... do you want me to witness something? To remember something?'

'No,' he replied curtly. 'What happens now happens privately, but I wanted you to know that, in part, it is because of you. When I return, if I feel it is appropriate, I will convey certain recollections to you. If that is acceptable.'

'I'm honoured, captain. I will await your pleasure.'

Loken nodded.

'Should I come with–' Memed began.

'No,' said the Luna Wolf.

'Right,' Memed said quickly, backing off. He went away to study a tree bole.

'You asked me the right questions, and so showed me I was asking the right questions too,' Loken told Mersadie.

'Did I? Did you answer them?'

'No,' he replied. 'Wait here, please,' he said, and walked away towards a box hedge trimmed by the finest topiarists into a thick, green bastion wall. He vanished from sight under a leafy arch.

Mersadie turned to the waiting soldiers.

'Know any games?' she asked.

They shrugged.

She plucked a deck of cards from her coat pocket. 'I've got one to show you,' she grinned, and sat down on the grass to deal.

The soldiers put down their rifles and grouped around her in the lengthening blue shadows.

'Soldiers love cards,' Ignace Karkasy had said to her before she left the flagship, right before he'd grinned and handed her the deck.

Beyond the high hedge, an ornamental water garden lay in shadowy ruin. The height of the hedge and the neighbouring trees, just now becoming spiky black shapes against the rose sky, screened out what was left of the direct sunlight. The gloom upon the gardens was almost misty.

The garden had once been composed of rectangular ouslite slabs laid like giant flagstones, surrounding a series of square, shallow basins where lilies and bright water flowers had flourished in pebbly sinks fed by some spring or water source. Frail ghost ferns and weeping trees had edged the pools.

During the assault of the High City, shells or airborne munitions had bracketed the area, felling many of the plants and shattering a great number of the blocks. Many of the ouslite slabs had been dislodged, and several of the pools greatly increased in breadth and depth by the addition of deep, gouging craters.

But the hidden spring had continued to feed the place, filling the shell holes, and pouring overflow between dislodged stones.

The whole garden was a shimmering, flat pool in the gloom, out of which tangled branches, broken root balls and asymmetric shards of rock stuck up in miniature archipelagos.

Some of the intact blocks, slabs two metres long and half a metre thick, had been rearranged, and not randomly by the blasts. They had been levered out to form a walkway into the pool area, a stone jetty sunk almost flush with the water's surface.

Loken stepped out onto the causeway and began to follow it. The air smelled damp, and he could hear the clack of amphibians and the hiss of evening flies. Water flowers, their fragile colours almost lost in the closing darkness, drifted on the still water either side of his path.

Loken felt no fear. He was not built to feel it, but he registered a trepidation, an anticipation that made his hearts beat. He was, he knew, about to pass a threshold in his life, and he held faith that what lay beyond that threshold would be provident. It also felt right that he was about to take a profound step forward in his career. His world, his life, had changed greatly of late, with the rise of the Warmaster and the consequent alteration of the crusade, and it was only proper that he changed with it. A new phase. A new time.

He paused and looked up at the stars that were beginning to light in the purpling sky. A new time, and a *glorious* new time at that. Like him, mankind was on a threshold, about to step forward into greatness.

He had gone deep into the ragged sprawl of the water garden, far beyond the lamps of the landing zone behind the hedge, far beyond the lights of the city. The sun had vanished. Blue shadows surrounded him.

The causeway path came to an end. Water gleamed beyond.

Ahead, across thirty metres of still pond, a little bank of weeping trees rose up like an atoll, silhouetted against the sky.

He wondered if he should wait. Then he saw a flicker of light amongst the trees across the water, a flutter of yellow flame that went as quickly as it came.

Loken stepped off the causeway into the water. It was shin deep. Ripples, hard black circles, radiated out across the reflective pool. He began to wade out towards the islet, hoping that his feet wouldn't suddenly encounter some unexpected depth of submerged crater and so lend comedy to this solemn moment.

He reached the bank of trees and stood in the shallows, gazing up into the tangled blackness.

'Give us your name,' a voice called out of the darkness. It spoke the words in Cthonic, his home-tongue, the battle-argot of the Luna Wolves.

'Garviel Loken is my name to give.'

'And what is your honour?'

'I am Captain of the Tenth Company of the Sixteenth Legio Astartes.'

'And who is your sworn master?'

'The Warmaster and the Emperor both.'

Silence followed, interrupted only by the splash of frogs and the noise of insects in the waterlogged thickets.

The voice spoke again. Two words. 'Illuminate him.'

There was a brief metallic scrape as the slot of a lantern was pulled open, and yellow flame-light shone out across him. Three figures stood on the tree-lined bank above him, one holding the lantern up.

Aximand. Torgaddon, lifting the lantern. Abaddon.

Like him, they wore their warrior armour, the dancing light catching bright off the curves of the plate. All were bareheaded, their crested helmets hung at their waists.

'Do you vouch that this soul is all he claims to be?' Abaddon asked. It seemed a strange question, as all three of them knew him well enough. Loken understood it was part of the ceremony.

'I so vouch,' Torgaddon said. 'Increase the light.'

Abaddon and Aximand stepped away, and began to open the slots of a dozen other lanterns hanging from the surrounding boughs. When they had finished, a golden light suffused them all. Torgaddon set his own lamp on the ground.

The trio stepped forward into the water to face Loken. Tarik Torgaddon was the tallest of them, his trickster grin never leaving his face. 'Loosen up, Garvi,' he chuckled. 'We don't bite.'

Loken flashed a smile back, but he felt unnerved. Partly, it was the high status of these three men, but he also hadn't expected the induction to be so ritualistic.

Horus Aximand, Captain of Fifth Company, was the youngest and shortest of them, shorter than Loken. He was squat and robust, like a guard dog. His head was shaved smooth, and oiled, so that the lamp-light gleamed off it. Aximand, like many in the younger generations of the Legion, had been named in honour of the commander, but only he used the name openly. His noble face, with wide-set eyes and firm, straight nose, uncannily resembled the visage of the Warmaster, and this had earned him the affectionate name 'Little Horus'. Little Horus Aximand, the devil-dog in war, the master strategist. He nodded greeting to Loken.

Ezekyle Abaddon, First Captain of the Legion, was a towering brute. Somewhere between Loken's height and Torgaddon's, he seemed greater than both due to the cresting top-knot adorning his otherwise shaved scalp. When his helm was off, Abaddon bound his mane of black hair up in a silver sleeve that made it stand proud like a palm tree or a fetish switch on his crown. He, like Torgaddon, had been in the Mournival from its inception. He, like Torgaddon and Aximand both, shared the same aspect of straight nose and wide-spaced eyes so reminiscent of the Warmaster, though only in Aximand were the features an actual likeness. They might have been brothers, actual womb brothers, if they had been sired in the old way. As it was, they were brothers in terms of gene-source and martial fraternity.

Now Loken was to be their brother too.

There was a curious incidence in the Luna Wolves Legion of Astartes bearing a facial resemblance to their primarch. This had been put down to conformities in the gene-seed, but still, those who echoed Horus in their features were considered especially lucky, and were known by all the men as 'the Sons of Horus'. It was a mark of honour, and it often seemed the case that 'Sons' rose faster and found better favour than the rest. Certainly, Loken knew for a fact, all the previous members of the Mournival had been 'Sons of Horus'. In this respect, he was unique. Loken owed his looks to an inheritance of the pale, craggy bloodline of Cthonia. He was the first non-'Son' to be elected to this elite inner circle.

Though he knew it couldn't be the case, he felt as if he had achieved this eminence through simple merit, rather than the atavistic whim of physiognomy.

'This is a simple act,' Abaddon said, regarding Loken. 'You have been vouched for here, and proposed by great men before that. Our lord, and the Lord Dorn have both put your name forward.'

'As have you, sir, so I understand,' Loken said.

Abaddon smiled. 'Few match you in soldiering, Garviel. I've had my eye on you, and you proved my interest when you took the palace ahead of me.'

'Luck.'

'There's no such thing,' said Aximand gruffly.

'He only says that because he never has any,' Torgaddon grinned.

'I only say that because there's no such thing,' Aximand objected. 'Science has shown us this. There is no luck. There is only success or the lack of it.'

'Luck,' said Abaddon. 'Isn't that just a word for modesty? Garviel is too modest to say "Yes, Ezekyle, I bested you, I won the palace, and triumphed where you did not," for he feels that would not become him. And I admire modesty in a man, but the truth is, Garviel, you are here because you are a warrior of superlative talent. We welcome you.'

'Thank you, sir,' Loken said.

'A first lesson, then,' Abaddon said. 'In the Mournival, we are equals. There is no rank. Before the men, you may refer to me as "sir" or "First Captain", but between us, there is no ceremony. I am Ezekyle.'

'Horus,' said Aximand.

'Tarik,' said Torgaddon.

'I understand,' Loken answered, 'Ezekyle.'

'The rules of our confraternity are simple,' Aximand said, 'and we will get to them, but there is no structure to the duties expected of you. You should prepare yourself to spend more time with the command staff, and function at the Warmaster's side. Have you a proxy in mind to oversee the Tenth in your absence?'

'Yes, Horus,' Loken said.

'Vipus?' Torgaddon smiled.

'I would,' Loken said, 'but the honour should be Jubal's. Seniority and rank.'

Aximand shook his head. 'Second lesson. Go with your heart. If you trust Vipus, make it Vipus. Never compromise. Jubal's a big boy. He'll get over it.'

'There will be other duties and obligations, special duties...' Abaddon said. 'Escorts, ceremonies, embassies, planning meetings. Are you sanguine about that? Your life will change.'

'I am sanguine,' Loken nodded.

'Then we should mark you in,' Abaddon said. He stepped past Loken and waded forward into the shallow lake, away from the light of the lamps. Aximand followed him. Torgaddon touched Loken on the arm and ushered him along as well.

They strode out into the black water and formed a ring. Abaddon bade them stand stock-still until the water ceased to lap and ripple. It became mirror-smooth. The bright reflection of the rising moon wavered on the water between them.

'The one fixture that has always witnessed an induction,' Abaddon said. 'The moon. Symbolic of our Legion name. No one has ever entered the Mournival, except by the light of a moon.'

Loken nodded.

'This seems a poor, false one,' Aximand muttered, looking up at the sky, 'but it will do. The image of the moon must also always be reflected. In the first days of the Mournival, close on two hundred years ago, it was favoured to have the chosen moon's image captured in a scrying dish or polished mirror. We make do now. Water suffices.'

Loken nodded again. His feeling of being unnerved had returned, sharp and unwelcome. This was a ritual, and it smacked dangerously of the practices of corpse-whisperers and spiritualists. The entire process seemed shot through with superstition and arcane worship, the sort of spiritual unreason Sindermann had taught him to rail against.

He felt he had to say something before it was too late. 'I am a man of faith,' he said softly, 'and that faith is the truth of the Imperium. I will not bow to any fane or acknowledge any spirit. I own only the empirical clarity of Imperial Truth.'

The other three looked at him.

'I told you he was straight up and down,' Torgaddon said.

Abaddon and Aximand laughed.

'There are no spirits here, Garviel,' Abaddon said, resting a hand reassuringly against Loken's arm.

'We're not trying to ensorcel you,' Aximand chuckled.

'This is just an old habit, a practice. The way it has always been done,' Torgaddon said. 'We keep it up for no other reason than it seems to make it matter. It's… pantomime, I suppose.'

'Yes, pantomime,' agreed Abaddon.

'We want this moment to be special to you, Garviel,' Aximand said. 'We want you to remember it. We believe it's important to mark an induction with a sense of ceremony and occasion, so we use the old ways. Perhaps that's just theatrical of us, but we find it reassuring.'

'I understand,' Loken said.

'Do you?' Abaddon asked. 'You're going to make a pledge to us. An oath as firm as any oath of moment you have ever undertaken. Man to man. Cold and clear and very, very secular. An oath of brothership, not some occult pact. We stand together in the light of a moon, and swear a bond that only death will break.'

'I understand,' Loken repeated. He felt foolish. 'I want to take the oath.'

Abaddon nodded. 'Let's mark you, then. Say the names of the others.'

Torgaddon bowed his head and recited nine names. Since the foundation of the Mournival, only twelve men had held the unofficial rank, and three of those were present. Loken would be the thirteenth.

'Keyshen. Minos. Berabaddon. Litus. Syrakul. Deradaeddon. Karaddon. Janipur. Sejanus.'

'Lost in glory,' Aximand and Abaddon said as one voice. 'Mourned by the Mournival. Only in death does duty end.'

A bond that only death will break. Loken thought about Abaddon's words. Death was the single expectation of each and every Astartes. Violent death. It was not an if, it was a when. In the service of the Imperium, each of them would eventually sacrifice his life. They were phlegmatic about it. It would happen, it was that simple. One day, tomorrow, next year. It would happen.

There was an irony, of course. To all intents and purposes, and by every measurement known to the gene-scientists and gerontologists, the Astartes, like the primarchs, were immortals. Age would not wither them, nor bring them down. They would live forever... five thousand years, ten thousand, beyond even that into some unimaginable millennium. Except for the scythe of war.

Immortal, but not invulnerable. Yes, they might live forever, but they would never get the chance. Immortality was a by-product of their Astartes strengths, but those strengths had been gene-built for combat. They had been born immortal only to die in war. That was the way of it. Brief, bright lives. Like Hastur Sejanus, the warrior Loken was replacing. Only the beloved Emperor, who had left the warring behind, would truly live forever.

Loken tried to imagine the future, but the image would not form. Death would wipe them all from history. Not even the great First Captain Ezekyle Abaddon would survive forever. There would be a time when Abaddon no longer waged bloody war across the territories of humanity.

Loken sighed. That would be a sad day indeed. Men would cry out for Abaddon's return, but he would never come.

He tried to picture the manner of his own death. Fabled, imaginary combats flashed through his mind. He imagined himself at the Emperor's side, fighting some great, last stand against an unknown foe. Primarch Horus would be there, of course. He had to be. It wouldn't be the same without him. Loken would battle, and die, and perhaps even Horus would die, to save the Emperor at the last.

Glory. Glory, like he'd never known. Such an hour would become so ingrained in the minds of men that it would be the cornerstone of all that came after. A great battle, upon which human culture would be based.

Then, briefly, he imagined another death. Alone, far away from his comrades and his Legion, dying from cruel wounds on some nameless rock, his passing as memorable as smoke.

Loken swallowed hard. Either way, his service was to the Emperor, and his service would be true to the end.

'The names are said,' Abaddon intoned, 'and of them, we hail Sejanus, latest to fall.'

'Hail, Sejanus!' Torgaddon and Aximand cried.

'Garviel Loken,' Abaddon said, looking at Loken. 'We ask you to take Sejanus's place. How say you?'

'I will do this thing gladly.'

'Will you swear an oath to uphold the confraternity of the Mournival?'

'I will,' said Loken.

'Will you accept our brothership and give it back as a brother?'

'I will.'

'Will you be true to the Mournival to the end of your life?'

'I will.'

'Will you serve the Luna Wolves for as long as they bear that proud name?'

'I will,' said Loken.

'Do you pledge to the commander, who is primarch over us all?' asked Aximand.

'I so pledge.'

'And to the Emperor above all primarchs, everlasting?'

'I so pledge.'

'Do you swear to uphold the truth of the Imperium of Mankind, no matter what evil may assail it?' Torgaddon asked.

'I swear,' said Loken.

'Do you swear to stand firm against all enemies, alien and domestic?'

'This I swear.'

'And in war, kill for the living and kill for the dead?'

'Kill for the living! Kill for the dead!' Abaddon and Aximand echoed.

'I swear.'

'As the moon lights us,' Abaddon said, 'will you be a true brother to your brother Astartes?'

'I will.'

'No matter the cost?'

'No matter the cost.'

'Your oath is taken, Garviel. Welcome into the Mournival. Tarik? Illuminate us.'

Torgaddon pulled a vapour flare from his belt and fired it off into the night sky. It burst in a bright umbrella of light, white and harsh.

As the sparks of it rained slowly down onto the waters, the four warriors hugged and whooped, clasping hands and slapping backs. Torgaddon, Aximand and Abaddon took turns to embrace Loken.

'You're one of us now,' Torgaddon whispered as he drew Loken close.

'I am,' said Loken.

Later, on the islet, by the light of the lanterns, they branded Loken's helm above the right eye with the crescent mark of the new moon. This was his badge of office. Aximand's helm bore the brand of the half moon, Torgaddon's the gibbous, and Abaddon's the full. The four stage cycle of a moon was shared between their wargear. So the Mournival was denoted.

They sat on the islet, talking and joking, until the sun rose again.

They were playing cards on the lawn by the light of chemical lanterns. The simple game Mersadie had proposed had long been eclipsed by a punitive betting game suggested by one of the soldiers. Then the iterator, Memed, had joined them, and taken great pains to teach them an old version of cups.

Memed shuffled and dealt the cards with marvellous dexterity. One of the soldiers whistled mockingly. 'A real card hand we have here,' the officer remarked.

'This is an old game,' Memed said, 'which I'm sure you will enjoy. It dates back a long way, its origins lost in the very beginnings of Old Night. I have researched it, and I understand it was popular amongst the peoples of Ancient Merica, and also the tribes of the Franc.'

He let them play a few dummy hands until they had the way

of it, but Mersadie found it hard to remember what spread won over what. In the seventh turn, believing she had the game's measure at last, she discarded a hand which she believed inferior to the cards Memed was holding.

'No, no,' he smiled. 'You win.'

'But you have four of a kind again.'

He laid out her cards. 'Even so, you see?'

She shook her head. 'It's all too confusing.'

'The suits correspond,' he said, as if beginning a lecture, 'to the layers of society back then. Swords stand for the warrior aristocracy; cups, or chalices, for the ancient priesthood; diamonds, or coins, for the merchant classes; and baton clubs for the worker caste...'

Some of the soldiers grumbled.

'Stop iterating to us,' Mersadie said.

'Sorry,' Memed grinned. 'Anyway, you win. I have four alike, but you have ace, monarch, empress and knave. A mournival.'

'What did you just say?' Mersadie Oliton asked, sitting up.

'Mournival,' Memed replied, reshuffling the old, square-cut cards. 'It's the old Franc word for the four royal cards. A winning hand.'

Behind them, away beyond a high wall of hedge invisible in the still night, a flare suddenly banged off and lit the sky white.

'A winning hand,' Mersadie murmured. Coincidence, and something she privately believed in, called fate, had just opened the future up to her.

It looked very inviting indeed.

FIVE

Peeter Egon Momus
Lectitio Divinitatus
Malcontent

Peeter Egon Momus was doing them a great honour. Peeter Egon Momus was deigning to share with them his visions for the new High City. Peeter Egon Momus, architect designate for the 63rd Expedition, was unveiling his preparatory ideas for the transformation of the conquered city into a permanent memorial to glory and compliance.

The trouble was, Peeter Egon Momus was just a figure in the distance and largely inaudible. In the gathered audience, in the dusty heat, Ignace Karkasy shifted impatiently and craned his neck to see.

The assembly had been gathered in a city square north of the palace. It was just after midday, and the sun was at its zenith, scorching the bare basalt towers and yards of the city. Though the high walls around the square offered some shade, the air was oven dry and stiflingly hot. There was a breeze, but even that was heated like exhaust vapour, and it did nothing but stir up fine grit in the air. Powder dust, the particulate residue of the great battle, was everywhere, hazing the bright air like smoke. Karkasy's throat was as arid as a river bed in drought. Around him, people in the crowd coughed and sneezed.

The crowd, five hundred strong, had been carefully vetted. Three-quarters of them were local dignitaries; grandees, nobles, merchants, members of the overthrown government,

representatives of that part of Sixty-Three Nineteen's ruling
classes who had pledged compliance to the new order. They
had been summoned by invitation so that they might partici-
pate, however superficially, in the renewal of their society.

The rest were remembrancers. Many of them, like Karkasy, had
been granted their first transit permit to the surface, at long last,
so they could attend. If this was what he had been waiting for,
Karkasy thought, they could keep it. Standing in a crowded kiln
while some old fart made incoherent noises in the background.

The crowd seemed to share his mood. They were hot and
despondent. Karkasy saw no smiles on the faces of the invited
locals, just hard, drawn looks of forbearance. The choice between
compliance or death didn't make compliance any more pleasurable. They were defeated, deprived of their culture and their
way of life, facing a future determined by alien minds. They
were simply, wearily enduring the indignity of this period of
transition into the Imperium of Man. From time to time, they
clapped in a desultory manner, but only when stirred up by the
iterators carefully planted in their midst.

The crowd had drawn up around the aprons of a metal stage
erected for the event. Upon it were arranged hololithic screens
and relief models of the city to be, as well as many of the extrav-
agantly complex brass and steel surveying instruments Momus
utilised in his work. Geared, spoked and meticulous, the instruments suggested to Karkasy's mind devices of torture.

Torture was right.

Momus, when he could be seen between the heads of the
crowd, was a small, trim man with over-dainty mannerisms. As
he explained his plans, the staff of iterators on stage with him
aimed live picters close up at relevant areas of the relief models, the images transferring directly to the screens, along with
graphic schematics. But the sunlight was too glaring for decent
hololithic projection, and the images were milked-out and hard
to comprehend. Something was wrong with the vox-mic Momus
was using too, and what little of his speech came through served
only to demonstrate the man had no gift whatsoever for public speaking.

'...always a heliolithic city, a tribute to the sun above, and we
may see this afternoon, indeed, I'm sure you will have noticed,
the glory of the light here. A city of light. Light out of darkness
is a noble theme, by which, of course, I mean the light of truth
shining upon the darkness of ignorance. I am much taken with
the local phototropic technologies I have found here, and intend
to incorporate them into the design...'

Karkasy sighed. He never thought he would find himself wishing for an iterator, but at least those bastards knew how to speak in public. Peeter Egon Momus should have left the talking to one of the iterators while he aimed the wretched picter wand for them.

His mind wandered. He looked up at the high walls around them, geometric slabs against the blue sky, baked pink in the sunlight, or smoke black where shadows slanted. He saw the scorch marks and dotted bolt craters that pitted the basalt like acne. Beyond the walls, the towers of the palace were in worse repair, their plasterwork hanging off like shed snakeskin, their missing windows like blinded eyes.

In a yard to the south of the gathering, a Titan of the Mechanicum stood on station, its grim humanoid form rising up over the walls. It stood perfectly still, like a piece of monumental martial statuary, instantly installed. Now that, thought Karkasy, was a far more appropriate celebration of glory and compliance.

Karkasy stared at the Titan for a little while. He'd never seen anything like it before in his life, except in picts. The awesome sight of it almost made the tedious outing worthwhile.

The more he stared at it, the more uncomfortable it made him feel. It was so huge, so threatening, and so very still. He knew it could move. He began to wish it would. He found himself yearning for it to suddenly turn its head or take a step, or otherwise rumble into animation. Its immobility was agonising.

Then he began to fear that if it did suddenly move, he would be quite unmanned, and might be forced to cry out in involuntary terror, and fall to his knees.

A burst of clapping made him jump. Momus had apparently said something apposite, and the iterators were stirring up the crowd in response. Karkasy slapped his sweaty hands together a few times obediently.

Karkasy was sick of it. He knew he couldn't bear to stand there much longer with the Titan staring at him.

He took one last look at the stage. Momus was rambling on, well into his fiftieth minute. The only other point of interest to the whole affair, as far as Karkasy was concerned, stood at the back of the podium behind Momus. Two giants in yellow plate. Two noble Astartes from the VII Legion, the Imperial Fists, the Emperor's Praetorians. They were presumably in attendance to lend Momus an appropriate air of authority. Karkasy guessed the VII had been chosen over the Luna Wolves because of their noted genius in the arts of fortification and defence. The Imperial Fists were fortress builders, warrior masons who raised such impenetrable redoubts that they could be held for eternity against any enemy. Karkasy smelled the artful handiwork of iterator propaganda: the architects of war watching over the architect of peace.

Karkasy had waited to see if either would speak, or come forward to remark upon Momus's plans, but they did not. They stood there, bolters across their broad chests, as static and unwavering as the Titan.

Karkasy turned away, and began to push his way out through the inflexible crowd. He headed towards the rear of the square.

Troopers of the Imperial army had been stationed around the hem of the crowd as a precaution. They had been required to wear full dress uniform, and they were so overheated that their sweaty cheeks were blanched a sickly green-white.

One of them noticed Karkasy moving out through the thinnest part of the audience, and came over to him.

'Where are you going, sir?' he asked.

'I'm dying of thirst,' Karkasy replied.

'There will be refreshments, I'm told, after the presentation,' the soldier said. His voice caught on the word 'refreshments' and Karkasy knew there would be none for the common soldiery.

'Well, I've had enough,' Karkasy said.

'It's not over.'

'I've had enough.'

The soldier frowned. Perspiration beaded at the bridge of his nose, just beneath the rim of his heavy fur shako. His throat and jowls were flushed pink and sheened with sweat.

'I can't allow you to wander away. Movement is supposed to be restricted to approved areas.'

Karkasy grinned wickedly. 'And I thought you were here to keep trouble out, not keep us in.'

The soldier didn't find that funny, or even ironic. 'We're here to keep you safe, sir,' he said. 'I'd like to see your permit.'

Karkasy took out his papers. They were an untidy, crumpled bundle, warm and damp from his trouser pocket. Karkasy waited, faintly embarrassed, while the soldier studied them. He had never liked barking up against authority, especially not in front of people, though the back of the crowd didn't seem to be at all interested in the exchange.

'You're a remembrancer?' the soldier asked.

'Yes. Poet,' Karkasy added before the inevitable second question got asked.

The soldier looked up from the papers into Karkasy's face, as if searching for some essential characteristic of poet-hood that might be discerned there, comparable to a Navigator's third eye or a slave-drone's serial tattoo. He'd likely never seen a poet before, which was all right, because Karkasy had never seen a Titan before.

'You should stay here, sir,' the soldier said, handing the papers back to Karkasy.

'But this is pointless,' Karkasy said. 'I have been sent to make a memorial of these events. I can't get close to anything. I can't even hear properly what that fool's got to say. Can you imagine the wrong-headedness of this? Momus isn't even history. He's just another kind of memorialist. I've been allowed here to remember his remembrance, and I can't even do that properly. I'm so far removed from the things I should be engaging with, I might as well have stayed on Terra and made do with a telescope.'

The soldier shrugged. He'd lost the thread of Karkasy's speech early on. 'You should stay here, sir. For your own safety.'

'I was told the city had been made safe,' Karkasy said. 'We're only a day or two from compliance, aren't we?'

The soldier leaned forward discreetly, so close that Karkasy could smell the stale odour of garbage the heat was infusing into his breath. 'Just between us, that's the official line, but there has been trouble. Insurgents. Loyalists. You always get it in a conquered city, no matter how clean the victory. The back streets are not secure.'

'Really?'

'They're saying loyalists, but it's just discontent, if you ask me. These bastards have lost it all, and they're not happy about it.'

Karkasy nodded. 'Thanks for the tip,' he said, and turned back to rejoin the crowd.

Five minutes later, with Momus still droning on and Karkasy close to despair, an elderly noblewoman in the crowd fainted, and there was a small commotion. The soldiers hurried in to take charge of the situation and carry her into the shade.

When the soldier's back was turned, Karkasy took himself off out of the square and into the streets beyond.

He walked for a while through empty courts and high-walled streets where shadows pooled like water. The day's heat was still pitiless, but moving around made it more bearable. Periodic breezes gusted down alleyways, but they were not at all relieving. Most were so full of sand and grit that Karkasy had to turn his back to them and close his eyes until they abated.

The streets were vacant, except for an occasional figure

hunched in the shadows of a doorway, or half-visible behind broken shutters. He wondered if anybody would respond if he approached them, but felt reluctant to try. The silence was penetrating, and to break it would have felt as improper as disturbing a mourning vigil.

He was alone, properly alone for the first time in over a year, and master of his own actions. It felt tremendously liberating. He could go where he pleased, and quickly began to exercise that privilege, taking street turns at random, walking where his feet took him. For a while, he kept the still-unmoving Titan in sight, as a point of reference, but it was soon eclipsed by towers and high roofs, so he resigned himself to getting lost. Getting lost would be liberating too. There were always the great towers of the palace. He could follow those back to their roots if necessary.

War had ravaged many parts of the city he passed through. Buildings had toppled into white and dusty heaps of slag, or been reduced to their very basements. Others were roofless, or burned out, or wounded in their structures, or simply rendered into facades, their innards blown out, standing like the wooden flats of stage scenery.

Craters and shell holes pock-marked certain pavements, or the surfaces of metalled roads, sometimes forming strange rows and patterns, as if their arrangement was deliberate, or concealed, by some secret code, great truths of life and death. There was a smell in the dry, hot air, like burning or blood or ordure, yet none of those things. A mingled scent, an afterscent. It wasn't burning he could smell, it was things burnt. It wasn't blood, it was dry residue. It wasn't ordure, it was the seeping consequence of sewer systems broken and cracked by the bombardment.

Many streets had stacks of belongings piled up along the pavements. Furniture, bundles of clothing, kitchenware. A great deal of it was in disrepair, and had evidently been recovered from ruined dwellings. Other piles seemed more intact, the items carefully packed in trunks and coffers. People were intending to quit the city, he realised. They had piled up their possessions in readiness while they tried to procure transportation, or perhaps the relevant permission from the occupying authorities.

Almost every street and yard bore some slogan or other notice upon its walls. All were hand written, in a great variety of styles and degrees of calligraphic skill. Some were daubed in pitch, others paint or dye, others chalk or charcoal – the latter, Karkasy reasoned, marks made by the employment of burnt sticks and splinters taken from the ruins. Many were indecipherable, or

unfathomable. Many were bold, angry graffiti, splenetically cursing the invaders or defiantly announcing a surviving spark of
resistance. They called for death, for uprising, for revenge.

Others were lists, carefully recording the names of the citizens
who had died in that place, or plaintive requests for news about
the missing loved ones listed below. Others were agonised state-
ments of lament, or minutely and delicately transcribed texts
of some sacred significance.

Karkasy found himself increasingly captivated by them, by
the variation and contrast of them, and the emotions they conveyed. For the first time, the first true and proper time since he'd
left Terra, he felt the poet in him respond. This feeling excited
him. He had begun to fear that he might have accidentally left
his poetry behind on Terra in his hurry to embark, or at least
that it malingered, folded and unpacked, in his quarters on the
ship, like his least favourite shirt.

He felt the muse return, and it made him smile, despite the
heat and the mummification of his throat. It seemed apt, after
all, that it should be words that brought words back into his
mind.

He took out his chapbook and his pen. He was a man of traditional inclinations, believing that no great lyric could ever be
composed on the screen of a data-slate, a point of variance that
had almost got him into a fist fight with Palisad Hadray, the
other 'poet of note' amongst the remembrancer group. That had
been near the start of their conveyance to join the expedition,
during one of the informal dinners held to allow the remembrancers to get to know one another. He would have won the
fight, if it had come to it. He was fairly sure of that. Even though
Hadray was an especially large and fierce woman.

Karkasy favoured notebooks of thick, cream cartridge paper,
and at the start of his long, feted career, had sourced a supplier
in one of Terra's arctic hives, who specialised in antique methods of paper manufacture. The firm was called Bondsman, and
it offered a particularly pleasing quarto chapbook of fifty leaves,
bound in a case of soft, black kid, with an elasticated strap to
keep it closed. The Bondsman Number 7. Karkasy, a sallow, raw-
headed youth back then, had paid a significant proportion of
his first royalty income for an order of two hundred. The volumes had come, packed head to toe, in a waxed box lined with
tissue paper, which had smelled, to him at least, of genius and
potential. He had used the books sparingly, leaving not one precious page unfilled before starting a new one. As his fame grew,
and his earnings soared, he had often thought about ordering

another box, but always stopped when he realised he had over half the original shipment still to use up. All his great works had been composed upon the pages of Bondsman Number 7's. His *Fanfare to Unity*, all eleven of his *Imperial Cantos*, his *Ocean Poems*, even the meritorious and much republished *Reflections and Odes*, written in his thirtieth year, which had secured his reputation and won him the Ethiopic Laureate.

The year before his selection to the role of remembrancer, after what had been, in all fairness, a decade of unproductive doldrums that had seen him living off past glories, he had decided to rejuvenate his muse by placing an order for another box. He had been dismayed to discover that Bondsman had ceased operation.

Ignace Karkasy had nine unused volumes left in his possession. He had brought them all with him on the voyage. But for an idiot scribble or two, their pages were unmarked.

On a blazing, dusty street corner in the broken city, he took the chapbook out of his coat pocket, and slid off the strap. He found his pen – an antique plunger-action fountain, for his traditionalist tastes applied as much to the means of marking as what should be marked – and began to write.

The heat had almost congealed the ink in his nib, but he wrote anyway, copying out such pieces of wall writing as affected him, sometimes attempting to duplicate the manner and form of their delineation.

He recorded one or two at first, as he moved from street to street, and then became more inclusive, and began to mark down almost every slogan he saw. It gave him satisfaction and delight to do this. He could feel, quite definitely, a lyric beginning to form, taking shape from the words he read and recorded. It would be superlative. After years of absence, the muse had flown back into his soul as if it had never been away.

He realised he had lost track of time. Though it was still stifling hot and bright, the hour was late, and the blazing sun had worked its way over, lower in the sky. He had filled almost twenty pages, almost half his chapbook.

He felt a sudden pang. What if he had only nine volumes of genius left in him? What if that box of Bondsman Number 7's, delivered so long ago, represented the creative limits of his career?

He shuddered, chilled despite the clinging heat, and put his chapbook and pen away. He was standing on a lonely, war-scabbed street-corner, persecuted by the sun, unable to fathom which direction to turn.

For the first time since escaping Peeter Egon Momus's presentation, Karkasy felt afraid. He felt that eyes were watching him from the blind ruins.

He began to retrace his steps, slouching through gritty shadow and dusty light. Only once or twice did a new graffito persuade him to stop and take out his chapbook again.

He'd been walking for some time, in circles probably, for all the streets had begun to look the same, when he found the eating house. It occupied the ground floor and basement of a large basalt tenement, and bore no sign, but the smell of cooking announced its purpose. Door-shutters had been opened onto the street, and there was a handful of tables set out. For the first time, he saw people in numbers. Locals, in dark sun cloaks and shawls, as unresponsive and indolent as the few souls he had glimpsed in doorways. They were sitting at the tables under a tattered awning, alone or in small, silent groups, drinking thimble glasses of liquor or eating food from finger bowls.

Karkasy remembered the state of his throat, and his belly remembered itself with a groan.

He walked inside, into the shade, nodding politely to the patrons. None responded.

In the cold gloom, he found a wooden bar with a dresser behind it, laden with glassware and spouted bottles. The hostel keeper, an old woman in a khaki wrap, eyed him suspiciously from behind the serving counter.

'Hello,' he said.

She frowned back.

'Do you understand me?' he asked.

She nodded slowly.

'That's good, very good. I had been told our languages were largely the same, but that there were some accent and dialect differences.' He trailed off.

The old woman said something that might have been 'What?' or might have been any number of curses or interrogatives.

'You have food?' he asked. Then he mimed eating.

She continued to stare at him.

'Food?' he asked.

She replied with a flurry of guttural words, none of which he could make out. Either she didn't have food, or was unwilling to serve him, or she didn't have any food for the likes of him.

'Something to drink then?' he asked.

No response.

He mimed drinking, and when that brought nothing, pointed at the bottles behind her.

She turned and took down one of the glass containers, select-
ing one as if he had indicated it directly instead of generally.
It was three-quarters full of a clear, oily fluid that roiled in the
gloom. She thumped it onto the counter, and then put a thimble glass beside it.

'Very good,' he smiled. 'Very, very good. Well done. Is this
local? Ah ha! Of course it is, of course it is. A local speciality?
You're not going to tell me, are you? Because you have no idea
what I'm actually saying, have you?'

She stared blankly at him.

He picked up the bottle and poured a measure into the glass.
The liquor flowed as slowly and heavily through the spout as
his ink had done from his pen in the street. He put the bottle
down and lifted the glass, toasting her.

'Your health,' he said brightly, 'and to the prosperity of your
world. I know things are hard now, but trust me, this is all for
the best. All for the very best.'

He swigged the drink. It tasted of liquorice and went down
very well, heating his dry gullet and lighting a buzz in his gut.

'Excellent,' he said, and poured himself a second. 'Very good
indeed. You're not going to answer me, are you? I could ask your
name and your lineage and anything at all, and you would just
stand there like a statue, wouldn't you? Like a Titan?'

He sank the second glass and poured a third. He felt very
good about himself now, better than he had done for hours,
better even than when the muse had flown back to him in the
streets. In truth, drink had always been a more welcome companion to Ignace Karkasy than any muse, though he would never
have been willing to admit it, or to admit the fact that his affection for drink had long weighed down his career, like rocks in
a sack. Drink and his muse, both beloved of him, each pulling
in opposite directions.

He drank his third glass, and tipped out a fourth. Warmth
infused him, a biological warmth much more welcome than the
brutal heat of the day. It made him smile. It revealed to him
how extraordinary this false Terra was, how complex and intoxicating. He felt love for it, and pity, and tremendous goodwill.
This world, this place, this hostelry, would not be forgotten.

Suddenly remembering something else, he apologised to the
old woman, who had remained facing him across the counter like a fugued servitor, and reached into his pocket. He had
currency – Imperial coin and plastek wafers. He made a pile of
them on the stained and glossy bartop.

'Imperial,' he said, 'but you take that. I mean, you're obliged to. I was told that by the iterators this morning. Imperial currency is legal tender now, to replace your local coin. Terra, you don't know what I'm saying, do you? How much do I owe you?'

No answer.

He sipped his fourth drink and pushed the pile of cash towards her. 'You decide, then. You tell me. Take for the whole bottle.' He tapped his finger against the side of the flask. 'The whole bottle? How much?'

He grinned and nodded at the money. The old woman looked at the heap, reached out a bony hand and picked up a five aquila piece. She studied it for a moment, then spat on it and threw it at Karkasy. The coin bounced off his belly and fell onto the floor.

Karkasy blinked and then laughed. The laughter boomed out of him, hard and joyous, and he was quite unable to keep it in. The old woman stared at him. Her eyes widened ever so slightly.

Karkasy lifted up the bottle and the glass. 'I tell you what,' he said. 'Keep it all. All of it.'

He walked away and found an empty table in the corner of the place. He sat down and poured another drink, looking about him. Some of the silent patrons were staring at him. He nodded back, cheerfully.

They looked so human, he thought, and realised it was a ridiculous thing to think, because they were without a doubt human. But at the same time, they weren't. Their drab clothes, their drab manner, the set of their features, their way of sitting and looking and eating. They seemed a little like animals, man-shaped creatures trained to ape human behaviour, yet not quite accomplished in that art.

'Is that what five thousand years of separation does to a species?' he asked aloud. No one answered, and some of his watchers turned away.

Was that what five thousand years did to the divided branches of mankind? He took another sip. Biologically identical, but for a few strands of genetic inheritance, and yet culturally grown so far apart. These were men who lived and walked and drank and shat, just as he did. They lived in houses and raised cities, and wrote upon walls and even spoke the same language, old women not withstanding. Yet time and division had grown them along alternate paths. Karkasy saw that clearly now. They were a graft from the rootstock, grown under another sun, similar yet alien. Even the way they sat at tables and sipped at drinks.

Karkasy stood up suddenly. The muse had abruptly jostled the pleasure of drink out of the summit of his mind. He bowed to the old woman as he collected up his glass and two-thirds empty bottle, and said, 'My thanks, madam.'

Then he teetered back out into the sunlight.

He found a vacant lot a few streets away that had been levelled to rubble by bombing, and perched himself on a chunk of basalt. Setting down the bottle and the glass carefully, he took out his half-filled Bondsman Number 7 and began to write again, forming the first few stanzas of a lyric that owed much to the writings on the walls and the insight he had garnered in the hostelry. It flowed well for a while, and then dried up.

He took another drink, trying to restart his inner voice. Tiny black ant-like insects milled industriously in the rubble around him, as if trying to rebuild their own miniature lost city. He had to brush one off the open page of his chapbook. Others raced exploratively over the toe-caps of his boots in a frenetic expedition.

He stood up, imagining itches, and decided this wasn't a place to sit. He gathered up his bottle and his glass, taking another sip once he'd fished out the ant floating in it with his finger.

A building of considerable size and magnificence faced him across the damaged lot. He wondered what it was. He stumbled over the rubble towards it, almost losing his footing on the loose rocks from time to time.

What was it – a municipal hall, a library, a school? He wandered around it, admiring the fine rise of the walls and the decorated headers of the stonework. Whatever it was, the building was important. Miraculously, it had been spared the destruction visited on its neighbouring lots.

Karkasy found the entrance, a towering arch of stone filled with copper doors. They weren't locked. He pushed his way in.

The interior of the building was so profoundly and refreshingly cool it almost made him gasp. It was a single space, an arched roof raised on massive ouslite pillars, the floor dressed in cold onyx. Under the end windows, some kind of stone structure rose.

Karkasy paused. He put down his bottle beside the base of one of the pillars, and advanced down the centre of the building with his glass in his hand. He knew there was a word for a place like this. He searched for it.

Sunlight, filleted by coloured glass, slanted through the thin windows. The stone structure at the end of the chamber was a carved lectern supporting a very massive and very old book.

Karkasy touched the crinkled parchment of the book's open

pages with delight. It appealed to him the same way as the pages of a Bondsman Number 7 did. The sheets were old, and faded, covered with ornate black script and hand-coloured images.

This was an altar, he realised. This place, a temple, a fane!

'Terra alive!' he declared, and then winced as his words echoed back down the cool vault. History had taught him about fanes and religious belief, but he had never before set foot inside such a place. A place of sprits and divinity. He sensed that the spirits were looking down on his intrusion with disapproval, and then laughed at his own idiocy. There were no spirits. Not anywhere in the cosmos. Imperial Truth had taught him that. The only spirits in this building were the ones in his glass and his belly.

He looked at the pages again. Here was the truth of it, the crucial mark of difference between his breed of man and the local variety. They were heathens. They continued to embrace the superstitions that the fundamental strand of mankind had set aside. Here was the promise of an afterlife, and an ethereal world. Here was the nonsense of a faith in the intangible.

Karkasy knew that there were some, many perhaps, amongst the population of the compliant Imperium, who longed for a return to those ways. God, in every incarnation and pantheon, was long perished, but still men hankered after the ineffable. Despite prosecution, new credos and budding religions were sprouting up amongst the cultures of Unified Man. Most vigorous of all was the Imperial Creed that insisted humanity adopt the Emperor as a divine being. A God-Emperor of Mankind.

The idea was ludicrous and, officially, heretical. The Emperor had always refused such adoration in the most stringent terms, denying his apotheosis. Some said it would only happen after his death, and as he was functionally immortal, that tended to cap the argument. Whatever his powers, whatever his capacity, whatever his magnificence as the finest and most gloriously total leader of the species, he was still just a man. The Emperor liked to remind mankind of this whenever he could. It was an edict that rattled around the bureaucracies of the expanding Imperium. The Emperor is the Emperor, and he is great and everlasting.

But he is not a god, and he refuses any worship offered to him.

Karkasy took a swig and put his empty thimble-glass down, at an angle on the edge of the lectern shelf. The Lectitio Divinitatus, that's what it was called. The missal of the underground wellspring that strove, in secret, to establish the Cult of the Emperor, against his will. It was said that even some of the upstanding members of the Council of Terra supported its aims.

The Emperor as god. Karkasy stifled a laugh. Five thousand years of blood, war and fire to expunge all gods from the culture, and now the man who achieved that goal supplants them as a new deity.

'How foolish is mankind?' Karkasy laughed, enjoying the way his words echoed around the empty fane. 'How desperate and flailing? Is it that we simply need a concept of god to fulfill us? Is that part of our make up?'

He fell silent, considering the point he had raised to himself. A good point, well-reasoned. He wondered where his bottle had gone.

It *was* a good point. Maybe that was mankind's ultimate weakness. Maybe it was one of humanity's basic impulses, the need to believe in another, higher order. Perhaps faith was like a vacuum, sucking up credulity in a frantic effort to fill its own void. Perhaps it was a part of mankind's genetic character to need, to hunger for, a spiritual solace.

'Perhaps we are cursed,' Karkasy told the empty fane, 'to crave something which does not exist. There are no gods, no spirits, no daemons. So we make them up, to comfort ourselves.'

The fane seemed oblivious to his ramblings. He took hold of his empty glass and wandered back to where he had left the bottle. Another drink.

He left the fane and threaded his way out into the blinding sunlight. The heat was so intense that he had to take another swig.

Karkasy wobbled down a few streets, away from the temple, and heard a rushing, roasting noise. He discovered a team of Imperial soldiers, stripped to the waist, using a flamer to erase anti-Imperial slogans from a wall. They had evidently been working their way down the street, for all the walls displayed swathes of heat burns.

'Don't do that,' he said.

The soldiers turned and looked at him, their flamer spitting. From his garments and demeanour, he was unmistakably not a local.

'Don't do that,' he said again.

'Orders, sir,' said one of the troopers.

'What are you doing out here?' asked another.

Karkasy shook his head and left them alone. He trudged through narrow alleys and open courts, sipping from the spout of the bottle.

He found another vacant lot very similar to the one he had sat down in before, and placed his rump upon a scalene block of basalt. He took out his chapbook and ran through the stanzas he had written.

They were terrible.

He groaned as he read them, then became angry and tore the precious pages out. He balled the thick, cream paper up and tossed it away into the rubble.

Karkasy suddenly became aware that eyes were staring at him from the shadows of doorways and windows. He could barely make out their shapes, but knew full well that locals were watching him.

He got up, and quickly retrieved the balls of crumpled paper he had discarded, feeling that he had no right to add in any way to the mess. He began to hurry down the street, as thin boys emerged from hiding to lob stones and jeers after him.

He found himself, unexpectedly, in the street of the hostelry again. It was uninhabited, but he was pleased to have found it as his bottle had become unaccountably empty.

He went into the gloom. There was no one around. Even the old woman had disappeared. His pile of Imperial currency lay where he had left it on the counter.

Seeing it, he felt authorised to help himself to another bottle from behind the bar. Clutching the bottle in his hand, he very carefully sat down at one of the tables and poured another drink.

He had been sitting there for an indefinite amount of time when a voice asked him if he was all right.

Ignace Karkasy blinked and looked up. The gang of Imperial army troops who had been burning clean the walls of the city had entered the hostelry, and the old woman had reappeared to fetch them drinks and food.

The officer looked down at Karkasy as his men took their seats.

'Are you all right, sir?' he asked.

'Yes. Yes, yes, yes,' Karkasy slurred.

'You don't look all right, pardon me for saying. Should you be out in the city?'

Karkasy nodded furiously, tucking into his pocket for his permit. It wasn't there. 'I'm meant to be here,' he said, instead. 'Meant to. I was ordered to come. To hear Eater Piton Momus. Shit, no, that's wrong. To hear Peeter Egon Momus present his plans for the new city. That's why I'm here. I'm meant to be.'

The officer regarded him cautiously. 'If you say so, sir. They say Momus has drawn up a wonderful scheme for the reconstruction.'

'Oh yes, quite wonderful,' Karkasy replied, reaching for his bottle and missing. 'Quite bloody wonderful. An eternal memorial to our victory here...'

'Sir?'

'It won't last,' Karkasy said. 'No, no. It won't last. It can't. Nothing lasts. You look like a wise man to me, friend, what do you think?'

'I think you should be on your way, sir,' the officer said gently.

'No, no, no... about the city! The city! It won't last, Terra take Peeter Egon Momus. To the dust, all things return. As far as I can see, this city was pretty wonderful before we came and hobbled it.'

'Sir, I think–'

'No, you don't,' Karkasy said, shaking his head. 'You don't, and no one does. This city was supposed to last forever, but we broke it and laid it in tatters. Let Momus rebuild it, it will happen again, and again. The work of man is destined to perish. Momus said he plans a city that will celebrate mankind forever. You know what? I bet that's what the architects who built this place thought too.'

'Sir–'

'What man does comes apart, eventually. You mark my words. This city, Momus's city. The Imperium–'

'Sir, you–'

Karkasy rose to his feet, blinking and wagging a finger. 'Don't "sir" me! The Imperium will fall asunder as soon as we construct it! You mark my words! It's as inevitable as–'

Pain abruptly splintered Karkasy's face, and he fell down, bewildered. He registered a frenzy of shouting and movement, then felt boots and fists slamming into him, over and over again. Enraged by his words, the troopers had fallen upon him. Shouting, the officer tried to pull them off.

Bones snapped. Blood spurted from Karkasy's nostrils.

'Mark my words!' he coughed. 'Nothing we build will last forever! You ask these bloody locals!'

A bootcap cracked into his sternum. Bloody fluid washed into his mouth.

'Get off him! Get off him!' the officer was yelling, trying to rein in his provoked and angry men.

By the time he managed to do so, Ignace Karkasy was no longer pontificating.

Or breathing.

SIX

Counsel
A question well answered
Two gods in one room

Torgaddon was waiting for him in the towering ante-hall behind the strategium.

'There you are,' he grinned.

'Here I am,' Loken agreed.

'There will be a question,' Torgaddon remarked, keeping his voice low. 'It will seem a minor thing, and will not be obviously directed to you but be ready to catch it.'

'Me?'

'No, I was talking to myself. Yes, you, Garviel! Consider it a baptismal test. Come on.'

Loken didn't like the sound of Torgaddon's words, but he appreciated the warning. He followed Torgaddon down the length of the ante-hall. It was a perilously tall, narrow place, with embossed columns of wood set into the walls that soared up and branched like carved trees to support a glass roof two hundred metres above them, through which the stars could be seen. Darkwood panels cased the walls between the columns, and they were covered with millions of lines of hand-painted names and numbers, all rendered in exquisite gilt lettering. They were the names of the dead: all those of the Legions, the army, the fleet and the Divisio Militaris who had fallen since the start of the Great Crusade in actions where this flagship vessel had been present. The names of immortal heroes were limned here on the walls, grouped in columns below header legends that proclaimed the world-sites of famous actions and hallowed conquests. From this display, the ante-hall earned its particular name: the Avenue of Glory and Lament.

The walls of fully two-thirds of the ante-hall were filled up with golden names. As the two striding captains in their glossy white plate drew closer to the strategium end, the wall boards became bare, unoccupied. They passed a group of hooded necrologists huddled by the last, half-filled panel, who were carefully stencilling new names onto the dark wood with gold-dipped brushes.

The latest dead. The roll call from the High City battle.

The necrologists stopped work and bowed their heads as the two captains went by. Torgaddon didn't spare them a second glance, but Loken turned to read the half-writ names. Some of them were brothers from Locasta he would never see again.

He could smell the tangy oil suspension of the gold-leaf the necrologists were using.

'Keep up,' Torgaddon grunted.

High doors, lacquered gold and crimson, stood closed at the end of the Avenue Hall. Before them, Aximand and Abaddon were waiting. They were likewise fully armoured, their heads bare, their brush-crested helms held under their left arms. Abaddon's great white shoulder plates were draped with a black wolf-pelt.

'Garviel,' he smiled.

'It doesn't do to keep him waiting,' Aximand grumbled. Loken wasn't sure if Little Horus meant Abaddon or the commander. 'What were you two gabbing about? Like fishwives, the pair of you.'

'I was just asking him if he'd settled Vipus in,' Torgaddon said simply.

Aximand glanced at Loken, his wide-set eyes languidly half-hooded by his lids.

'And I was reassuring Tarik that I had,' Loken added. Evidently, Torgaddon's quiet heads-up had been for his ears only.

'Let's enter,' Abaddon said. He raised his gloved hand and pushed the gold and crimson doors wide.

A short processional lay before them, a twenty-metre colonnade of ebon stone chased with a fretwork of silver wire. It was lined by forty Guardsmen of the Imperial army, members of Varvaras's own Byzant Janizars, twenty against each wall. They were splendidly appointed in full dress uniforms: long cream greatcoats with gold frogging, high-crowned chrome helms with basket visors and scarlet cockades, and matching sashes. As the

Mournival came through the doors, the Janizars brandished their ornate power lances, beginning with the pair directly inside the doorway. The polished blades of the weapons whirled up into place in series, like chasing dominoes along the processional, each facing pair of weapons locking into position just before the marching captains caught up with the ripple.

The final pair came to salute, eyes-front, in perfect discipline, and the Mournival stepped past them onto the deck of the strategium.

The strategium was a great, semicircular platform that projected like a lip out above the tiered theatre of the flagship's bridge. Far below lay the principal command level, thronging with hundreds of uniformed personnel and burnished aide servitors, tiny as ants. To either side, the beehive sub-decks of the secondary platforms, dressed in gold and black ironwork, rose up, past the level of the projecting strategium, up into the roof itself, each storey busy with Navy staff, operators, cogitation officers and astropaths. The front section of the bridge chamber was a great, strutted window, through which the constellations and the ink of space could be witnessed. The standards of the Luna Wolves and the Imperial Fists hung from the arching roof, either side of the staring eye banner of the Warmaster himself. That great banner was marked, in golden thread, with the decree: 'I am the Emperor's Vigilance and the Eye of Terra.'

Loken remembered the award of that august symbol with pride during the great triumph after Ullanor was done.

In all his decades of service, Loken had only been on the bridge of the *Vengeful Spirit* twice before: once to formally accept his promotion to captain, and then again to mark his elevation to the captaincy of the Tenth. The scale of the place took his breath away, as it had done both times before.

The strategium deck itself was an ironwork platform which supported, at its centre, a circular dais of plain, unfinished ouslite, one metre deep and ten in diameter. The commander had always eschewed any form of throne or seat. The ironwork walk space around the dais was half-shadowed by the overhang of tiered galleries that climbed the slopes of the chamber behind it. Glancing up, Loken saw huddles of senior iterators, tacticians, ship captains of the expedition fleet and other notables gathering to view the proceedings. He looked for Sindermann, but couldn't find his face.

Several attendant figures stood quietly around the edges of the dais. Lord Commander Hektor Varvaras, marshal of the expedition's army, a tall, precise aristocrat in red robes, stood discussing the content of a data-slate with two formally uniformed army aides. Boas Comnenus, Master of the Fleet, waited, drumming steel fingers on the edge of the ouslite plinth. He was a squat bear of a man, his ancient, flaccid body encased in a superb silver-and-steel exo-skeleton, further draped in robes of deep, rich, selpic blue. Neatly machined occular lenses whirred and exchanged in the augmetic frame that supplanted his long-dead eyes.

Ing Mae Sing, the expedition's Mistress of Astropaths, stood to the master's left, a gaunt, blind spectre in a hooded white gown, and, round from her, in order, the High Senior of the Navis Nobilite, Navigator Chorogus, the Master Companion of Vox, the Master Companion of Lucidation, the senior tacticae, the senior heraldists, and various gubernatorial legates.

Each one, Loken noticed, had placed a single personal item on the edge of the dais where they stood: a glove, a cap, a wand-stave.

'We stay in the shadows,' Torgaddon told him, bringing Loken up short under the edge of the shade cast by the balcony above. 'This is the Mournival's place, apart, yet present.'

Loken nodded, and remained with Torgaddon and Aximand in the symbolic shadow of the overhang. Abaddon stepped forward into the light, and took his place at the edge of the dais between Varvarus, who nodded pleasantly to him, and Comnenus, who didn't. Abaddon placed his helm upon the edge of the ouslite disc.

'An item placed on the dais registers a desire to be heard and noted,' Torgaddon told Loken. 'Ezekyle has a place by dint of his status as first captain. For now, he will speak as first captain, not as the Mournival.'

'Will I get the hang of this ever?' Loken asked.

'No, not at all,' Torgaddon said. Then he grinned. 'Yes, you will. Of course, you will!'

Loken noticed another figure, removed from the main assembly. The man, if it were a man, lurked at the rail of the strategium deck, gazing out across the chasm of the bridge. He was a machine, it seemed, much more a machine than a man. Vague relics of flesh and muscle remained in the skeletal fabric of his mechanical body, a fabulously wrought armature of gold and steel.

'Who is that?' Loken whispered.

'Regulus,' Aximand replied curtly. 'Adept of the Mechanicum.'

So that was what a Mechanicum adept looked like, Loken thought. That was the sort of being who could command the invincible Titans into war.

'Hush now,' Torgaddon said, tapping Loken on the arm.

Plated glass doors on the other side of the platform slid open, and laughter boomed out. A huge figure came out onto the strategium, talking and laughing animatedly, along with a diminutive presence who scuttled to keep up.

Everybody dropped in a bow. Loken, going down on one knee, could hear the rustle of others bowing in the steep balconies above him. Boas Comnenus did so slowly, because his exoskeleton was ancient. Adept Regulus did so slowly, not because his machine body was stiff, but rather because he was clearly reluctant.

Warmaster Horus looked around, smiled, and then leapt up onto the dais in a single bound. He stood at the centre of the ouslite disc, and turned slowly.

'My friends,' he said. 'Honour's done. Up you get.'

Slowly, they rose and beheld him.

He was as magnificent as ever, Loken thought. Massive and limber, a demigod manifest, wrapped in white-gold armour and pelts of fur. His head was bare. Shaven, sculptural, his face was noble, deeply tanned by multiple sunlights, his wide-spaced eyes bright, his teeth gleaming. He smiled and nodded to each and every one of them.

He had such vitality, like a force of nature – a tornado, a tempest, an avalanche – trapped in humanoid form and distilled, the potential locked in. He rotated slowly on the dais, grinning, nodding to some, pointing out certain friends with a familiar laugh.

The primarch looked at Loken, back in the shadows of the overhang, and his smile seemed to broaden for a second.

Loken felt a shudder of fear. It was pleasant and vigorous. Only the Warmaster could make an Astartes feel that.

'Friends,' Horus said. His voice was like honey, like steel, like a whisper, like all of those things mixed as one. 'My dear friends and comrades of the 63rd Expedition, is it really that time again?'

Laughter rippled around the deck, and from the galleries above.

'Briefing time,' Horus chuckled, 'and I salute you all for coming here to bear the tedium of yet another session. I promise I'll keep you no longer than is necessary. First though…'

Horus jumped back down off the dais and stooped to place a sheltering arm around the tiny shoulders of the man who had accompanied him out of the inner chamber, like a father showing off a small child to his brothers. So embraced, the man fixed a stiff, sickly grin upon his face, more a desperate grimace than a show of pleasure.

'Before we begin,' Horus said, 'I want to talk about my good friend Peeter Egon Momus here. How I deserved... pardon me, how *humanity* deserved an architect as fine and gifted as this, I don't know. Peeter has been telling me about his designs for the new High City here, and they are wonderful. Wonderful, wonderful.'

'Really, I don't know, my lord...' Momus harrumphed, his rictus trembling. The architect designate was beginning to shake, enduring direct exposure to such supreme attention.

'Our lord the Emperor himself sent Peeter to us,' Horus told them. 'He knew his worth. You see, I don't want to conquer. Conquest of itself is so messy, isn't it Ezekyle?'

'Yes, lord,' Abaddon murmured.

'How can we draw the lost outposts of man back into one harmonious whole if all we bring them is conquest? We are duty-bound to leave them better than we found them, enlightened by the communication of the Imperial Truth and dazzlingly made over as august provinces of our wide estate. This expedition – and all expeditions – must look to the future and be mindful that what we leave in our wake must stand as an enduring statement of our intent, especially upon worlds, as here, where we have been forced to inflict damage in the promulgation of our message. We must leave legacies behind us. Imperial cities, monuments to the new age, and fitting memorials to those who have fallen in the struggle to establish it. Peeter, my friend Peeter here, understands this. I urge you all to take the time to visit his workshops and review his marvellous schemes. And I look forward to seeing the genius of his vision gracing all the new cities we build in the course of our crusade.'

Applause broke out.

'A-all the new cities...' Momus coughed.

'Peeter is the man for the job,' Horus cried, ignoring the architect's muted gasp. 'I am at one with the way he perceives architecture as celebration. He understands, like no other, I believe, how the spirit of the crusade may be realised in steel and glass and stone. What we raise up is far more important than what we strike down. What we leave behind us, men must admire for eternity, and say "This was well done indeed. This is what the Imperium means, and without it we would be shadows". For that, Peeter's our man. Let's laud him now!'

A huge explosion of applause rang out across the vast chamber. Many officers in the command tiers below joined in. Peeter

Egon Momus looked slightly glazed as he was led off the strate-gium by an aide.

Horus leapt back onto the dais. 'Let's begin... my worthy adept?'

Regulus stepped towards the edge of the dais and put a pol-ished machine-cog down delicately on the lip of the ouslite. When he spoke, his voice was augmented and inhuman, like an electric wind brushing through the boughs of steel trees. 'My lord Warmaster, the Mechanicum is satisfied with this rock. We continue to study, with great interest, the technolo-gies captured here. The gravitic and phasic weapons are being reverse-engineered in our forges. At last report, three standard template construct patterns, previously unknown to us, have been recovered.'

Horus clapped his hands together. 'Glory to our brothers of the tireless Mechanicum! Slowly, we piece together the missing parts of humanity's knowledge. The Emperor will be delighted, as will, I'm sure, your Martian lords.'

Regulus nodded, lifting up the cog and stepping back from the dais.

Horus looked around. 'Rakris? My dear Rakris?'

Lord Governor Elect Rakris, a portly man in dove-grey robes, had already placed his sceptre-wand on the edge of the dais to mark his participation. Now he fiddled with it as he made his report. Horus heard him out patiently, nodding encouragingly from time to time. Rakris droned on, at unnecessary length. Loken felt sorry for him. One of Lord Commander Varvaras's generals, Rakris had been selected to remain at Sixty-Three Nine-teen as governor overseer, marshalling the occupation forces as the world transmuted into a full Imperial state. Rakris was a career soldier, and it was clear that, though he took his elec-tion as a signal honour, he was quite aghast at the prospect of being left behind. He looked pale and ill, brooding on the time, not long away, when the expedition fleet left him to manage the work alone. Rakris was Terran born, and Loken knew that once the fleet sailed on and left him to his job, Rakris would feel as abandoned as if he had been marooned. A governorship was intended to be the ultimate reward for a war-hero's service, but it seemed to Loken a quietly terrible fate: to be monarch of a world, and then cast away upon it.

Forever.

The crusade would not be back to visit conquered worlds in a hurry.

'...in truth, my commander,' Rakris was saying, 'it may be

many decades until this world achieves a state of equity with
the Imperium. There is great opposition.'

'How far are we from compliance?' Horus asked, looking
around.

Varvaras replied. 'True compliance, lord? Decades, as my good
friend Rakris says. Functional compliance? Well, that is different.
There is a seed of dissidence in the southern hemisphere that
we cannot quench. Until that is brought into line, this world
cannot be certified.'

Horus nodded. 'So we stay here, if we must, until the job is
done. We must hold over our plans to advance. Such a shame...'
The primarch's smile faded for a second as he pondered. 'Unless
there is another suggestion?'

He looked at Abaddon and let the words hang. Abaddon
seemed to hesitate, and glanced quickly back into the shadows behind him.

Loken realised that this was the question. This was a moment
of counsel when the primarch looked outside the official hierarchy of the expedition's command echelon for the informal
advice of his chosen inner circle.

Torgaddon nudged Loken, but the nudge was unnecessary. Loken had already stepped forward into the light behind
Abaddon.

'My lord Warmaster,' Loken said, almost startled by the sound
of his own voice.

'Captain Loken,' Horus said with a delighted flash of his
eyes. 'The thoughts of the Mournival are always welcome at
my counsel.'

Several present, including Varvaras, made approving sounds.

'My lord, the initial phase of the war here was undertaken
quickly and cleanly,' Loken said. 'A surgical strike by the speartip against the enemy's head to minimise the loss and hardship
that both sides would suffer in a longer, full-scale offensive. A
guerilla war against insurgents would inevitably be an arduous,
drawn out, costly affair. It could last for years without resolution,
eroding Lord Commander Varvaras's precious army resources
and blighting any good beginning of the Lord Governor Elect's
rule. Sixty-Three Nineteen cannot afford it, and neither can the
expedition. I say, and if I speak out of turn, forgive me, I say
that if the speartip was meant to conquer this world in one,
clean blow, it has failed. The work is not yet done. Order the
Legion to finish the job.'

Murmuring sprang up all around. 'You'd have me unleash the
Luna Wolves again, captain?' Horus asked.

Loken shook his head. 'Not the Legion as a whole, sir. Tenth Company. We were first in, and for that we have been praised, but the praise was not deserved, for the job is not done.'

Horus nodded, as if quite taken with this. 'Varvaras?'

'The army always welcomes the support of the noble Legion. The insurgent factions might plague my men for months, as the captain rightly points out, and make a great tally of killing before they are done with. A company of Luna Wolves could crush them utterly and end their mutiny.'

'Rakris?'

'An expedient solution would be a weight off my back, sir,' Rakris said. He smiled. 'It would be a hammer to crush a nut, perhaps, but it would be emphatic. The work would be done, and quickly.'

'First captain?'

'The Mournival speaks with one voice, lord,' Abaddon said. 'I urge for a swift conclusion to our business here, so that Sixty-Three Nineteen can get on with its life, and we can get on with the crusade.'

'So it shall be,' Horus said, smiling broadly again. 'So I make a command of it. Captain, have Tenth Company drawn ready and oathed to the moment. We will anticipate news of your success eagerly. Thank you for speaking your mind plainly, and for cutting to the quick of this thorny problem.'

There was a firm flutter of approving applause.

'Then possibilities open for us after all,' Horus said. 'We can begin to prepare for the next phase. When I signal him...' Horus looked at the blind Mistress of Astropaths, who nodded silently '...our beloved Emperor will be delighted to learn that our portion of the crusade is about to advance again. We should now discuss the options open to us. I thought to brief you on our findings concerning these myself, but there is another who positively insists he is fit to do it.'

Everyone present turned to look as the plate glass doors slid open for a second time. The primarch began to clap, and the applause gathered and swept around the galleries, as Maloghurst limped out onto the stage of the strategium. It was the equerry's first formal appearance since his recovery from the surface.

Maloghurst was a veteran Luna Wolf, and a 'Son of Horus' to boot. He had been in his time a company captain, and might even have risen to the first captaincy had he not been promoted to the office of equerry. A shrewd and experienced soul, Maloghurst's talents for intrigue and intelligence ideally served him in that role, and had long since earned him the title 'Twisted'.

He took no shame in this. The Legion might protect the Warmaster physically, but he protected him politically, guiding and advising, blocking and out-playing, aware and perfectly sensitive to every nuance and current in the expedition's hierarchy. He had never been well-liked, for he was a hard man to get close to, even by the intimidating standards of the Astartes, and he had never made any particular effort to be liked. Most thought of him as a neutral power, a facilitator, loyal only to Horus himself. No one was ever foolish enough to underestimate him.

But circumstance had suddenly made him popular. Beloved almost. Believed dead, he had been found alive, and in the light of Sejanus's death, this had been taken as some compensation. The work of the remembrancer Euphrati Keeler had cemented his new role as the noble, wounded hero as the picts of his unexpected rescue had flashed around the fleet. Now the assembly welcomed him back rapturously, cheering his fortitude and resolve. He had been reinvented through misfortune into an adored hero.

Loken was quite sure Maloghurst was aware of this ironic turn, and fully prepared to make the most of it.

Maloghurst came out into the open. His injuries had been so severe that he was not yet able to clothe himself in the armour of the Legion, and wore instead a white robe with the wolf's head emblem embroidered on the back. A gold signet in the shape of the Warmaster's icon, the staring eye, formed the cloak's clasp under his throat. He limped, and walked with the aid of a metal staff. His back bulged with a kyphotic misalignment. His face, drawn thin and pale since last it had been seen, was lined with effort, and waddings of synthetic skin-gel covered gashes upon his throat and the left side of his head.

Loken was shocked to see that he was now truly twisted. The old, mocking nickname suddenly seemed crass and indelicate.

Horus got down off the dais and threw his arms around his equerry. Varvaras and Abaddon both went over to greet him with warm embraces. Maloghurst smiled, and nodded to them, then nodded and waved up to the galleries around to acknowledge the welcome.

As the applause abated, Maloghurst leaned heavily against the side of the dais, and placed his staff upon it in the ceremonial manner. Instead of returning to his place, the Warmaster stood back, away from the circle, giving his equerry centre stage.

'I have enjoyed,' Maloghurst began, his voice hard, but brittle with effort, 'a certain luxury of relaxation in these last few days.' Laughter rattled out from all sides, and the clapping resumed for a moment.

'Bed rest,' Maloghurst went on, 'that bane of a warrior's life, has suited me well, for it has given me ample opportunity to review the intelligence gathered in these last few months by our advance scouts. However, bed rest, as a thing to be enjoyed, has its limits. I insisted that I be allowed to present this evidence to you today for, Emperor bless me, never in my dreams did I imagine I would die of inaction.'

More approving laughter. Loken smiled. Maloghurst really was making the best use of his new status amongst them. He was almost... likable.

'To review,' Maloghurst said, taking out a control wand and gesturing with it briefly. 'Three key areas are of interest to us at this juncture.' His gestures activated the underdeck hololithic projectors, and shapes of solid light came into being above the strategium, projected so that all in the galleries could see them. The first was a rotating image of the world they orbited, surrounded by graphic indicators of elliptical alignment and precession. The spinning world shrank rapidly until it became part of a system arrangement, similarly draped in schematic overlays, a turning, three-dimensional orrery suspended in the air. Then that too shrank and became a small, highlighted component in a mosaic of stars.

'First,' Maloghurst said, 'this area here, itemised eight fifty-eight one-seven, the cluster adjacent to our current locale.' A particular stellar neighbourhood on the light map glowed. 'Our most obvious and accessible next port of call. Scout ships report eighteen systems of interest, twelve of which promise fundamental worth in terms of elemental resource, but no signs of life or habitation. The searches are not yet conclusive, but at this early juncture might I be so bold as to suggest that this region need not concern the expedition. Subject to certification, these systems should be added to the manifest of the colonial pioneers who follow in our footsteps.'

He waved the wand again, and a different group of stars lit up. 'This second region, estimated as... Master?'

Boas Comnenus cleared his throat and obligingly said, 'Nine weeks, standard travel time to spinward of us, equerry.'

'Nine weeks to spinward, thank you,' Maloghurst replied. 'We have barely begun to scout this district, but there are early indications that some significant culture or cultures, of interstellar capability, exist within its bounds.'

'Currently functioning?' Abaddon asked. Too often, Imperial expeditions came upon the dry traces of long perished societies in the desert of stars.

'Too early to tell, first captain,' Maloghurst said. 'Though the scouts report some discovered relics bear similarities to those we found on seven ninety-three one-five half a decade ago.'

'So, not human?' Adept Regulus asked.

'Too early to tell, sir,' Maloghurst repeated. 'The region has an itemisation code, but I believe you'll all be interested to hear that it bears an Old Terran name. Sagittarius.'

'The Dreadful Sagittary,' Horus whispered, with a delighted grin.

'Quite so, my lord. The region certainly requires further examination.' The crippled equerry moved the wand again, and brought up a third coil of suns. 'Our third option, further to spinward.'

'Eighteen weeks, standard,' Boas Comnenus supplied before he had to be asked.

'Thank you, Master. Our scouts have yet to examine it, but we have received word from the 140th Expedition, commanded by Khitas Frome of the Blood Angels, that opposition to Imperial advance has been encountered there. Reports are patchy, but war has broken out.'

'Human resistance?' Varvaras asked. 'Are we talking about lost colonies?'

'Xenos, sir,' Maloghurst said, succinctly. 'Alien foes, of some capacity. I have sent a missive to the 140th asking if they require our support at this time. It is significantly smaller than ours. No reply has yet been received. We may consider it a priority to venture forward to this region to reinforce the Imperial presence there.'

For the first time since the briefing began, the smile had left the Warmaster's face. 'I will speak with my brother Sanguinius on this matter,' he said. 'I would not see his men perish, unsupported.' He looked at Maloghurst. 'Thank you for this, equerry. We appreciate your efforts, and the brevity of your summation.'

There was a ripple of applause.

'One last thing, my lord,' Maloghurst said. 'A personal matter I wish to clear up. I have become known, so I understand, as Maloghurst the Twisted, for reasons of… character that I know are not lost on any present. I have always rejoiced in the title, though some of you might think that odd. I relish the arts politic, and make no effort to hide that. Some of my aides, as I have learned, have made efforts to have the soubriquet quashed, believing it offends my altered state. They worry that I might find it cruel. A slur. I want all here assembled to know that I do not. My body is broken, but my mind is not. I would take offence if the name was to be dropped out of politeness. I don't value sympathy much, and I don't want pity. I am twisted in body now, but I am still complex in mind. Don't think you are somehow sparing my feelings. I wish to be known as I always was.'

'Well said,' Abaddon cried, and smacked his palms together. The assembly rose in a tumult as brisk as the one that had ushered Maloghurst on to the stage.

The equerry picked up his staff from the dais and, leaning upon it, turned to the Warmaster. Horus raised both hands to restore quiet.

'Our thanks to Maloghurst for presenting these options to us. There is much to consider. I dissolve this briefing now, but I request policy suggestions and remarks to my attention in the next day, ship-time. I urge you to study all possibilities and present your assessments. We will reconvene the day after tomorrow at this time. That is all.'

The meeting broke up. As the upper galleries emptied, buzzing with chatter, the parties on the strategium deck gathered in informal conference. The Warmaster stood in quiet conversation with Maloghurst and the Mechanicum Adept.

'Nicely done,' Torgaddon whispered to Loken.

Loken breathed out. He hadn't realised what a weight of tension had built up in him since his summons to the briefing had arrived.

'Yes, finely put,' said Aximand. 'I approve your commentary, Garviel.'

'I just said what I felt. I made it up as I went along,' Loken admitted.

Aximand frowned at him as if not sure whether he was joking or not.

'Are you not cowed by these circumstances, Horus?' Loken asked.

'At first, I suppose I must have been,' Aximand replied in an off-hand way. 'You get used to it, once you've been through one or two. I found it was helpful to look at his feet.'

'His feet?'

'The Warmaster's feet. Catch his eye and you'll quite forget what you were going to say.' Aximand smiled slightly. It was the first hint of any softening towards Loken that Little Horus had shown.

'Thanks. I'll remember that.'

Abaddon joined them under the shadow of the overhang. 'I knew we'd picked right,' he said, clasping Loken's hand in his own. 'Cut to the quick, that's what the Warmaster wants of us.

A clean appraisal. Good job, Garviel. Now just make sure it's a good job.'

'I will.'

'Need any help? I can lend you the Justaerin if you need them.'

'Thank you, but Tenth can do this.'

Abaddon nodded. 'I'll tell Falkus his widowmakers are superfluous to requirements.'

'Please don't do that,' Loken snapped, alarmed at the prospect of insulting Falkus Kibre, Captain of First Company's Terminator elite. The other three-quarters of the Mournival laughed out loud.

'Your face,' said Torgaddon.

'Ezekyle goads you so easily,' chuckled Aximand.

'Ezekyle knows he will develop a tough skin, soon enough,' Abaddon remarked.

'Captain Loken?' Lord Governor Elect Rakris was approaching them. Abaddon, Aximand and Torgaddon stood aside to let him through. 'Captain Loken,' Rakris said, 'I just wanted to say, sir, I just wanted to say how grateful I was. To take this matter upon yourself and your company. To speak out so very directly. Lord Varvaras's soldiers are trying their best, but they are just men. The regime here is doomed unless firm action is taken.'

'Tenth Company will deal with the problem, lord governor,' Loken said. 'You have my word as an Astartes.'

'Because the army can't hack it?' They looked around and found that the tall, princely figure of Lord Commander Varvaras had joined them too.

'I-I didn't mean to suggest...' Rakris blithered.

'No offence was intended, lord commander,' said Loken.

'And none taken,' Varvaras said, extending a hand towards Loken. 'An old custom of Terra, Captain Loken...'

Loken took his hand and shook it. 'One I have been reminded of lately,' he said.

Varvaras smiled. 'I wanted to welcome you into our inner circle, captain. And to assure you that you did not speak out of turn today. In the south, my men are being slaughtered. Day in, day out. I have, I believe, the finest army in all of the expeditions, but I know full well it is composed of men, and just men. I understand when a fighting man is needed and when an Astartes is needed. This is the latter time. Come to my war cabinet, at your convenience, and I'll be happy to brief you fully.'

'Thank you, lord commander. I will attend you this afternoon.' Varvaras nodded.

'Excuse me, lord commander,' Torgaddon said. 'The Mournival

is needed. The Warmaster is withdrawing and he has called for us.'

The Mournival followed the Warmaster through the plated glass doors into his private sanctum, a wide, well-appointed chamber built below the well of the audience galleries on the port side of the flagship. One wall was glass, open to the stars. Maloghurst and the Warmaster bustled in ahead of them, and the Mournival drew back into the shadows, waiting to be called upon.

Loken stiffened as three figures descended the ironwork screw stair into the room from the gallery above. The first two were Astartes of the Imperial Fists, almost glowing in their yellow plate. The third was much larger. Another god.

Rogal Dorn, primarch of the Imperial Fists, brother to Horus.

Dorn greeted the Warmaster warmly, and went to sit with him and Maloghurst upon the black leather couches facing the glass wall. Servitors brought them refreshments.

Rogal Dorn was a being as great in all measure as Horus. He, and his entourage of Imperial Fists, had been travelling with the expedition for some months, though they were expected to take their leave soon. Other duties and expeditions called. Loken had been told that Primarch Dorn had come to them at Horus's behest, so that the two of them might discuss in detail the obligations and remit of the role of Warmaster. Horus had solicited the opinions and advice of all his brother primarchs on the subject since the honour had been bestowed upon him. Being named Warmaster set him abruptly apart from them, and raised him up above his brothers, and there had been some stifled objections and discontent, especially from those primarchs who felt the title should have been theirs. The primarchs were as prone to sibling rivalry and petty competition as any group of brothers.

Guided, it was likely, by Maloghurst's shrewd hand, Horus had courted his brothers, stilling fears, calming doubts, reaffirming pacts and generally securing their cooperation. He wanted none to feel slighted, or overlooked. He wanted none to think they were no longer listened to. Some, like Sanguinius, Lorgar and Fulgrim, had acclaimed Horus's election from the outset. Others, like Angron and Perturabo, had raged biliously at the new order, and it had taken masterful diplomacy on the Warmaster's part to placate their choler and jealousy. A few, like Russ and the Lion, had been cynically resolved, unsurprised by the turn of events.

But others, like Guilliman, Khan and Dorn had simply taken

it in their stride, accepting the Emperor's decree as the right and obvious choice. Horus had ever been the brightest, the first and the favourite. They did not doubt his fitness for the role, for none of the primarchs had ever matched Horus's achievements, nor the intimacy of his bond with the Emperor. It was to these solid, resolved brothers that Horus turned in particular for counsel. Dorn and Guilliman both embodied the staunchest and most dedicated Imperial qualities, commanding their Legion expeditions with peerless devotion and military genius. Horus desired their approval as a young man might seek the quiescence of older, more accomplished brothers.

Rogal Dorn possessed perhaps the finest military mind of all the primarchs. It was as ordered and disciplined as Roboute Guilliman's, as courageous as the Lion's, yet still supple enough to allow for the flex of inspiration, the flash of battle zeal that had won the likes of Leman Russ and the Khan so many victory wreaths. Dorn's record in the crusade was second only to Horus's, but he was resolute where Horus was flamboyant, reserved where Horus was charismatic, and that was why Horus had been the obvious choice for Warmaster. In keeping with his patient, stony character, Dorn's Legion had become renowned for siegecraft and defensive strategies. The Warmaster had once joked that where he could storm a fortress like no other, Rogal Dorn could hold it. 'If I ever laid assault to a bastion possessed by you,' Horus had quipped at a recent banquet, 'then the war would last for all eternity, the best in attack matched by the best in defence.' The Imperial Fists were an immovable object to the Luna Wolves' unstoppable force.

Dorn had been a quiet, observing presence in his months with the 63rd Expedition. He had spent hours in close conference with the Warmaster, but Loken had seen him from time to time, watching drills and studying preparations for war. Loken had not yet spoken to him, or met him directly. This was the smallest place they had both been in at the same time.

He regarded him now, in calm discussion with the Warmaster; two mythical beings manifest in one room. Loken felt it an honour just to be in their presence, to see them talk, like men, in unguarded fashion. Maloghurst seemed a tiny form beside them.

Primarch Dorn wore a case of armour that was burnished and ornate like a tomb chest, dark red and copper-gold compared to Horus's white dazzle. Unfurled eagle wings, fashioned in metal, haloed his head and decorated his chest and shoulder plate, and aquilas and graven laurels embossed the armour sections of his limbs. A mantle of red velvet hung around his broad shoulders, trimmed in golden weave. His lean face was stern and unsmiling, even when the Warmaster raised a joke, and his hair was a shock of white, bleached like dead bones.

The two Astartes who had escorted him down from the gallery came over to wait with the Mournival. They were well known to Abaddon, Torgaddon and Aximand, but Loken had only yet seen them indirectly about the flagship. Abaddon introduced them as Sigismund, First Captain of the Imperial Fists, resplendent in black and white heraldry, and Efried, Captain of the Third Company. The Astartes made the sign of the aquila to one another in formal greeting.

'I approve of your direction,' Sigismund told Loken at once.

'I'm gratified. You were watching from the galleries?'

Sigismund nodded. 'Prosecute the foe. Get it over with. Get on. There is still so much to be done, we cannot afford delays or time wasting.'

'There are so many worlds still to be brought to compliance,' Loken agreed. 'One day, we will rest at last.'

'No,' Sigismund replied bluntly. 'The crusade will never end. Don't you know that?'

Loken shook his head, 'I wouldn't–'

'Not ever,' said Sigismund emphatically. 'The more we spread, the more we find. World after world. New worlds to conquer. Space is limitless, and so is our appetite to master it.'

'I disagree,' Loken said. 'War will end, one day. A rule of peace will be established. That is the very purpose of our efforts.'

Sigismund grinned. 'Is it? Perhaps. I believe that we have set ourselves an unending task. The nature of mankind makes it so. There will always be another goal, another prospect.'

'Surely, brother, you can conceive of a time when all worlds have been brought into one unity of Imperial rule. Isn't that the dream we strive to realise?'

Sigismund stared into Loken's face. 'Brother Loken, I have heard much about you, all of it good. I had not imagined I would discover such naivety in you. We will spend our lives fighting to secure this Imperium, and then I fear we will spend the rest of our days fighting to keep it intact. There is such involving darkness amongst the stars. Even when the Imperium is complete, there will be no peace. We will be obliged to fight on to preserve what we have fought to establish. Peace is a vain wish. Our crusade may one day adopt another name, but it will never truly end. In the far future, there will be only war.'

'I think you're wrong,' Loken said.

'How innocent you are,' Sigismund mocked, 'and I thought

the Luna Wolves were supposed to be the most aggressive of us all. That's how you like the other Legions to think of you, isn't it? The most feared of mankind's warrior classes?'

'Our reputation speaks for itself, sir,' said Loken.

'As does the reputation of the Imperial Fists,' Sigismund replied. 'Are we going to scrap about it now? Argue which Legion is toughest?'

'The answer, always, is the Wolves of Fenris,' Torgaddon put in, 'because they are clinically insane.' He grinned broadly, sensing the tension, and wishing to dispel it. 'If you're comparing sane Legions, of course, the question becomes more complex. Primarch Roboute's Ultramarines make a good show, but then there are so bloody many of them. The Word Bearers, the White Scars, the Imperial Fists, oh, all have fine records. But the Luna Wolves, ah me, the Luna Wolves. Sigismund, in a straight fight? Do you really think you'd have a hope? Honestly? Your yellow ragamuffins against the best of the best?'

Sigismund laughed. 'Whatever helps you sleep, Tarik. Terra bless us all it is a paradigm that will never be tested.'

'What brother Sigismund isn't telling you, Garviel,' Torgaddon said, 'is that his Legion is going to miss all the glory. It's to be withdrawn. He's quite miffed about it.'

'Tarik is being selective with the truth,' Sigismund snorted. 'The Imperial Fists have been commanded by the Emperor to return to Terra and establish a guard around him there. We are chosen as his Praetorians. Now who's miffed, Luna Wolf?'

'Not I,' said Torgaddon. 'I'll be winning laurels in war while you grow fat and lazy minding the home fires.'

'You're quitting the crusade?' Loken asked. 'I had heard something of this.'

'The Emperor wishes us to fortify the Palace of Terra and guard its bulwarks. This was his word at the Ullanor Triumph. We have been the best part of two years tying up our business so we might comply with his desires. Yes, we're going home to Terra. Yes, we will sit out the rest of the crusade. Except that I believe there will be plenty of crusade left once we have been given leave to quit Earth, our duty done. You won't finish this, Luna Wolves. The stars will have long forgotten your name when the Imperial Fists war abroad again.'

Torgaddon placed his hand on the hilt of his chainsword, playfully. 'Are you so keen to be slapped down by me for your insolence, Sigismund?'

'I don't know. Is he?'

Rogal Dorn suddenly towered behind them. 'Does Sigismund

deserve a slap, Captain Torgaddon? Probably. In the spirit of comradeship, let him be. He bruises easily.'

All of them laughed at the primarch's words. The barest hint of a smile flickered across Rogal Dorn's lips.

'Loken,' he said, gesturing. Loken followed the massive primarch to the far corner of the chamber. Behind them, Sigismund and Efried continued to sport with the others of the Mournival, and elsewhere Horus sat in intense conference with Maloghurst.

'We are charged to return to the homeworld,' Dorn said, conversationally. His voice was low and astonishingly soft, like the lap of water on a distant beach, but there was a strength running through it, like the tension of a steel cable. 'The Emperor has asked us to fortify the Imperial stronghold, and who am I to question the Emperor's needs? I am glad he recognises the particular talents of the VII Legion.'

Dorn looked down at Loken. 'You're not used to the likes of me, are you, Loken?'

'No, lord.'

'I like that about you. Ezekyle and Tarik, men like them have been so long in the company of your lord, they think nothing of it. You, however, understand that a primarch is not like a man, or even an Astartes. I'm not talking about strength. I'm talking about the weight of responsibilty.'

'Yes, lord.'

Dorn sighed. 'The Emperor has no like, Loken. There are no gods in this hollow universe to keep him company. So he made us, demigods, to stand beside him. I have never quite come to terms with my status. Does that surprise you? I see what I am capable of, and what is expected of me, and I shudder. The mere fact of me frightens me sometimes. Do you think your lord Horus ever feels that way?'

'I do not, lord,' Loken said. 'Self-confidence is one of his keenest qualities.'

'I think so too, and I am glad of it. There could be no better Warmaster than Horus, but a man, even a primarch, is only as good as the counsel he receives, especially if he is utterly self-confident. He must be tempered and guided by those close to him.'

'You speak of the Mournival, sir.'

Rogal Dorn nodded. He gazed out through the armoured glass wall at the scintillating expanse of the starfield. 'You know that I've had my eye on you? That I spoke in support of your election?'

'I have been told so, lord. It baffles and flatters me.'

'My brother Horus needs an honest voice in his ear. A voice that appreciates the scale and import of our undertaking. A voice that is not blasé in the company of demigods. Sigismund and Efried do this for me. They keep me honest. You should do the same for your lord.'

'I will endeavour to–' Loken began.

'They wanted Luc Sedirae or Iacton Qruze. Did you know that? Both names were considered. Sedirae is a battle-hungry killer, so much like Abaddon. He would say yes to anything, if it meant war-glory. Qruze – you call him the "Half-heard" I'm told?'

'We do, lord.'

'Qruze is a sycophant. He would say yes to anything if it meant he stayed in favour. The Mournival needs a proper, dissenting opinion.'

'A naysmith,' Loken said.

Dorn flashed a real smile. 'Yes, just so, like the old dynasts did! A naysmith. Your schooling's good. My brother Horus needs a voice of reason in his ear, if he is to rein in his eagerness and act in the Emperor's stead. Our other brothers, some of them quite demented by the choice of Horus, need to see he is firmly in control. So I vouched for you, Garviel Loken. I examined your record and your character, and thought you would be the right mix in the alloy of the Mournival. Don't be insulted, but there is something very human about you, Loken, for an Astartes.'

'I fear, my lord, that my helm will no longer fit me, you have swelled my head so with your compliments.'

Dorn nodded. 'My apologies.'

'You spoke of responsibility. I feel that weight suddenly, terribly.'

'You're strong, Loken. Astartes-built. Endure it.'

'I will, lord.'

Dorn turned from the armoured port and looked down at Loken. He placed his great hands gently on Loken's shoulders. 'Be yourself. Just be yourself. Speak your mind plainly, for you have been granted the rare opportunity to do so. I can return to Terra confident that the crusade is in safe hands.'

'I wonder if your faith in me is too much, lord,' Loken said. 'As fervent as Sedirae, I have just proposed a war–'

'I heard you speak. You made the case well. That is all part of your role now. Sometimes you must advise. Sometimes you must allow the Warmaster to use you.'

'Use me?'

'You understand what Horus had you do this morning?'

'Lord?'

'He had primed the Mournival to back him, Loken. He is cultivating the air of a peacemaker, for that plays well across the worlds of the Imperium. This morning, he wanted someone other than himself to suggest unleashing the Legions for war.'

SEVEN

Oaths of moment
Keeler takes a pict
Scare tactics

'Stay close, please,' the iterator said. 'No one wander away from the group, and no one make any record beyond written notes without prior permission. Is that clear?'

They all answered yes.

'We have been granted ten minutes, and that limit will be strictly observed. This is a real privilege.'

The iterator, a sallow man in his thirties called Emont, who despite his appearance possessed what Euphrati Keeler thought was a most beautiful speaking voice, paused and offered one last piece of advice to the group. 'This is also a hazardous place. A place of war. Watch your step, and be aware of where you are.'

He turned and led them down the concourse to the massive blast hatch. The rattle of machine tools echoed out to them. This was an area of the ship the remembrancers had never previously been allowed to visit. Most of the martial areas were off limits except by strict permission, but the embarkation deck was utterly forbidden at all times.

There were six of them in the group. Keeler, another imagist called Siman Sark, a painter called Fransisko Twell, a composer of symphonic patterns called Tolemew Van Krasten, and two documentarists called Avrius Carnis and Borodin Flora. Carnis and Flora were already bickering quietly about 'themes and approaches'.

All of the remembrancers wore durable clothing appropriate for bad weather, and all carried kit bags. Keeler was fairly sure they'd all prepared in vain. The permission they hoped for would not be issued. They were lucky to get this far.

She looped her own kit bag over her shoulder, and settled her favourite picter unit around her neck on its strap. At the head of the party, Emont came to a halt before the two fully armoured Luna Wolves standing watch at the hatch, and showed them the group's credentials.

'Approved by the equerry,' she heard him say. In his beige robes, Emont was a fragile figure compared to the two armoured giants. He had to lift his head to look up at them. The Astartes studied the paperwork, made comments to one another in brief clicks of inter-suit vox, and then nodded them through.

The embarkation deck – and Keeler had to remind herself that this was just *one* embarkation deck, for the flagship possessed six – was an immense space, a long, echoing tunnel dominated by the launch ramps and delivery trackways running its length. At the far end, half a kilometre away, open space was visible through the shimmer of integrity fields.

The noise was punishing. Motorised tools hammered and ratcheted, hoists whined, loading units trundled and rattled, hatches slammed, and reactive engines whooped and flared as they were tested. There was activity everywhere: deck crews hurrying into position, fitters and artificers making final checks and adjustments, servitors unlocking fuel lines. Munition carts hummed past in long sausage-chains. The air stank of heat, oil and exhaust fumes.

Six Stormbirds sat on launch carriages before them. Heavy, armoured delivery vehicles, they were void capable, but also honed and sleek for atmospheric work. They sat in two rows of three, wings extended, like hawks waiting to be thrown to the lure. They were painted white, and showed the wolf's head icon and the eye of Horus on their hulls.

'...known as Stormbirds,' the iterator was saying as he walked them forward. 'The actual pattern type is Warhawk VI. Most expedition forces are now reliant on the smaller, standard construct Thunderhawk pattern, examples of which you can see under covers to our left in the hardstand area, but the Legion has made an effort to keep these old, heavy-duty machines in service. They have been delivering the Luna Wolves into war since the start of the Great Crusade, since before that, actually. They were manufactured on Terra by the Yndonesic Bloc for use against the Panpacific tribes during the Unification Wars.

A dozen will be employed in this venture today. Six from this deck, six from Aft Embarkation 2.'

Keeler raised her picter and took several quick shots of the line of Stormbirds ahead. For the last, she crouched down to get a low, impressive angle down the row of their flared wings.

'I said no records!' Emont snapped, hurrying to her.

'I didn't think for a moment you were serious,' Keeler responded smoothly. 'We've got ten minutes. I'm an imagist. What the hell did you think I was going to do?'

Emont looked flustered. He was about to say something when he noticed that Carnis and Flora were wandering astray, locked in some petty squabble.

'Stay with the group!' Emont cried out, hurrying to shepherd them back.

'Get anything good?' Sark asked Keeler.

'*Please*, it's me,' she replied.

He laughed, and took out a picter of his own from his rucksack. 'I didn't have the balls, but you're right. What the hell are we doing here if not our job?'

He took a few shots. Keeler liked Sark. He was good company and had a decent track record of work on Terra. She doubted he would get much here. His eye for composition was fine when it came to faces, but this was very much her thing.

Both the documentarists had now cornered Emont and were grilling him with questions that he struggled to answer. Keeler wondered where Mersadie Oliton had got to. Competition amongst the remembrancers for these six places had been fierce, and Mersadie had won a slot thanks to Keeler's good word and, it was said, approval from someone high up in the Legion, but she had failed to show up on time that morning, and her place had been taken at the last minute by Borodin Flora.

Ignoring the iterator's instructions, she moved away from the group, and chased images with her picter. The Luna Wolf emblem stencilled on an erect braking flap; two servitors glistening with lubricant as they struggled to fix a faulty feed; deck crew panting and wiping sweat from their brows beside a munition trolley they had just loaded; the bare-metal snout of an underwing cannon.

'Are you trying to get me replaced?' Emont asked, catching up with her.

'No.'

'I really must ask you to keep in line, madam,' he said. 'I know you're in favour, but there is a limit. After that business on the surface...'

'What business?' she asked.

'A couple of days ago, surely you heard?'

'No.'

'Some remembrancer gave his minders the slip during a surface visit and got into a deal of trouble. Quite a scandal. It's annoyed the higher-ups. The Primary Iterator had to wrangle hard to prevent the remembrancer contingent being suspended from activity.'

'Was it that bad?'

'I don't know the details. Please, for me, stay in line.'

'You have a very lovely voice,' Keeler said. 'You could ask me to do anything. Of course I will.'

Emont blushed. 'Let's continue with the visit.'

As he turned, she took another pict, capturing the scruffy iterator, head down, against a backdrop of bustling crewmen and threatening ships.

'Iterator?' she called. 'Have we been granted permission to accompany the drop?'

'I don't believe so,' he said sadly. 'I'm sorry. I've not been told.'

A fanfare boomed out across the vast deck. Keeler heard – and felt – a beat like a heavy drum, like a warhammer striking again and again against metal.

'Come to one side. Now! To one side!' Emont called, trying to gather the group on the edge of the deck space.

The drumming grew closer and louder. It was feet. Steel-shod feet marching across decking.

Three hundred Astartes, in full armour and marching perfectly in step, advanced onto the embarkation deck between the waiting Stormbirds. At the front of them, a standard bearer carried the great banner of the Tenth Company.

Keeler gasped at the sight of them. So many, so perfect, so huge, so regimented. She raised her picter with trembling hands and began to shoot. Giants in white metal, assembling for war, uniform and identical, precise and composed.

Orders flew out, and the Astartes came to a halt with a crashing din of heels. They became statues, as equerries hurried through their files, directing and assigning men to their carriers.

Smoothly, units began to turn in fluid sequence, and filed onto the waiting vessels.

'They will have already taken their oaths of moment,' Emont was saying to the group in a hushed whisper.

'Explain,' Van Krasten requested.

Emont nodded. 'Every soldier of the Imperium is sworn to uphold his loyalty to the Emperor at the start of his commission, and the Astartes are no exception. No one doubts their continued devotion to the pledge, but before individual missions, the Astartes choose to swear an immediate oath, an "oath of moment", that binds them specifically to the matter at hand. They pledge to uphold the particular concerns of the enterprise before them. You may think of it as a reaffirmation, I suppose. It is a ritual re-pledging. The Astartes do love their rituals.'

'I don't understand,' said Van Krasten. 'They are already sworn but–'

'To uphold the truth of the Imperium and the light of the Emperor,' Emont said, 'but, as the name suggests, an oath of moment applies to an individual action. It is specific and precise.'

Van Krasten nodded.

'Who's that?' Twell asked, pointing. A senior Astartes, a captain by his cloak, was walking the lines of warriors as they streamed neatly onto the drop-ships.

'That's Loken,' Emont said.

Keeler raised her picter.

Loken's comb-crested helm was off. His fair, cropped hair framed his pale, freckled face. His grey eyes seemed immense. Mersadie had spoken to her of Loken. Quite a force now, if the rumours were true. One of the four.

She shot him speaking to a subordinate, and again, waving servitors clear of a landing ramp. He was the most extraordinary subject. She didn't have to compose around him, or shoot to crop later. He dominated every frame.

No wonder Mersadie was so taken with him. Keeler wondered again why Mersadie Oliton had missed this chance.

Now Loken turned away, his men all but boarded. He spoke with the standard bearer, and touched the hem of the banner with affection. Another fine shot. Then he swung round to face five armoured figures approaching across the suddenly empty deck.

'This is…' Emont whispered. 'This is quite something. I hope you all understand you're lucky to see this.'

'See what?' asked Sark.

'The captain takes his oath of moment last of all. It will be heard and sworn to by two of his fellow captains, but, oh my goodness, the rest of the Mournival have come to hear him pledge.'

'That's the Mournival?' Keeler asked, her picter shooting.

'First Captain Abaddon, Captain Torgaddon, Captain Aximand, and with them Captains Sedirae and Targost,' Emont breathed, afraid of raising his voice.

'Which one is Abaddon?' Keeler asked, aiming her picter.

✠ ✠ ✠

Loken knelt. 'There was no need–' he began.

'We wanted to do this right,' Torgaddon replied. 'Luc?'

Luc Sedirae, Captain of the Thirteenth Company, took out the seal paper on which the oath of moment was written. 'I am sent to hear you,' he said.

'And I am here to witness it,' Targost said.

'And we are here to keep you cheerful,' Torgaddon added. Abaddon and Little Horus chuckled.

Neither Targost nor Sedirae were Sons of Horus. Targost, Captain of the Seventh, was a blunt-faced man with a deep scar across his brow. Luc Sedirae, champion of so many wars, was a smiling rogue, blond and handsome, his eyes blue and bright, his mouth permanently half-open as if about to bite something. Sedirae raised the scrap of parchment.

'Do you, Garviel Loken, accept your role in this? Do you promise to lead your men into the zone of war, and conduct them to glory, no matter the ferocity or ingenuity of the foe? Do you swear to crush the insurgents of Sixty-Three Nineteen, despite all they might throw at you? Do you pledge to do honour to the XVI Legion and the Emperor?'

Loken placed his hand on the bolter Targost held out.

'On this matter and by this weapon, I swear.'

Sedirae nodded and handed the oath paper to Loken.

'Kill for the living, brother,' he said, 'and kill for the dead.' He turned to walk away. Targost holstered his bolter, made the sign of the aquila, and followed him.

Loken rose to his feet, securing his oath paper to the rim of his right shoulderguard.

'Do this right, Garviel,' Abaddon said.

'I'm glad you told me that,' Loken dead-panned. 'I'd been considering making a mess of it.'

Abaddon hesitated, wrong-footed. Torgaddon and Aximand laughed.

'He's growing that thick skin already, Ezekyle,' Aximand sniggered.

'You walked into that,' Torgaddon added.

'I know, I know,' Abaddon snapped. He glared at Loken. 'Don't let the commander down.'

'Would I?' Loken replied, and walked away to his Stormbird.

'Our time's up,' Emont said.

Keeler didn't care. That last pict had been exceptional. The Mournival, Sedirae and Targost, all in a solemn group, Loken on his knees.

Emont conducted the remembrancers out of the embarkation deck space to an observation deck, adjacent to the launch port from which they could watch the Stormbirds deploy. They could hear the rising note of the Stormbird engines behind them, trembling the embarkation deck as they fired up in pre-launch test. The roaring dulled away as they walked down the long access tunnel, hatches closing one by one after them.

The observation deck was a long chamber, one side of which was a frame of armoured glass. The deck's internal lighting had been switched low so that they could better see into the darkness outside.

It was an impressive view. They directly overlooked the yawning maw of the embarkation deck, a colossal hatch ringing with winking guide lights. The bulk of the flagship rose away above them, like a crenellated Gothic city. Beyond, lay the void itself.

Small service craft and cargo landers flitted past, some on local business, some heading out to other ships of the expedition fleet. Five of these could be seen from the observation deck, sleek monsters at high anchor several kilometres away. They were virtual silhouettes, but the distant sun caught them obliquely, and gave them hard, golden outlines along their ribbed upper hulls.

Below lay the world they orbited. Sixty-Three Nineteen. They were above its nightside, but there was a smoky grey crescent of radiance where the terminator crept forward. In the dark mass, Keeler could make out the faint light-glow of cities speckling the sleeping surface.

Impressive though the view was, she knew shots would be a waste of time. Between the glass, the distance and the odd light sources, resolution would be poor.

She found a seat away from the others, and began to review the picts she'd already taken, calling them up on the picter's viewscreen.

'May I see?' asked a voice.

She looked up and had to peer in the deck's gloom to identify the speaker. It was Sindermann, the Primary Iterator.

'Of course,' she said, rising to her feet and holding the picter so he could see the images as she thumbed them up one by one. He craned his head forward, curious.

'You have a wonderful eye, Mistress Keeler. Oh, that one is particularly fine! The crew working so hard. I find it striking because it is so natural, candid, I suppose. So very much of our pictorial record is arch and formally posed.'

'I like to get people when they're not aware of me.'

'This one is simply magnificent. You've captured Garviel perfectly there.'

'You know him personally, sir?'

'Why do you ask?'

'You called him by his forename, not by any honorific or rank.'

Sindermann smiled at her. 'I think Captain Loken might be considered a friend of mine. I'd like to think so, anyway. You never can tell with an Astartes. They form relationships with mortals in a curious way, but we spend time together and discuss certain matters.'

'You're his mentor?'

'His tutor. There is a great difference. I know things he does not, so I am able to expand his knowledge, but I do not presume to have influence over him. Oh, Mistress Keeler! This one is superb! The best, I should say.'

'I thought so. I was very pleased with it.'

'All of them together like that, and Garviel kneeling so humbly, and the way you've framed them against the company standard.'

'That was just happenstance,' Keeler said. 'They chose what they were standing beside.'

Sindermann placed his hand gently upon hers. He seemed genuinely grateful for the chance to review her work. 'That pict alone will become famous, I have no doubt. It will be reproduced in history texts for as long as the Imperium endures.'

'It's just a pict,' she chided.

'It is a witness. It is a perfect example of what the remembrancers can do. I have been reviewing some of the material produced by the remembrancers thus far, the material that's been added to the expedition's collective archive. Some of it is... patchy, shall I say? Ideal ammunition for those who claim the remembrancer project is a waste of time, funds and ship space, but some is outstanding, and I would class your work amongst that.'

'You're very kind.'

'I am honest, mistress. And I believe that if mankind does not properly document and witness his achievements, then only half of this undertaking has been made. Speaking of honest, come with me.'

He led her back to the main group by the window. Another figure had joined them on the observation deck, and stood talking to Van Karsten. It was the equerry, Maloghurst, and he turned as they approached.

'Kyril, do you want to tell them?'

'You engineered it, equerry. The pleasure's yours.'

Maloghurst nodded. 'After some negotiation with the expedition seniors, it has been agreed that the six of you can follow the strike force to the surface and observe the venture. You will travel down with one of the ancillary support vessels.'

The remembrancers chorused their delight.

'There's been a lot of debate about allowing remembrancers to become embedded in the layers of military activity,' Sindermann said, 'particularly concerning the issue of civilian welfare in a warzone. There is also, if I may be quite frank, some concern about what you will see. The Astartes in war is a shocking, savage sight. Many believe that such images are not for public distribution, as they might paint a negative picture of the crusade.'

'We both believe otherwise,' Maloghurst said. 'The truth can't be wrong, even if it is ugly or shocking. We need to be clear about what we are doing, and how we are doing it, and allow persons such as yourselves to respond to it. That is the honesty on which a mature culture must be based. We also need to celebrate, and how can you celebrate the courage of the Astartes if you don't see it? I believe in the strength of positive propaganda, thanks, in no small part, to Mistress Keeler here and her documenting of my own plight. There is a rallying power in images and reports of both Imperial victory and Imperial suffering. It communicates a common cause to bind and uplift our society.'

'It helps,' Sindermann put in, 'that this is a low-key action. An unusual use of the Astartes in a policing role. It should be over in a day or so, with little collateral risk. However, I wish to emphasise that this is still dangerous. You will observe instruction at all times, and never stray from your protection detail. I am to accompany you – this was one of the stipulations made by the Warmaster. Listen to me and do as I say at all times.'

So we're still to be vetted and controlled, Keeler thought. Shown only what they choose to show us. Never mind, this is still a great opportunity. One that I can't believe Mersadie has missed.

'Look!' cried Borodin Flora.

They all turned.

The Stormbirds were launching. Like giant steel darts they shot from the deck mouth, the sunlight catching their armoured flanks. Majestically, they turned in the darkness as they fell away, burners lighting up like blue coals as they dropped in formation towards the planet.

Bracing himself against the low, overhead handrails, Loken moved down the spinal aisle of the lead Stormbird. Luna

Wolves, impassive behind their visors, their weapons locked and stowed, sat in the rear-facing cage-seats either side of him. The bird rocked and shuddered as it cut its steep path through the upper atmosphere.

He reached the cockpit section and wrenched open the hatch to enter. Two flight officers sat back to back, facing wall panel consoles, and beyond them two pilot servitors lay, hardwired into forward-facing helm positions in the cone. The cockpit was dark, apart from the coloured glow of the instrumentation and the sheen of light coming in through the forward slit-ports.

'Captain?' one of the flight officers said, turning and looking up.

'What's the problem with the vox?' Loken asked. 'I've had several reports of comm faults from the men. Ghosting and chatter.'

'We're getting that too, sir,' the officer said, his hands playing over his controls. 'and I'm hearing similar reports from the other birds. We think it's atmospherics.'

'Disruption?'

'Yes, sir. I've checked with the flagship, and they haven't picked up on it. It's probably an acoustic echo from the surface.'

'It seems to be getting worse,' Loken said. He adjusted his helm and tried his link again. The static hiss was still there, but now it had shapes in it, like muffled words.

'Is that language?' he asked.

The officer shook his head. 'Can't tell, sir. It's just reading as general interference. Perhaps we're bouncing up broadcasts from one of the southern cities. Or maybe even army traffic.'

'We need clean vox,' Loken said. 'Do something.'

The officer shrugged and adjusted several dials. 'I can try purging the signal. I can wash it through the signal buffers. Maybe that will tidy up the channels...'

In Loken's ears, there was a sudden, seething rush of static, and then things became quieter suddenly.

'Better,' he said. Then he paused. Now the hiss was gone, he could hear the voice. It was tiny, distant, impossibly quiet, but it was speaking proper words.

'...only name you'll hear....'

'What is that?' Loken asked. He strained to hear. The voice was so very far away, like a rustle of silk.

The flight officer craned his neck, listening to his own headphones. He made minute adjustments to his dials.

'I might be able to...' he began. A touch of his hand had suddenly cleaned the signal to audibility.

'What in the name of Terra *is* that?' he asked.

Loken listened. The voice, like a gust of dry, desert wind, said, 'Samus. That's the only name you'll hear. Samus. It means the end and the death. Samus. I am Samus. Samus is all around you. Samus is the man beside you. Samus will gnaw upon your bones. Look out! Samus is here.'

The voice faded. The channel went dead and quiet, except for the occasional echo pop.

The flight officer took off his headset and looked at Loken. His face was wide-eyed and fearful. Loken recoiled slightly. He wasn't made to deal with fear. The concept disgusted him.

'I d-don't know what that was,' the flight officer said.

'I do,' said Loken. 'Our enemy is trying to scare us.'

EIGHT

One-way war
Sindermann in grass and sand
Jubal

Following the 'Emperor's' death and the fall of their ancient, centralised government, the insurgents had fled into the mountain massifs of the southern hemisphere, and occupied a fastness in a range of peaks, called the Whisperheads in the local language. The air was thin, for the altitude was very great. Dawn was coming up, and the mountains loomed as stern, misty steeples of pale green ice that reflected sun glare.

The Stormbirds dropped from the edge of space, out of the sky's dark blue mantle, trailing golden fire from their ablative surfaces. In the frugal habitations and villages in the foothills, the townsfolk, born into a culture of myth and superstition, saw the fiery marks in the dawn sky as an omen. Many fell to wailing and lamenting, or hurried to their village fanes.

The religious faith of Sixty-Three Nineteen, strong in the capital and the major cities, was distilled here into a more potent brew. These were impoverished backwaters, where the anachronistic beliefs of the society were heightened by a subsistence lifestyle and poor education. The Imperial army had already struggled to contain this primitive zealotry during its occupation. As the streaks of fire crossed the sky, they found themselves hard-pressed to control the mounting agitation in the villages.

The Stormbirds set down, engines screaming, on a plateau of dry, white lava-rock five thousand metres below the caps of the highest peaks where the rebel fastness lay. They whirled up clouds of pumice grit from their jets as they crunched in.

The sky was white, and the peaks were white against it, and white cloud softened the air. A series of precipitous rifts and ice canyons dropped away behind the plateau, wreathed in smoke-cloud, and the lower peaks gleamed in the rising light.

Tenth Company clattered out into the sparse, chilly air, weapons ready. They came to martial order, and disembarked as smoothly as Loken could have wished.

But the vox was still disturbed. Every few minutes, 'Samus' chattered again, like a sigh upon the mountain wind.

Loken called the senior squad leaders to him as soon as he had landed: Vipus of Locasta, Jubal of Hellebore, Rassek of the Terminator squad, Talonus of Pithraes, Kairus of Walkure, and eight more.

All grouped around, showing deference to Xavyer Jubal.

Loken, who had always read men well as a commander, needed none of his honed leadership skills to realise that Jubal wasn't wearing Vipus's elevation well. As the others of the Mournival had advised him, Loken had followed his gut and appointed Nero Vipus his proxy-commander, to serve when matters of state drew Loken apart from Tenth. Vipus was popular, but Jubal, as sergeant of the first squad, felt slighted. There was no rule that stated the sergeant of a company's first squad automatically followed in seniority. The sequencing was simply a numerical distinction, but there was a given order to things, and Jubal felt aggrieved. He had told Loken so, several times.

Loken remembered Little Horus's words. *If you trust Vipus, make it Vipus. Never compromise. Jubal's a big boy. He'll get over it.*

'Let's do this, and quickly,' Loken told his officers. 'The Terminators have the lead here. Rassek?'

'My squad is ready to serve, captain,' Rassek replied curtly. Like all the men in his specialist squad, Sergeant Rassek wore the titanic armour of a Terminator, a variant only lately introduced into the arsenal of the Astartes. By dint of their primacy, and the fact that their primarch was Warmaster, the Luna Wolves had been amongst the first Legions to benefit from the issue of Terminator plate. Some entire Legions still lacked it. The armour was designed for heavy assault. Thickly plated and consequently exaggerated in its dimensions, a Terminator suit turned an Astartes warrior into a slow, cumbersome, but entirely unstoppable humanoid tank. An Astartes clad in Terminator plate gave up all his speed, dexterity, agility and range of movement. What he got in return was the ability to shrug off almost any ballistic attack.

Rassek towered over them in his armour, dwarfing them as a primarch dwarfs Astartes, or an Astartes dwarfs mortal men. Massive weapons systems were built into his shoulders, arms and gauntlets.

'Lead off to the bridges and clear the way,' Loken said. He paused. Now was a moment for gentle diplomacy. 'Jubal, I want Hellebore to follow the Terminators in as the weight of the first strike.'

Jubal nodded, evidently pleased. The scowl of displeasure he had been wearing for weeks now lifted for a moment. All the officers were bare-headed for this briefing, despite the fact that the air was unbreathably thin by human standards. Their enhanced pulmonary systems didn't even labour. Loken saw Nero Vipus smile, and knew he understood the significance of this instruction. Loken was offering Jubal some measure of glory, to reassure him he was not forgotten.

'Let's go to it!' Loken cried. 'Lupercal!'

'Lupercal!' the officers answered. They clamped their helms into place.

Portions of the company began to move ahead towards the natural rock bridges and causeways that linked the plateau to the higher terrain.

Army regiments, swaddled in heavy coats and rebreathers against the cold, thin air, had moved up onto the plateau to meet them from the town of Kasheri in the lower gorge.

'Kasheri is at compliance, sir,' an officer told Loken, his voice muffled by his mask, his breathing pained and ragged. 'The enemy has withdrawn to the high fortress.'

Loken nodded, gazing up at the bright crags looming in the white light. 'We'll take it from here,' he said.

'They're well armed, sir,' the officer warned. 'Every time we've pushed to take the rock bridges, they've killed us with heavy cannon. We don't think they have much in the way of numerical weight, but they have the advantage of position. It's a slaughter ground, sir, and they have the cross-draw on us. We understand the insurgents are being led by an Invisible called Rykus or Ryker. We–'

'We'll take it from here,' Loken repeated. 'I don't need to know the name of the enemy before I kill him.'

He turned. 'Jubal. Vipus. Form up and move ahead!'

'Just like that?' the army officer asked sourly. 'Six weeks we've been here, slogging it out, the body toll like you wouldn't believe, and you–'

'We're Astartes,' Loken said. 'You're relieved.'

The officer shook his head with a sad laugh. He muttered something under his breath.

Loken turned back and took a step towards the man, causing him to start in alarm. No man liked to see the stern eye-slits of a Luna Wolf's impassive visor turn to regard him.

'What did you say?' Loken asked.

'I... I... nothing, sir.'

'What did you say?'

'I said... "and the place is haunted", sir.'

'If you believe this place is haunted, my friend,' Loken said, 'then you are admitting to a belief in spirits and daemons.'

'I'm not, sir! I'm really not!'

'I should think not,' Loken said. 'We're not barbarians.'

'All I mean,' said the soldier breathlessly, his face flushed and sweaty behind his breather mask, 'is that there's something about this place. These mountains. They're called the Whisperheads, and I've spoken to some of the locals in Katheri. The name's old, sir. Really old. The locals believe that a man might hear voices out here, calling to him, when there's no one around. It's an old tale.'

'Superstition. We know this world has temples and fanes. They are dark-age in their beliefs. Bringing light to that ignorance is part of why we're here.'

'So what are the voices, sir?'

'What?'

'Since we've been here, fighting our way up the valley, we've all heard them. I've heard them. Whispers. In the night, and sometimes in the bold brightness of day when there's no one about, and on the vox too. Samus has been talking.'

Loken stared at the man. The oath of moment fixed to his shoulder plate fluttered in the mountain wind. 'Who is Samus?'

'Damned if I know,' the officer shrugged. 'All I know for certain is the whole vox-net has been loopy these past few days. Voices on the line, all saying the same thing. A threat.'

'They're trying to scare us,' Loken said.

'Well, it worked then, didn't it?'

Loken walked out across the plateau in the biting wind, between the parked Stormbirds. Samus was muttering again, his voice a dry crackle in the background of Loken's open link.

'Samus. That's the only name you'll hear. I'm Samus. Samus is all around you. Samus is the man beside you. Samus will gnaw upon your bones.'

Loken was forced to admit the enemy propaganda was good.

It was unsettling in its mystery and its whisper. It had probably been highly effective in the past against other nations and cultures on Sixty-Three Nineteen. The 'Emperor' had most likely come to global power on the basis of malignant whispers and invisible warriors.

The Astartes of the true Emperor would not be gulled and unmanned by such simple tools.

Some of the Luna Wolves around him were standing still, listening to the mutter in their helm sets.

'Ignore it,' Loken told them. 'It's just a game. Let's move in.'

Rassek's lumbering Terminators approached the rock bridges, arches of granite and lava that linked the plateau to the fierce verticality of the peaks. These were natural spans left behind by the action of ancient glaciers.

Corpses, some of them reduced to desiccated mummies by the altitude, littered the plateau shelf and the rock bridges. The officer had not been lying. Hundreds of army troopers had been cut down in the various attempts to storm the high fortresses. The field of fire had been so intense, their comrades had not been able even to retrieve their bodies.

'Advance!' Loken ordered.

Raising their storm bolters, the Terminator squad began to crunch out across the rock bridges, dislodging white bone and rotten tunics with their immense feet. Gunfire greeted them immediately, blistering down from invisible positions up in the crags. The shots spanked and whined off the specialised armour. Heads set, the Terminators walked into it, shrugging it away, like men walking into a gale wind. What had kept the army at bay for weeks, and cost them dearly, merely tickled the Legion warriors.

This would be over quickly, Loken realised. He regretted the loyal blood that had been wasted needlessly. This had always been a job for the Astartes.

The front ranks of the Terminator squad, halfway across the bridges, began to fire. Bolters and inbuilt heavy weapon systems unloaded across the abyss, blitzing las shots and storms of explosive munitions at the upper slopes. Hidden positions and fortifications exploded, and limp, tangled bodies tumbled away into the chasm below in flurries of rock and ice.

'Samus' began his worrying again. 'Samus. That's the only name you'll hear. Samus. It means the end and the death. Samus. I am Samus. Samus is all around you. Samus is the man beside you. Samus will gnaw upon your bones. Look out! Samus is here.'

'Advance!' Loken cried, 'and please, someone, shut that bastard up!'

'And who's Samus?' Borodin Flora asked.

The remembrancers, with an escort of army troopers and servitors, had just disembarked from their lander into the bitter cold of a township called Kasheri. The cold mountains swooped up beyond them into the mist.

The area had been securely occupied by Varvaras's troopers and war machines. The party stepped into the light, all of them giddy and breathless from the altitude. Keeler was calibrating her picter against the harsh glare, trying to slow her desperate breath-rate. She was annoyed. They'd set down in a safe zone, a long way back from the actual fighting area. There was nothing to see. They were being handled.

The town was a bleak outcrop of longhouses in a lower gorge below the peaks. It looked like it hadn't changed much in centuries. There were opportunities for shots of rustic dwellings or parked army war machines, but nothing significant. The glaring light had a pure quality, though. There was a thin rain in it. Some of the servitors had been instructed to carry the remembrancers' bags, but the rest were fighting to keep parasol canopies upright over the heads of the party in the crosswind. Keeler felt they all looked like some idle gang of aristos on a grand tour, exposing themselves not to risk but to some vague, stage-managed version of danger.

'Where are the Astartes?' she asked. 'When do we approach the war zone?'

'Never mind that,' Flora interrupted. 'Who is Samus?'

'Samus?' Sindermann asked, puzzled. He had walked a short distance away from the group beside the lander into a scrubby stretch of white grass and sand, from where he could overlook the misty depth of the rainswept gorge. He looked small, as if he was about to address the canyon as an audience.

'I keep hearing it,' Flora insisted, following him. He was having trouble catching a breath. Flora wore an earplug so he could listen in to the military's vox traffic.

'I heard it too,' said one of the protection squad soldiers from behind his fogged rebreather.

'The vox has been playing up,' said another.

'All the way down to the surface,' said the officer in charge. 'Ignore it. Interference.'

'I've been told it's been happening for days here,' Van Krasten said.

'It's nothing,' said Sindermann. He looked pale and fragile, as if he might be about to faint from the airlessness.

'The captain says it's scare tactics,' said one of the troopers.

'The captain is surely right,' said Sindermann. He took out his data-slate, and connected it to the fleet archive base. As an afterthought, he uncoupled his rebreather mask and set it to his face, sucking in oxygen from the compact tank strapped to his hip.

After a few moments' consultation, he said, 'Oh, that's interesting.'

'What is?' asked Keeler.

'Nothing. It's nothing. The captain is right. Spread yourselves out, please, and look around. The soldiers here will be happy to answer any questions. Feel free to inspect the war machines.'

The remembrancers glanced at one another and began to disperse. Each one was followed by an obedient servitor with a parasol and a couple of grumpy soldiers.

'We might as well not have come,' Keeler said.

'The mountains are splendid,' Sark said.

'Bugger the mountains. Other worlds have mountains. Listen.'

They listened. A deep, distant booming rolled down the gorge to them. The sound of a war happening somewhere else.

Keeler nodded in the direction of the noise. 'That's where we ought to be. I'm going to ask the iterator why we're stuck here.'

'Best of luck,' said Sark.

Sindermann had walked away from the group to stand under the eaves of one of the mountain town's crude longhouse dwellings. He continued to study his slate. The mountain wind nodded the tusks of dry grass sprouting from the white sand around his feet. Rain pattered down.

Keeler went over to him. Two soldiers and a servitor with a parasol began to follow her. She turned to face them.

'Don't bother,' she said. They stopped in their tracks and allowed her to walk away, alone. By the time she reached the iterator, she was sucking on her own oxygen supply. Sindermann was entirely occupied with his data-slate. She held off with her complaint for a moment, curious.

'There's something wrong, isn't there?' she asked quietly.

'No, not at all,' Sindermann said.

'You've found out what Samus is, haven't you?'

He looked at her and smiled. 'Yes. You're very tenacious, Euphrati.'

'Born that way. What is it, sir?'

Sindermann shrugged. 'It's silly,' he said, showing her the screen of the data-slate. 'The background history we've already been able to absorb from this world features the name Samus, and the Whisperheads. It seems this is a sacred place to the people of Sixty-Three Nineteen. A holy, haunted place, where the alleged barrier between reality and the spirit world is at its most permeable. This is intriguing. I am endlessly fascinated by the belief systems and superstitions of primitive worlds.'

'What does your slate tell you, sir?' Keeler asked.

'It says… this is quite funny. I suppose it would be scary, if one actually believed in such things. It says that the Whisperheads are the one place on this world where the spirits walk and speak. It mentions Samus as chief of those spirits. Local, and very ancient, legend, tells how one of the emperors battled and restrained a nightmarish force of devilry here. The devil was called Samus. It is here in their myths, you see? We had one of our own, in the very antique days, called Seytan, or Tearmat. Samus is the equivalent.'

'Samus is a spirit, then?' Keeler whispered, feeling unpleasantly light-headed.

'Yes. Why do you ask?'

'Because,' said Keeler, 'I've heard him hissing at me since the moment we touched down. And I don't have a vox.'

Beyond the rock bridges, the insurgents had raised shield walls of stone and metal. They had heavy cannons covering the gully approaches to their fortress, wired munition charges in the narrow defiles, electrified razor wire, bolted storm-doors, barricades of rockcrete blocks and heavy iron poles. They had a few automated sentry devices, and the advantage of the sheer drop and unscalable ice all around. They had faith and their god on their side.

They had held off Varvaras's regiments for six weeks.

They had no chance whatsoever.

Nothing they did even delayed the advance of the Luna Wolves. Shrugging off cannon rounds and the backwash of explosives, the Terminators wrenched their way through the shield walls, and blasted down the storm-doors. They crushed the spark of electric life out of the sentry drones with their mighty claws, and pushed down the heaped barricades with their shoulders. The company flooded in behind them, firing their weapons into the rising smoke.

The fortress itself had been built into the mountain peak. Some sections of roof and battlement were visible from outside, but most of the structure lay within, thickly armoured by hundreds of metres of rock. The Luna Wolves poured in through the fortified gates. Assault squads rose up the mountain face on their jump packs and settled like flocks of white birds on the exposed roofs, ripping them apart to gain entry and drop in from above. Explosions ripped out the interior chambers of the fortress, opening them to the air, and sending rafts of dislodged ice and rock crashing down into the gorge.

The interior was a maze of wet-black rock tunnels and old tile work, through which the wind funnelled so sharply it seemed to be hyperventilating. The bodies of the slain lay everywhere, slumped and twisted, sprawled and broken. Stepping over them, Loken pitied them. Their culture had deceived them into this resistance, and the resistance had brought down the wrath of the Astartes on their heads. They had all but invited a catastrophic doom.

Terrible human screams echoed down the windy rock tunnels, punctuated by the door-slam bangs of bolter fire. Loken hadn't even bothered to keep a tally of his kills. There was little glory in this, just duty. A surgical strike by the Emperor's martial instruments.

Gunfire pinked off his armour, and he turned, without really thinking, and cut down his assailants. Two desperate men in mail shirts disintegrated under his fire and spattered across a wall. He couldn't understand why they were still fighting. If they'd ventured a surrender, he would have accepted it.

'That way,' he ordered, and a squad moved up past him into the next series of chambers. As he followed them, a body on the floor at his feet stirred and moaned. The insurgent, smeared in his own blood and gravely wounded, looked up at Loken with glassy eyes. He whispered something.

Loken knelt down and cradled his enemy's head in one massive hand. 'What did you say?'

'Bless me...' the man whispered.

'I can't.'

'Please, say a prayer and commend me to the gods.'

'I can't. There are no gods.'

'Please... the otherworld will shun me if I die without a prayer.'

'I'm sorry,' Loken said. 'You're dying. That's all there is.'

'Help me...' the man gasped.

'Of course,' Loken said. He drew his combat blade, the standard-issue short, stabbing sword, and activated the power cell. The grey blade glowed with force. Loken cut down and sharply back up again in the mercy stroke, and gently set the man's detached head on the ground.

The next chamber was vast and irregular. Meltwater trickled

down from the black ceiling, and formed spurs of glistening mineral, like silver whiskers, on the rocks it ran over. A pool had been cut in the centre of the chamber floor to collect the melt-water, probably as one of the fortress's primary water reserves. The squad he had sent on had come to a halt around its lip.

'Report,' he said.

One of the Wolves looked round. 'What is this, captain?' he asked.

Loken stepped forward to join them and saw that a great number of bottles and glass flasks had been set around the pool, many of them in the path of the trickling feed from above. At first, he assumed they were there to collect the water, but there were other items too: coins, brooches, strange doll-like figures of clay and the head bones of small mammals and lizards. The spattering water fell across them, and had evidently done so for some time, for Loken could see that many of the bottles and other items were gleaming and distorted with mineral deposits. On the overhang of rock above the pool, ancient, eroded script had been chiselled. Loken couldn't read the words, and realised he didn't want to. There were symbols there that made him feel curiously uneasy.

'It's a fane,' he said simply. 'You know what these locals are like. They believe in spirits, and these are offerings.'

The men glanced at one another, not really understanding.

'They believe in things that aren't real?' asked one.

'They've been deceived,' Loken said. 'That's why we're here. Destroy this,' he instructed, and turned away.

The assault lasted sixty-eight minutes, start to finish. By the end, the fastness was a smoking ruin, many sections of it blown wide to the fierce sunlight and mountain air. Not a single Luna Wolf had been lost. Not a single insurgent had survived.

'How many?' Loken asked Rassek.

'They're still counting bodies, captain,' Rassek replied. 'As it stands, nine hundred and seventy-two.'

In the course of the assault, something in the region of thirty meltwater fanes had been discovered in the labyrinthine fortress, pools surrounded by offerings. Loken ordered them all expunged.

'They were guarding the last outpost of their faith,' Nero Vipus remarked.

'I suppose so,' Loken replied.

'You don't like it, do you, Garvi?' Vipus asked.

'I hate to see men die for no reason. I hate to see men give their lives like this, for nothing. For a belief in nothing. It sickens me. This is what we were once, Nero. Zealots, spiritualists, believers in lies we'd made up ourselves. The Emperor showed us the path out of that madness.'

'So be of good humour that we've taken it,' Vipus said. 'And, though we spill their blood, be phlegmatic that we're at last bringing truth to our lost brothers here.'

Loken nodded. 'I feel sorry for them,' he said. 'They must be so scared.'

'Of us?'

'Yes, of course, but that's not what I mean. Scared of the truth we bring. We're trying to teach them that there are no greater forces at work in the galaxy than light, gravity and human will. No wonder they cling to their gods and spirits. We're removing every last crutch of their ignorance. They felt safe until we came. Safe in the custody of the spirits that they believed watched over them. Safe in the ideal that there was an afterlife, an otherworld. They thought they would be immortal, beyond flesh.'

'Now they have met real immortals,' Vipus quipped. 'It's a hard lesson, but they'll be better for it in the long run.'

Loken shrugged. 'I just empathise, I suppose. Their lives were comforted by mysteries, and we've taken that comfort away. All we can show them is a hard and unforgiving reality in which their lives are brief and without higher purpose.'

'Speaking of higher purpose,' Vipus said, 'you should signal the fleet and tell them we're done. The iterators have voxed us. They request permission to bring the observers up to the site here.'

'Grant it. I'll signal the fleet and give them the good news.'

Vipus turned away, then halted. 'At least that voice shut up,' he said.

Loken nodded. 'Samus' had quit his maudlin ramblings half an hour since, though the assault had failed to identify any vox system or broadcast device.

Loken's intervox crackled.

'Captain?'

'Jubal? Go ahead.'

'Captain, I'm...'

'What? You're what? Say again, Jubal.'

'Sorry, captain. I need you to see this. I'm... I mean, I need you to see this. It's Samus.'

'What? Jubal, where are you?'

'Follow my locator. I've found something. I'm... I've found something. Samus. It means the end and the death.'

'What have you found, Jubal?'

'I'm... I've found... Captain, Samus is here.'

Loken left Vipus to orchestrate the clean-up, and descended into the bowels of the fastness with Seventh Squad, following the pip of Jubal's locator. Seventh Squad, Brakespur Tactical Squad, was commanded by Sergeant Udon, one of Loken's most reliable warriors.

The locator led them down to a massive stone well in the very basement of the fortress, deep in the heart of the mountain. They gained access to it via a corroded iron gate built into a niche in the dark stone. The dank chamber beyond the gate was a natural, vertical split in the mountain rock, a slanting cavern that overlooked a deep fault where only blackness could be detected. A pier of old stone steps arced out over the abyss, which dropped away into the very bottom of the mountain. Meltwater sprinkled down the glistening walls of the cavern well.

The wind whined through invisible fissures and vents.

Xavyer Jubal was alone at the edge of the drop. As Loken and Seventh Squad approached, Loken wondered where the rest of Hellebore had gone.

'Xavyer?' Loken called.

Jubal looked around. 'Captain,' he said. 'I've found something wonderful.'

'What?'

'See?' Jubal said. 'See the words?'

Loken stared where Jubal was pointing. All he saw was water streaming down a calcified buttress of rock.

'No. What words?'

'There! There!'

'I see only water,' Loken said. 'Falling water.'

'Yes, yes! It's written in the water! In the falling water! There and gone, there and gone, You see? It makes words and they stream away, but the words come back.'

'Xavyer? Are you well? I'm concerned that–'

'Look, Garviel! Look at the words! Can't you hear the water speaking?'

'Speaking?'

'Drip drip drop. One name. Samus. That's the only name you'll hear.'

'Samus?'

'Samus. It means the end and the death. I'm...'

Loken looked at Udon and the men. 'Restrain him,' he said quietly.

Udon nodded. He and four of his men slung their bolters and stepped forward.

'What are you doing?' Jubal laughed. 'Are you threatening me? For Terra's sake, Garviel, can't you see? Samus is all around you!'

'Where's Hellebore, Jubal?' Loken snapped. 'Where's the rest of your squad?'

Jubal shrugged. 'They didn't see it either,' he said, and glanced towards the edge of the precipice. 'They couldn't see, I suppose. It's so clear to me. Samus is the man beside you.'

'Udon,' Loken nodded. Udon moved towards Jubal. 'Let's go, brother,' he said, kindly.

Jubal's bolter came up very suddenly. There was no warning. He shot Udon in the face, blowing gore and pulverised skull fragments out through the back of Udon's exploded helm. Udon fell on his face. Two of his men lunged forward, and the bolter roared again, punching holes in their chestplates and throwing them over onto their backs.

Jubal's visor swung to look at Loken. 'I'm Samus,' he said, chuckling. 'Look out! Samus is here.'

NINE

The unthinkable
Spirits of the Whisperheads
Compatible minds

Two days before the Legion's assault on the Whisperheads, Loken had consented to another private interview with the remembrancer Mersadie Oliton. It was the third such interview he had granted since his election to the Mournival, at which time his attitude towards her seemed to have substantially altered. Though the subject had not been mentioned formally, Mersadie had begun to feel that Loken had chosen her to be his particular memorialist. He had told her on the night of his election that he might choose to share his recollections with her, but she was now secretly astonished at the extent of his eagerness to do so. She had already recorded almost six hours of reminiscence – accounts of battles and tactics, descriptions of especially demanding military operations, reflections on the qualities of certain types of weapon, celebrations of notable deeds and triumphs accomplished by his comrades. In the time between interviews, she took herself to her room and processed the material, composing it into the skeleton of a long, fluid account. She hoped eventually to have a complete history of the expedition, and a more general record of the Great Crusade as witnessed by Loken during the other expeditions that had preceded the 63rd.

Indeed, the weight of anecdotal fact she was gathering was huge, but one thing was lacking, and that was Loken himself.

In the latest interview, she tried once again to draw out some spark of the man.

'As I understand it,' she said, 'you have nothing in you that we ordinary mortals might know as fear?'

Loken paused and frowned. He had been lapping a plate section of his armour. This seemed to be his favourite diversion when in her company. He would call her to his private arming chamber and sit there, scrupulously polishing his war harness while he spoke and she listened. To Mersadie, the particular smell of the lapping powder had become synonymous with the sound of his voice and the matter of his tales. He had well over a century of stories to tell.

'A curious question,' he said.

'And how curious is the answer?'

Loken shrugged lightly. 'The Astartes have no fear. It is unthinkable to us.'

'Because you have trained yourself to master it?' Mersadie asked.

'No, we are trained for discipline, but the capacity for fear is bred out of us. We are immune to its touch.'

Mersadie made a mental note to edit this last comment later. To her, it seemed to leach away some of the heroic mystique of the Astartes. To deny fear was the very character of a hero, but there was nothing courageous about being insensible to the emotion. She wondered too if it was possible to simply remove an entire emotion from what was essentially a human mind. Did that not leave a void? Were other emotions compromised by its lack? Could fear even be removed cleanly, or did its excision tear out shreds of other qualities along with it? It certainly might explain why the Astartes seemed larger than life in almost every aspect except their own personalities.

'Well, let us continue,' she said. 'At our last meeting, you were going to tell me about the war against the overseers. That was twenty years ago, wasn't it?'

He was still looking at her, eyes slightly narrowed. 'What?' he asked.

'I'm sorry?'

'What is it? You didn't like my answer just then.'

Mersadie cleared her throat. 'No, not at all. It wasn't that. I had just been...'

'What?'

'May I be candid?'

'Of course,' he said, patiently rubbing a nub of polishing fibre around the edges of a pot.

'I had been hoping to get something a little more personal. You have given me a great deal, sir, authentic details and points of fact that would make any history text authoritative. Posterity will know with precision, for instance, which hand Iacton Qruze carried his sword in, the colour of the sky over the Monastery Cities of Nabatae, the methodology of the White Scars' favoured pincer assault, the number of studs on the shoulder plate of a Luna Wolf, the number of axe blows, and from which angles, it took to fell the last of the Omakkad Princes...' She looked at him squarely, 'but nothing about you, sir. I know what you saw, but not what you felt.'

'What I felt? Why would anyone be interested in that?'

'Humanity is a sensible race, sir. Future generations, those that our remembrances are intended for, will learn more from any factual record if those facts are couched in an emotional context. They will care less for the details of the battles at Ullanor, for instance, than they will for a sense of what it felt like to be there.'

'Are you saying that I'm boring?' Loken asked.

'No, not at all,' she began, and then realised he was smiling. 'Some of the things you have told me sound like wonders, yet you do not yourself seem to wonder at them. If you know no fear, do you also not know awe? Surprise? Majesty? Have you not seen things so bizarre they left you speechless? Shocked you? Unnerved you even?'

'I have,' he said. 'Many times the sheer oddity of the cosmos has left me bemused or startled.'

'So tell me of those things.'

He pursed his lips and thought about it. 'Giant hats,' he began.

'I beg your pardon?'

'On Sarosel, after compliance, the citizens held a great carnival of celebration. Compliance had been bloodless and willing. The carnival ran for eight weeks. The dancers in the streets wore giant hats of ribbon and cane and paper, each one fashioned into some gaudy form: a ship, a sword and fist, a dragon, a sun. They were as broad across as my span.' Loken spread his arms wide. 'I do not know how they balanced them, or suffered their weight, but day and night they danced along the inner streets of the main city, these garish forms weaving and bobbing and circling, as if carried along on a slow flood, quite obscuring the human figures beneath. It was an odd sight.'

'I believe you.'

'It made us laugh. It made Horus laugh to see it.'

'Was that the strangest thing you ever knew?'

'No, no. Let's see... the method of war on Keylek gave us all

pause. This was eighty years ago. The keylekid were a groste-
que alien kind, of a manner you might describe as reptilian.
They were greatly skilled in the arts of combat, and rose against
us angrily the moment we made contact. Their world was a
harsh place. I remember crimson rock and indigo water. The
commander – this was long before he was made Warmaster –
expected a prolonged and brutal struggle, for the keylekid were
large and strong creatures. Even the least of their warriors took
three or four bolt rounds to bring down. We drew forth upon
their world to make war, but they would not fight us.'

'How so?'

'We did not comprehend the rules they fought by. As we
learned later, the keylekid considered war to be the most abhorrent activity a sentient race could indulge in, so they set upon it
tight controls and restrictions. There were large structures upon
the surface of their world, rectangular fields many kilometres
in dimension, covered with high, flat roofs and open at the
sides. We named them "slaughter-houses", and there was one
every few hundred kilometres. The keylekid would only fight
at these prescribed places. The sites were reserved for combat.
War was forbidden on any other part of their world's surface.
They were waiting for us to meet them at a slaughter-house and
decide the matter.'

'How bizarre! What was done about it?'

'We destroyed the keylekid,' he said, matter of factly.

'Oh,' she replied, with a tilt of her abnormally long head.

'It was suggested that we might meet them and fight them
by the terms of their rules,' Loken said. 'There may have been
some honour in that, but Maloghurst, I think it was, reasoned
that we had rules of our own which the enemy chose not to
recognise. Besides, they were formidable. Had we not acted deci-
sively, they would have remained a threat, and how long would
it have taken them to learn new rules or abandon old ones?'

'Is an image of them recorded?' Mersadie asked.

'Many, I believe. The preserved cadaver of one of their warriors is displayed in this ship's Museum of Conquest, and since
you ask what I feel, sometimes it is sadness. You mentioned the
overseers, a story I was going to tell. That was a long campaign,
and one which filled me with misery.'

As he told the story, she sat back, occasionally blink-clicking
to store his image. He was concentrating on the preparation
of his armour, but she could see sadness behind that concern.
The overseers, he explained, were a machine race and, as artificial sentients, quite beyond the limits of Imperial law. Machine

life untempered by organic components had long been out-
lawed by both the Imperial Council and the Mechanicum. The
overseers, commanded by a senior machine called the Arch-
droid, inhabited a series of derelict, crumbling cities on the
world of Dahinta. These were cities of fine mosaics, which had
once been very beautiful indeed, but extreme age and decay
had faded them. The overseers scuttled amongst the mouldering piles, fighting a losing battle of repair and refurbishment in
a single-minded obsession to keep the neglected cities intact.

The machines had eventually been destroyed after a last-
ing and brutal war in which the skills of the Mechanicum had
proved invaluable. Only then was the sad secret found.

'The overseers were the product of human ingenuity,' Loken
said.

'Humans made them?'

'Yes, thousands of years ago, perhaps even during the last Age
of Technology. Dahinta had been a human colony, home to a
lost branch of our race, where they had raised a great and marvellous culture of magnificent cities, with thinking machines
to serve them. At some time, and in a manner unknown to us,
the humans had become extinct. They left behind their ancient
cities, empty but for the deathless guardians they had made. It
was most melancholy, and passing strange.'

'Did the machines not recognise men?' she asked.

'All they saw was the Astartes, lady, and we did not look like
the men they had called master.'

She hesitated for a moment, then said, 'I wonder if I shall witness so many marvels as we make this expedition.'

'I trust you will, and I hope that many will fill you with joy
and amazement rather than distress. I should tell you sometime of the Great Triumph after Ullanor. That was an event that
should be remembered.'

'I look forward to hearing it.'

'There is no time now. I have duties to attend to.'

'One last story, then? A short one, perhaps? Something that
filled you with awe.'

He sat back and thought. 'There was a thing. No more than
ten years ago. We found a dead world where life had once been.
A species had lived there once, and either died out or moved
to another world. They had left behind them a honeycomb of
subterranean habitats, dry and dead. We searched them carefully, every last cave and tunnel, and found just one thing of
note. It was buried deepest of all, in a stone bunker ten kilometres under the planet's crust. A map. A great chart, in fact,

fully twenty metres in diameter, showing the geophysical relief of an entire world in extraordinary detail. We did not at first recognise it, but the Emperor, beloved of all, knew what it was.'

'What?' she asked.

'It was Terra. It was a complete and full map of Terra, perfect in every detail. But it was a map of Terra from an age long gone, before the rise of the hives or the molestation of war, with coastlines and oceans and mountains of an aspect long since erased or covered over.'

'That is… amazing,' she said.

He nodded. 'So many unanswerable questions, locked into one forgotten chamber. Who had made the map, and why? What business had brought them to Terra so long ago? What had caused them to carry the chart across half the galaxy, and then hide it away, like their most precious treasure, in the depths of their world? It was unthinkable. I cannot feel fear, Mistress Oliton, but if I could I would have felt it then. I cannot imagine anything ever unsettling my soul the way that thing did.'

Unthinkable.

Time had slowed to a pinprick point on which it seemed all the gravity in the cosmos was pressing. Loken felt lead-heavy, slow, out of joint, unable to frame a lucid response, or even begin to deal with what he was seeing.

Was this fear? Was he tasting it now, after all? Was this how terror cowed a mortal man?

Sergeant Udon, his helm a deformed ring of bloody ceramite, lay dead at his feet. Beside him sprawled two other battle-brothers, shot point-blank through the hearts, if not dead then fatally damaged.

Before him stood Jubal, the bolter in his hand.

This was madness. This could not be. Astartes had turned upon Astartes. A Luna Wolf had murdered his own kind. Every law of fraternity and honour that Loken understood and trusted had just been torn as easily as a cobweb. The insanity of this crime would echo forever.

'Jubal? What have you done?'

'Not Jubal. Samus. I am Samus. Samus is all around you. Samus is the man beside you.'

Jubal's voice had a catch to it, a dry giggle. Loken knew he was about to fire again. The rest of Udon's squad, quite as aghast as Loken, stumbled forward, but none raised their bolters. Even in the stark light of what Jubal had just done, not one of them could break the sworn code of the Astartes and fire upon one of their own.

Loken knew he certainly couldn't. He threw his bolter aside and leapt at Jubal.

Xavyer Jubal, commander of Hellebore squad and one of the finest file officers in the company, had already begun to fire. Bolt rounds screeched out across the chamber and struck into the hesitating squad. Another helmet exploded in a welter of blood, bone chips and armour fragments, and another battle-brother crashed to the cave floor. Two more were knocked down beside him as bolt rounds detonated against their torso armour.

Loken smashed into Jubal, and staggered him backwards, trying to pin his arms. Jubal thrashed, sudden fury in his limbs.

'Samus!' he yelled. 'It means the end and the death! Samus will gnaw upon your bones!'

They crashed against a rock wall together with numbing force, splintering stone. Jubal would not relinquish his grip on the murder weapon. Loken drove him backwards against the rock, the drizzle of meltwater spraying down across them both.

'Jubal!'

Loken threw a punch that would have decapitated a mortal man. His fist cracked against Jubal's helm and he repeated the action, driving his fist four or five times against the other's face and chest. The ceramite visor chipped. Another punch, his full weight behind it, and Jubal stumbled. Each stroke of Loken's fist resounded like a smith's hammer in the echoing chamber, steel against steel.

As Jubal stumbled, Loken grabbed his bolter and tore it out of his hand. He hurled it away across the deep stone well.

But Jubal was not yet done. He seized Loken and slammed him sideways into the rock wall. Lumps of stone flew out from the jarring impact. Jubal slammed him again, swinging Loken bodily into the rock, like a man swinging a heavy sack. Pain flared through Loken's head and he tasted blood in his mouth. He tried to pull away, but Jubal was throwing punches that ploughed into Loken's visor and bounced the back of his head off the wall repeatedly.

The other men were upon them, shouting and grappling to separate them.

'Hold him!' Loken yelled. 'Hold him down!'

They were Astartes, as strong as young gods in their power armour, but they could not do as Loken ordered. Jubal lashed out with a free fist and knocked one of them clean off his feet. Two of the remaining three clung to his back like wrestlers, like human cloaks, trying to pull him down, but he hoisted them up and twisted, throwing them off him.

Such strength. Such unthinkable strength that could shrug off Astartes like target dummies in a practice cage.

Jubal turned on the remaining brother, who launched himself forward to tackle the madman.

'Look out!' Jubal screamed with a cackle. 'Samus is here!'

His lancing right hand met the brother head on. Jubal struck with an open hand, fingers extended, and those fingers drove clean in through the battle-brother's gorget as surely as any speartip. Blood squirted out from the man's throat, through the puncture in the armour. Jubal ripped his hand out, and the brother fell to his knees, choking and gurgling, blood pumping in profuse, pulsing surges from his ruptured throat.

Beyond any thought of reason now, Loken hurled himself at Jubal, but the berserker turned and smacked him away with a mighty back-hand slap.

The power of the blow was stupendous, far beyond anything even an Astartes should have been able to wield. The force was so great that the armour of Jubal's gauntlet fractured, as did the plating of Loken's shoulder, which took the brunt. Loken blacked out for a split-second, then was aware that he was flying. Jubal had struck him so hard that he was sailing across the stone well and out over the abyssal fault.

Loken struck the arching pier of stone steps. He almost bounced off it, but he managed to grab on, his fingers gouging the ancient stone, his feet swinging above the drop. Meltwater poured down in a thin rain across him, making the steps slick and oily with mineral wash. Loken's fingers began to slide. He remembered dangling in a similar fashion over the tower lip in the 'Emperor's' palace, and snarled in frustrated rage.

Fury pulled him up. Fury, and an intense passion that he would not fail the Warmaster. Not in this. Not in the face of this terrible wrong.

He hauled himself upright on to the pier. It was narrow, no wider than a single path where men could not pass if they met. The gulf, black as the outer void, yawned below him. His limbs were shaking with effort.

He saw Jubal. He was charging forward across the cavern to the foot of the steps, drawing his combat blade. The sword glowed as it powered into life.

Loken wrenched out his own sword. Falling meltwater hissed and sparked as it touched the active metal of the short, stabbing blade.

Jubal bounded up the steps to meet him, slashing with his sword. He was raving still, in a voice that was in no way his own any longer. He struck wildly at Loken, who hopped back up the steps, and then began to deflect the strikes with his own weapon. Sparks flashed, and the blades struck one another like the tolling of a discordant bell. Height was not an advantage in this fight, as Loken had to hunch low to maintain his guard.

Combat swords were not duelling weapons. Short and double-edged, they were made for stabbing, for battlefield onslaught. They had no reach or subtlety. Jubal hacked with his like an axe, forcing Loken to defend. Their blades cut falling water as they scythed, sizzling and billowing steam into the air.

Loken prided himself on maintaining a masterful discipline and practice of all weapons. He regularly clocked six or eight hours at a time in the flagship's practice cages. He expected all of the men in his command to do likewise. Xavyer Jubal, he knew, was foremost a master with daggers and sparring axes, but no slouch with the sword.

Except today. Jubal had discarded all his skill, or had forgotten it in the flush of madness that had engulfed his mind. He attacked Loken like a maniac, in a frenzy of savage cuts and blows. Loken was likewise forced to dispense with much of his skill in an effort to block and parry. Three times, Loken managed to drive Jubal back down the pier a few steps, but always the other man retaliated and forced Loken higher up the arch. Once, Loken had to leap to avoid a low slice, and barely regained his footing as he landed. In the silver downpour, the steps were treacherous, and it was as much a fight to keep balance as to resist Jubal's constant assault.

It ended suddenly, like a jolt. Jubal passed Loken's guard and sunk the full edge of his blade into Loken's left shoulder plate.

'Samus is here!' he cried in delight, but his blade, flaring with power, was wedged fast.

'Samus is done,' Loken replied, and drove the tip of his sword into Jubal's exposed chest. The sword punched clean through, and the tip emerged through Jubal's back.

Jubal wavered, letting go of his own weapon, which remained transfixed through Loken's shoulder guard. With half-open, shuddering hands, he reached at Loken's face, not violently, but gently, as if imploring some mercy or even aid. Water splashed off them and streamed down their white plating.

'Samus...' he gasped. Loken wrenched his sword out.

Jubal staggered and swayed, the blood leaking out of the gash in his chestplate, diluting as soon as it appeared and mixing with the drizzle, covering his belly plate and thigh armour with a pink stain.

He toppled backwards, crashing over and over down the steps in a windmill of heavy, loose limbs. Five metres from the base of the pier, his headlong career bounced him half-off the steps, and he came to a halt, legs dangling, partly hanging over the chasm, gradually sliding backwards under his own weight. Loken heard the slow squeal of armour scraping against slick stone.

He leapt down the flight to reach Jubal's side. He got there just moments before Jubal slid away into oblivion. Loken grabbed Jubal by the edge of his left shoulder plate and slowly began to heave him back onto the pier. It was almost impossible. Jubal seemed to weigh a billion tonnes.

The three surviving members of Brakespur squad stood at the foot of the steps, watching him struggle.

'Help me!' Loken yelled.

'To save him?' one asked.

'Why?' asked another. 'Why would you want to?'

'Help me!' Loken snarled again. They didn't move. In desperation, Loken raised his sword and stabbed it down, spearing Jubal's right shoulder to the steps. So pinned, his slide was arrested. Loken hauled his body back onto the pier.

Panting, Loken dragged off his battered helm and spat out a mouthful of blood.

'Get Vipus,' he ordered. 'Get him now.'

By the time they were conducted up to the plateau, there wasn't much to see and the light was failing. Euphrati took a few random picts of the parked Stormbirds and the cone of smoke lifting off the broken crag, but she didn't expect much from any of them. It all seemed drab and lifeless up there. Even the vista of the mountains around them was insipid.

'Can we see the combat area?' she asked Sindermann.

'We've been told to wait.'

'Is there a problem?'

He shook his head. It was an 'I don't know' kind of shake. Like all of them, he was strapped into his rebreather, but he looked frail and tired.

It was eerily quiet. Groups of Luna Wolves were trudging back to the Stormbirds from the fastness, and army troops had secured the plateau itself. The remembrancers had been told that a solid victory had been achieved, but there was no sign of jubilation.

'Oh, it's a mechanical thing,' Sindermann said when Euphrati questioned him. 'This is just a routine exercise for the Legion. A low-key action, as I said before we set out. I'm sorry if you're disappointed.'

'I'm not,' she said, but in truth there was a sense of anticlimax about it all. She wasn't sure what she had been expecting, but the rush of the drop, and the strange circumstance at Kasheri had begun to thrill her. Now everything was done, and she'd seen nothing.

'Carnis wants to interview some of the returning warriors,' Siman Sark said, 'and he's asked me to pict them while he does. Would that be permissible?'

'I should think so,' Sindermann sighed. He called out for an army officer to guide Carnis and Sark to the Astartes.

'I think,' said Tolemew Van Krasten aloud, 'that a tone poem would be most appropriate. Full symphonic composition would overwhelm the atmosphere, I feel.'

Euphrati nodded, not really understanding.

'A minor key, I think. E, or A perhaps. I'm taken with the title "The Spirits of the Whisperheads", or perhaps, "The Voice of Samus". What do you think?'

She stared at him.

'I'm joking,' he said with a sad smile. 'I have no idea what I am supposed to respond to here, or how. It all seems so dour.'

Euphrati Keeler had supposed Van Krasten to be a pompous type, but now she warmed to him. As he turned away and gazed mournfully up at the smoking peak, she was seized by a thought and raised her picter.

'Did you just take my likeness?' he asked.

She nodded. 'Do you mind? You looking at the peak like that seemed to sum up how we all feel.'

'But I'm a remembrancer,' he said. 'Should I be in your record?'

'We're all in this. Witnesses or not, we're all here,' she replied. 'I take what I see. Who knows? Maybe you can return the favour? A little refrain of flutes in your next overture that represents Euphrati Keeler?'

They both laughed.

A Luna Wolf was approaching the huddle of them.

'Nero Vipus,' he said, making the sign of the aquila. 'Captain Loken presents his respects and wishes the attention of Master Sindermann at once.'

'I'm Sindermann,' the elderly man replied. 'Is there some problem, sir?'

'I've been asked to conduct you to the captain,' Vipus replied. 'This way, please.'

The pair of them moved away, Sindermann scurrying to keep up with Vipus's great strides.

'What is going on?' Van Krasten asked, his voice hushed.

'I don't know. Let's find out,' Keeler replied.

'Follow them? Oh, I don't think so.'

'I'm game,' said Borodin Flora. 'We haven't actually been told to stay here.'

They looked round. Twell had sat himself down beside the prow landing strut of a Stormbird and was beginning to sketch with charcoal sticks on a small pad. Carnis and Sark were busy elsewhere.

'Come on,' said Euphrati Keeler.

Vipus led Sindermann up into the ruined fastness. The wind moaned and whistled through the grim tunnels and chambers. Army troopers were clearing the dead from the entry halls and casting them into the gorge, but still Vipus had to steer the iterator past many crumpled, exploded corpses. He kept saying such things as, 'I'm sorry you had to see that, sir,' and, 'Look away to spare your sensibilities.'

Sindermann could not look away. He had iterated loyally for many years, but this was the first time he had walked across a fresh battlefield. The sights appalled him and burned themselves into his memory. The stench of blood and ordure assailed him. He saw human forms burst and brutalised, and burned beyond any measure he had imagined possible. He saw walls sticky with blood and brain-matter, fragments of exploded bone weeping marrow, body parts littering the blood-soaked floors.

'Terra,' he breathed, over and again. This was what the Astartes did. This was the reality of the Emperor's crusade. Mortal hurt on a scale that passed belief.

'Terra,' he whispered to himself. By the time he was brought to Loken, who awaited him in one of the fortress's upper chambers, the word had become 'terror' without him realising it.

Loken was standing in a wide, dark chamber beside some sort of pool. Water gurgled down one of the black-wet walls and the air smelled of damp and oxides. A dozen solemn Luna Wolves attended Loken, including one giant fellow in glowering Terminator armour, but Loken himself was bareheaded. His face was smudged with bruises. He'd removed his left shoulder guard, which lay beside him on the ground, stuck through with a short sword.

'You have done such a thing,' Sindermann said, his voice small. 'I don't think I'd quite understood what you Astartes were capable of, but now I–'

'Quiet,' Loken said bluntly. He looked at the Luna Wolves around him and dismissed them with a nod. They filed out past Sindermann, ignoring him.

'Stay close, Nero,' Loken called. Stepping out through the chamber door, Vipus nodded.

Now the room was almost empty, Sindermann could see that a body lay beside the pool. It was the body of a Luna Wolf, limp and dead, his helm off, his white armour mottled with blood. His arms had been lashed to his trunk with climbing cable.

'I don't...' Sindermann began. 'I don't understand, captain. I was told there had been no losses.'

Loken nodded slowly. 'That's what we're going to say. That will be the official line. The Tenth took this fortress in a clean strike, with no losses, and that's true enough. None of the insurgents scored any kills. Not even a wounding. We took a thousand of them to their deaths.'

'But this man...?'

Loken looked at Sindermann. His face was troubled, more troubled than the iterator had ever seen before. 'What is it, Garviel?' he asked.

'Something has happened,' Loken said. 'Something so... so unthinkable that I...'

He paused, and looked at Jubal's bound corpse. 'I have to make a report, but I don't know what to say. I have no frame of reference. I'm glad you are here, Kyril, you of all people. You have steered me well over the years.'

'I like to think that...'

'I need your counsel now.'

Sindermann stepped forward and placed his hand on the giant warrior's arm. 'You may trust me with any matter, Garviel. I'm here to serve.'

Loken looked down at him. 'This is confidential. Utterly confidential.'

'I understand.'

'There have been deaths today. Six brothers of Brakespur squad, including Udon. Another barely clinging to life. And Hellebore... Hellebore has vanished, and I fear they are dead too.'

'This can't be. The insurgents couldn't have–'

'They did nothing. This is Xavyer Jubal,' Loken said, pointing towards the body on the floor. 'He killed the men,' he said simply.

Sindermann rocked back as if slapped. He blinked. 'He what? I'm sorry, Garviel, I thought for a moment you said he–'

'He killed the men. Jubal killed the men. He took his bolter and his fists and he killed six of Brakespur right in front of my eyes, and he would have killed me too, if I hadn't run him through.'

Sindermann felt his legs tremble. He found a nearby rock and sat down abruptly. 'Terra,' he gasped.

'Terror is right. Astartes do not fight Astartes. Astartes do not kill their own. It is against all the rules of nature and man. It is counter to the very gene-code the Emperor fused into us when he wrought us.'

'There must be some mistake,' Sindermann said.

'No mistake. I saw him do it. He was a madman. He was possessed.'

'What? Steady, now. You look to old terms, Garviel. Possession is a spiritualist word that–'

'He was possessed. He claimed he was Samus.'

'Oh.'

'You've heard the name, then?'

'I've heard the whisper. That was just enemy propaganda, wasn't it? We were told to dismiss it as scare tactics.'

Loken touched the bruises on his face, feeling the ache of them. 'So I thought. Iterator, I'm going to ask you this once. Are spirits real?'

'No, sir. Absolutely not.'

'So we are taught and thus we are liberated, but could they exist? This world is lousy with superstition and temple-fanes. Could they exist here?'

'No,' Sindermann replied more firmly. 'There are no spirits, no daemons, no ghosts in the dark edges of the cosmos. Truth has shown us this.'

'I've studied the archive, Kyril,' Loken replied. 'Samus was the name the people of this world gave to their arch-fiend. He was imprisoned in these mountains, so their legends say.'

'Legends, Garviel. Only legends. Myths. We have learned much during our time amongst the stars, and the most pertinent of those things is that there is always a rational explanation, even for the most mysterious events.'

'An Astartes draws his weapon and kills his own, whilst claiming to be a daemon from hell? Rationalise *that*, sir.'

Sinderman rose. 'Calm yourself, Garviel, and I will.'

Loken didn't reply. Sindermann walked over to Jubal's body and stared at it. Jubal's open, staring eyes were rolled back in his skull and utterly bloodshot. The flesh of his face was drawn and shrivelled, as if he had aged ten thousand years. Strange patterns, like clusters of blemishes or moles, were visible on the painfully stretched skin.

'These marks,' said Sindermann. 'These vile signs of wasting. Could they be the traces of disease or infection?'

'What?' Loken asked.

'A virus, perhaps? A reaction to toxicity? A plague?'

'Astartes are resistant,' Loken said.

'To most things, but not to everything. I think this could be some contagion. Something so virulent that it destroyed Jubal's mind along with his body. Plagues can drive men insane, and corrupt their flesh.'

'Then why only him?' asked Loken.

Sindermann shrugged. 'Perhaps some tiny flaw in his gene-code?'

'But he behaved as if possessed,' Loken said, repeating the word with brutal emphasis.

'We've all been exposed to the enemy's propaganda. If Jubal's mind was deranged by fever, he might simply have been repeating the words he'd heard.'

Loken thought for a moment. 'You speak a lot of sense, Kyril,' he said.

'Always.'

'A plague,' Loken nodded. 'It's a sound explanation.'

'You've suffered a tragedy today, Garviel, but spirits and daemons played no part in it. Now get to work. You need to lock down this area in quarantine and get a medicae task force here. There may yet be further outbreaks. Non-Astartes, such as myself, might be less resistant, and poor Jubal's corpse may yet be a vector for disease.'

Sindermann looked back down at the body. 'Great Terra,' he said. 'He has been so ravaged. I weep to see this waste.'

With a creak of dried sinew, Jubal raised his head and stared up at Sindermann with blood-red eyes.

'Look out,' he wheezed.

Euphrati Keeler had stopped taking picts. She stowed away her picter. The things they were seeing in the narrow tunnels of the fortress went beyond all decency to record. She had never imagined that human forms could be dismantled so grievously, so totally. The stench of blood in the close, cold air made her gag, despite her rebreather.

'I want to go back now,' Van Krasten said. He was shaking and upset. 'There is no music here. I am sick to my stomach.'

Euphrati was inclined to agree.

'No,' said Borodin Flora in a muffled, steely voice. 'We must see it all. We are chosen remembrancers. This is our duty.'

Euphrati was quite sure Flora was making an effort not to throw up, but she warmed to the sentiment. This was their duty. This was the very reason they had been summoned. To record and commemorate the Crusade of Man. Whatever it looked like.

She tugged her picter back out of its carry-bag and took a few, tentative shots. Not of the dead, for that would be indecent, but of the blood on the walls, the smoke fuming in the wind along the narrow tunnels, the piles of scattered, spent shell cases littering the black-flecked ground.

Teams of army troopers moved past them, lugging bodies away for disposal. Some looked at the three of them curiously.

'Are you lost?' one asked.

'Not at all. We're allowed to be here,' Flora said.

'Why would you want to be?' the man wondered.

Euphrati took a series of long shots of troopers, almost in silhouette, gathering up body parts at a tunnel junction. It chilled her to see it, and she hoped her picts would have the same effect on her audience.

'I want to go back,' Van Krasten said again.

'Don't stray, or you'll get lost,' Euphrati warned.

'I think I might be sick,' Van Krasten admitted.

He was about to retch when a shrill, harrowing scream echoed down the tunnels.

'What the hell was that?' Euphrati whispered.

Jubal rose. The ropes binding him sheared and split, releasing his arms. He screamed, and then screamed again. His frantic wails soared and echoed around the chamber.

Sindermann stumbled backwards in total panic. Loken ran forward and tried to restrain the reanimating madman.

Jubal struck out with one thrashing fist and caught Loken in the chest. Loken flew backwards into the pool with a crash of water.

Jubal turned, hunched. Saliva dangled from his slack mouth, and his bloodshot eyes spun like compasses at true north.

'Please, oh please…' Sindermann gabbled, backing away.

'Look. Out.' The words crawled sluggishly out of Jubal's drooling mouth. He lumbered forward. Something was happening to him, something malign and catastrophic. He was bulging, expanding so furiously that his armour began to crack and shatter. Sections of broken plate split and fell away from him, exposing thick arms swollen with gangrene and fibrous growths. His taut flesh was pallid and blue. His face was distorted, puffy and livid, and his tongue flopped out of his rotting mouth, long and serpentine.

He raised his meaty, distended hands triumphantly, exposing fingernails grown into dark hooks and psoriatic claws.

'Samus is here,' he drawled.

Sindermann fell on his knees before the misshapen brute. Jubal reeked of corruption and sore wounds. He shambled forward. His form flickered and danced with blurry yellow light, as if he was not quite in phase with the present.

A bolter round struck him in the right shoulder and detonated against the rindy integument his skin had become. Shreds of meat and gobbets of pus sprayed in all directions. In the chamber doorway, Nero Vipus took aim again.

The thing that had once been Xavyer Jubal grabbed Sindermann and threw him at Vipus. The pair of them crashed backwards against the wall, Vipus dropping his weapon in an effort to catch and cushion Sindermann and spare the frail bones of the elderly iterator.

The Jubal-thing shuffled past them into the tunnel, leaving a noxious trail of dripped blood and wretched, discoloured fluid in its wake.

Euphrati saw the thing coming for them and tried to decide whether to scream or raise her picter. In the end, she did both. Van Krasten lost control of his bodily functions, and fell to the floor in a puddle of his own manufacture. Borodin Flora just backed away, his mouth moving silently.

The Jubal-thing advanced down the tunnel towards them. It was gross and distorted, its skin stretched by humps and swellings. It had become so gigantic that what little remained of its pearl-white armour dragged behind it like metal rags. Strange puncta and moles marked its flesh. Jubal's face had contorted into a dog snout, wherein his human teeth stuck out like stray ivory markers, displaced by the thin, transparent crop of needle fangs that now invested his mouth. There were so many fangs that his mouth could no longer close. His eyes were blood pools. Jerky, spasmodic flashes of yellow light surrounded him, making vague shapes and patterns. They caused Jubal's movements to seem wrong, as if he was a pict-feed image, badly cut and running slightly too fast.

He snatched up Tolemew Van Krasten and dashed him like a toy against the walls of the tunnel, back and forth, with huge, slamming, splattering effect, so that when he let go, little of Tolemew still existed above the sternum.

'Oh Terra!' Keeler cried, retching violently. Borodin Flora stepped past her to confront the monster, and made the defiant sign of the aquila.

'Begone!' he cried out. 'Begone!'

The Jubal-thing leaned forward, opened its mouth to a hitherto unimaginable width, revealing an unguessable number of needle teeth, and bit off Borodin Flora's head and upper body. The remainder of his form crumpled to the floor, ejecting blood like a pressure hose.

Euphrati Keeler sank to her knees. Terror had rendered her powerless to run. She accepted her fate, largely because she had no idea what it was to be. In the final moments of her life, she reassured herself that at least she hadn't added to brutal death the indignity of wetting herself in the face of such incomprehensible horror.

TEN

The Warmaster and his son
No matter the ferocity or ingenuity of the foe
Official denial

'You killed it?'

'Yes,' said Loken, gazing at the dirt floor, his mind somewhere else.

'You're sure?'

Loken looked up out of his reverie. 'What?'

'I need you to be sure,' Abaddon said. 'You killed it?'

'Yes.' Loken was sitting on a crude hardwood stool in one of the longhouses in Kasheri. Night had fallen outside, bringing with it a keening, malevolent wind that shrieked around the gorge and the Whisperhead peaks. A dozen oil lamps lit the place with a feeble ochre glow. 'We killed it. Nero and I together, with our bolters. It took ninety rounds at full auto. It burst and burned, and we used a flamer to cremate all that remained.'

Abaddon nodded. 'How many people know?'

'About that last act? Myself, Nero, Sindermann and the remembrancer, Keeler. We cut the thing down just before it bit her in half. Everyone else who saw it is dead.'

'What have you said?'

'Nothing, Ezekyle.'

'That's good.'

'I've said nothing because I don't know what to say.'

Abaddon scooped up another stool and brought it over to sit

down facing Loken. Both were in full plate, their helms removed. Abaddon hunched his head low to catch Loken's eyes.

'I'm proud of you, Garviel. You hear me? You dealt with this well.'

'What did I deal with?' Loken asked sombrely.

'The situation. Tell me, before Jubal rose again, who knew of the murders?'

'More. Those of Brakespur that survived. All of my officers. I wanted their advice.'

'I'll speak to them,' Abaddon muttered. 'This mustn't get out. Our line will be as you set it. Victory, splendid but unexceptional. The Tenth crushed the insurgents, though losses were taken in two squads. But that is war. We expect casualties. The insurgents fought bitterly and formidably to the last. Hellebore and Brakespur bore the brunt of their rage, but Sixty-Three Nineteen is advanced to full compliance. Glory the Tenth, and the Luna Wolves, glory the Warmaster. The rest will remain a matter of confidence within the inner circle. Can Sindermann be trusted to keep this close?'

'Of course, though he is very shaken.'

'And the remembrancer? Keener, was it?'

'Keeler. Euphrati Keeler. She's in shock. I don't know her. I don't know what she'll do, but she has no idea what it was that attacked her. I told her it was a wild beast. She didn't see Jubal… change. She doesn't know it was him.'

'Well, that's something. I'll place an injunction on her, if necessary. Perhaps a word will be sufficient. I'll repeat the wild beast story, and tell her we're keeping the matter confidential for morale's sake. The remembrancers must be kept away from this.'

'Two of them died.'

Abaddon got up. 'A tragic mishap during deployment. A landing accident. They knew the risks they were taking. It will be just a footnote blemish to an otherwise exemplary undertaking.'

Loken looked up at the first captain. 'Are we trying to forget this even happened, Ezekyle? For I cannot. And I will not.'

'I'm saying this is a military incident and will remain restricted. It's a matter of security and morale, Garviel. You are disturbed, I can see that plainly. Think what needless trauma this would cause if it got out. It would ruin confidence, break the spirit of the expedition, tarnish the entire crusade, not to mention the unimpeachable reputation of the Legion.'

The longhouse door banged open and the gale squealed in for a moment before the door closed again. Loken didn't look up. He was expecting Vipus back at any time with the muster reports.

'Leave us, Ezekyle,' a voice said.

It wasn't Vipus.

Horus was not wearing his armour. He was dressed in simple foul-weather clothes, a mail shirt and a cloak of furs. Abaddon bowed his head and quickly left the longhouse.

Loken had risen to his feet.

'Sit, Garviel,' Horus said softly. 'Sit down. Make no ceremony to me.'

Loken slowly sat back down and the Warmaster knelt beside him. He was so immensely made that kneeling, his head was on a level with Loken's. He plucked off his black leather gloves and placed his bare left hand on Loken's shoulder.

'I want you to let go of your troubles, my son,' he said.

'I try, sir, but they will not leave me alone.'

Horus nodded. 'I understand.'

'I have made a failure of this undertaking, sir,' Loken said. 'Ezekyle says we will put a brave face on it for appearance sake, but even if these events remain secret, I will bear the shame of failing you.'

'And how did you do that?'

'Men died. A brother turned upon his own. Such a manifest sin. Such a crime. You charged me to take this seat of resistance, and I have made such a mess of it that you have been forced to come here in person to–'

'Hush,' Horus whispered. He reached out and unfixed Loken's tattered oath of moment from his shoulder plate.

'Do you, Garviel Loken, accept your role in this?' The Warmaster read out. 'Do you promise to lead your men into the zone of war, and conduct them to glory, no matter the ferocity or ingenuity of the foe? Do you swear to crush the insurgents of Sixty-Three Nineteen, despite all they might throw at you? Do you pledge to do honour to the XVI Legion and the Emperor?'

'Fine words,' Loken said.

'They are indeed. I wrote them. Well, did you, Garviel?'

'Did I what, sir?'

'Did you crush the insurgents of Sixty-Three Nineteen, despite all they threw at you?'

'Well, yes–'

'And did you lead your men into the zone of war, and conduct them to glory, no matter the ferocity or ingenuity of the foe?'

'Yes…'

'Then I can't see how you've failed in any way, my son. Consider that last phrase particularly. "No matter the ferocity or ingenuity of the foe". When poor Jubal turned, did you give up?

Did you flee? Did you cast away your courage? Or did you fight against his insanity and his crime, despite your wonder at it?'

'I fought, sir,' Loken said.

'Throne of Earth, yes, you did. Yes, you did, Loken! You fought. Cast shame out. I will not have it. You served me well today, my son, and I am only sorry that the extent of your service cannot be more widely proclaimed.'

Loken started to reply, but fell silent instead. Horus rose to his feet and began to pace about the room. He found a bottle of wine amongst the clutter on a wall dresser and poured himself a glass.

'I spoke to Kyril Sindermann,' he said, and took a sip of the wine. He nodded to himself before continuing, as if surprised at its quality. 'Poor Kyril. Such a terrible thing to endure. He's even speaking of spirits, you know? Sindermann, the arch prophet of secular truth, speaking of spirits. I put him right, naturally. He mentioned spirits were a concern of yours too.'

'Kyril convinced me it was a plague, at first, but I saw a spirit… a daemon… take hold of Xavyer Jubal and remake his flesh into the form of a monster. I saw a daemon take hold of Jubal's soul and turn him against his own kind.'

'No, you didn't,' Horus said.

'Sir?'

Horus smiled. 'Allow me to illuminate you. I'll tell you what you saw, Garviel. It is a secret thing, known to a very few, though the Emperor, beloved of all, knows more than any of us. A secret, Garviel, more than any other secret we are keeping today. Can you keep it? I'll share it, for it will soothe your mind, but I need you to keep it solemnly.'

'I will,' Loken said.

The Warmaster took another sip. 'It was the warp, Garviel.'

'The… warp?'

'Of course it was. We know the power of the warp and the chaos it contains. We've seen it change men. We've seen the wretched things that infest its dark dimensions. I know you have. On Erridas. On Syrinx. On the bloody coast of Tassilon. There are entities in the warp that we might easily mistake for daemons.'

'Sir, I…' Loken began. 'I have been trained in the study of the warp. I am well-prepared to face its horrors. I have fought the foul things that pour forth from the gates of the empyrean, and yes, the warp can seep into a man and transmute him. I have seen this happen, but only in psykers. It is the risk they take. Not in Astartes.'

'Do you understand the full mechanism of the warp, Garviel?'
Horus asked. He raised the glass to the nearest light to examine the colour of the wine.

'No, sir. I don't pretend to.'

'Neither do I, my son. Neither does the Emperor, beloved by all. Not entirely. It pains me to admit that, but it is the truth, and we deal in truths above all else. The warp is a vital tool to us, a means of communication and transport. Without it, there would be no Imperium of Man, for there would be no quick bridges between the stars. We use it, and we harness it, but we have no absolute control over it. It is a wild thing that tolerates our presence, but brooks no mastery. There is power in the warp, fundamental power, not good, nor evil, but elemental and anathema to us. It is a tool we use at our own risk.'

The Warmaster finished his glass and set it down. 'Spirits. Daemons. Those words imply a greater power, a fiendish intellect and a purpose. An evil archetype with cosmic schemes and stratagems. They imply a god, or gods, at work behind the scenes. They imply the very supernatural state that we have taken great pains, through the light of science, to shake off. They imply sorcery and a palpable evil.'

He looked across at Loken. 'Spirits. Daemons. The supernatural. Sorcery. These are words we have allowed to fall out of use, for we dislike the connotations, but they are just words. What you saw today... call it a spirit. Call it a daemon. The words serve well enough. Using them does not deny the clinical truth of the universe as man understands it. There can be daemons in a secular cosmos, Garviel. Just so long as we understand the use of the word.'

'Meaning the warp?'

'Meaning the warp. Why coin new terms for its horrors when we have a bounty of old words that might suit us just as well? We use the words "alien" and "xenos" to describe the inhuman filth we encounter in some locales. The creatures of the warp are just "aliens" too, but they are not life forms as we understand the term. They are not organic. They are extra-dimensional, and they influence our reality in ways that seem sorcerous to us. Supernatural, if you will. So let's use all those lost words for them... daemons, spirits, possessors, changelings. All we need to remember is that there are no gods out there, in the darkness, no great daemons and ministers of evil. There is no fundamental, immutable evil in the cosmos. It is too large and sterile for such melodrama. There are simply inhuman things that oppose us, things we were created to battle and destroy. Orks. Gykon.

Tushepta. Keylekid. Eldar. Jokaero… and the creatures of the warp, which are stranger than all for they exhibit powers that are bizarre to us because of the otherness of their nature.'

Loken rose to his feet. He looked around the lamp-lit room and heard the moaning of the mountain wind outside. 'I have seen psykers taken by the warp, sir,' he said. 'I have seen them change and bloat in corruption, but I have never seen a sound man taken. I have never seen an Astartes so abused.'

'It happens,' Horus replied. He grinned. 'Does that shock you? I'm sorry. We keep it quiet. The warp can get into anything, if it so pleases. Today was a particular triumph for its ways. These mountains are not haunted, as the myths report, but the warp is close to the surface here. That fact alone has given rise to the myths. Men have always found techniques to control the warp, and the folk here have done precisely that. They let the warp loose upon you today, and brave Jubal paid the price.'

'Why him?'

'Why not him? He was angry at you for overlooking him, and his anger made him vulnerable. The tendrils of the warp are always eager to exploit such chinks in the mind. I imagine the insurgents hoped that scores of your men would fall under the power they had let loose, but Tenth Company had more resolve than that. Samus was just a voice from the Chaotic realm that briefly anchored itself to Jubal's flesh. You dealt with it well. It could have been far worse.'

'You're sure of this, sir?'

Horus grinned again. The sight of that grin filled Loken with sudden warmth. 'Ing Mae Sing, Mistress of Astropaths, informed me of a rapid warp spike in this region just after you disembarked. The data is solid and substantive. The locals used their limited knowledge of the warp, which they probably understood as magic, to unleash the horror of the empyrean upon you as a weapon.'

'Why have we been told so little about the warp, sir?' Loken asked. He looked directly into Horus's wide-set eyes as he asked the question.

'Because so little is known,' the Warmaster replied. 'Do you know why I am Warmaster, my son?'

'Because you are the most worthy, sir?'

Horus laughed and, pouring another glass of wine, shook his head. 'I am Warmaster, Garviel, because the Emperor is busy. He has not retired to Terra because he is weary of the crusade. He has gone there because he has more important work to do.'

'More important than the crusade?' Loken asked.

Horus nodded. 'So he said to me. After Ullanor, he believed the time had come when he could leave the crusading work in the hands of the primarchs so that he might be freed to undertake a still higher calling.'

'Which is?' Loken waited for an answer, expecting some transcendent truth.

What the Warmaster said was, 'I don't know. He didn't tell me. He hasn't told anyone.'

Horus paused. For what seemed like an age, the wind banged against the longhouse shutters. 'Not even me,' Horus whispered. Loken sensed a terrible hurt in his commander, a wounded pride that he, even he, had not been worthy enough to know this secret.

In a second, the Warmaster was smiling at Loken again, his dark mood forgotten. 'He didn't want to burden me,' he said briskly, 'but I'm not a fool. I can speculate. As I said, the Imperium would not exist but for the warp. We are obliged to use it, but we know perilously little about it. I believe that I am Warmaster because the Emperor is occupied in unlocking its secrets. He has committed his great mind to the ultimate mastery of the warp, for the good of mankind. He has realised that without final and full understanding of the immaterium, we will founder and fall, no matter how many worlds we conquer.'

'What if he fails?' Loken asked.

'He won't,' the Warmaster replied bluntly.

'What if we fail?'

'We won't,' Horus said, 'because we are his true servants and sons. Because we cannot fail him.' He looked at his half-drunk glass and put it aside. 'I came here looking for spirits,' he joked, 'and all I find is wine. There's a lesson for you.'

Trudging, unspeaking, the warriors of Tenth Company clambered from the cooling Stormbirds and streamed away across the embarkation deck towards their barracks. There was no sound save for the clink of their armour and the clank of their feet.

In their midst, brothers carried the biers on which the dead of Brakespur lay, shrouded in Legion banners. Four of them carried Flora and Van Krasten too, though no formal flags draped the coffins of the dead remembrancers. The Bell of Return rang out across the vast deck. The men made the sign of the aquila and pulled off their helms.

Loken wandered away towards his arming chamber, calling for the service of his artificers. He carried his left shoulder guard in his hands, Jubal's sword still stuck fast through it.

Entering the chamber, he was about to hurl the miserable memento away into a corner, but he pulled up short, realising he was not alone.

Mersadie Oliton stood in the shadows.

'Mistress,' he said, setting the broken guard down.

'Captain, I'm sorry. I didn't mean to intrude. Your equerry let me wait here, knowing you were about to return. I wanted to see you. I wanted to apologise.'

'For what?' Loken asked, hooking his battered helm on the top strut of his armour rack.

She stepped forward, the light glowing off her black skin and her long, augmented cranium. 'For missing the opportunity you gave me. You were kind enough to suggest me as a candidate to accompany the undertaking, and I did not attend in time.'

'Be grateful for that,' he said.

She frowned. 'I… there was a problem, you see. A friend of mine, a fellow remembrancer. The poet Ignace Karkasy. He finds himself in a deal of trouble, and I was taken up trying to assist him. It so detained me, I missed the appointment.'

'You didn't miss anything, mistress,' Loken said as he began to strip off his armour.

'I would like to speak with you about Ignace's plight. I hesitate to ask, but I believe someone of your influence might help him.'

'I'm listening,' Loken said.

'So am I, sir,' Mersadie said. She stepped forward and placed a tiny hand on his arm to restrain him slightly. He had been throwing off his armour with such vigorous, angry motions.

'I am a remembrancer, sir,' she said. 'Your remembrancer, if it is not too bold to say so. Do you want to tell me what happened on the surface? Is there any memory you would like to share with me?'

Loken looked down at her. His eyes were the colour of rain. He pulled away from her touch.

'No,' he said.

PART TWO
BROTHERHOOD IN SPIDERLAND

ONE

Loathe and love
This world is Murder
A hunger for glory

Even after he'd slain a fair number of them, Saul Tarvitz was still unable to say with any certainty where the biology of the meg-arachnid stopped and their technology began. They were the most seamless things, a perfect fusion of artifice and organism. They did not wear their armour or carry their weapons. Their armour was an integument bonded to their arthropod shells, and they possessed weapons as naturally as a man might own fingers or a mouth.

Tarvitz loathed them, and loved them too. He loathed them for their abominable want of human perfection. He loved them because they were genuinely testing foes, and in mastering them, the Emperor's Children would take another stride closer to attaining their full potential. 'We always need a rival,' his lord Eidolon had once said, and the words had stuck forever in Tar-vitz's mind, 'a true rival, of considerable strength and fortitude. Only against such a rival can our prowess be properly measured.'

There was more at stake here than the Legion's prowess, how-ever, and Tarvitz understood that solemnly. Brother Astartes were in trouble, and this was a mission – though no one had dared actually use the term – of rescue. It was thoroughly improper to openly suggest that the Blood Angels needed rescuing.

Reinforcement. That was the word they had been told to use, but it was hard to reinforce what you could not find. They had been on the surface of Murder for sixty-six hours, and had found no sign of the 140th Expedition forces.

Or even, for the most part, of each other.

Lord Commander Eidolon had committed the entire company to the surface drop. The descent had been foul, worse than the warnings they had been given prior to the drop, and the warnings had been grim enough. Nightmarish atmospherics had scattered their drop pods like chaff, casting them wildly astray from their projected landing vectors. Tarvitz knew it was likely many pods hadn't even made it to the ground intact. He found himself one of two captains in charge of just over thirty men, around one-third of the company force, and all that had been able to regroup after planetfall. Due to the storm-cover, they couldn't raise the fleet in orbit, nor could they raise Eidolon or any other part of the landing force.

Presuming Eidolon and any other part of the landing force had survived.

The whole situation smacked of abject failure, and failure was not a concept the Emperor's Children cared to entertain. To turn failure into something else, there was little choice but to get on with the remit of the undertaking, so they spread out in a search pattern to find the brothers they had come to help. On the way, perhaps, they might reunite with other elements of their scattered force, or even find some geographical frame of reference.

The dropsite environs was disconcerting. Under an enamel-white sky, fizzling and blemished by the megarachnid shield-storms, the land was an undulating plain of ferrous red dust from which a sea of gigantic grass stalks grew, grey-white like dirty ice. Each stalk, as thick as a man's plated thigh, rose up straight to a height of twenty metres: tough, dry and bristly. They swished gently in the radioactive wind, but such was their size, at ground level, the air was filled with the creaking, moaning sound of their structures in motion. The Astartes moved through the groaning forest of stalks like lice in a wheatfield.

There was precious little lateral visibility. High above their heads, the nodding vertical shoots soared upwards and pointed incriminatingly at the curdled glare of the sky. Around them, the stalks had grown so close together that a man could see only a few metres in any direction.

The bases of most of the grass stalks were thick with swollen, black larvae: sack-things the size of a man's head, clustered tumorously to the metre or so of stalk closest to the ground. The larvae did nothing but cling and, presumably, drink. As they did so, they made a weird hissing, whistling noise that added to the eerie acoustics of the forest floor.

Bulle had suggested that the larvae might be infant forms of the enemy, and for the first few hours, they had systematically destroyed all they'd found with flamers and blades, but the work was wearying and unending. There were larvae everywhere, and eventually they had chosen to forget it and ignore the hissing sacks. Besides, the foetid ichor that burst from the larvae when they were struck was damaging the edges of their weapons and scarring their armour where it splashed.

Lucius, Tarvitz's fellow captain, had found the first tree, and called them all close to inspect it. It was a curious thing, apparently made of a calcified white stone, and it dwarfed the surrounding sea of stalks. It was shaped like a wide-capped mushroom: a fifty-metre dome supported on a thick, squat trunk ten metres broad. The dome was an intricate hemisphere of sharp, bone-white thorns, tangled and sharply pointed, the barbs some two or three metres in length.

'What is it for?' Tarvitz wondered.

'It's not for anything,' Lucius replied. 'It's a tree. It has no purpose.'

In that, Lucius was wrong.

Lucius was younger than Tarvitz, though they were both old enough to have seen many wonders in their lives. They were friends, except that the balance of their friendship was steeply and invisibly weighted in one direction. Saul and Lucius represented the bipolar aspect of their Legion. Like all of the Emperor's Children, they devoted themselves to the pursuit of martial perfection, but Saul was diligently grounded where Lucius was ambitious.

Saul Tarvitz had long since realised that Lucius would one day outstrip him in honour and rank. Lucius would perhaps become a lord commander in due course, part of the aloof inner circle at the Legion's traditionally hierarchical core. Tarvitz didn't care. He was a file officer, born to the line, and had no desire for elevation. He was content to glorify the primarch and the Emperor, beloved of all, by knowing his place, and keeping it with unstinting devotion.

Lucius mocked him playfully sometimes, claiming Tarvitz courted the common ranks because he couldn't win the respect of the officers. Tarvitz always laughed that off, because he knew Lucius didn't properly understand. Saul Tarvitz followed the code exactly, and took pride in that. He knew his perfect destiny was as a file officer. To crave more would have been overweening and imperfect. Tarvitz had standards, and despised anyone who cast their own standards aside in the hunt for inappropriate goals.

It was all about purity, not superiority. That's what the other Legions always failed to understand.

Barely fifteen minutes after the discovery of the tree – the first of many they would find scattered throughout the creaking grasslands – they had their first dealings with the megarachnid.

The enemy's arrival had been announced by three signs: the larvae nearby had suddenly stopped hissing; the towering grass stalks had begun an abrupt shivering vibration, as if electrified; then the Astartes had heard a strange, chittering noise, coming closer.

Tarvitz barely saw the enemy warriors during that first clash. They had come, thrilling and clattering, out of the grass forest, moving so fast they were silver blurs. The fight lasted twelve chaotic seconds, a period filled to capacity with gunshots and shouts, and odd, weighty impacts. Then the enemy had vanished again, as fast as they had come, the stalks had stilled, and the larvae had resumed their hissing.

'Did you see them?' asked Kercort, reloading his bolter.

'I saw something…' Tarvitz admitted, doing the same.

'Durellen's dead. So is Martius,' Lucius announced casually, approaching them with something in his hand.

Tarvitz couldn't quite believe what he had been told. 'They're dead? Just… dead?' he asked Lucius. The fight surely hadn't lasted long enough to have included the passing of two veteran Astartes.

'Dead,' nodded Lucius. 'You can look upon their cadavers if you wish. They're over there. They were too slow.'

Weapon raised, Tarvitz pushed through the swaying stalks, some of them broken and snapped over by frantic bolter fire. He saw the two bodies, tangled amid fallen white shoots on the red earth, their beautiful purple and gold armour sawn apart and running with blood.

Dismayed, he looked away from the butchery. 'Find Varras,' he told Kercort, and the man went off to locate the Apothecary.

'Did we kill anything?' Bulle asked.

'I hit something,' Lucius said proudly, 'but I cannot find the body. It left this behind.' He held out the thing in his hand.

It was a limb, or part of a limb. Long, slender, hard. The main part of it, a metre long, was a gently curved blade, apparently made of brushed zinc or galvanised iron. It came to an astonishingly sharp point. It was thin, no thicker than a grown man's wrist. The long blade ended in a widening joint, which attached it to a thicker limb section. This part was also armoured with mottled grey metal, but came to an abrupt end where Lucius's shot had blown it off. The broken end, in cross-section, revealed a skin of metal surrounding a sleeve of natural, arthropoid chitin around an inner mass of pink, wet meat.

'Is it an arm?' Bulle asked.

'It's a sword,' Katz corrected.

'A sword with a joint?' Bulle snorted. 'And meat inside?'

Lucius grasped the limb, just above the joint, and brandished it like a sabre. He swung it at the nearest stalk, and it went clean through. With a lingering crash, the massive dry shoot toppled over, tearing into others as it fell.

Lucius started laughing, then he cried out in pain and dropped the limb. Even the base part of the limb, above the joint, had an edge, and it was so sharp that the force of his grip had bitten through his gauntlet.

'It has cut me,' Lucius complained, poking at his ruptured glove.

Tarvitz looked down at the limb, bent and still on the red soil. 'Little wonder they can slice us to ribbons.'

Half an hour later, when the stalks shivered again, Tarvitz met his first megarachnid face to face. He killed it, but it was a close-run thing, over in a couple of seconds.

From that encounter, Saul Tarvitz began to understand why Khitas Frome had named the world Murder.

The great warship exploded like a breaching whale from the smudge of un-light that was its retranslation point, and returned to the silent, physical cosmos of real space again with a shivering impact. It had translated twelve weeks earlier, by the ship-board clocks, and had made a journey that ought to have taken eighteen weeks. Great powers had been put into play to expedite the transit, powers that only a Warmaster could call upon.

It coasted for about six million kilometres, trailing the last, luminous tendrils of plasmic flare from its immense bulk, like remorae, until strobing flashes of un-light to stern announced the belated arrival of its consorts: ten light cruisers and five mass conveyance troop ships. The stragglers lit their real space engines and hurried wearily to join formation with the huge flagship. As they approached, like a school of pups swimming close to their mighty parent, the flagship ignited its own drives and led them in.

Towards One Forty Twenty. Towards Murder.

Forward arrayed detectors pinged as they tasted the magnetic and energetic profiles of other ships at high anchor around the system's fourth planet, eighty million kilometres ahead. The local sun was yellow and hot, and billowed with loud, charged particles.

As it advanced at the head of the trailing flotilla, the flagship broadcast its standard greeting document, in vox, vox-supplemented pict, War Council code, and astrotelepathic forms.

'This is the *Vengeful Spirit*, of the 63rd Expedition. This vessel approaches with peaceful intent, as an ambassador of the Imperium of Man. House your guns and stand to. Make acknowledgement.'

On the bridge of the *Vengeful Spirit*, Master Comnenus sat at his station and waited. Given its great size and number of personnel, the bridge around him was curiously quiet. There was just a murmur of low voices and the whir of instrumentation. The ship itself was protesting loudly. Undignified creaks and seismic moans issued from its immense hull and layered decks as the superstructure relaxed and settled from the horrendous torsion stresses of warp translation.

Boas Comnenus knew most of the sounds like old friends, and could almost anticipate them. He'd been part of the ship for a long time, and knew it as intimately as a lover's body. He waited, braced, for erroneous creaks, for the sudden chime of defect alarms.

So far, all was well. He glanced at the Master Companion of Vox, who shook his head. He switched his gaze to Ing Mae Sing who, though blind, knew full well he was looking at her.

'No response, master,' she said.

'Repeat,' he ordered. He wanted that signal response, but more particularly, he was waiting for the fix. It was taking too long. Comnenus drummed his steel fingers on the edge of his master console, and deck officers all around him stiffened. They knew, and feared, that sign of impatience.

Finally, an adjutant hurried over from the navigation pit with the wafer slip. The adjutant might have been about to apologise for the delay, but Comnenus glanced up at him with a whir of augmetic lenses. The whir said, 'I do not expect you to speak.' The adjutant simply held the wafer out for inspection.

Comnenus read it, nodded, and handed it back.

'Make it known and recorded,' he said. The adjutant paused long enough for another deck officer to copy the wafer for the principal transit log, then hurried up the rear staircase of the bridge to the strategium deck. There, with a salute, he handed it to the duty master, who took it, turned, and walked twenty paces to the plated glass doors of the sanctum, where he handed it in turn to the master bodyguard. The master bodyguard, a massive Astartes in gold custodes armour, read the wafer quickly, nodded, and opened the doors. He passed the wafer to the solemn, robed figure of Maloghurst, who was waiting just inside.

Maloghurst read the wafer too, nodded in turn, and shut the doors again.

'Location is confirmed and entered into the log,' Maloghurst announced to the sanctum. 'One Forty Twenty.'

Seated in a high-backed chair that had been drawn up close to the window ports to afford a better view of the starfield outside, the Warmaster took a deep, steady breath. 'Determination of passage so noted,' he replied. 'Let my acknowledgement be a matter of record.' The twenty waiting scribes around him scratched the details down in their manifests, bowed and withdrew.

'Maloghurst?' The Warmaster turned his head to look at his equerry. 'Send Boas my compliments, please.'

'Yes, lord.'

The Warmaster rose to his feet. He was dressed in full ceremonial wargear, gleaming gold and frost white, with a vast mantle of purple scale-skin draped across his shoulders. The eye of Terra stared from his breastplate. He turned to face the ten Astartes officers gathered in the centre of the room, and each one of them felt that the eye was regarding him with particular, unblinking scrutiny.

'We await your orders, lord,' said Abaddon. Like the other nine, he was wearing battle plate with a floor-length cloak, his crested helm carried in the crook of his left arm.

'And we're where we're supposed to be,' said Torgaddon, 'and alive, which is always a good start.'

A broad smile crossed the Warmaster's face. 'Indeed it is, Tarik.' He looked into the eyes of each officer in turn. 'My friends, it seems we have an alien war to contest. This pleases me. Proud as I am of our accomplishments on Sixty-Three Nineteen, that was a painful fight to prosecute. I can't derive satisfaction from a victory over our own kind, no matter how wrong-headed and stubborn their philosophies. It limits the soldier in me, and inhibits my relish of war, and we are all warriors, you and I. Made for combat. Bred, trained and disciplined. Except you pair,' Horus smirked, nodding at Abaddon and Luc Sedirae. 'You kill until I have to tell you to stop.'

'And even then you have to raise your voice,' added Torgaddon. Most of them laughed.

'So an alien war is a delight to me,' the Warmaster continued, still smiling. 'A clear and simple foe. An opportunity to wage war without restraint, regret or remorse. Let us go and be warriors for a while, pure and undiluted.'

'Hear, hear!' cried the ancient Iacton Qruze, businesslike and sober, clearly bothered by Torgaddon's constant levity. The other nine were more modest in their assent.

Horus led them out of the sanctum onto the strategium deck, the four captains of the Mournival and the company commanders: Sedirae of the Thirteenth, Qruze of the Third, Targost of the Seventh, Marr of the Eighteenth, Moy of the Nineteenth, and Goshen of the Twenty-Fifth.

'Let's have tactical,' the Warmaster said.

Maloghurst was waiting, ready. As he motioned with his control wand, detailed hololithic images shimmered into place above the dais. They showed a general profile of the system, with orbital paths delineated, and the position and motion of tracked vessels. Horus gazed up at the hololithic graphics and reached out. Actuator sensors built into the fingertips of his gauntlets allowed him to rotate the hololithic display and bring certain segments into magnification. 'Twenty-nine craft,' he said. 'I thought the 140th was eighteen vessels strong?'

'So we were told, lord,' Maloghurst replied. As soon as they had stepped out of the sanctum, they had started conversing in Cthonic, so as to preserve tactical confidence whilst in earshot of the bridge personnel. Though Horus had not been raised on Cthonia – uncommonly, for a primarch, he had not matured on the cradle-world of his Legion – he spoke it fluently. In fact, he spoke it with the particular hard palatal edge and rough vowels of a Western Hemispheric ganger, the commonest and roughest of Cthonia's feral castes. It had always amused Loken to hear that accent. Early on, he had assumed it was because that's how the Warmaster had learned it, from just such a speaker, but he doubted that now. Horus never did anything by accident. Loken believed that the Warmaster's rough Cthonic accent was a deliberate affectation so that he would seem, to the men, as honest and low-born as any of them.

Maloghurst had consulted a data-slate provided by a waiting deck officer. 'I confirm the 140th Expedition was given a complement of eighteen vessels.'

'Then what are these others?' asked Aximand. 'Enemy ships?'

'We're awaiting sensor profile analysis, captain,' ⸻ replied, 'and there has been no response to our sign⸻

'Tell Master Comnenus to be… more emphatic,' the ⸻ ter told his equerry.

'Should I instruct him to form our components into a ⸻ line, lord?' Maloghurst asked.

'I'll consider it,' the Warmaster said. Maloghurst limped away down the platform steps onto the main bridge to speak to Boas Comnenus.

'Should we form a battle line?' Horus asked his commanders.

'Could the additional profiles be alien vessels?' Qruze wondered.

'It doesn't look like a battle spread, Iacton,' Aximand replied, 'and Frome said nothing about enemy vessels.'

'They're ours,' said Loken.

The Warmaster looked over at him. 'You think so, Garviel?'

'It seems evident to me, sir. The hits show a spread of ships at high anchor. Imperial anchorage formation. Others must have responded to the call for assistance…' Loken trailed off, and suddenly fought back an embarrassed smile. 'You knew that all along, of course, my lord.'

'I was just wondering who else might have been sharp enough to recognise the pattern,' Horus smiled. Qruze shook his head with a grin, sheepish at his own mistake.

The Warmaster nodded towards the display. 'So, what's this big fellow here? That's a barge.'

'The *Misericord*?' suggested Qruze.

'No, no, *that's* the *Misericord*. And what's *this* about?' Horus leaned forwards, and ran his fingers across the hard light display. 'It looks like… music. Something like music. Who's transmitting music?'

'Outstation relays,' Abaddon said, studying his own data-slate. 'Beacons. The 140th reported thirty beacons in the system grid. Xenos. Their broadcasts are repeating and untranslatable.'

'Really? They have no ships, but they have outstation beacons?' Horus reached out and changed the display to a close breakdown of scatter patterns. 'This is untranslatable?'

'So the 140th said,' said Abaddon.

'Have we taken their word for that?' asked the Warmaster.

'I imagine we have,' said Abaddon.

'There's sense in this,' Horus decided, peering at the luminous graphics. 'I want this run. I want us to run it. Start with standard numeric blocks. With respect to the 140th, I don't intend to take their word for anything. Cursed awful job they've done here so far.'

Abaddon nodded, and stepped aside to speak to one of the waiting deck officers and have the order enacted.

'You said it looks like music,' Loken said.

'What?'

'You said it looks like music, sir,' Loken repeated. 'An interesting word to choose.'

The Warmaster shrugged. 'It's mathematical, but there's a sequential rhythm to it. It's not random. Music and maths, Garviel. Two sides of a coin. This is deliberately structured. Lord knows which idiot in the 140th Fleet decided this was untranslatable.'

Loken nodded. 'You see that, just by looking at it?' he asked.

'Isn't it obvious?' Horus replied.

Maloghurst returned. 'Master Comnenus confirms all contacts are Imperial,' he said, holding out another wafer slip of print out. 'Other units have been arriving these last few weeks, in response to the calls for aid. Most of them are Imperial army conveyances en route to Carollis Star, but the big vessel is the *Proudheart*. Third Legion, the Emperor's Children. A full company, under the command privilege of Lord Commander Eidolon.'

'So, they beat us to it. How are they doing?'

Maloghurst shrugged. 'It would seem… not well, lord,' he said.

The planet's official designation in the Imperial Registry was One Hundred and Forty Twenty, it being the twentieth world subjected to compliance by the fleet of the 140th Expedition. But that was inaccurate, as clearly the 140th had not achieved anything like compliance. Still, the Emperor's Children had used the number to begin with, for to do otherwise would have been an insult to the honour of the Blood Angels.

Prior to arrival, Lord Commander Eidolon had briefed his Astartes comprehensively. The initial transmissions of the 140th Expedition had been clear and succinct. Khitas Frome, captain of the three Blood Angels companies that formed the marrow of the 140th, had reported xenos hostilities a few days after his forces had touched down on the world's surface. He had described 'very capable things, like upright beetles, but made of, or shod in, metal. Each one is twice the height of a man and very belligerent. Assistance may be required if their numbers increase.'

After that, his relayed communiqués had been somewhat patchy and intermittent. Fighting had 'grown thicker and more savage' and the xenos forms 'appeared not to lack in numbers'. A week later, and his transmissions were more urgent. 'There is a race here that resists us, and which we cannot easily overcome. They refuse to admit communication with us, or any parlay. They spill from their lairs. I find myself admiring their mettle, though they are not made as we are. Their martial schooling is fine indeed. A worthy foe, one that might be written about in our annals.'

A week after that, the expedition's messages had become rather more simple, sent by the Master of the Fleet instead of Frome. 'The enemy here is formidable, and quite outweighs us. To take this world, the full force of the Legio is required. We humbly submit a request for reinforcement at this time.'

Frome's last message, relayed from the surface a fortnight later by the expedition fleet, had been a tinny rasp of generally indecipherable noise. All the articulacy and purpose of his words had been torn apart by the feral distortion. The only cogent thing that had come through was his final utterance. Each word had seemed to be spoken with inhuman effort.

'This. World. Is. Murder.'

And so they had named it.

The task force of the Emperor's Children was comparatively small in size: just a company of the Legion's main strength, conveyed by the battle-barge *Proudheart*, under the command of Lord Eidolon. After a brief, peace-keeping tour of newly compliant worlds in the Satyr Lanxus Belt, they had been en route to rejoin their primarch and brethren companies at Carollis Star to begin a mass advance into the Lesser Bifold Cluster. However, during their transit, the 140th Expedition had begun its requests for assistance. The task force had been the closest Imperial unit fit to respond. Lord Eidolon had requested immediate permission from his primarch to alter course and go to the expedition's aid.

Fulgrim had given his authority at once. The Emperor's Children would never leave their Astartes brothers in jeopardy. Eidolon had been given his primarch's instant, unreserved blessing to reroute and support the beleaguered expedition. Other forces were rushing to assist. It was said a detachment of Blood Angels was on its way, as was a heavyweight response from the Warmaster himself, despatched from the 63rd Expedition.

At best, the closest of them was still many days off. Lord Eidolon's task force was the interim measure: critical response, the first to the scene.

Eidolon's battle-barge had joined with the operational vessels of the 140th Expedition at high anchor above One Forty

Twenty. The 140th Expedition was a small, compact force of eighteen carriers, mass conveyances and escorts supporting the noble battle-barge *Misericord*. Its martial composition was three companies of Blood Angels under Captain Frome, and four thousand men of the Imperial army, with allied armour, but no Mechanicum force.

Mathanual August, Master of the 140th Fleet, had welcomed Eidolon and his commanders aboard the barge. Tall and slender, with a forked white beard, August was fretful and nervous. 'I am gratified at your quick response, lord,' he'd told Eidolon.

'Where is Frome?' Eidolon had asked bluntly.

August had shrugged, helplessly.

'Where is the commander of the army divisions?'

A second pitiful shrug. 'They are all down there.'

Down there. On Murder. The world was a hazy, grey orb, mottled with storm patterning in the atmosphere. Drawn to the lonely system by the curious, untranslatable broadcasts of the outstation beacons, a clear and manifest trace of sentient life, the 140th Expedition had focussed its attentions on the fourth planet, the only orb in the star's orbit with an atmosphere. Sensor sweeps had detected abundant vital traces, though nothing had answered their signals.

Fifty Blood Angels had dropped first, in landers, and had simply disappeared. Previously calm weather cycles had mutated into violent tempests the moment the landers had entered the atmosphere, like an allergic reaction, and swallowed them up. Due to the suddenly volatile climate, communication with the surface was impossible. Another fifty had followed, and had similarly vanished.

That was when Frome and the fleet officers had begun to suspect that the life forms of One Forty Twenty somehow commanded their own weather systems as a defence. The immense storm fronts, later dubbed 'shield-storms', that had risen up to meet the surface-bound landers, had probably obliterated them. After that, Frome had used drop pods, the only vehicles that seemed to survive the descent. Frome had led the third wave himself, and only partial messages had been received from him subsequently, even though he'd taken an astrotelepath with him to counter the climatic vox-interference.

It was a grim story. Section by section, August had committed the Astartes and army forces in his expedition to surface drops in a vain attempt to respond to Frome's broken pleas for support. They had either been destroyed by the storms or lost in the impenetrable maelstrom below. The shield-storms, once roused, would not die away. There were no clean surface picts, no decent topographic scans, no uplinks or viable communication lines. One Forty Twenty was an abyss from which no one returned.

'We'll be going in blind,' Eidolon had told his officers. 'Drop pod descent.'

'Perhaps you should wait, lord,' August had suggested. 'We have word that a Blood Angels force is en route to relieve Captain Frome, and the Luna Wolves are but four days away. Combined, perhaps, you might better–'

That had decided it. Tarvitz knew Lord Eidolon had no intention of sharing any glory with the Warmaster's elite. His lord was relishing the prospect of demonstrating the excellence of his company, by rescuing the cohorts of a rival Legion... whether the word 'rescuing' was used or not. The nature of the deed, and the comparisons that it made, would speak for themselves.

Eidolon had sanctioned the drop immediately.

TWO

The nature of the enemy
A trace
The purpose of trees

The megarachnid warriors were three metres tall, and possessed eight limbs. They ambulated, with dazzling speed, on their four hindmost limbs, and used the other four as weapons. Their bodies, one third again as weighty and massive as a human's, were segmented like an insect's: a small, compact abdomen hung between the four, wide-spread, slender walking limbs; a massive, armoured thorax from which all eight limbs depended; and a squat, wide, wedge-shaped head, equipped with short, rattling mouthparts that issued the characteristic chittering noise, a heavy, ctenoid comb of brow armour, and no discernible eyes. The four upper limbs matched the trophy Lucius had taken in the first round: metal-cased blades over a metre in length beyond the joint. Every part of the megarachnid appeared to be thickly plated with mottled, almost fibrous grey armour, except the head crests, which seemed to be natural, chitinous growths, rough, bony and ivory.

As the fighting wore on, Tarvitz thought he identified a status in those crests. The fuller the chitin growths, the more senior – and larger – the warrior.

Tarvitz made his first kill with his bolter. The megarachnid lunged out of the suddenly vibrating stalks in front of them, and decapitated Kercort with a flick of its upper left blade. Even stationary, it was a hyperactive blur, as if its metabolism, its very

life, moved at some rate far faster than that of the enhanced
gene-seed warriors of Chemos. Tarvitz had opened fire, dent-
ing the centre line of the megarachnid's thorax armour with
three shots, before his fourth obliterated the thing's head in a
shower of white paste and ivory crest shards. Its legs stumbled
and scrabbled, its blade arms waved, and then it fell, but just
before it did, there was another crash.

The crash was the sound of Kercort's headless body finally
hitting the red dust, arterial spray jetting from his severed neck.

That was how fast the encounter had passed. From first strike
to clean kill, poor Kercort had only had time to fall down.

A second megarachnid appeared behind the first. Its flickering limbs had torn Tarvitz's bolter out of his hands, and set a
deep gouge across the facing of his breastplate, right across the
palatine aquila displayed there. That was a great crime. Alone
amongst the Legions, only the Emperor's Children had been
permitted, by the grace of the Emperor himself, to wear that
symbol upon their chestplates. Backing away, hearing bolter fire
and yells from the shivering thickets all around him, Tarvitz had
felt stung by genuine insult, and had unslung his broadsword,
powered it, and struck downwards with a two-handed cut. His
long, heavy blade had glanced off the alien's headcrest, chip-
ping off flecks of yellowish bone, and Tarvitz had been forced
to dance back out of the reach of the four, slicing limb-blades.

His second strike had been better. His sword missed the bone
crest and instead hacked deeply into the megarachnid's neck, at
the joint where the head connected to the upper thorax. He had
split the thorax wide open to the centre, squirting out a gush
of glistening white ichor. The megarachnid had trembled, fidg-
eting, slowly understanding its own death as Tarvitz wrenched
his blade back out. It took a moment to die. It reached out with
its quivering blade-limbs, and touched the tips of them against
Tarvitz's recoiling face, two on either side of the visor. The touch
was almost gentle. As it fell, the four points made a shrieking
sound as they dragged backwards across the sides of his visor,
leaving bare metal scratches in the purple gloss.

Someone was screaming. A bolter was firing on full auto, and
debris from exploded grass stalks was spilling up into the air.

A third hostile flickered at Tarvitz, but his blood was up.
He swung at it, turning his body right around, and cut clean
through the mid line of the thorax, between upper arms and
lower legs.

Pale liquid spattered into the air, and the top of the alien fell
away. The abdomen, and the half-thorax remaining, pumping

milky fluid, continued to scurry on its four legs for a moment before it collided with a grass stalk and toppled over.

And that was the fight done. The stalks ceased their shivering, and the wretched grubs started to whistle and buzz again.

When they had been on the ground for ninety hours, and had engaged with the megarachnid twenty-eight times in the dense thickets of the grass forests, seven of their meagre party were dead and gone. The process of advance became mechanical, almost trance-like. There was no guiding narrative, no strategic detail. They had established no contact with the Blood Angels, or their lord, or any segments of other sections of their company. They moved forwards, and every few kilometres fighting broke out.

This was an almost perfect war, Saul Tarvitz decided. Simple and engrossing, testing their combat skills and physical prowess to destruction. It was like a training regime made lethal. Only days afterwards did he appreciate how truly focussed he had become during the undertaking. His instincts had grown as sharp as the enemy limb-blades. He was on guard at all times, with no opportunity to slacken or lose concentration, for the megarachnid ambushes were sudden and ferocious, and came out of nowhere. The party moved, then fought, moved, then fought, without space for rest or reflection. Tarvitz had never known, and would never know again, such pure martial perfection, utterly uncomplicated by politics or beliefs. He and his fellows were weapons of the Emperor, and the megarachnid were the unqualified quintessence of the hostile cosmos that stood in man's way.

Almost all of the gradually dwindling Astartes had switched to their blades. It took too many bolter rounds to bring a megarachnid down. A blade was surer, provided one was quick enough to get the first stroke in, and strong enough to ensure that stroke was a killing blow.

It was with some surprise that Tarvitz discovered his fellow captain, Lucius, thought differently. As they pushed on, Lucius boasted that he was playing the enemy.

'It's like duelling with four swordsmen at once,' Lucius crowed. Lucius was a bladesman. To Tarvitz's knowledge, Lucius had never been bested in swordplay. Where Tarvitz, and men like him, rotated through weapon drills to extend perfection in all forms and manners, Lucius had made a single art of the sword. Frustratingly, his firearms skill was such that he never seemed to need to hone it on the ranges. It was Lucius's proudest claim to have 'personally worn out' four practice cages. Sometimes, the Legion's other sword-masters, warriors like Ekhelon and Brazenor, sparred with Lucius to improve their technique. It was said, Eidolon himself often chose Lucius as a training partner.

Lucius carried an antique long sword, a relic of the Unification Wars, forged in the smithies of the Urals by artisans of the Terrawatt Clan. It was a masterpiece of perfect balance and temper. Usually, he fought with it in the old style, with a combat shield locked to his left arm. The sword's wire-wound handle was unusually long, enabling him to change from a single to a double grip, to spin the blade one-handed like a baton, and to slide the pressure of his grip back and forth: back for a looping swing, forwards for a taut, focussed thrust.

He had his shield strapped across his back, and carried the megarachnid blade-limb in his left hand as a secondary sword. He had bound the base of the severed limb with strips of steel paper from the liner of his shield to prevent the edge from further harming his grip. Head low, he paced forwards through the endless avenues of stalks, hungry for any opportunity to deal death.

During the twelfth attack, Tarvitz witnessed Lucius at work for the first time. Lucius met a megarachnid head on, and set up a flurry of dazzling, ringing blows, his two blades against the creature's four. Tarvitz saw three opportunities for straight kill strokes that Lucius didn't so much miss as choose not to take. He was enjoying himself so much that he didn't want the game to end too soon.

'We will take one or two alive later,' he told Tarvitz after the fight, without a hint of irony. 'I will chain them in the practice cages. They will be useful for sparring.'

'They are xenos,' Tarvitz scolded.

'If I am going to improve at all, I need decent practice. Practice that will test me. Do you know of a man who could push me?'

'They are xenos,' Tarvitz said again.

'Perhaps it is the Emperor's will,' Lucius suggested. 'Perhaps these things have been placed in the cosmos to improve our war skills.'

Tarvitz was proud that he didn't even begin to understand how xenos minds worked, but he was also confident that the purpose of the megarachnid, if they had some higher, ineffable purpose, was more than to give mankind a demanding training partner. He wondered, briefly, if they had language, or culture, culture as a man might recognise it. Art? Science? Emotion? Or were those things as seamlessly and exotically bonded into them as their technologies, so that mortal man might not differentiate or identify them?

Were they driven by some emotive cause to attack the Emperor's Children, or were they simply responding to trespass, like a mound of drone insects prodded with a stick? It occurred to him that the megarachnid might be attacking because, to them, the humans were hideous and xenos.

It was a terrible thought. Surely the megarachnid could see the superiority of the human design compared with their own? Maybe they fought because of jealousy?

Lucius was busy droning on, delightedly explaining some new finesse of wrist-turn that fighting the megarachnid had already taught him. He was demonstrating the technique against the bole of a stalk.

'See? A lift and turn. Lift and turn. The blow comes down and in. It would be of no purpose against a man, but here it is essential. I think I will compose a treatise on it. The move should be called "the Lucius", don't you think? How fine does that sound?'

'Very fine,' Tarvitz replied.

'Here is something!' a voice exclaimed over the vox. It was Sakian. They hurried to him. He had found a sudden and surprising clearing in the grass forest. The stalks had stopped, exposing a broad field of bare, red earth many kilometres square.

'What is this?' asked Bulle.

Tarvitz wondered if the space had been deliberately cleared, but there was no sign that stalks had ever sprouted there. The tall, swishing forest surrounded the area on all sides.

One by one, the Astartes stepped out into the open. It was unsettling. Moving through the grass forest, there had been precious little sense of going anywhere, because everywhere looked the same. This gap was suddenly a landmark. A disconcerting difference.

'Look here,' Sakian called. He was twenty metres out in the barren plain, kneeling to examine something. Tarvitz realised he had called out because of something more specific than the change in environs.

'What is it?' Tarvitz asked, trudging forwards to join Sakian.

'I think I know, captain,' Sakian replied, 'but I don't like to say it. I saw it here on the ground.'

Sakian held the object out so that Tarvitz could inspect it.

It was a vaguely triangular, vaguely concave piece of tinted glass, with rounded corners, roughly nine centimetres on its longest side. Its edges were lipped, and machine formed. Tarvitz

knew what it was at once, because he was staring at it through
two similar objects.

It was a visor lens from an Astartes helmet. What manner of
force could have popped it out of its ceramite frame?

'It's what you think it is,' Tarvitz told Sakian.

'Not one of ours.'

'No. I don't think so. The shape is wrong. This is Mark III.'

'The Blood Angels, then?'

'Yes. The Blood Angels.' The first physical proof that anyone
had been here before them.

'Look around!' Tarvitz ordered to the others. 'Search the dirt!'

The troop spent ten minutes searching. Nothing else was discovered. Overhead, an especially fierce shield-storm had begun
to close in, as if drawn to them. Furious ripples of lightning striated the heavy clouds. The light grew yellow, and the storm's
distortions whined and shrieked intrusively into their vox-links.

'We're exposed out here,' Bulle muttered. 'Let's get back into
the forest.'

Tarvitz was amused. Bulle made it sound as if the stalk thickets were safe ground.

Giant forks of lightning, savage and yellow-white phosphorescent, were searing down into the open space, explosively
scorching the earth. Though each fork only existed for a nano-
second, they seemed solid and real, like fundamental, physical
structures, like upturned, thorny trees. Three Astartes, including
Lucius, were struck. Secure in their Mark IV plate, they shrugged
off the massive, detonating impacts and laughed as aftershock
electrical blooms crackled like garlands of blue wire around
their armour for a few seconds.

'Bulle's right,' Lucius said, his vox signal temporarily mauled
by the discharge dissipating from his suit. 'I want to go back
into the forest. I want to hunt. I haven't killed anything in
twenty minutes.'

Several of the men around roared their approval at Lucius's
wilfully belligerent pronouncement. They slapped their fists
against their shields.

Tarvitz had been trying to contact Lord Eidolon again, or
anyone else, but the storm was still blocking him. He was concerned that the few of them still remaining should not separate,
but Lucius's bravado had annoyed him.

'Do as you see fit, captain. I want to find out what that is,' he
said to Lucius, petulantly. He pointed. On the far side of the
cleared space, three or four kilometres away, he could make out
large white blobs in the far thickets.

'More trees,' Lucius said.

'Yes, but–'

'Oh, very well,' Lucius conceded.

There were now just twenty-two warriors in the group led by Lucius and Tarvitz. They spread out in a loose line and began to cross the open space. The clearing, at least, afforded them time to see any megarachnid approach.

The storm above grew still more ferocious. Five more men were struck. One of them, Ulzoras, was actually knocked off his feet. They saw fused, glassy craters in the ground where lightning had earthed with the force of penetrator missiles. The shield-storm seemed to be pressing down on them, like a lid across the sky, pressurising the air, and squeezing them in an atmospheric vice.

When the megarachnid appeared, they showed themselves in ones or twos at first. Katz saw them initially, and called out. The grey things were milling in and out of the edges of the stalk forest. Then they began to emerge en masse and move across the open ground towards the Astartes war party.

'Terra!' Lucius clucked. '*Now* we have a battle.'

There were more than a hundred of the aliens. Chittering, they closed on the Astartes from all sides, an accelerating ring of onrushing grey, closing faster and faster, a blur of scurrying limbs.

'Form a ring,' Tarvitz instructed calmly. 'Bolters.' He stuck his broadsword, tip down, into the red earth beside him and unslung his firearm. Others did likewise. Tarvitz noticed that Lucius kept his grip on his paired blades.

The flood of megarachnid swallowed up the ground, and closed in a concentric ring around the circle of the Emperor's Children.

'Ready yourselves,' Tarvitz called. Lucius, his swords raised by his sides, was evidently happy for Tarvitz to command the action.

They could hear the dry, febrile chittering as it came closer. The drumming of four hundred rapid legs.

Tarvitz nodded to Bulle, who was the best marksman in the troop. 'The order is yours,' he said.

'Thank you, sir.' Bulle raised his bolter and yelled, 'At ten metres! Shoot till you're dry!'

'Then blades!' Tarvitz bellowed.

When the tightening wave of megarachnid warriors was ten and a half metres away, Bulle yelled, 'Fire!' and the firm circle of Astartes opened up.

Their weapons made a huge, rolling noise, despite the storm. All around them, the front ranks of the enemy buckled and toppled, some splintering apart, some bursting. Pieces of thorny, zinc-grey metal spun away into the air.

As Bulle had instructed, the Astartes fired until their weapons were spent, and then hefted their blades up in time to meet the onrushing foe. The megarachnid broke around them like a wave around a rock. There was a flurried, multiplied din of metal-on-metal impacts as human and alien blades clashed. Tarvitz saw Lucius rush forwards at the last minute, swords swinging, meeting the megarachnid host head on, severing and hacking.

The battle lasted for three minutes. Its intensity should have been spread out across an hour or two. Five more Astartes died. Dozens of megarachnid things fell, broken and rent, onto the red earth. Reflecting upon the encounter later, Tarvitz found he could not remember any single detail of the fight. He'd dropped his bolter and raised his broadsword, and then it had all become a smear of bewildering moments. He found himself, standing there, his limbs aching from effort, his sword and armour dripping with stringy, white matter. The megarachnid were falling back, pouring back, as rapidly as they had advanced.

'Regroup! Reload!' Tarvitz heard himself yelling.

'Look!' Katz called out. Tarvitz looked.

There was something in the sky, objects sweeping down out of the molten, fracturing air above them.

The megarachnid had more than one biological form.

The flying things descended on long, glassy wings that beat so furiously they were just flickering blurs that made a strident thrumming noise. Their bodies were glossy black, their abdomens much fuller and longer than those of their land-bound cousins. Their slender black legs were pulled up beneath them, like wrought-iron undercarriages.

The winged clades took men from the air, dropping sharply and seizing armoured forms in the hooked embrace of their dark limbs. Men fought back, struggled, fired their weapons, but within seconds four or five warriors had been snatched up and borne away into the tumultuous sky, writhing and shouting.

Unit cohesion broke. The men scattered, trying to evade the things swooping out of the air. Tarvitz yelled for order, but knew it was futile. He was forced to duck as a winged shape rushed over him, making a reverberative, chopping drone. He caught a glimpse of a head crest formed into a long, dark, malevolent hook.

Another passed close by. Boltguns were pumping. Tarvitz lashed out with his sword, striking high, trying to drive the creature back. The thrumming of its wings was distressingly loud and made his diaphragm quiver. He jabbed and thrust with his blade, and the thing bobbed backwards across the soil, effortless and light. With a sharp, sudden movement, it turned away, took hold of another man, and lifted him into the sky.

Another of the winged things had seized Lucius. It had him by the back and was taking him off the ground. Lucius, twisting like a maniac, was trying to stab his swords up behind himself, to no avail.

Tarvitz sprang forwards and grabbed hold of Lucius as he left the ground. Tarvitz thrust up past him with his broadsword, but a hooked black leg struck him, and his broadsword tumbled away out of his hand. He held on to Lucius.

'Drop! Drop!' Lucius yelled.

Tarvitz could see that the thing held Lucius by the shield strapped to his back. Swinging, he wrenched out his combat knife, and hacked at the straps. They sheared away, and Lucius and Tarvitz fell from the thing's clutches, plummeting ten metres onto the red dust.

The flying clades made off, taking nine of the Astartes with them. They were heading in the direction of the white blobs in the far thickets. Tarvitz didn't need to give an order. The remaining warriors took off across the ground as fast as they could, chasing after the retreating dots.

They caught up with them at the far edge of the clearing. The white blobs had indeed been more trees, three of them, and now Lucius discovered they had a purpose after all.

The bodies of the taken Astartes were impaled upon the thorns of the trees, rammed onto the stone spikes, their armoured shapes skewered into place, allowing the winged megarachnid to feed upon them. The creatures, their wings now stilled and quiet and extended, long and slender, out behind their bodies like bars of stained glass, were crawling over the stone trees, gnawing and biting, using their hooked head crests to break open thorn-pinned armour to get at the meat within.

Tarvitz and the others came to a halt and watched in sick dismay. Blood was dripping from the white thorns and streaming down the squat, chalky trunks.

Their brothers were not alone amongst the thorns. Other cadavers hung there, rotten and rendered down to bone and dry gristle. Pieces of red armour plate hung from the reduced bodies, or littered the ground at the foot of the trees.

At last, they had found out what had happened to the Blood Angels.

THREE

During the voyage
Bad poetry
Secrets

During the twelve-week voyage between Sixty-Three Nineteen and One Forty Twenty, Loken had come to the conclusion that Sindermann was avoiding him.

He finally located him in the endless stacks of Archive Chamber Three. The iterator was sitting in a stilt-chair, examining ancient texts secured on one of the high shelves of the archive's gloomiest back annexes. There was no bustle of activity back here, no hurrying servitors laden with requested books. Loken presumed that the material catalogued in this area was of little interest to the average scholar.

Sindermann didn't hear him approach. He was intently studying a fragile old manuscript, the stilt-chair's reading lamp tilted over his left shoulder to illuminate the pages.

'Hello?' Loken hissed.

Sindermann looked down and saw Loken. He started slightly, as if woken from a deep sleep.

'Garviel,' he whispered. 'One moment.' Sindermann put the manuscript back on the shelf, but several other books were piled up in the chair's basket rack. As he re-shelved the manuscript, Sindermann's hands seemed to tremble. He pulled a brass lever on the chair's armrest and the stilt legs telescoped down with a breathy hiss until he was at ground level.

Loken reached out to steady the iterator as he stepped out of the chair.

'Thank you, Garviel.'

'What are you doing back here?' Loken asked.

'Oh, you know. Reading.'

'Reading what?'

Sindermann cast what Loken judged to be a slightly guilty look at the books in his chair's rack. Guilty, or embarrassed. 'I confess,' Sindermann said, 'I have been seeking solace in some old and terribly unfashionable material. Pre-Unification fiction, and some poetry. Just desolate scraps, for so little remains, but I find some comfort in it.'

'May I?' Loken asked, gesturing to the basket.

'Of course,' said Sindermann.

Loken sat down in the brass chair, which creaked under his weight, and took some of the old books out of the side basket to examine them. They were frayed and foxed, even though some of them had evidently been rebound or sleeved from earlier bindings prior to archiving.

'*The Golden Age of Sumaturan Poetry*?' Loken said. '*Folk Tales of Old Muscovy*? What's this? *The Chronicles of Ursh*?'

'Boisterous fictions and bloody histories, with the occasional smattering of fine lyric verse.'

Loken took out another, heavy book. '*Tyranny of the Panpacific*,' he read, and flipped open the cover to see the title page. '"An Epic Poem in Nine Cantos, Exalting the Rule of Narthan Dume"… it sounds rather dry.'

'It's raw-headed and robust, and quite bawdy in parts. The work of over-excited poets trying to turn the matter of their own, wretched times into myth. I'm rather fond of it. I used to read such things as a child. Fairy tales from another time.'

'A better time?'

Sindermann baulked. 'Oh, Terra, no! An awful time, a murderous, rancorous age when we were sliding into species doom, not knowing that the Emperor would come and apply the brakes to our cultural plummet.'

'But they comfort you?'

'They remind me of my boyhood. That comforts me.'

'Do you need comforting?' Loken asked, putting the books back in the basket and looking up at the old man. 'I've barely seen you since–'

'Since the mountains,' Sindermann finished, with a sad smile.

'Indeed. I've been to the school on several occasions to hear you brief the iterators, but always there's someone standing in for you. How are you?'

Sindermann shrugged. 'I confess, I've been better.'

'Your injuries still–'

'I've healed in body, Garviel, but…' Sindermann tapped his temple with a gnarled finger. 'I'm unsettled. I haven't felt much like speaking. The fire's not in me just now. It will return. I've kept my own company, and I'm on the mend.'

Loken stared at the old iterator. He seemed so frail, like a baby bird, pale and skinny necked. It had been nine weeks since the bloodshed at the Whisperheads, and most of that time they had spent in warp transit. Loken felt he had begun to come to terms with things himself, but seeing Sindermann, he realised how close to the surface the hurt lay. He could block it out. He was Astartes. But Sindermann was a mortal man, and nothing like as resilient.

'I wish I could–'

Sindermann held up a hand. 'Please. The Warmaster himself was kind enough to speak with me about it, privately. I understand what happened, and I am a wiser man for it.'

Loken got out of the chair and allowed Sindermann to take his place. The iterator sat down, gratefully.

'He keeps me close,' Loken said.

'Who does?'

'The Warmaster. He brought me and the Tenth with him on this undertaking, just to keep me by him. So he could watch me.'

'Because?'

'Because I've seen what few have seen. Because I've seen what the warp can do if we're not careful.'

'Then our beloved commander is very wise, Garviel. Not only has he given you something to occupy your mind with, he's offering you the chance to reforge your courage in battle. He still needs you.'

Sindermann got to his feet again and limped along the book stacks for a moment, tracing his thin hand across the spines. From his gait, Loken knew he hadn't healed anything like as well as he'd claimed. He seemed occupied with the books once more.

Loken waited for a moment. 'I should go,' he said. 'I have duties to attend to.'

Sindermann smiled and waved Loken on his way with eyelash blinks of his fingers.

'I've enjoyed talking with you again,' Loken said. 'It's been too long.'

'It has.'

'I'll come back soon. A day or two. Hear you brief, perhaps?'

'I might be up to that.'

Loken took a book out of the basket. 'These comfort you, you say?'

'Yes.'

'May I borrow one?'

'If you bring it back. What have you there?' Sindermann shuffled over and took the volume from Loken. 'Sumaturan poetry?
I don't think that's you. Try this–'

He took one of the other books out of the chair's rack. *The
Chronicles of Ursh.* Forty chapters, detailing the savage reign
of Kalagann. You'll enjoy that. Very bloody, with a high body
count. Leave the poetry to me.'

Loken scanned the old book and then put it under his arm.
'Thanks for the recommendation. If you like poetry, I have some
for you.'

'Really?'

'One of the remembrancers–'

'Oh yes,' Sindermann nodded. 'Karkasy. I was told you'd
vouched for him.'

'It was a favour, to a friend.'

'And by friend, you mean Mersadie Oliton?'

Loken laughed. 'You told me you'd kept your own company
these last few months, yet you still know everything about
everything.'

'That's my job. The juniors keep me up to speed. I understand you've indulged her a little. As your own remembrancer.'

'Is that wrong?'

'Not at all!' Sindermann smiled. 'That's the way it's supposed
to work. Use her, Garviel. Let her use you. One day, perhaps,
there will be far finer books in the Imperial archives than these
poor relics.'

'Karkasy was going to be sent away. I arranged probation,
and part of that was for him to submit all his work to me. I
can't make head nor tail of it. Poetry. I don't do poetry. Can I
give it to you?'

'Of course.'

Loken turned to leave. 'What was the book you put back?'
he asked.

'What?'

'When I arrived, you had volumes in your basket there, but
you were also studying one, intently, it seemed to me. You put
it back on the shelves. What was it?'

'Bad poetry,' said Sindermann.

The fleet had embarked for Murder less than a week after the
Whisperheads incident. The transmitted requests for assistance
had become so insistent that any debate as to what the 63rd

Expedition undertook next became academic. The Warmaster had ordered the immediate departure of ten companies under his personal command, leaving Varvaras behind with the bulk of the fleet to oversee the general withdrawal from Sixty-Three Nineteen.

Once Tenth Company had been chosen as part of the relief force, Loken had found himself too occupied with the hectic preparations for transit to let his mind dwell on the incident. It was a relief to be busy. There were squad formations to be reassigned, and replacements to be selected from the Legion's novitiate and Scout auxiliaries. He had to find men to fill the gaps in Hellebore and Brakespur, and that meant screening young candidates and making decisions that would change lives forever. Who were the best? Who should be given the chance to advance to full Astartes status?

Torgaddon and Aximand assisted Loken in this solemn task, and he was thankful for their contributions. Little Horus, in particular, seemed to have extraordinary insight regarding candidates. He saw true strengths in some that Loken would have dismissed, and flaws in others that Loken liked the look of. Loken began to appreciate that Aximand's place in the Mournival had been earned by his astonishing analytical precision.

Loken had elected to clear out the dormitory cells of the dead men himself.

'Vipus and I can do that,' Torgaddon said. 'Don't bother yourself.'

'I want to do it,' Loken replied. 'I should do it.'

'Let him, Tarik,' said Aximand. 'He's right. He should.' Loken found himself truly warming to Little Horus for the first time. He had not imagined they would ever be close, but what had at first seemed to be quiet, reserved and stern in Little Horus Aximand was proving to be plain-spoken, empathic and wise.

When he came to clean out the modest, spartan cells, Loken made a discovery. The warriors had little in the way of personal effects: some clothing, some select trophies, and little, tightly bound scrolls of oath papers, usually stored in canvas cargo sacks beneath their crude cots. Amongst Xavyer Jubal's meagre effects, Loken found a small, silver medal, unmounted on any chain or cord. It was the size of a coin, a wolf's head set against a crescent moon.

'What is this?' Loken asked Nero Vipus, who had come along with him.

'I can't say, Garvi.'

'I think I know what it is,' Loken said, a little annoyed at his friend's blank response, 'and I think you do too.'

'I really can't say.'

'Then guess,' Loken snapped. Vipus suddenly seemed very caught up in examining the way the flesh of his wrist was healing around the augmetic implant he had been fitted with.

'Nero...'

'It could be a lodge medal, Garvi,' Vipus replied dismissively. 'I can't say for sure.'

'That's what I thought,' Loken said. He turned the silver medal over in his palm. 'Jubal was a lodge member, then, eh?'

'So what if he was?'

'You know my feelings on the subject,' Loken replied.

Officially, there were no warrior lodges, or any other kind of fraternities, within the Adeptus Astartes. It was common knowledge that the Emperor frowned on such institutions, claiming they were dangerously close to cults, and only a step away from the Imperial creed, the Lectitio Divinitatus, that supported the notion of the Emperor, beloved by all, as a god.

But fraternal lodges did exist within the Astartes, occult and private. According to rumours, they had been active in the XVI Legion for a long time. Some six decades earlier, the Luna Wolves, in collaboration with the XVII Legion, the Word Bearers, had undertaken the compliance of a world called Davin. A feral place, Davin had been controlled by a remarkable warrior caste, whose savage nobility had won the respect of the Astartes sent to pacify their warring feuds. The Davinite warriors had ruled their world through a complex structure of warrior lodges, quasi-religious societies that had venerated various local predators. By cultural osmosis, the lodge practices had been quietly absorbed by the Legions.

Loken had once asked his mentor, Sindermann, about them. 'They're harmless enough,' the iterator had told him. 'Warriors always seek the brotherhood of their kind. As I understand it, they seek to promote fellowship across the hierarchies of command, irrespective of rank or position. A kind of internal bond, a ribwork of loyalty that operates, as it were, perpendicular to the official chain of command.'

Loken had never been sure what something that operated perpendicular to the chain of command might look like, but it sounded wrong to him. Wrong, if nothing else, in that it was deliberately secret and thus deceitful. Wrong, in that the Emperor, beloved by all, disapproved of them.

'Of course,' Sindermann had added, 'I can't actually say if they exist.'

Real or not, Loken had made it plain that any Astartes

intending to serve under his captaincy should have nothing to do with them.

There had never been any sign that anyone in the Tenth was involved in lodge activities. Now the medal had turned up. A lodge medal, belonging to the man who had turned into a daemon and killed his own.

Loken was greatly troubled by the discovery. He told Vipus that he wanted it made known that any man in his command who had information concerning the existence of lodges should come forwards and speak with him, privately if necessary. The next day, when Loken came to sort through the personal effects he had gathered, one last time, he found the medal had disappeared.

In the last few days before departure, Mersadie Oliton had come to him several times, pleading Karkasy's case. Loken remembered her talking to him about it on his return from the Whisperheads, but he had been too distracted then. He cared little about the fate of a remembrancer, especially one foolish enough to anger the expedition authorities.

But it was another distraction, and he needed as many as he could get. After consulting with Maloghurst, he told her he would intervene.

Ignace Karkasy was a poet and, it appeared, an idiot. He didn't know when to shut up. On a surface visit to Sixty-Three Nineteen, he had wandered away from the legitimate areas of visit, got drunk, and then shot his mouth off to such an extent he had received a near-fatal beating from a crew of army troopers.

'He is going to be sent away,' Mersadie said. 'Back to Terra, in disgrace, his certification stripped away. It's wrong, captain. Ignace is a good man...'

'Really?'

'No, all right. He's a lousy man. Uncouth. Stubborn. Annoying. But he is a great poet, and he speaks the truth, no matter how unpalatable that is. Ignace didn't get beaten up for lying.'

Recovered enough from his beating to have been transferred from the flagship's infirmary to a holding cell, Ignace Karkasy was a dishevelled, unedifying prospect.

He rose as Loken walked in and the stab lights came on.

'Captain, sir,' he began. 'I am gratified you take an interest in my pathetic affairs.'

'You have persuasive friends,' Loken said. 'Oliton, and Keeler too.'

'Captain Loken, I had no idea I had persuasive friends. In point of fact, I had little notion I had friends at all. Mersadie is kind, as I'm sure you've realised. Euphrati… I heard there was some trouble she was caught up in.'

'There was.'

'Is she well? Was she hurt?'

'She's fine,' Loken replied, although he had no idea what state Keeler was in. He hadn't seen her. She'd sent him a note, requesting his intervention in Karkasy's case. Loken suspected Mersadie Oliton's influence.

Ignace Karkasy was a big man, but he had suffered a severe assault. His face was still puffy and swollen, and the bruises had discoloured his skin yellow like jaundice. Blood vessels had burst in his hang-dog eyes. Every movement he made seemed to give him pain.

'I understand you're outspoken,' Loken said. 'Something of an iconoclast?'

'Yes, yes,' Karkasy said, shaking his head, 'but I'll grow out of it, I promise you.'

'They want rid of you. They want to send you home,' said Loken. 'The senior remembrancers believe you're giving the order a bad name.'

'Captain, I could give someone a bad name just by standing next to them.'

That made Loken smile. He was beginning to like the man.

'I've spoken with the Warmaster's equerry about you, Karkasy,' Loken said. 'There is a potential for probation here. If a senior Astartes, such as myself, vouches for you, then you could stay with the expedition.'

'There'd be conditions?' Karkasy asked.

'Of course there would, but first of all I have to hear you tell me that you want to stay.'

'I want to stay. Great Terra, captain, I made a mistake, but I want to stay. I want to be part of this.'

Loken nodded. 'Mersadie says you should. The equerry, too, has a soft spot for you. I think Maloghurst likes an underdog.'

'Sir, never has a dog been so much under.'

'Here are the conditions,' Loken said. 'Stick to them, or I will withdraw my sponsorship of you entirely, and you'll be spending a cold forty months lugging your arse back to Terra. First, you reform your habits.'

'I will, sir. Absolutely.'

'Second, you report to me every three days, my duties permitting, and copy me with everything you write. Everything, do you understand? Work intended for publication and idle scribbles. Nothing goes past me. You will show me your soul on a regular basis.'

'I promise, captain, though I warn you it's an ugly, cross-eyed, crook-backed, club-footed soul.'

'I've seen ugly,' Loken assured him. 'The third condition. A question, really. Do you lie?'

'No, sir, I don't.'

'This is what I've heard. You tell the truth, unvarnished and unretouched. You are judged a scoundrel for this. You say things others dare not.'

Karkasy shrugged – with a groan brought about by sore shoulders. 'I'm confused, captain. Is saying yes to that going to spoil my chances?'

'Answer anyway.'

'Captain Loken, I always, always tell the truth as I see it, though it gets me beaten to a pulp in army bars. And, with my heart, I denounce those who lie or deliberately blur the whole truth.'

Loken nodded. 'What did you say, remembrancer? What did you say that provoked honest troopers so far they took their fists to you?'

Karkasy cleared his throat and winced. 'I said... I said the Imperium would not endure. I said that nothing lasts forever, no matter how surely it has been built. I said that we will be fighting forever, just to keep ourselves alive.'

Loken did not reply.

Karkasy rose to his feet. 'Was that the right answer, sir?'

'Are there any right answers, sir?' Loken replied. 'I know this... a warrior-officer of the Imperial Fists said much the same thing to me not long ago. He didn't use the same words, but the meaning was identical. He was not sent home.' Loken laughed to himself. 'Actually, as I think of it now, he was, but not for that reason.'

Loken looked across the cell at Karkasy.

'The third condition, then. I will vouch for you, and stand in recognisance for you. In return, you must continue to tell the truth.'

'Really? Are you sure about that?'

'Truth is all we have, Karkasy. Truth is what separates us from the xenos-breeds and the traitors. How will history judge us fairly if it doesn't have the truth to read? I was told that was what the remembrancer order was for. You keep telling the truth, ugly and unpalatable as it might be, and I'll keep sponsoring you.'

Following his strange and disconcerting conversation with Kyril Sindermann in the archives, Loken walked along to the gallery

chamber in the flagship's midships where the remembrancers
had taken to gathering.

As usual, Karkasy was waiting for him under the high arch
of the chamber's entrance. It was their regular, agreed meeting
place. From the broad chamber beyond the arch floated sounds
of laughter, conversation and music. Figures, mostly remembrancers, but also some crew personnel and military aides, bustled in
and out through the archway, many in noisy, chattering groups.

The gallery chamber, one of many aboard the massive flagship
designed for large assembly meetings, addresses and military
ceremonies, had been given over to the remembrancers' use once
it had been recognised that they could not be dissuaded from
social gathering and conviviality. It was most undignified and
undisciplined, as if a small carnival had been permitted to pitch
in the austere halls of the grand warship. All across the Imperium, warships were making similar accommodations as they
adjusted to the uncomfortable novelty of carrying large communities of artists and freethinkers with them. By their very nature,
the remembrancers could not be regimented or controlled the
way the military complements of the ship could. They had an
unquenchable desire to meet and debate and carouse. By giving
them a space for their own use, the masters of the expedition
could at least ring-fence their boisterous activities.

The chamber had become known as the Retreat, and it had
acquired a grubby reputation. Loken had no wish to go inside,
and always arranged to meet Karkasy at the entrance. It felt so
odd to hear unrestrained laughter and jaunty music in the solemn depths of the *Vengeful Spirit*.

Karkasy nodded respectfully as the captain approached him.
Seven weeks of voyage time had seen his injuries heal well, and
the bruises on his flesh were all but gone. He presented Loken
with a printed sheaf of his latest work. Other remembrancers,
passing by in little social cliques, eyed the Astartes captain with
curiosity and surprise.

'My most recent work,' Karkasy said. 'As agreed.'

'Thank you. I'll see you here in three days.'

'There's something else, captain,' Karkasy said, and handed
Loken a data-slate. He thumbed it to life. Picts appeared on
the screen, beautifully composed picts of him and Tenth Company, assembling for embarkation. The banner. The files. Here
he was swearing his oath of moment to Targost and Sedirae.
The Mournival.

'Euphrati asked me to give you this,' Karkasy said.

'Where is she?' Loken asked.

'I don't know, captain,' Karkasy said. 'No one's seen her about much. She has become reclusive since...'

'Since?'

'The Whisperheads.'

'What has she told you about that?'

'Nothing, sir. She says there's nothing to tell. She says the first captain told her there was nothing to tell.'

'She's right about that. These are fine images. Thank you, Ignace. Thank Keeler for me. I will treasure these.'

Kakasy bowed and began to walk back into the Retreat.

'Karkasy?'

'Sir?'

'Look after Keeler, please. For me. You and Oliton. Make sure she's not alone too often.'

'Yes, captain. I will.'

Six weeks into the voyage, while Loken was drilling his new recruits, Aximand came to him.

'*The Chronicles of Ursh*?' he muttered, noticing the volume Loken had left open beside the training mat.

'It pleases me,' Loken replied.

'I enjoyed it as a child,' Aximand replied. 'Vulgar, though.'

'I think that's why I like it,' Loken replied. 'What can I do for you?'

'I wanted to speak to you,' Aximand said, 'on a private matter.'

Loken frowned. Aximand opened his hand and revealed a silver lodge medal.

'I would like you to give this a fair hearing,' Aximand said, once they had withdrawn to the privacy of Loken's arming chamber. 'As a favour to me.'

'You know how I feel about lodge activities?'

'It's been made known to me. I admire your purity, but there's no hidden malice in the lodge. You have my word, and I hope, by now, that's worth something.'

'It is. Who told you of my interest?'

'I can't say. Garviel, there is a lodge meeting tonight, and I would like you to attend it as my guest. We would like to embrace you to our fraternity.'

'I'm not sure I want to be embraced.'

Aximand nodded his head. 'I understand. There would be no duress. Come, attend, see for yourself and decide for yourself. If you don't like what you find, then you're free to leave and disassociate yourself.'

Loken made no response.

'It is simply a band of brothers,' Aximand said. 'A fraternity of warriors, bi-partisan and without rank.'

'So I've heard.'

'Since the Whisperheads, we have had a vacancy. We'd like you to fill it.'

'A vacancy?' Loken said. 'You mean Jubal? I saw his medal.'

'Will you come with me?' asked Aximand.

'I will. Because it's you who's asking me,' said Loken.

FOUR

Felling the Murder trees
Megarachnid industry
Pleased to know you

Their brothers on the tree were already dead, past saving, but Tarvitz could not leave them skewered and unavenged. The ruination of their proud, perfect forms insulted his eyes and the honour of his Legion.

He gathered all the explosives carried by the remaining men, and moved forwards towards the trees with Bulle and Sakian.

Lucius stayed with the others. 'You're a fool to do that,' he told Tarvitz. 'We might yet need those charges.'

'What for?' Tarvitz asked.

Lucius shrugged. 'We've a war to win here.'

That almost made Saul Tarvitz laugh. He wanted to say that they were already dead. Murder had swallowed the companies of Blood Angels and now, thanks to Eidolon's zeal for glory, it had swallowed them too. There was no way out. Tarvitz didn't know how many of the company were still alive on the surface, but if the other groups had suffered losses commensurate to their own, the full number could be little higher than fifty.

Fifty men, fifty Astartes even, against a world of numberless hostiles. This was not a war to win; this was just a last stand, wherein, by the Emperor's grace, they might take as many of the foe with them as they could before they fell.

He did not say this to Lucius, but only because others were in earshot. Lucius's brand of courage admitted no reality, and if Tarvitz had been plain about their situation, it would have led to an argument. The last thing the men needed now was to see their officers quarrelling.

'I'll not suffer those trees to stand,' Tarvitz said.

With Bulle and Sakian, he approached the white stone trees, running low until they were in under the shadows of their grim, rigid canopies. The winged megarachnid up among the thorns ignored them. They could hear the cracking, clicking noises of the insects' feeding, and occasional trickles of black blood spattered down around them.

They divided the charges into three equal amounts, and secured them to the boles of the trees. Bulle set a forty-second timer.

They began to run back towards the edge of the stalk forest where Lucius and the rest of the troop lay in cover.

'Move it, Saul,' Lucius's voice crackled over the vox.

Tarvitz didn't reply.

'Move it, Saul. Hurry. Don't look back.'

Still running, Tarvitz looked behind him. Two of the winged clades had disengaged themselves from the feeding group and had taken to the air. Their beating wings were glass-blurs in the yellow light, and the lightning flash glinted off their polished black bodies. They circled up away from the thorn trees and came on in the direction of the three figures, wings throcking the air like the buzz of a gnat slowed and amplified to gargantuan, bass volumes.

'Run!' said Tarvitz.

Sakian glanced back. He lost his footing and fell. Tarvitz skidded to a halt and turned back, dragging Sakian to his feet. Bulle had run on. 'Twelve seconds!' he yelled, turning and drawing his bolter. He kept backing away, but trained his weapon at the oncoming forms.

'Come on!' he yelled. Then he started to fire and shouted 'Drop! Drop!'

Sakian pushed them both down, and he and Tarvitz sprawled onto the red dirt as the first winged clade went over them, so low the downdraft of its whirring wings raised dust.

It rose past them and headed straight for Bulle, but veered away as he struck it twice with bolter rounds.

Tarvitz looked up and saw the second megarachnid drop straight towards him in a near stall, the kind of pounce-dive that had snared so many of his comrades earlier.

He tried to roll aside. The black thing filled the entire sky.

A bolter roared. Sakian had cleared his weapon and was firing upwards, point blank. The shots tore through the winged clade's thorax in a violent puff of smoke and chitin shards, and the thing fell, crushing them both beneath its weight.

It twitched and spasmed on top of them, and Tarvitz heard Sakian cry out in pain. Tarvitz scrabbled to heave it away, his hands sticky with its ichor.

The charges went off.

The shockwave of flame rushed out across the red dirt in all directions. It scorched and demolished the nearby edge of the stalk forest, and lifted Tarvitz, Sakian and the thing pinning them, into the air. It blew Bulle off his feet, throwing him backwards. It caught the flying thing, tore off its wings, and hurled it into the thickets.

The blast levelled the three stone trees. They collapsed like buildings, like demolished towers, fracturing into brittle splinters and white dust as they fell into the fireball. Two or three of the winged clades feeding on the trees took off, but they were on fire, and the heat-suck of the explosion tumbled them back into the flames.

Tarvitz got up. The trees had been reduced to a heap of white slag, burning furiously. A thick pall of ash-white dust and smoke rolled off the blast zone. Burning, smouldering scads, like volcanic out-throw, drizzled down over him.

He hauled Sakian upright. The creature's impact on them had broken Sakian's right upper arm, and that break had been made worse when they had been thrown by the blast. Sakian was unsteady, but his genhanced metabolism was already compensating.

Bulle, unhurt, was getting up by himself.

The vox stirred. It was Lucius. 'Happy now?' he asked.

Beyond revenge and honour, Tarvitz's action had two unexpected consequences. The second did not become evident for some time, but the first was apparent in less than thirty minutes.

Where the vox had failed to link the scattered forces on the surface, the blast succeeded. Two other troops, one commanded by Captain Anteus, the other by Lord Eidolon himself, detected the considerable detonation, and followed the smoke plume to its source. United, they had almost fifty Astartes between them.

'Make report to me,' Eidolon said. They had taken up position at the edge of the clearing, some half a kilometre from the destroyed trees, near the hem of the stalk forest. The open ground afforded them ample warning of the approach of the

megarachnid scurrier-clades, and if the winged forms reappeared, they could retreat swiftly into the cover of the thickets
and mount a defence.

Tarvitz outlined all that had befallen his troop since landfall
as quickly and clearly as possible. Lord Eidolon was one of the
primarch's most senior commanders, the first chosen to such
a role, and brooked no familiarity, even from senior line officers like Tarvitz. Saul could tell from his manner that Eidolon
was seething with anger. The undertaking had not gone at all
to his liking. Tarvitz wondered if Eidolon might ever admit he
was wrong to have ordered the drop. He doubted it. Eidolon,
like all the elite hierarchy of the Emperor's Children, somehow
made pride a virtue.

'Repeat what you said about the trees,' Eidolon prompted.

'The winged forms use them to secure prey for feeding, lord,'
Tarvitz said.

'I understand that,' Eidolon snapped. 'I've lost men to the
winged things, and I've seen the thorn trees, but you say there
were other bodies?'

'The corpses of Blood Angels, lord,' Tarvitz nodded, 'and men
of the Imperial army force too.'

'We've not seen that,' Captain Anteus remarked.

'It might explain what happened to them,' Eidolon replied.
Anteus was one of Eidolon's chosen circle and enjoyed a far
more cordial relationship with his lord than Tarvitz did.

'Have you proof?' Anteus asked Tarvitz.

'I destroyed the trees, as you know, sir,' Tarvitz said.

'So you don't have proof?'

'My word is proof,' said Tarvitz.

'And good enough for me,' Anteus nodded courteously. 'I
meant no offence, brother.'

'And I took none, sir.'

'You used all your charges?' Eidolon asked.

'Yes, lord.'

'A waste.'

Tarvitz began to reply, but stifled the words before he could
say them. If it hadn't been for his use of the explosives, they
wouldn't have reunited. If it hadn't been for his use of the explosives, the ragged corpses of fine Emperor's Children would have
hung from stone gibbets in ignominious disarray.

'I told him so, lord,' Lucius remarked.

'Told him what?'

'That using all our charges was a waste.'

'What's that in your hand, captain?' Eidolon asked.

Lucius held up the limb-blade.

'You taint us,' Anteus said. 'Shame on you. Using an enemy's claw like a sword...'

'Throw it away, captain,' Eidolon said. 'I'm surprised at you.'

'Yes, lord.'

'Tarvitz?'

'Yes, my lord?'

'The Blood Angels will require some proof of their fallen. Some relic they can honour. You say shreds of armour hung from those trees. Go and retrieve some. Lucius can help you.'

'My lord, should we not secure this–'

'I gave you an order, captain. Execute it please, or does the honour of our brethren Legion mean nothing to you?'

'I only thought to–'

'Did I ask for your counsel? Are you a lord commander, and privy to the higher links of command?'

'No, lord.'

'Then get to it, captain. You too, Lucius. You men, assist them.'

The local shield-storm had blown out. The sky over the wide clearing was surprisingly clear and pale, as if night was finally falling. Tarvitz had no idea of Murder's diurnal cycle. Since they had made planetfall, night and day periods must surely have passed, but in the stalk forests, lit by the storm flare, such changes had been imperceptible.

Now it seemed cooler, stiller. The sky was a washed-out beige, with filaments of darkness threading through it. There was no wind, and the flicker of sheet lightning came from many kilometres away. Tarvitz thought he could even glimpse stars up there, in the darker patches of the open sky.

He led his party out to the ruins of the trees. Lucius was grumbling, as if it was all Tarvitz's fault.

'Shut up,' Tarvitz told him on a closed channel. 'Consider this ample payback for your kiss-arse display to the lord commander.'

'What are you talking about?' Lucius asked.

'I told him it was a waste, lord,' Tarvitz answered, mimicking Lucius's words in an unflattering voice.

'I did tell you!'

'Yes, you did, but there's such a thing as solidarity. I thought we were friends.'

'We are friends,' Lucius said, hurt.

'And that was the act of a friend?'

'We are the Emperor's Children,' Lucius said solemnly. 'We seek perfection, we don't hide our mistakes. You made a mistake.

Acknowledging our failures is another step on the road to perfection. Isn't that what our primarch teaches?'

Tarvitz frowned. Lucius was right. Primarch Fulgrim taught that only by imperfection could they fail the Emperor, and only by recognising those failures could they eradicate them. Tarvitz wished someone would remind Eidolon of that key tenet of their Legion's philosophy.

'I made a mistake,' Lucius admitted. 'I used that blade thing. I relished it. It was xenos. Lord Eidolon was right to reprimand me.'

'I told you it was xenos. Twice.'

'Yes, you did. I owe you an apology for that. You were right, Saul. I'm sorry.'

'Never mind.'

Lucius put his hand on Tarvitz's plated arm and stopped him.

'No, it's not. I'm a fine one to talk. You are always so grounded, Saul. I know I mock you for that. I'm sorry. I hope we're still friends.'

'Of course.'

'Your steadfast manner is a true virtue,' Lucius said. 'I become obsessive sometimes, in the heat of things. It is an imperfection of my character. Perhaps you can help me overcome it. Perhaps I can learn from you.' His voice had that childlike tone in it that had made Tarvitz like him in the first place. 'Besides,' Lucius added, 'you saved my life. I haven't thanked you for that.'

'No, you haven't, but there's no need, brother.'

'Then let's get this done, eh?'

The other men had waited while Tarvitz and Lucius conducted their private, vox-to-vox conversation. The pair hurried over to rejoin them.

The men Eidolon had picked to go with them were Bulle, Pherost, Lodoroton and Tykus, all men from Tarvitz's squad. Eidolon was so clearly punishing the troop, it wasn't funny. Tarvitz hated the fact that his men suffered because he was not in favour.

And Tarvitz had a feeling they weren't being punished for wasting charges. They were suffering Eidolon's opprobrium because they had achieved more of significance than either of the other groups since the drop.

They reached the ruined trees and crunched up the slopes of smouldering white slag. Remnants of stone thorns stuck out of the heap, like the antlers of bull deer, some blackened with charred scraps of flesh.

'What do we do?' asked Tykus.

Tarvitz sighed, and knelt down in the white spoil. He began to sift aside the chalky debris with his gloved hands. 'This,' he said.

They worked for an hour or two. Some kind of night began to fall, and the air temperature dropped sharply as the light drained out of the sky. Stars came out, properly, and distant lightning played across the endless grass forests ringing the clearing.

Immense heat was issuing from the heart of the slag heap, and it made the cold air around them shimmer. They sifted the dusty slag piece by piece, and retrieved two battered shoulder plates, both Blood Angels issue, and an Imperial army cap.

'Is that enough?' asked Lodoroton.

'Keep going,' replied Tarvitz. He looked out across the dim clearing to where Eidolon's force was dug in. 'Another hour, maybe, and we'll stop.'

Lucius found a Blood Angels helmet. Part of the skull was still inside it. Tykus found a breastplate belonging to one of the lost Emperor's Children.

'Bring that too,' Tarvitz said.

Then Pherost found something that almost killed him.

It was one of the winged clades, burned and buried, but still alive. As Pherost pulled the calcified cinders away, the crumpled black thing, wingless and ruptured, reared up and stabbed at him with its hooked headcrest.

Pherost stumbled, fell, and slithered down the slag slope on his back. The clade struggled after him, dragging its damaged body, its broken wing bases vibrating pointlessly.

Tarvitz leapt over and slew it with his broadsword. It was so near death and dried out that its body crumpled like paper under his blade, and only a residual ichor, thick like glue, oozed out.

'All right?' Tarvitz asked.

'Just took me by surprise,' Pherost replied, laughing it off.

'Watch how you go,' Tarvitz warned the others.

'Do you hear that?' asked Lucius.

It had become very still and dark, like a true and proper night fall. Amping their helmet acoustics, they could all hear the chittering noise Lucius had detected. In the edges of the thickets, starlight flashed off busy metallic forms.

'They're back,' said Lucius, looking round at Tarvitz.

'Tarvitz to main party,' Tarvitz voxed. 'Hostile contact in the edges of the forest.'

'We see it, captain,' Eidolon responded immediately. 'Hold your position until we–'

The link cut off abruptly, like it was being jammed.

'We should go back,' Lucius said.

'Yes,' Tarvitz agreed.

A sudden light and noise made them all start. The main party, half a kilometre away, had opened fire. Across the distance, they heard and saw bolters drumming and flashing in the darkness. Distant zinc-grey forms danced and jittered in the strobing light of the gunfire.

Eidolon's position had been attacked.

'Come on!' Lucius cried.

'And do what?' Tarvitz asked. 'Wait! Look!'

The six of them scrambled down into cover on one side of the spoil heap. Megarachnid were approaching from the edges of the forest, their marching grey forms almost invisible except where they caught the starlight and the distant blink of lightning. They were streaming towards the tree mound in their hundreds, in neat, ordered lines. Amongst them, there were other shapes, bigger shapes, massive megarachnid forms. Another clade variant.

Tarvitz's party slid down the chalky rubble and backed away into the open, the expanse of the clearing behind them, keeping low. To their right, Lord Eidolon's position was engulfed in loud, furious combat.

'What are they doing?' asked Bulle.

'Look,' said Tarvitz.

The columns of megarachnid ascended the heap of rubble. Warrior forms, equipped with quad-blades, took station around the base, on guard. Others mounted the slopes and began to sort the spoil, clearing it with inhuman speed and efficiency. Tarvitz saw warrior forms doing this work, and also clades of a similar design, but which possessed spatulate shovel limbs in place of blades. With minute precision, the megarachnid began to disassemble the rubble heap, and carry the loose debris away into the thickets. They formed long, mechanical work gangs to do this. The more massive forms, the clades Tarvitz had not seen before, came forwards. They were superheavy monsters with short, thick legs and gigantic abdomens. They moved ponderously, and began to gnaw and suck on the loose rubble with ghastly, oversized mouth-parts. The smaller clades scurried around their hefty forms, pulling skeins of white matter from their abdominal spinnerets with curiously dainty, weaving motions of their upper limbs. The smaller clades carried this fibrous, stiffening matter back into the increasingly cleared site and began to plaster it together.

'They're rebuilding the trees,' Bulle whispered.

It was an extraordinary sight. The massive clades, weavers, were consuming the broken scraps of the trees Tarvitz had felled, and turning them into fresh new material, like gelling concrete. The smaller clades, busy and scurrying, were taking the material and forming new bases with it in the space that others of their kind had cleared.

In less than ten minutes, much of the area had been picked clean, and the trunks of three new trees were being formed. The scurrying builders brought limb-loads of wet, milk white matter to the bases, and then regurgitated fluid onto them so as to mix them as cement. Their limbs whirred and shaped like the trowels of master builders.

Still, the battle behind them roared. Lucius kept glancing in the direction of the fight.

'We should go back,' he whispered. 'Lord Eidolon needs us.'

'If he can't win without the six of us,' Tarvitz said, 'he can't win. I felled these trees. I'll not see them built again. Who's with me?'

Bulle answered 'Aye.' So did Pherost, Lodoroton and Tykus.

'Very well,' said Lucius. 'What do we do?'

But Tarvitz had already drawn his broadsword and was charging the megarachnid workers.

The fight that followed was simple insanity. The six Astartes, blades out, bolters ready, rushed the megarachnid work gangs and made war upon them in the cold night air. Picket clades, warrior forms drawn up as sentinels around the edge of the site, alerted to them first and rushed out in defence. Lucius and Bulle met them and slaughtered them, and Tarvitz and Tykus ploughed on into the main site to confront the industrious builder forms. Pherost and Lodoroton followed them, firing wide to fend off flank strikes.

Tarvitz attacked one of the monster 'weaver' forms, one of the builder clades, and split its massive belly wide open with his sword. Molten cement poured out like pus, and it began to claw at the sky with its short, heavy limbs. Warrior forms leapt over its stricken mass to attack the Imperials. Tykus shot two out of the air and then decapitated a third as it pounced on him. The megarachnid were everywhere, milling like ants.

Lodoroton had slain eight of them, including another monster clade, when a warrior form bit off his head. As if unsatisfied with that, the warrior form proceeded to flense Lodoroton's body apart with its four limb-blades. Blood and meat particles spumed into the cold air. Bulle shot the warrior clade dead with a single bolt round. It dropped on its face.

Lucius hacked his way through the outer guards, which were closing on him in ever increasing numbers. He swung his sword, no longer playing, no longer toying. This was test enough.

He'd killed sixteen megarachnid by the time they got him. A clade with spatulate limbs, bearing a cargo of wet milky cement, fell apart under his sword strokes, and dying, dumped its payload on him. Lucius fell, his arms and legs glued together by the wet load. He tried to break free, but the organic mulch began to thicken and solidify. A warrior clade pounced on him and made to skewer him with its four blade arms.

Tarvitz shot it in the side of the body and knocked it away. He stood over Lucius to protect him from the xenos scum. Bulle came to his side, shooting and chopping. Pherost fought his way to join them, but fell as a limb-blade punched clean through his torso from behind. Tykus backed up close. The three remaining Emperor's Children blazed and sliced away at the enclosing foe. At their feet, Lucius struggled to free himself and get up.

'Get this off me, Saul!' he yelled.

Tarvitz wanted to. He wanted to be able to turn and hack free his stricken friend, but there was no space. No time. The megarachnid warrior clades were all over them now, chittering and slashing. If he broke off even for a moment, he would be dead.

Thunder boomed in the clear night sky. Caught up in the fierce warfare, Tarvitz paid it no heed. Just the shield-storm returning.

But it wasn't.

Meteors were dropping out of the sky into the clearing around them, impacting hard and super-hot in the red dirt, like lightning strikes. Two, four, a dozen, twenty.

Drop pods.

The noise of fresh fire rang out above the din of the fight. Bolters boomed. Plasma weapons shrieked. The drop pods kept falling like bombs.

'Look!' Bulle cried out. 'Look!'

The megarachnid were swarming over them. Tarvitz had lost his bolter and could barely swing his broadsword, such was the density of enemies upon him. He felt himself slowly being borne over by sheer weight of numbers.

'–hear me?' The vox squealed suddenly.

'W-what? Say again!'

'I said, we are Imperial! Do we have brothers in there?'

'Yes, in the name of Terra–'

An explosion. A series of rapid gunshots. A shockwave rocked through the enemy masses.

'Follow me in,' a voice was yelling, commanding and deep. 'Follow me in and drive them back!'

More searing explosions. Grey bodies blew apart in gouts of flame, spinning broken limbs into the air like matchwood. One whizzing limb smacked into Tarvitz's visor and knocked him onto his back. The world, scarlet and concussed, spun for a second.

A hand reached down towards Tarvitz. It swam into his field of view. It was an Astartes gauntlet. White, with black edging.

'Up you come, brother.'

Tarvitz grabbed at it and felt himself hauled upright.

'My thanks,' he yelled, mayhem still raging all around him. 'Who are you?'

'My name is Tarik, brother,' said his saviour. 'Pleased to meet you.'

FIVE

Informal formalities
The war dogs' rebuke
I can't say

It was a little cruel, in Loken's opinion. Someone, somewhere –
and Loken suspected the scheming of Maloghurst – had omitted
to tell the officers of the 140th Expedition Fleet exactly who
they were about to welcome on board.

The *Vengeful Spirit*, and its attendant fleet consorts, had drawn
up majestically into high anchorage alongside the vessels of the
140th and the other ships that had come to the expedition's
aid, and an armoured heavy shuttle had transferred from the
flagship to the battle-barge *Misericord*.

Mathanual August and his coterie of commanders, including Eidolon's equerry Eshkerrus, had assembled on one of the
Misericord's main embarkation decks to greet the shuttle. They
knew it was bearing the commanders of the relief task force
from the 63rd Expedition, and that inevitably meant officers
of the XVI Legion. With the possible exception of Eshkerrus,
they were all nervous. The arrival of the Luna Wolves, the most
famed and feared of all Astartes divisions, was enough to tension any man's nerve strings.

When the shuttle's landing ramp extended and ten Luna Wolves
descended through the clearing vapour, there had been silence,
and that silence had turned to stifled gasps when it became apparent these were not the ten brothers of a captain's ceremonial
detail, but ten captains themselves in full, formal wargear.

The first captain led the party, and made the sign of the aquila to Mathanual August.

'I am–' he began.

'I know who you are, lord,' August said, and bowed deeply, trembling. There were few in the Imperium who didn't recognise or fear First Captain Abaddon. 'I welcome you and–'

'Hush, master,' Abaddon said. 'We're not there yet.'

August looked up, not really understanding. Abaddon stepped back into his place, and the ten, cloaked captains, five on each side of the landing ramp, formed an honour guard and snapped to attention, visors front and hands on the pommels of their sheathed swords.

The Warmaster emerged from the shuttle. Everyone, apart from the ten captains and Mathanual August, immediately prostrated themselves on the deck.

The Warmaster stepped slowly down the ramp. His very presence was enough to inspire total and unreserved attention, but he was, quite calculatedly, doing the one thing that made matters even worse. He wasn't smiling.

August stood before him, his eyes wide open, his mouth opening and closing wordlessly, like a beached fish.

Eshkerrus, who had himself gone quite green, glanced up and yanked at the hem of August's robes. 'Abase yourself, fool!' he hissed.

August couldn't. Loken doubted the veteran fleet master could have even recalled his own name at that moment. Horus came to a halt, towering over him.

'Sir, will you not bow?' Horus inquired.

When August finally replied, his voice was a tiny, embryonic thing. 'I can't,' he said. 'I can't remember how.'

Then, once again, the Warmaster showed his limitless genius for leadership. He sank to one knee and bowed to Mathanual August.

'I have come, as fast as I was able, to help you, sir,' he said. He clasped August in an embrace. The Warmaster was smiling now. 'I like a man who's proud enough not to bend his knees to me,' he said.

'I would have bent them if I had been able, my lord,' August said. Already August was calmer, gratefully put at his ease by the Warmaster's informality.

'Forgive me, Mathanual… may I call you Mathanual? *Master* is so stiff. Forgive me for not informing you that I was coming in person. I detest pomp and ceremony, and if you'd known I was coming, you'd have gone to unnecessary lengths. Soldiers in dress regs, ceremonial bands, bunting. I particularly despise bunting.'

Mathanual August laughed. Horus rose to his feet and looked around at the prone figures covering the wide deck. 'Rise, please. Please. Get to your feet. A cheer or a round of applause will do me, not this futile grovelling.'

The fleet officers rose, cheering *and* applauding. He'd won them over. Just like that, thought Loken, he'd won them over. They were his now, forever.

Horus moved forwards to greet the officers and commanders individually. Loken noticed Eshkerrus, in his purple and gold robes and half-armour, taking his greeting with a bow. There was something sour about the equerry, Loken thought. Something definitely put out.

'Helms!' Abaddon ordered, and the company commanders removed their helmets. They moved forwards, more casually now, to escort their commander through the press of applauding figures.

Horus whispered an aside to Abaddon as he took greeting kisses and bows from the assembly. Abaddon nodded. He touched his link, activating the privy channel, and spoke, in Cthonic, to the other three members of the Mournival. 'War council in thirty minutes. Be ready to play your parts.'

The other three knew what that meant. They followed Abaddon into the greeting crowd.

They assembled for council in the strategium of the *Misericord*, a massive rotunda situated behind the barge's main bridge. The Warmaster took the seat at the head of the long table, and the Mournival sat down with him, along with August, Eshkerrus and nine senior ship commanders and army officers. The other Luna Wolf captains sat amongst the crowds of lesser fleet officers filling the tiered seating in the panelled galleries above them.

Master August called up hololithic displays to illuminate his succinct recap of the situation. Horus regarded each one in turn, twice asking August to go back so he could study details again.

'So you poured everything you had into this death trap?' Torgaddon began bluntly, once August had finished.

August recoiled, as if slapped. 'Sir, I did as–'

The Warmaster raised his hand. 'Tarik, too much, too stern. Master August was simply doing as Captain Frome told him.'

'My apologies, lord,' Torgaddon said. 'I withdraw the comment.'

'I don't believe Tarik should have to,' Abaddon cut in. 'This was a monumental misuse of manpower. Three companies? Not to mention the army units...'

'It wouldn't have happened under my watch,' murmured Torgaddon. August blinked his eyes very fast. He looked like he was attempting not to tear up.

'It's unforgivable,' said Aximand. 'Simply unforgivable.'

'We will forgive him, even so,' Horus said.

'Should we, lord?' asked Loken.

'I've shot men for less,' said Abaddon.

'Please,' August said, pale, rising to his feet. 'I deserve punishment. I implore you to–'

'He's not worth the bolt,' muttered Aximand.

'Enough,' Horus smoothed. 'Mathanual made a mistake, a command mistake. Didn't you, Mathanual?'

'I believe I did, sir.'

'He drip-fed his expedition's forces into a danger zone until they were all gone,' said Horus. 'It's tragic. It happens sometimes. We're here now, that's all that matters. Here to rectify the problem.'

'What of the Emperor's Children?' Loken put in. 'Did they not even consider waiting?'

'For what, exactly?' asked Eshkerrus.

'For us,' smiled Aximand.

'An entire expedition was in jeopardy,' replied Eshkerrus, his eyes narrowing. 'We were first on scene. A critical response. We owed it to our Blood Angels brothers to–'

'To what? Die too?' Torgaddon asked.

'Three companies of Blood Angels were–' Eshkerrus exclaimed.

'Probably dead already,' Aximand interrupted. 'They'd showed you the trap was there. Did you just think you'd walk into it too?'

'We–' Eshkerrus began.

'Or was Lord Eidolon simply hungry for glory?' asked Torgaddon.

Eshkerrus rose to his feet. He glared across the table at Torgaddon. 'Captain, you offend the honour of the Emperor's Children.'

'That may indeed be what I'm doing, yes,' Torgaddon replied.

'Then, sir, you are a base and low-born–'

'Equerry Eshkerrus,' Loken said. 'None of us like Torgaddon much, except when he is speaking the truth. Right now, I like him a great deal.'

'That's enough, Garviel,' Horus said quietly. 'Enough, all of you. Sit down, equerry. My Luna Wolves speak harshly because they are dismayed at this situation. An Imperial defeat. Companies lost. An implacable foe. This saddens me, and it will sadden the Emperor too, when he hears of it.'

Horus rose. 'My report to him will say this. Captain Frome was right to assault this world, for it is clearly a nest of xenos filth. We applaud his courage. Master August was right to support the captain, even though it meant he spent the bulk of his military formation. Lord Commander Eidolon was right to engage, without support, for to do otherwise would have been cowardly when lives were at stake. I would also like to thank all those commanders who rerouted here to offer assistance. From this point on, we will handle it.'

'How will you handle it, lord?' Eshkerrus asked boldly.

'Will you attack?' asked August.

'We will consider our options and inform you presently. That's all.'

The officers filed out of the strategium, along with Sedirae, Marr, Moy, Goshen, Targost and Qruze, leaving the Warmaster alone with the Mournival.

Once they were alone, Horus looked at the four of them. 'Thank you, friends. Well played.'

Loken was fast learning both how the Warmaster liked to employ the Mournival as a political weapon, and what a masterful political animal the Warmaster was. Aximand had quietly briefed Loken on what would be required of him just before they boarded the shuttle on the *Vengeful Spirit*. 'The situation here is a mess, and the commander believes that mess has in part been caused by incompetence and mistakes at command level. He wants all the officers reprimanded, rebuked so hard they smart with shame, but... if he's going to pull the 140th Expedition back together again and make it viable, he needs their admiration, their respect and their unswerving loyalty. None of which he will have if he marches in and starts throwing his weight around.'

'So the Mournival does the rebuking for him?'

'Just so,' Aximand had smiled. 'The Luna Wolves are feared anyway, so let them fear us. Let them hate us. We'll be the mouthpiece of discontent and rancour. All accusations must come from us. Play the part, speak as bluntly and critically as you like. Make them squirm in discomfort. They'll get the message, but at the same time, the Warmaster will be seen as a benign conciliator.'

'We're his war dogs?'

'So he doesn't have to growl himself. Exactly. He wants us to give them hell, a dressing down they'll remember and learn from. That allows him to seem the peacemaker. To remain beloved, adored, a voice of reason and calm. By the end, if we do things properly, they'll all feel suitably admonished, and simultaneously they'll all love the Warmaster for showing mercy and calling us off. Everyone thinks the Warmaster's keenest talent is as a warrior. No one expects him to be a consummate politician. Watch him and learn, Garvi. Learn why the Emperor chose him as his proxy.'

'Well played indeed,' Horus said to the Mournival with a smile. 'Garviel, that last comment was deliciously barbed. Eshkerrus was quite incandescent.'

Loken nodded. 'From the moment I laid eyes on him, he struck me as man eager to cover his arse. He knew mistakes had been made.'

'Yes, he did,' Horus said. 'Just don't expect to find many friends amongst the Emperor's Children for a while. They are a proud bunch.'

Loken shrugged. 'I have all the friends I need, sir,' he said.

'August, Eshkerrus and a dozen others may, of course, be formally cautioned and charged with incompetence once this is done,' Horus said lightly, 'but only once this is done. Now, morale is crucial. Now we have a war to design.'

It was about half an hour later when August summoned them to the bridge. A sudden and unexpected hole had appeared in the shield-storms of One Forty Twenty, an abrupt break in the fury, and quite close to the supposed landing vectors of the Emperor's Children.

'At last,' said August, 'a gap in that storm.'

'Would that I had Astartes to drop into it,' Eshkerrus muttered to himself.

'But you don't, do you?' Aximand remarked snidely. Eshkerrus glowered at Little Horus.

'Let's go in,' Torgaddon urged the Warmaster. 'Another hole might be a long time coming.'

'The storm might close in again,' Horus said, pointing to the radiating cyclonics on the lith.

'You want this world, don't you?' said Torgaddon. 'Let me take the speartip down.' The lots had already been drawn. The speartip was to be Torgaddon's company, along with the companies of Sedirae, Moy and Targost.

'Orbital bombardment,' Horus said, repeating what had already been decided as the best course of action.

'Men might yet live,' Torgaddon said.

The Warmaster stepped aside, and spoke quietly, in Cthonic, to the Mournival.

'If I authorise this, I echo August and Eidolon, and I've just had you take them to task for that very brand of rash mistake.'

'This is different,' Torgaddon replied. 'They went in blind, wave after wave. I'd not advocate duplicating that stupidity, but that break in the weather... it's the first they've detected in months.'

'If there are brothers still alive down there,' Little Horus said, 'they deserve one last chance to be found.'

'I'll go in,' said Torgaddon. 'See what I can find. Any sign that the weather is changing, I'll pull the speartip straight back out and we can open up the fleet batteries.'

'I still wonder about the music,' the Warmaster said. 'Anything on that?'

'The translators are still working,' Abaddon replied.

Horus looked at Torgaddon. 'I admire your compassion, Tarik, but the answer is a firm no. I'm not going to repeat the errors that have already been made and pour men into–'

'Lord?' August had come over to them again, and held out a data-slate.

Horus took it and read it.

'Is this confirmed?'

'Yes, Warmaster.'

Horus regarded the Mournival. 'The Master of Vox has detected trace vox traffic on the surface, in the area of the storm break. It does not respond or recognise our signals, but it is active. Imperial. It looks like squad to squad, or brother to brother transmissions.'

'There are men still alive,' said Abaddon. He seemed genuinely relieved. 'Great Terra and the Emperor! There are men still alive down there.'

Torgaddon stared at the Warmaster steadily and said nothing. He'd already said it.

'Very well,' said Horus to Torgaddon. 'Go.'

The drop pods were arranged down the length of the *Vengeful Spirit*'s fifth embarkation deck in their launch racks, and the warriors of the speartip were locking themselves into place. Lid doors, like armoured petals, were closing around them, so the drop-pods resembled toughened, black seed cases ready for autumn. Klaxons sounded, and the firing coils of the launchers were beginning to charge. They made a harsh, rising whine and a stink of ozone smouldered like incense in the deck air.

The Warmaster stood at the side of the vast deck space, watching the hurried preparations, his arms folded across his chest.

'Climate update?' he snapped.

'No change in the weather break, my lord,' Maloghurst replied, consulting his slate.

'How long's it been now?' Horus asked.

'Eighty-nine minutes.'

'They've done a good job pulling this together in such a short time,' Horus said. 'Ezekyle, commend the unit officers, please. Make it known I'm proud of them.'

Abaddon nodded. He held the papers of four oaths of moment in his armoured hands. 'Aximand?' he suggested.

Little Horus stepped forwards.

'Ezekyle?' Loken said. 'Could I?'

'You want to?'

'Luc and Serghar heard and witnessed mine before the Whisperheads. And Tarik is my friend.'

Abaddon looked sidelong at the Warmaster, who gave an almost imperceptible nod. Abaddon handed the parchments to Loken.

Loken strode out across the deck, Aximand at his side, and heard the four captains take their oaths. Little Horus held out the bolter on which the oaths were sworn.

When it was done, Loken handed the oath papers to each of them.

'Be well,' he said to them, 'and commend your unit commanders. The Warmaster personally admired their work today.'

Verulam Moy made the sign of the aquila. 'My thanks, Captain Loken,' he said, and walked away towards his pod, shouting for his unit seconds.

Serghar Targost smiled at Loken, and clasped his fist, thumb around thumb. By his side, Luc Sedirae grinned with his ever half-open mouth, his eyes a murderous blue, eager for war.

'If I don't see you next on this deck...' Sedirae began.

'...let it be at the Emperor's side,' Loken finished.

Sedirae laughed and ran, whooping, towards his pod. Targost locked on his helm and strode away in the opposite direction.

'Luc's blood is up,' Loken said to Torgaddon. 'How's yours?'

'My humours are all where they should be,' Torgaddon replied. He hugged Loken, with a clatter of plate, and then did the same to Aximand.

'Lupercal!' he bellowed, punching the air with his fist, and turned away, running to his waiting drop pod.

'Lupercal!' Loken and Aximand shouted after him.

The pair turned and walked back to join Abaddon, Maloghurst and the Warmaster.

'I'm always a little jealous,' Little Horus muttered to Loken as they crossed the deck.

'Me too.'

'I always want it to be me.'

'I know.'

'Going into something like that.'

'I know. And I'm always just a little afraid.'

'Of what, Garviel?'

'That we won't see them again.'

'We will.'

'How can you be so sure, Horus?' Loken wondered.

'I can't say,' replied Aximand, with a deliberate irony that made Loken laugh.

The observing party withdrew behind the blast shields. A sudden, volatile pressure change announced the opening of the deck's void fields. The firing coils accelerated to maximum charge, shrieking with pent up energy.

'The word is given,' Abaddon instructed above the uproar.

One by one, each with a concussive bang, the drop pods fired down through the deck slots like bullets. It was like the ripple of a full broadside firing. The embarkation deck shuddered as the drop pods ejected free.

Then they were all gone, and the deck was suddenly quiet, and tiny armoured pellets, cocooned in teardrops of blue fire, sank away towards the planet's surface.

I can't say.

The phrase had haunted Loken since the sixth week of the voyage to Murder. Since he had gone with Little Horus to the lodge meeting.

The meeting place had been one of the aft holds of the flagship, a lonely, forgotten pocket of the ship's superstructure. Down in the dark, the way had been lit by tapers.

Loken had come in simple robes, as Aximand had instructed him. They'd met on the fourth midships deck, and taken the rail carriage back to the aft quarters before descending via dark service stairwells.

'Relax,' Aximand kept telling him.

Loken couldn't. He'd never liked the idea of the lodges, and the discovery that Jubal had been a member had increased his disquiet.

'This isn't what you think it is,' Aximand had said.

And what did he think it was? A forbidden conclave. A cult of the Lectitio Divinitatus. Or worse. A terrible assembly. A worm in the bud. A cancer at the heart of the Legion.

As he walked down the dim, metal deckways, part of him

hoped that what awaited him would be infernal. A coven. Proof
that Jubal had already been tainted by some manufacture of the
warp before the Whisperheads. Proof that would reveal a source
of evil to Loken that he could finally strike back at in open retribution, but the greater part of him willed it to be otherwise.
Little Horus Aximand was party to this meeting. If it was tainted,
then Aximand's presence meant that taint ran profoundly deep.
Loken didn't want to have to go head to head with Aximand. If
what he feared was true, then in the next few minutes he might
have to fight and kill his Mournival brother.

'Who approaches?' asked a voice from the darkness. Loken
saw a figure, evidently an Astartes by his build, shrouded in a
hooded cloak.

'Two souls,' Aximand replied.

'What are your names?' the figure asked.

'I can't say.'

'Pass, friends.'

They entered the aft hold. Loken hesitated. The vast,
scaffold-framed area was eerily lit by candles and a vigorous
fire in a metal canister. Dozens of hooded figures stood around.
The dancing light made weird shadows of the deep hold's structural architecture.

'A new friend comes,' Aximand announced.

The hooded figures turned. 'Let him show the sign,' said one
of them in a voice that seemed familiar.

'Show it,' Aximand whispered to Loken.

Loken slowly held out the medal Aximand had given him. It
glinted in the fire light. Inside his robe, his other hand clasped
the grip of the combat knife he had concealed.

'Let him be revealed,' a voice said.

Aximand reached over and drew Loken's hood down.

'Welcome, brother warrior,' the others said as one.

Aximand pulled down his own hood. 'I speak for him,' he
said.

'Your voice is noted. Is he come of his own free will?'

'He is come because I invited him.'

'No more secrecy,' the voice said.

The figures removed their hoods and showed their faces in
the glow of the candles. Loken blinked.

There was Torgaddon, Luc Sedirae, Nero Vipus, Kalus Ekaddon, Verulam Moy and two dozen other senior and junior
Astartes.

And Serghar Targost, the hidden voice. Evidently the lodge
master.

'You'll not need the blade,' Targost said gently, stepping forwards and holding out his hand for it. 'You are free to leave at any time, unmolested. May I take it from you? Weapons are not permitted within the bounds of our meetings.'

Loken took out the combat knife and passed it to Targost. The lodge master placed it on a wall strut, out of the way.

Loken continued to look from one face to another. This wasn't like anything he had expected.

'Tarik?'

'We'll answer any question, Garviel,' Torgaddon said. 'That's why we brought you here.'

'We'd like you to join us,' said Aximand, 'but if you choose not to, we will respect that too. All we ask, either way, is that you say nothing about what and who you see here to anyone outside.'

Loken hesitated. 'Or… '

'It's not a threat,' said Aximand. 'Nor even a condition. Simply a request that you respect our privacy.'

'We've known for a long time,' Targost said, 'that you have no interest in the warrior lodge.'

'I'd perhaps have put it more strongly than that,' said Loken.

Targost shrugged. 'We understand the nature of your opposition. You're far from being the only Astartes to feel that way. That is why we've never made any attempt to induct you.'

'What's changed?' asked Loken.

'You have,' said Aximand. 'You're not just a company officer now, but a Mournival lord. And the fact of the lodge has come to your attention.'

'Jubal's medal…' said Loken.

'Jubal's medal,' nodded Aximand. 'Jubal's death was a terrible thing, which we all mourn, but it affected you more than anyone. We see how you strive to make amends, to whip your company into tighter and finer form, as you blame yourself. When the medal turned up, we were concerned that you might start to make waves. That you might start asking open questions about the lodge.'

'So this is self-interest?' Loken asked. 'You thought you'd gang up on me and force me into silence?'

'Garviel,' said Luc Sedirae, 'the last thing the Luna Wolves need is an honest and respected captain, a member of the Mournival no less, campaigning to expose the lodge. It would damage the entire Legion.'

'Really?'

'Of course,' said Sedirae. 'The agitations of a man like you would force the Warmaster to act.'

'And he doesn't want to do that,' Torgaddon said.

'He... knows?' Loken asked.

'You seemed shocked,' said Aximand. 'Wouldn't you be more shocked to learn the Warmaster *didn't* know about the quiet order within his Legion? He knows. He's always known, and he turns a blind eye, provided we remain closed and confidential in our activities.'

'I don't understand...' Loken said.

'That's why you're here,' said Moy. 'You speak out against us because you don't understand. If you wish to oppose what we do, then at least do so from an informed position.'

'I've heard enough,' said Loken, turning away. 'I'll leave now. Don't worry, I'll say nothing. I'll make no waves, but I'm disappointed in you all. Someone can return my blade to me tomorrow.'

'Please,' Aximand began.

'No, Horus! You meet in secret, and secrecy is the enemy of truth. So we are taught! Truth is everything we have! You hide yourselves, you conceal your identities... for what? Because you are ashamed? Hell's teeth, you should be! The Emperor himself, beloved by all, has ruled on this. He does not sanction this kind of activity!'

'Because he doesn't understand!' Torgaddon exclaimed.

Loken turned back and strode across the chamber until he was nose to nose with Torgaddon. 'I can hardly believe I heard you say that,' he snarled.

'It's true,' said Torgaddon, not backing down. 'The Emperor isn't a god, but he might as well be. He's so far removed from the rest of mankind. Unique. Singular. Who does he call brother? No one! Even the blessed primarchs are only sons to him. The Emperor is wise beyond all measure, and we love him and would follow him until the crack of doom, but he doesn't understand brotherhood, and that is *all* we meet for.'

There was silence for a moment. Loken turned away from Torgaddon, unwilling to look upon his face. The others stood in a ring around them.

'We are warriors,' said Targost. 'That is all we know and all we do. Duty and war, war and duty. Thus it has been since we were created. The only bond we have that is not prescribed by duty is that of brotherhood.'

'That is the purpose of the lodge,' said Sedirae. 'To be a place where we are free to meet and converse and confide, outside the strictures of rank and martial order. There is only one qualification a man needs to be a part of our quiet order. He must be a warrior.'

'In this company,' said Targost, 'a man of any rank can meet and speak openly of his troubles, his doubts, his ideas, his dreams, without fear of scorn, or monition from a command-ing officer. This is a sanctuary for our spirit as men.'

'Look around,' Aximand invited, stepping forwards, gesturing with his hands. 'Look at these faces, Garviel. Company cap-tains, sergeants, file warriors. Where else could such a mix of men meet as equals? We leave our ranks at the door when we come in. Here, a senior commander can talk with a junior initi-ate, man to man. Here, knowledge and experience is passed on, ideas are circulated, commonalities discovered. Serghar holds the office of lodge master only so that a function of order may be maintained.'

Targost nodded. 'Horus is right. Garviel, do you know how old the quiet order is?'

'Decades...'

'No, older. Perhaps thousands of years older. There have been lodges in the Legions since their inception, and allied orders in the army and all other branches of the martial divisions. The lodge can be traced back into antiquity, before even the Uni-fication Wars. It's not a cult, nor a religious obscenity. Just a fraternity of warriors. Some Legions do not practise the habit. Some do. Ours always has done. It lends us strength.'

'How?' asked Loken.

'By connecting warriors otherwise divorced by rank or station. It makes bonds between men who would otherwise not even know one another's name. We thrive, like all Legions, from our firm hierarchy of formal authority, the loyalty that flows down from a commander through to his lowest soldier. Loyal to a squad, to a section, to a company. The lodge reinforces com-plementary links *across* that structure, from squad to squad, company to company. It could be said to be our secret weapon. It is the true strength of the Luna Wolves, strapping us together, side to side, where we are already bound up top to toe.'

'You have a dozen spears to carry into war,' said Torgaddon quietly. 'You gather them, shaft to shaft, as a bundle, so they are easier to bear. How much easier is that bundle to carry if it is tied together around the shafts?'

'If that was a metaphor,' Loken said, 'it was lousy.'

'Let me speak,' said another man. It was Kalus Ekaddon. He stepped forwards to face Loken.

'There's been bad blood between us, Loken,' he said bluntly.

'There has.'

'A little matter of rivalry on the field. I admit it. After the High

City fight, I hated your guts. So, in the field, though we served the same master and followed the same standard, there'd always be friction between us. Competition. Am I right?'

'I suppose…'

'I've never spoken to you,' Ekaddon said. 'Never, informally. We don't meet or mix. But I tell you this much: I've heard you tonight, in this place, amongst friends. I've heard you stand up for your beliefs and your point of view, and I've learned respect for you. You speak your mind. You have principles. Tomorrow, Loken, no matter what you decide tonight, I'll see you in a new light. You'll not get any grief from me any more, because I know you now. I've seen you as the man you are.' He laughed, raw and loud. 'Terra, it's a crude example, Loken, for I'm a crude fellow, but it shows what the lodge can do.'

He held out his hand. After a moment, Loken took it.

'There's a thing at least,' said Ekaddon. 'Now get on, if you're going. We've talking and drinking to do.'

'Or will you stay?' asked Torgaddon.

'For now, perhaps,' said Loken.

The meeting lasted for two hours. Torgaddon had brought wine, and Sedirae produced some meat and bread from the flagship's commissary. There were no crude rituals or daemonic practices to observe. The men – the brothers – sat around and talked in small groups, then listened as Aximand recounted the details of a xenos war that he had participated in, which he hoped might give them insight into the fight ahead. Afterwards, Torgaddon told some jokes, most of them bad.

As Torgaddon rambled on with a particularly involved and vulgar tale, Aximand came over to Loken.

'Where do you suppose,' he began quietly, 'the notion of the Mournival came from?'

'From this?' Loken asked.

Aximand nodded. 'The Mournival has no legitimate standing or powers. It's simply an informal organ, but the Warmaster would not be without it. It was created originally as a visible extension of the invisible lodge, though that link has long since gone. They're both informal bodies interlaced into the very formal structures of our lives. For the benefit of all, I believe.'

'I imagined so many horrors about the lodge,' said Loken.

'I know. All part of that straight up and down thing you do so well, Garvi. It's why we love you. And the lodge would like to embrace you.'

'Will there be formal vows? All the theatrical rigmarole of the Mournival?'

Aximand laughed. 'No! If you're in, you're in. There are only very simple rules. You don't talk about what passes between us here to any not of the lodge. This is downtime. Free time. The men, especially the junior ranks, need to be confident they can speak freely without any comeback. You should hear what some of them say.'

'I think I might like to.'

'That's good. You'll be given a medal to carry, just as a token. And if anyone asks you about any lodge confidence, the answer is "I can't say". There's nothing else really.'

'I've misjudged this thing,' Loken said. 'I made it quite a daemon in my head, imagining the worst.'

'I understand. Particularly given the matter of poor Jubal. And given your own staunch character.'

'Am I... to replace Jubal?'

'It's not a matter of replacement,' Little Horus said, 'and anyway, no. Jubal was a member, though he hadn't attended any meetings in years. That's why we forgot to palm away his medal before your inspection. There's your danger sign, Garvi. Not that Jubal was a member, but that he was a member and had seldom attended. We didn't know what was going on in his head. If he'd come to us and shared, we might have pre-empted the horror you endured at the Whisperheads.'

'But you told me I was to replace someone,' Loken said.

'Yes. Udon. We miss him.'

'Udon was a lodge member?'

Aximand nodded. 'A long-time brother, and, by the way, go easy on Vipus.'

Loken went over to where Nero Vipus was sitting, beside the canister fire. The lively yellow flames jumped into the dark air and sent stray sparks oscillating away into the black. Vipus looked uncomfortable, toying with the heal-seam of his new hand.

'Nero?'

'Garviel. I was bracing myself for this.'

'Why?'

'Because you... because you didn't want anyone in your command to...'

'As I understand it,' Loken said, 'and forgive me if I'm wrong, because I'm new to this, but as I understand it, the lodge is a place for free speech and openness. Not discomfort.'

Nero smiled and nodded. 'I was a member of the lodge long

before I came into your command. I respected your wishes, but I couldn't leave the brotherhood. I kept it hidden. Sometimes, I thought about asking you to join, but I knew you'd hate me for it.'

'You're the best friend I have,' Loken said. 'I couldn't hate you for anything.'

'The medal though. Jubal's medal. When you found it, you wouldn't let the matter go.'

'And all you said was "I can't say". Spoken like a true lodge member.'

Nero sniggered.

'By the way,' Loken said. 'It was you, wasn't it?'

'What?'

'Who took Jubal's medal.'

'I told Captain Aximand about your interest, just so he knew, but no, Garvi. I didn't take the medal.'

When the meeting closed, Loken walked away along one of the vast service tunnels that ran the length of the ship's bilges. Water dripped from the rusted roof, and oil rainbows shone on the dirty lakes across the deck.

Torgaddon ran to catch up with him.

'Well?' he asked.

'I was surprised to see you there,' said Loken.

'I was surprised to see you there,' Torgaddon replied. 'A starch-arse like you?'

Loken laughed. Torgaddon ran ahead and leapt up to slap his palm against a pipe high overhead. He landed with a splash.

Loken chuckled, shook his head, and did the same, slapping higher than Torgaddon had managed.

The pipe clang echoed away from them down the tunnel.

'Under the engineerium,' Torgaddon said, 'the ducts are twice as high, but I can touch them.'

'You lie.'

'I'll prove it.'

'We'll see.'

They walked on for a while. Torgaddon whistled the Legion March loudly and tunelessly.

'Nothing to say?' he asked at length.

'About what?'

'Well, about that.'

'I was misinformed. I understand better now.'

'And?'

Loken stopped and looked at Torgaddon. 'I have only one

worry,' he said. 'The lodge meets in secret, so, logically, it is good at keeping itself secret. I have a problem with secrets.'

'Which is?'

'If you get good at keeping them, who knows what kind you'll end up keeping.'

Torgaddon maintained a straight face for as long as possible and then exploded in laughter. 'No good,' he spluttered. 'I can't help it. You're so straight up and down.'

Loken smiled, but his voice was serious. 'So you keep telling me, but I mean it, Tarik. The lodge hides itself so well. It's become used to hiding things. Imagine what it could hide if it wanted to.'

'The fact that you're a starch-arse?' Torgaddon asked.

'I think that's common knowledge.'

'It is. It so is!' Torgaddon chuckled. He paused. 'So... will you attend again?'

'I can't say,' Loken replied.

SIX

Chosen instrument
Rare picts
The Emperor protects

Four full companies of the Luna Wolves had dropped into the clearing, and the megarachnid forces had perished beneath their rapacious onslaught, those that had not fled back into the shivering forests. A block of smoke, as black and vast as a mountainside, hung over the battlefield in the cold night air. Xenos bodies covered the ground, curled and shrivelled like metal shavings.

'Captain Torgaddon,' the Luna Wolf said, introducing himself formally and making the sign of the aquila.

'Captain Tarvitz,' Tarvitz responded. 'My thanks and respect for your intervention.'

'The honour's mine, Tarvitz,' Torgaddon said. He glanced around the smouldering field. 'Did you really assault here with only six men?'

'It was the only workable option in the circumstances,' Tarvitz replied.

Nearby, Bulle was freeing Lucius from the wad of megarachnid cement.

'Are you alive?' Torgaddon asked, looking over.

Lucius nodded sullenly, and set himself apart while he picked the scabs of cement off his perfect armour. Torgaddon regarded him for a moment, then turned his attention to the vox intel.

'How many with you?' Tarvitz asked.

'A speartip,' said Torgaddon. 'Four companies. A moment, please. Second Company, form up on me! Luc, secure the perimeter. Bring up the heavies. Serghar, cover the left flank! Verulam... I'm waiting! Front up the right wing.'

The vox crackled back.

'Who's the commander here?' a voice demanded.

'I am,' said Torgaddon, swinging round. Flanked by a dozen of the Emperor's Children, the tall, proud figure of Lord Eidolon crunched towards them across the fuming white slag.

'I am Eidolon,' he said, facing Torgaddon.

'Torgaddon.'

'Under the circumstances,' Eidolon said, 'I'll understand if you don't bow.'

'I can't for the life of me imagine any circumstances in which I would,' Torgaddon replied.

Eidolon's bodyguards wrenched out their combat blades.

'What did you say?' demanded one.

'I said you boys should put those pig sticks away before I hurt somebody with them.'

Eidolon raised his hand and the men sheathed their swords. 'I appreciate your intervention, Torgaddon, for the situation was grave. Also, I understand that the Luna Wolves are not bred like proper men, with proper manners. So I'll overlook your comment.'

'That's *Captain* Torgaddon,' Torgaddon replied. 'If I insulted you, in any way, let me assure you, I meant to.'

'Face to face with me,' Eidolon growled, and tore off his helm, forcing his genhanced biology to cope with the atmosphere and the radioactive wind. Torgaddon did the same. They stared into each other's eyes.

Tarvitz watched the confrontation in mounting disbelief. He'd never seen anyone stand up to Lord Eidolon.

The pair were chestplate to chestplate, Eidolon slightly taller. Torgaddon seemed to be smirking.

'How would you like this to go, Eidolon?' Torgaddon inquired. 'Would you, perhaps, like to go home with your head stuck up your arse?'

'You are a base-born cur,' Eidolon hissed.

'Just so you know,' replied Torgaddon, 'you'll have to do an awful lot better than that. I'm a base-born cur and proud of it. You know what that is?'

He pointed up at one of the stars above them.

'A star?' asked Eidolon, momentarily wrong-footed.

'Yes, probably. I haven't the faintest idea. The point is, I'm

the designated commander of the Luna Wolves speartip, come
to rescue your sorry backsides. I do this by warrant of the Warmaster himself. He's up there, in one of those stars, and right
now he thinks you're a cretin. And he'll tell Fulgrim so, next
time he meets him.'

'Do not speak my primarch's name so irreverently, you bastard. Horus will–'

'There you go again,' Torgaddon sighed, pushing Eidolon away
from him with a two-handed shove to the lord's breastplate.
'He's the Warmaster.' Another shove. 'The Warmaster. *Your* Warmaster. Show some cursed respect.'

Eidolon hesitated. 'I, of course, recognise the majesty of the
Warmaster.'

'Do you? Do you, Eidolon? Well, that's good, because I'm
it. I'm his chosen instrument here. You'll address me as if I
were the Warmaster. You'll show me some respect too! Warmaster Horus believes you've made some shit-awful mistakes
in your prosecution of this theatre. How many brothers did
you drop here? A company? How many left? Serghar? Head
count?'

'Thirty-nine live ones, Tarik,' the vox answered. 'There may be
more. Lots of body piles to dig through.'

'Thirty-nine. You were so hungry for glory you wasted more
than half a company. If I was... *Primarch* Fulgrim, I'd have your
head on a pole. The Warmaster may yet decide to do just that.
So, *Lord* Eidolon, are we clear?'

'We...' Eidolon replied slowly, '...are clear, captain.'

'Perhaps you'd like to go and undertake a review of your
forces?' Torgaddon suggested. 'The enemy will be back soon,
I'm sure, and in greater numbers.'

Eidolon gazed venomously at Torgaddon for a few seconds
and then replaced his helm. 'I will not forget this insult, captain,' he said.

'Then it was worth the trip,' Torgaddon replied, clamping on
his own helmet.

Eidolon crunched away, calling to his scattered troops. Torgaddon turned and found Tarvitz looking at him.

'What's on your mind, Tarvitz?' he asked.

I've been wanting to say that for a long time, Tarvitz wished to
say. Out loud, he said, 'What do you need me to do?'

'Gather up your squad and stand ready. When the shit comes
down next, I'd like to know you're with me.'

Tarvitz made the sign of the aquila across his chest. 'You can
count on it. How did you know where to drop?'

Torgaddon pointed at the calm sky. 'We came in where the storm had gone out,' he said.

Tarvitz hoisted Lucius to his feet. Lucius was still picking at his ruined armour.

'That Torgaddon is an odious rogue,' he said. Lucius had over-heard the entire confrontation.

'I rather like him.'

'The way he spoke to our lord? He's a dog.'

'I like dogs,' Tarvitz said.

'I believe I will kill him for his insolence.'

'Don't,' Tarvitz said. 'That would be wrong, and I'd have to hurt you if you did.'

Lucius laughed, as if Tarvitz had said something funny.

'I mean it,' Tarvitz said.

Lucius laughed even more.

It took a little under an hour to assemble their forces in the clearing. Torgaddon established contact with the fleet via the astrotelepath he had brought with him. The shield-storms raged with dreadful fury over the surrounding stalk forests, but the sky directly above the clearing remained calm.

As he marshalled the remains of his force, Tarvitz observed Torgaddon and his fellow captains conducting a further angry debate with Eidolon and Anteus. There were apparently some differences of opinion as to what their course of action should be.

After a while, Torgaddon walked away from the argument. Tarvitz guessed he was recusing himself from the quarrel before he said something else to infuriate Eidolon.

Torgaddon walked the line of the picket, stopping to talk to some of his men, and finally arrived at Tarvitz's position.

'You seem like a decent sort, Tarvitz,' he remarked. 'How do you stand that lord of yours?'

'It is my duty to stand him,' Tarvitz replied. 'It is my duty to serve. He is my lord commander. His combat record is glorious.'

'I doubt he'll be adding this endeavour to his triumph roll,' Torgaddon said. 'Tell me, did you agree with his decision to drop here?'

'I neither agreed nor disagreed,' Tarvitz replied. 'I obeyed. He is my lord commander.'

'I know that.' Torgaddon sighed. 'All right, just between you and me, Tarvitz. Brother to brother. Did you like the decision?'

'I really–'

'Oh, come on. I just saved your life. Answer me candidly and we'll call it quits.'

Tarvitz hesitated. 'I thought it a little reckless,' he admitted. 'I thought it was prompted by ambitious notions that had little to do with the safety of our company or the salvation of the missing forces.'

'Thank you for speaking honestly.'

'May I speak honestly a little more?' Tarvitz asked.

'Of course.'

'I admire you, sir,' Tarvitz said. 'For both your courage and your plain speaking. But please, remember that we are the Emperor's Children, and we are very proud. We do not like to be shown up, or belittled, nor do we like others... even other Astartes of the most noble Legions... diminishing us.'

'When you say "we" you mean Eidolon?'

'No, I mean we.'

'Very diplomatic,' said Torgaddon. 'In the early days of the crusade, the Emperor's Children fought alongside us for a time, before you had grown enough in numbers to operate autonomously.'

'I know, sir. I was there, but I was just a file trooper back then.'

'Then you'll know the esteem with which the Luna Wolves regarded your Legion. I was a junior officer back then too, but I remember distinctly that Horus said... what was it? That the Emperor's Children were the living embodiment of the Adeptus Astartes. Horus enjoys a special bond with your primarch. The Luna Wolves have cooperated militarily with just about every other Legion during this great war. We still regard yours as about the best we've ever had the honour of serving with.'

'It pleases me to hear you say so, sir,' Tarvitz replied.

'Then... how have you changed so?' Torgaddon asked. 'Is Eidolon typical of the command echelon that rules you now? His arrogance astounds me. So damned superior...'

'Our ethos is not about superiority, captain,' Tarvitz answered. 'It is about purity. But one is often mistaken for the other. We model ourselves on the Emperor, beloved by all, and in seeking to be like him, we can seem aloof and haughty.'

'Did you ever think,' asked Torgaddon, 'that while it's laudable to emulate the Emperor as much as possible, the one thing that you cannot and should not aspire to is his supremacy? He is the Emperor. He is singular. Strive to be like him in all ways, by all means, but do not presume to be on his level. No one belongs there. No one is alike to him.'

'My Legion understands that,' Tarvitz said. 'Sometimes, though, it doesn't translate well to others.'

'There's no purity in pride,' Torgaddon said. 'Nothing pure or admirable in arrogance or over-confidence.'

'My lord Eidolon knows this.'

'He should show he knows it. He led you into a disaster, and he won't even apologise for it.'

'I'm sure, in due course, my lord will formally acknowledge your efforts in relieving us and–'

'I don't want any credit,' Torgaddon said. 'You were brothers in trouble, and we came to help. That's the start and finish of it. But I had to face down the Warmaster to get permission to drop, because he believed it was insanity to send any more men to their deaths in an unknowable place against an unknowable foe. That's what Eidolon did. In the name, I imagine, of honour and pride.'

'How did you convince the Warmaster?' Tarvitz wondered.

'I didn't,' said Torgaddon. 'You did. The storm had gone out over this area, and we detected your vox scatter. You proved you were still alive down here, and the Warmaster immediately sanctioned the speartip to come and pull you out.'

Torgaddon looked up at the misty stars. 'The storms are their best weapon,' he mused. 'If we're going to wrestle this world to compliance, we'll have to find a way to beat them. Eidolon suggested the trees might be key. That they might act as generators or amplifiers for the storm. He said that once he'd destroyed the trees, the storm in this locality collapsed.'

Tarvitz paused. 'My Lord Eidolon said that?'

'Only piece of sense I've heard out of him. He said that as soon as he set charges to the trees and demolished them, the storm went out. It's an interesting theory. The Warmaster wants me to use the storm-break to pull everyone here out, but Eidolon is dead set on finding more trees and levelling them, in the hope that we can break a hole in the enemy's cover. What do you think?'

'I think... my Lord Eidolon is wise,' said Tarvitz.

Bulle had been stationed nearby, and had overheard the exchange. He could not contain himself any longer.

'Permission to speak, captain,' he said.

'Not now, Bulle,' Tarvitz said.

'Sir, I–'

'You heard him, Bulle,' Lucius cut in, walking up to them.

'What's your name, brother?' Torgaddon asked.

'Bulle, sir.'

'What did you want to say?'

'It's not important,' Lucius snorted. 'Brother Bulle speaks out of turn.'

'You are Lucius, right?' Torgaddon asked.

'Captain Lucius.'

'And Bulle was one of the men who stood over you and fought to keep you alive?'

'He did. I am honoured by his service.'

'Maybe you could let him talk, then?' Torgaddon suggested.

'It would be inappropriate,' said Lucius.

'Tell you what,' Torgaddon said. 'As commander of the spear-tip, I believe I have authority here. I'll decide who talks and who doesn't. Bulle? Let's hear you, brother.'

Bulle looked awkwardly at Lucius and Tarvitz.

'That was an order,' said Torgaddon.

'My Lord Eidolon did not destroy the trees, sir. Captain Tarvitz did it. He insisted. My Lord Eidolon then chastised him for the act, claiming it was a waste of charges.'

'Is this true?' Torgaddon asked.

'Yes,' said Tarvitz.

'Why did you do it?'

'Because it didn't seem right for the bodies of our dead to hang in such ignominy,' Tarvitz said.

'And you'd let Eidolon take the credit and not say anything?'

'He is my lord.'

'Thank you, brother,' Torgaddon said to Bulle. He glanced at Lucius. 'Reprimand him or punish him in any way for speaking out and I'll have the Warmaster himself personally deprive you of your rank.'

Torgaddon turned to Tarvitz. 'It's a funny thing. It shouldn't matter, but it does. Now I know you felled the trees, I feel better about pursuing that line of action. Eidolon clearly knows a good idea when someone else has it. Let's go cut down a few more trees, Tarvitz. You can show me how it's done.'

Torgaddon walked away, shouting out orders for muster and movement. Tarvitz and Lucius exchanged long looks, and then Lucius turned and walked away.

The armed force moved away from the clearing and back into the thickets of the stalk forest. They passed back into the embrace of the storm cover. Torgaddon had his Terminator squads lead the way. The man-tanks, under the command of Trice Rokus, ignited their heavy blades, and cut a path, felling the stalks to clear a wide avenue into the forest swathe.

They pressed on beneath the wild storms for twenty kilometres. Twice, megarachnid skirmish parties assaulted their lines, but the speartip drew its phalanxes close and, with the advantage of range created by the cleared avenue, slaughtered the attackers with their bolters.

The landscape began to change. They were apparently reaching the edge of a vast plateau, and the ground began to slope away steeply before them. The stalk growth became more patchy and sparse, clinging to the rocky, ferrous soil of the descent. A wide basin spread out below them, a rift valley. Here, the spongy, marshy ground was covered with thousands of small, coned trees, rising some ten metres high, which dotted the terrain like fungal growths. The trees, hard and stony and composed of the same milky cement from which the murder trees had been built, peppered the depression like armour studs.

As they descended onto it, the Astartes found the land at the base of the rift swampy and slick, decorated with long, thin lakes of water stained orange by the iron content of the soil. The flash of the overhead storms scintillated in reflection from the long, slender pools. They looked like claw wounds in the earth.

The air was busy with fibrous grey bugs that milled and swirled interminably in the stagnant atmosphere. Larger flying things, flitting like bats, hunted the bugs in quick, sharp swoops.

At the mouth of the rift, they discovered six more thorn trees arranged in a silent grove. Reduced cadavers and residual meat and armour adorned their barbs. Blood Angels, and Imperial army. There was no sign of the winged clades, though fifty kilometres away, over the stalk forests, black shapes could be seen, circling madly in the lightning-washed sky.

'Lay them low,' Torgaddon ordered. Moy nodded and began to gather munitions. 'Find Captain Tarvitz,' Torgaddon called. 'He'll show you how to do it.'

Loken remained on the strategium for the first three hours after the drop, long enough to celebrate Torgaddon's signal from the surface. The speartip had secured the dropsite, and formed up with the residue of Lord Eidolon's company. After that, the atmosphere had become, strangely, more tense. They were waiting to hear Torgaddon's field decision. Abaddon, cautious and closed, had already ordered Stormbirds prepped for extraction flights. Aximand paced, silently. The Warmaster had withdrawn into his sanctum with Maloghurst.

Loken leant at the strategium rail for a while, overlooking the bustle of the vast bridge below, and discussed tactics with

Tybalt Marr. Marr and Moy were both Sons of Horus, cast in his image so firmly that they looked like identical twins. At some point in the Legion's history, they had earned the nicknames 'the Either' and the 'the Or', referring to the fact that they were almost interchangeable. It was often hard to distinguish between them, they were so alike. One might do as well as the other.

Both were competent field officers, with a rack of victories each that would make any captain proud, though neither had attained the glories of Sedirae or Abaddon. They were precise, efficient and workmanlike in their leadership, but they were Luna Wolves, and what was workmanlike to that fratery was exemplary to any other regiment.

As Marr spoke, it became clear to Loken that he was envious of his 'twin's' selection to the undertaking. It was Horus's habit to send both or neither. They worked well together, complementing one another, as if somehow anticipating one another's decisions, but the ballot for the speartip had been democratic and fair. Moy had won a place. Marr had not.

Marr rattled on to Loken, evidently sublimating his worries about his brother's fate. After a while, Qruze came over to join them at the rail.

Iacton Qruze was an anachronism. Ancient and rather tiresome, he had been a captain in the Legion since its inception, his prominence entirely eclipsed once Horus had been repatriated and given command by the Emperor. He was the product of another era, a throwback to the years of the Unification Wars and the bad old times, stubborn and slightly cantankerous, a vestigial trace of the way the Legion had gone about things in antiquity.

'Brothers,' he greeted them as he came up. Qruze still had a habit, perhaps unconscious, of making the salute of the single clenched fist against his breast, the old pre-Unity symbol, rather than the double-handed eagle. He had a long, tanned face, deeply lined with creases and folds, and his hair was white. He spoke softly, expecting others to make the effort to listen, and believed that it was his quiet tone that had, over the years, earned him the nickname 'the Half-heard'.

Loken knew this wasn't so. Qruze's wits were not as sharp as they'd once been, and he often appeared tired or inappropriate in his commentary or advice. He was known as 'the Half-heard' because his pronouncements were best not listened to too closely.

Qruze believed he stood as a wise father-figure to the Legion, and no one had the spite to inform him otherwise. There had been several quiet attempts to deprive him of company command, just as Qruze had made several attempts to become elected to the first captaincy.

By duration of service, he should have been so long since. Loken believed that the Warmaster regarded Qruze with some pity and couldn't abide the idea of retiring him. Qruze was an irksome relic, regarded by the rest of them with equal measures of affection and frustration, who could not accept that the Legion had matured and advanced without him.

'We will be out of this in a day,' he announced categorically to Loken and Marr. 'You mark my words, young men. A day, and the commander will order extraction.'

'Tarik is doing well,' Loken began.

'The boy Torgaddon has been lucky, but he cannot press this to a conclusion. You mark my words. In and out, in a day.'

'I wish I was down there,' Marr said.

'Foolish thoughts,' Qruze decided. 'It's only a rescue run. I cannot for the life of me imagine what the Emperor's Children thought they were doing, going into this hell. I served with them, in the early days, you know? Fine fellows. Very proper. They taught the Wolves a thing or two about decorum, thank you very much! Model soldiers. Put us to shame on the Eastern Fringe, so they did, but that was back then.'

'It certainly was,' said Loken.

'It most certainly was,' agreed Qruze, missing the irony entirely. 'I can't imagine what they thought they were doing here.'

'Prosecuting a war?' Loken suggested.

Qruze looked at him diffidently. 'Are you mocking me, Garviel?'

'Never, sir. I would never do that.'

'I hope we're deployed,' Marr grumbled, 'and soon.'

'We won't be,' Qruze declared. He rubbed the patchy grey goatee that decorated his long, lined face. He was most certainly not a Son of Horus.

'I've business to attend to,' Loken said, excusing himself. 'I'll take my leave, brothers.'

Marr glared at Loken, annoyed to be left alone with the Half-heard. Loken winked and wandered off, hearing Qruze embark on one of his long and tortuous 'stories' to Marr.

Loken went downship to the barrack decks of Tenth Company. His men were waiting, half-armoured, weapons and kit spread out for fitting. Apprenta and servitors manned portable lathes and forge carts, making final, precise adjustments to plate segments. This was just displacement activity: the men had been battle-ready for weeks.

Loken took the time to appraise Vipus and the other squad leaders of the situation, and then spoke briefly to some of the new blood warriors they'd raised to company service during the voyage. These men were especially tense. One Forty Twenty might see their baptism as full Astartes.

In the solitude of his arming chamber, Loken sat for a while, running through certain mental exercises designed to promote clarity and concentration. When he grew bored of them, he took up the book Sindermann had loaned him.

He'd read a good deal less of *The Chronicles of Ursh* during the voyage than he'd intended. The commander had kept him busy. He folded the heavy, yellowed pages open with ungloved hands and found his place.

The *Chronicles* were as raw and brutal as Sindermann had promised. Long-forgotten cities were routinely sacked, or burned, or simply evaporated in nuclear storms. Seas were regularly stained with blood, skies with ash, and landscapes were often carpeted with the bleached and numberless bones of the conquered. When armies marched, they marched a billion strong, the ragged banners of a million standards swaying above their heads in the atomic winds. The battles were stupendous maelstroms of blades and spiked black helms and baying horns, lit by the fires of cannons and burners. Page after page celebrated the cruel practices and equally cruel character of the despot Kalagann.

It amused Loken, for the most part. Fanciful logic abounded, as did an air of strained realism. Feats of arms were described that no pre-Unity warriors could have accomplished. These, after all, were the feral hosts of techno-barbarians that the proto-Astartes, in their crude thunder armour, had been created to bring to heel. Kalagann's great generals, Lurtois and Sheng Khal and, later, Quallodon, were described in language more appropriate to primarchs. They carved, for Kalagann, an impossibly vast domain during the latter part of the Age of Strife.

Loken had skipped ahead once or twice, and saw that later parts of the work recounted the fall of Kalagann, and described the apocalyptic conquest of Ursh by the forces of Unity. He saw passages referring to enemy warriors bearing the thunderbolt and lightning emblem, which had been the personal device of the Emperor before the eagle of the Imperium was formalised. These men saluted with the fist of unity, as Qruze still did, and were clearly arrayed in thunder armour. Loken wondered if the Emperor himself would be mentioned, and in what terms, and wanted to look to see if he could recognise the names of any of the proto-Astartes warriors.

But he felt he owed it to Kyril Sindermann to read the thing thoroughly, and returned to his original place and order. He quickly became absorbed by a sequence detailing Shang Khal's campaigns against the Nordafrik Conclaves. Shang Khal had assembled a significant horde of irregular levies from the southern client states of Ursh, and used them to support his main armed strengths, including the infamous Tupelov Lancers and the Red Engines, during the invasion.

The Nordafrik technogogues had preserved a great deal more high technology for the good of their conclaves than Ursh possessed, and sheer envy, more than anything, motivated the war. Kalagann was hungry for the fine instruments and mechanisms the conclaves owned.

Eight epic battles marked Shang Khal's advance into the Nord-afrik zones, the greatest of them being Xozer. Over a period of nine days and nights, the war machines of the Red Engines blasted their way across the cultivated agroponic pastures and reduced them back to the desert, from which they had originally been irrigated and nurtured. They cut through the laserthorn hedges and the jewelled walls of the outer conclave, and unleashed dirty atomics into the heart of the ruling zone, before the Lancers led a tidal wave of screaming berserkers through the breach into the earthly paradise of the gardens at Xozer, the last fragment of Eden on a corrupted planet.

Which they, of course, trampled underfoot.

Loken felt himself skipping ahead again, as the account bogged down in interminable lists of battle glories and honour rolls. Then his eyes alighted on a strange phrase, and he read back. At the heart of the ruling zone, a ninth, minor battle had marked the conquest, almost as an afterthought. One bastion had remained, the *murengon*, or walled sanctuary, where the last hierophants of the conclaves held out, practising, so the text said, their 'sciomancy by the flame lyght of their burning realm'.

Shang Khal, wishing swift resolution to the conquest, had sent Anult Keyser to crush the sanctuary. Keyser was lord martial of the Tupelov Lancers and, by various bonds of honour, could call freely upon the services of the Roma, a squadron of mercenary fliers whose richly decorated interceptors, legend said, never landed or touched the earth, but lived eternally in the scope of the air. During the advance on the murengon, Keyser's oneirocriticks – and by that word, Loken understood the text meant 'interpreters of dreams' – had warned of the hierophants' sciomancy, and their phantasmagorian ways.

When the battle began, just as the oneirocriticks had warned, majiks were unleashed. Plagues of insects, as thick as monsoon rain and so vast in their swirling masses that they blacked out the sun, fell upon Keyser's forces, choking air intakes, weapon ports, visors, ears, mouths and throats. Water boiled without fire. Engines overheated or burned out. Men turned to stone, or their bones turned to paste, or their flesh succumbed to boils and buboes and flaked off their limbs. Others went mad. Some became daemons and turned upon their own.

Loken stopped reading and went back over the sentences again. '...and where the plagueing ynsects did nott crawle, or madness lye, so men did blister and recompose them ownselves ynto the terrible likeness of daimons, such foule pests as the afreet and the d'genny that persist in the silent desert places. In such visage, they turned uponn theyr kin and gnawed then upon their bloody bones...'

Some became daemons and turned upon their own.

Anult Keyser himself was slain by one such daemon, which had, just hours previously, been his loyal lieutenant, Wilhym Mardol.

When Shang Khal heard the news, he flew into a fury, and went at once to the scene, bringing with him what the text described as his 'wrathsingers', who appeared to be magi of some sort. Their leader, or master, was a man called Mafeo Orde, and somehow, Orde drew the wrathsingers into a kind of remote warfare with the hierophants. The text was annoyingly vague about exactly what occurred next, almost as if it was beyond the understanding of the writer. Words such as 'sorcery' and 'majik' were employed frequently, without qualification, and there were invocations to dark, primordial gods that the writer clearly thought his audience would have some prior knowledge of. Since the start of the text, Loken had seen references to Kalagann's 'sorcerous' powers, and the 'invisibles artes' that formed a key part of Ursh's power, but he had taken them to be hyperbole. This was the first time sorcery had appeared on the page, as a kind of fact.

The earth trembled, as if afraid. The sky tore like silk. Many in the Urshite force heard the voices of the dead whispering to them. Men caught fire, and walked around, bathed in lambent flames that did not consume them, pleading for help. The remote war between the wrathsingers and the hierophants lasted for six days, and when it ended, the ancient desert was thick with snow, and the skies had turned blood red. The air formations of the Roma had been forced to flee, lest their craft be torn from the heavens by screaming angels and dashed down upon the ground.

At the end of it, all the wrathsingers were dead, except Orde himself. The murengon was a smoking hole in the ground, its stone walls so hideously melted by heat they had become slips of glass. And the hierophants were extinct.

The chapter ended. Loken looked up. He had been so enthralled, he wondered if he had missed an alert or a summons. The arming chamber was quiet. No signal runes blinked on the wall panel.

He began to read the next part, but the narrative had switched to a sequence concerning some northern war against the nomadic caterpillar cities of the Taiga. He skipped a few pages, hunting for further mention of Orde or sorcery, but could detect none. Frustrated, he set the book aside.

Sindermann… had he given Loken this work deliberately? To what end? A joke? Some veiled message? Loken resolved to study it, section by section, and take his questions to his mentor.

But he'd had enough of it for the time being. His mind was clouded and he wanted it clear for combat. He walked to the vox-plate beside the chamber door and activated it.

'Officer of the watch. How can I serve, captain?'

'Any word from the speartip?'

'I'll check, sir. No, nothing routed to you.'

'Thank you. Keep me appraised.'

'Sir.'

Loken clicked the vox off. He walked back to where he had left the book, picked it up, and marked his page. He was using a thin sliver of parchment torn from the edge of one of his oath papers as a marker. He closed the book, and went to put it away in the battered metal crate where he kept his belongings. There were precious few items in there, little to show for such a long life. It reminded him of Jubal's meagre effects. If I die, Loken thought, who will clean this out? What will they preserve? Most of the bric-a-brac was worthless trophies, stuff that only meant something to him: the handle of a combat knife he'd broken off in the gullet of a greenskin warboss; long feathers, now musty and threadbare, from the hatchet-beak that had almost killed him on Balthasar, decades earlier; a piece of dirty, rusted wire, knotted at each end, which he'd used to garrote a nameless eldar champion when all other weapons had been lost to him.

That had been a fight. A real test. He decided he ought to tell Oliton about it, sometime. How long ago was it? Ages past, though the memory was as fresh and heavy as if it had been yesterday. Two warriors, deprived of their common arsenals by the circumstance of war, stalking one another through the fluttering leaves of a wind-lashed forest. Such skill and tenacity. Loken had almost wept in admiration for the opponent he had slain.

All that was left was the wire and the memory, and when Loken passed, only the wire would remain. Whoever came here after his death would likely throw it out, assuming it to be a twist of rusty wire and nothing more.

His rummaging hands turned up something that would not be cast away. The data-slate Karkasy had given him. The data-slate from Keeler.

Loken sat back and switched it on, flicking through the picts again. Rare picts. Tenth Company, assembled on the embarkation deck for war. The company banner. Loken himself, framed against the bold colour of the flag. Loken taking his oath of moment. The Mournival group: Abaddon, Aximand, Torgaddon and himself, with Targost and Sedirae.

He loved the picts. They were the most precious material gift he'd ever received, and the most unexpected. Loken hoped that, through Oliton, he might leave some sort of useful legacy. He doubted it would be anything like as significant as these images.

He scrolled the picts back into their file, and was about to de-activate the slate when he saw, for the first time, there was another file lodged in the memory. It was stored, perhaps deliberately, in an annex to the slate's main data folder, hidden from cursory view. Only a tiny icon digit '2' betrayed that the slate was loaded with more than one file of material.

It took him a moment to find the annex and open it. It looked like a folder of deleted or discarded images, but there was a tag caption attached to it that read 'IN CONFIDENCE'.

Loken cued it. The first pict washed into colour on the slate's small screen. He stared at it, puzzled. It was dark, unbalanced in colour or contrast, almost unreadable. He thumbed up the next, and the next.

And stared in horrid fascination.

He was looking at Jubal, or rather the thing that Jubal had become in the final moments. A rabid, insane mass, ploughing down a dark hallway towards the viewer.

There were more shots. The light, the sheen of them, seemed unnatural, as if the picter unit that had captured them had found difficulty reading the image. There were clear, sharp-focused droplets of gore and sweat frozen in the air as they splashed out in the foreground. The thing behind them, the thing that had shaken the droplets out, was fuzzy and imprecise, but never less than abominable.

Loken switched the slate off and began to strip off his armour as quickly as he could. When he was down to the thick, mimetic polymers of his sub-suit bodyglove, he stopped, and pulled on a long, hooded robe of brown hemp. He took up the slate, and a vox-cuff, and went outside.

'Nero!'

Vipus appeared, fully plated except for his helm. He frowned in confusion at the sight of Loken's attire.

'Garvi? Where's your armour? What's going on?'

'I've an errand to run,' Loken replied quickly, clasping on the vox-cuff. 'You have command here in my absence.'

'I do?'

'I'll return shortly.' Loken held up the cuff, and allowed it to auto-sync channels with Vipus's vox system. Small notice lights on the cuff and the collar of Vipus's armour flashed rapidly and then glowed in unison.

'If the situation changes, if we're called forwards, vox me immediately. I'll not be derelict of my duties. But there's something I must do.'

'Like what?'

'I can't say,' Loken said.

Nero Vipus paused and nodded. 'Just as you say, brother. I'll cover for you and alert you of any changes.' He stood watching as his captain, hooded and hurrying, slipped away down an access tunnel and was swallowed by the shadows.

The game was going so badly against him that Ignace Karkasy decided it was high time he got his fellow players drunk. Six of them, with a fairly disinterested crowd of onlookers, occupied a table booth at the forward end of the Retreat, under the gilded arches. Beyond them, remembrancers and off-duty soldiers, along with ship personnel relaxing between shifts, and a few iterators (one could never tell if an iterator was on duty or off) mingled in the long, crowded chamber, drinking, eating, gaming and talking. There was a busy chatter, laughter, the clink of glasses. Someone was playing a viol. The Retreat had become quite the social focus of the flagship.

Just a week or two before, a sozzled second engineer had explained to Karkasy that there had never been any gleeful society aboard the *Vengeful Spirit*, nor on any other line ship in his experience. Just quiet after-shift drinking and sullen gambling schools. The remembrancers had brought their bohemian habits to the warship, and the crewmen and soldiery had been drawn to its light.

The iterators, and some senior ship officers, had clucked

disapprovingly at the growing, casual conviviality, but the mingling was permitted. When Comnenus had voiced his objections to the unlicensed carousing the *Vengeful Spirit* was now host to, someone – and Karkasy suspected the commander himself – had reminded him that the purpose of the remembrancers was to meet and fraternise. Soldiers and Navy adepts flocked to the Retreat, hoping to find some poor poet or chronicler who would record their thoughts and experiences for posterity. Though mostly, they came to get a skinful, play cards and meet girls.

It was, in Karkasy's opinion, the finest achievement of the remembrancer programme to date: to remind the expedition warriors they were human, and to offer them some fun.

And to win rudely from them at cards.

The game was *targe main*, and they were playing with a pack of square-cut cards that Karkasy had once lent to Mersadie Oliton. There were two other remembrancers at the table, along with a junior deck officer, a sergeant-at-arms and a gunnery oberst. They were using, as bidding tokens, scurfs of gilt that someone had cheerfully scraped off one of the stateroom's golden columns. Karkasy had to admit that the remembrancers had abused their facilities terribly. Not only had the columns been half-stripped to the ironwork, the murals had been written on and painted over. Verses had been inscribed in patches of sky between the shoulders of ancient heroes, and those ancient heroes found themselves facing eternity wearing comical beards and eye patches. In places, walls and ceilings had been whitewashed, or lined with gum-paper, and entire tracts of new composition inscribed upon them.

'I'll sit this hand out,' Karkasy announced, and pushed back his chair, scooping up the meagre handful of scraped gilt flecks he still owned. 'I'll find us all some drinks.'

The other players murmured approval as the sergeant-at-arms dealt the next hand. The junior deck officer, his head sunk low and his eyes hooded, thumped the heels of his hands together in mock applause, his elbows on the table top, his hands fixed high above his lolling head.

Karkasy moved off through the crowd to find Zinkman. Zinkman, a sculptor, had drink, an apparently bottomless reserve of it, though where he sourced it from was anyone's guess. Someone had suggested Zinkman had a private arrangement with a crewman in climate control who distilled the stuff. Zinkman owed Karkasy at least one bottle, from an unfinished game of *merci merci* two nights earlier.

He asked for Zinkman at two or three tables, and also made

inquiries with various groups standing about the place. The viol
music had stopped for the moment, and some around were
clapping as Carnegi, the composer, clambered up onto a table.
Carnegi owned a half-decent baritone voice, and most nights he
could be prevailed upon to sing popular opera or take requests.

Karkasy had one.

A squall of laughter burst from nearby, where a small, lively
group had gathered on stools and recliners to hear a remembrancer give a reading from his latest work. In one of the wall
booths formed by the once golden colonnade, Karkasy saw
Ameri Sechloss carefully inscribing her latest remembrance in
red ink over a wall she'd washed white with stolen hull paint.
She'd masked out an image of the Emperor triumphant at Cyclo-
nis. Someone would complain about that. Parts of the Emperor,
beloved by all, poked out from around the corners of her white
splash.

'Zinkman? Anyone? Zinkman?' he asked.

'I think he's over there,' one of the remembrancers watching
Sechloss suggested.

Karkasy turned, and stood on tiptoe to peer across the press.
The Retreat was crowded tonight. A figure had just walked in
through the chamber's main entrance. Karkasy frowned. He
didn't need to be on tiptoe to spot this newcomer. Robed and
hooded, the figure towered over the rest of the crowd, by far
and away the tallest person in the busy room. Not a human's
build at all. The general noise level did not drop, but it was
clear the newcomer was attracting attention. People were whispering, and casting sly looks in his direction.

Karkasy edged his way through the crowd, the only person in
the chamber bold enough to approach the visitor. The hooded
figure was standing just inside the entrance arch, scanning the
crowd in search of someone.

'Captain?' Karkasy asked, coming forwards and peering up
under the cowl. 'Captain Loken?'

'Karkasy.' Loken seemed very uncomfortable.

'Were you looking for me, sir? I didn't think we were due to
meet until tomorrow.'

'I was… I was looking for Keeler. Is she here?'

'Here? Oh no. She doesn't come here. Please, captain, come
with me. You don't want to be in here.'

'Don't I?'

'I can read the discomfort in your manner, and when we meet,
you never step inside the archway. Come on.'

They went back out through the arched entranceway into the

cool, gloomy quiet of the corridor outside. A few people passed them by, heading into the Retreat.

'It must be important,' Karkasy said, 'for you to set foot in there.'

'It is,' Loken replied. He kept the hood of his robe up, and his manner remained stiff and guarded. 'I need to find Keeler.'

'She doesn't much frequent the common spaces. She's probably in her quarters.'

'Where's that?'

'You could have asked the watch officer for her billet reference.'

'I'm asking you, Ignace.'

'That important, and that private,' Karkasy remarked. Loken made no reply. Karkasy shrugged. 'Come with me and I'll show you.'

Karkasy led the captain down into the warren of the residential deck where the remembrancers were billeted. The echoing metal companionways were cold, the walls brushed steel and marked with patches of damp. This area had once been a billet for army officers but, like the Retreat, it had ceased to feel anything like the interior of a military vessel. Music echoed from some chambers, often through half-open hatches. The sound of hysterical laughter came from one room, and from another the din of a man and a woman having a ferocious quarrel. Paper notices had been pasted to the walls: slogans and verses and essays on the nature of man and war. Murals had also been daubed in places, some of them magnificent, some of them crude. There was litter on the deck, an odd shoe, an empty bottle, scraps of paper.

'Here,' said Karkasy. The shutter of Keeler's billet was closed. 'Would you like me to…?' Karkasy asked, gesturing to the door.

'Yes.'

Karkasy rapped his fist against the shutter and listened. After a moment, he rapped again, harder. 'Euphrati? Euphrati, are you there?'

The shutter slid open, and the scent of body warmth spilled out into the cool corridor. Karkasy was face to face with a lean young man, naked but for a pair of half-buttoned army fatigue pants. The man was sinewy and tough, hard-bodied and hard-faced. He had numerical tattoos on his upper arms, and metal tags on a chain around his neck.

'What?' he snapped at Karkasy.

'I want to see Euphrati.'

'Piss off,' the soldier replied. 'She doesn't want to see you.'

Karkasy backed away a step. The soldier was physically intimidating.

'Cool down,' said Loken, looming behind Karkasy and lowering his hood. He stared down at the soldier. 'Cool down, and I won't ask your name and unit.'

The soldier looked up at Loken with wide eyes. 'She... she's not here,' he said.

Loken pushed past him. The soldier tried to block him, but Loken caught his right wrist in one hand and turned it neatly so that the man suddenly found himself contorted in a disabling lock.

'Don't do that again,' Loken advised, and released his hold, adding a tiny shove that dropped the soldier onto his hands and knees.

The room was quite small, and very cluttered. Discarded clothes and rumpled bedding littered the floor space, and the shelves and low table were covered with bottles and unwashed plates.

Keeler stood on the far side of the room, beside the unmade cot. She had pulled a sheet around her slim, naked body and stared at Loken with disdain. She looked weary, unhealthy. Her hair was tangled and there were dark shadows under her eyes.

'It's all right, Leef,' she told the soldier. 'I'll see you later.'

Still wary, the soldier pulled on his vest and boots, snatched up his jacket, and left, casting one last murderous look at Loken.

'He's a good man,' Keeler said. 'He cares for me.'

'Army?'

'Yes. It's called fraternisation. Does Ignace have to be here for this?'

Karkasy was hovering in the doorway. Loken turned. 'Thank you for your help,' he said. 'I'll see you tomorrow.'

Karkasy nodded. 'All right,' he said. Reluctantly, he walked away. Loken closed the shutter. He looked back at Keeler. She was pouring clear liquor from a flask into a shot glass.

'Can I interest you?' she asked, gesturing with the flask. 'In the spirit of hospitality?'

He shook his head.

'Ah. I suppose you Astartes don't drink. Another biological flaw ironed out of you.'

'We drink well enough, under certain circumstances.'

'And this isn't one, I suppose?' Keeler put the flask down and took up her glass. She walked back to the cot, holding the sheet around her with one hand and sipping from the glass held in the other. Holding her drink out steady, she settled herself down on the cot, drawing her legs up and folding the sheet modestly over herself.

'I can imagine why you're here, captain,' she said. 'I'm just amazed. I expected you weeks ago.'

'I apologise. I only found the second file tonight. I obviously hadn't looked carefully enough.'

'What do you think of my work?'

'Astonishing. I'm flattered by the picts you shot on the embarkation deck. I meant to send you a note, thanking you for copying them to me. Again, I apologise. The second file, however, is...'

'Problematic?' she suggested.

'At the very least,' he said.

'Why don't you sit down?' she asked. Loken shrugged off his robe and sat carefully on a metal stool beside the cluttered table.

'I wasn't aware any picts existed of that incident,' Loken said.

'I didn't know I'd shot them,' Keeler replied, taking another sip. 'I'd forgotten, I think. When the first captain asked me at the time, I said no, I hadn't taken anything. I found them later. I was surprised.'

'Why did you send them to me?' he asked.

She shrugged. 'I don't really know. You have to understand, sir, that I was... traumatised. For a while, I was in a very bad way. The shock of it all. I was a mess, but I got through it. I'm content now, stable, centred. My friends helped me through it. Ignace, Sadie, some others. They were kind to me. They stopped me from hurting myself.'

'Hurting yourself?'

She fiddled with her glass, her eyes focused on the floor. 'Nightmares, Captain Loken. Terrible visions, when I was asleep and when I was awake. I found myself crying for no reason. I drank too much. I acquired a small pistol, and spent long hours wondering if I had the strength to use it.'

She looked up at him. 'It was in that... that pit of despair that I sent you those picts. It was a cry for help, I suppose. I don't know. I can't remember. Like I said, I'm past that now. I'm fine, and feel a little foolish for bothering you, especially as my efforts took so long to reach you. You wasted a visit.'

'I'm glad you feel better,' Loken said, 'but I haven't wasted anything. We need to talk about those images. Who's seen them?'

'No one. You and me. No one else.'

'Did you not think it wise to inform the first captain of their existence?'

Keeler shook her head. 'No. No, not at all. Not back then. If I'd gone to the authorities, they'd have confiscated them... destroyed them, probably, and told me the same story about a

wild beast. The first captain was very certain it was a wild beast,
some xenos creature, and he was very certain I should keep my
mouth shut. For the sake of morale. The picts were a lifeline
for me, back then. They proved I wasn't going mad. That's why
I sent them to you.'

'Am I not part of the authorities?'

She laughed. 'You were there, Loken. You were there. You saw
it. I took a chance. I thought you might respond and–'

'And what?'

'Tell me the truth of it.'

Loken hesitated.

'Oh, don't worry,' she admonished, rising to refill her glass. 'I
don't want to know the truth now. A wild beast. A wild beast.
I've got over it. This late in the day, captain, I don't expect you
to break loyalty and tell me something you're sworn not to tell.
It was a foolish notion, which I now regret. My turn to apologise to you.'

She looked over at him, tugging up the edge of the sheet to
cover her bosom. 'I've deleted my copies. All of them. You have
my word. The only ones that exist are the ones I sent to you.'

Loken took out the data-slate and placed it on the table. He
had to push dirty crockery aside to make a space for it. Keeler
looked at the slate for a long while, and then knocked back her
glass and refilled it.

'Imagine that,' she said, her hand trembling as it lifted the
flask. 'I'm terrified even to have them back in the room.'

'I don't think you're as over it as you like to pretend,' Loken
said.

'Really?' she sneered. She put down her glass and ran the fingers of her free hand through her short blonde hair. 'Hell with
it, then, since you're here. Hell with it.'

She walked over and snatched up the slate. 'Wild beast, eh?
Wild beast?'

'Some form of vicious predator indigenous to the mountain
region that–'

'Forgive me, that's so much shit,' she said. She snapped the
slate into the reader slot of a compact edit engine on the far side
of the room. Some of her picters and spare lenses littered the
bench beside it. The engine whirred into life, and the screen lit
up, cold and white. 'What did you make of the discrepancies?'

'Discrepancies?' Loken asked.

'Yes.' She expertly tapped commands into the engine's controls, and selected the file. With a stab of her index finger, she
opened the first image. It bloomed on the screen.

'Terra, I can't look at it,' she said, turning away.

'Switch it off, Keeler.'

'No, you look at it. Look at the visual distortion there. Surely you noticed that? It's like it's there and yet not there. Like it's phasing in and out of reality.'

'A signal error. The conditions and the poor light foxed your picter's sensors and–'

'I know how to use a picter, captain, and I know how to recognise poor exposure, lens flare, and digital malformance. That's not it. Look.'

She punched up the second pict, and half-looked at it, gesturing with her hand. 'Look at the background. And the droplets of blood in the foreground there. Perfect pict capture. But the thing itself. I've never seen anything create that effect on a high-gain instrument. That "wild beast" is out of sync with the physical continuity around it. Which is, captain, exactly as I saw it. You've studied these closely, no doubt?'

'No,' said Loken.

Keeler pulled up another image. She stared at it fully this time, and then looked away. 'There, you see? The afterimage? It's on all of them, but this is the clearest.'

'I don't see...'

'I'll boost the contrast and lose a little of the motion blurring.' She fiddled with the engine's controls. 'There. See now?'

Loken stared. What had at first seemed to be a frothy, milky ghost blurring across the image of the nightmare thing had resolved clearly thanks to her manipulation. Superimposed on the fuzzy abomination was a semi-human shape, echoing the pose and posture of the creature. Though it was faint, there was no mistaking the shrieking face and wracked body of Xavyer Jubal.

'Know him?' she asked. 'I don't, but I recognise the physiognomy and build of an Astartes when I see it. Why would my picter register that, unless...'

Loken didn't reply.

Keeler switched the screen off, popped out the slate and tossed it back to Loken. He caught it neatly. She went back over to the cot and flopped down.

'That's what I wanted you to explain to me,' she said. 'That's why I sent you the picts. When I was in my deepest, darkest pits of madness, that's what I was hoping you'd come and explain to me, but don't worry. I'm past that now. I'm fine. A wild beast, that's all it was. A wild beast.'

Loken gazed at the slate in his hand. He could barely imagine what Keeler had been through. It had been bad enough for the rest of them, but he and Nero and Sindermann had all enjoyed the benefit of proper closure. They'd been told the truth. Keeler hadn't. She was smart and bright and clever, and she'd seen the holes in the story, the awful inconsistencies that proved there had been more to the event than the first captain's explanation. And she'd managed with that knowledge, coped with it, alone.

'What did you think it was?' he asked.

'Something awful that we should never know about,' she replied. 'Throne, Loken. Please don't take pity on me now. Please don't decide to tell me.'

'I won't,' he said. 'I can't. It was a wild beast. Euphrati, how did you deal with it?'

'What do you mean?'

'You say you're fine now. How are you fine?'

'My friends helped me through. I told you.'

Loken got up, picked up the flask, and went over to the cot. He sat down on the end of the mattress and refilled the glass she held out.

'Thank you,' she said. 'I've found strength. I've found–'

For a moment, Loken was certain she had been about to say 'faith'.

'What?'

'Trust. Trust in the Imperium. In the Emperor. In you.'

'In me?'

'Not you, personally. In the Astartes, in the Imperial army, in every branch of mankind's warrior force that is dedicated to the protection of us mere mortals.' She took a sip and sniggered. 'The Emperor, you see, protects.'

'Of course he does,' said Loken.

'No, no, you misunderstand,' said Keeler, folding her arms around her raised, sheet-covered knees. 'He actually does. He protects mankind, through the Legions, through the martial corps, through the war machines of the Mechanicum. He understands the dangers. The inconsistencies. He uses you, and all the instruments like you, to protect us from harm. To protect our physical bodies from murder and damage, to protect our minds from madness, to protect our souls. This is what I now understand. This is what this trauma has taught me, and I am thankful for it. There are insane dangers in the cosmos, dangers that mankind is fundamentally unable to comprehend, let alone survive. So he protects us. There are truths out there that would drive us mad by one fleeting glimpse of them. So he chooses not to share them with us. That's why he made you.'

'That's a glorious concept,' Loken admitted.

'In the Whisperheads, that day… You saved me, didn't you? You shot that thing apart. Now you save me again, by keeping the truth to yourself. Does it hurt?'

'Does what hurt?'

'The truth you keep hidden?'

'Sometimes,' he said.

'Remember, Garviel. The Emperor is our truth and our light. If we trust in him, he will protect.'

'Where did you get that from?' Loken asked.

'A friend. Garviel, I have only one concern. A lingering thing that will not quit my mind. You Astartes are loyal, through and through. You keep to your own, and never break confidence.'

'And?'

'Tonight, I really believe you would have told me something, but for the loyalty you keep with your brothers. I admire that, but answer me this. How far does your loyalty go? Whatever it was happened to us in the Whisperheads, I believe an Astartes brother was part of it. But you close ranks. What has to happen before you forsake your loyalty to the Legion and recognise your loyalty to the rest of us?'

'I don't know what you mean,' he said.

'Yes, you do. If a brother turns on his brothers again, will you cover that up too? How many have to turn before you act? One? A squad? A company? How long will you keep your secrets? What will it take for you to cast aside the fraternal bonds of the Legion and cry out "This is wrong!"?'

'You're suggesting an impossible–'

'No, I'm not. You, of all people, know I'm not. If it can happen to one, it can happen to others. You're all so drilled and perfect and identical. You march to the same beat and do whatever is asked of you. Loken, do you know of any Astartes who would break step? Would you?'

'I…'

'Would you? If you saw the rot, a hint of corruption, would you step out of your regimented life and stand against it? For the greater good of mankind, I mean?'

'It's not going to happen,' Loken said. 'That would never happen. You're suggesting civil disunity. Civil war. That is against every fibre of the Imperium as the Emperor has created it. With Horus as Warmaster, as our guiding light, such a possibility is beyond countenance. The Imperium is firm and strong, and of one purpose. There are inconsistencies, Euphrati, just like there are wars and plagues and famines. They hurt us, but they do not kill us. We rise above them and move onwards.'

'It rather depends,' she remarked, 'where those inconsistencies occur.'

Loken's vox-cuff suddenly began to bleat. Loken raised his wrist, and thumbed the call stud. 'I'm on my way,' he said. He looked back at her.

'Let's talk again, Euphrati,' he said.

She nodded. He leant forwards and kissed her on the forehead. 'Be well. Be better. Look to your friends.'

'Are you my friend?' she asked.

'Know it,' he said. He got up and retrieved his robe from the floor.

'Garviel,' she called from the cot.

'Yes?'

'Delete those images, please. For me. They don't need to exist.'

He nodded, opened the shutter, and stepped out into the chill of the hall.

Once the shutter had closed, Keeler got up off the cot and let the sheet fall from her. Naked, she padded over to a cupboard, knelt and opened its doors. From inside, she took out two candles and a small figurine of the Emperor. She placed them on the top of the cupboard, and lit the candles with an igniter. Then she rummaged in the cupboard and pulled out the dog-eared pamphlet that Leef had given her. It was a cheap, crude thing, badly pressed from a mechanical bulk-printer. There were ink soils along its edges, and rather a lot of spelling mistakes in the text.

Keeler didn't care. She opened the first page and, bowed before the makeshift shrine, she began to read.

'The Emperor of Mankind is the Light and the Way, and all his actions are for the benefit of mankind, which is his people. The Emperor is God and God is the Emperor, so it is taught in the Lectitio Divinitatus, and above all things, the Emperor will protect...'

Loken ran down the companionways of the remembrancers' billet wing, his cloak billowing out behind him. Sirens were sounding. Men and women peered out of doorways to look at him as he passed by.

He raised his cuff to his mouth. 'Nero. Report! Is it Tarik? Has something happened?'

The vox crackled and Vipus's voice issued tinnily from the cuff speaker. 'Something's happened all right, Garvi. Get back here.'

'What? What's happened?'

'A ship, that's what. A battle-barge has just translated in-system behind us. It's Sanguinius. Sanguinius himself has come.'

SEVEN

Lord of the Angels
Brotherhood in Spiderland
Interdiction

Just a week or so earlier, during one of their regular, private interviews, Loken had finally told Mersadie Oliton about the Great Triumph after Ullanor.

'You cannot imagine it,' he said.

'I can try.'

Loken smiled. 'The Mechanicum had planed smooth an entire continent as a stage for the event.'

'Planed smooth? What?'

'With industrial meltas and geoformer engines. Mountains were erased and their matter used to infill valleys. The surface was left smooth and endless, a vast table of dry, polished rock chippings. It took months to accomplish.'

'It ought to have taken centuries!'

'You underestimate the industry of the Mechanicum. They sent four labour fleets to undertake the work. They made a stage worthy of an Emperor, so broad it could know midnight at one end and midday at the other.'

'You exaggerate!' she cried, with a delighted snort.

'Maybe I do. Have you known me do that before?'

Oliton shook her head.

'You have to understand, this was a singular event. It was a Triumph to mark the turn of an era, and the Emperor, beloved of all, knew it. He knew it had to be remembered. It was the end of the Ullanor campaign, the end of the crusade, the coronation of the Warmaster. It was a chance for the Astartes to say farewell to the Emperor before his departure to Terra, after two centuries of personal leadership. We wept as he announced his retirement from the field. Can you picture that, Mersadie? A hundred thousand warriors, weeping?'

She nodded. 'I think it was a shame no remembrancers were there to witness it. It was a moment that comes only once every epoch.'

'It was a private affair.'

She laughed again. 'A hundred thousand present, a continent levelled for the event, and it was a private affair?'

Loken looked at her. 'Even now, you don't understand us, do you? You still think on a very human scale.'

'I stand corrected,' she replied.

'I meant no offence,' he said, noticing her expression, 'but it was a private affair. A ceremony. A hundred thousand Astartes. Eight million army regulars. Legions of Titan war machines, like forests of steel. Armour units by the hundred, formations of tanks, thousands upon thousands. Warships filling the low orbit, eclipsed by the squadrons of aircraft flying over in unending echelons. Banners and standards, so many banners and standards.'

He fell silent for a moment, remembering. 'The Mechanicum had made a roadway. Half a kilometre wide, and five hundred kilometres long, a straight line across the stage they had levelled. On each side of this road, every five metres, was an iron post topped with the skull of a greenskin, trophies of the Ullanor war. Beyond the roadway, to either hand, promethium fires burned in rockcrete basins. For five hundred kilometres. The heat was intense. We marched along the roadway in review, passing below the dais on which the Emperor stood, beneath a steel-scale canopy. The dais was the only raised structure the Mechanicum had left, the root of an old mountain. We marched in review, and then assembled on the wide plain below the dais.'

'Who marched?'

'All of us. Fourteen Legions were represented, either in total or by a company. The others were engaged in wars too remote to allow them to attend. The Luna Wolves were there en mass, of course. Nine primarchs were there, Mersadie. Nine. Horus, Dorn, Angron, Fulgrim, Lorgar, Mortarion, Sanguinius, Magnus, the Khan. The rest had sent ambassadors. Such a spectacle. You cannot imagine.'

'I'm still trying.'

Loken shook his head. 'I'm still trying to believe I was there.'

'What were they like?'

'You think I met them? I was just another brother-warrior marching in the file. In my life, lady, I have seen almost all of the primarchs at one time or another, but mostly from a distance. I've personally spoken to two of them. Until my election to the Mournival, I didn't move in such elevated circles. I know the primarchs as distant figures. At the Triumph, I could barely believe so many were present.'

'But still, you had impressions?'

'Indelible impressions. Each one, so mighty, so huge and so proud. They seemed to embody human characteristics. Angron, red and angry; Dorn solid and implacable; Magnus, veiled in mystery, and Sanguinius, of course. So perfect. So charismatic.'

'I've heard this of him.'

'Then you've heard the truth.'

His long black hair was pressed down by the weight of the shawl of gold chain he wore across his head. The edges of it framed his solemn features. He had marked his cheeks with grey ash in mourning.

An attendant stood by with ink pot and brush to paint the ritual tears of grief on his cheeks, but Primarch Sanguinius shook his head, making the chain shawl clink. 'I have real tears,' he said.

He turned, not to his brother Horus, but to Torgaddon.

'Show me, Tarik,' he said.

Torgaddon nodded. The wind moaned around the still figures assembled on the lonely hillside, and rain pattered off their armour plate. Torgaddon gestured, and Tarvitz, Bulle and Lucius stepped forwards, holding out the dirty relics.

'These men, my lord,' Torgaddon said, his voice unusually shaky, 'these Children of the Emperor, recovered these remains selflessly, and it is fit they offer them to you themselves.'

'You did this honour?' Sanguinius asked Tarvitz.

'I did, my lord.'

Sanguinius took the battered Astartes helm from Tarvitz's hands and studied it. He towered over the captain, his golden plate badged with rubies and bright jewels, and marked, like the armour of the Warmaster, with the unblinking eye of Terra. Sanguinius's vast wings, like the pinions of a giant eagle, were furled against his back, and hung with silver bands and loops of pearls.

Sanguinius turned the helm over in his hands, and regarded the armourer's mark inside the rim.

'Eight knight leopard,' he said.

At his side, Chapter Master Raldoron began to inspect the manifest.

'Don't trouble yourself, Ral,' Sanguinius told him. 'I know the mark. Captain Thoros. He will be missed.'

Sanguinius handed the helm to Raldoron and nodded to Tarvitz. 'Thank you for this kindness, captain,' he said. He looked across at Eidolon. 'And to you, sir, my gratitude that you came to Frome's help so urgently.'

Eidolon bowed, and seemed to ignore the dark glare the Warmaster was casting in his direction.

Sanguinius turned to Torgaddon. 'And to you, Tarik, most of all. For breaking this nightmare open.'

'I do only what my Warmaster instructs me,' Torgaddon replied.

Sanguinius looked over at Horus. 'Is that right?'

'Tarik had some latitude,' Horus smiled. He stepped forwards and embraced Sanguinius to his breast. No two primarchs were as close as the Warmaster and the Angel. They had barely been out of each other's company since Sanguinius's arrival.

The majestic Lord of the Blood Angels, the IX Legion Astartes, stepped back, and looked out across the forlorn landscape. Around the base of the ragged hill, hundreds of armoured figures waited in silence. The vast majority wore either the hard white of the Luna Wolves or the arterial red of the Angels, save for the remnants of the detachment of Emperor's Children, a small knot of purple and gold. Behind the Astartes, the war machines waited in the rain, silent and black, ringing the gathering like spectral mourners. Beyond them, the hosts of the Imperial army stood in observance, banners flapping sluggishly in the cold breeze. Their armoured vehicles and troop carriers were drawn up in echelon, and many of the soldiers had clambered up to stand on the hulls to get a better view of the proceedings.

Torgaddon's speartip had razed a large sector of the landscape, demolishing stone trees wherever they could be found, and thus taming the formidable weather in this part of Murder. The sky had faded to a mottled powder-grey, run through with thin white bars of cloud, and rain fell softly and persistently, reducing visibility in the distances to a foggy blur. At the Warmaster's command, the main force of the assembled Imperial ships had made planetfall in the comparative safety of the storm-free zone.

'In the old philosophies of Terra,' Sanguinius said, 'so I have read, vengeance was seen as a weak motive and a flaw of the spirit. It is hard for me to feel so noble today. I would cleanse this rock in the memory of my lost brothers, and their kin who died trying to save them.'

The Angel looked at his primarch brother. 'But that is not necessary. Vengeance is not necessary. There is xenos here, implacable alien menace that rejects any civilised intercourse with mankind, and has greeted us with murder and murder alone. That suffices. As the Emperor, beloved by all, has taught us, since the start of our crusade, what is anathema to mankind must be dealt with directly to ensure the continued survival of the Imperium. Will you stand with me?'

'We will murder Murder together,' Horus replied.

Once those words were spoken, the Astartes went to war for six months. Supported by the army and the devices of the Mechanicum, they assaulted the bleak, shivering latitudes of the world called Murder, and laid waste the megarachnid.

It was a glorious war, in many ways, and not an easy one. No matter how many of them were slaughtered, the megarachnid did not cower or turn in retreat. It seemed as if they had no will, nor any spirit, to be broken. They came on and on, issuing forth from cracks and crevasses in the ruddy land, day after day, set for further dispute. At times, it felt as if there was an endless reserve of them, as if unimaginably vast nests of them infested the mantle of the planet, or as if ceaseless subterranean factories manufactured more and yet more of them every day to replace the losses delivered by the Imperial forces. For their own part, no matter how many of them they slaughtered, the warriors of the Imperium did not come to underestimate the megarachnid. They were lethal and tough, and so numerous as to put a man out of countenance. 'The fiftieth beast I killed,' Little Horus remarked at one stage, 'was as hard to overcome as the first.'

Loken, like many of the Luna Wolves present, personally rejoiced in the circumstances of the conflict, for it was the first time since his election as Warmaster that the commander had led them on the field. Early on, in the command habitent one rainy evening, the Mournival had gently tried to dissuade Horus from field operations. Abaddon had attempted, deftly, to portray the Warmaster's role and importance as a thing of a much higher consequence than martial engagement.

'Am I not fit for it?' Horus had scowled, the rain drumming on the canopy overhead.

'I mean you are too precious for it, lord,' Abaddon had countered. 'This is one world, one field of war. The Emperor has charged you with the concerns of all worlds and all fields. Your scope is–'

'Ezekyle...' The Warmaster's tone had betrayed a warning note, and he had switched to Cthonic, a clear sign his mind was on war and nothing else, '...do not presume to instruct me on my duties.'

'Lord, I would not!' Abaddon exclaimed immediately, with a respectful bow.

'Precious is the word,' Aximand had put in quickly, coming to Abaddon's aid. 'If you were to be wounded, to fall even, it would–'

Horus rose, glaring. 'Now you deride my abilities as a warrior, little one? Have you grown soft since my ascendance?'

'No, my lord, no...'

Only Torgaddon, it seemed, had noticed the glimmer of amusement behind the Warmaster's pantomime of anger.

'We're only afraid you won't leave any glory for us,' he said.

Horus began to laugh. Realising he had been playing with them, the members of the Mournival began to laugh too. Horus cuffed Abaddon across the shoulder and pinched Aximand's cheek.

'We'll war this together, my sons,' he said. 'That is how I was made. If I had suspected, back at Ullanor, that the rank of Warmaster would require me to relinquish the glories of the field forever, I would not have accepted it. Someone else could have taken the honour. Guilliman or the Lion, perhaps. They ache for it, after all.'

More loud amusement followed. The laughter of Cthonians is dark and hard, but the laughter of Luna Wolves is a harder thing altogether.

Afterwards, Loken wondered if the Warmaster had not been using his sly political skills yet again. He had avoided the central issue entirely, and deflected their concerns with good humour and an appeal to their code as warriors. It was his way of telling them that, for all their good counsel, there were some matters on which his mind would not be swayed. Loken was sure that Sanguinius was the reason. Horus could not bring himself to stand by and watch his dearest brother go to war. Horus could not resist the temptation of fighting shoulder to shoulder with Sanguinius, as they had done in the old days.

Horus would not let himself be outshone, even by the one he loved most dearly.

To see them together on the battlefield was a heart-stopping thing. Two gods of war, raging at the head of a tide of red and white. Dozens of times, they accomplished victories in partnership on Murder that should, had what followed been any different, become deeds as lauded and immortal as Ullanor or any other great triumph.

Indeed the war as a whole produced many extraordinary feats that posterity ought to have celebrated, especially now the remembrancers were amongst them.

Like all her kind, Mersadie Oliton was not permitted to descend to the surface with the fighting echelons, but she absorbed every detail transmitted back from the surface, the daily ebb and flow of the brutal warfare, the losses and the gains. When, periodically, Loken returned with his company to the flagship to rest, repair and re-arm, she quizzed him furiously, and made him describe all he had seen. Horus and Sanguinius, side by side, was what interested her the most, but she was captivated by all his accounts.

Many battles had been vast, pitched affairs, where thousands of Astartes led tens of thousands of army troopers against endless files of the megarachnid. Loken struggled to find the language to describe it, and sometimes felt himself, foolishly, borrowing lurid turns of phrase he had picked up from *The Chronicles of Ursh*. He told her of the great things he had witnessed, the particular moments. How Luc Sedirae had led his company against a formation of megarachnid twenty-five deep and one hundred across, and splintered it in under half an hour. How Sacrus Carminus, Captain of the Blood Angels Third Company, had held the line against a buzzing host of winged clades through one long, hideous afternoon. How Iacton Qruze, despite his stubborn, tiresome ways, had broken the back of a surprise megarachnid assault, and proved there was mettle in him still. How Tybalt Marr, 'the Either', had taken the low mountains in two days and elevated himself at last into the ranks of the exceptional. How the megarachnid had revealed more, and yet more nightmarish biological variations, including massive clades that strode forwards like armoured war machines, and how the Titans of the Mechanicum, led at the van by the *Dies Irae* of the Legio Mortis, smote them apart and trampled their blackened wing cases underfoot. How Saul Tarvitz, fighting at Torgaddon's side rather than in the cohort of his arrogant lord Eidolon, renewed the Luna Wolves' respect for the Emperor's Children through several feats of arms.

Tarvitz and Torgaddon had achieved a brotherhood during the

war and eased the discontent between the two Legions. Loken had heard rumours that Eidolon was initially displeased with Tarvitz's deportment, until he recognised how simple brotherhood and effort was redeeming his mistake. Eidolon, though he would never admit it, realised full well he was out of favour with the Warmaster, but as time passed, he found he was at least tolerated within the bounds of the commander's war-tent, and consulted along with the other officers.

Sanguinius had also smoothed the way. He knew his brother Horus was keen to rebuke Fulgrim for the high-handed qualities his Astartes had lately displayed. Horus and Fulgrim were close, almost as close as Sanguinius and the Warmaster. It dismayed the Lord of Angels to see a potential rift in the making.

'You cannot afford dissent,' Sanguinius had said. 'As Warmaster, you must have the undivided respect of the primarchs, just as the Emperor had. Moreover, you and Fulgrim are too long bound as brothers for you to fall to bickering.'

The conversation had taken place during a brief hiatus in the fighting, during the sixth week, when Raldoron and Sedirae were leading the main force west into a series of valleys and narrow defiles along the foothills of a great bank of mountains. The two primarchs had rested for a day in a command camp some leagues behind the advance. Loken remembered it well. He and the others of the Mournival had been present in the main war-tent when Sanguinius brought the matter up.

'I don't bicker,' Horus said, as his armourers removed his heavy, mud-flecked wargear and bathed his limbs. 'The Emperor's Children have always been proud, but that pride is becoming insolence. Brother or not, Fulgrim must know his place. I have trouble enough with Angron's bloody rages and Perturabo's damn petulence. I'll not brook disrespect from such a close ally.'

'Was it Fulgrim's error, or his man Eidolon's?' Sanguinius asked.

'Fulgrim made Eidolon lord commander. He favours his merits, and evidently trusts him, and approves of his manner. If Eidolon embodies the character of the III Legion, then I have issue with it. Not just here. I need to know I can rely upon the Emperor's Children.'

'And why do you think you can't?'

Horus paused while an attendant washed his face, then spat sidelong into a bowl held ready by another. 'Because they're too damn proud of themselves.'

'Are not all Astartes proud of their own cohort?' Sanguinius took a sip of wine. He looked over at the Mournival. 'Are you not proud, Ezekyle?'

'To the ends of creation, my lord,' Abaddon replied.

'If I may, sir,' said Torgaddon, 'there is a difference. There is a man's natural pride and loyalty to his own Legion. That may be a boastful pride, and the source of rivalry between Astartes. But the Emperor's Children seem particularly haughty, as if above the likes of us. Not all of them, I hasten to add.'

Listening, Loken knew Torgaddon was referring to Tarvitz and the other friends he had made amongst Tarvitz's unit.

Sanguinius nodded. 'It is their mindset. It has always been so. They seek perfection, to be the best they can, to echo the perfection of the Emperor himself. It is not superiority. Fulgrim has explained this to me himself.'

'And Fulgrim may believe so,' Horus said, 'but superiority is how it manifests amongst some of his men. There was once mutual respect, but now they sneer and condescend. I fear it is my new rank that they resent. I'll not have it.'

'They don't resent you,' Sanguinius said.

'Maybe, but they resent the role my rank invests upon my Legion. The Luna Wolves have always been seen as rude barbarians. The flint of Cthonia is in their hearts, and the smudge of its dirt upon their skins. The Children regard the Luna Wolves as peers only by dint of my Legion's record in war. The Wolves sport no finery or elegant manners. We are cheerfully raw where they are regal.'

'Then maybe it is time to consider doing what the Emperor suggested,' Sanguinius said.

Horus shook his head emphatically. 'I refused that on Ullanor, honour though it was. I'll not contemplate it again.'

'Things change. You are Warmaster now. All the Legions Astartes must recognise the preeminence of the XVI Legion. Perhaps some need to be reminded.'

Horus snorted. 'I don't see Russ trying to clean up his berserk horde and rebrand them to court respect.'

'Leman Russ is not Warmaster,' said Sanguinius. 'Your title changed, brother, at the Emperor's command, so that all the rest of us would be in no mistake as to the power you wield and the trust the Emperor placed in you. Perhaps the same thing must happen to your Legion.'

Later, as they trudged west through the drizzle, following the plodding Titans across red mudflats and skeins of surface water, Loken asked Abaddon what the Lord of Angels had meant.

'At Ullanor,' the first captain answered, 'the beloved Emperor advised our commander to rename the XVI Legion, so there might be no mistake as to the power of our authority.'

'What name did he wish us to take?' Loken asked.

'The Sons of Horus,' Abaddon replied.

The sixth month of the campaign was drawing to a close when the strangers arrived.

Over the period of a few days, the vessels of the expedition, high in orbit, became aware of curious signals and etheric displacements that suggested the activity of starships nearby, and various attempts were made to locate the source. Advised of the situation, the Warmaster presumed that other reinforcements were on the verge of arrival, perhaps even additional units from the Emperor's Children. Patrolling scout ships, sent out by Master Comnenus, and cruisers on picket control, could find no concrete trace of any vessels, but many reported spectral readings, like the precursor field elevations that announced an imminent translation. The expedition fleet left high anchor and took station on a battle-ready grid, with the *Vengeful Spirit* and the *Proudheart* in the vanguard, and the *Misericord* and the *Red Tear*, Sanguinius's flagship, on the trailing flank.

When the strangers finally appeared, they came in rapidly and confidently, gunning in from a translation point at the system edges: three massive capital ships, of a build pattern and drive signature unknown to Imperial records.

As they came closer, they began to broadcast what seemed to be challenge signals. The nature of these signals was remarkably similar to the repeat of the outstation beacons, untranslatable and, according to the Warmaster, akin to music.

The ships were big. Visual relay showed them to be bright, sleek and silver-white, shaped like royal sceptres, with heavy prows, long, lean hulls and splayed drive sections. The largest of them was twice the keel length of the *Vengeful Spirit*.

General alert was sounded throughout the fleet, shields raised and weapons unshrouded. The Warmaster made immediate preparations to quit the surface and return to his flagship. Engagements with the megarachnid were hastily broken off, and the ground forces recalled into a single host. Horus ordered Comnenus to make hail, and hold fire unless fired upon. There seemed a high probability that these vessels belonged to the megarachnid, come from other worlds in support of the nests on Murder.

The ships did not respond directly to the hails, but continued to broadcast their own, curious signals. They prowled in close, and halted within firing distance of the expedition formation.

Then they spoke. Not with one voice, but with a chorus of voices, uttering the same words, overlaid with more of the curious musical transmissions. The message was received cleanly by the Imperial vox, and also by the astrotelepaths, conveyed with such force and authority, Ing Mae Sing and her adepts winced.

They spoke in the language of mankind. 'Did you not see the warnings we left?' they said. 'What have you done here?'

PART THREE

THE DREADFUL SAGITTARY

ONE

Make no mistakes
Cousins far removed
Other ways

As an unexpected sequel to the war on Murder, they became the guests of the interex, and right from the start of their sojourn, voices had begun to call for war.

Eidolon was one, and a vociferous one at that, but Eidolon was out of favour and easy to dismiss. Maloghurst was another, and so too were Sedirae and Targost, and Goshen, and Raldoron of the Blood Angels. Such men were not so easy to ignore.

Sanguinius kept his counsel, waiting for the Warmaster's decision, understanding that Horus needed his brother primarch's unequivocal support.

The argument, best summarised by Maloghurst, ran as follows: the people of the interex are of our blood and we descend from common ancestry, so they are lost kin. But they differ from us in fundamental ways, and these are so profound, so inescapable, that they are cause for legitimate war. They contradict absolutely the essential tenets of Imperial culture as expressed by the Emperor, and such contradictions cannot be tolerated.

For the while, Horus tolerated them well enough. Loken could understand why. The warriors of the interex were easy to admire, easy to like. They were gracious and noble, and once the misunderstanding had been explained, utterly without hostility.

It took a strange incident for Loken to learn the truth behind the Warmaster's thinking. It took place during the voyage, the nine-week voyage from Murder to the nearest outpost world of the interex, the mingled ships of the expedition and its hangers-on trailing the sleek vessels of the interex flotilla.

The Mournival had come to Horus's private staterooms, and a bitter row had erupted. Abaddon had been swayed by the arguments for war. Both Maloghurst and Sedirae had been whispering in his ear. He was convinced enough to face the Warmaster and not back down. Voices had been raised. Loken had watched in growing amazement as Abaddon and the Warmaster bellowed at each other. Loken had seen Abaddon wrathful before, in the heat of combat, but he had never seen the commander so ill-tempered. Horus's fury startled him a little, almost scared him.

As ever, Torgaddon was trying to diffuse the confrontation with levity. Loken could see that even Tarik was dismayed by the anger on show.

'You have no choice!' Abaddon snarled. 'We have seen enough already to know that their ways are in opposition to ours! You must–'

'Must?' Horus roared. 'Must I? You are Mournival, Abaddon! You advise and you counsel, and that is your place! Do not imagine you can tell me what to do!'

'I don't have to! There is no choice, and you know what must be done!'

'Get out!'

'You know it in your heart!'

'Get out!' Horus yelled, and cast aside his drinking cup with such force it shattered on the steel deck. He glared at Abaddon, teeth clenched. 'Get out, Ezekyle, before I look to find another first captain!'

Abaddon glowered back for a moment, spat on the floor and stormed from the chamber. The others stood in stunned silence.

Horus turned, his head bowed. 'Torgaddon?' he said quietly.

'Lord, yes?'

'Go after him, please. Calm him down. Tell him if he craves my forgiveness in an hour or two, I might soften enough to hear him, but he'd better be on his knees when he does it, and his voice had better not rise above a whisper.'

Torgaddon bowed and left the chamber immediately. Loken and Aximand glanced at one another, made an awkward salute, and turned to follow him out.

'You two stay,' Horus growled.

They stopped in their tracks. When they turned back, they saw the Warmaster was shaking his head, wiping a hand across his mouth. A kind of smile informed his wide-set eyes. 'Throne, my sons. How the molten core of Cthonia burns in us sometimes.'

Horus sat down on one of the long, cushioned couches, and waved to them with a casual flick of his hand. 'Hard as a rock, Cthonia, hot as hell in the heart. Volcanic. We've all known the heat of the deep mines. We all know how the lava spurts up sometimes, without warning. It's in us all, and it wrought us all. Hard as rock with a burning heart. Sit, sit. Take wine. Forgive my outburst. I'd have you close. Half a Mournival is better than nothing.'

They sat on the couch facing him. Horus took up a fresh cup, and poured wine from a silver ewer. 'The wise one and the quiet one,' he said. Loken wasn't sure which the Warmaster thought he was. 'Counsel me, then. You were both entirely too silent during that debate.'

Aximand cleared his throat. 'Ezekyle had... a point,' he began. He stiffened as he saw the Warmaster raise his eyebrows.

'Go on, little one.'

'We... that is to say... we prosecute this crusade according to certain doctrines. For two centuries, we have done so. Laws of life, laws on which the Imperium is founded. They are not arbitrary. They were given to us, to uphold, by the Emperor himself.'

'Beloved of all,' Horus said.

'The Emperor's doctrines have guided us since the start. We have never disobeyed them.' Aximand paused, then added, 'Before.'

'You think this is disobedience, little one?' Horus asked. Aximand shrugged. 'What about you, Garviel?' Horus asked. 'Are you with Aximand on this?'

Loken looked back into the Warmaster's eyes. 'I know why we ought to make war upon the interex, sir,' he said. 'What interests me is why you think we shouldn't.'

Horus smiled. 'At last, a thinking man.' He rose to his feet and, carrying his cup carefully, walked across to the right-hand wall of the stateroom, a section of which had been richly decorated with a mural. The painting showed the Emperor, ascendant above all, catching the spinning constellations in his outstretched hand. 'The stars,' Horus said. 'See, there? How he scoops them up? The zodiacs swirl into his grasp like fireflies. The stars are mankind's birthright. That's what he told me. That's one of the first things he told me when we met. I was like a child then, raised up from nothing. He set me at his side, and pointed to the heavens. Those points of light, he said, are what we have been waiting generations to master. Imagine, Horus, every one

a human culture, every one a realm of beauty and magnificence, free from strife, free from war, free from bloodshed and
the tyrannous oppression of alien overlords. Make no mistake,
he said, and they will be ours.'

Horus slowly traced his fingers across the whorl of painted
stars until his hand met the image of the Emperor's hand. He
took his touch away and looked back at Aximand and Loken.
'As a foundling, on Cthonia, I saw the stars very infrequently.
The sky was so often thick with foundry smoke and ash, but
you remember, of course.'

'Yes,' said Loken. Little Horus nodded.

'On those few nights when the stars were visible, I wondered
at them. Wondered what they were and what they meant. Little,
mysterious sparks of light, they had to have some purpose in
being there. I wondered such things every day of my life until
the Emperor came. I was not surprised when he told me how
important they were.'

'I'll tell you a thing,' said Horus, walking back to them and
resuming his seat. 'The first thing my father gave me was an
astrological text. It was a simple thing, a child's primer. I have it
here somewhere. He noted my wonder in the stars, and wished
me to learn and understand.'

He paused. Loken was always captivated whenever Horus
began to refer to the Emperor as 'my father'. It had happened a
few times since Loken had been part of the inner circle, and on
every occasion it had led to unguarded revelations.

'There were zodiac charts in it. In the text.' Horus took a sip
of his wine and smiled at the memory. 'I learned them all. In
one evening. Not just the names, but the patterns, the associations, the structure. All twenty signs. The next day, my father
laughed at my appetite for knowledge. He told me the zodiac
signs were old and unreliable models, now that the explorator
fleets had begun detailed cosmological mapping. He told me
that the twenty signs in the heavens would one day be matched
by twenty sons like me. Each son would embody the character
and notion of a particular zodiac group. He asked me which
one I liked the best.'

'What did you answer?' Loken asked.

Horus sat back, and chuckled. 'I told him I liked all the patterns they made. I told him I was glad to finally have names
for the sparks of light in the sky. I told him I liked Leos, naturally, for his regal fury, and Skorpos, for his armour and warlike
blade. I told him that Tauromach appealed to my sense of stub-
bornness, and Arbitos to my sense of fairness and balance.' The

Warmaster shook his head, sadly. 'My father said he admired my choices, but was surprised I had not picked another in particular. He showed me again the horseman with the bow, the galloping warrior. The dreadful Sagittary, he said. Most warlike of all. Strong, relentless, unbridled, swift and sure of his mark. In ancient times, he told me, this was the greatest sign of all. The centaur, the horse-man, the hunter-warrior, had been beloved in the old ages. In Anatoly, in his own childhood, the centaur had been a revered symbol. A rider upon a horse, so he said, armed with a bow. The most potent martial instrument of its age, conquering all before it. Over time, myth had blended horseman and steed into one form. The perfect synthesis of man and war machine. That is what you must learn to be, he told me. That is what you must master. One day, you must command my armies, my instruments of war, as if they were an extension of your own person. Man and horse, as one, galloping the heavens, submitting to no foe. At Ullanor, he gave me this.'

Horus set down his cup, and leaned forward to show them the weathered gold ring he wore on the smallest finger of his left hand. It was so eroded by age that the image was indistinct. Loken thought he could detect hooves, a man's arm, a bent bow.

'It was made in Persia, the year before the Emperor was born. The dreadful Sagittary. This is you now, he said to me. My Warmaster, my centaur. Half man, half army, embedded in the Legions of the Imperium. Where you turn, so the Legions turn. Where you move, so they move. Where you strike, so they strike. Ride on without me, my son, and the armies will ride with you.'

There was a long silence. 'So you see,' Horus smiled. 'I am predisposed to like the dreadful Sagittary, now we meet him, face to face.'

His smile was infectious. Both Loken and Aximand nodded and laughed.

'Now tell them the real reason,' a voice said.

They turned. Sanguinius stood in an archway at the far end of the chamber, behind a veil of white silk. He had been listening. The Lord of Angels brushed the silk hanging aside, and stepped into the stateroom, the crests of his wings brushing the glossy material. He was dressed in a simple white robe, clasped at the waist with a girdle of gold links. He was eating fruit from a bowl.

Loken and Aximand stood up quickly.

'Sit down,' Sanguinius said. 'My brother's in the mood to open his heart, so you had better hear the truth.'

'I don't believe–' Horus began.

Sanguinius scooped one of the small, red fruits from his bowl and threw it at Horus.

'Tell them the rest,' he sniggered.

Horus caught the thrown fruit, gazed at it, then bit into it. He wiped the juice off his chin with the back of his hand and looked across at Loken and Aximand.

'Remember the start of my story?' he asked. 'What the Emperor said to me about the stars? *Make no mistake, and they will be ours.*'

He took another two bites, threw the fruit stone away, and swallowed the flesh before he continued. 'Sanguinius, my dear brother, is right, for Sanguinius has always been my conscience.'

Sanguinius shrugged, an odd gesture for a giant with furled wings.

'*Make no mistake,*' Horus continued. 'Those three words. Make no mistake. I am Warmaster, by the Emperor's decree. I cannot fail him. I cannot make mistakes.'

'Sir?' Aximand ventured.

'Since Ullanor, little one, I have made two. Or been party to two, and that is enough, for the responsibility for all expedition mistakes falls to me in the final count.'

'What mistakes?' asked Loken.

'Mistakes. Misunderstandings.' Horus stroked his hand across his brow. 'Sixty-Three Nineteen. Our first endeavour. My first as Warmaster. How much blood was spilt there, blood from misunderstanding? We misread the signs and paid the price. Poor, dear Sejanus. I miss him still. That whole war, even that nightmare up on the mountains you had to endure, Garviel... a mistake. I could have handled it differently. Sixty-Three Nineteen could have been brought to compliance without bloodshed.'

'No, sir,' said Loken emphatically. 'They were too set in their ways, and their ways were set against us. We could not have made them compliant without a war.'

Horus shook his head. 'You are kind, Garviel, but you are mistaken. There were ways. There should have been ways. I should have been able to sway that civilisation without a shot being fired. The Emperor would have done so.'

'I don't believe he would,' Aximand said.

'Then there's Murder,' Horus continued, ignoring Little Horus's remark. 'Or Spiderland, as the interex has it. What is the way of their name for it again?'

'Urisarach,' Sanguinius said, helpfully. 'Though I think the word only works with the appropriate harmonic accompaniment.'

'Spiderland will suffice, then,' said Horus. 'What did we waste there? What misunderstandings did we make? The interex left us warnings to stay away, and we ignored them. An embargoed world, an asylum for the creatures they had bested in war, and we walked straight in.'

'We weren't to know,' Sanguinius said.

'We should have known!' Horus snapped.

'Therein lies the difference between our philosophy and that of the interex,' Aximand said. 'We cannot endure the existence of a malign alien race. They subjugate it, but refrain from annihilating it. Instead, they deprive it of space travel and exile it to a prison world.'

'We annihilate,' said Horus. 'They find a means around such drastic measures. Which of us is the most humane?'

Aximand rose to his feet. 'I find myself with Ezekyle on this. Tolerance is weakness. The interex is admirable, but it is forgiving and generous in its dealings with xenos breeds who deserve no quarter.'

'It has brought them to book, and learned to live in sympathy,' said Horus. 'It has trained the kinebrach to–'

'And that's the best example I can offer!' Aximand replied. 'The kinebrach. It embraces them as part of its culture.'

'I will not make another rash or premature decision,' Horus stated flatly. 'I have made too many, and my Warmastery is threatened by my mistakes. I will understand the interex, and learn from it, and parlay with it, and only then will I decide if it has strayed too far. They are a fine people. Perhaps we can learn from them for a change.'

The music was hard to get used to. Sometimes it was magisterial and loud, especially when the meturge players struck up, and sometimes it was just a quiet whisper, like a buzz, like tinnitus, but it seldom went away. The people of the interex called it the aria, and it was a fundamental part of their communication. They still used language – indeed, their spoken language was an evolved human dialect closer in form to the prime language of Terra than Cthonic – but they had long ago formulated the aria as an accompaniment and enhancement of speech, and as a mode of translation.

Scrutinised by the iterators during the voyage, the aria proved to be hard to define. Essentially, it was a form of high mathematics, a universal constant that transcended linguistic barriers, but the mathematical structures were expressed through specific harmonic and melodic modes which, to the untrained ear, sounded like music. Strands of complex melody rang in the background of all the interex's vocal transmissions, and when one of their kind spoke face to face, it was usual to have one or more of the

meturge players accompany his speech with their instruments.
The meturge players were the translators and envoys.

Tall, like all the people of the interex, they wore long coats of
a glossy, green fibre, laced with slender gold piping. The flesh
of their ears was distended and splayed, by genetic and surgical enhancement, like the ears of bats or other nocturnal fliers.
Comm technology, the equivalent of vox, was laced around the
high collars of their coats, and each one carried an instrument
strapped across his chest, a device with amplifiers and coiled
pipes, and numerous digital keys on which the meturge player's nimble fingers constantly rested. A swan-necked mouthpiece
rose from the top of each instrument, enabling the player to
blow, hum, or vocalise into the device.

The first meeting between Imperium and interex had been
formal and cautious. Envoys came aboard the *Vengeful Spirit*,
escorted by meturge players and soldiers. The envoys were uni-
formly handsome and lean, with piercing eyes. Their hair was
dressed short, and intricate dermatoglyphics – Loken suspected
permanent tattoos – decorated either the left or right-hand sides
of their faces. They wore knee-length robes of a soft, pale blue
cloth, under which they were dressed in close-fitting clothing
woven from the same, glossy fibre that composed the meturge
players' coats.

The soldiers were impressive. Fifty of them, led by officers,
had descended from their shuttle. Taller than the envoys, they
were clad from crown to toe in metal armour of burnished silver and emerald green with aposematic chevrons of scarlet.
The armour was of almost delicate design, and sheathed their
bodies tightly; it was in no way as massive or heavy-set as the
Astartes' plate. The soldiers – variously gleves or sagittars, Loken
learned – were almost as tall as the Astartes, but with their far
more slender build and more closely fitted armour, they seemed
slight compared to the Imperial giants. Abaddon, at the first
meeting, muttered that he doubted their fancy armour would
stand even a slap.

Their weapons caused more remarks. Most of the soldiers
had swords sheathed across their backs. Some, the gleves, carried long-bladed metal spears with heavy ball counterweights
on the base ends. The others, the sagittars, carried recurve bows
wrought from some dark metal. The sagittars had sheaves of
long, flightless darts laced to their right thighs.

'Bows?' Torgaddon whispered. 'Really? They stun us with the
power and scale of their vessels, then come aboard carrying bows?'

'They're probably ceremonial,' Aximand murmured.

The soldier officers wore serrated half-discs across the skulls of their helmets. The visors of their close-fitting helms were all alike: the metal modelled to the lines of brow and cheekbone and nose, with simple oval eyeslits that were backlit blue. The mouth and chin area of each visor was built out, like a thrusting, pugnacious jaw, containing a communication module.

Behind the slender soldiers, as a further escort, came heavier forms. Shorter, and far more thick-set, these men were similarly armoured, though in browns and golds. Loken supposed them to be heavy troopers, their bodies gene-bred for bulk and muscle, designed for close combat, but they carried no weapons. There were twenty of them, and they flanked five robotic creatures, slender, silver quadrupeds of intricate and elegant design, made to resemble the finest Terra-stock horses, except that they possessed no heads or necks.

'Artificials,' Horus whispered aside to Maloghurst. 'Make sure Master Regulus is observing this via the pict feed. I'll want his notes later.'

One of the flagship's embarkation decks had been entirely cleared for the ceremonial meeting. Imperial banners had been hung along the vault, and the whole of First Company assembled in full plate as an honour guard. The Astartes formed two unwavering blocks of white figures, rigid and still, their front rows a glossy black line of Justaerin Terminators. In the aisle between the two formations, Horus stood with the Mournival, Maloghurst and other senior officials like Ing Mae Sing. The Warmaster and his lieutenants wore full armour and cloaks, though Horus's head was bare.

They watched the heavy interex shuttle move ponderously down the lighted runway of the deck, and settle on polished skids. Then hatch-ramps in its prow opened, the white metal unfolding like giant origami puzzles, and the envoys and their escorts disembarked. In total, with the soldiers and the meturge players, there were over one hundred of them. They came to a halt, with the envoys in a line at the front and the escort arranged in perfect symmetry behind. Forty-eight hours of intense intership communication had preceded that cautious moment. Forty-eight hours of delicate diplomacy.

Horus gave a nod, and the men of First Company chested their weapons and bowed their heads in one, loud, unified motion. Horus himself stepped forward and walked alone down the aisle space, his cloak billowing behind him.

He came face to face with what seemed to be the senior envoy, made the sign of the aquila, and bowed.

'I greet you on–' he began.

The moment he started speaking, the meturge players began sounding their instruments softly. Horus stopped.

'Translation form,' the envoy said, his own words accompanied by meturge playing.

'It is disconcerting,' Horus smiled.

'For purposes of clarity and comprehension,' the envoy said.

'We appear to understand each other well enough,' Horus smiled.

The envoy nodded curtly. 'Then I will tell the players to stop,' he said.

'No,' said Horus. 'Let us be natural. If this is your way.'

Again, the envoy nodded. The exchange continued, surrounded by the oddly melodied playing.

'I greet you on behalf of the Emperor of Mankind, beloved by all, and in the name of the Imperium of Terra.'

'On behalf of the society of the interex, I accept your greetings and return them.'

'Thank you,' said Horus.

'Of the first thing,' the envoy said. 'You are from Terra?'

'Yes.'

'From old Terra, that was also called Earth?'

'Yes.'

'This can be verified?'

'By all means,' smiled Horus. 'You know of Terra?'

An odd expression, like a pang, crossed the envoy's face, and he glanced round at his colleagues. 'We are from Terra. Ancestrally. Genetically. It was our origin world, eons ago. If you are truly of Terra, then this is a momentous occasion. For the first time in thousands of years, the interex has established contact with its lost cousins.'

'It is our purpose in the stars,' Horus said, 'to find all the lost families of man, cast away so long ago.'

The envoy bowed his head. 'I am Diath Shehn, abbrocarius.'

'I am Horus, Warmaster.'

The music of the meturge players made a slight, but noticeably discordant sound as it expressed 'Warmaster'.

Shehn frowned.

'Warmaster?' he repeated.

'The rank given to me personally by the Emperor of Mankind, so that I may act as his most senior lieutenant.'

'It is a robust title. Bellicose. Is your fleet a military undertaking?'

'It has a military component. Space is too dangerous for us to roam unarmed. But from the look of your fine soldiers, abbro-carius, so does yours.'

Shehn pursed his lips. 'You laid assault to Urisarach, with great aggression and vehemence, and in disregard to the advisory beacons we had positioned in the system. It would appear your military component is a considerable one.'

'We will discuss this in detail later, abbrocarius. If an apology needs to be made, you will hear it directly from me. First, let me welcome you in peace.'

Horus turned, and made a signal. The entire company of Astartes, and the plated officers, locked off their weapons and removed their helms. Human faces, row after row. Openness, not hostility.

Shehn and the other envoys bowed, and made a signal of their own, a signal supported by a musical sequence. The warriors of the interex removed their visors, displaying clean, hard-eyed faces.

Except for the squat figures, the heavy troops in brown and gold. When their helmets came off, they revealed faces that weren't human at all.

They were called the kinebrach. An advanced, mature species, they had been an interstellar culture for over fifteen thousand years. They had already founded a strong, multi-world civilisation in the local region of space before Terra had entered its First Age of Technology, an era when humanity was only just feeling its way beyond the Solar system in sub-light vehicles.

By the time the interex encountered them, their culture was aging and fading. A territorial war developed after initial contact, and lasted for a century. Despite the kinebrach's superior technology, the humans of the interex were victorious, but, in victory, they did not annihilate the aliens. Rapprochement was achieved, thanks in part to the interex's willingness to develop the aria to facilitate a more profound level of inter-species communication. Faced with options including further warfare and exile, the kinebrach elected to become client citizens of the expanding interex. It suited them to place their tired, flagging destiny in the charge of the vigorous and progressive humans. Culturally bonded as junior partners in society, the kinebrach shared their technological advances by way of exchange. For three thousand years, the interex humans had successfully co-existed with the kinebrach.

'Conflict with the kinebrach was our first significant alien war,' Diath Shehn explained. He was seated with the other envoys in the Warmaster's audience chamber. The Mournival was present, and meturge players lined the walls, gently accompanying the talks. 'It taught us a great deal. It taught us about our place in the cosmos, and certain values of compassion, understanding and empathy. The aria developed directly from it, as a tool for use in further dealings with non-human parties. The war made us realise that our very humanity, or at least our trenchant dependance on human traits, such as language, was an obstacle to mature relations with other species.'

'No matter how sophisticated the means, abbrocarius,' Abaddon said, 'sometimes communication is not enough. In our experience, most xenos types are wilfully hostile. Communication and bargaining is not an option.' The first captain, like many present, was uncomfortable. The entire interex party had been permitted to enter the audience chamber, and the kine-brach were attending at the far end. Abaddon kept glancing at them. They were hefty, simian things with eyes so oddly sunken beneath big brow ridges that they were just sparks in shadows. Their flesh was blue-black, and deeply creased, with fringes of russet hair, so fine it was almost like feather-down, surrounding the bases of their heavy, angular craniums. Mouth and nose was one organ, a trifold split at the end of their blunt jaw-snouts, capable of peeling back, wet and pink, to sniff, or opening laterally to reveal a comb of small, sharp teeth like a dolphin's beak. There was a smell to them, a distinctive earthy smell that wasn't exactly unpleasant, except that it was entirely and completely not human.

'This we have found ourselves,' Shehn agreed, 'though it would seem less frequently than you. Sometimes we have encountered a species that has no wish to exchange with us, that approaches us with predatory or invasive intent. Sometimes conflict is the only option. Such was the case with the... What did you say you called them again?'

'Megarachnid,' Horus smiled.

Shehn nodded and smiled. 'I see how that word is formed, from the old roots. The megarachnid were highly advanced, but not sentient in a way we could understand. They existed only to reproduce and develop territory. When we first met them, they infested eight systems along the Shartiel Edge of our provinces, and threatened to invade and choke two of our populated worlds. We went to war, to safeguard our own interests. In the end, we were victorious, but there was still no opportunity for rapprochement or peace terms. We gathered all the megarachnid remaining into captivity, and transported them to Urisarach.

We also deprived them of all their interstellar technology, or the means to manufacture the same. Urisarach was created as a reservation for them, where they might exist without posing a threat to ourselves or others. The interdiction beacons were established to warn others away.'

'You did not consider exterminating them?' Maloghurst asked.

Shehn shook his head. 'What right do we have to make another species extinct? In most cases, an understanding can be reached. The megarachnid were an extreme example, where exile was the only humane option.'

'The approach you describe is a fascinating one,' Horus said quickly, seeing that Abaddon was about to speak again. 'I believe it is time for that apology, abbrocarius. We misunderstood your methods and purpose on Urisarach. We violated your reservation. The Imperium apologises for its transgression.'

TWO

Envoys and delegations
Xenobia
Hall of Devices

Abaddon was furious. Once the interex envoys had returned to their vessels, he withdrew with the others of the Mournival and vented his feelings.

'Six months! Six months warring on Murder! How many great deeds, how many brothers lost? And now he apologises? As if it was an error? A mistake? These xenos-loving bastards even admit themselves the spiders were so dangerous they had to lock them away!'

'It's a difficult situation,' Loken said.

'It's an insult to the honour of our Legion! And to the Angels too!'

'It takes a wise and strong man to know when to apologise,' remarked Aximand.

'And only a fool appeases aliens!' Abaddon snarled. 'What has this crusade taught us?'

'That we're very good at killing things that disagree with us?' suggested Torgaddon.

Abaddon glared at him. 'We know how brutal this cosmos is. How cruel. We must fight for our place in it. Name one species we have met that would not rejoice to see mankind vanished in a blink.'

None of them could answer that.

'Only a fool appeases aliens,' Abaddon repeated, 'or appeases those who seek such appeasement.'

'Are you calling the Warmaster a fool?' Loken asked.

Abaddon hesitated. 'No. No, I'm not. Of course. I serve at his will.'

'We have one duty,' Aximand said, 'as the Mournival, we must speak with one mind when we advise him.'

Torgaddon nodded.

'No,' said Loken. 'That's not why he values us. We must tell him what we think, each one of us, even if we disagree. And let him decide. That is our duty.'

Meetings with the various interex envoys continued over a period of days. Sometimes the interex ships sent a mission to the *Vengeful Spirit*, sometimes an Imperial embassy crossed to their command ship and was entertained in glittering chambers of silver and glass where the aria filled the air.

The envoys were hard to read. Their behaviour often seemed superior or condescending, as if they regarded the Imperials as crude and unsophisticated. But still, clearly, they were fascinated. The legends of old Terra and the human bloodline had long been a central tenet of their myths and histories. However disappointing the reality, they could not bear to break off contact with their treasured ancestral past.

Eventually, a summit was proposed, whereby the Warmaster and his entourage would travel to the nearest interex outpost world, and conduct more detailed negotiations with higher representatives than the envoys.

The Warmaster took advice from all quarters, though Loken was sure he had already made up his mind. Some, like Abaddon, counselled that links should be broken, and the interex held at abeyance until sufficient forces could be assembled to annex their territories. There were other matters at hand that urgently demanded the Warmaster's attention, matters that had been postponed for too long while he indulged in the six-month spider-war on Murder. Petitions and salutations were being received on a daily basis. Five primarchs had requested his personal audience on matters of general crusade strategy or for councils of war. One, the Lion, had never made such an approach before, and it was a sign of a welcome thawing in relations, one that Horus could not afford to overlook. Thirty-six expedition fleets had sent signals asking for advice, tactical determination or outright martial assistance. Matters of state also mounted. There was now a vast body of bureaucratic material relayed from the Council of Terra that required the Warmaster's direct attention. He had been putting it off for too long, blaming the demands of the crusade.

Accompanying the Warmaster on most of his daily duties, Loken began to see plainly what a burden the Emperor had placed on Horus's broad shoulders. He was expected to be all things: a commander of armies, a mastermind of compliance, a judge, a decider, a tactician, and the most delicate of diplomats.

During the six-month war, more ships had arrived at high anchor above Murder, gathering around the flagship like supplicants. The rest of the 63rd Expedition had translated, under Varvarus's charge, Sixty-Three Nineteen having at last been left in the lonely hands of poor Rakris. Fourteen vessels of the 88th Expedition had also appeared, under the command of Trajus Boniface of the Alpha Legion. Boniface claimed they had come in response to the 140th's plight, and hoped to support the war action on Murder, but it rapidly emerged he hoped to use the opportunity to convince Horus to lend the 63rd's strengths to a proposed offensive into ork-held territories in the Kayvas Belt. This was a scheme his primarch, Alpharius, had long cherished and, like the Lion's advances, was a sign that Alpharius sought the approval and comradeship of the new Warmaster.

Horus studied the plans in private. The Kayvas Belt offensive was a projected five-year operation, and required ten times the manpower the Warmaster could currently muster.

'Alpharius is dreaming,' he muttered, showing the scheme to Loken and Torgaddon. 'I cannot commit myself to this.'

One of Varvaras's ships had brought with it a delegation of eaexector tributi administrators from Terra. This was perhaps the most galling of all the voices baying for the Warmaster's attention. On the instruction of Malcador the Sigillite, and countersigned by the Council of Terra, the eaexectors had been sent throughout the spreading territories of the Imperium, in a programme of general dispersal that made the mass deployment of the remembrancers look like a modest operation.

The delegation was led by a high administrix called Aenid Rathbone. She was a tall, slender, handsome woman with red hair and pale, high-boned features, and her manner was exacting. The Council of Terra had decreed that all expedition and crusade forces, all primarchs, all commanders, and all governors of compliant world-systems should begin raising and collecting taxes from their subject planets in order to bolster the increasing fiscal demands of the expanding Imperium. All she insisted on talking about was the collection of tithes.

'One world cannot support and maintain such a gigantic undertaking singlehanded,' she explained to the Warmaster in slightly over-shrill tones. 'Terra cannot shoulder this burden alone. We are masters of a thousand worlds now, a thousand thousand. The Imperium must begin to support itself.'

'Many worlds are barely in compliance, lady,' Horus said gently. 'They are recovering from the damage of war, rebuilding, reforming. Taxation is a blight they do not need.'

'The Emperor has insisted this be so.'

'Has he?'

'Malcador the Sigillite, beloved by all, has impressed this upon me and all of my rank. Tribute must be collected, and mechanisms established so that such tribute is routinely and automatically gathered.'

'The world governors we have put in place will find this too thankless a task,' Maloghurst said. 'They are still legitimising their rule and authority. This is premature.'

'The Emperor has insisted this be so,' she repeated.

'That's the Emperor, beloved by all?' Loken asked. His comment made Horus smile broadly.

Rathbone sniffed. 'I'm not sure what you're implying, captain,' she said. 'This is my duty, and this is what I must do.'

When she had retired from the room with her staff, Horus sat back, alone amongst his inner circle. 'I have often thought,' he remarked, 'that it might be the eldar who unseat us. Though fading, they are the most ingenious creatures, and if any could over-master mankind and break our Imperium apart, it would likely be them. At other times, I have fancied that it would be the greenskins. No end of numbers and no end of brute strength, but now, friends, I am certain it will be our own tax collectors who will do us in.'

There was general laughter. Loken thought of the poem in his pocket. Most of Karkasy's output he handed on to Sindermann for appraisal, but at their last meeting, Karkasy had introduced 'something of the doggerel'. Loken had read it. It had been a scurrilous and mordant stanza about tax collectors that even Loken could appreciate. He thought about bringing it out for general amusement, but Horus's face had darkened.

'I only half joke,' Horus said. 'Through the eaxectors, the Council places a burden on the fledgling worlds that is so great it might break us. It is too soon, too comprehensive, too stringent. Worlds will revolt. Uprisings will occur. Tell a conquered man he has a new master, and he'll shrug. Tell him his new master wants a fifth of his annual income, and he'll go and find his pitchfork. Aenid Rathbone, and administrators like her, will be the undoing of all we have achieved.'

More laughter echoed round the room.

'But it is the Emperor's will,' Torgaddon remarked.

Horus shook his head. 'It is not, for all she says. I know him as a son knows his father. He would not agree to this. Not now, not this early. He must be too bound up in his work to know of it. The Council is making decisions in his absence. The Emperor understands how fragile things are. Throne, this is what happens when an empire forged by warriors devolves executive power to civilians and clerics.'

They all looked at him.

'I'm serious,' he said. 'This could trigger civil war in certain regions. At the very least, it could undermine the continued work of our expeditions. The eaexectors need to be... sidelined for the moment. They should be given terrific weights of material to pore through to determine precise tribute levels, world by world, and bombarded with copious additional intelligence concerning each world's status.'

'It won't slow them down forever, lord,' Maloghurst said. 'The Administration of Terra has already determined systems and measures by which tribute should be calculated, pro rata, world by world.'

'Do your best, Mal,' Horus said. 'Delay that woman at least. Give me breathing space.'

'I'll get to it,' Maloghurst said. He rose and limped from the chamber.

Horus turned to the assembled circle and sighed. 'So...' he said. 'The Lion calls for me. Alpharius too.'

'And other brothers and numerous expeditions,' Sanguinius remarked.

'And it seems my wisest option is to return to Terra and confront the Council on the issue of taxation.'

Sanguinius sniggered.

'I was not wrought to do that,' Horus said.

'Then we should consider the interex, lord,' said Erebus.

Erebus, of the Word Bearers Legion, the XVII, had joined them a fortnight earlier as part of the contingent brought by Varvaras. In his stone-grey Mark IV plate, inscribed with bas-relief legacies of his deeds, Erebus was a sombre, serious figure. His rank in the XVII was first chaplain, roughly equivalent to that of Abaddon or Eidolon. He was a senior commander of that Legion, close to Kor Phaeron and the primarch, Lorgar, himself. His quiet manner and soft, composed voice commanded instant respect from all who met him, but the Luna Wolves had embraced him anyway. The Wolves had historically enjoyed a

relationship with the Bearers as close as the one they had formed
with the Emperor's Children. It was no coincidence that Horus
counted Lorgar amongst his most intimate brothers, alongside
Fulgrim and Sanguinius.

Erebus, who time had fashioned as much into a statesman
as a warrior, both of which duties he performed with superlative skill, had come to find the Warmaster at the behest of his
Legion. Evidently, he had a favour to crave, a request to make.
One did not send Erebus except to broker terms.

However, on his arrival, Erebus had understood immediately
the pressure laid at Horus's door, the countless voices screaming
for attention. He had shelved his reason for coming, wishing
to add nothing to the Warmaster's already immense burden,
and had instead acted as a solid counsel and advisor with no
agenda of his own.

For this, the Mournival had admired him greatly, and welcomed him, like Raldorus, into the circle. Abaddon and Aximand
had served alongside Erebus in numerous theatres. Torgaddon
knew him of old. All three spoke in nothing but the highest
terms of First Chaplain Erebus.

Loken had needed little convincing. From the outset, Erebus had made a particular effort to establish good terms with
Loken. Erebus's record and heritage were such that he seemed
to Loken to carry the weight of a primarch with him. He was,
after all, Lorgar's chosen mouthpiece.

Erebus had dined with them, counselled with them, sat easy
after hours and drunk with them, and, on occasions, had entered
the practice cages and sparred with them. In one afternoon, he
had bested Torgaddon and Aximand in quick bouts, then tal-
lied long with Saul Tarvitz before dumping him on the mat.
Tarvitz and his comrade Lucius had been brought along at Torgaddon's invitation.

Loken had wanted to test his hand against Erebus, but Lucius
had insisted he was next. The Mournival had grown to like
Tarvitz, their impression of him favourably influenced by Torgaddon's good opinions, but Lucius remained a separate entity,
too much like Lord Eidolon for them to warm to him. He always
appeared plaintive and demanding, like a spoilt child.

'You go, then,' Loken had waved, 'if it matters so much.' It was
clear that Lucius strained to restore the honour of his Legion,
an honour lost, as he saw it, the moment Erebus had dropped
Tarvitz with a skillful slam of his sword.

Drawing his blade, Lucius had entered the practice cage facing
Erebus. The iron hemispheres closed around them. Lucius took

up a straddled stance, his broadsword held high and close. Erebus kept his own blade extended low. They circled. Both Astartes were stripped to the waist, the musculature of their upper bodies rippling. This was play, but a wrong move could maim. Or kill.

The bout lasted sixteen minutes. That in itself would have made it one of the longest sparring sessions any of them had ever known. What made it more remarkable was the fact that in that time, there was no pause, no hesitation, no cessation. Erebus and Lucius flew at one another, and rang blows off one another's blades at a rate of three or four a second. It was relentless, extraordinary, a dizzying blur of dancing bodies and gleaming swords that rang on and on like a dream.

Abaddon, Tarvitz, Torgaddon, Loken and Aximand closed around the cage in fascination, beginning to clap and yell in thorough approval of the amazing skill on display.

'He'll kill him!' Tarvitz gasped. 'At that speed, unprotected. He'll kill him!'

'Who will?' asked Loken.

'I don't know, Garvi. Either one!' Tarvitz exclaimed.

'Too much, too much!' Aximand laughed.

'Loken fights the winner,' Torgaddon cried.

'I don't think so!' Loken rejoined. 'I've seen winner and loser!'

Still they duelled on. Erebus's style was defensive, low, repeating and changing each parry like a mechanism. Lucius's style was full of attack, furious, brilliant, dextrous. The play of them was hard to follow.

'If you think I'm taking on either of them after this,' Loken began.

'What? Can't you do it?' Torgaddon mocked.

'No.'

'You go in next,' chuckled Abaddon, clapping his hands. 'We'll give you a bolter to even it up.'

'How very humorous, Ezekyle.'

At the fifty-ninth second of the sixteenth minute, according to the practice cage chron, Lucius scored his winning blow. He hooked his broadsword under Erebus's guard and wrenched the Word Bearer's blade out of his grip. Erebus fell back against the bars of the practice cage, and found Lucius's blade edge at his throat.

'Whoa! Whoa now, Lucius!' Aximand cried, triggering the cage open.

'Sorry,' said Lucius, not sorry at all. He withdrew his broadsword and saluted Erebus, sweat beading his bare shoulders

'A good match. Thank you, sir.'

'My thanks to you,' Erebus smiled, breathing hard. He bent to pick up his blade. 'Your skill with a sword is second to none, Captain Lucius.'

'Out you come, Erebus,' Torgaddon called. 'It's Garvi's turn.'

'Oh no,' Loken said.

'You're the best of us with a blade,' Little Horus insisted. 'Show him how the Luna Wolves do it.'

'Skill with a blade isn't everything,' Loken protested.

'Just get in there and stop shaming us,' Aximand hissed. He looked over at Lucius, who was wiping his torso down with a cloth. 'You ready for another, Lucius?'

'Bring it on.'

'He's mad,' Loken whispered.

'Legion honour,' Abaddon muttered back, pushing Loken forward.

'That's right,' crowed Lucius. 'Anyway you want me. Show me how a Luna Wolf fights, Loken. Show me how you win.'

'It's not just about the blade,' Loken said.

'However you want it,' Lucius snorted.

Erebus stood up from the corner of the platform and tossed his blade to Loken. 'It sounds like it's your turn, Garviel,' he said.

Loken caught the sword, and tested it through the air, back and forth. He stepped up into the cage and nodded. The hemispheres of bars closed around him and Lucius.

Lucius spat and shook out his shoulders. He turned his sword and began to dance around Loken.

'I'm no swordsman,' Loken said.

'Then this will be over quickly.'

'If we spar, it won't be just about the blade.'

'Whatever, whatever,' Lucius called, jumping back and forth. 'Just get on and fight me.'

Loken sighed. 'I've been watching you, of course, the attacking strokes. I can read you.'

'You wish.'

'I can read you. Come for me.'

Lucius lunged at Loken. Loken side-stepped, blade down, and punched Lucius in the face. Lucius fell on his back, hard.

Loken dropped Erebus's sword onto the mat. 'I think I made my point. That's how a Luna Wolf fights. Understand your foe and do whatever is necessary to bring him down. Sorry, Lucius.'

Spitting blood, Lucius's response was incoherent.

'I said we should consider the interex, sir,' Erebus pressed.

'We should,' Horus replied, 'and my mind is made up. All

these voices calling for my attention, pulling me this way and that. They can't disguise the fact that the interex is a significant new culture, occupying a significant region of space. They're human. We can't ignore them. We can't deny their existence. We must deal with them directly. Either they are friends, potential allies, or they are enemies. We cannot turn our attention elsewhere and expect them to stay put. If they are enemies, if they are against us, then they could pose a threat as great as the greenskins. I will go to the summit and meet their leaders.'

Xenobia was a provincial capital on the marches of interex territory. The envoys had been guarded in revelations of the precise size and extent of the interex, but their cultural holdings evidently occupied in excess of thirty systems, with the heartworlds some forty weeks from the advancing edge of Imperial influence. Xenobia, a gateway world and a sentinel station on the edge of interex space, was chosen as the site for the summit.

It was a place of considerable wonder. Escorted from mass anchorage points in the orbit of the principal satellite, the Warmaster and his representatives were conducted to Xenobia Principis, a wealthy, regal city on the shores of a wide, ammonia sea. The city was set into the slopes of a wide bay, so that it shelved down the ramparts of the hills to sea level. The continental region behind it was sheathed in verdant rainforest, and this lush growth spilled down through the city too, so that the city structures – towers of pale grey stone and turrets of brass and silver – rose up out of the thick canopy like hilltop peaks. The vegetation was predominately dark green, indeed so dark in colour it seemed almost black in the frail, yellow daylight. The city was structured in descending tiers under the trees, where arched stone viaducts and curved street galleries stepped down to the shoreline in the quiet, mottled shadow of the greenery. Where the grey towers and ornate campaniles rose above the forest, they were often capped in polished metal, and adorned with high masts from which flags and standards hung in the warm air.

It was not a fortress city. There was little evidence of defences either on the ground or in local orbit. Horus was in no doubt that the place could protect itself if necessary. The interex did not wear its martial power as obviously as the Imperium, but its technology was not to be underestimated.

The Imperial party was over five hundred strong and included Astartes officers, escort troops and iterators, as well as a selection of remembrancers. Horus had authorised the latter's inclusion.

This was a fact-finding mission, and the Warmaster thought the eager, inquisitive remembrancers might gather a great deal of supplementary material that would prove valuable. Loken believed that the Warmaster was also making an effort to establish a rather different impression than before. The envoys of the interex had seemed so disdainful of the expedition's military bias. Horus came to them now, surrounded as much by teachers, poets and artists as he was warriors.

They were provided with excellent accommodation in the western part of the city, in a quarter known as the *Extranus*, where, they were politely informed, all 'strangers and visitors' were reserved and hosted. Xenobia Principis was a place designed for trade delegations and diplomatic meetings, with the Extranus set aside to keep guests reserved in one place. They were handsomely provided with meturge players, household servants, and court officers to see to their every need and answer any questions.

Under the guided escort of abbrocarii, the Imperials were allowed beyond the shaded compound of the Extranus to visit the city. In small groups, they were shown the wonders of the place: halls of trade and industry, museums of art and music, archives and libraries. In the green twilight of the galleried streets, under the hissing canopy of the trees, they were guided along fine avenues, through splendid squares, and up and down endless flights of steps. The city was home to buildings of exquisite design, and it was clear the interex possessed great skill in both the old crafts of stonemasonry and metalwork, and the newer crafts of technology. Pavements abounded with gorgeous statuary and tranquil water fountains, but also with modernist public sculpture of light and sonics. Ancient lancet window slits were equipped with glass panels reactive to light and heat. Doors opened and closed via automatic body sensors. Interior light levels could be adjusted by a wave of the hand. Everywhere, the soft melody of the aria played.

The Imperium possessed many cities that were larger and grander and more cyclopean. The super-hives of Terra and the silver spires of Prospero both were stupendous monuments to cultural advancement that quite diminished Xenobia Principis. But the interex city was every bit as refined and sophisticated as any conurbation in Imperial space, and it was merely a border settlement.

On the day of their arrival, the Imperials were welcomed by a great parade, which culminated in their presentation to the senior royal officer of Xenobia, a 'general commander' named

Jephta Naud. There were high-ranking civil officers in the interex party too, but they had decided to allow a military leader to oversee the summit. Just as Horus had diluted the martial composition of his embassy to impress the interex, so it had brought its military powers to the fore.

The parade was complex and colourful. Meturge players marched in great numbers, dressed in rich formal robes, and performed skirling anthems that were as much non-verbal messages of welcome as they were mood-setting music. Gleves and sagittars strode in long, uniform columns, their armour polished brightly and dressed with garlands of ribbons and leaves. Behind the human soldiery came the kinebrach auxiliaries, armoured and lumbering, and glittering formations of robotic cavalry. The cavalry was made up of hundreds of the headless artificial horses that had featured in the envoys' honour guard. They were headless no longer. Sagittars and gleves had mounted the quadruped frames, seating themselves where the base of the neck would have been. Warrior armour and robot technology had fused smoothly, locking the 'riders' in place, their legs folded into the breastbones of the steeds. They were centaurs now, man and device linked as one, myths given technological reality.

The citizenry of Xenobia Principis came out in force for the parade, and cheered and sang, and strewed the route of the procession with petals and strips of ribbon.

The parade's destination was a building called the Hall of Devices, a place which apparently had some military significance to the interex. Old, and of considerable size, the hall resembled a museum. Built into a steep section of the bay slopes, the hall enclosed many chambers that were more than two or three storeys high. Plunging display vaults, some of great size, showed off assemblies of weapons, from forests of ancient swords and halberds to modern motorised cannons, all suffused in the pale blue glow of the energy fields that secured them.

'The hall is both a museum of weapons and war devices, and an armoury,' Jephta Naud explained as he greeted them. Naud was a tall, noble creature with complicated dermatoglyphics on the right side of his face. His eyes were the colour of soft gold, and he wore silver armour and a cloak of scalloped red metal links that made a sound like distant chimes when he moved. An armoured officer walked at his side, carrying Naud's crested warhelm.

Though the Astartes had come armoured, the Warmaster had chosen to wear robes and furs rather than his battle-plate. He showed great and courteous interest as Naud led them through the deep vaults, commenting on certain devices, remarking with delight when archaic weapons revealed a shared ancestry.

'They're trying to impress us,' Aximand murmured to his brothers. 'A museum of weapons? They're as good as telling us they are so advanced... so beyond war... they've been able to retire it as a curiosity. They're mocking us.'

'No one mocks me,' Abaddon grunted.

They were entering a chamber where, in the chilly blue field light, the artifacts were a great deal stranger than before.

'We hold the weapons of the kinebrach here,' Naud said, to meturge accompaniment. 'Indeed, we preserve here, in careful stasis, examples of the weapons used by many of the alien species we have encountered. The kinebrach have, as a sign of service to us, foresworn the bearing of arms, unless under such circumstances as we grant them said use in time of war. Kinebrach technology is highly advanced, and many of their weapons are deemed too lethal to be left beyond securement.'

Naud introduced a hulking, robed kinebrach called Asherot, who held the rank of Keeper of Devices, and was the trusted curator of the hall. Asherot spoke the human tongue in a lisping manner, and for the first time, the Imperials were grateful for the meturge accompaniment. The baffling cadences of Asherot's speech were rendered crystal clear by the aria.

Most of the kinebrach weapons on display didn't resemble weapons at all. Boxes, odd trinkets, rings, hoops. Naud clearly expected the Imperials to ask questions about the devices, and betray their warmongering appetites, but Horus and his officers affected disinterest. In truth, they were uneasy in the society of the indentured alien.

Only Sindermann expressed curiosity. A very few of the kinebrach weapons looked like weapons: long daggers and swords of exotic design.

'Surely, general commander, a blade is just a blade?' Sindermann asked politely. 'These daggers here, for instance. How are these weapons "too lethal to be left beyond securement"?'

'They are tailored weapons,' Naud replied. 'Blades of sentient metal, crafted by the kinebrach metallurgists, a technique now utterly forbidden. We call them anathames. When such a blade is selected for use against a specific target, it becomes that target's nemesis, utterly inimical to the person or being chosen.'

'How?' Sindermann pressed.

Naud smiled. 'The kinebrach have never been able to explain it to us. It is a factor of the forging process that defies technical evaluation.'

'Like a curse?' prompted Sindermann. 'An enchantment?'

The aria generated by the meturge players around them hiccupped slightly over those words. To Sindermann's surprise, Naud replied, 'I suppose that is how you could describe it, iterator.'

The tour moved on. Sindermann drew close to Loken, and whispered, 'I was joking, Garviel, about the curse, I mean, but he took me seriously. They are enjoying treating us as unsophisticated cousins, but I wonder if their superiority is misplaced. Do we detect a hint of pagan superstition?'

THREE

Impasse
Illumination
The wolf and the moon

They all rose as the Warmaster entered the room. It was a large chamber in the Extranus compound where the Imperials met for their regular briefings. Large shield-glass windows overlooked the tumbling terraces of the forested city and the glittering ocean beyond.

Horus waited silently while six officers and servitors from the Master of Vox's company finished their routine sweep for spyware, and only spoke once they had activated the portable obscurement device in the corner of the room. The distant melodies of the aria were immediately blanked out.

'Two weeks without solid agreement,' Horus said, 'nor even a mutually acceptable scheme of how to continue. They regard us with a mixture of curiosity and caution, and hold us at arm's length. Any commentary?'

'We've exhausted all possibilities, lord,' Maloghurst said, 'to the extent that I fear we are wasting our time. They will admit to nothing but a willingness to open and pursue ambassadorial links, with a view to trade and some cultural exchange. They will not be led on the subject of alliance.'

'Or compliance,' Abaddon remarked quietly.

'An attempt to enforce our will here,' said Horus, 'would only confirm their worst opinions of us. We cannot force them into compliance.'

'We can,' Abaddon said.

'Then I'm saying we shouldn't,' Horus replied.

'Since when have we worried about hurting people's feelings, lord?' Abaddon asked. 'Whatever our differences, these are humans. It is their duty and their destiny to join with us and stand with us, for the primary glory of Terra. If they will not...'

He let the words hang. Horus frowned. 'Someone else?'

'It seems certain that the interex has no wish to join us in our work,' said Raldoron. 'They will not commit to a war, nor do they share our goals and ideals. They are content with pursuing their own destiny.'

Sanguinius said nothing. He allowed his Chapter Master to weigh in with the opinion of the Blood Angels, but kept his own considerable influence for Horus's ears alone.

'Maybe they fear we will try to conquer them,' Loken said.

'Maybe they're right,' said Abaddon. 'They are deviant in their ways. Too deviant for us to embrace them without forcing change.'

'We will not have war here,' Horus said. 'We cannot afford it. We cannot afford to open up a conflict on this front. Not at this time. Not on the vast scale subduing the interex would demand. If they even need subduing.'

'Ezekyle has a valid point,' said Erebus quietly. 'The interex, for good reasons, I'm sure, have built a society that is too greatly at variance to the model of human culture that the Emperor has proclaimed. Unless they show a willingness to adapt, they must by necessity be regarded as enemies to our cause.'

'Perhaps the Emperor's model is too stringent,' the Warmaster said flatly.

There was a pause. Several of those present glanced at each other in quiet unease.

'Oh, come on!' Sanguinius exclaimed, breaking the silence. 'I see those looks. Are you honestly nursing concerns that our Warmaster is contemplating defiance of the Emperor? His father?' He laughed aloud at the very notion, and forced a few smiles to surface.

Abaddon was not smiling. 'The Emperor, beloved of all,' he began, 'enfranchised us to do his bidding and make known space safe for human habitation. His edicts are unequivocal. We must suffer not the alien, nor the uncontrolled psyker, safeguard against the darkness of the warp, and unify the dislocated pockets of mankind. That is our charge. Anything else is sacrilege against his wishes.'

'And one of his wishes,' said Horus, 'was that I should be

Warmaster, his sole regent, and strive to make his dreams reality. The crusade was born out of the Age of Strife, Ezekyle. Born out of war. Our ruthless approach of conquest and cleansing was formulated in a time when every alien form we met was hostile, every fragment of humanity that was not with us was profoundly opposed to us. War was the only answer. There was no room for subtlety, but two centuries have passed, and different problems face us. The bulk of war is over. That is why the Emperor returned to Terra and left us to finish the work. Ezekyle, the people of the interex are clearly not monsters, nor resolute foes. I believe that if the Emperor were with us today, he would immediately embrace the need for adaptation. He would not want us to wantonly destroy that which there is no good reason to destroy. It is precisely to make such choices that he has placed his trust in me.'

He looked round at them all. 'He trusts me to make the decisions he would make. He trusts me to make no mistakes. I must be allowed the freedom to interpret policy on his behalf. I will not be forced into violence simply to satisfy some slavish expectation.'

A chill evening had covered the tiers of the city, and under layers of foliage stirred by the ocean's breath, the walkways and pavements were lit with frosty white lamps.

Loken's duty for that part of the night was as perimeter bodyguard. The commander was dining with Jephta Naud and other worthies at the general commander's palatial house. Horus had confided to the Mournival that he hoped to use the occasion to informally press Naud for some more substantial commitments, including the possibility that the interex might, at least in principle for now, recognise the Emperor as the true human authority. Such a suggestion had not yet been risked in formal talks, for the iterators had predicted it would be rejected out of hand. The Warmaster wanted to test the general commander's feelings on the subject in an atmosphere where any offence could be smoothed over as conjecture. Loken didn't much like the idea, but trusted his commander to couch it delicately. It was an uneasy time, well into the third week of their increasingly fruitless visit. Two days earlier, Primarch Sanguinius had finally taken his leave and returned to Imperial territory with the Blood Angels contingents.

Horus clearly hated to see him go, but it was a prudent move, and one Sanguinius had chosen to make simply to buy his brother more time with the interex. Sanguinius was returning to deal directly with some of the matters most urgently requiring the Warmaster's attention, and thus mollify the many voices pleading for his immediate recall.

Naud's house was a conspicuously vast structure near the centre of the city. Six storeys high, it overhung one of the grander civic tiers and was formed from a great black-iron frame infilled with mosaics of varnished wood and coloured glass. The interex did not welcome armed foreigners abroad in their city, but a small detail of bodyguards was permitted for so august a personage as the Warmaster. Most of the substantial Imperial contingent was sequestered in the Extranus compound for the night. Torgaddon, and ten hand-picked men from his company, were inside the dining hall, acting as close guard, while Loken, with ten men of his own, roamed the environs of the house.

Loken had chosen Tenth Company's Sixth Squad, Walkure Tactical Squad, to stand duty with him. Through its veteran leader, Brother-Sergeant Kairus, he'd spread the men out around the entry areas of the hall, and formulated a simple period of patrol.

The house was quiet, the city too. There was the sound of the soft ocean breeze, the hissing of the overgrowth, the splash and bell-tinkle of ornamental fountains, and the background murmur of the aria. Loken strolled from chamber to chamber, from shadow to light. Most of the house's public spaces were lit from sources within the walls, so they played matrices of shade and colour across the interior, cast by the inset wall panels of rich wood and coloured gem-glass. Occasionally, he encountered one of Walkure on a patrol loop, and exchanged a nod and a few quiet words. Less frequently, he saw scurrying servants running courses to and from the closed dining hall, or crossed the path of Naud's own sentries, mostly armoured gleves, who said nothing, but saluted to acknowledge him.

Naud's house was a treasure trove of art, some of it mystifyingly alien to Loken's comprehension. The art was elegantly displayed in lit alcoves and on free-standing plinths with their own shimmering field protection. He understood some of it. Portraits and busts, paintings and light sculptures, pictures of interex nobles and their families, studies of animals or wildflowers, mountain scenes, elaborate and ingenious models of unnamed worlds opened in mechanical cross-section like the layers of an onion.

In one lower hallway in the eastern wing of the house, Loken came upon an artwork that especially arrested him. It was a book, an old book, large, rumpled, illuminated, and held within its own box field. The lurid woodcut illuminations caught his eye first, the images of devils and spectres, angels and cherubs. Then he saw it was written in the old text of Terra, the language and form that had survived from prehistory to *The Chronicles of Ursh* that lay, still unfinished, in his arming chamber. He peered at it. A wave of his hand across the field's static charge turned the pages. He turned them right back to the front and read the title page in its bold woodblock.

A Marvelous Historie of Eevil; Being a warninge to Man Kind on the Abuses of Sorcerie and the Seduction of the Daemon.

'That has taken your eye, has it?'

Loken rose and turned. A royal officer of the interex stood nearby, watching him. Loken knew the man, one of Naud's subordinate commanders, by the name of Mithras Tull. What he didn't know was how Tull had managed to come up on him without Loken noticing.

'It is a curious thing, commander,' he said.

Tull nodded and smiled. A gleve, his weighted spear was leant against a pillar behind him, and he had removed his visor to reveal his pleasant, honest face. 'A likeness,' he said.

'A what?'

'Forgive me, that is the word we have come to use to refer to things that are old enough to display our common heritage. A likeness. That book means as much to you as it does to us, I'm sure.'

'It is curious, certainly,' Loken admitted. He unclasped his helm and removed it, out of politeness. 'Is there a problem, commander?'

Tull made a dismissive gesture. 'No, not at all. My duties are akin to yours tonight, captain. Security. I'm in charge of the house patrols.'

Loken nodded. He gestured back at the ancient book on display. 'So tell me about this piece. If you've the time?'

'It's a quiet night,' Tull smiled again. He came forward, and brushed the field with his metal-sleeved fingers to flip the pages. 'My lord Jephta adores this book. It was composed during the early years of our history, before the interex was properly founded, during our outwards expansion from Terra. Very few copies remain. A treatise against the practice of sorcery.'

'Naud adores it?' Loken asked.

'As a... what was your word again? A curiosity?' There was something strange about Tull's voice, and Loken finally realised what it was. This was the first conversation he'd had with a representative of the interex without meturge players producing the aria in the background. 'It's such a woe-begotten, dark age piece,' Tull continued. 'So doomy and apocalyptic. Imagine,

captain... men of Terra, voyaging out into the stars, equipped
with great and wonderful technologies, and fearing the dark so
much they have to compose treatises on daemons.'

'Daemons?'

'Indeed. This warns against witches, gross practices, familiars,
and the arts by which a man might transform into a daemon
and prey upon his own kind.'

Some became daemons and turned upon their own.

'So... you regard it as a joke? An odd throwback to unen-
lightened days?'

Tull shrugged. 'Not a joke, captain. Just an old-fashioned,
alarmist approach. The interex is a mature society. We understand the threat of Kaos well enough, and set it in its place.'

'Chaos?'

Tull frowned. 'Yes, captain. *Kaos*. You say the word like you've
never heard it before.'

'I know the word. You say it like it has a specific connotation.'

'Well, of course it has,' Tull said. 'No star-faring race in the cosmos can operate without understanding the nature of Kaos. We
thank the eldar for teaching us the rudiments of it, but we would
have recognised it soon enough without their help. Surely, one
can't use the immaterium for any length of time without coming to terms with Kaos as a...' his voice trailed off. 'Great and
holy heavens! You don't know, do you?'

'Don't know what?' Loken snapped.

Tull began to laugh, but it wasn't mocking. 'All this time,
we've been pussyfooting around you and your great Warmaster, fearing the worst...'

Loken took a step forward. 'Commander,' he said, 'I will own
up to ignorance and embrace illumination, but I will not be
laughed at.'

'Forgive me.'

'Tell me why I should. Illuminate me.'

Tull stopped laughing and stared into Loken's face. His blue
eyes were terribly cold and hard. 'Kaos is the damnation of all
mankind, Loken. Kaos will outlive us and dance on our ashes.
All we can do, all we can strive for, is to recognise its menace
and keep it at bay, for as long as we persist.'

'Not enough,' said Loken.

Tull shook his head sadly. 'We were so wrong,' he said.

'About what?'

'About you. About the Imperium. I must go to Naud at once
and explain this to him. If only the substance of this had come
out earlier...'

'Explain it to me first. Now. Here.'

Tull gazed at Loken for a long, silent moment, as if judging his options. Finally, he shrugged and said, 'Kaos is a primal force of the cosmos. It resides within the immaterium… what you call the warp. It is a source of the most malevolent and complete corruption and evil. It is the greatest enemy of mankind – both interex and Imperial, I mean – because it destroys from within, like a canker. It is insidious. It is not like a hostile alien form to be defeated or expunged. It spreads like a disease. It is at the root of all sorcery and magic. It is…'

He hesitated and looked at Loken with a pained expression. 'It is the reason we have kept you at arm's length. You have to understand that when we first made contact, we were exhilarated, overjoyed. At last. At last! Contact with our lost kin, contact with Terra, after so many generations. It was a dream we had all cherished, but we knew we had to be careful. In the ages since we last had contact with Terra, things might have changed. An age of strife and damnation had passed. There was no guarantee that the men, who looked like men, and claimed to come from Terra in the name of a new Terran Emperor, might not be agents of Kaos in seemly guise. There was no guarantee that while the men of the interex remained pure, the men of Terra might have become polluted and transformed by the ways of Kaos.'

'We are not–'

'Let me finish, Loken. Kaos, when it manifests, is brutal, rapacious, warlike. It is a force of unquenchable destruction. So the eldar have taught us, and the kinebrach, and so the pure men of the interex have stood to check Kaos wherever it rears its warlike visage. Tell me, captain, how warlike do you appear? Vast and bulky, bred for battle, driven to destroy, led by a man you happily title Warmaster? *War* master? What manner of rank is that? Not Emperor, not commander, not general, but Warmaster. The bluntness of the term reeks of Kaos. We want to embrace you, yearn to embrace you, to join with you, to stand shoulder to shoulder with you, but we fear you, Loken. You resemble the enemy we have been raised from birth to anticipate. The all-conquering, unrelenting daemon of Kaos-war. The bloody-handed god of annihilation.'

'That is not us,' said Loken, aghast.

Tull nodded eagerly. 'I know it. I see it now. Truly. We have made a mistake in our delays. There is no taint in you. There is only the most surprising innocence.'

'I'll try not to be offended.'

Tull laughed and clasped his hands around Loken's right fist. 'No need, no need. We can show you the dangers to watch for. We can be brothers and–'

He paused suddenly, and took his hands away.

'What is it?' Loken asked.

Tull was listening to his comm-relay. His face darkened. 'Understood,' he said to his collar mic. 'Action at once.'

He looked back at Loken. 'Security lock-down, captain. Would… I'm sorry, this seems very blunt after what we've just been saying… but would you surrender your weapons to me?'

'My weapons?'

'Yes, captain.'

'I'm sorry, commander. I can't do that. Not while my commander is in the building.'

Tull cleared his throat and carefully fitted his visor plate to his armour. He reached out and carefully took hold of his spear. 'Captain Loken,' he said, his voice now gusting from his audio relays, 'I demand you turn your weapons over to me at this time.'

Loken took a step back. 'For what reason?'

'I don't have to give a reason, dammit! I'm officer of the watch, on interex territory. Hand over your weapons!'

Loken clamped his own helm in place. The visor screens were alarmingly blank. He checked sub-vox and security channels, trying to reach Kairus, Torgaddon or any of the bodyguard detail. His suit systems were being comprehensively blocked.

'Are you damping me?' he asked.

'City systems are damping you. Hand me your sidearm, Loken.'

'I'm afraid I can't. My priority is to safeguard my commander.'

Tull shook his armoured head. 'Oh, you're clever. Very clever. You almost had me there. You almost had me believing you were innocent.'

'Tull, I don't know what's going on.'

'Naturally you don't.'

'Commander Tull, we had reached an understanding, man to man. Why are you doing this?'

'Seduction. You almost had me. It was very good, but you got the timing off. You showed your hand too soon.'

'Hand? What hand?'

'Don't pretend. The Hall of Devices is burning. You've made your move. Now the interex replies.'

'Tull,' Loken warned, placing his hand firmly on the pommel of his blade. 'Don't make me fight you.'

With a snarl of disappointed rage, Tull swung his spear at Loken.

The interex officer moved with astounding speed. Even with his hand on his blade, Loken had no time to draw it. He managed to snatch up his plated arms to fend off the blow, and the two that followed it. The lightweight armour of the interex soldiery seemed to facilitate the most dazzling motion and dexterity, perhaps even augmenting the user's natural abilities. Tull's attack was fluent and professional, slicing in blows with the long spear blade designed to force Loken back and down into submission. The microfine edge of the blade hacked several deep gouges into Loken's plating.

'Tull! Stop!'

'Surrender to me now!'

Loken had no wish to fight, and scarcely any clue as to what had turned Tull so suddenly and completely, but he had no intention of surrendering. The Warmaster was on site, exposed. As far as Loken knew, all Imperial agents in the area had been deprived of vox and sensor links. There was no cue to the Warmaster's party, or to the Extranus compound, and certainly none to the fleet. He knew his priority was simple. He was a weapon, an instrument, and he had one simply defined purpose: protect the life of the Warmaster. All other issues were entirely secondary and moot.

Loken focussed. He felt the power in his limbs, in the suddenly warming, suddenly active flex of the polymer muscles in his suit's inner skin. He felt the throb of the power unit against the small of his back as it obeyed his instincts and yielded full power. He'd been swatting away the spear blows, allowing Tull to disfigure his plate.

No more.

He swung out, met the next blow, and smashed the blade aside with the ball of his fist. Tull travelled with the recoil expertly, spinning and using the momentum to drive a thrust directly at Loken's chest. It never landed. Loken caught the spear at the base of the blade with his left hand, moving as quickly and dazzlingly as the interex officer, and stopped it dead. Before Tull could pull free, Loken punched with his right fist against the flat of the blade and broke the entire blade-tip off the spear. It spun away, end over end.

Tull rallied, and rotated the broken weapon to drive the weighted base-end at Loken like a long club. Loken guarded off two heavy blows from the ball-end with the edges of his gauntlets. Tull twisted his grip, and the spear suddenly became charged with dancing blue sparks of electrical charge. He slammed the crackling ball at Loken again and there was a

loud bang. The discharging force of the spear was so powerful
that Loken was thrown bodily across the chamber. He landed on
the polished floor and slid a few metres, dying webs of charge
flickering across his chestplate. He tasted blood in his mouth,
and felt the brief, quickly-occluded pain of serious bruising to
his torso.

Loken scissored his back and legs, and sprang up on to his
feet as Tull closed in. Now he brought his sword out. In the
multi-coloured light, the white-steel blade of his combat sword
shone like a spike of ice in his fist.

He offered Tull no opportunity to renew the bout as aggres-
sor. Loken launched forward at the charging man and swung
hammer blows with his sword. Tull recoiled, forced to use the
remains of the spear as a parrying tool, the Imperial blade biting chips out of its haft.

Tull leapt back, and drew his own sword over his shoulder
from the scabbard over his back. He clutched the long, silver sword – a good ten fingers longer than Loken's utilitarian
blade – in his right hand, and the spear/club in his left. When
he came in again, he was swinging blows with both.

Loken's Astartes-born senses predicted and matched all of
the strikes. His blade flicked left and right, spinning the club
back and parrying the sword with two loud chimes of metal.
He forced his way into Tull's bodyline guard and pressed his
sword aside long enough to shoulder-barge the royal officer in
the chest. Tull staggered back. Loken gave him no respite. He
swung again and tore the club out of Tull's left hand. It bounced
across the floor, sparking and firing.

Then they closed, blade on blade, The exchange was furious. Loken had no doubts about his own ability: he'd been
tested too many times of late, and not found wanting. But Tull
was evidently a master swordsman and, more significantly, had
learned his art via some entirely different school of bladesman-
ship. There was no common language in their fight, no shared
basis of technique. Every blow and parry and riposte, each one
essayed was inexplicable and foreign to the other. Every milli-
second of the exchange was a potentially lethal learning curve.

It was almost enjoyable. Fascinating. Inventive. Illuminating.
Loken believed Lucius would have enjoyed such a match, so
many new techniques to delight at.

But it was wasting time. Loken parried Tull's next quicksil-
ver slice, captured his right wrist firmly in his left hand, and
struck off Tull's sword-arm at the elbow with a neat and deliberate chop.

Tull rocked backwards, blood venting from his stump. Loken tossed the sword and severed limb aside. He grabbed Tull by the face and was about to perform the mercy stroke, the quick, down-up decapitation, then thought better of it. He smashed Tull in the side of the head with his sword instead, using the flat.

Tull went flying. His body cartwheeled clumsily across the floor and came to rest against the foot of one of the display plinths. Blood leaked out of it in a wide pool.

'This is Loken, Loken, Loken!' Loken yelled in the link. Nothing but dead patterns and static. Switching his blade to his left hand, he drew his bolter and ran forward. He'd gone three steps when the two sagittars bounded into the chamber. They saw him, and their bows were already drawn to fire.

Loken put a bolt round into the wall behind them and made them flinch.

'Drop the bows!' he ordered via his helmet speakers. The bolter in his hand told them not to argue. They threw aside the bows and shafts with a clatter. Loken nodded his head at Tull, his gun still covering them both. 'I've no wish to see him die,' he said. 'Bind his arm quickly before he bleeds out.'

They wavered and then ran to Tull's side. When they looked up again, Loken had gone.

He ran down a hallway into an adjoining colonnade, hearing what was certainly bolter fire in the distance. Another sagittar appeared ahead, and fired what seemed like a laser bolt at him. The shot went wide past his left shoulder. Loken aimed his bolter and put the warrior on his back, hard.

No room for compassion now.

Two more interex soldiers came into view, another sagittar and a gleve. Loken, still running, shot them both before they could react. The force of his bolts, both torso-shots, threw the soldiers back against the wall, where they slithered to the ground. Abaddon had been wrong. The armour of the interex warriors was masterful, not weak. His rounds hadn't penetrated the chest-plates of either of the men, but the sheer, concussive force of the impacts had taken them out of the fight, probably pulping their innards.

He heard footsteps and turned. It was Kairus and one of his men, Oltrentz. Both had weapons drawn.

'What the hell's happening, captain?' Kairus yelled.

'With me!' Loken demanded. 'Where's the rest of the detail?'

'I have no idea,' Kairus complained. 'The vox is dead!'

'We're being damped,' Oltrentz added.

'Priority is the Warmaster,' Loken assured them. 'Follow me and–'

More flashes, like laser fire. Projectiles, moving so fast they were just lines of light, zipped down the colonnade, faster than Loken could track. Oltrentz dropped onto his knees with a heavy clang, transfixed by two flightless arrows that had cut clean through his Mark IV plate.

Clean through. Loken could still remember Torgaddon's amusement and Aximand's assurance... *They're probably ceremonial.*

Oltrentz fell onto his face. He was dead, and there was no time, and no Apothecary, to make his death fruitful.

Further shafts flashed by. Loken felt an impact. Kairus staggered as a sagittar's dart punched entirely through his torso and embedded itself in the wall behind him.

'Kairus!'

'Keep on, captain!' Kairus drawled, in pain. 'Too clean a shot. I'll heal!'

Kairus rose and opened up with his storm bolter, firing on auto. He hosed the colonnade ahead of them, and Loken saw three sagittars crumble and explode under the thunderous pummel of the weapon. Now their armour broke. Under six of seven consecutive explosive penetrators, *now* their armour broke.

How we have underestimated them, Loken thought. He moved on, with Kairus limping behind him. Already Kairus had stopped bleeding. His genhanced body had self-healed the entry and exit wounds, and whatever the sagittar dart had skewered between those two points was undoubtedly being compensated for by the built-in redundancies of the Astartes's anatomy.

Together, they kicked their way into the main dining hall. The room was chaotic. Torgaddon and the rest of his detail were covering the Warmaster as they led him towards the south exit. There was no sign of Naud, but interex soldiers were firing at Torgaddon's group from a doorway on the far side of the chamber. Bolter fire lit up the air. Several bodies, including that of a Luna Wolf, lay twisted amongst the overturned chairs and banquet tables. Loken and Kairus trained their fire on the far doorway.

'Tarik!'

'Good to see you, Garvi!'

'What the hell is this?'

'A mistake,' Horus roared, his voice cracking with despair. 'This is wrong! Wrong!'

Brilliant shafts of light stung into the wall alongside them.

Sagittar darts sliced through the smoky air. One of Torgaddon's men buckled and fell, a dart speared through his helm.

'Mistake or not, we have to get clear. Now!' Loken yelled.

'Zakes! Cyclos! Regold!' Torgaddon yelled, firing. 'Close with Captain Loken and see us out!'

'With me!' Loken shouted.

'No!' bellowed the Warmaster. 'Not like this! We can't–'

'Go!' Loken screamed at his commander.

The fight to extricate themselves from Naud's house lasted ten furious minutes. Loken and Kairus led the rearguard with the brothers Torgaddon had appointed to them, while Torgaddon himself ferried the Warmaster out through the basement loading docks onto the street. Twice, Horus insisted on going back in, not wanting to leave anyone, especially not Loken, behind. Somehow, using words Torgaddon never shared with Loken, Torgaddon persuaded him otherwise.

By the time they had come out into the street, the remainder of Loken's outer guard had formed up with them, adding to the armour wall around the Warmaster, all except Jaeldon, whose fate they never learned.

The rearguard was a savage action. Backing metre by metre through the exit hall and the loading dock, Loken's group came under immense fire, most of it dart-shot from sagittars, but also some energised beams from heavy weapons. Bells and sirens were ringing everywhere. Zakes fell in the loading dock, his head shorn away by a blue-white beam of destruction that scorched the walls. Cyclos, his body a pincushion of darts, dropped at the doors of the exit hall. Prone, bleeding furiously, he tried to fire again, but two more shafts impaled his skull and nailed him to the door. Kairus took another dart through the left thigh as he gave Loken cover. Regold was felled by an arrow that pierced his right eyeslit, and got up in time to be finished by another through the neck.

Firing behind him, Loken dragged Kairus out through the dock area onto the street.

They were out into the city evening, the dark canopy hissing in the breeze over their heads. Lamps twinkled. In the distance, a ruddy glow backlit the clouds, spilling up from a building in the lower depths of the tiered city. Sirens wailed around them.

'I'm all right,' Kairus said, though it was clear he was having trouble standing. 'Close, that one, captain.'

He reached up and plucked out a sagittar shaft that had stuck through Loken's right shoulder plate. In the colonnade, the impact he'd felt.

'Not close enough, brother,' Loken said.

'Come on, if you're coming!' Torgaddon yelled, approaching them and spraying bolter fire back down the dock.

'This is a mess,' Loken said.

'As if I hadn't noticed!' Torgaddon spat. He uncoupled a charge pack from his belt and hurled it down the dockway.

The blast sent smoke and debris tumbling out at them.

'We have to get the Warmaster to safety,' Torgaddon said. 'To the Extranus.'

Loken nodded. 'We have to–'

'No,' said a voice.

They looked round. Horus stood beside them. His face was sidelit by the burning dock. His wide-set eyes were fierce. He had dressed for dinner that night, not for war. He was wearing a robe and a wolf-pelt. It was clear from his manner that he itched for armour plate and a good sword.

'With respect, sir,' Torgaddon said. 'We are drawn bodyguard. You are our responsibility.'

'No,' Horus said again. 'Protect me by all means, but I will not go quietly. Some terrible mistake has been made tonight. All we have worked for is overthrown.'

'And so, we must get you out alive,' Torgaddon said.

'Tarik's right, lord,' Loken added. 'This is not a situation that–'

'Enough, enough, my son,' Horus said. He looked up at the sighing black branches above them. 'What has gone so wrong? Naud took such great and sudden offence. He said we had transgressed.'

'I spoke with a man,' Loken said. 'Just when things turned sour. He was telling me of Chaos.'

'What?'

'Of Chaos, and how it is our greatest common foe. He feared it was in us. He said that is why they had been so careful with us, because they feared we had brought Chaos with us. Lord, what did he mean?'

Horus looked at Loken. 'He meant Jubal. He meant the Whisperheads. He meant the warp. Have you brought the warp here, Garviel Loken?'

'No, sir.'

'Then the fault is within them. The great, great fault that the Emperor himself, beloved by all, told me to watch for, foremost of all things. Oh gods, I wished this place to be free of it. To be clean. To be cousins we could hug to our chests. Now we know the truth.'

Loken shook his head. 'Sir, no. I don't think that's what was meant. I think these people despise Chaos... the warp... as much as we do. I think they only fear it in us, and tonight, something has proved that fear right.'

'Like what?' Torgaddon snapped.

'Tull said the Hall of Devices was on fire.'

Horus nodded. 'This is what they accused us of. Robbery. Deceit. Murder. Apparently someone raided the Hall of Devices tonight and slew the curator. Weapons were stolen.'

'What weapons, sir?' Loken asked.

Horus shook his head. 'Naud didn't say. He was too busy accusing me over the dinner table. That's where we should go now.'

Torgaddon laughed derisively. 'Not at all. We have to get you to safety, sir. That is our priority.'

The Warmaster looked at Loken. 'Do you think this also?'

'Yes, lord.'

'Then I am troubled that I will have to countermand you both. I respect your efforts to safeguard me. Your strenuous loyalty is noted. Now take me to the Hall of Devices.'

The hall was on fire. Bursting fields exploded through the lower depths of the place and cascaded flames up into the higher galleries. A meturge player, blackened by smoke, limped out to greet them.

'Have you not sinned enough?' he asked, venomously.

'What is it you think we have done?' Horus asked.

'Petty murder. Asherot is dead. The hall is burning. You could have asked to know of our weapons. You had no need to kill to win them.'

Horus shook his head. 'We have done nothing.'

The meturge player laughed, then fell.

'Help him,' Horus said.

Scads of ash were falling on them, drizzling from a choking black sky. The blaze had spread to the oversweeping forest, and the street was flame lit. There was a rank smell of burning vegetation. On lower street tiers, hundreds of figures gathered, looking up at the fire. A great panic, a horror was spreading through Xenobia Principis.

'They feared us from the start,' the Warmaster said. 'Suspected us. Now this. They will believe they were right to do so.'

'Enemy warriors are gathering on the approach steps,' Kairus called out.

'Enemy?' Horus laughed. 'When did they become the enemy? They are men like us.' He glared up at the night sky, threw back his head and screamed a curse at the stars. Then his voice fell to a whisper. Loken was close enough to hear his words.

'Why have you tasked me with this, father? Why have you forsaken me? Why? It is too hard. It is too much. Why did you leave me to do this on my own?'

Interex formations were approaching. Loken heard hooves clattering on the flagstones, and saw the shapes of mounted sagittars bobbing black against the fires. Darts, like bright tears, began to drizzle through the night. They struck the ground and the walls nearby.

'My lord, no more delays,' Torgaddon urged. Gleves were massing too, their moving spears black stalks against the orange glow. Sparks flew up like lost prayers into the sky.

'Hold!' Horus bellowed at the advancing soldiers. 'In the name of the Emperor of Mankind! I demand to speak to Naud. Fetch him now!'

The only reply was another flurry of shafts. The Luna Wolf beside Torgaddon fell dead, and another staggered back, wounded. An arrow had embedded itself in the Warmaster's left arm. Without wincing, he dragged it out, and watched his blood spatter the flagstones at his feet. He walked to the fallen Astartes, bent down, and gathered up the man's bolter and sword.

'Their mistake,' he said to Loken and Torgaddon. 'Their damn mistake. Not ours. If they're going to fear us, let us give them good reason.' He raised the sword in his fist.

'For the Emperor!' he yelled in Cthonic. 'Illuminate them!'

'Lupercal! Lupercal!' answered the handful of warriors around him.

They met the charging sagittars head on, bolter fire strobing the narrow street. Robot steeds shattered and tumbled, men falling from them, arms spread wide. Horus was already moving to meet them, ripping his sword into steel flanks and armoured chests. His first blow knocked a man-horse clear into the air, hooves kicking, crashing it back over onto the ranks behind it.

'Lupercal!' Loken yelled, coming to the Warmaster's right side, and swinging his sword double-handed. Torgaddon covered the left, striking down a trio of gleves, then using a lance taken from one of them to smite the pack that followed. Interex soldiers, some screaming, were forced back down the steps, or toppled over the stone railing of the street to plunge onto the tier beneath.

Of all the battles Loken had fought at his commander's side, that was the fiercest, the saddest, the most vicious. Teeth bared in the firelight, swinging his blade at the foe on all sides, Horus seemed more noble than Loken had ever known. He would remember that moment, years later, when fate had played its cruel trick and sense had turned upside down. He would remember Horus, Warmaster, in that narrow firelit street, defining the honour and unyielding courage of the Imperium of Man.

There should have been frescoes painted, poems written, symphonies composed, all to celebrate that instant when Horus made his most absolute statement of devotion to the Throne.

And to his father.

There would be none. The hateful future swallowed up such possibilities, swallowed the memories too, until the very fact of that nobility became impossible to believe.

The enemy warriors, and they were enemy warriors now, choked the street, driving the Warmaster and his few remaining bodyguards into a tight ring. A last stand. It was oddly as he had imagined it, that night in the garden, making his oath. Some great, last stand against an unknown foe, fighting at Horus's side.

He was covered in blood, his suit gouged and dented in a hundred places. He did not falter. Through the smoke above, Loken glimpsed a moon, a small moon glowing in the corner of the alien sky.

Appropriately, it was reflected in the glimmering mirror of ocean out in the bay.

'Lupercal!' screamed Loken.

FOUR

Parting shots
The Sons of Horus
Anathame

'What was taken?' Mersadie Oliton asked.

'A weapon, so they claim.'

'One weapon?'

'We didn't take it,' Loken said, stripping off the last of his battered armour. 'We took nothing. The killing was for nothing.'

She shrugged. She took a sheaf of papers from her gown. They were Karkasy's latest offerings, and she had come to the arming chamber on the pretence of delivering them. In truth, she was hoping to learn what had befallen on Xenobia.

'Will you tell me?' she asked. He looked up. There was dried blood on his face and hands.

'Yes,' he said.

The battle of Xenobia Principis lasted until dawn, and engulfed much of the city. At the first sign of commotion, unable to establish contact with either the Warmaster or the fleet, Abaddon and Aximand had mobilised the two companies of Luna Wolves garrisoned at the Extranus. In the streets surrounding the compound area, the people of the interex got their first taste of the power of the Imperial Astartes. In the years to come, they would experience a good deal more. Abaddon was in wrathful mood, so much so that Aximand had to rein him back on several occasions.

It was Aximand's units that first reached the embattled War-master on the upper tier near the Hall of Devices, and fought a route to him through the cream of Naud's army. Abaddon's forces had struck at several of the city's control stations, and restored communications. The fleet was already moving in, in response to the apparent threat to the Warmaster and the Impe-rial parties on the ground. As interex warships moved to engage, landing assaults began, led by Sedirae and Targost.

With communications restored, a fullscale extraction was coor-dinated, drawing all Imperial personnel from the Extranus, and from fighting zones in the streets.

Horus sent one final communiqué to the interex. He expected no response, and received none. Far too much blood had been spilled and destruction wrought for relations to be soothed by diplo-macy. Nevertheless, Horus expressed his bitter regret at the turn of events, lamented the interex for acting with such a heavy hand, and repeated once again his unequivocal denial that the Impe-rium had committed any of the crimes of which it stood accused.

When the ships of the expedition returned to Imperial space, some weeks later, the Warmaster had a decree proclaimed. He told the Mournival that, upon reflection, he had reconsidered the importance of defining his role, and the relationship of the XVI Legion to that role. Henceforth, the Luna Wolves would be known as the Sons of Horus.

The news was well-received. In the quiet corners of the flagship archives, Kyril Sindermann was told by some of his iterators, and approved the decision, before turning back to books that he was the first person to read in a thousand years. In the bustle of the Retreat, the remembrancers – many of whom had been extracted from the Extranus by the Astartes efforts – cheered and drank to the new name. Ignace Karkasy sank a drink to the hon-our of the Legion, and Captain Loken in particular, and then had another one just to be sure.

In her private room, Euphrati Keeler knelt by her secret shrine and thanked her god, the Emperor of Mankind, in the simple terms of the Lectitio Divinitatus, praising him for giving strong and honourable men to protect them. Sons of Horus, all.

Air hummed down rusting ducts and flues. Darkness pooled in the belly vaults of the *Vengeful Spirit*, in the bilges where even the lowliest ratings and proto-servitors seldom strayed. Only vermin lived here, insect lice and rats, gnawing a putrid exist-ence in the corroded bowels of the ancient ship.

By the light of a single candle, he held the strange blade up and watched how the glow coruscated off its edge. The blade was rippled along its length, grey like napped flint, and caught the light with a glitter like diamond. A fine thing. A beautiful thing. A cosmos-changing thing.

He could feel the promise within it breathing. The promise and the curse.

Slowly, Erebus lowered the anathame, placed it in its casket, and closed the lid.

'And that is all?'

'We tried,' said Loken. 'We tried to bond with them. It was a brave thing, a noble thing to attempt. War would have been easier. But it failed.'

'Yes,' he said. Loken had taken up the lapping powder and a cloth, and was working at the scratches and gouges on his breastplate, knowing full well the scars were too deep this time. He'd have to fetch the armourers.

'So it was a tragedy?' she asked.

'Yes,' he nodded, 'but not of our making. I've never... I've never felt so sure.'

'Of what?' she asked.

'Horus, as Warmaster. As the Emperor's proxy. I've never questioned it. But seeing him there, seeing what he was trying to do. I've never felt so sure the Emperor made the right choice.'

'What happens now?'

'With the interex? I imagine attempts will be made to broker peace. The priority will be low, for the interex are marginal and show no inclination to get involved in our affairs. If peace fails, then, in time, a military expedition will be drawn up.'

'And for us? Are you allowed to tell me the expedition's orders?'

Loken smiled and shrugged. 'We're due to rendezvous with the 203rd Fleet in a month, at Sardis, prior to a campaign of compliance in the Caiades Cluster, but on the way, a brief detour. We're to settle a minor dispute. An old tally, if you will. First Chaplain Erebus has asked the Warmaster to intercede. We'll be there and gone again in a week or so.'

'Intercede where?' she asked.

'A little moon,' Loken said, 'in the Davin System.'

Graham McNeill

FALSE GODS

The heresy takes root

~ DRAMATIS PERSONAE ~

The XVI Legion 'Sons of Horus'

HORUS	Warmaster
EZEKYLE ABADDON	First Captain
TARIK TORGADDON	Captain, Second Company
IACTON QRUZE	'The Half-heard', captain, Third Company
HASTUR SEJANUS	Captain, Fourth Company (Deceased)
HORUS AXIMAND	'Little Horus', captain, Fifth Company
SERGHAR TARGOST	Captain, Seventh Company, lodge master
GARVIEL LOKEN	Captain, Tenth Company
LUC SEDIRAE	Captain, 13th Company
TYBALT MARR	'The Either', captain, 18th Company
VERULAM MOY	'The Or', captain, 19th Company
KALUS EKADDON	Captain, Catulan Reaver Squad
FALKUS KIBRE	'Widowmaker', captain, Justaerin Terminator Squad
NERO VIPUS	Sergeant, Locasta Tactical Squad
MALOGHURST	'The Twisted', equerry to the Warmaster

The Primarchs

ANGRON
Primarch of the
World Eaters

FULGRIM
Primarch of the
Emperor's Children

Other Space Marines

EREBUS
First Chaplain of the
Word Bearers

KHÂRN
Captain, Eighth Assault
Company of the
World Eaters

The Legio Mortis

ESAU TURNET
Princeps of the *Dies Irae*,
an Imperator-class Titan

CASSAR
Moderati Primus, one of
the senior crew of
the *Dies Irae*

ARUKEN
Moderati Primus. Another
of the *Dies Irae*'s crew

The Davinites

AKSHUB
Priestess, Leader of the
Lodge of the Serpent

TSI REKH
Davinite liaison

TSEPHA
A cultist of Davin and
facilitator for Akshub

Non-Astartes Imperials

PETRONELLA VIVAR   Palatina Majoria of House Carpinus – one of the scions of a wealthy noble family of Terra

MAGGARD   Bodyguard to Petronella

VARVARAS   Lord Commander of Imperial Army forces attached to Horus's Legion

REGULUS   Mechanicum representative to Horus

PART ONE
THE BETRAYER

I was there the day that Horus fell...

'It is the folly of men to believe that they are great players on the stage of history, that their actions might affect the grand procession that is the passage of time. It is an insulating conceit a powerful man might clasp tight to his bosom that he might sleep away the night, safe in the knowledge that, but for his presence, the world would not turn, the mountains would crumble and the seas dry up. But if the remembrance of history has taught us anything, it is that, in time, all things will pass. Unnumbered civilisations before ours are naught but dust and bones, and the greatest heroes of their age are forgotten legends. No man lives forever and even as memory fades, so too will any remembrance of him.

'It is a universal truth and an unavoidable law that cannot be denied, despite the protestations of the vain, the arrogant and the tyrannical.

'Horus was the exception.'

– Kyril Sindermann, *Preface to the Remembrancers*

'It would take a thousand clichés to describe the Warmaster, each one truer than the last.'

– Petronella Vivar,
Palatina Majoria of House Carpinus

'Everything degenerates in the hands of men.'

– Ignace Karkasy, *Meditations on the Elegiac Hero*

ONE

Scion of Terra
Colossi
Rebel moon

Cyclopean Magnus, Rogal Dorn, Leman Russ: names that rang with history, names that *shaped* history. Her eyes roamed further up the list: Corax, Night Haunter, Angron... and so on through a legacy of heroism and conquest, of worlds reclaimed in the name of the Emperor as part of the ever-expanding Imperium of Man.

It thrilled her just to hear the names in her head.

But greater than any of them was the name at the top of the list.

Horus: the Warmaster.

Lupercal, she heard his soldiers now called him – an affectionate nickname for their beloved commander. It was a name earned in the fires of battle: on Ullanor, on Murder, on Sixty-Three Nineteen, – a world the deluded inhabitants had, in their ignorance, known as Terra – and a thousand other battles she had not yet committed to her mnemonic implants.

The thought that she was so very far from the sprawling family estates of Kairos and would soon set foot on the *Vengeful Spirit* to record living history took her breath away. But she was here to do more than simply record history unfolding; she knew, deep in her soul, that Horus *was* history.

She ran a hand through her long, midnight black hair, swept up in a style considered chic in the Terran court – not that anyone this far out in space would know, allowing her finger-nails to trace a path down her smooth, unblemished skin. Her olive skinned features had been carefully moulded by a life of wealth and facial sculpting to be regal and distinguished, with just the fashionable amount of aloofness crafted into the proud sweep of her jawline.

Tall and striking, she sat at her maplewood escritoire, a fam-ily heirloom her father proudly boasted had been a gift from the Emperor to his great-great-grandmother after the great oath-taking in the Urals. She tapped on her data-slate with a gold tipped mnemo-quill, its reactive nib twitching in response to her excitement. Random words crawled across the softly glowing surface, the quill's organic stem-crystals picking up the surface thoughts from her frontal lobes.

Crusade… Hero… Saviour… Destroyer.

She smiled and erased the words with a swipe of an elegantly manicured nail, the edge smooth down to the fractal level, and began to write with pronounced, cursive sweeps of the quill.

It is with great heart and a solemn sense of honour that I, Pet-ronella Vivar, Palatina Majoria of House Carpinus, do pen these words. For many a long year I have journeyed from Terra, enduring many travails and inconveniences…

Petronella frowned and quickly erased the words she had writ-ten, angry at having copied the unnatural affectedness that so infuriated her in the remembrancers' scripts that had been sent back from the leading edge of the Great Crusade.

Sindermann's texts in particular irritated her, though of late they had become few and far between. Dion Phraster produced some passable symphonics – nothing that would enjoy more than a day or so of favour in the Terran ballrooms – but pleas-ing enough; and the landscapes of Keland Roget were certainly vibrant, but possessed a hyperbole of brush stroke that she felt was unwarranted.

Ignace Karkasy had written some passable poems, but they painted a picture of the Great Crusade she often thought unflat-tering to such a wondrous undertaking (especially *Blood Through Misunderstanding*) and she often asked herself why the Warmas-ter allowed him to pen such words. She wondered if perhaps the subtexts of the poetry went over his head, and then laughed at the thought that anything could get past one such as Horus.

She sat back on her chair and placed the quill in the Lethe-well as a sudden, treacherous doubt gnawed at her. She was so crit-ical of the other remembrancers, but had yet to test her own mettle amongst them.

Could she do any better? Could she meet with the greatest hero of the age – a god some called him, although that was a ridiculous, outmoded concept these days – and achieve what they had, in her opinion, singularly failed to do? Who was she to believe that her paltry skill could do justice to the mighty tales the Warmaster was forging, hot on the anvil of battle?

Then she remembered her lineage and her posture straightened. Was she not of House Carpinus, finest and most influential of the noble houses in Terran aristocracy? Had not House Carpinus chronicled the rise of the Emperor and his domain throughout the Wars of Unification, watching it grow from a planet-spanning empire to one that was even now reaching from one side of the galaxy to the other to reclaim mankind's lost realm?

As though seeking further reassurance, Petronella opened a flat blotting folder with a monogrammed leather cover and slid a sheaf of papers from inside it. At the top of the pile was a pict image of a fair-haired Astartes in burnished plate, kneeling before a group of his peers as one of them presented a long, trailing parchment to him. Petronella knew that these were called oaths of moment, vows sworn by warriors before battle to pledge their skill and devotion to the coming fight. An intertwined 'EK' device in the corner of the pict identified it as one of Euphrati Keeler's images, and though she was loath to give any of the remembrancers credit, this piece was simply wondrous.

Smiling, she slid the pict to one side, to reveal a piece of heavy grain cartridge paper beneath. The paper bore the familiar double-headed eagle watermark, representing the union of the Mechanicum of Mars and the Emperor, and the script was written in the short, angular strokes of the Sigillite's hand, the quick pen strokes and half-finished letters speaking of a man writing in a hurry. The upward slant to the tails of the high letters indicated that he had a great deal on his mind, though why that should be so, now that the Emperor had returned to Terra, she did not know.

She smiled as she studied the letter for what must have been the hundredth time since she had left the port at Gyptus, knowing that it represented the highest honour accorded to her family.

A shiver of anticipation travelled along her spine as she heard far distant klaxons, and a distorted automated voice, coming from the gold-rimmed speakers in the corridor outside her suite, declared that her vessel had entered high anchor around the planet.

She had arrived.

Petronella pulled a silver sash beside the escritoire and, barely a moment later, the door chime rang and she smiled, knowing without turning that only Maggard would have answered her summons so quickly. Though he never uttered a word in her presence – nor ever would, thanks to the surgery she'd had the family chaperones administer – she always knew when he was near by the agitated jitter of her mnemo-quill as it reacted to the cold steel bite of his mind.

She spun around in her deeply cushioned chair and said, 'Open.'

The door swung smoothly open and she let the moment hang as Maggard waited for permission to stand in her presence.

'I give you leave to enter,' she said and watched as her dour bodyguard of twenty years smoothly crossed the threshold into her frescoed suite of gold and scarlet. His every move was controlled and tight, as though his entire body – from the hard, sculpted muscles of his legs, to his wide, powerful shoulders – was in tension.

He moved to the side as the door shut behind him, his dancing, golden eyes sweeping the vaulted, filigreed ceiling and the adjacent anterooms in a variety of spectra for anything suspect. He kept one hand on the smooth grip of his pistol, the other on the grip of his gold-bladed Kirlian rapier. His bare arms bore the faint scars of augmetic surgery, pale lines across his dark skin, as did the tissue around his eyes where house chirurgeons had replaced them with expensive biometric spectral enhancers to enable him better to protect the scion of House Carpinus.

Clad in gold armour of flexing, ridged bands and silver mail, Maggard nodded in unsmiling acknowledgement that all was clear, though Petronella could have told him that without all his fussing. But since his life was forfeit should anything untoward befall her, she supposed she could understand his caution.

'Where is Babeth?' asked Petronella, slipping the Sigillite's letter back into the blotter and lifting the mnemo-quill from the Lethe-well. She placed the nib on the data-slate and cleared her mind, allowing Maggard's thoughts to shape the words his throat could not, frowning as she read what appeared.

'She has no business being asleep,' said Petronella. 'Wake her. I am to be presented to the mightiest hero of the Great Crusade and I'm not going before him looking as though I've just come from some stupid pilgrim riot on Terra. Fetch her and have her bring the velveteen gown, the crimson one with the high collars. I'll expect her within five minutes.'

Maggard nodded and withdrew from her presence, but not before she felt the delicious thrill of excitement as the mnemo-quill twitched in her grip and scratched a last few words on the data-slate.

...ing bitch...

In one of the ancient tongues of Terra its name meant 'Day of Wrath' and Jonah Aruken knew that the name was well deserved. Rearing up before him like some ancient god of a forgotten time, the *Dies Irae* stood as a vast monument to war and destruction, its armoured head staring proudly over the assembled ground crew that milled around it like worshippers.

The Imperator-class Titan represented the pinnacle of the Mechanicum's skill and knowledge, the culmination of millennia of war and military technology. The Titan had no purpose other than to destroy, and had been designed with all the natural affinity for the business of killing that mankind possessed. Like some colossal armoured giant of steel, the Titan stood forty-three metres tall on crenellated bastion legs, each one capable of mounting a full company of soldiers and their associated supporting troops.

Jonah watched as a long banner of gold and black was unfurled between the Titan's legs, like the loincloth of some feral savage, emblazoned with the death's head symbol of the Legio Mortis. Scores of curling scrolls, each bearing the name of a glorious victory won by the Warmaster, were stitched to the honour banner and Jonah knew that there would be many more added before the Great Crusade was over.

Thick, ribbed cables snaked from the shielded power cores in the hangar's ceiling towards the Titan's armoured torso, where the mighty war engine's plasma reactor was fed with the power of a caged star.

Its adamantine hull was scarred and pitted with the residue of battle, the tech-adepts still patching it up after the fight against the megarachnid. Nevertheless, it was a magnificent and humbling sight, though not one that could dull the ache in his head and the churning in his belly from too much amasec the night before.

Giant, rumbling cranes suspended from the ceiling lifted massive hoppers of shells and long, snub-nosed missiles into the launch bays of the Titan's weapon mounts. Each gun was the size of a hab-block, massive rotary cannons, long-range howitzers and a monstrous plasma cannon with the power to level cities. He watched the ordnance crews prep the weapons, feeling the familiar flush of pride and excitement as he made his way towards the Titan, and smiled at the obvious masculine symbolism of a Titan being made ready for war.

He jumped as a gurney laden with Vulkan bolter shells sped past him, just barely avoiding him as it negotiated its way at speed through the organised chaos of ground personnel, Titan crews and deck hands. It squealed to a halt and the driver's head snapped around.

'Watch where the hell you're going, you damn fool!' shouted the driver, rising from his seat and striding angrily towards him. 'You Titan crewmen think you can swan about like pirates, well this is my–'

The words died in the man's throat and he snapped to attention as he saw the garnet studs and the winged skull emblem on the shoulder boards of Jonah's uniform jacket that marked him as a moderati primus of the *Dies Irae*.

'Sorry,' smiled Jonah, spreading his arms in a gesture of amused apology as he watched the man fight the urge to say more. 'Didn't see you there, chief, got a hell of a hangover. Anyway, what the devil are you doing driving so fast? You could have killed me.'

'You just walked out in front of me, sir,' said the man, staring fixedly at a point just over Jonah's shoulder.

'Did I? Well… just… be more careful next time,' said Jonah, already walking away.

'Then watch where you're going…' hissed the man under his breath, before climbing back onto his gurney and driving off.

'You be careful now!' Jonah called after the driver, imagining the colourful insults the man would already be cooking up about 'those damned Titan crewmen' to tell his fellow ground staff.

The hangar, though over two kilometres in length, felt cramped to Jonah as he made his way towards the *Dies Irae*, the scent of engine oil, grease and sweat not helping one whit with his hangover.

A host of Battle Titans of the Legio Mortis stood ready for war: fast, mid-range Reavers, snarling Warhounds and the mighty Warlords – as well as some newer Night Gaunt-class Titans – but none could match the awesome splendour of an Imperator-class Titan. The *Dies Irae* dwarfed them all in size, power and magnificence, and Jonah knew there was nothing in the galaxy that could stand against such a terrifying war machine.

Jonah adjusted his collar and fastened the brass buttons of his jacket, straightening it over his stocky frame before he reached the Titan's wide feet. He ran his hands through his shoulder-length black hair, trying to give the impression, at least, that he hadn't slept in his clothes. He could see the thin, angular form of Titus Cassar, his fellow moderati primus, working behind a monitoring terminal, and had no wish to endure another lecture on the ninety-nine virtues of the Emperor.

Apparently, smartness of appearance was one of the most important.

'Good morning, Titus,' he said, keeping his tone light.

Cassar's head bobbed up in surprise and he quickly slid a folded pamphlet beneath a sheaf of readiness reports.

'You're late,' he said, recovering quickly. 'Reveille was an hour ago and punctuality is the hallmark of the pious man.'

'Don't start with me, Titus,' said Jonah, reaching over and snatching the pamphlet that Cassar had been so quick to conceal. Cassar made to stop him, but Jonah was too quick, brandishing the pamphlet before him.

'If Princeps Turnet catches you reading this, you'll be a gunnery servitor before you know what's hit you.'

'Give it back, Jonah, please.'

'I'm not in the mood for another sermon from this damned Lectitio Divinitatus chapbook.'

'Fine, I'll put it away, just give it back, all right?'

Jonah nodded and held the well-thumbed paper out to Cassar, who snatched it back and quickly slid it inside his uniform jacket.

Rubbing his temples with the heel of his palms, Jonah said, 'Anyway, what's the rush? It's not as though the old girl's even ready for the pre-deployment checks, is she?'

'I pray you'll stop referring to it as a she, Jonah, it smacks of pagan anthropomorphising,' said Cassar. 'A Titan is a war machine, nothing more: steel, adamantine and plasma with flesh and blood controlling it.'

'How can you say that?' asked Aruken, sauntering over to a steel plated leg section and climbing the steps to the arched gates that led within. He slapped his palm on the thick metal and said, 'She's obviously a she, Titus. Look at the shapely legs, the curve of the hips, and doesn't she carry us within her like a mother protecting her unborn children?'

'In mockery are the seeds of impiety sown,' said Cassar without a trace of irony, 'and I will not have it.'

'Oh, come on, Titus,' said Aruken, warming to his theme. 'Don't you feel it when you're inside her? Don't you hear the beat of her heart in the rumble of her reactor, or feel the fury of her wrath in the roar of her guns?'

Cassar turned back to the monitoring panel and said, 'No, I do not, and I do not wish to hear any more of your foolishness, we are already behind on our pre-deployment checks. Princeps Turnet will have our hides nailed to the hull if we are not ready.'

'Where is the princeps?' asked Jonah, suddenly serious.

'With the War Council,' said Cassar.

Aruken nodded and descended the steps of the Titan's foot, joining Cassar at the monitoring station and letting fly with one last jibe. 'Just because you've never had the chance to enjoy a woman doesn't mean I'm not right.'

Cassar gave him a withering glare, and said, 'Enough. The War Council will be done soon, and I'll not have it said that the Legio Mortis wasn't ready to do the Emperor's bidding.'

'You mean Horus's bidding,' corrected Jonah.

'We have been over this before, my friend,' said Cassar. 'Horus's authority comes from the Emperor. We forget that at our peril.'

'That's as maybe, but it's been many a dark and bloody day since we've fought with the Emperor beside us, hasn't it? But hasn't Horus always been there for us on every battlefield?'

'Indeed he has, and for that I'd follow him into battle beyond the Halo Stars,' nodded Cassar. 'But even the Warmaster has to answer to the God-Emperor.'

'God-Emperor?' hissed Jonah, leaning in close as he saw a number of the ground crew turn their heads towards them. 'Listen, Titus, you have to stop this God-Emperor rubbish. One day you're going to say that to the wrong person and you'll get your skull cracked open. Besides, even the Emperor himself says he's not a god.'

'Only the truly divine deny their divinity,' said Cassar, quoting from his book.

Jonah raised his hands in surrender and said, 'All right, have it your way, Titus, but don't say I didn't warn you.'

'The righteous have nothing to fear from the wicked, and–'

'Spare me another lesson on ethics, Titus,' sighed Jonah, turning away and watching as a detachment of Imperial Army soldiers marched into the hangar, lasrifles on canvas slings hanging from their shoulders.

'Any word yet on what we're going to be fighting on this rock?' asked Jonah, changing the subject. 'I hope it's the greenskin. We still owe them for the destruction of *Vulkas Tor* on Ullanor. Do you think it will be the greenskin?'

Cassar shrugged. 'I don't know, Jonah. Does it matter? We fight who we are ordered to fight.'

'I just like to know.'

'You will know when Princeps Turnet returns,' said Cassar. 'Speaking of which, hadn't you better prepare the command deck for his return?'

Jonah nodded, knowing that his fellow moderati was right and that he'd wasted enough time in baiting him. Senior Princeps Esau Turnet's reputation as a feared, ruthless warrior was well deserved and he ran a tight ship on the *Dies Irae*. Titan crews might be permitted more leeway in their behaviour than the common soldiery, but Turnet brooked no such laxity in the crew of his Titan.

'You're right, Titus, I'm sorry.'

'Don't be sorry,' said Cassar, pointing to the gateway in the Titan's leg. 'Be ready.'

Jonah sketched a quick salute and jogged up the steps, leaving Cassar to finish prepping the Titan for refuelling. He made his way past embarking soldiers who grumbled as he pushed them aside. Some raised their voices, but upon seeing his uniform, and knowing that their lives might soon depend on him, they quickly silenced their objections.

Jonah halted at the entrance to the Titan, taking a second to savour the moment as he stood at the threshold. He tilted his head back and looked up the height of the soaring machine, taking a deep breath as he passed through the tall, eagle and lightning bolt wreathed gateway and entered the Titan.

He was bathed in red light as he entered the cold, hard interior of the Titan and began threading his way through the low-ceilinged corridors with a familiarity borne of countless hours learning the position of every rivet and bolt that held the *Dies Irae* together. There wasn't a corner of the Titan that Jonah didn't know: every passageway, every hatch and every secret the old girl had in her belonged to him. Even Titus and Princeps Turnet didn't know the *Dies Irae* as well as he did.

Reaching the end of a narrow corridor, Jonah approached a thick, iron door guarded by two soldiers in burnished black breastplates over silver mail shirts. Each wore a mask fashioned in the shape of the Legio's death's head and was armed with a short jolt-stick and a holstered shock-pistol. They tensed as he came into view, but relaxed a fraction as they recognised him.

Jonah nodded to the soldiers and said, 'Moderati primus moving from lower levels to mid levels.'

The nearest soldier nodded and indicated a glassy, black panel beside the door as the other drew his pistol. Its muzzle was slightly flared, and two silver steel prongs protruded threateningly, sparks of blue light flickering between them. Arcs of light could leap out and sear the flesh from a man's bones in a burst of lightning, but wouldn't dangerously ricochet in the cramped confines of a Titan's interior.

Jonah pressed his palm against the panel and waited as the yellow beam scanned his hand. A light above the door flashed green and the nearest soldier reached over and turned a hatch wheel that opened the door.

'Thanks,' said Jonah and passed through, finding himself in one of the screw-stairs that climbed the inside of the Titan's leg. The narrow iron mesh stairs curled around thick, fibre-bundle muscles and throbbing power cables wreathed in a shimmering energy field, but Jonah paid them no mind, too intent on his roiling stomach as he climbed the hot, stuffy stairs. He had to pause to catch his breath halfway up, and wiped a hand across his sweaty brow before reaching the next level.

This high up, the air was cooler as powerful recyc-units dispersed the heat generated by the venting of plasma gasses from the reactor. Hooded adepts of the Mechanicum tended to flickering control panels as they carefully built up the plasma levels in the reactor. Crewmen passed him along the cramped confines of the Titan's interior, saluting as they passed him. Good men crewed the *Dies Irae*, they had to be good – Princeps Turnet would never have picked them otherwise. All the men and women onboard the Titan had been chosen personally for their expertise and dedication.

Eventually, Jonah reached the Moderati Chambers in the heart of the Titan and slid his authenticator into the slot beside the door.

'Moderati Primus Jonah Aruken,' he said.

The lock mechanism clicked and, with a chime, the door slid open. Inside was a brilliant domed chamber with curving walls of shining metal and half a dozen openings spaced evenly throughout the ceiling.

Jonah stood in the centre of the room and said, 'Command Bridge, Moderati Primus Jonah Aruken.'

The floor beneath him shimmered and rippled like mercury, a perfectly circular disc of mirror-like metal forming beneath his feet and lifting him from the ground. The thin disc climbed into the air and Jonah rose through a hole in the ceiling, passing along the transport tube towards the summit of the Titan. The walls of the tube glowed with their own inner light, and Jonah stifled a yawn as the silver disc came to a halt and he emerged onto the command deck.

The interior of the *Dies Irae*'s head section was wide and flat, with recessed bays in the floor to either side of the main gangway, where hooded adepts and servitors interfaced directly with the deep core functions of the colossal machine.

'And how is everyone this fine morning?' he asked no one in particular. 'Ready to take the fight to the heathens once more?'

As usual, no one answered him and Jonah shook his head with a smile as he made his way to the front of the bridge, already feeling his hangover receding at the thought of meshing with the command interface. Three padded chairs occupied a raised dais before the glowing green tactical viewer, each with thick bundles of insulated cables trailing from the arms and headrests.

He slid past the central chair, that of Princeps Turnet, and sat in the chair to the right, sliding into the comfortable groove he'd worn in the creaking leather over the years.

'Adepts,' he said. 'Link me.'

Red-robed adepts of the Mechanicum appeared, one on either side of him, their movements slow and in perfect concert with one another, and slotted fine micro-cellular gauntlets over his hands, the inner, mnemonic surfaces meshing with his skin and registering his vital signs. Another adept lowered a silver lattice of encephalographic sensors onto his head, and the touch of the cool metal against his skin was a welcome sensation.

'Hold still, moderati,' said the adept behind him, his voice dull and lifeless. 'The cortical-dendrites are ready to deploy.'

Jonah heard the hiss of the neck clamps as they slid from the side of the headrest, and, from the corners of his eyes, he could see slithering slivers of metal emerging from the clamps. He braced himself for the momentary pain of connection as they slid across his cheek like silver worms reaching towards his eyes.

Then he could see them fully: incredibly fine silver wires, each no thicker than a human hair, yet capable of carrying vast amounts of information.

The clamps gripped his head firmly as the silver wires descended and penetrated the corners of his eyes, worming down past his optic nerve and into his brain, where they finally interfaced directly with his cerebral cortex.

He grunted as the momentary, icy pain of connection passed through his brain, but relaxed as he felt the body of the Titan become one with his own. Information flooded through him, the cortical-dendrites filtering it through portions of his brain that normally went unused, allowing him to feel every part of the gigantic machine as though it were an extension of his own flesh.

Within microseconds, the post-hypnotic implants in the subconscious portions of his brain were already running the pre-deployment checks, and the insides of his eyeballs lit up with telemetry data, weapon readiness status, fuel levels and a million other nuggets of information that would allow him to command this beautiful, wonderful Titan.

'How do you feel?' asked the adept, and Jonah laughed.

'It's good to be the king,' he said.

As the first pinpricks of light flared in the sky, Akshub knew that history had come to her world. She gripped her fetish-hung staff tightly in her clawed hand, knowing that a moment in time had dawned that mankind would never forget, heralding a day when the gods themselves would step from myth and legend to hammer out the future in blood and fire.

She had waited for this day since the great warriors from the sky had brought word of the sacred task appointed to her when she was little more than a babe in arms. As the great red orb of the sun rose in the north, hot, dry winds brought the sour fragrance of bitter blossoms from the tomb-littered valleys of long-dead emperors.

Standing high in the mountains, she watched this day of days unfold below her, tears of rapture spilling down her wrinkled cheeks from her black, oval eyes, as the pinpricks of light became fiery trails streaking across the clouds towards the ground.

Below her, great herds of horned beasts trekked across the verdant savannah, sweeping towards their watering holes in the south before the day grew too hot for them to move and the swift, razor-fanged predators emerged from their rocky burrows. Flocks of wide-pinioned birds wheeled over the highest peaks of the mountains above her, their cries raucous, yet musical, as this momentous day grew older.

All the multitudinous varieties of life carried on in their usual ways, oblivious to the fact that events that would change the fate of the galaxy were soon to unfold on this unremarkable world.

On this day of days, only she truly appreciated it.

The first wave of drop pods landed around the central massif at exactly 16:04 zulu time, the screaming jets of their retros bringing them in on fiery pillars as they breached the lower atmosphere. Stormbirds followed, like dangerously graceful birds of prey swooping in on some hapless victim.

Black and scorched by the heat of re-entry, the thirty drop pods sent up great clouds of dust and earth from their impacts, their wide doors opening with percussive booms and clanging down on the steppe.

Three hundred warriors in thick, plate armour swiftly disembarked from the drop pods and fanned out with mechanical precision, quickly linking up with other squads, and forming a defensive perimeter around an unremarkable patch of ground in the centre of their landing pattern. Stormbirds circled above in overlapping racetrack patterns, as though daring anything to approach.

At some unseen signal, the Stormbirds broke formation and rose into the sky as the boxy form of a Thunderhawk descended from the clouds, its belly blackened and trailing blue-white contrails. The larger craft surrounded the smaller one, like mother hens protecting a chick, escorting it to the surface, where it landed in a billowing cloud of red dust.

The Stormbirds screamed away on prescribed patrol circuits as the forward ramp of the Thunderhawk groaned open, the hiss of pressurised air gusting from within. Ten warriors clad in the comb-crested helms and shimmering plate armour of the Sons of Horus marched from the gunship, cloaks of many colours billowing at their shoulders.

Each carried a golden bolter across his chest, and their heads turned from left to right as they searched for threats.

Behind them came a living god, his armour gleaming gold and ocean green, with a cloak of regal purple framing him perfectly. A single, carved red eye stared out from his breastplate and a wreath of laurels sat upon his perfect brow.

'Davin,' sighed Horus. 'I never thought I'd see this place again.'

TWO

You bleed
A good war
Until the galaxy burns
A time to listen

Mersadie Oliton forced herself to watch the blade stab towards Loken, knowing that this strike must surely end his life. But, as always, he swayed aside from the lethal sweep with a speed that belied his massive Astartes frame, and raised his sword in time to block yet another stabbing cut. A heavy cudgel looped down at his head, but he had obviously anticipated the blow and ducked as it slashed over him.

The armatures of the practice cage clattered as the weapons swung, stabbed and slashed through the air, mindlessly seeking to dismember the massive Astartes warrior who fought within. Loken grunted, his hard-muscled body shining with a gleaming layer of sweat as a blade scored his upper arm, and Mersadie winced as a thin line of blood ran from his bicep.

As far as she could remember, it was the first time she had ever seen him wounded in the practice cages.

The smirking blond giant, Sedirae, and Loken's friend Vipus had long ago left the training halls, leaving her alone with the Captain of Tenth Company. Flattered as she was that he'd asked her to watch him train, she soon found herself wishing that he would finish this punishing ritual so that they could talk about what had happened on Davin and the events that now led them to war on its moon. Sitting on the cold, iron benches outside the practice cages, she had already blink-clicked more images to store in her memory coils than she would ever need.

Moreover, if she was honest, the sheer... obsessiveness of Loken's desperate sparring was somehow unsettling. She had watched him spar before, but it had always been an adjunct to their normal discussions, never the focus. This... this was something else. It was as though the captain of the Luna Wolves–

No, not the Luna Wolves, she reminded herself: the Sons of Horus.

As Loken deflected yet another slashing blade, she checked her internal chronometer again and knew that she would have to leave soon. Karkasy wouldn't wait, his prodigious appetite outweighing any notion of courtesy towards her, and he would head for the Iterators' Luncheon in the ship's staterooms without her. There would be copious amounts of free wine there and, despite Ignace's newfound dedication to the cause of remembrance, she did not relish the thought of such a smorgasbord of alcohol landing in his path again.

She pushed thoughts of Karkasy aside as the hissing mechanical hemispheres of the sparring cage withdrew and a bell began chiming. Loken stepped from the cage, his fair hair, longer than she had seen it before, plastered to his scalp, and his lightly freckled face flushed with exertion.

'You're hurt,' she said, passing him a towel from the bench.

He looked down, as though unaware of the wound.

'It's nothing,' he said, wiping away the already clotted blood. His breathing came in short bursts and she tried to mask her surprise. To see an Astartes out of breath was utterly alien to her. How long had he been training before she had arrived in the halls?

Loken wiped the sweat from his face and upper body as he made his way to his personal arming chamber. Mersadie followed him and, as usual, could not help but admire the sheer physical perfection of his enhanced physique. The ancient tribes of the Olympian Hegemony were said to have called such specimens of physical perfection Adonian, and the word fit Loken like a masterfully crafted suit of Mark IV plate. Almost without thinking, Mersadie blink-clicked the image of his body.

'You're staring,' said Loken, without turning.

Momentarily flustered, she said, 'Sorry, I didn't mean–'

He laughed. 'I'm teasing. I don't mind. If I am to be remembered, I'd like it to be when I was at my peak rather than as a toothless old man drooling into my gruel.'

'I didn't realise Astartes aged,' she replied, regaining her composure.

Loken shrugged, picking up a carved vambrace and a polishing cloth. 'I don't know if we do either. None of us has ever lived long enough to find out.'

Her sense for things unsaid told her that she could use this angle in a chapter of her remembrances, if he would talk more on the subject. The melancholy of the immortal, or the paradox of an ageless being caught in the flux of constantly changing times – struggling flies in the clotting amber of history.

She realised she was getting ahead of herself and asked, 'Does that bother you, not getting old? Is there some part of you that wants to?'

'Why would I want to get old?' asked Loken, opening his tin of lapping powder and applying it to the vambrace, its new colour, a pale, greenish hued metallic still unfamiliar to her. 'Do you?'

'No,' she admitted, unconsciously reaching up to touch the smooth black skin of her hairless augmetic scalp. 'No, I don't. To be honest, it scares me. Does it scare you?'

'No. I've told you, I'm not built to feel like that. I am powerful now, strong. Why would I want to change that?'

'I don't know. I thought that if you aged maybe you'd be able to, you know, retire one day. Once the Great Crusade is over I mean.'

'Over?'

'Yes, once the fighting is done and the Emperor's realm is restored.'

Loken didn't answer immediately, instead continuing to polish his armour. She was about to ask the question again when he said, 'I don't know that it ever will be over, Mersadie. Since I joined the Mournival, I've spoken to a number of people who seem to think we'll never finish the Great Unification. Or if we do, that it won't last.'

She laughed. 'Sounds like you've been spending too much time with Ignace. Has his poetry taken a turn for the maudlin again?'

He shook his head. 'No.'

'Then what is it? What makes you think like this? Those books you've been borrowing from Sindermann?'

'No,' repeated Loken, his pale grey eyes darkening at the mention of the venerable primary iterator, and she sensed that he would not be drawn any further on the subject. Instead, she stored this conversation away for another time, one when he might be more forthcoming on these uncharacteristically gloomy thoughts.

She decided to ask another question and steer the conversation in a more upbeat direction, when a looming shadow fell over the pair of them and she turned to see the massive, slab-like form of First Captain Abaddon towering over her.

As usual, his long hair was pulled up in its silver-sheathed top-knot, the rest of his scalp shaved bare. The captain of the First Company of the Sons of Horus was dressed in simple sparring fatigues and carried a monstrous sword with a toothed edge.

He glared disapprovingly at Mersadie.

'First Captain Abaddon–' she began, bowing her head, but he cut her off.

'You bleed?' said Abaddon and took Loken's arm in his powerful grip, the sonorous tone of his voice only accentuating his massive bulk. 'The sparring machine drew Astartes blood?'

Loken glanced at the bulging muscle where the blade had cut across the black, double-headed eagle tattoo there. 'Yes, Ezekyle, it was a long session and I was getting tired. It's nothing.'

Abaddon grunted and said, 'You're getting soft, Loken. Perhaps if you spent more time in the company of warriors than troublesome poets and inquisitive scriveners you'd be less inclined to such tiredness.'

'Perhaps,' agreed Loken, and Mersadie could sense the crackling tension between the two Astartes. Abaddon nodded curtly to Loken and gave her a last, barbed glance before turning away to the sparring cages, his sword buzzing into throaty life.

Mersadie watched Loken's eyes as they followed Abaddon, and saw something she never expected to see there: wariness.

'What was all that about?' she asked. 'Did it have anything to do with what happened on Davin?'

Loken shrugged. 'I can't say.'

Davin. The melancholy ruins scattered throughout its deserts told of its once civilised culture, but the anarchy of Old Night had destroyed whatever society had once prospered many centuries before. Now Davin was a feral world swept by hot, arid winds and baking under the baleful red eye of a sun. It had been six decades since Loken had last set foot on Davin, though back then it had been known as Sixty-Three Eight, being the eighth world brought into compliance by the 63rd Expeditionary force.

Compliance had not improved it much in his opinion.

Its surface was hard, baked clay clumped with scrubby vegetation and forests of tall, powerfully scented trees. Habitation was limited to primitive townships along the fertile river valleys, though there were many nomadic tribes that made their lonely way across the mighty, serpent-infested deserts.

Loken well remembered the battles they'd fought to bring this world into compliance, short sharp conflicts with the auto-chthonic warrior castes who made war upon one another, and whose internecine conflicts had almost wiped them out. Though outnumbered and hopelessly outclassed, they had fought with great courage, before offering their surrender after doing all that honour demanded.

The Luna Wolves had been impressed by their courage and willingness to accept the new order of their society and the commander – not yet the Warmaster – had decreed that his warriors could learn much from these brave opponents.

Though the tribesmen were separated from the human genome by millennia of isolation, and shared few physical traits with the settlers that came after the Astartes, Horus had allowed the feral tribesmen to remain, in light of their enthusiastic embracing of the Imperial way of life.

Iterators and remembrancers had not yet become an official part of the Crusade fleets, but the civilians and scholars who hung on the coattails of the expeditionary forces moved amongst the populace and promulgated the glory and truth of the Imperium. They had been welcomed with open arms, thanks largely to the dutiful work undertaken by the Chaplains of the XVII Legion, the Word Bearers, in the wake of the conquest.

It had been a good war; won rapidly and, for the Luna Wolves, bloodlessly. The defeated foe was brought into compliance quickly and efficiently, allowing the commander to leave Kor Phaeron of the Word Bearers to complete the task of bringing the light of truth and enlightenment to Davin.

Yes, it had been a good war, or so he had thought.

Sweat trickled down the back of his head and ran down the inside of his armour, its greenish, metallic sheen still new and startling to him, even though it had been months since he had repainted it. He could have left the job to one of the Legion's many artificers, but had known on some bone-deep level that he must look to his battle gear himself, and thus had painstakingly repainted each armoured segment single-handedly. He missed the pristine gleam of his white plate, but the Warmaster had decreed that the new colour be adopted to accompany the Legion's new name: the Sons of Horus.

Loken remembered the cheers and the cries of adoration laid at the feet of the Warmaster as his announcement had spread through the Expedition. Fists punched the air and throats were shouted hoarse with jubilation. Loken had joined in with the rest of his friends, but a ripple of unease had passed through him upon hearing his beloved Legion's new name.

Torgaddon, ever the joker, had noticed the momentary shadow pass over his face and said, 'What's the matter, you wanted it to be the Sons of Loken?'

Loken had smiled and said, 'No, it's just–'

'Just what? Don't we deserve this? Hasn't the commander earned this honour?'

'Of course, Tarik,' nodded Loken, shouting to be heard over the deafening roar of the Legion's cheers. 'More than anyone, he has earned it, but don't you think the name carries a whiff of self-aggrandisement to it?'

'Self-aggrandisement?' laughed Torgaddon. 'Those remembrancers that follow you around like whipped dogs must be teaching you new words. Come on, enjoy this and don't be such a starch arse!'

Tarik's enthusiasm had been contagious and Loken had found himself once again cheering until his throat was raw.

He could almost feel that rawness again as he took a deep breath of the sour, acrid winds of Davin that blew from the far north, wishing he could be anywhere else right now. It was not a world without beauty, but Loken did not like Davin, though he could not say what exactly bothered him about it. A sour unease had settled in his belly on the journey from Xenobia to Davin, but he had pushed it from his thoughts as he marched ahead of the commander onto the planet's surface.

To someone from the nightmarish, industrial caverns of Cthonia, Loken could not deny that Davin's wide-open spaces were intoxicatingly beautiful. To the west of them, soaring mountain peaks seemed to scrape the stars and further north, Loken knew that there were valleys that plumbed the very depths of the earth, and fantastical tombs of ancient kings.

Yes, they had waged a good war on Davin.

Why then had the Word Bearers brought them here again?

Some hours before, on the bridge of the *Vengeful Spirit*, Maloghurst had activated the data-slate he held in his twisted claw of a hand; the skin fused and wet pink, despite the best efforts of the Legion Apothecaries to restore it. He had scanned the contents of the communiqué within the slate once more, angry at the turn of phrase used by the petitioner.

He did not relish the prospect of showing the message to the Warmaster and briefly wondered if he could ignore it or pretend the missive had never come before him, but Maloghurst had not risen to become the Warmaster's equerry by insulating him from bad news. He sighed; these days the words of bland administrators carried the weight of the Emperor and, as much as Maloghurst wanted to, he could not ignore this message in particular.

The Warmaster would never agree to it, but Maloghurst had to tell him. In a moment of weakness, Maloghurst turned and limped across the strategium deck towards the Warmaster's sanctum chamber. He would leave the slate on the Warmaster's table, for him to find in his own time.

The sanctum doors slid smoothly aside, revealing the dark and peaceful interior.

Maloghurst enjoyed the solitude of the sanctum, the coolness of the air easing the pain of his raw skin and twisted spine. The only sound that broke the stillness of the sanctum was the breath rasping in his throat, the abnormal rearward curvature of his spine placing undue pressure on his lungs.

Maloghurst shuffled painfully along the length of the smooth surfaced oval table, reaching out to place the slate at its head, where the Warmaster sat.

It has been too long since the Mournival gathered here, thought Maloghurst.

'Evening, Mal,' said a voice from the shadows, sombre and tired.

Maloghurst turned in surprise towards the source of the voice, dropping the slate to the table, ready to rebuke whoever had seen fit to violate the Warmaster's sanctum. A shape resolved out of the darkness and he relaxed as he saw the familiar features of the commander, eerily red-lit from below by the light of his gorget.

Fully armoured in his battle-plate, the Warmaster sat at the back of the darkened sanctum, his elbows resting on his knees and his head held in his hands.

'My lord,' said Maloghurst. 'Is everything all right?'

Horus stared at the terrazzo-tiled floor of the sanctum and rubbed the heels of his palms across his shaved skull. His noble, tanned face and wide spaced eyes were deep in shadow and Maloghurst waited patiently for the Warmaster's answer.

'I don't know anymore, Mal,' said Horus.

Maloghurst felt a shiver travel down his ruined spine at the Warmaster's words. Surely, he had misheard. To imagine that the Warmaster did not know something was inconceivable.

'Do you trust me?' asked Horus suddenly.

'Of course, sir,' answered Maloghurst without pause.

'Then what do you leave here for me that you don't dare bring me directly?' asked Horus, moving to the table and lifting the fallen data-slate.

Maloghurst hesitated. 'Another burden you do not need, my lord. A remembrancer from Terra, one with friends in high places it would seem: the Sigillite for one.'

'Petronella Vivar of House Carpinus,' said Horus, reading the contents of the slate. 'I know of her family. Her ancestors chronicled my father's rise, back in the days before Unification.'

'What she demands,' spat Maloghurst, 'is ridiculous.'

'Is it, Maloghurst? Am I so insignificant that I don't require remembrance?'

Maloghurst was shocked. 'Sir, what are you talking about? You are the Warmaster, chosen by the Emperor, beloved by all, to be his regent in this great endeavour. The remembrancers of this fleet may record every fact they witness, but without you, they are nothing. Without you, all of it is meaningless. You are above all men.'

'Above all men,' chuckled Horus. 'I like the sound of that. All I've ever wanted to do was to lead this Crusade to victory and complete the work my father left me.'

'You are an example to us all, sir,' said Maloghurst, proudly.

'I suppose that's all a man can hope for during his lifetime,' nodded Horus, 'to set an example, and when he is dead, to be an inspiration for history. Perhaps she will help me with that noble ideal.'

'Dead? You are a god amongst men, sir: immortal and beloved by all.'

'I know!' shouted Horus, and Maloghurst recoiled before his sudden, volcanic rage. 'Surely the Emperor would not have created such a being as me, with the ability to grasp the infinite, to exist only for this short span! You're right, Mal, you and Erebus both. My father made me for immortality and the galaxy should know of me. Ten thousand years from now I want my name to be known all across the heavens.'

Maloghurst nodded, the Warmaster's furious conviction intoxicating, and dropped painfully to one knee in supplication.

'What would you have me do, my lord?'

'Tell this Petronella Vivar that she may have her audience, but it must be now,' said Horus, his fearsome outburst quite forgotten, 'and tell her that if she impresses me, I will allow her to be my personal documentarist for as long as she desires it.'

'Are you sure about this, sir?'

'I am, my friend,' smiled Horus. 'Now get up off your knees, I know it pains you.'

Horus helped Maloghurst rise to his feet and gently placed his armoured gauntlet on his equerry's shoulder.

'Will you follow me, Mal?' asked the Warmaster. 'No matter what occurs?'

'You are my lord and master, sir,' swore Maloghurst. 'I will follow you until the galaxy burns and the stars themselves go out.'

'That's all I ask, my friend,' smiled Horus. 'Now let's get ready to see what Erebus has to say for himself. Davin, eh? Who'd have thought we'd ever be back here?'

Two hours after making planetfall on Davin.

The communication from Erebus of the Word Bearers that had brought the 63rd Expedition to Davin had spoken of an old tally, the settling of a dispute, but had said nothing of its cause or participants.

After the carnage on Murder and the desperate extraction from the Extranus, Loken had expected a warzone of unremitting ferocity, but this warzone, if indeed it could be called that, was deathly quiet, hot and... peaceful.

He didn't know whether to be disappointed or relieved.

Horus had come to the same conclusion not long after they had landed, sniffing the air of Davin with a look of recognition.

'There is no war here,' he had said.

'No war?' Abaddon had asked. 'How can you tell?'

'You learn, Ezekyle,' said Horus. 'The smell of burnt meat and metal, the fear and the blood. There is none of that on this world.'

'Then why are we here?' asked Aximand, reaching up to lift his plumed helmet clear of his head.

'It would seem we are here because we have been summoned,' replied Horus, his tone darkening, and Loken had not liked the sound of the word 'summoned' coming from the Warmaster's lips.

Who would dare to summon the Warmaster?

The answer had come when a column of dust grew on the eastern horizon and eight boxy, tracked vehicles rumbled across the steppe towards them. Shadowed by the Stormbirds that had flown in with the Warmaster, the dark, brushed steel vehicles trailed guidons from their vox-antenna, emblazoned with the heraldry of an Astartes Legion.

From the lead Rhino, a great, devotional trophy rack stood proud of the armoured glacis, hung with golden eagles and books, and sporting jagged lightning bolts picked out in lapis lazuli.

'Erebus,' spat Loken.

'Hold your tongue,' warned Horus as the Rhinos had drawn closer, 'and let me do the talking.'

Bizarrely, the yurt smelled of apples, although Ignace Karkasy could see no fruit in any of the carved wooden trays, just heaped cuts of meat that looked a little on the raw side for his epicurean palate. He could swear he smelled apples. He glanced around the interior of the yurt, wondering if perhaps there was some local brew of cider on offer. A hairy-faced local with impene-trable black eyes had already offered him a shallow bowl of the local liquor, a foul-looking brew that smelled like curdled milk, but after catching a pointed glance from Euphrati Keeler he'd politely declined.

Like the drink, the yurt was crude, but had a primitive maj-esty to it that appealed to the romantic in him, though he was savvy enough to know that primitive was all very well and good unless you had to live there. Perhaps a hundred people filled the yurt – army officers, strategium adepts, a few remembranc-ers, scribes and military aides.

All come for the commander's War Council.

Casting his gaze around the smoky interior, Karkasy had seen that he was in illustrious company indeed: Hektor Varvarus, Lord Commander of the Army, stood next to a hunched Asta-rtes giant swathed in cream coloured robes who Karkasy knew must be the Warmaster's equerry, Maloghurst.

An unsmiling figure in the black uniform of a Titan com-mander stood to attention at the forefront of the gathering, and Karkasy recognised the jowly features of Princeps Esau Turnet, commander of the Imperator Titan, *Dies Irae*. Turnet's Titan had led the armada of enormous battle machines into the heart of the megarachnid territory on Murder and had earned the Legio Mortis the lion's share of the glory.

Karkasy remembered the huge Titan that towered over the architectural presentation that Peeter Egon Momus had given back on Sixty-Three Nineteen, and shivered. Even motionless, it had provoked an intense reaction in him, and the thought of such incredible destructive power being unleashed didn't bear thinking about.

The hissing collection of silver struts and whirling cogs that encased scraps of flesh in a vaguely humanoid form must be the Mechanicum adept, Regulus, and Karkasy saw enough brass and medals hanging from puffed out, uniformed chests to equip a battalion.

Despite the presence of such luminaries, Karkasy found himself stifling a yawn as he and the rest of the audience listened to the Davinite lodge master, Tsi Rekh, performing an elaborate chant in the local tongue. As interesting as it had been to see the bizarre, almost-human locals, Karkasy knew that simply bearing witness to this interminable ceremony of welcome couldn't be the reason why Captain Loken had authorised his presence at the War Council.

A bland-faced iterator named Yelten translated the lodge priest's speech into Imperial Gothic, the precisely modulated timbre of his voice carrying the words to the very edges of the yurt.

Say what you like about the iterators, thought Karkasy, they can certainly enunciate to the back row.

'How much longer is this going to go on for?' whispered Euphrati Keeler, leaning towards him. Dressed in her ubiquitous combat fatigues, chunky army boots and tight white vest top, Keeler looked every inch the spunky frontierswoman. 'When is the Warmaster going to get here?'

'No idea,' said Ignace, sneaking a look down her cleavage. A thin silver chain hung around her neck, whatever was hanging on it, hidden beneath the fabric of her top.

'My face is up here, Ignace,' said Euphrati.

'I know, my dear Euphrati,' he said, 'but I'm terribly bored now and this view is much more to my liking.'

'Give it up, Ignace, it's never going to happen.'

He shrugged. 'I know, but it is a pleasant fiction, my dear, and the sheer impossibility of a quest is no reason to abandon it.'

She smiled, and Ignace knew that he was probably a little in love with Euphrati Keeler, though the time since the xeno beast had attacked her in the Whisperheads had been hard for her, and to be honest, he was surprised to see her here. She'd lost weight and wore her blonde hair scraped back in a tight ponytail, still beautifully feminine, despite her best attempts to disguise the fact. He'd once written an epic poem for the marchioness Xorianne Delaquis, one of the supposed great beauties of the Terran court – a despicable commission that he'd loathed, but one that had paid handsomely – but her beauty was artificial and hollow compared to the vitality he now saw in Keeler's face, like someone born anew.

Well out of his league, he knew, what with his generously proportioned physique, hangdog eyes and plain, round face; but his looks had never deterred Ignace Karkasy from attempting to seduce beautiful women – they just made it more of a challenge.

He had made some conquests by riding the adulation for his earlier work, *Reflections and Odes* garnering him several notable carnal tales, while other, more easily impressed members of the opposite sex had been seduced by his witty badinage.

He already knew that Euphrati Keeler was too smart to fall for such obvious flattery, and contented himself with counting her simply as a friend. He smiled as he realised that he didn't think he'd ever had a woman as a friend before.

'To answer your question seriously, my dear,' he said. 'I hope the Warmaster will be here soon. My mouth's as dry as a Tallarn's sandal and I could use a bloody drink.'

'Ignace...' said Euphrati.

'Spare us from those of moral fibre,' he sighed. 'I didn't mean anything alcoholic, though I could fair sink a bottle of that swill they drank on Sixty-Three Nineteen right about now.'

'I thought you hated that wine,' said Keeler. 'You said it was tragic.'

'Ah, yes, but when you've been reduced to drinking the same vintage for months, it's surprising what you'll be willing to drink for a change.'

She smiled, placing her hand over whatever lay at the end of the chain around her neck and said, 'I'll pray for you, Ignace.'

He felt a flicker of surprise at her choice of words, and then saw an expression of rapt adoration settle over her as she raised her picter at something behind him. He turned to see the door flap of the yurt pushed aside and the massive bulk of an Astartes duck down as he entered. Karkasy did a slow double take as he saw that the warrior's shining plate armour was not that of the Sons of Horus, but was the carved granite grey of the Word Bearers. The warrior carried a staff crowned with a book draped in oath paper, over which wound a long sash of purple cloth. He had his helmet tucked into the crook of his arm, and seemed surprised to see all the remembrancers there.

Karkasy could see that the Astartes's wide-featured face was earnest and serious, his skull shaved and covered with intricate scriptwork. One shoulder guard of his armour was draped in heavy parchment, rich with illuminated letters, while the other bore the distinctive icon of a book with a flame burning in its centre. Though he knew it symbolised enlightenment springing forth from the word, Karkasy instinctively disliked it.

It spoke to his poet's soul of the Death of Knowledge, a terrible time in the history of ancient Terra when madmen and demagogues burned books, libraries and wordsmiths for fear of the ideas they might spread with their artistry. By Karkasy's

way of thinking, such symbols belonged to heathens and phil-
istines, not Astartes charged with expanding the frontiers of
knowledge, progress and enlightenment.

He smiled to himself at this delicious heresy, wondering if he
could work it into a poem without Captain Loken realising, but
even as the rebellious thought surfaced, he quashed it. Karkasy
knew that his patron was showing his work to the increasingly
reclusive Kyril Sindermann. For all his dreariness, Sindermann
was no fool when it came to the medium, and he would surely
spot any risqué references.

In that case, Karkasy would quickly find himself on the next
bulk hauler on its way back to Terra, regardless of his Astartes
sponsorship.

'So who's that?' he asked Keeler, returning his attention to the
new arrival as Tsi Rekh stopped his chanting and bowed towards
the newcomer. The warrior in turn raised his long staff in greeting.

Keeler gave him a sidelong glance, looking at him as though
he had suddenly sprouted another head.

'Are you serious?' she hissed.

'Never more so, my dear, who is he?'

'That,' she said proudly, snapping off another pict of the Astartes warrior, 'is Erebus, First Chaplain of the Word Bearers.'

And suddenly, with complete clarity, Ignace Karkasy knew
why Captain Loken had wanted him here.

Stepping onto the dusty hardpan of Davin, Karkasy had been
reminded of the oppressive heat of Sixty-Three Nineteen. Moving clear of the propwash of the shuttle's atmospheric rotors,
he'd half run, half stumbled from beneath its deafening roar
with his exquisitely tailored robes flapping around him.

Captain Loken had been waiting for him, resplendent in his
armour of pale green and apparently untroubled by the heat
or the swirling vortices of dust.

'Thank you for coming at such short notice, Ignace.'

'Not at all, sir,' said Karkasy, shouting over the noise of the
shuttle's engines as it lifted off the ground. 'I'm honoured, and
not a little surprised, if I'm honest.'

'Don't be. I told you I wanted someone familiar with the
truth, didn't I?'

'Yes, sir, indeed you did, sir,' beamed Karkasy. 'Is that why
I'm here now?'

'In a manner of speaking,' agreed Loken. 'You're an inveterate
talker, Ignace, but today I need you to listen. Do you understand me?'

'I think so. What do you want to me to listen to?'

'Not what, but who.'

'Very well. Who do you want me to listen to?'

'Someone I don't trust,' said Loken.

THREE

A sheet of glass
A man of fine character
Hidden words

On the day before making planetfall to the surface of Davin, Loken sought out Kyril Sindermann in Archive Chamber Three to return the book he had borrowed from him. He made his way through the dusty stacks and piles of yellowed papers, lethargic globes of weak light bobbing just above head height, his heavy footsteps echoing loudly in the solemn hush. Here and there, a lone scholar clicked through the gloom in a tall stilt chair, but none was his old mentor.

Loken travelled through yet another dizzyingly tall lane of manuscripts and leather bound tomes with names like *Canticles of the Omniastran Dogma*, *Meditations on the Elegiac Hero* and *Thoughts and Memories of Old Night*. None of them was familiar, and he began to despair of ever finding Sindermann amidst this labyrinth of the arcane, when he saw the iterator's familiar, stooped form hunched over a long table and surrounded by collections of loose parchment bound with leather cords, and piles of books.

Sindermann had his back to him and was so absorbed in his reading that, unbelievably, he didn't appear to have heard Loken's approach.

'More bad poetry?' asked Loken from a respectful distance.

Sindermann jumped and looked over his shoulder with an expression of surprise and the same furtiveness he had displayed when Loken had first met him here.

'Garviel,' said Sindermann, and Loken detected a note of relief in his tone.

'Were you expecting someone else?'

'No. No, not at all. I seldom encounter others in this part of the archive. The subject matter is a little lurid for most of the serious scholars.'

Loken moved around the table and scanned the papers spread before Sindermann – tightly curled, unintelligible script, sepia woodcuts depicting snarling monsters and men swathed in flames. His eyes flicked to Sindermann, who chewed his bottom lip nervously at Loken's scrutiny.

'I must confess to have taken a liking to the old texts,' explained Sindermann. 'Like *The Chronicles of Ursh* I loaned you, it's bold, bloody stuff. Naïve and overly hyperbolic, but stirring nonetheless.'

'I have finished reading it, Kyril,' said Loken, placing the book before Sindermann.

'And?'

'As you say, it's bloody, garish and sometimes given to flights of fantasy...'

'But?'

'But I can't help thinking that you had an ulterior motive in giving me this book.'

'Ulterior motive? No, Garviel, I assure you there was no such subterfuge,' said Sindermann, though Loken could not be sure that he believed him.

'Are you sure? There are passages in there that I think have more than a hint of truth to them.'

'Come now, Garviel, surely you can't believe that,' scoffed Sindermann.

'The murengon,' stated Loken. 'Anult Keyser's final battle against the Nordafrik conclaves.'

Sindermann hesitated. 'What about it?'

'I can see from your eyes that you already know what I'm going to say.'

'No, Garviel, I don't. I know the passage you speak of and, while it's certainly an exciting read, I hardly think you can take its prose too literally.'

'I agree,' nodded Loken. 'All the talk of the sky splitting like silk and the mountains toppling is clearly nonsense, but it talks of men becoming daemons and turning on their fellows.'

'Ah... now I see. You think that this is another clue as to what happened to Xavyer Jubal?'

'Don't you?' asked Loken, turning one of the yellowed

parchments around to point at a fanged daemon figure clothed in fur with curling ram's horns and a bloody, skull-stamped axe.

'Jubal turned into a daemon and tried to kill me! Just as happened to Anult Keyser himself. One of his lieutenants, a man called Wilhym Mardol, became a daemon and killed him. Doesn't that sound familiar?'

Sindermann leaned back in his chair and closed his eyes. Loken saw how tired he looked, his skin the colour of the parchments he perused and his clothes hanging from his body as though draped across his bare bones.

Loken realised that the venerable iterator was exhausted.

'I'm sorry, Kyril,' he said, also sitting back. 'I didn't come here to pick a fight with you.'

Sindermann smiled, reminding Loken of how much he had come to rely on his wise counsel. Though not a tutor as such, Sindermann had filled the role of Loken's mentor and instructor for some time, and it had come as a great shock to discover that Sindermann did not have all the answers.

'It's all right, Garviel, it's good that you have questions, it shows you are learning that there is often more to the truth than what we see at first. I'm sure the Warmaster values that aspect of you. How is the commander?'

'Tired,' admitted Loken. 'The demands of those crying for his attention grow more strident every day. Communiqués from every expedition in the Crusade seek to pull him in all directions, and insulting directives from the Council of Terra seek to turn him into a damned administrator instead of the Warmaster. He carries a huge burden, Kyril; but don't think you can change the subject that easily.'

Sindermann laughed. 'You are becoming too quick for me, Garviel. Very well, what is it you want to know?'

'The men in the book who were said to use sorcerous powers, were they warlocks?'

'I don't know,' admitted Sindermann. 'It's certainly possible. The powers they used certainly do not sound natural.'

'But how could their leaders have sanctioned the use of such powers? Surely they must have seen how dangerous it was?'

'Perhaps, but think on this: we know so little on the subject and we have the light of the Emperor's wisdom and science to guide us. How much less must they have known?'

'Even a barbarian must know that such things are dangerous,' said Loken.

'Barbarian?' said Sindermann. 'A pejorative term indeed, my

friend. Do not be so quick to judge, we are not so different from the tribes of Old Earth as you might think.'

'Surely you're not serious,' asked Loken. 'We are as different from them as a star from a planet.'

'Are you so sure, Garviel? You believe that the wall, separating civilisation from barbarism is as solid as steel, but it is not. I tell you the division is a thread, a sheet of glass. A touch here, a push there, and you bring back the reign of pagan superstition, fear of the dark and the worship of fell beings in echoing fanes.'

'You exaggerate.'

'Do I?' asked Sindermann, leaning forward. 'Imagine a newly compliant world that experiences a shortage of some vital resource, such as fuel, water or food, how long would it take before civilised behaviour broke down and barbaric behaviour took over? Would human selfishness cause some to fight to get that resource at all costs, even if it meant harm to others and trafficking with evil? Would they deprive others of this resource, or even destroy them in an effort to keep it for themselves? Common decency and civil behaviour are just a thin veneer over the animal at the core of mankind that gets out whenever it has the chance.'

'You make it sound like there's no hope for us.'

'Far from it, Garviel,' said Sindermann, shaking his head. 'Mankind continually stands bewildered in the presence of its own creation, but, thanks to the great works of the Emperor, I firmly believe that the time will come when we will rise to mastery of all before us. The time that has passed since civilisation began is but a fragment of the duration of our existence, and but a fragment of the ages yet to come. The rule of the Emperor, brotherhood in society, equality in rights and privileges, and universal education foreshadow the higher plane of society to which our experience, intelligence and knowledge are steadily tending. It will be a revival, in a higher form, of the liberty, equality and fraternity of the ancient tribes of Man before the rise of warlords like Kalagann or Narthan Dume.'

Loken smiled, 'And to think I thought you were in despair.'

Sindermann returned Loken's smile and said, 'No, Garviel, far from it. I admit I was shaken after the Whisperheads, but the more I read, the more I see how far we have come and how close we are to achieving everything we ever dreamed of. Each day, I am thankful that we have the light of the Emperor to guide us into this golden future. I dread to think what might become of us were he to be taken from us.'

'Don't worry,' said Loken. 'That will never happen.'

✠ ✠ ✠

Aximand looked through a gap in the netting and said, 'Erebus is here.'

Horus nodded and turned to face the four members of the Mournival. 'You all know what to do?'

'No,' said Torgaddon. 'We've completely forgotten. Why don't you remind us.'

Horus's eyes darkened at Tarik's levity and he said, 'Enough, Tarik. There is a time for jokes, and this isn't it, so keep your mouth shut.'

Torgaddon looked shocked at the Warmaster's outburst, and shot a hurt glance at his fellows. Loken was less shocked, having witnessed the commander raging at subordinates many times in the weeks since they had departed the marches of the interex. Horus had known no peace since the terrible bloodshed amid the House of Devices on Xenobia, and the deaths and the missed opportunity of unification with the interex haunted him still.

Since the debacle with the interex, the Warmaster had withdrawn into a sullen melancholy, remaining more and more within his inner sanctum, with only Erebus to counsel him. The Mournival had barely seen their commander since returning to Imperial space and they all keenly felt their exclusion from his presence.

Where once they had offered the Warmaster their guidance, now, only Erebus whispered in his ear.

Thus, it was with some relief that the Mournival heard that Erebus would take his leave of the Expedition and journey ahead with his own Legion to Davin.

Even while en route to the Davin system, the Warmaster had not had a moment's peace. Repeated requests for aid or tactical assistance came to him from all across the galaxy, from brother primarchs, Army commanders and, most loathed of all, the army of civil administrators who followed in the wake of their conquests.

The eaxectors from Terra, led by a high administratrix called Aenid Rathbone, plagued the Warmaster daily for assistance in their dispersal throughout the compliant territories to begin the collection of the Emperor's Tithe. Everyone with an ounce of common sense knew that such a measure was premature, and Horus had done all he could to stall Rathbone and her eaxectors, but there was only so long they could be kept at bay.

'If I had my choice,' Horus had told Loken one evening as they had discussed fresh ways of delaying the taxation of compliant worlds, 'I would kill every eaxector in the Imperium, but I'm sure we would be getting tax bills from hell before breakfast.'

Loken had laughed, but the laughter had died in his throat when he realised that Horus was serious.

They had reached Davin, and there were more important matters to deal with.

'Remember,' said Horus. 'This plays out exactly as I have told you.'

A revered hush fell on the assemblage and every person present dropped to one knee as the Emperor's chosen proxy made his entrance. Karkasy felt faint at the sight of the living god, arrayed as he was in a magnificent suit of plate armour the colour of a distant ocean and a cloak of deepest purple. The eye of Terra shone on his breast, and Karkasy was overcome by the magisterial beauty of the Warmaster.

To have spent so long in the 63rd Expedition and only now to lay eyes upon the Warmaster seemed the grossest waste of his time, and Karkasy resolved to tear out the pages he'd written in the Bondsman Number 7 this week and compose an epic soliloquy on the nobility of the commander.

The Mournival followed him, together with a tall, statuesque woman in a crimson velveteen gown with high collars and puffed sleeves, her long hair worn in an impractical looking coiffure. He felt his indignation rise as he realised this must be Vivar, the remembrancer from Terra that they had heard about.

Horus raised his arms and said, 'Friends, I keep telling you that no one need kneel in my presence. Only the Emperor is deserving of such an honour.'

Slowly, as though reluctant to cease their veneration of this living god, the crowd rose to its feet as Horus passed amongst those closest to him, shaking hands and dazzling them with his easy charm and spontaneous wit. Karkasy watched the faces of those the Warmaster spoke to, feeling intense jealousy swell within his breast at the thought of not being so favoured.

Without thinking, he began pushing his way through the crowd towards the front, receiving hostile glares and the odd elbow to the gut for his troubles. He felt a tug on the collar of his robe and craned his neck to rebuke whoever had thought to handle his expensive garments so roughly. He saw Euphrati Keeler behind him and, at first, thought she was attempting to pull him back, but then he saw her face and smiled as he realised that she was coming with him, using his bulk like a plough.

He managed to get within six or seven people of the front, when he remembered why he had been allowed within this august body in the first place. He tore his eyes from the Warmaster to watch Erebus of the Word Bearers.

Karkasy knew little of the XVII Legion, save that its prima-rch, Lorgar, was a close and trusted brother of Horus. Both Legions had fought and shed their blood together many times for the glory of the Imperium. The members of the Mournival came forward and, one by one, embraced Erebus as a long lost brother. They laughed and slapped each other's armour in wel-come, though Karkasy saw a measure of reticence in the embrace between Loken and Erebus.

'Focus, Ignace, focus...' he whispered to himself as he found his gaze straying once again to the glory of the Warmaster. He tore his eyes from Horus in time to see Abaddon and Ere-bus shake hands one last time and saw a gleam of silver pass between their palms. He couldn't be sure, it had happened so fast, but it had looked like a coin or medal of some sort.

The Mournival and Vivar then took up positions a respect-ful distance behind the Warmaster, as Maloghurst assumed his place at his master's side. Horus lifted his arms and said, 'You must bear with me once again, my friends, as we gather to dis-cuss our plans to bring truth and light to the dark places.'

Polite laughter and clapping spread towards the edges of the yurt as Horus continued. 'Once again we return to Davin, site of a great triumph and the eighth world brought into compli-ance. Truly it is–'

'Warmaster,' came a voice from the centre of the yurt.

The word was spoken softly, and the audience let out a col-lective gasp at such a flagrant breach of etiquette.

Karkasy saw the Warmaster's expression turn thunderous, understanding that he was obviously unused to being inter-rupted, before switching his scrutiny back to the speaker.

The crowd drew back from Erebus, as though afraid that mere proximity to him might somehow taint them with his temerity.

'Erebus,' said Maloghurst. 'You have something to say.'

'Merely a correction, equerry,' explained the Word Bearer.

Karkasy saw Maloghurst give the Warmaster a wary sidelong glance. 'A correction you say. What would you have corrected?'

'The Warmaster said that this world is compliant,' said Erebus.

'Davin is compliant,' growled Horus.

Erebus shook his head sadly and, for the briefest instant, Karkasy detected a trace of dark amusement in his next pronouncement.

'No,' said Erebus. 'It is not.'

Loken felt his choler rise at this affront to their honour and sensed the anger of the Mournival in the stiffening of their backs. Surprisingly, Aximand went so far as to reach for his sword, but Torgaddon shook his head and Little Horus reluctantly removed his hand from his weapon.

He had known Erebus for only a short time, but Loken had seen the respect and esteem the softly spoken Chaplain of the Word Bearers commanded. His counsel had been sage, his manner easy and his faith in the Warmaster unshakeable; but Erebus's subtle infiltration to the Warmaster's side had unsettled Loken in ways beyond simple jealousy. Since taking counsel from the First Chaplain, the commander had become sullen, needlessly argumentative and withdrawn. Maloghurst himself had expressed his concern to the Mournival over the Word Bearer's growing influence upon the Warmaster.

After a conversation with Erebus in the *Vengeful Spirit's* forward observation deck, Loken had known that there was more to the First Chaplain than met the eye. Seeds of suspicion had been planted in his heart that day, and Erebus's words were now like fresh spring rain upon them.

After the influence he had accumulated since Xenobia, Loken could hardly believe that Erebus would now choose to behave in such a boorish manner.

'Would you care to elaborate on that?' asked Maloghurst, visibly struggling to keep his temper. Loken had never admired the equerry more.

'I would,' said Erebus, 'but perhaps these might be matters best discussed in private.'

'Say what you have to say, Erebus, this is the War Council and there are no secrets here,' said Horus, and Loken knew that whatever role the Warmaster had planned for them was an irrelevance now. He saw that the other members of the Mournival realised this too.

'My lord,' began Erebus, 'I apologise if–'

'Save your apology, Erebus,' said Horus. 'You have a nerve to come before me like this. I took you in and gave you a place at my War Council and this is how you repay me, with dishonour? With insolence? I'll not stand for it, I'll tell you that right now. Do you understand me?'

'I do, my lord, and no dishonour was intended. If you would allow me to continue, you will see that I mean no insult.'

A crackling tension filled the yurt, and Loken silently willed the Warmaster to put an end to this farce and retire to somewhere more secluded, but he could see the Warmaster's blood was up and there would be no backing down from this confrontation.

'Go on,' said Horus through gritted teeth.

'As you know, we left here six decades ago, my lord. Davin was compliant and seemed as though it would become an enlightened part of the Imperium. Sadly that has not proven to be the case.'

'Get to the point, Erebus,' said Horus, his fists clenching in murderous balls.

'Of course. En route to Sardis and our rendezvous with the 203rd fleet, the revered Lord Kor Phaeron bade me detour to Davin that I might ensure the Word of the Emperor, beloved by all, was being maintained by Commander Temba and the forces left with him.'

'Where is Temba anyway?' demanded Horus. 'I gave him enough men to pacify any last remnants of resistance. Surely if this world was no longer compliant I would have heard about it?'

'Eugan Temba is a traitor, my lord,' said Erebus. 'He is on the moon of Davin and no longer recognises the Emperor as his lord and master.'

'Traitor?' shouted Horus. 'Impossible. Eugan Temba was a man of fine character and admirable martial spirit, I chose him personally for this honour. He would never turn traitor!'

'Would that that were true, my lord,' said Erebus, sounding genuinely regretful.

'Well, what in the name of the Emperor is he doing on the moon?' asked Horus.

'The tribes on Davin itself were honourable and readily accepted compliance, but those on the moon did not,' explained Erebus. 'Temba led his men in a glorious, but ultimately foolhardy, expedition to the moon to bring the tribes there into line.'

'Why foolhardy? Such is the duty of an Imperial commander.'

'It was foolhardy, my lord, for the tribes of the moon do not understand respect as we do and it appears that when Temba attempted an honourable parley with them, they employed... means to twist the perceptions of our men and turn them against you.'

'Means? Speak plainly, man!' said Horus.

'I hesitate to name them, my lord, but they are what might be described in the ancient texts as, well, sorcery.'

Loken felt the humours in his blood swing wildly out of balance at this mention of sorcery, and a gasp of disbelief swept around the yurt at such a notion.

'Temba now serves the master of Davin's moon and has spat on his oaths of loyalty to the Emperor. He names you as the lackey of a fallen god.'

Loken had never met Eugan Temba, but he felt his hatred of the man rise like a sickness in his gorge at this terrible insult to the Warmaster's honour. An astonished wailing swept round the yurt as the assembled warriors felt this insult as keenly as he did.

'He will pay for this!' roared Horus. 'I will tear his head off and feed his body to the crows. By my honour I swear this!'

'My lord,' said Erebus. 'I am sorry to be the bearer of such ill news, but surely this is a matter best left to those appointed beneath you.'

'You would have me despatch others to avenge this stain upon my honour, Erebus?' demanded Horus. 'What sort of a warrior do you take me for? I signed the Decree of Compliance here and I'll be damned if the only world to backslide from the Imperium is one that I conquered!'

Horus turned to the Mournival. 'Ready a speartip – now!'

'Very well, my lord,' said Abaddon. 'Who shall lead it?'

'I will,' said Horus.

The War Council was dismissed; all other concerns and matters due before it shelved by this terrible development. A frantic vigour seized the 63rd Expedition as commanders returned to their units and word spread of Eugan Temba's treachery.

Amid the urgent preparations for departure, Loken found Ignace Karkasy in the yurt so recently vacated by the incensed War Council. He sat with an open book before him, writing with great passion and pausing only to sharpen his nib with a small pocket knife.

'Ignace,' said Loken.

Karkasy looked up from his work, and Loken was surprised at the amusement he saw in the remembrancer's face. 'Quite a meeting, eh? Are they all that dramatic?'

Loken shook his head. 'No, not usually. What are you writing?'

'This, oh, just a quick poem about the vile Temba,' said Karkasy. 'Nothing special, just a stream of consciousness kind of thing. I thought it appropriate given the mood of the expedition.'

'I know. I just can't believe anyone could say such a thing.'

'Nor I, and I think that's the problem.'

'What do you mean?'

'I'll explain,' said Karkasy, rising from his seat and making his way towards the untouched bowls of cold meat and helping himself to a plateful. 'I remember a piece of advice I heard about the Warmaster. It was said that a good trick upon meeting him was to look at his feet, because if you caught his eye you'd quite forget what it was you were going to say.'

'I have heard that too. Aximand told me the same thing.'

'Well it's obviously a good piece of advice, because I was quite taken aback when I saw him up close for the first time: quite magnificent. Almost forgot why I was there.'

'I'm not sure I understand,' said Loken, shaking his head as Karkasy offered him some meat from the plate.

'Put it this way, can you imagine anyone who had actually met Horus – may I call him Horus? I hear you're not too fond of us mere mortals calling him that – saying such a thing as this Temba person is supposed to have said?'

Loken struggled to keep up with Karkasy's rapid delivery, realising that his anger had blinded him to the simple fact of the Warmaster's glory.

'You're right, Ignace. No one who'd met the Warmaster could say such things.'

'So the question then becomes, why would Erebus say that Temba had said it?'

'I don't know. Why would he?'

Karkasy swallowed some of the meat on his plate and washed it down with a drink of the white liquor.

'Why indeed?' asked Karkasy, warming to the weaving of his tale. 'Tell me, have you had the "pleasure" of meeting Aeliuta Hergig? She's a remembrancer – one of the dramatists – and pens some dreadfully overwrought plays. Tedious things if you ask me, but I can't deny that she has some skill in treading the boards herself. I remember watching her play Lady Ophelia in *The Tragedy of Amleti* and she was really rather good, though–'

'Ignace,' warned Loken. 'Get to the point.'

'Oh, yes, of course. My point is that as talented an actress as Ms Hergig is, she couldn't hold a candle to the performance given by Erebus today.'

'Performance?'

'Indeed. Everything he did from the moment he entered this yurt was a performance. Didn't you see it?'

'No, I was too angry,' admitted Loken. 'That's why I wanted you there. Explain it to me simply and without digressions, Ignace.'

Karkasy beamed in pride before continuing.

'Very well. When he first spoke of Davin's non-compliance, Erebus suggested taking the matter somewhere more private, yet he had just broached this highly provocative subject in a room full of people. And did you notice? Erebus said that Temba had turned against him, Horus, not the Emperor: Horus. He made it personal. '

'But why would he seek to provoke the Warmaster so?'

'Perhaps to unbalance his humour in order to bring his choler to the fore, it's not like he wouldn't have known what his reaction would be. I think Erebus wanted the Warmaster in a position where he wasn't thinking clearly.'

'Be careful, Ignace. Are you suggesting that the Warmaster does not think clearly?'

'No, no, no,' said Karkasy. 'Only that with his humours out of balance, Erebus was able to manipulate him.'

'Manipulate him to what end?'

Karkasy shrugged. 'I don't know, but what I do know is that Erebus *wants* Horus to go to Davin's moon.'

'But he counselled against going there. He even had the nerve to suggest that others go in the Warmaster's place.'

Karkasy shook his hand dismissively. 'Only so as to look like he had tried to stop him from his course of action, while knowing full well that the Warmaster couldn't back down from this insult to his honour.'

'And nor should he, remembrancer,' said a deep voice at the entrance to the yurt.

Karkasy jumped, and Loken turned at the sound of the voice to see the First Captain of the Sons of Horus resplendent and huge in his plate armour.

'Ezekyle,' said Loken. 'What are you doing here?'

'Looking for you,' said Abaddon. 'You should be with your company. The Warmaster himself is to lead the speartip, and you waste time with scriveners who call into question the word of an honourable Astartes.'

'First Captain Abaddon,' breathed Karkasy, lowering his head. 'I meant no disrespect. I was just apprising Captain Loken of my impressions of what I heard.'

'Be silent, worm,' snapped Abaddon. 'I should kill you where you stand for the dishonour you do to Erebus.'

'Ignace was just doing what I asked him to do,' Loken pointed out.

'You put him up to this, Garviel?' asked Abaddon. 'I'm disappointed in you.'

'There's something not right about this, Ezekyle,' said Loken. 'Erebus isn't telling us everything.'

Abaddon shook his head. 'You would take this fool's word over that of a brother Astartes? Your dalliance with petty wordsmiths has turned your head around, Loken. The commander shall hear of this.'

'I sincerely hope so,' said Loken, his anger growing at

Abaddon's easy dismissal of his concerns. 'I will be standing next to you when you tell him.'

The First Captain turned on his heel and made to leave the yurt.

'First Captain Abaddon,' said Karkasy. 'Might I ask you a question?'

'No, you may not,' snarled Abaddon, but Karkasy asked anyway.

'What was the silver coin you gave Erebus when you met him?'

FOUR

Secrets and hidden things
Chaos
Spreading the word
Audience

Abaddon froze at Karkasy's words.

Loken recognised the signs and quickly moved to stand between the First Captain and the remembrancer.

'Ignace, get out of here,' he shouted, as Abaddon turned and lunged for Karkasy.

Abaddon roared in anger and Loken grabbed his arms, holding him at bay as Karkasy squealed in terror and bolted from the yurt. Abaddon pushed Loken back, the First Captain's massive strength easily greater than his; Loken tumbled away, but he had achieved his objective in redirecting Abaddon's wrath.

'You would raise arms against a brother, Loken?' bellowed Abaddon.

'I just saved you from making a big mistake, Ezekyle,' replied Loken as he climbed to his feet. He could see that Abaddon's blood was up and knew that he must tread warily. Aximand had told him of Abaddon's berserk rages during the desperate extraction of the commander from the Extranus, and his temper was becoming more and more unpredictable.

'A mistake? What are you talking about?'

'Killing Ignace,' said Loken. 'Think what would have happened if you'd killed him. The Warmaster would have had your head for that. Imagine the repercussions if an Astartes murdered a remembrancer in cold blood.'

Abaddon furiously paced the interior of the yurt like a caged animal, but Loken could see that his words had penetrated the red mist of his friend's anger.

'Damn it, Loken... Damn it,' hissed Abaddon.

'What was Ignace talking about, Ezekyle? Was it a lodge medal that passed between you and Erebus?'

Abaddon looked directly at Loken and said, 'I can't say.'

'Then it was.'

'I. Can't. Say.'

'Damn you, Ezekyle. Secrets and hidden things, my brother, I can't abide them. This is exactly why I can't return to the warrior lodge. Aximand and Torgaddon have both asked me to, but I won't, not now. Tell me: is Erebus part of the lodge now? Was he always part of it or did you bring him in on the journey here?'

'You heard Serghar's words at the meeting. You know I can't speak of what happens within the circles of the lodge.'

Loken stepped in close to Abaddon, chestplate to chestplate, and said, 'You'll tell me now, Ezekyle. I smell something rank here and I swear if you lie to me I'll know.'

'You think to bully me, little one?' laughed Abaddon, but Loken saw the lie in his bluster.

'Yes, Ezekyle, I do. Now tell me.'

Abaddon's eyes flickered to the entrance of the yurt.

'Very well,' he said. 'I'll tell you, but what I say goes no further.'

Loken nodded and Abaddon said, 'We did not bring Erebus into the lodge.'

'No?' asked Loken, his disbelief plain.

'No,' repeated Abaddon. 'It was Erebus who brought us in.'

Erebus, brother Astartes, First Chaplain of the Word Bearers...

Trusted counsellor of the Warmaster...

Liar.

No matter how much he tried to blot the word out with his battle meditation it kept coming back to haunt him. In response, Euphrati Keeler's words, from the last time they had spoken, swirled around his head, over and over.

She had stared him down and asked, 'If you saw the rot, a hint of corruption, would you step out of your regimented life and stand against it?'

Keeler had been suggesting the impossible, and he had denied that anything like what she was suggesting could ever take place. Yet here he was entertaining the possibility that a brother Astartes – someone the Warmaster valued and trusted – was lying to them for reasons unknown.

Loken had tried to find Kyril Sindermann to broach the subject with him, but the iterator was nowhere to be found and so Loken had returned to the training halls despondent. The smiling killer, Luc Sedirae, was cleaning the dismantled parts of his bolter; the 'twins', Moy and Marr, were conducting a sword drill; and Loken's oldest friend, Nero Vipus, sat on the benches polishing his breastplate, working out the scars earned on Murder.

Sedirae and Vipus nodded in acknowledgement as he entered.

'Garvi,' said Vipus. 'Something on your mind?'

'No, why?'

'You look a little strung out, that's all.'

'I'm fine,' snapped Loken.

'Fine, fine,' muttered Vipus. 'What did I do?'

'I'm sorry, Nero,' Loken said. 'I'm just...'

'I know, Garvi. The whole company's the same. They can't wait to get in theatre and be the first to get to grips with that bastard, Temba. Luc's already bet me he'll be the one to take his head.'

Loken nodded noncommittally and said, 'Have either of you seen First Captain Abaddon?'

'No, not since we got back,' replied Sedirae without looking up from his work. 'That remembrancer, the black girl, she was looking for you though.'

'Oliton?'

'Aye, that's her. Said she'd come back in an hour or so.'

'Thank you, Luc,' said Loken, turning back to Vipus, 'and again, I'm sorry I snapped at you, Nero.'

'Don't worry,' laughed Vipus. 'I'm a big boy now and my skin's thick enough to withstand your bad moods.'

Loken smiled at his friend and opened his arming cage, stripping off his armour and carefully peeling away the thick, mimetic polymers of his sub-suit body glove until he was naked but for a pair of fatigues. He lifted his sword and stepped towards the training cage, activating the weapon as the iron-grey hemispheres lifted aside and the tubular combat servitor descended from the centre of the dome's top.

'Combat drill Epsilon nine,' he said. 'Maximum lethality.'

The combat machine hummed to life, long blade limbs unfolding from its sides in a manner that reminded him of the winged clades of Murder. Spikes and whirring edges sprouted from the contraption's body and Loken swivelled his neck and arms in readiness for the coming fight.

He needed a clear head if he was to think through all that had happened, and there was no better way to achieve purity of thought than through combat. The battle machine began a soft countdown and Loken dropped into a fighting crouch as his thoughts once again turned to the First Chaplain of the Word Bearers.

Liar...

It had been on the fifteenth day since leaving interex space, and a week before reaching Davin, that Loken finally had the chance to speak with Erebus alone. He awaited the First Chaplain of the Word Bearers in the forward observation deck of the *Vengeful Spirit*, watching smudges of black light and brilliant darkness slide past the great, armoured viewing bay.

'Captain Loken?'

Loken turned, seeing Erebus's open, serious face. His shaved, tattooed skull gleamed in the swirling vortices of coloured light shining through the glass of the observation bay; rendering his armour with the patina of an artist's palette.

'First Chaplain,' replied Loken, bowing low.

'Please, my given name is Erebus; I would be honoured if you would call me by it. We have no need of such formality here.'

Loken nodded as Erebus joined him in front of the great, multi-coloured vista laid out before them.

'Beautiful, isn't it?' said Erebus.

'I used to think so,' nodded Loken. 'But in truth I can't look on it now without dread.'

'Dread? Why so?' asked Erebus, placing his hand on Loken's shoulder. 'The warp is simply the medium through which our ships travel. Did not the Emperor, beloved by all, reveal the ways and means by which we might make use of it?'

'Yes, he did,' agreed Loken, glancing at the tattooed script on Erebus's skull, though the words were in a language he did not understand.

'They are the pronouncements of the Emperor as interpreted in the *Book of Lorgar* and rendered in the language of Colchis,' said Erebus, answering Loken's unasked question. 'They are as much a weapon as my bolter and blade.'

Seeing Loken's incomprehension, Erebus said, 'On the battlefield I must be a figure of awe and majesty, and by bearing the Word of the Emperor upon my very flesh, I cow the xeno and unbeliever before me.'

'Unbeliever?'

'A poor choice of word,' shrugged Erebus dismissively, 'perhaps misanthrope would be a better term, but I suspect that you did not ask me here to admire the view or my scripture.'

Loken smiled and said, 'No, you're right, I didn't. I asked to speak to you because I know the Word Bearers to be a Legion with many scholars among their ranks. You have sought out many worlds that were said to be seats of learning and knowledge and brought them to compliance.'

'True,' agreed Erebus slowly. 'Though we destroyed much of that knowledge as profane in the fires of war.'

'But you are wise in matters esoteric and I desired your counsel on a… a matter I thought best spoken of privately.'

'Now I am intrigued,' said Erebus. 'What is on your mind?'

Loken pointed towards the pulsing, spectral light of the warp on the other side of the observation bay's glass. Clouds of many colours and spirals of darkness spun and twisted like blooms of ink in water, constantly churning in a maelstrom of light and shadow. No coherent forms existed in the mysterious otherworld beyond the ship, which, but for the power of the Geller field, would destroy the Warmaster's vessel in the blink of an eye.

'The warp allows us to travel from one side of the galaxy to the other, but we don't really understand it at all, do we?' asked Loken. 'What do we really know about the things that lurk in its depths? What do we know of Chaos?'

'Chaos?' repeated Erebus, and Loken detected a moment of hesitation before the Word Bearer answered. 'What do you mean by that term?'

'I'm not sure,' admitted Loken. 'It was something Mithras Tull said to me back on Xenobia.'

'Mithras Tull? I don't know the name.'

'He was one of Jephta Naud's subordinate commanders,' explained Loken. 'I was speaking to him when everything went to hell.'

'What did he say, Captain Loken? Exactly.'

Loken's eyes narrowed at the First Chaplain's tone and he said, 'Tull spoke of Chaos as though it were a distinct force, a primal presence in the warp. He said that it was the source of the most malevolent corruption imaginable and that it would outlive us all and dance on our ashes.'

'He used a colourful turn of phrase.'

'That he did, but I believe he was serious,' said Loken, gazing out into the depths of the warp.

'Trust me: Loken; the warp is nothing more than mindless energy churning in constant turmoil. That is all there is to it. Or is there something else that makes you believe his words?'

Loken thought of the slavering creature that had taken the flesh of Xavyer Jubal in the water fane under the mountains of Sixty-Three Nineteen. That had not been mindless warp energy given form. Loken had seen a monstrous, thirsting intelligence lurking within the horrid deformity that Jubal had become.

Erebus was staring at him expectantly and as much as the Word Bearer had been welcomed within the ranks of the Sons of Horus, Loken wasn't yet ready to share the horror beneath the Whisperheads with an outsider.

Hurriedly he said, 'I read of battles between the tribes of men on old Terra, before the coming of the Emperor, and they were said to use powers that were–'

'Was this in *The Chronicles of Ursh*?' asked Erebus.

'Yes. How did you know?'

'I too have read it and I know of the passages to which you refer.'

'Then you also know that there was talk of dark, primordial gods and invocations to them.'

Erebus smiled indulgently. 'Yes, and it is the work of outrageous taletellers and incorrigible demagogues to make their farragoes as exciting as possible, is it not? *The Chronicles of Ursh* is not the only text of that nature. Many such books were written before Unification and each writer filled page after page with the most outrageous, blood-soaked terrors in order to outdo his contemporaries, resulting in some works of... dubious value.'

'You don't think there's anything to it then?'

'Not at all,' said Erebus.

'Tull said that the immaterium, as he called it, was the root of sorcery and magic.'

'Sorcery and magic?' laughed Erebus before locking his gaze with Loken. 'He lied to you, my friend. He was a fraterniser with xenos breeds and an abomination in the sight of the Emperor. You know the word of an enemy cannot be trusted. After all, did the interex not falsely accuse us of stealing one of the kinebrach's swords from the Hall of Devices? Even after the Warmaster himself vouchsafed that we did not?'

Loken said nothing as ingrained bonds of brotherhood warred with the evidence of his own senses. Everything Erebus was saying reinforced his long held beliefs in the utter falsehood of sorcery, spirits and daemons.

Yet he could not ignore what his instincts screamed at him: *that Erebus was lying to him and the threat of Chaos was horribly real.*

Mithras Tull had become an enemy and Erebus was a brother

Astartes, and Loken was astonished to find that he more readily believed the warrior of the interex.

'As you have described it to me, there is no such thing as Chaos,' promised Erebus.

Loken nodded in agreement, but despaired as he realised that no one, not even the interex, had said exactly what kind of weapon had been stolen from the Hall of Devices.

'Did you hear?' asked Ignace Karkasy, pouring yet another glass of wine. 'She's got full access... to the Warmaster! It's disgraceful. Here's us, breaking our backs to create art worthy of the name, in the hope of catching the eye of someone important enough to matter, and she bloody swans in without so much as a by your leave and gets an audience with the Warmaster!'

'I heard she has connections,' nodded Wenduin, a petite woman with red hair and an hourglass figure that ship scuttlebutt had down as a firecracker between the sheets. Karkasy had gravitated towards her as soon as he had realised she was hanging on his every bitter word. He'd forgotten exactly what it was she did, though he vaguely remembered something about 'compositions of harmonic light and shade' – whatever that meant.

Honestly, he thought, they'll let anyone be a remembrancer these days.

The Retreat was, as usual, thick with remembrancers: poets, dramatists, artists and composers, which had made for a bohemian atmosphere, while off-duty Army officers, naval ratings and crew were there for the civilians to impress with tales of books published, opening night ovations and scurrilous backstage hedonistic excess.

Without its audience, the Retreat revealed itself as an uncomfortably vandalised, smoky bar filled with people who had nothing better to do. The gamblers had scraped the arched columns bare of gilt to make gambling chips (of which Karkasy now had quite a substantial pile back in his cabin) and the artists had whitewashed whole areas of the walls for their own daubings – most of which were either lewd or farcical.

Men and women filled all the available tables, playing hands of merci merci while some of the more enthusiastic remembrancers planned their next compositions. Karkasy and Wenduin sat in one of the padded booths along the wall and the low buzz of conversation filled the Retreat.

'Connections,' repeated Wenduin sagely.

'That's it exactly,' said Karkasy, draining his glass. 'I heard the Council of Terra – the Sigillite too.'

'Throne! How'd she get them?' asked Wenduin. 'The connections I mean?'

Karkasy shook his head. 'Don't know.'

'It's not like you don't have connections either. You could find out,' Wenduin pointed out, filling his glass once more. 'I don't know what you have to be worried about anyway. You have one of the Astartes looking after you. You're a fine one to be casting aspersions!'

'Hardly,' snorted Karkasy, slapping a palm on the table. 'I have to show him everything I damn well write. It's censorship, that's what it is.'

Wenduin shrugged. 'Maybe it is, maybe it isn't, but you got to go to the War Council didn't you? A little censorship's worth that, I'll bet.'

'Maybe,' said Karkasy, unwilling to be drawn on the subject of the events on Davin and his terror at the sight of an enraged First Captain Abaddon coming to tear his head off.

In any event, Captain Loken had later found him, trembling and afraid, in the commissariat tent, making inroads into a bottle of distilac. It had been a little ridiculous really. Loken had ripped a page from the Bondsman Number 7 and written on it in large, blocky letters before handing it to him.

'This is an oath of moment, Ignace,' Loken had said. 'Do you know what that means?'

'I think so,' he had replied, reading the words Loken had written.

'It is an oath that applies to an individual action. It is very specific and very precise,' Loken had explained. 'It is common for an Astartes to swear such an oath before battle when he vows to achieve a certain objective or uphold a certain ideal. In your case, Ignace, it will be to keep what passed here tonight between us.'

'I will, sir.'

'You must swear, Ignace. Place your hand on the book and the oath and swear the words.'

He had done so, placing a shaking hand atop the page, feeling the heavy texture of the page beneath his sweating palm.

'I swear not to tell another living soul what passed between us,' he said.

Loken had nodded solemnly and said, 'Do not take this lightly, Ignace. You have just made an oath with the Astartes and you must never break it. To do so would be a mistake.'

He'd nodded and made his way to the first transport off Davin.

Karkasy shook his head clear of the memory, any warmth or comfort the wine had given him suddenly, achingly, absent.

'Hey,' said Wenduin. 'Are you listening to me? You looked a million miles away there.'

'Yes, sorry. What were you saying?'

'I was asking if there was any chance you could put in a good word for me to Captain Loken? Maybe you could tell him about my compositions? You know, how good they are.'

Compositions?

What did that mean? He looked into her eyes and saw a dreadful avarice lurking behind her façade of interest, now seeing her for the self-interested social climber she was. Suddenly all he wanted to do was get away.

'Well? Could you?'

He was saved from thinking of an answer by the arrival of a robed figure at the booth.

Karkasy looked up and said, 'Yes? Can I help–' but his words trailed off as he eventually recognised Euphrati Keeler. The change in her since the last time he had seen her was remarkable. Instead of her usual ensemble of boots and fatigues, she wore the beige robe of a female remembrancer, and her long hair had been cut into a modest fringe.

Though more obviously feminine, Karkasy was disappointed to find that the change was not to his liking, preferring her aggressive stylings to the strange sexless quality this attire granted her.

'Euphrati? Is that you?'

She simply nodded and said, 'I'm looking for Captain Loken. Have you seen him today?'

'Loken? No, well, yes, but not since Davin. Won't you join us?' he said, ignoring the viperous glare Wenduin cast in his direction.

His hopes of rescue were dashed when Euphrati shook her head and said, 'No, thank you. This place isn't really for me.'

'Nor me, but here I am,' smiled Karkasy. 'You sure I can't tempt you to some wine or a round of cards?'

'I'm sure, but thanks anyway. See you around, Ignace, and have a good night,' said Keeler with a knowing smile. Karkasy gave her a lopsided grin and watched her as she made her way from booth to booth before leaving the Retreat.

'Who was that?' asked Wenduin, and Karkasy was amused at the professional jealousy he heard in her voice.

'That was a very good friend of mine,' said Karkasy, enjoying the sound of the words.

Wenduin nodded curtly.

'Listen, do you want to go to bed with me or not?' she asked, all pretence of actual interest in him discarded in favour of blatant ambition.

Karkasy laughed. 'I'm a man. Of course I do.'

'And you'll tell Captain Loken of me?'

If you're as good as they say you are, you can bet on it, he thought.

'Yes, my dear, of course I will,' said Karkasy, noticing a folded piece of paper on the edge of the booth. Had it been there before? He couldn't remember. As Wenduin eased herself from the booth, he picked up the paper and unfolded it. At the top was some kind of symbol, a long capital 'I' with a haloed star at its centre. He had no idea what it meant and began to skim the words, thinking it might be some remembrancer's discarded scribblings.

Such thoughts faded, however, as he read the words written on the paper.

'The Emperor of Mankind is the Light and the Way, and all his actions are for the benefit of mankind, which is his people. The Emperor is God and God is the Emperor, so it is taught in this, the…'

'What's that?' asked Wenduin.

Karkasy ignored her, pushing the paper into his pocket and leaving the booth. He looked around the Retreat and saw several identical pamphlets on various tables around the room. Now he was convinced that the paper hadn't been on his table before Euphrati's visit and he began making his way around the bar, gathering up as many of the dog-eared papers as he could find.

'What are you doing?' demanded Wenduin, watching him with her arms folded impatiently across her chest.

'Piss off!' snarled Karkasy, heading for the exit. 'Find some other gullible fool to seduce. I don't have time.'

If he hadn't been so preoccupied, he might have enjoyed her look of surprise.

Some minutes later, Karkasy stood before Euphrati Keeler's billet, deep in the labyrinth of arched companionways and dripping passages that made up the residential deck. He noticed the symbol from the pamphlet etched on the bulkhead beside her billet and hammered his fist on her shutter until at last it opened. The smell of scented candles wafted into the corridor.

She smiled, and he knew she had been expecting him.

'Lectitio Divinitatus?' he said, holding up the pile of pamphlets he'd gathered from the Retreat. 'We need to talk.'

'Yes, Ignace, we do,' she said, turning and leaving him standing at the threshold.

He went inside after her.

Horus's personal chambers were surprisingly modest, thought Petronella, simple and functional with only a few items that might be considered personal. She hadn't expected lavish ostentation, but had thought to see more than could be found in any Army soldier's billet. A stack of yellowed oath papers filled a footlocker against one wall and some well-thumbed books sat on the shelves beside the cot bed, its length and breadth massive to her, but probably barely sufficient for a being with the inhuman scale of a primarch.

She smiled at the idea of Horus sleeping, wondering what mighty visions of glory and majesty one of the Emperor's sons might dream. The idea of a primarch sleeping was distinctly humanising, though it had never crossed her mind that one such as Horus would even need to rest. Petronella had assumed that, as well as never aging, the primarchs did not tire either. She decided the bed was an affectation, a reminder of his humanity.

In deference to her first meeting with Horus, Petronella wore a simple dress of emerald green, its skirts hung with silver and topaz netting, and a scarlet bodice with a scandalous décolletage. She carried her data-slate and gold tipped mnemo-quill in a demure reticule of gold cord draped over her shoulder, and her fingers itched to begin their work. She had considered leaving Maggard outside the chambers, but she knew the thought of being denied the chance to stand in the presence of such a sublime warrior as Horus would be galling to him. Being in such close proximity to the Astartes had been a powerful intoxicant to her bodyguard, who she could tell looked up to them as gods. She regarded his pleasure at being amongst such powerful warriors as quietly endearing.

She ran her fingertips across the wooden surface of Horus's desk, anxious to begin this first session of documenting him. The desk's proportions were as enlarged as those of his bed, and she smiled as she imagined the many great campaigns he had planned here, and the commands for war signed upon its stained and faded surface.

Had he written the order granting her previous audience here, she wondered?

She remembered well receiving that instruction to attend upon the Warmaster immediately; she remembered her terror and elation as Babeth was run ragged with half a dozen rapid changes of costume for her. In the end she had settled for something elegant yet demure – a cream dress with an ivory panelled bodice that pushed her bosom up, and a webbed necklace of red gold that reached up her neck before curling over her forehead in a dripping cascade of pearls and sapphires. Eschewing the Terran custom of powdering her face, she opted instead for a subtle blend of powdered antimony sulphide to darken the rims of her eyes and a polychromatic lip-gloss.

Horus had obviously appreciated her sartorial restraint, smiling broadly as she was ushered into his presence. Her breath, had it not already been largely stolen by the constriction of her bodice, would have been snatched away by the glory of the Warmaster's physical perfection and palpable charisma. His hair was short, and his face open and handsome, with dazzling eyes that fixed her with a stare that told her she was the most important thing to him right now. She felt giddy, like a debutante at her first ball.

He wore gleaming battle armour the colour of a winter sky, its rims formed of beaten gold, and bas-relief text filling each shoulder guard. Bright against his chestplate was a staring red eye, like a drop of blood on virgin snow, and she felt transfixed by its unflinching gaze.

Maggard stood behind her, resplendent in brightly polished gold plate and silver mail. Of course, he carried no weapons, his swords and pistols already surrendered to Horus's bodyguards.

'My lord,' she began, bowing her head and making an elaborate curtsey, her hand held palm down before him in expectation of a kiss.

'So you are of House Carpinus?' asked Horus.

She recovered quickly, disregarding the Warmaster's breach of etiquette in ignoring her hand and asking her a question before formal introductions had been made. 'I am indeed, my lord.'

'Don't call me that,' said the Warmaster.

'Oh… of course… how should I address you?'

'Horus would be a good start,' he said, and she looked up to see him smiling broadly. The warriors behind him tried unsuccessfully to hide their amusement, and Petronella realised that Horus was toying with her. She forced herself to return his smile, masking her annoyance at his informality, and said, 'Thank you. I shall.'

'So you want to be my documentarist, do you?' asked Horus.

'If you will permit me to fulfil such a role, yes.'

'Why?'

Of all the questions she'd anticipated, this simple query was one she hadn't been expecting to be thrown so baldly at her.

'I feel this is my vocation, my lord,' she began. 'It is my destiny as a scion of House Carpinus to record great things and mighty deeds, and to encapsulate the glory of this war – the heroism, the danger, the violence and the full fury of battle. I desire to–'

'Have you ever seen a battle, girl?' asked Horus suddenly.

'Well, no. Not as such,' she said, her cheeks flushing angrily at the term 'girl'.

'I thought not,' said Horus. 'It is only those who have neither fired a shot nor heard the shrieks and groans of the dying who cry aloud for blood, vengeance and desolation. Is that what you want? Is that your "vocation"?'

'If that is what war is, then yes,' she said, unwilling to be cowed before his boorish behaviour. 'I want to see it all. See it all and record the glory of Horus for future generations.'

'The glory of Horus,' repeated the Warmaster, obviously relishing the phrase.

He held her pinned by his gaze and said, 'There are many remembrancers in my fleet, Miss Vivar. Tell me why I should give you this honour.'

Flustered by his directness once more, she searched for words, and the Warmaster chuckled at her awkwardness. Her irritation rose to the surface again and, before she could stop herself she said, 'Because no one else in the ragtag band of remembrancers you've managed to accumulate will do as good a job as I will. I will immortalise you, but if you think you can bully me with your bad manners and high and mighty attitude then you can go to hell... sir.'

A thunderous silence descended.

Then Horus laughed, the sound hard, and she knew that, in one flash of anger, she had destroyed her chances of being able to accomplish the task she had appointed herself.

'I like you, Petronella Vivar of House Carpinus,' he said. 'You'll do.'

Her mouth fell open and her heart fluttered in her breast.

'Truly?' she asked, afraid that the Warmaster was playing with her again.

'Truly,' agreed Horus.

'But I thought...'

'Listen, lass, I usually make up my mind about a person within ten seconds and I very rarely change it. The minute you walked in, I saw the fighter in you. There is something of the wolf in you, girl, and I like that. Just one thing...'

'Yes?'

'Not so formal next time,' he smirked. 'We are a ship of war, not the parlours of Merica. Now I fear I must excuse myself, as I have to head planetside to Davin for a council of war.'

And with that, she had been appointed.

It still amazed her that it had been so easy, though it meant most of the formal gowns she had brought now seemed wholly inappropriate, forcing her to dress in unbearably prosaic dresses more at home in the alms houses of the Gyptus spires. The dames of society wouldn't recognise her now.

She smiled at the memory as her trailing fingers reached the end of the desk and rested on an ancient tome with a cracked leather binding and faded gilt lettering. She opened the book and idly flipped a couple of pages, stopping at one showing a complex astrological diagram of the orbits of planets and conjunctions, below which was the image of some mythical beast, part man, part horse.

'My father gave me that,' said a powerful voice behind her.

She turned, guiltily snatching her hand back from the book.

Horus stood behind her, his massive form clad in battle-plate. As ever, he was almost overwhelmingly intimidating, physical and masculine, and the thought of sharing a room with such a powerful specimen of manhood in the absence of a chaperone gave her guilt a delicious edge.

'Sorry,' she said. 'That was impolite of me.'

Horus waved his hand. 'Don't worry,' he said. 'If there was anything I didn't want you to see I wouldn't have left it out.'

Despite his easy reassurance, he gathered up the book and slipped it onto the shelves above his bed. She immediately sensed great tension in him, and though he appeared outwardly clam, her heart raced as she felt his furious anger. It bubbled beneath his skin like the fires of a once dormant volcano on the verge of unleashing its terrible fury.

Before she could say anything in reply, he said, 'I'm afraid I can't sit and speak to you today, Miss Vivar. Matters have arisen on Davin's moon that require my immediate attention.'

She tried to cover her disappointment, saying, 'No matter, we can reschedule a meeting for when you have more time.'

He laughed, the sound harsh and, she thought, a little too sad to be convincing.

'That may not be for a while,' he warned.

'I'm not someone who gives up easily,' she promised. 'I can wait.'

Horus considered her words for a moment, and then shook his head.

'No, that won't be necessary,' he said with a smile. 'You said you wanted to see war?'

She nodded enthusiastically and he said, 'Then accompany me to the embarkation deck and I'll show you how the Astartes prepare for war.'

FIVE

Our people
A leader
Speartip

The bridge of the *Vengeful Spirit* bustled with activity, the business of ferrying troops and war machines back from the surface of Davin complete, and plans now drawn for the extermination of Eugan Temba's rebellious forces.

Extermination. That was the word they used, not subjugation, not pacification: extermination.

And the Legion was more than ready to carry out that sentence.

Sleek and deadly warships broke anchor with Davin under the watchful gaze of the Master of the Fleet, Boas Comnenus. Moving such a fleet even a short distance in formation was no small undertaking, but the ship's masters appointed beneath him knew their trade and the withdrawal from Davin was accomplished with the precision of a surgeon wielding a scalpel.

Not all the Expedition fleet vacated Davin's orbit, but enough followed the course of the *Vengeful Spirit* to ensure that nothing would be able to stand before the Astartes speartip.

The journey was a mercifully short one, Davin's moon a dirty, yellow brown smudge of reflected light haloed against the distant red sun.

To Boas Comnenus their destination looked like a terrible, bloated pustule against the heavens.

✠ ✠ ✠

Feverish activity filled the embarkation deck as fitters, deck hands and Mechanicum adepts made last minute pre-flight checks to the growling Stormbirds. Engines flared and strobing arc lights bathed the enormous, echoing deck in a pale, washed out industrial glow. Hatches were slammed shut, arming pins were removed from warheads, and fuel lines were disconnected from rumbling engines. Six of the monstrous flyers sat hunched at the end of their launch rails, cranes delivering the last of their ordnance payloads, while gunnery servitors calibrated the cannons slung beneath the cockpit.

The captains and warriors selected to accompany the Warmaster's speartip followed ground crews around the Stormbirds, checking and rechecking their machines. Their lives would soon depend on these aircraft and no one wanted to wind up dead thanks to something as trivial as mechanical failure. Along with the Mournival, Luc Sedirae, Nero Vipus and Verulam Moy – together with specialised squads from their companies – would travel to Davin's moon to fight once more in the name of the Imperium.

Loken was ready. His mind was full of new and disturbing thoughts, but he pushed them to one side in preparation for the coming fight. Doubt and uncertainty clouded the mind and an Astartes could afford neither.

'Throne, I'm ready for this,' said Torgaddon, clearly relishing the prospect of battle.

Loken nodded. Something still felt terribly wrong to him, but he too longed for the purity of real combat, the chance to test his warrior skills against a living opponent. Though if their intelligence was correct, all they would be facing was perhaps ten thousand rebellious Army soldiers, no match for even a quarter this many Astartes.

The Warmaster, however, had demanded the utter destruction of Temba's forces, and five companies of Astartes, a detachment of Varvarus's Byzant Janizars and a battle group of Titans from the Legio Mortis were to unleash his fiery wrath. Princeps Esau Turnet had pledged the *Dies Irae* itself.

'I've not seen a gathering of might like this since before Ullanor,' said Torgaddon. 'Those rebels on the moon are already as good as dead.'

Rebels…

Whoever thought to hear such a word?

Enemies yes, but rebels… never.

The thought soured his anticipation of battle as they made their way to where Aximand and Abaddon checked the arms inventory of their Stormbird, arguing over which munitions would be best suited to the mission.

'I'm telling you, the subsonic shells will be better,' said Aximand.

'And what if they have armour like those interex bastards?' demanded Abaddon.

'Then we use mass reactive. Tell him, Loken!'

Abaddon turned at Loken and Torgaddon's approach and nodded curtly.

'Aximand's right,' Loken said. 'Supersonic shells will pass through a man before they have time to flatten and create a killing exit wound. You might fire three of these through a target and still not put him down.'

'Just because the last few fights have been against armoured warriors, Ezekyle wants them,' said Aximand, 'but I keep telling him that this battle will be fought against men no more armoured than our own Army soldiers.'

'And let's face it,' sniggered Torgaddon. 'Ezekyle needs all the help he can get putting an enemy down.'

'I'll bloody well put you down, Tarik,' said Abaddon, his grim exterior finally cracking into a smile. The First Captain's hair was pulled back in a long scalp lock in preparation for donning his helmet, and Loken could see that he too was fiercely anticipating the coming bloodshed.

'Doesn't this bother any of you?' asked Loken, unable to contain himself any longer.

'What?' asked Aximand.

'This,' said Loken, waving an arm around the deck at the preparations for war that were being made all around them. 'Don't you realise what we're about to do?'

'Of course we do, Garvi,' bellowed Abaddon. 'We're going to kill some damned fool that insulted the Warmaster!'

'No,' said Loken. 'It's more than that, don't you see? These people we're going to kill, they're not some xenos empire or a lost strand of humanity that doesn't want to be brought to compliance. They're ours; it's our people we'll be killing.'

'They're traitors,' said Abaddon, needlessly emphasising the last word. 'That's all there is to it. Don't you see? They have turned their back on the Warmaster and the Emperor, and for that reason, their lives are forfeit.'

'Come on, Garvi,' said Torgaddon. 'You're worrying about nothing.'

'Am I? What do we do if it happens again?'

The other members of the Mournival looked at one another in puzzlement.

'If what happens again?' asked Aximand finally.

'What if another world rebels in our wake, then another and another after that? This is Army, but what happens if Astartes rebel? Would we still take the fight to them?'

The three of them laughed at that, but Torgaddon answered. 'You have a fine sense of humour, my brother. You know that could never happen. It's unthinkable.'

'And unseemly,' said Aximand, his face solemn. 'What you suggest might be considered treason.'

'What?'

'I could report you to the Warmaster for this sedition.'

'Aximand, you know I would never...'

Torgaddon was the first to crack. 'Oh, Garvi, you're too easy!' he said, and they all laughed. 'Even Aximand can get you now. Throne, you're so straight up and down.'

Loken forced a smile and said, 'You're right. I'm sorry.'

'Don't be sorry,' said Abaddon. 'Be ready to kill.'

The First Captain held his hand out into the middle of the group and said, 'Kill for the living.'

'Kill for the dead,' said Aximand, placing his hand on top of Abaddon's.

'To hell with the living and the dead,' said Torgaddon, following suit. 'Kill for the Warmaster.'

Loken felt a great love for his brothers and nodded, placing his hand into the circle, the confraternity of the Mournival filling him with pride and reassurance.

'I will kill for the Warmaster,' he promised.

The scale of it took her breath away. Her own vessel boasted three embarkation decks, but they were poor things compared to this, capable of handling only skiffs, cutters and shuttles.

To see so much martial power on display was humbling.

Hundreds of Astartes surrounded them, standing before their allocated Stormbirds – monstrous, fat-bodied flyers with racks of missiles slung under each wing and wide, rotary cannons seated in forward pintle mounts. Engines screamed as last minute adjustments were carried out, and each group of Astartes warriors, massive and powerful, began final weapons checks.

'I never dreamed it could be like this,' said Petronella, watching as the gargantuan blast door at the far end of the launch rails deafeningly rumbled open in preparation for the launch. Through the shimmering integrity field, she could see the leprous glow of Davin's moon against a froth of stars, as blackened jet blast deflectors rose up from the floor on hissing pneumatic pistons.

'This?' said Horus. 'This is nothing. At Ullanor, six hundred
vessels anchored above the planet of the greenskin. My entire
Legion went to war that day, girl. We covered the land with our
soldiers: over two million Army soldiers, a hundred Titans of
the Mechanicum and all the slaves we freed from the greenskin labour camps.'

'And all led by the Emperor,' said Petronella.

'Yes,' said Horus. 'All led by the Emperor...'

'Did any other Legions fight on Ullanor?'

'Guilliman and the Khan, their Legions helped clear the outer
systems with diversionary attacks, but my warriors won the day,
the best of the best slogging through blood and dirt. It was I
who led the Justaerin speartip to final victory.'

'It must have been incredible.'

'It was,' agreed Horus. 'Only Abaddon and I walked away
from the fight against the greenskin warlord. He was a tough
bastard, but I illuminated him and then threw his body from
the highest tower.'

'This was before the Emperor granted you the title of Warmaster?' asked Petronella, her mnemo-quill frantically trying to
keep up with Horus's rapid delivery.

'Yes.'

'And you led this... what did you call it? Speartip?'

'Yes, a speartip. A precision strike to tear out the enemy's
throat and leave him leaderless and blind.'

'And you'll lead it again here?'

'I will.'

'Is that not a little unusual?'

'What?'

'Someone of such high rank taking to the field of battle?'

'I have had this same argum... discussion with the Mournival,' said Horus, ignoring her look of confusion at the term. 'I
am the Warmaster and I did not attain such a title by keeping
myself away from battle. For men to follow me and obey my
orders without question as the Astartes do, they must see that
I am right there with them, sharing the danger. How can any
warrior trust me to send him into battle if he feels that all I do
is sign orders, without appreciating the dangers he must face?'

'Surely there comes a time when considerations of rank must
necessarily remove you from the battlefield? If you were to fall–'

'I will not.'

'But if you did.'

'I will not,' repeated Horus, and she could feel the force of
his conviction in every syllable. His eyes, always so bright and

full of power met hers and she felt the light of her belief in him
swell until it illuminated her entire body.

'I believe you,' she said.

'Tell me, would you like to meet the Mournival?'

'The what?'

Horus smiled. 'I'll show you.'

'Another damned remembrancer,' sneered Abaddon, shaking
his head as he saw Horus and a woman in a green and red
dress enter the embarkation deck. 'It's bad enough you've got
a gaggle of them hanging round you, Loken, but the Warmaster? It's disgraceful.'

'Why don't you tell him that yourself?' asked Loken.

'I will, don't worry,' said Abaddon.

Aximand and Torgaddon said nothing, knowing when to leave
the First Captain to his choler and when to back off. Loken,
however, was still relatively new to regular contact with Abaddon, and his anger with him over his defence of Erebus was
still raw.

'You don't feel the remembrancer program has any merit at
all?'

'Pah, it's a waste of our time to babysit them. Didn't Leman
Russ say something about giving them all a gun? That sounds
a damn sight more sensible to me than having them write stupid poems or paint pictures.'

'It's not about poems and pictures, Ezekyle, it's about capturing the spirit of the age. It's about history that we are writing.'

'We're not here to write history,' answered Abaddon, 'We're
here to make it.'

'Exactly. And they will tell it.'

'Well what use is that to us?'

'Perhaps it's not for us,' said Loken. 'Did you ever think of
that?'

'Then who's it for?' demanded Abaddon.

'It's for the generations who come after us,' said Loken. 'For
the Imperium yet to be. You can't imagine the wealth of information the remembrancers are gathering: libraries worth of
achievements chronicled, galleries worth of artistry and countless cities raised for the glory of the Imperium. Thousands of
years from now, people will look back at these times and they
will know us and understand the nobility of what we set out to
do. Ours will be an age of enlightenment that men will weep to
know they were not a part of it. All that we have achieved will
be celebrated and people will remember the Sons of Horus as

the founders of a new age of illumination and progress. Think of that, Ezekyle, the next time you dismiss the remembrancers so quickly.'

He locked eyes with Abaddon, daring him to contradict him.

The First Captain met his gaze then laughed. 'Maybe I should get one too. Wouldn't want anyone to forget my name in the future, eh?'

Torgaddon clapped both of them on the shoulders and said, 'No, who'd want to know about you, Ezekyle? It's me they'll remember, the hero of Spiderland who saved the Emperor's Children from certain death at the hands of the megarachnids. That's a tale worth telling twice, eh, Garvi?'

Loken smiled, glad of Tarik's intervention. 'It's a grand tale right enough, Tarik.'

'I wish it was only twice we had to hear it,' put in Aximand. 'I've lost count of how many times I've heard you tell that tale. It's getting to be as bad as that joke you tell about the bear.'

'Don't,' warned Loken, seeing Torgaddon about to launch into a rendition of the joke.

'There was this bear, the biggest bear you can imagine,' started Torgaddon. 'And a hunter...'

The others didn't give him a chance to continue, bundling him with shouts and whoops of laughter.

'This is the Mournival,' said a powerful voice and their play fighting ceased immediately.

Loken released Torgaddon from a headlock and straightened before the sound of the Warmaster's voice. The remainder of the Mournival did likewise, guiltily standing to attention before the commander. The dark complexioned woman with the black hair and fanciful dress stood at his side, and though she was tall for a mortal, she still only just reached the lower edges of his chest-plate. She stared at them in confusion, no doubt wondering what she had just seen.

'Are your companies ready for battle?' demanded Horus.

'Yes, sir,' they chorused.

Horus turned to the woman and said, 'This is Petronella Vivar of House Carpinus. She is to be my documentarist and I, unwisely it seems now, decided it was time for her to meet the Mournival.'

The woman took a step towards them and gave an elaborate and uncomfortable looking curtsey, Horus waiting a little behind her. Loken caught the amused glint concealed behind his brusqueness and said, 'Well are you going to introduce us, sir? She can't very well chronicle you without us can she?'

'No, Garviel,' smiled Horus. 'I wouldn't want the chronicles of Horus to exclude you, would I? Very well, this insolent young pup is Garviel Loken, recently elevated to the lofty position of the Mournival. Next to him is Tarik Torgaddon, a man who tries to turn everything into a joke, but mostly fails. Aximand is next. "Little Horus" we call him, since he is lucky enough to share some of my most handsome features. And finally, we come to Ezekyle Abaddon, Captain of my First Company.'

'The same Abaddon from the tower at Ullanor?' asked Petronella, and Abaddon beamed at her recognition.

'Yes, the very same,' answered Horus, 'though you wouldn't think it to look at him now.'

'And this is the Mournival?'

'They are, and for all their damned horseplay, they are invaluable to me. They are a voice of reason in my ear when all around me is confusion. They are as dear to me as my brother primarchs and I value their counsel above all others. In them are the humours of choler, phlegm, melancholia and sanguinity mixed in exactly the right amount I need to keep me on the side of the angels.'

'So they are advisors?'

'Such a term is too bland for the place they have in my heart. Learn this, Petronella Vivar, and your time with me will not have been in vain: without the Mournival, the office of Warmaster would be a poor thing indeed.'

Horus stepped forward and pulled something from his belt, something with a long strip of parchment drooping from it.

'My sons,' said Horus, dropping to one knee and holding the waxen token towards the Mournival. 'Would you hear my oath of moment?'

Stunned by the magnanimity of such an act, none of the Mournival dared move. The other Astartes on the embarkation deck saw what was happening and a hush spread throughout the chamber. Even the background noise of the deck seemed to diminish at the incredible sight of the Warmaster kneeling before his chosen sons.

Eventually, Loken reached out a trembling gauntlet and took the seal from the Warmaster's hand. He glanced over at Torgaddon and Aximand either side of him, quite dumbfounded by the Warmaster's humility.

Aximand nodded and said, 'We will hear your oath, Warmaster.'

'And we will witness it,' added Abaddon, unsheathing his sword and holding it out before the Warmaster.

Loken raised the oath paper and read the words the commander had written.

'Do you, Horus, accept your role in this? Will you take your vengeance to those who defy you and turn from the glory of all you have helped create? Do you swear that you shall leave none alive who stand against the future of humanity and do you pledge to do honour to the XVI Legion?'

Horus looked up into Loken's eyes and removed his gauntlet, clenching his bare fist around the blade Abaddon held out.

'On this matter and by this weapon, I swear,' said Horus, dragging his hand along the sword blade and opening the flesh of his palm. Loken nodded and handed the wax seal to the Warmaster as he rose to his feet.

Blood welled briefly from the cut and Horus dipped the oath paper in the clotting red fluid before affixing the oath paper to his breastplate and grinning broadly at them all.

'Thank you, my sons,' he said, coming forward to embrace them all one by one.

Loken felt his admiration for the Warmaster fill his heart, all the hurt at their exclusion from his deliberations on the way here forgotten as he held each of them close.

How could they ever have doubted him?

'Now, we have a war to wage, my sons,' shouted Horus. 'What say you?'

'Lupercal!' yelled Loken, punching the air.

The others joined in and the chant spread until the embarkation deck reverberated with the deafening roars of the Sons of Horus.

'Lupercal! Lupercal! Lupercal! Lupercal!'

The Stormbirds launched in sequence, the Warmaster's bird streaking from its launch rails like a predator unleashed. At intervals of seven seconds, each Stormbird fired until all six were launched. The pilots kept them close to the *Vengeful Spirit*, waiting for the remaining assault craft to launch from the other embarkation decks. So far, there had been no sign of the *Glory of Terra*, Eugan Temba's flagship, or any of the other vessels left behind, but no one was taking any chances that there might be wolf pack squadrons of cruisers or fighters lurking nearby.

Presently, another twelve Stormbirds of the Sons of Horus took up position with the Warmaster's squadron as well as two belonging to the Word Bearers. The formation complete, the Astartes craft banked sharply, altering course to take them to the surface of Davin's moon. The mighty, cliff-like flanks of the Warmaster's flagship receded and, like swarms of bright insects,

hundreds of Army drop-ships detached from their bulk transporters – each one carrying a hundred armed men.

But greatest of all were the lander vessels of the Mechanicum.

Vast, monolithic structures as big as city blocks, they resembled
snub-nosed tubes fitted with a wealth of heat resistant technologies and recessed deceleration burners. Inertial dampening
fields held their cargoes secure and explosive bolts on internal
anti-motion scaffolding were primed to release on impact.

In the wake of the militant arm of the launch came the logis-
tics of an invasion, ammunition carriers, food and water tankers,
fuel haulers and a myriad other support vessels essential for the
maintenance of offensive operations.

Such was the proliferation of craft heading for the surface
that no one could keep track of them all, not even the bridge
crew under Boas Comnenus, and thus the gold-skinned landing skiff that launched from the civilian bay of the *Vengeful
Spirit* went unnoticed.

The invasion fleet mustered in low orbit, orbital winds clutching at streamers of atmospheric gases and spinning them in lazy
coils beneath the vessels.

As always, it was the Astartes who led the invasion.

The way in was rough. Atmospheric disturbances and storms
wracked the skies and the Astartes Stormbirds were tossed like
leaves in a hurricane. Loken felt the craft vibrate wildly around
him, grateful for the restraint harness that held him fast to his
cage seat. His bolter was stowed above him and there was nothing to do but wait until the Stormbird touched down and the
attack began. He slowed his breathing and cleared his mind
of all distractions, feeling a hot energy suffuse his limbs as his
armour prepared his metabolism for imminent battle.

The warriors of Nero Vipus's Locasta squad and Brakespur
squad surrounded him, immobile, yet representing the peak of
humanity's martial prowess. He loved them all dearly and knew
that they wouldn't let him down. Their conduct on Murder and
Xenobia had been exemplary and many of the newly elevated
novitiates had been blooded on those desperate battlefields.

His company was battle tested and sure.

'Garviel,' said Vipus over the inter-armour link. 'There's something you should hear.'

'What is it?' asked Loken, detecting a tone of warning in his
friend's voice.

'Switch to channel seven,' said Vipus. 'I've isolated it from the
men, but I think you ought to hear this.'

Loken switched internal channels, hearing nothing but a wash of grainy static, warbling and constant. Pops and crackles punctuated the hiss, but he could hear nothing else.

'I don't hear anything,'

'Wait. You will,' promised Vipus.

Loken concentrated, listening for whatever Nero was hearing. And then he heard it.

Faint, as though coming from somewhere impossibly far away was a voice, a gargling, wet voice.

'...the ways of man. Folly... seek... doom of all things. In death and rebirth shall mankind live forever...'

Though he was not built to feel fear, Loken was suddenly and horribly reminded of the approach to the Whisperheads when the air had been thick with the taunting hiss of the thing called Samus.

'Oh no...' whispered Loken as the watery, rasping voice came again. 'Thus do I renounce the ways of the Emperor and his lackey the Warmaster of my own free will. If he dares come here, he will die. And in death shall he live forever. Blessed be the hand of Nurgh-leth. Blessed be. Blessed be...'

Loken hammered his fist against the release bolt on his cage seat and rose to his feet, swaying slightly as he felt a strange nausea cramp his belly. His genhanced body allowed him to compensate for the wild motion of the Stormbird, and he made his way swiftly along the ribbed decking towards the pilots' compartment, determined that they wouldn't walk blind into the same horror as had been waiting for them on Sixty-Three Nineteen.

He pulled open the hatch where the flight officers and hard-wired pilots fought to bring them in through the swirling yellow storm clouds. He could hear the same, repeating phrase coming over the internal speakers here.

'Where's it coming from?' he demanded.

The nearest flight officer turned and said, 'It's a vox, plain and simple, but...'

'But?'

'It's coming from a ship vox,' said the man, pointing at a wavering green waveform on the waterfall display before him. 'From the patterning it's one of ours. And it's a powerful one, a transmitter designed for inter-ship communication between fleets.'

'It's an actual vox transmission?' said Loken, relieved it wasn't ghost chatter like the hateful voice of Samus.

'Seems to be, but a ship's vox unit that size shouldn't be anywhere near the surface of a planet. Ships that big don't come this far down into the atmosphere. Leastways if they want to keep flying they don't.'

'Can you jam it?'

'We can try, but like I said, it's a powerful signal, it could burn through our jamming pretty quickly.'

'Can you trace where it's coming from?'

The flight officer nodded. 'Yes, that won't be a problem. A signal that powerful we could have traced from orbit.'

'Then why didn't you?'

'It wasn't there before,' protested the officer. 'It only started once we hit the ionosphere.'

Loken nodded. 'Jam it as best you can. And find the source.'

He turned back to the crew compartment, unsettled by the uncanny similarities between this development and the approach to the Whisperheads.

Too similar to be accidental, he thought.

He opened a channel to the other members of the Mournival, receiving confirmation that the signal was being heard throughout the speartip.

'It's nothing, Loken,' came the voice of the Warmaster from the Stormbird at the leading edge of the speartip. 'Propaganda.'

'With respect, sir, that's what we thought in the Whisperheads.'

'So what are you suggesting, Captain Loken? That we turn around and head back to Davin? Ignore this stain on my honour?'

'No, sir,' replied Loken. 'Just that we ought to be careful.'

'Careful?' laughed Abaddon, his hard Cthonic laughter grating even over the vox. 'We are Astartes. Others should be careful around us.'

'The First Captain is right,' said Horus. 'We will lock onto this signal and destroy it.'

'Sir, that might be exactly what our enemies want us to try.'

'Then they'll soon realise their error,' snapped Horus, shutting off the connection.

Moments later, Loken heard the Warmaster's orders come through the vox and felt the deck shift under him as the Stormbirds smoothly changed course like a pack of hunting birds.

He made his way back to his cage seat and strapped himself in, suddenly sure that they were walking into a trap.

'What's going on, Garvi?' asked Vipus.

'We're going to destroy that voice,' said Loken, repeating the Warmaster's orders. 'It's nothing, just a vox transmitter. Propaganda.'

'I hope that's all it is.'

So do I, thought Loken.

✠ ✠ ✠

The Stormbird touched down with a hard slam, lurching as its skids hit soft ground and fought for purchase. The harness restraints disengaged and the warriors of Locasta smoothly rose from their cage seats and turned to retrieve their stowed weaponry as the disembarking ramp dropped from the rear of the Stormbird.

Loken led his men from their transport, hot steam and noxious fumes fogging the air as the blue glow of the Stormbird's shrieking engines filled the air with noise. He stepped from the hard metal of the ramp and splashed down onto the boggy surface of Davin's moon. His armoured weight sank up to mid calf, an abominable stench rising from the wet ground underfoot.

The Astartes of Locasta and Brakespur dispersed from the Stormbird with expected efficiency, spreading out to form a perimeter and link up with the other squads from the Sons of Horus.

The noise of the Stormbirds diminished as their engines spooled down and the blue glow faded from beneath their wings. The billowing clouds of vapour they threw up began to disperse and Loken had his first view of Davin's moon.

Desolate moors stretched out as far as the eye could see, which wasn't far thanks to the rolling banks of yellow mist clinging to the ground and moist fog that restricted visibility to less than a few hundred metres. The Sons of Horus were forming up around the magnificent figure of the Warmaster, ready to move out, and spots of light in the yellow sky announced the imminent arrival of the Army drop-ships.

'Nero, get some men forward to scout the edges of the mist,' Loken ordered. 'I don't want anything coming at us without prior warning.'

Vipus nodded and set about establishing scouting parties as Loken opened a channel to Verulam Moy. The Captain of the Nineteenth Company had volunteered some of his heavy weapon squads and Loken knew he could rely on their steady aim and cool heads. 'Verulam? Make sure your Devastators are ready and have good fields of fire, they won't get much of a warning through this fog.'

'Indeed, Captain Loken,' replied Moy. 'They are deploying as we speak.'

'Good work, Verulam,' he said, shutting off the vox and studying the landscape in more detail. Wretched bogs and dank fens rendered the landscape a uniform brown and sludgy green, with the occasional blackened and withered tree silhouetted against the sky. Clouds of buzzing insects hovered in thick swarms over the black waters.

Loken tasted the atmosphere via his armour's external senses, gagging on the rank smell of excrement and rotten meat. The senses in his armour's helmet quickly filtered them out, but the breath he'd taken told him that the atmosphere was polluted with the residue of decaying matter, as though the ground beneath him was slowly rotting away. He took a few ungainly steps through the swampy ground, each step sending up a bubbling ripple of burps and puffs of noxious gasses.

As the noise of the Stormbirds faded, the silence of the moon became apparent. The only sounds were the splashing of the Astartes through the swampy bogs and the insistent buzz of the insects.

Torgaddon splashed towards him, his armour stained with mud and slime from the swamps and even though his helmet obscured his features, Loken could feel his friend's annoyance at this dismal location.

'This place reeks worse than the latrines of Ullanor,' he said.

Loken had to agree with him; the few breaths he'd taken before his armour had isolated him from the atmosphere still lingered in the back of his throat.

'What happened here?' wondered Loken. 'The briefing texts didn't say anything about the moon being like this.'

'What did they say?'

'Didn't you read them?'

Torgaddon shrugged. 'I figured I'd see what kind of place it was once we landed.'

Loken shook his head, saying, 'You'll never make an Ultramarine, Tarik.'

'No danger of that,' replied Torgaddon. 'I prefer to form plans as I go and Guilliman's lot are even more starch-arsed than you. But leaving my cavalier attitude to mission briefings aside, what's this place supposed to look like then?'

'It's supposed to be climatologically similar to Davin – hot and dry. Where we are now should be covered in forests.'

'So what happened?'

'Something bad,' said Loken, staring out into the foggy depths of the moon's marshy landscape. 'Something very bad.'

PART TWO
PLAGUE MOON

SIX

Land of decay
Dead things
Glory of Terra

The Astartes spread out through the fog, moving as swiftly as the boggy conditions allowed and following the source of the vox signal. Horus led from the front, a living god marching tall through the stinking quagmires and rank swamps of Davin's moon, untroubled by the noxious atmosphere. He disdained the wearing of a helmet, his superhuman physique easily able to withstand the airborne poisons.

Four blocks of Astartes marched, phalanx-like, into the mists, with each member of the Mournival leading nearly two hundred warriors. Behind them came the soldiers of the Imperial Army, company after company of red-jacketed warriors with gleaming lasguns and silver tipped lances. Each man was equipped with a rebreather apparatus after it was discovered that their mortal constitutions were unable to withstand the moon's toxic atmosphere. Initial landings of armour proved to be disastrous, as tanks sank into the marshland and drop-ships found themselves caught in the sucking mud.

Though the greatest of all the engines of war were those that emerged from the Mechanicum landers. Even the Astartes had paused in their advance to watch the descent of the three monstrously huge craft. Slowly dropping through the yellow skies in defiance of gravity like great primeval monoliths, the blackened hulks travelled on smoking pillars of fire as their colossal

retros fought to slow them down. Even with such fiery deceleration, the ground shook with the hammerblow of their impacts,
geysers of murky water thrown hundreds of metres into the air
along with blinding clouds as the swamps flashed to steam.
Massive hatches blew open and the motion resistant scaffolding
fell away as the Titans of the Legio Mortis stepped from their
landing craft and onto the moon's surface.

The *Dies Irae* led the *Death's Head* and *Xestor's Sword*, Warlord
Titans with long, fluttering honour rolls hung from their armoured
thorax. Each thunderous footstep of the mighty Titans sent shock-
waves through the swamps for kilometres in all directions, their
bastion legs sinking several metres through the marshy ground to
the bedrock beneath. Their steps churned huge gouts of mud and
water, their appearance that of awesome gods of war come to smite
the Warmaster's enemies beneath their mighty tread.

Loken watched the arrival of the Titans with a mixture of awe
and unease: awe for the majesty of their colossal appearance,
unease for the fact that the Warmaster felt it necessary to deploy
such powerful engines of destruction.

The advance was slow going, trudging through clinging mud and
stinking, brackish water, all the while unable to see much more
than a few dozen metres. The thick fog banks deadened sound
such that something close by might be inaudible while Loken
could clearly hear the splash of warriors from Luc Sedirae's
men, far to his right. Of course he couldn't see them through
the yellow mist, so each company kept in regular vox contact
to try and ensure they weren't separating.

Loken wasn't sure it was helping though. Strange groans and
hisses, like the expelled breath of a corpse, bubbled from the
ground and blurred shadow forms moved in the mist. Each time
he raised his bolter to take aim in readiness, the mist would
part and an armoured figure in the green of the Sons of Horus
or the steel grey of the Word Bearers would be revealed. Erebus
had led his warriors to Davin's moon in support of the Warmaster and Horus had welcomed their presence.

The mist gathered in thickness with unsettling speed, slowly
swallowing them up until all Loken could see were warriors
from his own company. They passed through a dark forest of
leafless, dead trees, the bark glistening and wet looking. Loken
paused to examine one, pressing his gauntlet against the tree's
surface and grimacing as its bark sloughed off in wet chunks.
Writhing maggots and burrowing creatures curled and wriggled
within the rotten sapwood.

'These trees...' he said.

'What about them?' asked Vipus.

'I thought they were dead, but they're not.'

'No?'

'They're diseased. Rotten with it.'

Vipus shrugged and carried onwards, and once again Loken was struck by the certainty that something terrible had happened here. And looking at the diseased heartwood of the tree, he wasn't sure that it was over. He wiped his stained gauntlet on his leg armour and set off after Vipus.

The eerily silent march continued through the fog and, assisted by the servo muscles of their armour, the Astartes quickly began to outpace the soldiers of the Imperial Army, who were finding the going much more difficult.

'Mournival,' said Loken over the inter-suit link. 'We need to slow our advance, we're leaving too big a gap between ourselves and the Army detachments.'

'Then they need to pick up the pace,' returned Abaddon. 'We don't have time to wait for lesser men. We're almost at the source of the vox.'

'Lesser men,' said Aximand. 'Be careful, Ezekyle, you're starting to sound a little like Eidolon now.'

'Eidolon? That fool would have come down here on his own to gain glory,' snarled Abaddon. 'I'll not be compared to him!'

'My apologies, Ezekyle. You're obviously nothing like him,' deadpanned Aximand.

Loken listened with amusement to his fellow Mournival's bantering, which, together with the quiet of Davin's moon began to reassure him that his concerns over their deployment here might be unfounded. He lifted his armoured boot from the swamp and took another step forward, this time feeling something crack under his step. Glancing down, he saw something round and greenish white bob upwards in the water.

Even without turning it over he could see it was a skull, the paleness of bone wreathed in necrotic strands of rotted flesh and muscle. A pair of shoulders rose from the depths behind it, the spinal column exposed beneath a layer of bloated green flesh.

Loken's lip curled in disgust as the decomposed corpse rolled onto its back, its sightless eye sockets filled with mud and weeds. Even as he saw the rotted cadaver, more bobbed to the surface, no doubt disturbed from their resting places on the bottom of the swamps by the footfalls of the Titans.

He called a halt and opened the link to his fellow commanders once again as yet more bodies, hundreds now, floated to the surface of the swamp. Grey and lifeless meat still clung to their bones and the impacts of the Titans' footfalls gave their dead limbs a horrid animation.

'This is Loken,' he said. 'I've found some bodies.'

'Are they Temba's men?' asked Horus.

'I can't tell, sir,' answered Loken. 'They're too badly decomposed. It's hard to tell. I'm checking now.'

He slung his bolter and leaned forwards, gripping the nearest corpse and lifting it from the water. Its bloated, rancid flesh was alive with wriggling motion, burrowing carrion insects and larvae nesting within it. Sure enough, mouldering scraps of a uniform hung from it and Loken wiped a smear of mud from its shoulder.

Barely legible beneath the scum and filth of the swamps he found a sewn patch bearing the number sixty-three emblazoned over the outline of a snarling wolf's head.

'Yes, 63rd Expedition,' confirmed Loken. 'They're Temba's, but I–'

Loken never finished the sentence as the bloated body suddenly reached up and fastened its bony fingers around his neck, its eyes filled with lambent green fire.

'Loken?' said Horus as the link was suddenly cut off. 'Loken?'

'Something amiss?' asked Torgaddon.

'I don't know yet, Tarik,' answered the Warmaster.

Suddenly the hard bangs of bolter fire and the whoosh of flame units could be heard from all around them.

'Second Company!' shouted Torgaddon. 'Stand to, weapons free!'

'Where's it coming from?' bellowed Horus.

'Can't say,' replied Torgaddon. 'The mist's playing merry hell with the acoustics.'

'Find out,' ordered the Warmaster.

Torgaddon nodded, demanding contact reports from all companies. Garbled shouts of impossible things came over the link, along with the louder bark of heavy bolter fire.

Gunfire sounded to his left and he spun to face it, his bolter raised before him. He could see nothing but the staccato flashes of weapon fire and the occasional blue streak of a plasma shot. Even the external senses of his armour were unable to penetrate the creeping mist.

'Sir, I think we–'

Without warning the swamp exploded as something vast and bloated erupted from the water before him. Its gangrenous, rotten flesh barrelled into him, its bulk sufficient to knock him onto his back and into the swamp.

Before he went under the dark water, Torgaddon had the fleeting impression of a yawning mouth filled with hundreds of fangs and a glaucous, cyclopean eye beneath a horn of yellowed bone.

'I don't know. The command net just went crazy,' said Moderati Primus Aruken in response to Princeps Turnet's question. The external surveyors had suddenly and shockingly filled with returns that hadn't been there a second ago and his princeps had demanded to know what was going on.

'Well find out, damn you!' ordered Turnet. 'The Warmaster's out there.'

'Main guns spooled up and ready to fire,' reported Moderati Primus Titus Cassar.

'We need a damn target first, I'm not about to fire into that mess without knowing what I'm shooting at,' said Turnet. 'If it was Army I'd risk it, but not Astartes.'

The bridge of the *Dies Irae* was bathed in a red light, its three command officers seated upon their control seats on a raised dais before the green glow of the tactical plot. Wired into the very essence of the Titan, they could feel its every motion as though it were their own.

Despite the mighty war machine beneath him, Jonah Aruken suddenly felt powerless as this unknown enemy arose to engulf the Sons of Horus. Expecting armoured opposition and an enemy they could see, they had been little more than a focus for the Imperial forces to rally around so far. For all the Titan's overwhelming superiority in firepower, there was little they could do to aid their fellows.

'Getting something,' reported Cassar. 'Incoming signal.'

'What is it? I need better information than that, damn you,' shouted Turnet.

'Aerial contact. Signal's firming up. Fast moving and heading towards us.'

'Is it a Stormbird?'

'No, sir. All Stormbirds are accounted for in the deployment zone and I'm not picking up any military transponder signals.'

Turnet nodded. 'Then it's hostile. Do you have a solution, Aruken?'

'Running it now, princeps.'

'Range six hundred metres and closing,' said Cassar. 'God-Emperor protect us, it's coming right for us.'

'Aruken! That's too damn close, shoot it down.'

'Working on it, sir.'

'Work faster!'

The dense mists made looking through the frontal windshield pointless; nevertheless, there was an irresistible fascination in looking out at an alien world – not that there was much, or indeed anything, to see. Thus, Petronella's first impressions upon breaching the upper atmosphere were of disappointment, having expected exotic vistas of unimaginable alien strangeness.

Instead, they had been buffeted by violent storm winds and could see nothing but the yellow skies and banks of fog that seemed to be gathered around another unremarkable patch of brown swampland ahead.

Though the Warmaster had politely, but firmly, declined her request to travel to the surface with the warriors of the spear-tip, she had been sure there was a glint of mischief in his eye. Taking that for a sign of tacit approval, she had immediately gathered Maggard and her flight crew in the shuttle bay in preparation for descent to the moon below.

Her gold-skinned landing skiff launched in the wake of the Army drop-ships, losing itself in the mass of assault craft heading to the moon's surface. Unable to keep pace with the invasion force, they had been forced to follow the emission trails and now found themselves circling deep in a soup of impenetrable fog that rendered the ground below virtually invisible.

'Getting some returns from up ahead, my lady,' said the first officer. 'I think it's the speartip.'

'At last,' she said. 'Get as close as you can then set us down. I want to get out of this mist so I can see something worth writing about.'

'Yes, ma'am.'

Petronella settled back into her seat as the skiff angled its course towards the source of the surveyor return, irritably altering the position of her restraint harness to try to avoid creasing the folds of her dress. She gave up, deciding that the dress was beyond saving, and returned her gaze to the windshield as the pilot gave a sudden yell of terror.

Hot fear seethed in her veins as the mist before them cleared and she saw a huge mechanical giant before them, its proportions massive and armoured. Saw-toothed bastions and towers filled her vision, massive cannons and a terrible, snarling face of dark iron.

'Throne!' cried the pilot, hauling on the controls in a desperate evasive manoeuvre as roaring fire and light horrifyingly filled the windshield.

Petronella's world exploded in pain and broken glass as the guns of the *Dies Irae* opened fire and blasted her skiff from the yellow skies.

Loken surged backwards in horror and disgust as the cadaver attempted to strangle the life from him with its slimy fingers. For something as apparently fragile as a rotted corpse, the thing was possessed of a fearsome strength and he was dragged to his knees by the weight and power of the creature.

With a thought, he flooded his metabolism with battle stimms and fresh strength surged into his limbs. He gripped the arms of his attacker and pulled them from its reeking torso in a flood of dead fluids and a wash of brackish blood. The fire died in the thing's eyes and it flopped lifeless to the swamp.

He pushed himself to his feet and took stock of the situation, his Astartes training suppressing any notion of panic or disorientation. From all around them, the bodies he had previously thought to be lifeless were rising from the dark waters and launching themselves at his warriors.

Bolters blasted chunks of mouldered flesh from their bodies or tore limbs from putrefied torsos, but still they kept coming, tearing at the Astartes with diseased, yellowed claws. More of the things were rising all around them and Loken shot three down with as many shots, shattering skulls and exploding chests with mass-reactive shells.

'Sons of Horus, on me!' he yelled. 'Form on me.'

The warriors of Tenth Company calmly began falling back to their captain, firing as they went at the necrotic horrors rising from the swamp like creatures from their worst nightmares. Hundreds of dead things surrounded them, mouldering corpses and bloated, muttering abominations, each with a single milky, distended eye and a scabrous horn sprouting from its forehead.

What were they? Monstrous xeno creatures with the power to reanimate dead flesh or something far worse? Thick, buzzing clouds of flies flew round them, and Loken saw an Astartes go down, the feeds on his helmet thick with fat bodied insects. The warrior frenziedly tore his helmet off and Loken was horrified to see his flesh rotting away with an unnatural rapidity, his skin greying and peeling away to reveal the liquefying tissue beneath.

The bark of bolter fire focussed him and he returned his attention to the battle before him, emptying magazine after magazine into the shambling mass of repulsive creatures before him.

'Head shots only!' he cried as he put another of the dead things down, its skull a ruin of blackened bone and sloshing ooze. The tide of the battle began to turn as more and more of the shambling horrors went down and stayed down. The green-fleshed things with grotesquely distended bellies took more killing, though it seemed to Loken that they dissolved into stinking matter as they fell into the water of the swamp.

More shapes moved through the mist as a thunderous roar of heavy cannon fire came from behind them, followed by the bright flare of an explosion high above. Loken looked up to see a golden landing skiff trailing smoke and fire wobble in the sky, though he had not the time to wonder what a civilian craft was doing in a warzone as yet more of the dead things climbed from the water.

Too close for bolters, he drew his sword and brought the monstrously toothed blade to life with a press of the activation stud. A ghastly thing of decomposed flesh and rotten meat hurled itself at him and he swung his blade two-handed for its skull.

The blade roared as it slew, gobbets of wet, grey meat spattering his armour as he ripped the sword through from brainpan to groin. He swung at another creature, the green fire of its eyes flickering out as he hacked it in two. All about him, Sons of Horus went toe to toe with the terrible creatures that had once been members of the 63rd Expedition.

Rotted hands clamped onto his armour from beneath the water and Loken felt himself being dragged down. He roared and reversed his grip on his sword, stabbing it straight down into leering skulls and rotted faces, but incredibly their strength was the greater and he could not resist their pull.

'Garvi!' shouted Vipus, hacking enemies from his path as he forged through the swamp towards him.

'Luc! Help me!' cried Vipus, grabbing onto Loken's outstretched arm. Loken gripped onto his friend's hand as he felt another set of hands grip him around his chest and haul backwards.

'Let go, you bastards!' roared Luc Sedirae, hauling with all his might.

Loken felt himself rising and kicked out as the swamp creatures finally released him. He scrambled back and clambered to his feet. Together, he, Luc and Nero fought with bludgeoning ferocity, although there was no shape to the battle now, if there ever had been. It was nothing more than butcher work, requiring no swordsmanship or finesse, just brute strength and a determination not to fall. Bizarrely, Loken thought of Lucius, the swordsman of the Emperor's Children Legion, and of how he would have hated this inelegant form of war.

Loken returned his attention to the battle and, with Luc Sedirae and Nero Vipus in the fight, he was able to gain some space and time to reorganise.

'Thanks, Luc, Nero. I owe you,' he said in a lull in the fighting. The Sons of Horus reloaded bolters and cleaned chunks of dead flesh from their swords. Sporadic bursts of gunfire still sounded from the swamp and strobing flashes lit the fog with firefly bursts. Off to their left Loken saw a burning pyre where the skiff had come down, its flames acting as a beacon in the midst of the obscuring fog.

'No problem, Garvi,' said Sedirae, and Loken knew that he was grinning beneath his helmet. 'You'll do the same for me before we're out of this shit-storm, I'll wager.'

'You're probably right, but let's hope not.'

'What's the plan, Garvi?' asked Vipus.

Loken held up his hand for silence as he attempted to make contact with his Mournival brothers and the Warmaster once more. Static and desperate cries filled the vox, terrified voices of army soldiers and the damned, gurgling voices that kept saying, 'Blessed be Nurgh-leth...' over and over.

Then a voice cut across every channel and Loken almost cried aloud in relief to hear it.

'All Sons of Horus, this is the Warmaster. Converge on this signal. Head for the flames!'

At the sound of the Warmaster's voice, fresh energy filled the tired limbs and hearts of the Astartes, and they moved off in good order towards the burning pillar of fire coming from the wrecked skiff they had seen earlier. Loken killed with a methodical precision, each shot felling an opponent. He began to feel that they finally had the measure of this grotesque enemy.

Whatever fell energy bestowed animation upon these diseased nightmares was clearly incapable of giving them much more than basic motor functions and an unremitting hostility.

Loken's armour was covered in deep gouges and he wished he knew how many men he had lost to the loathsome hunger of the dead things.

He vowed that this Nurgh-leth would pay dearly for each of their deaths.

She could barely breathe, her chest hiking as she drew in convulsive gulps of air from the respirator Maggard was pushing against her face. Petronella's eyes stung, tears of pain coursing down her cheeks as she tried to push herself into a sitting position.

All she remembered was a fury of noise and light, a metallic shriek and a bone jarring impact as the skiff crashed and broke into pieces. Blood filled her senses and she felt excruciating pain all down her left side. Flames leapt around her, and her vision blurred with the sting of the atmosphere and smoke.

'What happened?' she managed, her voice muffled through the respirator's mouthpiece.

Maggard didn't answer, but then she remembered that he couldn't and twisted her head around to gain a better appreciation of their current situation. Torn up bodies clothed in her livery littered the ground – the pilots and flight crew of her skiff – and there was a lot of blood covering the wreckage. Even through the respirator, she could smell the gore.

Cloying banks of leprous fog surrounded them, though the heat of the flames appeared to be clearing it in their immediate vicinity. Shambling shapes surrounded them and relief flooded her as she realised that they would soon be rescued.

Maggard spun, drawing his sword and pistol, and Petronella tried to shout at him that he must stand down, that these were their rescuers.

Then the first shape emerged from the smoke and she screamed as she saw its diseased flesh and the rotted innards hanging from its opened belly. Nor was it the worst of the approaching things. A cavalcade of cadavers with bloated, ruptured flesh and putrid, diseased bodies sloshed through the mud and wreckage towards them, clawed hands outstretched.

The green fire in their eyes spoke of monstrous appetites and Petronella felt a gut-wrenching terror greater than anything she had ever known.

Only Maggard stood between her and the walking, diseased corpses, and he was but one man. She had watched him train in the gymnasia of Kairos many times, but she had never seen him draw his weapons in anger.

Maggard's pistol barked and each shot blasted one of the shambling horrors from its feet, neat holes drilled in its forehead. He fired and fired until his pistol was empty, and then holstered it and drew a long, triangular bladed dagger.

As the horde approached, her bodyguard attacked.

He leapt, feet first, at the nearest corpse and a neck snapped beneath his boot heel. Maggard spun as he landed, his sword decapitating a pair of the monsters, and his dagger ripping the throat from another. His Kirlian rapier darted like a silver snake, its glowing edge stabbing and cutting with incredible speed. Whatever it touched dropped instantly to the muddy ground like a servitor with its dotrina wafer pulled.

His body was always in motion, leaping, twisting and dodging away from the clutching hands of his diseased attackers. There was no pattern to their assault, simply a mindless host of dead things seeking to envelop them. Maggard fought like nothing she had ever seen, his augmetic muscles bulging and flexing as he cut down his foes with quick, lethal strokes.

No matter how many he killed, there were always more pressing in and they steadily forced him back a step at a time. The horde of creatures began to surround them, and Petronella saw that Maggard couldn't possibly hold them all back. He staggered towards her, bleeding from a score of minor wounds. His flesh was blistered and weeping around the cuts and there was an unhealthy pallor to his skin, despite his respirator gear.

She wept bitter tears of horror as the monsters closed in, jaws opening wide to devour her flesh, and grasping hands ready to tear her perfect skin and feast on her innards. This wasn't how it was supposed to be. The Great Crusade wasn't supposed to end in failure and death!

A corpse with mouldering, sagging skin lurched past Maggard, his blade lodged in the belly of a giant, necrotic thing with green flesh that was thick with flies.

She screamed as it reached for her.

Deafening bangs thundered behind her and the creature disintegrated in an explosion of wet meat and bone. Petronella covered her ears as the thunderous roar of gunfire came again and her attackers were torn apart in a series of rancid explosions, falling back into the fires of the skiff and burning with stinking green flames.

She rolled onto her side, crying in pain and fear as the terrifyingly close volleys continued, clearing a path for the massive, armoured warriors of the Sons of Horus.

A giant towered above her, reaching for her with his armoured gauntlet.

He wore no helmet and was silhouetted by a terrible red glow, his awesome bulk haloed by blazing plumes of fire and pillars of black smoke. Even through her tears, the Warmaster's beauty and physical perfection rendered her speechless. Though blood and dark slime covered his armour and his cloak was torn and tattered, Horus towered like a war god unleashed, his face a mask of terrifying power.

He lifted her to her feet as easily as one might lift a babe in arms, while his warriors continued the slaughter of the monstrous dead things. More and more Sons of Horus were converging on the crash site, guns firing to drive the enemy back and forming a protective cordon around the Warmaster.

'Miss Vivar,' demanded Horus. 'What in the name of Terra are you doing here? I ordered you to stay aboard the *Vengeful Spirit*.'

She struggled for words, still in awe of his magnificent presence. He had saved her. The Warmaster had personally saved her and she wept to know his touch.

'I had to come. I had to see–'

'Your curiosity almost got you killed,' raged Horus. 'If your bodyguard had been less capable, you'd already be dead.'

She nodded dumbly, holding onto a twisted spar of metal to keep from collapsing as the Warmaster stepped through the debris towards Maggard. The gold armoured warrior held himself erect, despite the pain of his wounds.

Horus lifted Maggard's sword arm, examining the warrior's blade.

'What's your name, warrior?' asked the Warmaster.

Maggard, of course, did not answer, looking over at Petronella for help in answering.

'He cannot answer you, my lord,' said Petronella.

'Why not? Doesn't he speak Imperial Gothic?'

'He does not speak at all, sir. House Carpinus chaperones removed his vocal chords.'

'Why would they do that?'

'He is an indentured servant of House Carpinus and it is not a bodyguard's place to speak in the presence of his mistress.'

Horus frowned, as though he did not approve of such things, and said, 'Then you tell me what his name is.'

'He is called Maggard, sir.'

'And this blade he wields? How is it that the slightest touch of its edge slays one of these creatures?'

'It is a Kirlian blade, forged on ancient Terra and said to be able to sever the connection between the soul and the body, though I have never seen it used before today.'

'Whatever it is, I think it saved your life, Miss Vivar.'

She nodded as the Warmaster turned to face Maggard once more and made the sign of the aquila before saying, 'You fought with great courage, Maggard. Be proud of what you did here today.'

Maggard nodded and dropped to his knees with his head bowed, tears streaming from his eyes at being so honoured by the Warmaster.

Horus bent down and placed the palm of his hand on the bodyguard's shoulder, saying, 'Rise, Maggard. You have proven yourself to be a warrior, and no warrior of such courage should kneel before me.'

Maggard stood, smoothly reversing the grip of his sword and offering it, hilt first, to the Warmaster.

The yellow sky reflected coldly in his golden eyes, and Petronella shivered as she saw a newfound devotion in her bodyguard's posture, an expression of faith and pride that frightened her with its intensity.

The meaning of the gesture was clear. It said what Maggard himself could not.

I am yours to command.

Thus assembled, the Astartes took stock of their situation. All four phalanxes had rendezvoused around the crash site as the attacks from the diseased and dead things ceased for the time being. The speartip was blunted, but it was still an awesome fighting force and easily capable of destroying what remained of Temba's paltry detachment.

Sedirae volunteered his men to secure the perimeters, and Loken simply waved his assent, knowing that Luc was hungry for more battle and for a chance to shine in front of the Warmaster. Vipus re-formed the scouting parties and Verulam Moy set up fire positions for his Devastators.

Loken was relieved beyond words to see that all four members of the Mournival had survived the fighting, though Torgaddon and Abaddon had both lost their helmets in the furious mêlées. Aximand's armour had been torn open across his side and a splash of red, shockingly bright against the green of his armour, stained his thigh.

'Are you all right?' Torgaddon asked him, his armour stained and blistered, as though someone had poured acid over its plates.

'Just about,' nodded Loken. 'You?'

'Yes, though it was a close run thing,' conceded Torgaddon. 'Bastard got me underwater and was choking the life out of me. Tore my helmet right off and I think I must have drunk about a bucket of that swamp water. Had to gut him with my combat knife. Messy.'

Torgaddon's genhanced body would be unharmed by swallowing the water, no matter what toxins it carried, but it was a stark reminder of the power of these creatures that a warrior as fearsome as him could almost be overcome. Abaddon and

Aximand had similar tales of close run things, and Loken desperately wanted the fight to be over. The longer the mission went on, the more it reminded him of Eidolon's abortive first strike on Murder.

Restored communications revealed that the Byzant Janizars had suffered terribly under the assault from the swamp and had hunkered down in defensive positions. Not even the electro-scythes of their discipline masters were able to coerce them forward. The horrific enemy had melted back into the fog, but no one could say with any certainty where the creatures had gone.

The Titans of the Legio Mortis towered over the Astartes; the *Dies Irae* reassuring the assembled warriors by the simple virtue of is immensity.

It was left to Erebus to point the way onwards, he and his depleted warriors staggering into the circle of light surrounding Petronella Vivar's crashed skiff. The First Chaplain's armour was stained and battered, its many seals and scripture papers torn from it.

'Warmaster, I believe we have found the source of the transmissions,' reported Erebus. 'There is a… structure up ahead.'

'Where is it and how close?' demanded the Warmaster.

'Perhaps another kilometre to the west.'

Horus raised his sword and shouted, 'Sons of Horus, we have been grossly wronged here and some of our brothers are dead. It is time we avenge them.'

His voice easily carried over the dead waters of the swamps, his warriors roaring their assent and following the Warmaster, as Erebus and the Word Bearers set off into the mists.

Fired with furious energy, the Astartes ploughed through the sodden ground, ready to enact the Warmaster's wrath upon the vile foe that had unleashed such horrors upon them. Maggard and Petronella went with them, none of the Astartes willing to retreat and escort them back to the Army positions. Legion Apothecaries tended their wounds and helped them through the worst of the terrain.

Eventually, the mists began to thin and Loken could make out the more distant figures of Astartes warriors through the smudges of fog. The further they marched, the more solid the ground underfoot became, and as Erebus led them onwards, the mist became thinner still.

Then, as quickly as a man might step from one room to another, they were out of it.

Behind them, the banks of fog gathered and coiled, like a

theatre curtain in a playhouse waiting to unveil some wondrous marvel.

Before them was the source of the vox transmission, rearing
up from the muddy plain like a colossal iron mountain.

Eugan Temba's flagship, the *Glory of Terra*.

SEVEN

Watch our backs

Collapse

The betrayer

Rusted and dead nearly six decades, the vessel lay smashed and ruined on the cratered mudflats, its once mighty hull torn open and buckled almost beyond recognition. Its towering gothic spires, like the precincts of a mighty city, lay fallen and twisted, its buttresses and archways hung with decaying fronds of huge web-like vines. Its keel was broken, as though it had struck the moon's surface, belly first, and many of the upper surfaces had caved in, the decks below open to the elements.

Swathes of mossy greenery covered the hull and her command spire speared into the sky; warp vanes and tall vox masts bending in the moaning wind.

Loken thought the scene unbearably sad. That this should be the final resting place of such a magnificent vessel seemed utterly wrong to him.

Pieces of debris spotted the landscape, twisted hunks of rusted metal and incongruous personal items that must have belonged to the ship's crew and had been ejected during the massive impact with the ground.

'Throne…' breathed Abaddon.

'How?' was all Aximand could manage.

'It's the *Glory of Terra* all right,' said Erebus. 'I recognise the warp array configuration of the command deck. It's Temba's flagship.'

'Then Temba's already dead,' said Abaddon in frustration. 'Nothing could have survived that crash.'

'Then who's broadcasting that signal?' asked Horus.

'It could have been automated,' suggested Torgaddon. 'Maybe it's been going for years.'

Loken shook his head. 'No, the signal only started once we breached the atmosphere. Someone here activated it when they knew we were coming.'

The Warmaster stared at the massive shape of the wrecked spaceship, as if by staring hard enough he could penetrate its hull and discern what lay within.

'Then we should go in,' urged Erebus. 'Find whoever is inside and kill them.'

Loken rounded on the First Chaplain. 'Go inside? Are you mad? We don't have any idea what might be waiting for us. There could be thousands more of those... things inside, or something even worse.'

'What is the matter, Loken?' snarled Erebus. 'Are the Sons of Horus now afraid of the dark?'

Loken took a step towards Erebus and said, 'You dare insult us, Word Bearer?'

Erebus stepped to meet Loken's challenge, but the Mournival took up position behind their newest member and their presence gave the First Chaplain pause. Instead of pursuing the matter, Erebus bowed his head and said, 'I apologise if I spoke out of turn, Captain Loken. I sought only to erase the gross stain on the Legion's honour.'

'The Legion's honour is our own to uphold, Erebus,' said Loken. 'It is not for you to tell us how we must act.'

Horus decided the matter before further harsh words could be exchanged.

'We're going in,' he said.

The rippling fog bank followed the Astartes as they advanced towards the crashed ship and the Titans of the Legio Mortis followed behind, their legs still wreathed in the mists. Loken kept his bolter at the ready, conscious of the sounds of splashing water behind them, though he told himself that they were just the normal sounds of this world – whatever that meant.

As they closed the gap, he drew level with the Warmaster and said, 'Sir, I know what you will say, but I would be remiss if I didn't speak up.'

'Speak up about what, Garviel?' asked Horus.

'About this. About you leading us into the unknown.'

'Haven't I been doing that for the last two centuries?' asked Horus. 'All the time we've been pushing out into space, hasn't it been to push back the unknown? That's what we're here for, Garviel, to render that which is unknown as known.'

Loken sensed the commander's superlative skills of misdirection at work and kept himself focused on the point. The Warmaster had an easy way of steering conversations away from issues he didn't want to talk about.

'Sir, do you value the Mournival as counsel?' asked Loken, taking a different tack.

Horus paused in his advance and turned to face Loken, his face serious. 'You heard what I told that remembrancer in the embarkation deck, didn't you? I value your counsel above all things, Garviel. Why would you even ask such a question?'

'Because so often you simply use us as your war dogs, always baying for blood. Having us play a role, instead of allowing us to keep you true to your course.'

'Then say what you have to say, Garviel, and I swear I will listen,' promised Horus.

'With respect, sir, you should not be here leading this speartip and we should not be going into that vessel without proper reconnaissance. We have three of the Mechanicum's greatest war machines behind us. Can we not at least let them soften up the target first with their cannons?'

Horus chuckled. 'You have a thinker's head on you, my son, but wars are not won by thinkers, they are won by men of action. It has been too long since I wielded a blade and fought in such a battle – against abominations that seek nothing more than our utter destruction. I told you on Murder that had I felt I could not take to the field of battle again, I would have refused the position of Warmaster.'

'The Mournival would have done this thing for you, sir,' said Loken. 'We carry your honour now.'

'You think my shoulders so narrow that I cannot bear it alone?' asked Horus, and Loken was shocked to see genuine anger in his stare.

'No, sir, all I mean is that you don't need to bear it alone.'

Horus laughed and broke the tension. His anger quite forgotten, he said, 'You're right of course, my son, but my glory days are not over, for I have many laurels yet to earn.'

The Warmaster set off once more. 'Mark my words, Garviel Loken, everything achieved thus far in this Crusade will pale into insignificance compared to what I am yet to do.'

✠ ✠ ✠

Despite the Warmaster's insistence on leading the Astartes into the wreck, he consented to Loken's plan of allowing the Titans of the Legio Mortis to engage the target first. All three mighty war engines braced themselves and, at a command from the Warmaster, unleashed a rippling salvo of missiles and cannon fire into the massive ship. Flaring blooms of light and smoke rippled across the ship's immensity and it shuddered with each concussive impact. Fires caught throughout its hull, and thick plumes of acrid black smoke twisted skyward like signal beacons, as though the ship were trying to send a message to its former masters.

Once again, the Warmaster led from the front, the mist following them in like a smoggy cape of yellow. Loken could still hear noises from behind them, but with the thunderous footfalls of the Titans, the crackling of the burning ship and their own splashing steps, it was impossible to be sure what he was hearing.

'Feels like a damned noose,' said Torgaddon, looking over his shoulder and mirroring Loken's thoughts perfectly.

'I know what you mean.'

'I don't like the thought of going in there, I can tell you that.'

'You're not afraid are you?' asked Loken, only half joking.

'Don't be flippant, Garvi,' said Torgaddon. 'For once I think you're right. There's something not right about this.'

Loken saw genuine concern in his friend's face, unsettled at seeing the joker Torgaddon suddenly serious. For all his bluster and informality, Tarik had good instincts and they had saved Loken's life on more than one occasion.

'What's on your mind?' he asked.

'I think this is a trap,' said Torgaddon. 'We're being funnelled here and it feels like it's to get us inside that ship.'

'I said as much to the Warmaster.'

'And what did he say?'

'What do you think?'

'Ah,' nodded Torgaddon. 'Well, you didn't seriously expect to change the commander's mind did you?'

'I thought I might have given him pause, but it's as if he's not listening to us any more. Erebus has made the commander so angry at Temba, he won't even consider any other option than going in and killing him with his bare hands.'

'So what do we do?' asked Torgaddon, and once again, Loken was surprised.

'We watch our backs, my friend. We watch our backs.'

'Good plan,' said Torgaddon. 'I hadn't thought of that. And

here I was all set to walk into a potential trap with my guard down.'

That was the Torgaddon that Loken knew and loved.

The rear quarter of the crashed *Glory of Terra* reared up before them, its command decks pitched upwards at an angle, blotting out the diseased sky. It enveloped them in its dark, cold shadow, and Loken saw that getting into the ship would not be difficult. The gunfire from the Titans had blasted huge tears in its hull, and piles of debris had spilled from inside, forming great ramps of buckled steel like the rocky slopes before the walls of a breached fortress.

The Warmaster called a halt and began issuing his orders.

'Captain Sedirae, you and your assaulters will form the vanguard.'

Loken could practically feel Luc's pride at such an honour.

'Captain Moy, you will accompany me. Your flame and melta units will be invaluable in case we need to quickly cleanse an area or breach bulkheads.'

Verulam Moy nodded, his quiet reserve more dignified than Luc's eagerness to impress the Warmaster with his ardour.

'What are your orders, Warmaster?' asked Erebus, his grey armoured Word Bearers at attention behind their First Chaplain. 'We stand ready to serve.'

'Erebus, take your warriors over to the other side of the ship. Find a way in and then rendezvous with me in the middle. If that bastard Temba tries to run, I want him crushed between us.'

The First Chaplain nodded his understanding and led his warriors off into the shadow of the mighty vessel. Then the Warmaster turned to the Mournival.

'Ezekyle, use the signal locator on my armour to form overlapping echelons around my left. Little Horus, take my right. Torgaddon and Loken, form the rear. Secure this area and our line of withdrawal. Understood?'

The Warmaster delivered the orders with his trademark efficiency, but Loken was aghast at being left to cover the rear of their advance. He could see that the others of the Mournival, especially Torgaddon, were similarly surprised. Was this the Warmaster's way of punishing him for daring to question his orders or for suggesting that he should not be leading the speartip? To be left behind?

'Understood?' repeated Horus and all four members of the Mournival nodded their assent.

'Then let's move out,' snarled the Warmaster. 'I have a traitor to kill.'

✠ ✠ ✠

Luc Sedirae led the assaulters, the bulky back burners of their jump packs easily carrying them up towards the black tears in the side of the ship. As Loken expected, Luc was first inside, vanishing into the darkness with barely a pause. His warriors followed him and were soon lost to sight, as Abaddon and Aximand found other ways inside, clambering up the debris to reach the still smoking holes that the Titans had torn. Aximand gave him a quick shrug as he led his own squads upwards, and Loken watched them go, unable to believe that he would not be fighting alongside his brothers as they went into battle.

The Warmaster himself strode up the piled debris as easily as a man might ascend a gently sloping hill, Verulam Moy and his weapons specialists following in his wake.

Within moments, they were alone on the desolate mudflats, and Loken could sense the confusion in his warriors. They stood awkwardly, awaiting orders to send them into the fight, but he had none to give them.

Torgaddon saved him from his stupefaction, bellowing out commands and lighting a fire under the Astartes left behind. They spread out to form a cordon around their position, Nero Vipus's scouts taking up position at the edge of the mist, and Brakespur climbing up the slopes to guard the entrances to the *Glory of Terra*.

'Just what exactly did you say to the commander?' asked Torgaddon, squelching back through the mud towards him.

Loken cast his mind back to the words that had passed between himself and the Warmaster since they had set foot on Davin's moon, searching for some offence that he might have given. He could find nothing serious enough to warrant his and Torgaddon's exclusion from the battle against Temba.

'Nothing,' he said, 'just what I told you.'

'This doesn't make any sense,' said Torgaddon, attempting to wipe some mud from his face, but only serving to spread it further across his features. 'I mean, why leave us out of all the fun. I mean, come on, Moy?'

'Verulam's a competent officer,' said Loken.

'Competent?' scoffed Torgaddon. 'Don't get me wrong, Garvi, I love Verulam like a brother, but he's a file officer. You know it and I know it; and while there's nothing wrong with that and Emperor knows we need good file officers, he's not the sort the Warmaster should have at his side at a time like this.'

Loken couldn't argue with Tarik's logic, having had the same reaction upon hearing the Warmaster's orders. 'I don't know what to tell you, Tarik. You're right, but the commander has given his orders and we are pledged to obey him.'

'Even when we know those orders make no sense?'

Loken had no answer to that.

The Warmaster and Verulam Moy led the van of the speartip through the dark and oppressive interior of the *Glory of Terra*, its arched passageways canted at unnatural angles and its bulkheads warped and rusted with decay. Brackish water dripped through sections open to the elements, and a reeking wind gusted through the creaking hallways like a cadaver's breath. Diseased streamers of black fungus and dangling fronds of rotted matter brushed against their heads and helmets, leaving slimy trails of sticky residue behind.

The perforated floors were treacherous and uneven, but the Astartes made good time, pushing ever upwards through the halls of putrefaction towards the command decks.

Regular, static-laced communication with Sedirae's vanguard informed them of his progress ahead of them, the ship apparently lifeless and deserted. Even though the vanguard was relatively close, Sedirae's voice was chopped with interference, every third word or so unintelligible.

The deeper into the ship they penetrated, the worse it got.

'Ezekyle?' said the Warmaster, opening the vox-mic on his gorget. 'Progress report.'

Abaddon's voice was barely recognisable, as crackling pops and wet hissing overlaid it with meaningless babble.

'Moving... th... gh the lowe... rat... decks... keep... We have... flank... master.'

Horus tapped his gorget. 'Ezekyle? Damn it.'

The Warmaster turned to Verulam Moy and said, 'Try and raise Erebus,' before returning to his own attempts at communication. 'Little Horus, can you hear me?'

More static followed, uninterrupted save for a faint voice. '...ordnance deck... slow... shells. Making safe... but... make... gress.'

'Nothing from Erebus,' reported Moy, 'but he may be on the other side of the ship by now. If the interference we are getting between our own warriors is anything to go by, it is unlikely our armour links will be able to reach him.'

'Damn it,' repeated the Warmaster. 'Well, let's keep going.'

'Sir,' ventured Moy. 'Might I make a suggestion?'

'If it's that we turn back, forget it, Verulam. My honour and that of the Crusade has been impugned and I'll not have it said that I turned my back on it.'

'I know that, sir, but I believe Captain Loken is correct. We are taking a needless risk here.'

'Life is a risk, my friend. Every day we spend away from Terra is a risk. Every decision I make is a risk. We cannot avoid risk, my friend, for if we do, we achieve nothing. If the highest aim of a captain were to preserve his ship, he would keep it in port forever. You are a fine officer, Verulam, but you do not see heroic opportunities as I do.'

'But, sir,' protested Moy, 'we cannot maintain contact with our warriors and we have no idea what might be waiting for us in this ship. Forgive me if I speak out of turn, but delving into the unknown like this does not feel like heroism. It feels like guesswork.'

Horus leaned in close to Moy and said, 'Captain, you know as well as I do that the whole art of war consists of guessing what is on the other side of the hill.'

'I understand that, sir–' began Moy, but Horus was in no mood for interruptions.

'Ever since the Emperor appointed me in the role of Warmaster, people have been telling me what I can and cannot do, and I tell you I am sick and tired of it,' snapped Horus. 'If people don't like my opinions, then that's their problem. I am the Warmaster and I have made up my mind. We go on.'

A squealing shriek of static abruptly sliced through the darkness and Luc Sedirae's voice came over the armour link as clearly as if he stood next to them.

'Throne! They're here!' shouted Sedirae.

Then everything turned upside down.

Loken felt it through the soles of his boots as a tremendous rumbling that seemed to come from the very foundations of the moon. He turned in horror, hearing metal grind on metal with a deafening screech, and watching geysers of mud spout skyward as buried portions of the starship tore themselves free of the sucking mud. The upper sections of the vessel plummeted towards the ground and the entire ship began tipping over, the colossal rear section arcing downwards with a terrible inevitability.

'Everyone get clear!' bellowed Loken as the massive weight of metal gathered speed.

Astartes scattered from the falling wreck, and Loken felt its massive shadow like a shroud as his armour's senses shut out the roaring noise of the starship's collapse.

He looked back in time to see the wreckage slam into the ground with the force of an orbital strike, the superstructure crumpling under the impact of its own weight and hurling lakes of muddy water through the air. Loken was tossed like a leaf by the shockwave, landing waist deep in a stagnant pool of greenish scum and disappearing beneath the surface.

Rolling to his knees, he saw tsunamis of mud rippling out from the vessel, and watched as dozens of his warriors were buried beneath the brownish sludge. The power of the wrecked starship's impact spread from the crater it had gouged in the mud. A brackish rain of muddy water drizzled down, smearing his helmet's visor and reducing visibility to no more than a few hundred metres.

Loken climbed to his feet, clearing the action of his bolter as he realised the shockwave had dispersed the sulphurous fog that had been their constant companion since landing on this accursed moon.

'Sons of Horus, stand ready!' he shouted, seeing what lay beyond the fog.

Hundreds of the dead things marched relentlessly towards them.

Not even the armour of a primarch could withstand the impact of a falling starship, and Horus grunted as he pulled a twisted spar of jagged iron from his chest. Sticky blood coated his armour, the wound sealing almost as soon as he had withdrawn the metal. His genhanced body could easily withstand such trivial punishment, and despite the spinning fall through the decks of the ship, he remained perfectly orientated and in balance on the sloping deck.

He remembered the sound of tearing metal, the clang of metal on armour and the sharp crack of bones snapping as Astartes warriors were thrown around like children in a funhouse.

'Sons of Horus!' he shouted. 'Verulam!'

Only mocking echoes answered him, and he cursed as he realised he was alone. The vox mic on his gorget was shattered, brass wires hanging limply from the empty socket, and he angrily ripped them away.

Verulam Moy was nowhere to be seen, and his squad members were similarly scattered beyond sight. Quickly taking stock of his surroundings, Horus could see that he lay partially buried in metal debris on the armorium vestibule, its ceiling bulging and cracked. Icy water dripped in a cold rain, and he tipped his head back to let it pour over his face.

He was close to the bridge of the ship, assuming it hadn't sheared off on impact with the ground – for surely there could be no other explanation for what had happened. Horus hauled

himself from beneath the wreckage and checked to make sure
that he was still armed, finding his sword hilt protruding from
the detritus of the vestibule.

Pulling the weapon clear, its golden blade caught what little light there was and shone as though an inner fire burned
within its core. Forged by his brother, Ferrus Manus of the Tenth
Legion, the Iron Hands, it had been a gift to commemorate
Horus's investiture as Warmaster.

He smiled as he saw that the weapon remained as unblemished as the day Ferrus had held it out to him, the light of
adoration in his steel-grey eyes, and Horus had never been more
thankful for his brother's skill at the forge's anvil.

The deck creaked beneath his weight, and he suddenly began
to question the wisdom of leading this assault. Despite that, he
still seethed with molten rage for Eugan Temba, a man whose
character he had believed in, and whose betrayal cut his heart
with searing knives.

What manner of a man could betray the oath of loyalty to
the Imperium?

What manner of base cur would dare to betray *him*?

The deck shifted again, Horus easily compensating for the
lurching motion. He used his free hand to haul himself up
towards the gaping doorway that led to the warren of passageways that riddled a ship this size. Horus had set foot on the *Glory
of Terra* only once before, nearly seventy years ago, but remembered its layout as though it had been yesterday. Beyond this
doorway lay the upper gantries of the armorium and beyond
that, the central spine of the ship that led through several defensive choke points to the bridge.

Horus grunted as he felt a sharp pain in his chest and realised that the iron spar must have torn through one of his lungs.
Without hesitation, he switched his breathing pattern and carried on without pause, his eyesight easily piercing the darkness
of the vessel's interior.

This close to the bridge, Horus could see the terrible changes
wrought upon the ship, its walls coated in loathsome bacterial slime that ate at the metal like an acidic fungus. Dripping
fronds of waving, leech-like organisms suckled at oozing pus-
tules of greenish brown matter, and an unremitting stench of
decay hung in the air.

Horus wondered what had happened to this ship. Had the
tribes of the moon unleashed some kind of deadly plague on
the crew? Were these the means that Erebus had spoken of?

He could taste that the air was thick with lethal bacterial filth and biological contaminants, though none were even close to virulent enough to trouble his incredible metabolism. With the golden light of his sword to illuminate the way, Horus negotiated a path around the gantry, listening out for any signs of his warriors. The occasional distant crack of gunfire or clang of metal told him that he wasn't completely alone, but the whereabouts of the battles was a mystery. The corrupted inner structure of the ship threw phantom echoes and faraway shouts all around him until he decided to ignore them and press on alone.

Horus passed through the armorium and into the starship's central spine, the deck warped and canted at an unnatural angle. Flickering glow-globes and sputtering power conduits sparked and lit the arched passageway with blue electrical fire. Broken doors clanged against their frames with the rocking motion of the ship, making a sound like funeral bells.

Ahead he could hear a low moaning and the shuffle of callused feet, the first sounds he could clearly identify. They came from beyond a wide hatchway, toothed blast doors juddering open and closed like the jaws of some monstrous beast. Crushed debris prevented the doors from closing completely, and Horus knew that whatever was making the noises stood between him and his ultimate destination.

Some trick of the diffuse, strobing light threw jittering shadows from the mouth of the hatchway, and flickering after-images danced on his retinas as though the light came from a pict projector running in slow motion.

As the hatchway rumbled closed once more, a clawed hand reached out and gripped the smeared metal. Long, dripping yellow talons sprouted from the hand, the flesh of the wasted arm maggot-ridden and leprous. Another hand pushed through and clamped onto the metal, wrenching open the blast doors with a strength that belied the frailness of the arms.

The sensation of fear was utterly alien to Horus, but when the horrifying source of the sounds was revealed, he was suddenly seized with the conviction that perhaps his captains had been right after all.

A shambling mob of rotten–fleshed famine victims appeared, their shuffling gaits carrying them forwards in a droning phalanx of corruption. A creeping sensation of hidden power pulsed from their hunger-wasted bodies and swollen bellies, and buzzing clouds of flies surrounded their cyclopean, horned heads. Sonorous doggerel spilled from bloated and split lips, though Horus could make no sense of the words. Green flesh hung from exposed bones, and although they moved with the leaden monotony of the dead things, Horus could see coiled strength in their limbs and a terrible hunger in each monster's cataracted eyeball.

The creatures were less than a dozen metres from him, but their images were blurred and wavering, as though tears misted his vision. He blinked rapidly to clear it, and saw their swords, rusted and dripped with contagion.

'Well you're a handsome bunch and no mistake,' said Horus, raising his sword and throwing himself forward.

His golden sword clove into the monsters like a fiery comet, each blow hacking down a dozen or more without effort. Spatters of diseased meat caked the walls, and the air was thick with the stench of faecal matter as each monster exploded with rotten bangs of flesh at his every blow. Filthy claws tore at Horus, but his every limb was a weapon. His elbow smashed skulls from shoulders, his knees and feet shattered spines, and his sword struck his foes down as if they were the mindless automatons in the training cages.

Horus did not know what manner of creatures these were, but they had obviously never faced a being as mighty as a primarch. He pushed further up the central spine of the starship, hacking a path through hundreds of organ-draped beasts. Behind him lay the ruin of his passing, shredded meat that reeked of decay and pestilence. Before him lay scores more of the creatures, and the bridge of the *Glory of Terra*.

He lost track of time, the primal brutality of the fight capturing the entirety of his attention, his sword strikes mechanical and bludgeoning. Nothing could stand before him, and with each blow, the Warmaster drew closer to his goal. The corridor grew wider as he pushed through the heaving mass of cyclopean monsters, the golden sheen of his sword and the flickering, uncertain lights of the corridor making it appear that his enemies were becoming less substantial.

His sword chopped through a distended belly, ripping it wide open in a gush of stinking fluids, but instead of bursting open, the meat of the creature simply vanished like greasy smoke in the wind. Horus took another step forwards, but instead of meeting his foes head on with brutal ferocity, the corridor was suddenly and inexplicably empty. He looked around, and where once there had been a host of diseased creatures bent on his death, now there were only the reeking remains of hacked up corpses.

Even they were dissolving like fat on a griddle, vanishing in hissing streamers of green smoke so dark it was almost black.

'Throne,' hissed Horus, revolted by the sickening sight of the liquefying meat, and finally recognising the taint within the ship for what it was – a charnel house of the warp: a spawning ground of the immaterium.

Horus felt fresh resolve fill his limbs as he drew closer to the multiple blast doors that protected the bridge, more certain than ever that he must destroy Eugan Temba. He expected yet more legions of the warp-spawned things, but the way was eerily quiet, the silence punctuated only by the sounds of more gunfire (which he was now sure was coming from beyond the hull) and the patter of black water on his armour.

Horus made his way forward cautiously, brushing sparking cables from his path as, one by one, the sealed blast doors slowly rumbled open at his approach. The whole thing reeked of a trap, but nothing could deny him his vengeance now, and he pressed onwards.

Stepping onto the bridge of the *Glory of Terra*, Horus saw that its colonnaded immensity had been changed from a place of command to something else entirely. Mouldering banners hung from the highest reaches, with long dead corpses stitched into the torn fabric of each one. Even from here, Horus could see that they wore the lupine grey uniforms of the 63rd Expedition, and he wondered if these poor souls had stayed true to their oaths of loyalty.

'You will be avenged, my friends,' he whispered as he stepped further into the bridge.

The tiered workstations were smashed and broken, their inner workings ripped out and rewired in some bizarre new way, metres-thick bundles of coiled wire rising into the darkness of the arched ceiling.

Throbbing energy pulsed from the cables and Horus realised that he was looking at the source of the vox signal that had so perturbed Loken on the way in.

Indeed, he fancied he could still hear the words of that damned voice whispering on the air like a secret that would turn your tongue black were you to tell it.

Nurgh-leth, it hissed, over and over...

Then he realised that it wasn't some auditory echo from the ship's vox, but a whisper from a human throat.

Horus's eyes narrowed as he sought the source of the voice, his lip curling in revulsion as he saw the massively swollen figure of a man standing before the captain's throne. Little more than a heaving mass of corpulent flesh, a terrific stench of rank meat rose from his fleshy immensity.

Flying things with glossy black bodies infested every fold of his skin, and scraps of grey cloth were stuck to his green grey flesh, gold epaulettes glinting and silver frogging hanging limply over his massive belly.

One hand rested in the glutinous mess of an infected wound in his chest, while the other held a sword with a glitter-sheen like diamond.

Horus dropped to his knees in anger and sorrow as he saw the slumped corpse of an Astartes warrior sprawled before the decayed splendour of the bloated figure.

Verulam Moy, his neck obviously broken and his sightless eyes fixed upon the decaying corpses hanging from the banners.

Even before Horus lifted his gaze to Moy's killer, he knew who it would be: Eugan Temba...

The Betrayer.

EIGHT

Fallen god

Loken could scarcely remember a fight where he and his warriors had expended all their ammunition. Each Astartes carried enough shells to sustain them for most types of engagement, since no shot was wasted and each target would normally fall to a single bolt.

The ammo hoppers were back at the dropsite and there was no way they could get through to them. The Warmaster's resolute advance had seen to that.

Loken's full capacity of bolter rounds had long been expended, and he was thankful for Aximand's insistence on subsonic rounds, as they made satisfyingly lethal explosions within the bodies of the dead things.

'Throne, don't they ever stop?' gasped Torgaddon. 'I must have killed a hundred or more of the damned things.'

'You probably keep killing the same one,' replied Loken, shaking his sword free of grey matter. 'If you don't destroy the head, they get back up again. I've cut down half a dozen or more with bolter wounds in them.'

Torgaddon nodded and said, 'Hold on, the Legio's coming again.'

Loken gripped onto a more solid piece of debris, as the Titans began yet another deadly strafing run through the mass of rotted monsters. Like the monstrous giants said to haunt the mists of Barbarus, the Titans emerged from the fog with fists of thunder and fire. Wet explosions mushroomed from the swamp as high explosives hurled the cadavers into the air and the crashing steps of the mighty war machines crushed them to ooze beneath their hammer-blow footsteps.

The very air thrummed with the vibrations of the Titans' attack, avalanches of debris and mud sliding from the *Glory of Terra* with each explosion and titanic footstep. The dead things had gained the slopes of rubble and detritus that led into the starship three times; and three times had they sent them back, first with gunfire, and, when the ammunition had run out, with blades and brute strength. Each time they killed hundreds of their enemies, but each time a handful of Astartes was dragged down and pulled beneath the waters of the swamp.

Under normal circumstances, the Astartes would have had no trouble in dealing with these abominations, but with the Warmaster's fate unknown they were brittle and on edge, unable to think or fight with their customary ferocity. Loken knew exactly what they were feeling, because he felt it too.

Unable to raise the Warmaster, Aximand or Abaddon, the warriors outside the hulk were left paralysed and in disarray without their beloved leader.

'Temba,' said the Warmaster, rising to his feet and marching towards his erstwhile planetary governor. With each step, he saw further evidence of Eugan Temba's treachery, clotted blood on the edge of his sword and a fierce grin of anticipation. Where once had been the loyal and upright follower, Horus now saw only a filthy traitor who deserved the most painful of deaths. A fell light grew around Temba, further revealing the corruption of his flesh, and Horus knew that nothing of his former friend was left in the diseased shell that stood before him.

Horus wondered if this was what Loken had experienced beneath the mountains of Sixty-Three Nineteen: the horror of a former comrade succumbing to the warp. Horus had known of the bad blood between Jubal and Loken, now understanding that such enmity, however trivial, had been the chink in Jubal's armour by which the warp had taken him.

What flaw had been Temba's undoing? Pride, ambition, jealousy?

The bloated monster that had once been Eugan Temba looked up from the corpse of Verulam Moy and smiled, thoroughly pleased with its work.

'Warmaster,' said Temba, each syllable glottal and wet, as though spoken through water.

'Do not dare to address me by such a title, abomination.'

'Abomination?' hissed Temba, shaking his head. 'Don't you recognise me?'

'No,' said Horus. 'You're not Temba, you're warp-spawned filth, and I'm here to kill you.'

'You are wrong, Warmaster,' it laughed. 'I am Temba. The so-called friend you left behind. I am Temba, the loyal follower of Horus you left to rot on this backwater world while you went on to glory.'

Horus approached the dais of the captain's throne and dragged his eyes from Temba to the body of Verulam Moy. Blood streamed from a terrible wound in his side, pumping energetically onto the stained floor of the bridge. The flesh of his throat was purple and black, a lump of broken bone pushing at the bruised skin where his neck had been snapped.

'A pity about Moy,' said Temba. 'He would have been a fine convert.'

'Don't say his name,' warned Horus. 'You are not fit to give it voice.'

'If it consoles you, he was loyal until the end. I offered him a place at my side, with the power of Nurgh-leth filling his veins with its immortal necrosis, but he refused. He felt the need to try to kill me; foolish really. The power of the warp fills me and he had no chance at all, but that didn't stop him. Admirable loyalty, even if it was misplaced.'

Horus placed a foot on the first step of the dais, his golden sword held out before him, his fury at this beast drowning out all other concerns. All he wanted to do was throttle the life from this treacherous bastard with his bare hands, but he retained enough sense to know that if Moy had been killed with such apparent ease, then he would be a fool to discard his weapon.

'We don't have to be enemies, Horus,' said Temba. 'You have no idea of the power of the warp, old friend. It is like nothing we ever saw before. It's beautiful really.'

'It is power,' agreed Horus, climbing another step, 'elemental and uncontrollable and therefore not to be trusted.'

'Elemental? Perhaps, but it is far more than that,' said Temba. 'It seethes with life, with ambition and desire. You think it's a wasteland of raging energy that you bend to your will, but you have no idea of the power that lies there: the power to dominate, to control and to rule.'

'I have no desire for such things,' said Horus.

'You lie,' giggled Temba. 'I can see it in your eyes, old friend. Your ambition is a potent thing, Horus. Do not be afraid of it. Embrace it and we will not be enemies, we will be allies, embarking upon a course that will see us masters of the galaxy.'

'This galaxy already has a master, Temba. He is called the Emperor.'

'Then where is he? He blundered across the cosmos in the manner of the barbarian tribes of ancient Terra, destroying any-one who would not submit to his will, and then left you to pick up the pieces. What manner of leader is that? He is but a tyrant by another name.'

Horus took another step, and was almost at the top of the dais, almost within striking distance of this traitor who dared to profane the name of the Emperor.

'Think about it, Horus,' urged Temba. 'The whole history of the galaxy has been the gradual realisation that events do not happen in an arbitrary manner, but that they reflect an under-lying destiny. That destiny is Chaos.'

'Chaos?'

'Yes!' shouted Temba. 'Say it again, my friend. Chaos is the first power in the universe and it will be the last. When the first ape creatures bashed each other's brains out with bones, or cried to the heavens in the death throes of plague, they fed and nurtured Chaos. The blissful release of excess and the glee of intrigue – all is grist for the soul mills of Chaos. So long as Man endures, so too does Chaos.'

Horus reached the top of the dais and stood face to face with Temba, a man he had once counted as his friend and comrade in this great undertaking. Though the thing spoke with Temba's voice and its stretched features were still those of his comrade, there was nothing left of that fine man, only this wretched crea-ture of the warp.

'You have to die,' said Horus.

'No, for that is the glory of Nurgh-leth,' chuckled Temba. 'I will never die.'

'We'll soon see about that,' snarled Horus, and drove his sword into Temba's chest, the golden blade easily sliding through the layers of blubber towards the traitor's heart.

Horus ripped his sword free in a wash of black blood and stinking pus, the stench almost too much for even him to bear. Temba laughed, apparently untroubled by such a mortal wound, and brought up his own sword, its glinting, fractured blade like patterned obsidian.

He brought the blade to his blue lips and said, 'The War-master Horus.'

With a speed that was unnatural in its swiftness, the tip of the blade speared for the Warmaster's throat.

Horus threw up his sword, deflecting Temba's weapon barely a centimetre from his neck, and took a step backwards as the traitor lurched towards him. Recovering from the surprise attack, Horus gripped his sword two-handed, blocking every lethal thrust and cut that Temba made.

Horus fought like never before, his every move to parry and defend. Eugan Temba had never been a swordsman, so where this sudden, horrifying skill came from Horus had no idea. The two men traded blows back and forth across the command deck, the bloated form of Eugan Temba moving with a speed and dexterity quite beyond anything that should have been possible for someone of such vast bulk. Indeed, Horus had the distinct impression that it was not Temba's skill with a blade that he was up against, but the blade itself.

He ducked beneath a decapitating strike and spun inside Temba's guard, slashing his sword through his opponent's belly, a thick gruel of infected blood and fat spilling onto the deck. The dark blade darted out and struck his shoulder guard, ripping it from his armour in a flash of purple sparks.

Horus danced back from the blow as the return stroke arced towards his head. He dropped and rolled away as Temba turned his bloody, carven body back towards him. Any normal man would have died a dozen times or more, but Temba seemed untroubled by such killing wounds.

Temba's face shone with glistening sweat, and Horus blinked as the monster's outline wavered, like those of the cyclopean monsters that he had fought in the ship's central spine. Frantic motion shimmered and he could see something deep within the monstrously swollen body, the faint outline of a screaming man, his hands clasped to his ears and his face twisted in a rictus grin of horror.

Trailing his innards like gooey ropes, Eugan Temba descended the steps of the dais like a socialite making her entrance at one of the Merican balls. Horus saw the cursed sword gleaming with a terrible hunger, its edges twitching in Temba's hand, as though aching to bury itself in his flesh.

'It doesn't have to end this way, Horus,' gurgled Temba. 'We need not be enemies.'

'Yes,' said Horus. 'We do. You killed my friend and you betrayed the Emperor. It can be no other way.'

Even before the words were out of his mouth, the smoky grey blade streaked towards him, and Horus threw himself back as the razor-sharp edge grazed his breastplate and cut into the ceramite. Horus backed away from Temba, hearing twin cracks as the monstrously bloated traitor's anklebones finally snapped under his weight.

Horus watched as Temba dragged himself forwards unsteadily, the splintered ends of bone jutting from the bloody flesh of his ankles. No normal man could endure such agony, and Horus felt a flickering ember of compassion for his former friend stir within his breast. No man deserved to be abused so, and Horus vowed to end Temba's suffering, seeing again the jagged after-image sputtering within the alien flesh of the warp.

'I should have listened to you, Eugan,' he whispered.

Temba didn't reply. The glimmering blade wove bright patterns in the air, but Horus ignored it, too seasoned a warrior to be caught by such an elementary trick.

Once again, Temba's blade reached out for him, but Horus was now gaining a measure of its hunger to do him harm. It attacked without thought or reason, only the simple lust to destroy. He looped his own blade around the quillons of Temba's sword and swept his arm out in a disarming move, before closing to deliver the deathblow.

Instead of releasing the blade for fear of a shattered wrist, however, Temba retained his grip on the sword, its tip twisting in the air and plunging towards Horus's shoulder.

Both blades pierced flesh at the same instant, Horus's tearing through his foe's chest and into his heart and lungs, as Temba's stabbed into the muscle of Horus's shoulder where his armour had been torn away.

Horus yelled in sudden pain, his arm burning with the shimmering sword's touch, and reacted with all the speed the Emperor had bred into him. His golden sword slashed out, severing Temba's arm just above the elbow and the sword clanged to the deck where it twitched in the grip of the severed arm with a loathsome life of its own.

Temba wavered and fell to his knees with a cry of agony, and Horus reared above his foe with his sword upraised. His shoulder ached and bled, but victory was now his and he roared with anger, as he stood ready to enact his vengeance.

Through the red mist of anger and hurt, he saw the pathetic, weeping and soiled form of Eugan Temba stripped of the loathsome power of the warp that had claimed him. Still bloated and massive, the dark light in his eyes was gone, replaced by tears and pain as the enormity of his betrayal crashed down upon him.

'What have I done?' asked Temba, his voice little more than a whisper.

The anger went out of Horus in an instant and he lowered his sword, kneeling beside the dying man that had once been his trusted friend.

Juddering sobs of agony and remorse wracked Temba's body and he reached up with his remaining hand to grip the Warmaster's armour.

'Forgive me, my friend,' he said. 'I didn't know. None of us did.'

'Hush now, Eugan,' soothed Horus. 'It was the warp. The tribes of the moon must have used it against you. They would have called it magic.'

'No... I'm so sorry,' wept Temba, his eyes dimming as death reached up to claim him. 'They showed us what it could do and I saw the power of it. I saw beyond and into the warp. I saw the powers that dwell there and, Emperor forgive me, I still said yes to it.'

'There are no powers that dwell there, Eugan,' said Horus. 'You were deceived.'

'No!' said Temba, gripping Horus's arm tightly. 'I was weak and I fell willingly, but it is done with me now. There is great evil in the warp and I need you to know the truth of Chaos before the galaxy is condemned to the fate that awaits it.'

'What are you talking about? What fate?'

'I saw it, Warmaster, the galaxy as a wasteland, the Emperor dead and mankind in bondage to a nightmarish hell of bureaucracy and superstition. All is grim darkness and all is war. Only you have the power to stop this future. You must be strong, Warmaster. Never forget that...'

Horus wanted to ask more, but watched impotently as the spark of life fled Eugan Temba.

His shoulder still burning with fire, Horus rose to his feet and marched over to the rewired consoles and the throbbing bundle of cables that reached up to the chamber's roof.

With an aching cry of loss and anger, he severed the cables with one mighty blow of his sword. They flopped and spun like landed fish, sparks and green fluids spurting from internal tubes and cables, and Horus could tell that the damnable vox transmission had ceased.

Horus dropped his sword and, clutching his injured shoulder, sat on the deck next to Eugan Temba's dead body and wept for his lost friend.

✠ ✠ ✠

Loken hacked his sword through another corpse's neck, drop-ping the mouldering revenant to the ground as still more pressed in behind it. He and Torgaddon fought back to back, their swords coated in the flesh of the dead things as they were pushed further and further up the slopes of metal that led inside the starship. Their warriors fought desperately, each blow leaden and exhausted. The Titans of the Legio Mortis crushed what they could and sporadically raked the base of the rubble with sprays of gunfire, but there was no stopping the horde.

Dozens of Astartes were dead, and there was still no word from the forces that had entered the *Glory of Terra*.

Garbled vox transmissions from the Byzant Janizars seemed to indicate that they were finally moving forward, but no one could be sure as to where exactly they were moving.

Loken fought with robotic movements, his every blow struck with mechanical regularity rather than skill. His armour was dented and torn in a dozen places, but still he fought for vic-tory, despite the utter desperation of their cause.

That was what Astartes did: they triumphed over insurmount-able odds. Loken had lost track of how long they had been fighting, the brutal sensations of this combat having dulled his senses to all but his next attacker.

'We'll have to pull back into the ship!' he shouted.

Torgaddon and Nero Vipus nodded, too busy with their own immediate situations to respond verbally, and Loken turned and began issuing orders across the inter-suit vox, receiving acknowledgements from all his surviving squad commanders.

He heard a cry of anger and, recognising it as belonging to Torgaddon, turned with his sword raised. A mob of stinking cadavers swamped the top of the slopes, overwhelming the Asta-rtes gathered there in a frenzy of clawing hands and biting jaws. Torgaddon was borne to the ground, and the mouths of the corpses fastened on his neck and arms were dragging him down.

'No!' shouted Loken as he leapt towards the furious com-bat. He shoulder charged in amongst them, sending bodies flying down the slopes. His fists crushed skulls and his sword hacked dead things in two. A gauntleted fist thrust up through grey flesh and he grabbed it, feeling the weight of an armoured Astartes behind it.

'Hold on, Tarik!' he ordered, hauling on his friend's arm. Despite his strength, he couldn't free Torgaddon and felt grasping limbs envelop his legs and waist. He clubbed with his free hand, but he couldn't kill enough of them. Hands tore at his head, smearing blood across his visor and blinding him as he felt himself falling.

Loken thrashed in vain, breaking dead things apart, but unable to prevent himself and Torgaddon from being pulled apart. Claws tore at his armour, the unnatural strength of their enemies piercing his flesh and drawing his precious blood. A grinning, skull faced monster landed on his chest, face to face with him, and its jaws snapped shut on his visor. Unable to penetrate the armoured glass, rivulets of muddy saliva blurred his vision as its jaws worked up and down.

Loken head-butted the thing from his chest and rolled onto his front to gain some purchase. He lost his grip on his sword and bellowed in anger as he finally began to free himself from their intolerable grip. Loken fought with every ounce of his strength, finally gaining a respite and rising to his feet.

All around him, warriors of the Astartes struggled with the dead things, and he knew that they were undone.

Then, at a stroke, every one of the dead things dropped to the ground with a soft sigh of release.

Where seconds before the area around the starship had been a furious battlefield of warriors locked in life or death struggles, now it was an eerily silent graveyard. Bewildered Astartes picked themselves up and looked around at the inert, lifeless bodies surrounding them.

'What just happened?' asked Nero Vipus, disentangling himself from a pile of bludgeoned corpses. 'Why have they stopped?'

Loken shook his head. He had no answer to give him. 'I don't know, Nero.'

'It doesn't make any sense.'

'You'd rather they got back up?'

'No, don't be dense. I just mean that if someone was animating these things, then why stop now? They had us.'

Loken shuddered. For someone to wield a power that could defeat the Astartes was a sobering thought. All the time they had crusaded through the galaxy there had been nothing that could stand against them for long – eventually the enemy's will would break in the face of the overwhelming superiority of the Space Marines.

Would this happen when they met a foe with a will as implacable as their own?

Shaking himself free of such gloomy thoughts, he began issuing orders to dispose of the dead things, and they began hurling them from the wreckage, hacking or tearing heads from shoulders lest they reanimate.

Eventually Aximand and Abaddon led their warriors from the wreckage, battered and bloody from the ship's fall, but otherwise unharmed. Erebus too returned, his Word Bearers similarly abused, but also largely unharmed.

There was still no sign of Sedirae's men or the Warmaster.

'We're going back in there for the Warmaster,' said Abaddon. 'I'll lead.'

Loken was about to protest, but nodded as he saw the unshakable resolve in Ezekyle's face.

'We'll all go,' he said.

They found Luc Sedirae and his men trapped in one of the lower decks, hemmed in by fallen bulkheads and tonnes of debris. It took the better part of an hour to move enough of it to grant Luc's assaulters their freedom. On pulling Sedirae from his prison, all he could say was, 'They were here. Monsters with one eye... came out of nowhere, but we killed them, all of them. Now they're gone.'

Luc had suffered casualties; seven of his men were dead and his perpetual grin was replaced by a vengeful expression that reminded Loken of a defiant young boy's. Black, stinking residue coated the walls, and Sedirae had a haunted look to him that Loken did not like at all. It reminded him of Euphrati Keeler in the moments after the warp thing that had taken Jubal almost killed her.

With Sedirae and his warriors in tow, the Mournival pressed on with Loken leading the way, finding signs of battle scattered throughout the ship, bolter impacts and sword cuts that led inexorably towards the ship's bridge.

'Loken,' whispered Aximand. 'I fear what we may find ahead. You should prepare yourself.'

'No,' said Loken. 'I know what you are suggesting, but I won't think of that. I can't.'

'We have to be prepared for the worst.'

'No,' said Loken, louder than he had intended. 'We would know if—'

'If what?' asked Torgaddon.

'If the Warmaster was dead,' said Loken finally.

Thick silence enveloped them as they struggled to come to terms with such a hideous idea.

'Loken's right,' said Abaddon. 'We would know if the Warmaster was dead. You know we would. You of all of us would feel it, Little Horus.'

'I hope you're right, Ezekyle.'

'Enough of this damned misery,' said Torgaddon. 'All this talk of death and we haven't found hide nor hair of the Warmaster yet. Save your gloomy thoughts for the dead that we already know about. Besides, we all know that if the Warmaster was dead, the sky would have fallen, eh?'

That lightened their mood a little and they pressed on, making their way along the central spine of the ship, passing through juddering bulkheads and along corridors with flickering lights, until they reached the blast doors that led to the bridge.

Loken and Abaddon led the way, with Aximand, Torgaddon and Sedirae bringing up the rear.

Inside it was almost dark, only a soft light from ruptured consoles providing any illumination.

The Warmaster sat with his back to them, his glorious plate armour dented and filthy, cradling something vast and bloated in his lap.

Loken drew level with the Warmaster, grimacing as he saw a grotesquely swollen human head in his commander's lap. A great puncture wound pierced the Warmaster's breastplate and a bloody stab wound on his shoulder leaked blood down the armour of his arm.

'Sir?' said Loken. 'Are you all right?'

The Warmaster didn't answer, instead cradling the head of what Loken could only assume was Eugan Temba. His bulk was immense, and Loken wondered how such a monstrously fat creature could possibly have moved under his own strength.

The Mournival joined Loken, shocked and horrified at the Warmaster's appearance, and at this terrible place. They looked at one another with a growing unease, none quite knowing what to make of this bizarre scene.

'Sir?' said Aximand, kneeling before the weeping Warmaster.

'I failed him,' said Horus. 'I failed them all. I should have listened, but I didn't and now they're all dead. It's too much.'

'Sir, we're going to get you out of here. The dead things have stopped attacking. We don't know how long that's going to last, so we need to get out of this place and regroup.'

Horus shook his head slowly. 'They won't be attacking again. Temba's dead and I cut the vox signal. I don't know how exactly, but I think it was part of what was animating those poor souls.'

Abaddon pulled Loken aside and hissed, 'We need to get him out of here, and we can't let anyone see the state he's in.'

Loken knew that Abaddon was right. To see the Warmaster like this would break the spirit of every Astartes who saw him. The Warmaster was an invincible god of war, a towering figure of legend that could never be brought low.

To see him humbled so would be a blow to morale that the
63rd Expedition might never recover from.

Gently, they prised Eugan Temba's massive body away from
the Warmaster and lifted their commander to his feet. Loken
slung the Warmaster's arm over his shoulder, feeling a warm
wetness against his face from the blood that still dripped from
Horus's arm.

Between them, he and Abaddon walked the Warmaster from
the bridge.

'Wait,' said the Warmaster, his voice weak and low. 'I'll walk
out of this place on my own.'

Reluctantly, they let him go, and though he swayed a little,
the Warmaster kept his feet, despite the ashen pallor of his face
and the obvious pain he was in.

The Warmaster spared a last look at Eugan Temba and said,
'Gather up Verulam and let's get out of here, my sons.'

Maggard slumped against the steel bulkhead of the *Glory of
Terra*, his sword covered in black fluids from the dead things.
Petronella fought to hold back tears at the thought of how
close they had all come to death on this bleak, Emperor forsaken moon.

Sheltered behind the bulkhead where Maggard had thrust her,
she had heard rather than seen the desperate conflict that raged
outside – the war cries, the sound of motorised blades tearing
into wet meat, the percussive booms and explosive flashes of
light from the Titans' weapons.

Her imagination filled in the blanks and though a
gut-loosening terror filled her from head to toe, she pictured
glorious combats and heroic duels between the towering Astartes giants and the corrupt foes that sought their destruction.

Her breathing came in short, convulsive gasps as she realised
she had just survived her first battle, but with that realisation
came a strange calm: her limbs stopped shaking and she wanted
to smile and laugh. She wiped her hand across her eyes, smearing the kohl that lined them across her cheeks like tribal war
paint.

Petronella looked over at Maggard, seeing him now for the
great warrior he truly was, barbaric and bloody, and magnificent. She pushed herself to her feet and leaned out beyond her
sheltering bulkhead to look at the battlefield below.

It was like a scene from one of Keland Roget's landscapes,
and the sublime vision took her breath away. The fog and mist
had lifted and the sun was already breaking through to bathe

the landscape in its ruddy red glow. The pools of swamp water glittered like shards of broken glass spread across the landscape. The three magnificent Titans of the Legio Mortis watched over squads of Astartes, armed with flamers, putting the corpses of the dead things to the torch, and pyres of the fallen monsters burned with a blue green light.

She was already forming the metaphors and imagery she would use: the Emperor's warriors taking his light into the dark places of the galaxy, or perhaps that the Astartes were his Angels of Death bringing his retribution to the unrighteous.

The words had the right epic tone, but she sensed that such imagery still lacked some fundamental truth, sounding more like propaganda slogans than anything else.

This was what the Great Crusade was all about and the fear of the last few hours was washed away in a swelling wave of admiration for the Astartes and the men and women of the 63rd Expedition.

She turned as she heard heavy footfalls. The officers of the Mournival were marching towards her, a plate armoured body borne upon their shoulders, and the levity she had witnessed in them earlier now utterly absent. Each one's face, even the joker Torgaddon's, was serious and grim.

The cloaked figure of the Warmaster himself followed behind them, and she was shocked rigid at his beaten appearance. His armour was torn and gashed with foulness, and blood spatters matted his face and arm.

'What happened?' she asked as Captain Loken passed her. 'Whose body is that?'

'Be silent,' he snapped, 'and be gone.'

'No,' said the Warmaster. 'She is my documentarist and if that is to mean anything then she must see us at our worst as well as our best.'

'Sir–' began Abaddon, but Horus cut him off.

'I'll not be argued with on this, Ezekyle. She comes with us.'

Petronella felt her heart leap at this inclusion and fell into step with the Warmaster's party as they began their descent to the ground.

'The body is that of Verulam Moy, Captain of my Nineteenth Company,' said Horus, his voice weary and filled with pain. 'He fell in the line of duty and will be honoured as such.'

'You have my deepest sorrows, my lord,' said Petronella, her heart aching to see the Warmaster in such pain.

'Was it Eugan Temba?' she asked, fishing out her data-slate and mnemo-quill. 'Did he kill Captain Moy?'

Horus nodded, too weary even to answer her.

'And Temba is dead? You killed him?'

'Eugan Temba is dead,' answered Horus. 'I think he died a long time ago. I don't know exactly what I killed in there, but it wasn't him.'

'I don't understand.'

'I'm not sure I do either,' said Horus, stumbling as he reached the bottom of the slope of debris. She reached out a hand to steady him, before realising what a ridiculous idea that was. Her hand came away bloody and wet, and she saw that the Warmaster still bled from a wound in his shoulder.

'I ended the life of Eugan Temba, but damn me if I didn't weep for him afterwards.'

'But wasn't he an enemy?'

'I have no trouble with my enemies, Miss Vivar,' said Horus. 'I can take care of my enemies in a fight. But my so-called allies, my damned allies, they're the ones who keep me walking the floors at night.'

Legion Apothecaries made their way towards the Warmaster as she tried to make sense of what he was saying. She allowed the mnemo-quill to inscribe his words anyway. She saw the looks she was getting from the Mournival, but ignored them.

'Did you speak to him before you slew him? What did he say?'

'He said... that only I had the power... to stop the future...' said the Warmaster, his voice suddenly faint and echoing as though coming from the other end of a long tunnel.

Puzzled, she looked up in time to see the Warmaster's eyes roll back in their sockets and his legs buckle beneath him. She screamed, reaching out with her hand towards him, knowing that she was powerless to help him, but needing to try to prevent his fall.

Like a slow moving avalanche or a mountain toppling, the Warmaster collapsed.

The mnemo-quill scratched at the data-slate and she wept as she read the words there.

I was there the day that Horus fell.

NINE

Silver towers
A bloody return
The veil grows thin

From here, he could see the pyramid roof of the Athenaeum, the low evening sun reflecting on its gold panels as if it were ablaze, and even though Magnus knew he used but a colourful metaphor, the very idea gave him a pang of loss. To imagine that vast repository of knowledge lost in the flames was abhorrent and he turned his cyclopean gaze from the pyramid of crystal glass and gold.

Tizca, the so-called City of Light, stretched out before him, its marble colonnades and wide boulevards tree-lined and peaceful. Soaring towers of silver and gold reared above a city of gilded libraries, arched museums and sprawling seats of learning. The bulk of the city was constructed of white marble and gold-veined ouslite, shining like a bejewelled crown in the sun. Its architecture spoke of a time long passed, its buildings shaped by craftsmen who had honed their trades for centuries under the tutelage of the Thousand Sons.

From his balcony on the Pyramid of Photep, Magnus the Red, Primarch of the Thousand Sons, contemplated the future of Prospero. His head still hurt from the ferocity of the nightmare and his eye throbbed painfully in its enlarged socket. He gripped the marble balustrade of the balcony, trying to wish away the visions that assailed him in the night and now chased him into the daylight. Mysteries of the night were revealed in the light of day, but these visions of darkness could not be dragged out so easily.

For as long as Magnus could remember, he had been cursed and blessed with a measure of foresight, and his allegorical interpretation of the Athanaeum ablaze troubled him more than he liked to admit.

He poured himself some wine from a silver pitcher, rubbing a copper-skinned hand through his mane of fiery red hair. The wine helped dull the ache in his heart as well as his head, but he knew it was only a temporary solution. Events were now in motion that he had the power to shape and though much of what he had seen was madness and turmoil, and made no sense, he could make out enough to know that he had to make a decision soon – before events spiralled out of control.

Magnus turned from the view over Tizca and made his way back inside the pyramid, pausing as he caught sight of his reflection in the gleaming silver panels. Huge and red-skinned, Magnus was a towering giant with a lustrous mane of red hair. His patrician features were noble and just, his single eye golden and flecked with crimson. Where his other eye would have sat was blank and empty, though a thin scar ran from the bridge of his nose to the edge of his cheekbone.

Cyclopean Magnus they called him, or worse. Since their inception, the Thousand Sons had been viewed with suspicion for embracing powers that others were afraid of. Powers that, because they were not understood, were rejected as being somehow unclean: rejected ever since the Council of Nikaea.

Magnus threw down his goblet, angry at the memory of his humbling at the feet of the Emperor, when he had been forced to renounce the study of all things sorcerous for fear of what he might learn. Such a notion was surely ridiculous, for was his father's realm not founded on the pursuit of knowledge and reason? What harm could study and learning do?

Though he had retreated to Prospero and sworn to renounce such pursuits, the Planet of the Sorcerers had one vital attribute that made it the perfect place for such studies – it was far from the prying eyes of those who said he dabbled with powers beyond his control.

Magnus smiled at the thought, wishing he could show his persecutors the things he had seen, the wonders and the beauty of what lived beyond the veil of reality. Notions of good and evil fell by the wayside next to such power as dwelled in the warp, for they were the antiquated concepts of a religious society, long cast aside.

He stooped to retrieve his goblet and filled it once more before returning to his chambers and taking a seat at his desk. Inside it was cool and the scent of various inks and parchments made him smile. The wide chamber was walled with book-shelves and glass cabinets, filled with curios and remnants of lost knowledge gleaned from conquered worlds. Magnus him-self had penned many of the texts in this room, though others had contributed to this most personal of libraries – Phosis T'kar, Ahriman and Uthizzar to name but a few.

Knowledge had always been a refuge for Magnus, the intoxi-cating thrill of rendering the unknown down to its constituent parts and, by doing so, rendering it knowable. Ignorance of the universe's workings had created false gods in man's ancient past, and the understanding of them was calculated to destroy them. Such was Magnus's lofty goal.

His father denied such things, kept his people ignorant of the true powers that existed in the galaxy, and though he promulgated a doctrine of science and reason, it was naught but a lie, a comfort-ing blanket thrown over humanity to shield them from the truth.

Magnus had looked deep into the warp, however, and knew different.

He closed his eye, seeing again the darkness of the corrupt chamber, the glitter sheen of the sword, and the blow that would change the fate of the galaxy. He saw death and betrayal, heroes and monsters. He saw loyalty tested, and found wanting and standing firm in equal measure. Terrible fates awaited his broth-ers and, worst of all, he knew that his father was utterly ignorant of the doom that threatened the galaxy.

A soft knocking came at his door and the red-armoured fig-ure of Ahriman entered, holding before him a long staff topped with a single eye.

'Have you decided yet, my lord?' asked his Chief Librarian, without preamble.

'I have, my friend,' said Magnus.

'Then shall I gather the coven?'

'Yes,' sighed Magnus, 'in the catacombs beneath the city. Order the thralls to assemble the conjunction and I shall be with you presently.'

'As you wish, my lord,' said Ahriman.

'Something troubles you?' asked Magnus, detecting an edge of reticence in his old friend's tone.

'No, my lord, it is not my place to say.'

'Nonsense. If you have a concern then I give you leave to voice it.'

'Then may I speak freely?'

'Of course,' nodded Magnus. 'What troubles you?'

Ahriman hesitated before answering. 'This spell you propose is dangerous, very dangerous. None of us truly understand its subtleties and there may be consequences we do not yet foresee.'

Magnus laughed. 'I've not known you shirk from the power of a spell before, Ahriman. When manipulating power of this magnitude there will always be unknowns, but only by wielding it can we bring it to heel. Never forget that we are the masters of the warp, my friend. It is strong, yes, and great power lives within it, but we have the knowledge and means to bend it to our will, do we not?'

'We do, my lord,' agreed Ahriman. 'Why then do we use it to warn the Emperor of what is to come when he has forbidden us to pursue such matters?'

Magnus rose from his seat, his copper skin darkening in anger. 'Because when my father sees that it is our sorcery that has saved his realm, he will not be able to deny that what we do here is important, nay, vital to the Imperium's survival!'

Ahriman nodded, fearful of his primarch's rage, and Magnus softened his tone. 'There is no other way, my friend. The Emperor's palace is warded against the power of the warp and only a conjuration of such power will breach those wards.'

'Then I will gather the coven immediately,' said Ahriman.

'Yes, gather them, but await my arrival before beginning. Horus may yet surprise us.'

Panic, fear, indecision: three emotions previously unknown to Loken seized him as Horus fell. The Warmaster crashed to the ground in slow motion, splashing into the mud as his body went completely limp. Shouts of alarm went up, but a paralysis of inaction held those closest to the Warmaster tightly in its grip, as though time itself had slowed.

Loken stared at the Warmaster lying on the ground before him, inert and corpse-like, unable to believe what he was seeing. The rest of the Mournival stood similarly immobile, rooted to the spot in disbelief. He felt as though the air had become thick and cloying, the cries of fear that spread outwards echoing and distant as though from a holo-picter running too slow.

Only Petronella Vivar seemed unaffected by the inaction that held Loken and his brothers firm. Down on her knees in the mud next to the Warmaster, she was weeping and wailing at him to get back up again.

The knowledge that his commander was down and a mortal

woman had reacted before any of the Sons of Horus shamed Loken into action and he dropped to one knee alongside the fallen Horus.

'Apothecary!' shouted Loken, and time snapped back with a crash of shouts and cries.

The Mournival dropped to the ground beside him.

'What's wrong?' demanded Abaddon.

'Commander!' shouted Torgaddon.

'Lupercal!' cried Aximand.

Loken ignored them and forced himself to focus.

This is a battlefield injury and I will treat it as such, he thought.

He scanned the Warmaster's body as the others put their hands on him, pushing the remembrancer out of the way as each struggled to wake their lord and master. Too many hands were interfering, and Loken yelled, 'Stop. Get back!'

The Warmaster's armour was beaten and torn, but Loken could see no other obvious breaches in the armoured plates save where the shoulder guard had been torn away, and where the gaping puncture wound oozed in his chest.

'Help me get his armour off!' he shouted.

The Mournival, bound together as brothers, nodded and, grateful to have a focus for their efforts, instantly obeyed Loken's command. Within moments, they had removed Horus's breastplate and pauldrons and were unstrapping his remaining shoulder guard.

Loken tore off his helmet and cast it aside, pressing his ear to the Warmaster's chest. He could hear the Warmaster's hearts, pounding in a deathly slow double beat.

'He's still alive!' he cried.

'Get out of the way!' shouted a voice behind him, and he turned to rebuke this newcomer before seeing the double helix caduceus symbol on his armour plates. Another Apothecary joined the first and the Mournival was unceremoniously pushed aside as they went to work, hissing narthecium stabbing into the Warmaster's flesh.

Loken stood watching them, impotent and helpless as they fought to stabilise the Warmaster. His eyes filled with tears and he looked around in vain for something to do, something to make him feel he was helping. There was nothing, and he felt like crying out to the heavens for making him so powerful and yet so useless.

Abaddon wept openly, and to see the First Captain so unmanned made Loken's fear for the Warmaster all the more terrible. Aximand watched the Apothecaries work with a grim stoicism, while Torgaddon chewed his bottom lip and prevented the remembrancer from getting in the way.

The Warmaster's skin was ashen, his lips blue and his limbs rigid, and Loken knew that they must destroy whatever power had felled Horus. He turned and began marching back towards the *Glory of Terra*, determined that he would take the stricken craft apart, piece by piece if need be.

'Captain!' called one of the Apothecaries, a warrior Loken knew as Vaddon. 'Get a Stormbird here now! We need to get him to the *Vengeful Spirit*!'

Loken stood immobile, torn between his desire for vengeance and his duty to the Warmaster.

'Now, captain!' yelled the Apothecary, and the spell was broken.

He nodded dumbly and opened a channel to the captains of the Stormbirds, grateful to have a purpose in this maelstrom of confusion. Within moments, one of the medical craft was inbound and Loken watched, mesmerised, as the Apothecaries fought to save the Warmaster.

He could see from the frantic nature of their ministrations that they were fighting an uphill battle, their narthecium whirring miniature centrifuges of blood and dispensing patches of syn-skin to treat his wounds. Their conversations passed over him, but he caught the odd familiar word here and there.

'Larraman cells ineffective...'

'Hypoxic poisoning...'

Aximand appeared at his side and placed his hand on Loken's shoulder.

'Don't say it, Little Horus,' warned Loken.

'I wasn't going to, Garviel,' said Aximand. 'He'll be all right. There's nothing this place could throw at the Warmaster that'll keep him down for long.'

'How do you know?' asked Loken, his voice close to breaking.

'I just do. I have faith.'

'Faith?'

'Yes,' answered Aximand. 'Faith that the Warmaster is too strong and too stubborn to be brought low by something like this. Before you know it we'll be his war dogs once again.'

Loken nodded as the howling downdraught of a Stormbird snatched his breath away.

The screaming craft hovered overhead, throwing up sheets of water as it circled on its descent. Landing skids deployed and the craft came down amid a spray of muddy water.

Before it had touched down, the Mournival and Apothecaries

had lifted Horus between them. Even as the assault ramp came down, they were rushing inside, placing the Warmaster on one of the gurneys as the Stormbird's jets fired to lift it from Davin's moon.

The assault ramp clanged shut behind them, and Loken felt the aircraft lurch as the pilot aimed it for the skies. The Apothecaries hooked the Warmaster up to medicae machines, jamming needles and hissing tubes into his arms, and placing a feed line of oxygen over his mouth and nose.

Suddenly superfluous, Loken slumped into one of the armoured bucket seats against the fuselage of the aircraft and held his head in his hands.

Across from him, the Mournival did the same.

To say that Ignace Karkasy was not a happy man was an understatement. His lunch was cold, Mersadie Oliton was late and the wine he was drinking wasn't fit to lubricate the gears of an engine. To top it all off, his pen tapped on the thick paper of the Bondsman Number 7 without any inspiration flowing. He'd taken to avoiding the Retreat, partly for fear of running into Wenduin again, but mostly because it just depressed him too much. The vandalism done to the bar lent it an incredibly sad and gloomy aspect and, while some of the remembrancers needed the squalor to inspire their work, Karkasy wasn't one of them.

Instead, he relaxed in the sub-deck where most of the remembrancers gathered for their meals, but which was empty for the better part of the day. The solitude was helping him to deal with all that had happened since he'd challenged Euphrati Keeler about her distributing the Lectitio Divinitatus pamphlets – though it certainly wasn't helping him compose any poetry.

She'd been unrepentant when he'd confronted her, urging him to join her in prayer to the God-Emperor, before some kind of makeshift shrine.

'I can't,' he had said. 'It's ridiculous, Euphrati, can't you see that?'

'What's so ridiculous about it, Ig?' she'd asked. 'Think about it, we've embarked upon the greatest crusade known to man. A crusade: a war motivated by religious beliefs!'

'No, no,' he protested, 'it's not that at all. We've moved beyond the need for the crutch of religion, Euphrati and we didn't set out from Terra to take a step backwards into such outmoded concepts of belief. It's only by dispelling the clouds and superstitions of religion that we discover truth, reason and morality.'

'It's not superstition to believe in a god, Ignace,' said Euphrati, holding out another of the Lectitio Divinitatus pamphlets. 'Look, read this and then make up your mind.'

'I don't need to read it,' he snapped, throwing the pamphlet to the deck. 'I know what it will say and I'm not interested.'

'But you have no idea, Ignace. It's all so clear to me now. Ever since that thing attacked me, I've been hiding. In my billet and in my head, but I realise now that all I had to do was allow the light of the Emperor into my heart and I would be healed.'

'Didn't Mersadie and I have anything to do with that?' sneered Karkasy. 'All those hours we spent with you weeping on our shoulders?'

'Of course you did,' smiled Euphrati, coming forward and placing her hands on his cheeks. 'That's why I wanted to give you the message and tell you what I'd realised. It's very simple, Ignace. We create our own gods and the blessed Emperor is the Master of Mankind.'

'Create our own gods?' said Karkasy, pulling away from her. 'No, my dear, ignorance and fear create the gods, enthusiasm and deceit adorn them, and human weakness worships them. It's been the same throughout history. When men destroy their old gods they find new ones to take their place. What makes you think this is any different?'

'Because I feel the Emperor's light within me.'

'Oh, well, I can't argue with that, can I?'

'Spare me your sarcasm, Ignace,' said Euphrati, suddenly hostile. 'I thought you might be open to hearing the good word, but I can see you're just a close-minded fool. Get out, Ignace, I don't want to see you again.'

Thus dismissed, he'd found himself outside in the companionway alone, bereft of a friend he'd only just managed to make. That had been the last time she'd spoken to him. He'd seen her only once since then, and she had ignored his greeting.

'Lost in thought, Ignace?' asked Mersadie Oliton, and he looked up in surprise, shaken from his miserable reverie by her sudden appearance.

'Sorry, my dear,' he said. 'I didn't hear you approach. I was miles away; composing another verse for Captain Loken to misunderstand and Sindermann to discard.'

She smiled, instantly lifting his spirits. It was impossible to be too maudlin around Mersadie, she had a way of making a man realise that it was good to be alive.

'Solitude suits you, Ignace, you're far less susceptible to temptation.'

'Oh I don't know,' he said, holding up the bottle of wine.

'There's always room in my life for temptation. I count it a bad day if I'm not tempted by something or other.'

'You're incorrigible, Ignace,' she laughed, 'but enough of that, what's so important that you drag me away from my transcripts to meet here? I want to be up to date by the time the speartip gets back from the moon.'

Flustered by her directness, Karkasy wasn't sure where to begin and thus opted for the softly-softly approach. 'Have you seen Euphrati around recently?'

'I saw her yesterday evening, just before the Stormbirds launched. Why?'

'Did she seem herself?'

'Yes, I think so. I was a little surprised by the change in her appearance, but she's an imagist. I suppose it's what they do every now and again.'

'Did she try to give you anything?'

'Give me anything? No. Look, what's this all about?'

Karkasy slipped a battered pamphlet across the table towards Mersadie, watching her expression change as she read it and recognised it for what it was.

'Where did you get this?' she asked when she'd finished reading it.

'Euphrati gave it to me,' he replied. 'Apparently she wants to spread the word of the God-Emperor to us first because we helped her when she needed support.'

'God-Emperor? Has she taken leave of her senses?'

'I don't know, maybe,' he said, pouring himself a drink. Mersadie pushed over a glass and he filled that too. 'I don't think she was over her experience in the Whisperheads, even if she made out that she was.'

'This is insane,' said Mersadie. 'She'll have her certification revoked. Did you tell her that?'

'Sort of,' said Karkasy. 'I tried to reason with her, but you know how it is with those religious types, never any room for a dissenting opinion.'

'And?'

'And nothing, she threw me out of her billet after that.'

'So you handled it with your usual tact then?'

'Perhaps I could have been more delicate,' agreed Karkasy, 'but I was shaken to know that a woman of intelligence could be taken in by such nonsense.'

'So what do we do about it?'

'You tell me. I don't have a clue. Do you think we should tell someone about Euphrati?'

Mersadie took a long drink of the wine and said, 'I think we have to.'

'Any ideas who?'

'Sindermann maybe?'

Karkasy sighed. 'I had a feeling you were going to suggest him. I don't like the man, but he's probably the best bet these days. If anyone can talk Euphrati around it's an iterator.'

Mersadie sighed and poured another couple of drinks. 'Want to get drunk?'

'Now you're talking my language,' said Karkasy.

They swapped stories and memories of less complicated times for an hour, finishing the bottle of wine and sending a servitor to fetch more when it ran out. By the time they'd drained half the second one, they were already planning a great symphonic work of her documentarist findings embellished with his verse.

They laughed and studiously avoided any talk of Euphrati Keeler and the betrayal they were soon to visit upon her.

Their thoughts were immediately dispelled as chiming alarm bells rang out, and the corridor beyond began to fill with hurrying people. At first, they ignored the noise, but as the number of people grew, they decided to find out what was going on. Picking up the bottle and glasses, Karkasy and Mersadie unsteadily made their way to the hatchway where they saw a scene of utter bedlam.

Soldiers and civilians, remembrancers and ship's crew, were heading for the embarkation decks in a hurry. They saw faces streaked with tears, and huddled weeping figures consoling one another in their shared misery.

'What's going on?' shouted Karkasy, grabbing a passing soldier.

The man rounded on him angrily. 'Get off me, you old fool.'

'I just want to know what's happening,' said Karkasy, shocked at the man's venom.

'Haven't you heard?' wept the soldier. 'It's all over the ship.'

'What is?' demanded Mersadie.

'The Warmaster...'

'What about him? Is he all right?'

The man shook his head. 'Emperor save us, but the Warmaster is dead!'

The bottle slipped from Karkasy's hands, shattering on the floor, and he was instantly sober. The Warmaster dead? Surely, there had to be some kind of mistake. Surely, Horus was beyond such concerns as mortality. He faced Mersadie and could see exactly the same thoughts running through her head. The soldier he'd stopped shrugged off his grip and ran down the corridor, leaving the two of them standing there, aghast at such a horrific prospect.

'It can't be true,' whispered Mersadie. 'It just can't be.'

'I know. There must be some mistake.'

'What if there isn't?'

'I don't know,' said Karkasy, 'but we have to find out more.'

Mersadie nodded and waited for him to collect the Bondsman before they joined the hurrying throng as it made its mob-like way towards the embarkation decks. Neither of them spoke during the journey, too busy trying to process the impact of the Warmaster's death. Karkasy felt the muse stir within him at such weighty subject matter, and tried not to despise the fact that it came at such a terrible time.

He spotted the corridor leading to the observation deck adjacent to the launch port from where Stormbirds could be seen deploying, or returning. She resisted his pull until he explained his plan.

'There's no way they're going to let us in,' said Karkasy, out of breath from his exertions. 'We can watch the Stormbirds arrive from here and there's an observation gantry that overlooks the deck itself.'

They darted from the human river making its way to the embarkation deck and followed the arched corridor that led to the observation deck. Inside the long chamber, the wide armoured glass wall showed smudges of starlight and the glinting hulls of distant bulk cruisers belonging to the Army and the Mechanicum. Below them was the chasm-like opening of the embarkation deck, its blinking locator lights flashing an angry red.

Mersadie dimmed the lighting, and the details beyond the glass became clearer.

The yellow brown swell of Davin's moon curved away from them, its surface grimy and smeared with clouds. A hazy corona of sickly light haloed the moon and, from here, it looked peaceful.

'I don't see anything,' said Mersadie.

Karkasy pressed himself against the glass to eliminate reflections and tried to see something other than himself and Mersadie. Then he saw it. Like a glimmering firefly, a distant speck of fire was rising out of the moon's corona and heading towards the *Vengeful Spirit*.

'There!' he said, pointing towards the approaching light.

'Where? Oh, wait, I see it!' said Mersadie, blink-clicking the image of the approaching craft.

Karkasy watched as the light drew nearer, resolving itself into the shape of a speeding Stormbird as it angled its approach to the embarkation deck. Even though Karkasy was no pilot, he could tell that its approach was recklessly rapid, the craft's wings folding in at the last moment as it aimed for the yawning, red-lit hatch.

'Come on!' he said, taking Mersadie's hand and leading the way up the steps to the observation gantry. The steps were steep and narrow, and Karkasy had to stop to get his breath back before he reached the top. By the time they reached the gantry, the Stormbird had already been recovered and its assault ramp was descending.

A host of Astartes gathered around the craft as the Bell of Return began ringing and four warriors emerged, the plates of their armour dented and bloodstained. Between them, they carried a body draped in a Legion banner. Karkasy's breath caught in his throat and he felt his heart turn to stone at the sight.

'The Mournival,' said Mersadie. 'Oh no…'

The four warriors were quickly followed by an enormous gurney upon which lay a partially armoured warrior of magnificent stature.

Even from here, Karkasy could tell that the figure upon the gurney was the Warmaster and though tears leapt unbidden to his eyes at the sight of such a superlative warrior laid low, he rejoiced that the shrouded corpse was not the Warmaster. He heard Mersadie blink-clicking the images even though he knew there would be no point; her eyes were similarly misted with tears. Behind the gurney came the remembrancer woman, Vivar, her dress torn and bloody, the fine fabric mud stained and ragged, but Karkasy pushed her from his mind as he saw more warriors rush towards the gurney. Armoured in white plate, they surrounded the Warmaster as he was wheeled through the embarkation deck with great haste, and Karkasy's heart leapt as he recognised them as Legion Apothecaries.

'He's still alive…' he said.

'What? How do you know?'

'The Apothecaries are still working on him,' laughed Karkasy, the relief tasting like the sweetest wine. They threw themselves into each other's arms, embracing with the sheer relief of the Warmaster's survival.

'He's alive,' sobbed Mersadie. 'I knew he had to be. He couldn't be dead.'

'No,' agreed Karkasy. 'He couldn't.'

They broke apart and sagged against the railings as the Astartes escorted the fallen Warmaster across the deck. As the huge blast doors rumbled open, the masses of people gathered outside surged through in a great wave, their cries of loss and pain audible even through the armoured glass of the observation gantry.

'No,' whispered Karkasy. 'No, no, no.'

The Astartes were in no mood to be slowed by this mass of people, and brutally clubbed them aside as they forced a path through the crowd. The Mournival led the gurney through the crowds, mercilessly clearing a bloody path through the people before them. Karkasy saw men and women cast down, trampled underfoot, and their screams were pitiful to hear.

Mersadie held his arm as they watched the Astartes bludgeon their way from the embarkation deck. They vanished through the blast door and were lost to sight as they rushed towards the medical deck.

'Those poor people...' cried Mersadie, sinking to her knees and looking down on a scene like the aftermath of a battle: wounded soldiers, remembrancers and civilians lay where they had fallen, bleeding and broken, simply because they were unlucky enough to be in the path of the Astartes.

'They didn't care,' said Karkasy, still unable to believe the bloody scenes that he'd just witnessed. 'They've killed those people. It was like they didn't care.'

Still in shock at the casual ease with which the Astartes had punched through the crowd, Karkasy gripped the railings, his knuckles white and his jaw clenched with outrage.

'How dare they?' he hissed. 'How *dare* they?'

His anger at the scenes below still seethed close to the surface; however, he noticed a robed figure making her way through the carnage below, reaching out to the injured and stunned.

His eyes narrowed, but he recognised the shapely form of Euphrati Keeler.

She was handing out Lectitio Divinitatus pamphlets, and she wasn't alone.

Maloghurst watched the recording from the embarkation deck with a grim expression, watching his fellow Sons of Horus batter their way through the crowds that swarmed around the Warmaster's wracked body. The pict replayed again on the viewer set into the table in the Warmaster's sanctum, and each time he watched it, he willed it to be different, but each time the flickering images remained resolutely the same.

'How many dead?' asked Hektor Varvarus, standing at Maloghurst's shoulder.

'I don't have the final figures yet, but at least twenty-one are dead, and many more are badly injured or won't wake from the comas they're in.'

He cursed Loken and the others for their heavy handedness as the image played again, but supposed he couldn't blame them for their ardour. The Warmaster was in a critical condition and no one knew if he would live, so their desperation to reach the medical decks was forgivable, even if many might say that their actions were not.

'A bad business, Maloghurst,' said Varvarus needlessly. 'The Astartes will not come out of this well.'

Maloghurst sighed, and said, 'They thought the Warmaster was dying and acted accordingly.'

'Acted accordingly?' repeated Varvarus. 'I do not think many people will accept that, my friend, once word of this gets out, it will be a crippling blow to morale.'

'It will not get out,' assured Maloghurst. 'I am rounding up everyone who was on that deck and have shut down all non-command vox traffic from the ship.'

Tall and precise, Hektor Varvarus was rake-thin and angular, and his every movement was calculated – traits he carried over into his role as Lord Commander of the Army forces of the 63rd Expedition.

'Trust me, Maloghurst, this will get out. One way or another, it will get out. Nothing remains secret forever. Such things have a habit of wanting to be told and this will be no different.'

'Then what do you suggest, lord commander?' asked Maloghurst.

'Are you genuinely asking me, Mal, or are you just observing a courtesy because I am here?'

'I was genuinely asking,' said Maloghurst, smiling as he realised that he meant it. Varvarus was a canny soldier who understood the hearts and minds of mortal men.

'Then you have to tell people what happened. Be honest.'

'Heads will need to roll,' cautioned Maloghurst. 'People will demand blood for this.'

'Then give it to them. If that's what it takes, give it to them. Someone has to be seen to pay for this atrocity.'

'Atrocity? Is that what we're calling it now?'

'What else would you call it? Astartes warriors have committed murder.'

The enormity of what Varvarus was suggesting staggered Maloghurst, and he lowered himself slowly into one of the chairs at the Warmaster's table.

'You would have me give up an Astartes warrior for this? I cannot do it.'

Varvarus leaned over the table, the decorations and medals of his dress uniform reflecting like gold suns in its black surface.

'Innocent blood has been spilled, and while I can understand the reasons behind the actions of your men, it changes nothing.'

'I can't do it, Hektor,' said Maloghurst, shaking his head.

Varvarus moved to stand next to him. 'You and I both swore the oath of loyalty to the Imperium did we not?'

'We did, but what has that to do with anything?'

The old general locked eyes with Maloghurst and said, 'We swore that we would uphold the ideals of nobility and justice that the Imperium stands for, yes?'

'Yes, but this is different. There were extenuating circumstances...'

'Irrelevant,' snapped Varvarus. 'The Imperium must stand for something, or it stands for nothing. If you turn away from this, then you betray that oath of loyalty. Are you willing to do that, Maloghurst?'

Before he could answer, there was a soft knocking on the glass of the sanctum and Maloghurst turned to see who disturbed them.

Ing Mae Sing, Mistress of Astropathy, stood before them like a skeletal ghost in a hooded white robe, the upper portions of her face shrouded in shadows.

'Mistress Sing,' said Varvarus, bowing deeply towards the telepath.

'Lord Varvarus,' she replied, her voice soft and feather-light. She returned the lord commander's bow and despite her blindness, inclined her head in precisely the right direction – a talent that never failed to unnerve Maloghurst.

'What is it, Mistress Sing?' he asked, though in truth, he was glad of the interruption.

'I bring tidings that must concern you, Sire Maloghurst,' she said, turning her blind gaze upon him. 'The astropathic choirs are unsettled. They sense a powerful surge in the currents of the warp: powerful and growing.'

'What does that mean?' he asked.

'That the veil between worlds grows thin,' said Ing Mae Sing.

TEN

Apothecarion
Prayers
Confession

Stripped out of his armour and wearing bloody surgical robes, Vaddon was as close to desperate as he had ever been in his long experience as an Apothecary of the Sons of Horus. The Warmaster lay before him on the gurney, his flesh exposed to his knives and to the probes of the medicae machines. Oxygen was fed to the Warmaster through a mask, and saline drips pumped fluids into his body in an attempt to normalise his blood pressure. Medicae servitors brought fresh blood for immediate transfusions and the entire theatre fizzed with tension and frantic activity.

'We're losing him!' shouted Apothecary Logaan, watching the heart monitors. 'Blood pressure is dropping rapidly, heart rate spiking. He's going to arrest!'

'Damn it,' cursed Vaddon. 'Get me more Larraman serum, his blood won't clot, and fix up another fluid line.'

A whirring surgical narthecium swung down from the ceiling, multiple limbs clattering as they obeyed Vaddon's shouted commands. Fresh Larraman cells were pumped directly into Horus's shoulder and the bleeding slowed, though Vaddon could see it still wasn't stopping completely. Thick needles jabbed into the Warmaster's arms, filling him with super-oxygenated blood, but their supply was dwindling faster than he would have believed possible.

'Stabilising,' breathed Logaan. 'Heart rate slowing and blood pressure is up.'

'Good,' said Vaddon. 'We've got some breathing room then.'

'He can't take much more of this,' said Logaan. 'We're running out of things we can do for him.'

'I'll not hear that in my theatre, Logaan,' snapped Vaddon. 'We're not going to lose him.'

The Warmaster's chest hiked as he clung to life, his breathing coming in short, hyperventilating gasps, more blood pumping from the wound in his shoulder.

Of the two wounds the Warmaster had suffered, it seemed the least severe, but Vaddon knew it was the one that was killing him. The puncture wound in his chest had practically healed already, ultra-sonograms showing that his lung had sealed itself off from the pulmonary system while it repaired itself. The Warmaster's secondary lungs were sustaining him for now.

The Mournival hovered like expectant fathers as the Apothecaries worked harder than they had ever worked before. Vaddon had never expected to have the Warmaster for a patient. The primarch's biology was as far beyond that of a normal Astartes warrior as his own was from a mortal man, and Vaddon knew that he was out of his depth. Only the Emperor himself had the knowledge to delve into the body of a primarch with confidence, and the enormity of what was occurring was not lost on him.

A green light winked into life on the narthecium machine and he lifted the data-slate from the port in its silver steel surface. Numbers and text scrolled across its glossy surface and though much of it made no sense to him, he felt his spirits fall as what he could comprehend sank in.

Seeing that the Warmaster was stable, he circled the operating slab and joined the Mournival, wishing he had better news for them.

'What's wrong with him?' demanded Abaddon. 'Why is he still lying there?'

'Honestly, First Captain, I don't know.'

'What do you mean, "You don't know"?' shouted Abaddon, grabbing Vaddon and slamming him against the theatre wall. Silver trays laden with scalpels, saws and forceps clattered to the tiled floor. 'Why don't you know?'

Loken and Aximand grappled with the First Captain as Vaddon felt Abaddon's enormous strength slowly crushing his neck.

'Let go of him, Ezekyle!' cried Loken. 'This isn't helping!'

'You won't let him die!' snarled Abaddon, and Vaddon was

amazed to see a terrible fear in the First Captain's eyes. 'He is the Warmaster!'

'You think I don't know that?' gasped Vaddon as the others prised Abaddon's grip from his neck. He slid down the wall, already able to feel the swelling in his bruised throat.

'Emperor damn you if you let him die,' hissed Abaddon, stalking the theatre with predatory strides. 'If he dies, I will kill you.'

Aximand led the First Captain away from him, speaking soothing words as Loken and Torgaddon helped him to his feet.

'The man's a maniac,' hissed Vaddon. 'Get him out of my theatre, now!'

'He's not himself, Apothecary,' explained Loken. 'None of us are.'

'Just keep him away from my team, captain,' warned Vaddon. 'He's not in control of himself, and that makes him dangerous.'

'We will,' Torgaddon promised him. 'Now what can you tell us? Will he survive?'

Vaddon took a moment to compose himself before answering, picking up his fallen data-slate. 'As I said before, I just don't know. We're like children trying to repair a logic engine that's been dropped from orbit. We don't understand even a fraction of what his body is capable of or how it works. I can't even begin to guess what kind of damage it's suffered to have caused this.'

'What's actually happening to him?' asked Loken.

'It's the wound in his shoulder; it won't clot. It's bleeding out and we can't stop it. We found some degraded genetic residue in the wound that might be some kind of poison, but I can't be sure.'

'Might it be a bacteriological or a viral infection?' asked Torgaddon. 'The water on Davin's moon was thick with contaminants. I ought to know, I swallowed a flagon's worth of it.'

'No,' said Vaddon. 'The Warmaster's body is, for all intents and purposes, immune to such things.'

'Then what is it?'

'This is a guess, but it looks like this particular poison induces a form of anaemic hypoxia. Once it enters the bloodstream, it's absorbed exponentially by the red blood cells, in preference to oxygen. With the Warmaster's accelerated metabolism, the toxin was carried efficiently around his system, damaging his tissue cells as it went, so they were unable to make proper use of the reduced oxygen content.'

'So where did it come from?' asked Loken. 'I thought you said the Warmaster was immune to such things.'

'And so he is, but this is like nothing I've ever seen before...'

it's as though it's been specifically designed to kill him. It's got precisely the right genetic camouflage to fool his enhanced biological defences and allow it to do the maximum amount of damage. It's a primarch killer – pure and simple.'

'So how do we stop it?'

'This isn't an enemy you can take a bolter or sword to, Captain Loken. It's a poison,' he said. 'If I knew the source of the poisoning, we might be able to do something.'

'Then if we found the weapon that did this, would that be of some help?' asked Loken.

Seeing the desperate need for hope in the captain's eyes, Vaddon nodded. 'Maybe. From the wound shape, it looks like a stab wound from a sword. If you can retrieve the blade, then maybe we can do something for him.'

'I'll find it,' swore Loken. He turned from Vaddon and made his way to the theatre door.

'You're going back there?' asked Torgaddon, running to catch up with him.

'Yes, and don't try to stop me,' warned Loken.

'Stop you?' said Torgaddon. 'Don't be such a drama queen, Garvi. I'm coming with you.'

Recovering a Titan after action in the field was a long and arduous process, full of technical, logistical and manual difficulties. Entire fleets of vessels came down from orbit, bringing huge lifters, enormous diggers and loading machines. The delivery vessels had to be dug from their impact craters, and an army of Mechanicum servitors were required to facilitate the process.

Titus Cassar was exhausted. He'd spent the better part of the day prepping the Titan for its recovery and everything was in readiness for their return to the fleet. Until they were recovered, there wasn't much to do except wait, and that had become the hardest part of all for the men left behind on Davin's moon.

With time to wait, there was time to think; and with time to think, the human mind could conjure all manner of things from the depths of its imagination. Titus still couldn't believe that Horus had fallen. A being of such power, like unto a Titan himself, was not meant to fall in battle – he was invincible, the son of a god.

In the shadow of the *Dies Irae*, Titus fished out his Lectitio Divinitatus chapbook and, once he was satisfied he was alone, began to read the words there. The badly printed scripture gave him comfort, turning his mind to the glory of the divine Emperor of Mankind.

'Oh Emperor, who is lord and god above us all, hear me in this hour of need. Your servant lies with death's cold touch upon him and I ask you to turn your beneficent gaze his way.'

He fished out a pendant from beneath his uniform jacket as he read. It was a delicately wrought thing of silver and gold that he'd had one of the blank-faced servitors fashion for him. A silver capital 'I' with a golden starburst at its centre, it represented hope and the promise of a better future.

He held it clasped to his breast as he recited more of the words of the Lectitio Divinitatus, feeling a familiar warmth suffuse him as he repeated the words.

Titus sensed the presence of other people behind him a second too late and turned to see Jonah Aruken and a group of the Titan's crew.

Like him, they were dirty and tired after the fight against the monsters of this place, but unlike him they did not have faith.

Guiltily, he closed his chapbook and waited for Jonah's inevitable barb. No one said anything, and as he looked closer, he saw a brittle edge of sorrow and the need for comfort in the faces of the men before him.

'Titus,' said Jonah Aruken. 'We... uh... that is... the Warmaster. We wondered if...'

Titus smiled in welcome as understood what they'd come for.

He opened his chapbook again and said, 'Let us pray, brothers.'

The medical deck was a sterile, gleaming wilderness of tiled walls and brushed steel cabinets, a warren of soulless glass rooms and laboratories. Petronella had completely lost all sense of direction, bewildered by the hasty summons that had brought her from the moon's surface back to the *Vengeful Spirit*.

Passing through the bloody embarkation deck, she saw that the upper levels of the ship were in pandemonium as word of the Warmaster's death had spread from vessel to vessel with all the fearsome rapidity of an epidemic.

Maloghurst the Twisted had issued a fleet-wide communiqué denying that the Warmaster was dead, but hysteria and paranoia had a firm head start on his words. Riots had taken hold aboard several ships as doomsayers and demagogues had arisen proclaiming that these were now the end times. Army units had been ruthlessly quashing such malcontents, but more sprang up faster then they could stop them.

It had been scant hours since the Warmaster's fall, but the 63rd Expedition was already beginning to tear itself apart without him.

Maggard followed Petronella, his wounds bound and sealed with syn-skin by a Legion Apothecary on the journey back to the Warmaster's flagship. His skin still had an unhealthy pallor and his armour was dented and torn, but he was alive and magnificent. Maggard was only an indentured servant, but he had impressed her and she resolved to treat him with the respect his talents deserved.

A helmeted Astartes warrior led her through the confusing maze of the medicae deck, eventually indicating that she should enter a nondescript white door marked with a winged staff wrapped in a pair of twisting serpents.

Maggard opened the door for her and she entered a gleaming operating theatre, its circular walls covered, to waist height, in green enamelled tiles. Silver cabinets and hissing, pumping machines surrounded the Warmaster, who lay on the operating slab with a tangled web of tubes and wires attached to his flesh. A stool of gleaming metal sat next to the slab.

Medicae servitors lurked around the circumference of the room, set into niches around the wall, and a gurgling machine suspended above the Warmaster fed fluid and blood into his body.

Her eyes misted to see the Warmaster brought so low, and tears came at this violation of the natural order of things. A giant Astartes warrior in hooded surgical robes approached her and said, 'My name is Apothecary Vaddon, Miss Vivar.'

She brushed her hands across her eyes, conscious of how she must look – her dress torn and caked with mud, her eyes blackened with smudged make-up. She started to hold her hand out for a kiss, but realised how foolish that would be and simply nodded.

'I am Petronella Vivar,' she managed. 'I am the Warmaster's documentarist.'

'I know,' said Vaddon. 'He asked for you by name.'

Sudden hope flared in her breast. 'He's awake?'

Vaddon nodded. 'He is. If it was up to me, you would not be here now, but I do not disobey the word of the commander, and he desires to speak with you.'

'How is he?' she asked.

The Apothecary shook his head. 'He fades in and out of lucidity, so do not expect too much of him. If I decide it is time for you to leave, then you leave. Do you understand me?'

'I do,' she said, 'but please, may I speak with him now?'

Vaddon seemed reluctant to let her near the Warmaster, but moved aside and let her pass. She nodded her thanks and took a faltering step towards the operating slab, eager to see the War-master, but afraid of what she might find.

Petronella's hand leapt to her mouth to stifle an involuntary gasp at the sight of him. The Warmaster's cheeks were sunken and hollow, his eyes dull and listless. Grey flesh hung from his skull, wrinkled and ancient looking, and his lips were the blue of a corpse.

'Do I look that bad?' asked Horus, his voice rasping and distant.

'No,' she stammered. 'Not at all, I...'

'Don't lie to me, Miss Vivar. If you're to hear my valediction then there must be no deceit between us.'

'Valediction? No! I won't. You have to live.'

'Believe me, there's nothing I'd like more,' he wheezed, 'but Vaddon tells me there's not much chance of that, and I don't intend to leave this life without a proper legacy: a record that says the things that must be said before the end.'

'Sir, your deeds alone stand as an eternal legacy, please don't ask this of me.'

Horus coughed a froth of blood onto his chest, gathering his strength before speaking once more, and his voice was the strong and powerful one she remembered. 'You told me that it was your vocation to immortalise me, to record the glory of Horus for future generations, did you not?'

'I did,' she sobbed.

'Then do this last thing for me, Miss Vivar,' he said.

She swallowed hard and then fished out the data-slate and mnemo-quill from her reticule, before sitting on the high stool next to the operating slab.

'Very well,' she said at last. 'Let's start at the beginning.'

'It was too much,' began Horus. 'I promised my father I would make no mistakes, and now we have come to this.'

'Mistakes?' asked Petronella, though she suspected she knew the Warmaster's meaning.

'Temba, giving him lordship over Davin,' said Horus. 'He begged me not to leave him behind, claimed it was too much for him. I should have listened, but I was too eager to be away on some fresh conquest.'

'Temba's weakness is not your fault, sir,' she said.

'It is good of you to say that, Miss Vivar, but I appointed him,' said Horus. 'The responsibility lies with me. Throne! Guilli-man will laugh when he hears of this: him and the Lion both. They will say that I was not fit to be Warmaster since I could not read the hearts of men.'

'Never!' cried Petronella. 'They wouldn't dare.'

'Oh, they will, girl, believe me. We are brothers, yes, but like all brothers we squabble and seek to outdo one another.'

Petronella could think of nothing to say; the idea of the super-human primarchs squabbling quite beyond her.

'They were jealous, all of them,' continued Horus. 'When the Emperor named me Warmaster, it was all some of them could do to congratulate me. Angron especially, he was a wild one, and even now I can barely keep him in check. Guilliman wasn't much better. I could tell he thought it should have been him.'

'They were jealous of you?' asked Petronella, unable to believe what the Warmaster was telling her, the mnemo-quill scratching across the data-slate in response to her thoughts.

'Oh yes,' nodded Horus bitterly. 'Only a few of my brothers were gracious enough to bow their heads and mean it. Lorgar, Mortarion, Sanguinius, Fulgrim and Dorn – they are true brothers. I remember watching the Emperor's Stormbird leaving Ullanor and weeping to see him go, but most of all I remember the knives I felt in my back as he went. I could hear their thoughts as clearly as though they spoke them aloud: why should I, Horus, be named Warmaster when there were others more worthy of the honour?'

'You were made Warmaster *because* you were the most worthy, sir,' said Petronella.

'No,' said Horus. 'I was not. I was simply the one who most embodied the Emperor's need at that time. You see, for the first three decades of the Great Crusade I fought alongside the Emperor, and I alone felt the full weight of his ambition to rule the galaxy. He passed that vision to me and I carried it with me in my heart as we forged our path across the stars. It was a grand adventure we were on, system after system reunited with the Master of Mankind. You cannot imagine what it was like to live in such times, Miss Vivar.'

'It sounds magnificent.'

'It was,' said Horus. 'It was, but it couldn't last. Soon we were being drawn to other worlds where we discovered my brother primarchs. We had been scattered throughout the galaxy not long after our birth and, one by one, the Emperor recovered us all.'

'It must have been strange to be reunited with brothers you had never known.'

'Not as strange as you might think. As soon as I met each one, I had an immediate kinship with him, a bond that not even time or distance had broken. I won't deny that some were harder to like than others. If you ever meet Night Haunter you'll understand what I mean. Moody bastard, but handy in a tight spot when you need some alien empire shitting in its breeches before you attack.

'Angron's not much better, mind; he's got a temper on him like you've never seen. You think you know anger, I tell you now that you don't know anything until you've seen Angron lose his temper. And don't get me started on the Lion.'

'Of the Dark Angels? His is the First Legion is it not?'

'It is,' replied Horus, 'and doesn't he just love to remind everyone of that. I could see in his eyes that he thought he should have been Warmaster because his Legion was the first. Did you know he'd grown up living like an animal in the wilds, little better than a feral savage? I ask you, is that the sort of man you want as your Warmaster?'

'No it's not,' said Horus, answering his own question.

'Then who would you have picked to be Warmaster if not you?' asked Petronella.

Horus appeared to be momentarily perturbed by her question, but said, 'Sanguinius. It should have been him. He has the vision and strength to carry us to victory, and the wisdom to rule once that victory is won. For all his aloof coolness, he alone has the Emperor's soul in his blood. Each of us carries part of our father within us, whether it is his hunger for battle, his psychic talent or his determination to succeed. Sanguinius holds it all. It should have been his...'

'And what part of the Emperor do you carry, sir?'

'Me? I carry his ambition to rule. While the conquest of the galaxy lay before us that was enough, but now we are nearing the end. There is a Kretan proverb that says that peace is always "over there", but that is no longer true: it is within our grasp. The job is almost done and what is left for a man of ambition when the work is over?'

'You are the Emperor's right hand, sir,' protested Petronella. 'His favoured son.'

'No more,' said Horus sadly. 'Petty functionaries and administrators have supplanted me. The War Council is no more and I receive my orders from the Council of Terra now. Once everything in the Imperium was geared for war and conquest, but now we are burdened with eaxectors, scribes and scriveners who demand to know the cost of everything. The Imperium is changing and I'm not sure I know how to change with it.'

'In what way is the Imperium changing?'

'Bureaucracy and officialdom are taking over, Miss Vivar. Red tape, administrators and clerks are replacing the heroes of the age and unless we change our ways and our direction, our greatness as an empire will soon be a footnote in the history books. Everything I have achieved will be a distant memory of former glory, lost in the mists of time like the civilisations of ancient Terra, remembered kindly for their noble past.'

'But surely the Crusade was but the first step towards creating a new Imperium for mankind to rule the galaxy. In such a galaxy we will need administrators, laws and scribes.'

'And what of the warriors who conquered it for you?' snarled Horus. 'What becomes of us? Are we to become gaolers and peacekeepers? We were bred for war and we were bred to kill. That is what we were created for, but we have become so much more than that. *I* am more than that.'

'Progress is hard, my lord, and people must always adapt to changing times,' said Petronella, uneasy at this change of temper in the Warmaster.

'It is not strange to mistake change for progress, Miss Vivar,' said Horus. 'I was bred with wondrous powers encoded into my very flesh, but I did not dream myself into the man I am today; I hammered and forged myself upon the anvil of battle and conquest. All that I have achieved in the last two centuries will be given away to weak men and women who were not here to shed their blood with us in the dark places of the galaxy. Where is the justice in that? Lesser men will rule what I have conquered, but what will be my reward once the fighting is done?'

Petronella glanced away at Apothecary Vaddon, but he simply watched impassively as she took down Horus's words. She wondered briefly if he was as upset as she was at the Warmaster's anger.

As shocked as she was, her ambitious core realised that she had the makings of the most sensational remembrance imaginable, one that would dispel forever the myth of the Crusade as a united band of brothers forging their destiny among the stars. Horus's words painted a picture of mistrust and disunion that no one had ever dreamed of.

Seeing her expression, Horus reached up with a shaking hand and touched her arm.

'I am sorry, Miss Vivar. My thoughts are not as clear as they ought to be.'

'No,' she said. 'I think they're clearer than ever now.'

'I can tell I'm shocking you. I'm sorry if I have shattered your illusions.'

'I admit I am... surprised by much of what you're saying, sir.'

'But you like it, yes? It's what you came here for?'

She tried to deny it, but the sight of the dying primarch gave her pause and she nodded.

'Yes,' she said. 'It's what I came here for. Will you tell me everything?'

He looked up and met her stare.

'Yes,' he said. 'I will.'

ELEVEN

Answers
A devil's bargain
Anathame

The Thunderhawk's armoured flanks were not as sleek as those of a Stormbird, but it was functional and would take them back to Davin's moon more swiftly than the bigger craft. Tech servitors and Mechanicum flight crew prepped it for launch and Loken willed them to hurry. Each passing second brought the Warmaster closer to death and he wasn't going to allow that to happen.

Several hours had passed since they had brought the Warmaster aboard, but he hadn't cleaned his armour or weapons, preferring to go back the way he'd come out, though he had replenished his ammunition supply. The deck was still slick with the blood of those they had battered from their path and only now, with time to reflect on what they had done, did Loken feel ashamed.

He couldn't remember any of the faces, but he remembered the crack of skulls and the cries of pain. All the noble ideals of the Astartes... What did they mean when they could be so easily cast off? Kyril Sindermann was right, common decency and civil behaviour were just a thin veneer over the animal core that lurked in the hearts of all men... even Astartes.

If the mores of civilised behaviour could so easily be forgotten, what else might be betrayed with impunity in difficult circumstances?

Looking around the deck, Loken could sense a barely perceptible difference. Though hammers still beat, hatches still banged and gurneys laden with ordnance curled through the deck spaces, there was a subdued atmosphere to the embarkation deck, as though the memory of what had happened still lingered on the air.

The blast doors of the deck were shut tight, but Loken could still hear the muffled chants and songs of the crowds gathered outside.

Hundreds of people maintained a candlelit vigil in the wide corridors surrounding the embarkation deck, and filled the observation bays. Perhaps three score watched him from the windowed gantry above. They carried offerings and votive papers inscribed with pleas for the Warmaster's survival, random scribbles and outpourings of feelings.

Quite who these entreaties were directed at was a mystery, but it seemed to give people a purpose, and Loken could appreciate the value of purpose in these dark hours.

The men of Locasta were already onboard, though their journey to the embarkation deck had nearly sparked a stampede of terrified people – the memory of the last time the Astartes had marched through them still fresh and bloody.

Torgaddon and Vipus performed the last pre-launch checks on their men, and all that remained for him to do was to give the word.

He heard footsteps behind him and turned to see the armoured figure of Tybalt Marr, Captain of the Eighteenth Company, approaching him. Sometimes known as 'the Either' due to his uncanny resemblance to Verulam Moy – who had been known as 'the Or' – he was cast so firmly in the image of the Warmaster that Loken's breath caught in his throat. He bowed as his fellow captain approached.

'Captain Loken,' said Marr, returning the bow. 'Might I have a word?'

'Of course, Tybalt,' he said. 'I'm sorry about Verulam. He was a brave man.'

Marr nodded curtly and Loken could only imagine the pain he must be going through.

Loken had grieved for fallen brothers before, but Moy and Marr had been inseparable, enjoying a symbiotic relationship not unlike identical twins. As friends and brothers, they had fought best as a pair, but once again, Moy had been lucky enough to gain a place in the speartip, and Marr had not.

This time Moy had paid for that luck with his life.

'Thank you, Captain Loken. I appreciate the sentiment,' replied Marr.

'Was there something you wanted, Tybalt?'

'Are you returning to the moon?' asked Marr, and Loken knew exactly why Marr was here. He nodded. 'We are. There may be something there that will help the Warmaster. If there is, we will find it.'

'Is it in the place where Verulam died?'

'Yes,' said Loken. 'I think so.'

'Could you use another sword arm? I want to see where... where it happened.'

Loken saw the aching grief in Marr's eyes and said. 'Of course we could.'

Marr nodded his thanks and they marched up the assault ramp as the Thunderhawk's engines powered up with the shrieking of a banshee's wail.

Aximand watched Abaddon punch the sparring servitor's shoulder, tearing off its sword limb before closing to deliver a series of rapid hammer blows to its torso. Flesh caved beneath the assault, bone and steel broke, and the construct collapsed in a splintered mess of meat and metal.

It was the third servitor Abaddon had destroyed in the last thirty minutes. Ezekyle had always worked through his angst with his fists and this time was no different. Violence and killing was what the First Captain had been bred for, but it had become such a way of life to him that it was the only way he knew how to express his frustrations.

Aximand himself had dismantled and reassembled his bolter six times, slowly and methodically laying each part on an oiled cloth before cleaning it meticulously. Where Abaddon unleashed his pain through violence, Aximand preferred to detach his mind through familiar routines. Powerless to do anything constructive to help the commander, they had both retreated to the things they knew best.

'The Master of Armouries will have your head for destroying his servitors like that,' said Aximand, looking up as Abaddon pummelled what was left of the servitor to destruction.

Sweating and breathing hard, Abaddon stepped from the training cage, sweat lathering his body in gleaming sheets and his silver-wrapped topknot slick with sweat. Even for an Astartes, he was huge, muscular and solid as stone. Torgaddon often teased Abaddon, joking that he left leadership of the Justaerin to Falkus Kibre because he was too big to fit in a suit of Terminator armour.

'It's what they're for,' snapped Abaddon.

'I'm not sure you're meant to be that hard on them.'

Abaddon shrugged, lifted a towel from his arming chamber and hung it around his shoulders. 'How can you be calm at a time like this?'

'Trust me, I'm not calm, Ezekyle.'

'You look calm.'

'Just because I'm not smashing things with my fists doesn't mean I'm not choleric.'

Abaddon picked up a piece of his armour, and began polishing it, before hurling it aside with an angry snarl.

'Centre your humours, Ezekyle,' advised Aximand. 'It's not good to go too far out of balance, you might not come back.'

'I know,' sighed Abaddon. 'But I'm all over the place: choleric, melancholic, saturnine; all of them at the same time. I can't sit still for a second. What if he doesn't make it, Little Horus? What if he dies?'

The First Captain stood and paced the arming chambers, wringing his hands, and Aximand could see the blood rising in his cheeks as his anger and frustration grew once more.

'It's not fair,' growled Abaddon. 'It shouldn't be like this. The Emperor wouldn't let this happen. He shouldn't let this happen.'

'The Emperor hasn't been here for a long time, Ezekyle.'

'Does he even know what's happened? Does he even care anymore?'

'I don't know what to tell you, my friend,' said Aximand, picking up his bolter once more and pressing the catch that released the magazine, seeing that Abaddon had a new target for his impotent rage.

'It's not been the same since he left us after Ullanor,' raged Abaddon. 'He left us to clean up what he couldn't be bothered to finish, and for what? Some damn project on Terra that's more important than us?'

'Careful, Ezekyle,' warned Aximand. 'You're in dangerous territory.'

'It's true though isn't it? Don't tell me you don't feel the same, I know you do.'

'It's... different now, yes,' conceded Aximand.

'We're out here fighting and dying to conquer the galaxy for him and he won't even stand with us out on the frontier. Where is his honour? Where is his pride?'

'Ezekyle!' said Aximand, throwing down his bolter and rising to his feet. 'Enough. If you were anyone else, I would strike you down for those words. The Emperor is our lord and master. We are sworn to obey him.'

'We are pledged to the commander. Don't you remember your Mournival oath?'

'I remember it well enough, Ezekyle,' retorted Aximand, 'better than you it seems, for we also pledged to the Emperor above all primarchs.'

Abaddon turned away and gripped the wire mesh of the training cage, his muscles bulging and his head bowed. With a cry of animal rage, he tore the mesh panel from the cage and hurled it across the training halls, where it landed at the armoured feet of Erebus, who stood silhouetted in the doorway.

'Erebus,' said Aximand in surprise. 'How long have you been standing there?'

'Long enough, Little Horus, long enough.'

Aximand felt a dagger of unease settle in his heart and said, 'Ezekyle was just angry and upset. His humours are out of balance. Don't–'

Erebus waved his hand to brush off Aximand's words, the dim light reflecting from the brushed steel plates of his armour. 'Fear not, my friend, you know how it is between us. We are all lodge members here. If anyone were to ask me what I heard here today, you know what I would tell them, don't you?'

'I can't say.'

'Exactly,' smiled Erebus, but far from being reassured, Aximand suddenly felt beholden to the First Chaplain of the Word Bearers, as though his silence were some kind of bargaining chip.

'Did you come for anything, Erebus?' demanded Abaddon, his choler still to the fore.

'I did,' nodded Erebus, holding out his palm to reveal his silver lodge medal. 'The Warmaster's condition is deteriorating and Targost has called a meeting.'

'Now?' asked Aximand. 'Why?'

Erebus shrugged. 'I can't say.'

They gathered once more in the aft hold of the flagship, travelling the lonely service stairwells to the deep decks of the *Vengeful Spirit*. Tapers again lit the way and Aximand found himself desperate to get this over with. The Warmaster was dying and they were holding a meeting?

'Who approaches?' asked a hooded figure from the darkness.

'Three souls,' Erebus replied.

'What are your names?' the figure asked.

'Do we need to bother with this now?' snapped Aximand. 'You know it's us, Sedirae.'

'What are your names?' repeated the figure.

'I can't say,' said Erebus.

'Pass, friends.'

They entered the aft hold, Aximand shooting a venomous glance at the hooded Luc Sedirae, who simply shrugged and followed them in. Candles lit the vast, scaffold-framed area as usual, but instead of the lively banter of warriors, a subdued, solemn atmosphere shrouded the hold. All the usual suspects were there: Serghar Targost, Luc Sedirae, Kalus Ekaddon, Falkus Kibre and many more officers and file troopers he knew or recognised... and Maloghurst the Twisted.

Erebus led the way into the hold, moving to stand in the centre of the group as Aximand nodded towards the Warmaster's equerry.

'It's been some time since I've seen you at a meeting,' said Aximand.

'It has indeed,' agreed Maloghurst. 'I have neglected my duties as a lodge member, but there are matters before us that demand my attendance.'

'Brothers,' said Targost, beginning the meeting. 'We live in grim times.'

'Get to the point, Serghar,' snarled Abaddon. 'We don't have time for this.'

The lodge master glared at Abaddon, but saw the First Captain's lurking temper and nodded rather than confront him. Instead, he gestured towards Erebus and addressed the lodge as a whole. 'Our brother of the XVII Legion would speak to us. Shall we hear him?'

'We shall,' intoned the Sons of Horus.

Erebus bowed and said, 'Brother Ezekyle is right, we do not have time to stand on ceremony so I will be blunt. The Warmaster is dying and the fate of the Crusade stands on a knife-edge. We alone have the power to save it.'

'What does that mean, Erebus?' asked Aximand.

Erebus paced around the circumference of the circle as he spoke. 'The Apothecaries can do nothing for the Warmaster. For all their dedication, they cannot cure him of this sickness. All they can do is keep him alive, and they cannot do that for much longer. If we do not act now, it will be too late.'

'What do you propose, Erebus?' asked Targost.

'The tribes on Davin,' said Erebus.

'What of them?' asked the lodge master.

'They are a feral people, controlled by warrior castes, but then we all know this. Our own quiet order bears the hallmarks of their warrior lodges in its structure and practices. Each of their lodges venerates one of the autochthonic predators of their lands, and this is where our order differs. In my time on Davin during its compliance, I studied the lodges and their ways in search of corruption or religious profanity. I found nothing of that, but in one lodge I found what I believe might be our only hope of saving the Warmaster.'

Despite himself, Aximand became caught up in Erebus's words, his oratory worthy of the iterators, with the precise modulation of tone and timbre to entrance his audience.

'Tell us!' shouted Luc Sedirae.

The lodge took up the cry until Serghar Targost was forced to restore order with a bellowed command.

'We must take the Warmaster to the Temple of the Serpent Lodge on Davin,' declared Erebus. 'The priests there are skilled in the mystic arts of healing, and I believe they offer the best chance of saving the Warmaster.'

'Mystic arts?' asked Aximand. 'What does that mean? It sounds like sorcery.'

'I do not believe it is,' said Erebus, rounding on him, 'but what if it was, Brother Horus? Would you refuse their aid? Would you allow the Warmaster to die just so we can feel pure? Is the Warmaster's life not worth a little risk?'

'Risk, yes? But this feels wrong.'

'Wrong would be not doing all that we could to save the commander,' said Targost.

'Even if it means tainting ourselves with impure magick?'

'Don't get all high and mighty, Aximand,' said Targost. 'We do this for the Legion. There is no other choice.'

'Then is it already decided?' demanded Aximand, pushing past Erebus to stand in the centre of the circle. 'If so, then why this charade of debate? Why bother even summoning us here?'

Maloghurst limped from Targost's side and shook his head. 'We must all be in accord here, Brother Horus. You know how the lodge operates. If you do not agree to this, then we will go no further and the Warmaster will remain here, but he will die if we do nothing. You know that to be true.'

'You cannot ask this of me,' pleaded Aximand.

'I have to, my brother,' said Maloghurst. 'There is no other way.'

Aximand felt the responsibility of the decision before him crushing him to the floor as every eye in the chamber turned upon him. His eyes met Abaddon's and he saw that Ezekyle was clearly in favour of doing whatever it took to save the Warmaster.

'What of Torgaddon and Loken?' asked Aximand, trying to buy some time to think. 'They are not here to speak.'

'Loken is not one of us!' shouted Kalus Ekaddon, Captain of the Reaver squad. 'He had his chance to join us, but turned his back on our order. As for Tarik, he will follow our lead in this. There is no time to seek him out.'

Aximand looked into the faces of the men around him, and realised he had no choice. He never had from the moment he had walked into the room.

Whatever it took, the Warmaster had to live. It was that simple.

He knew there would be consequences. There always were in a devil's bargain like this, but any price was worth paying if it would save the commander.

He was damned if he would be remembered as the warrior who stood by and let the Warmaster die.

'Very well,' he said at last. 'Let the Lodge of the Serpent do what it can.'

The difference in Davin's moon in the few hours since they had last set foot on it was incredible, thought Loken. The cloying mists and fogs had vanished and the sky was lightening from a musky yellow to bleached white. The stench was still there, but it too was lessened, now just unpleasant rather than overpowering. Had the death of Temba broken some kind of power that held the moon locked in a perpetual cycle of decay?

As the Thunderhawk had skimmed the marshes, Loken had seen that the diseased forests were gone, their trunks collapsed in on themselves without the life-giving corruption holding them together. Without the obscuring mists, it was easy to find the *Glory of Terra*, though thankfully there was no deathly message coming over the vox this time.

They touched down and Loken led Locasta squad, Torgaddon, Vipus and Marr from the Thunderhawk with the confident strides of a natural leader. Though Torgaddon and Marr had held their captaincies longer than Loken, both instinctively deferred to him on this mission.

'What do you expect to find here, Garvi?' asked Torgaddon, squinting up at the collapsed hulk of the ship. He hadn't bothered to find a new helmet and his nose wrinkled at the stench of the place.

'I'm not sure,' he answered. 'Answers, maybe; something to help the Warmaster.'

Torgaddon nodded. 'Sounds good to me. What about you, Marr? What are you looking for?'

Tybalt Marr didn't answer, racking the slide of his bolter and marching towards the crashed vessel. Loken caught up with him and grabbed his shoulder guard.

'Tybalt, am I going to have a problem with you here?'

'No. I just want to see where Verulam died,' said Marr. 'It won't be real until I've seen the place. I know I saw him in the mortuary, but that wasn't a dead man. It was just like looking in a mirror. You understand?'

Loken didn't, but he nodded anyway. 'Very well, take up position in the file.'

They marched towards the dead ship, clambering up the broken ramps of debris to the gaping holes torn in its side.

'Damn, but it feels like a lifetime since we were fighting here,' said Torgaddon.

'It was only three or four hours ago, Tarik,' Loken pointed out.

'I know, but still…'

Eventually they reached the top of the ramp and penetrated the darkness of the ship, the memory of the last time he had done this and what he had found at the end of the journey still fresh in Loken's mind.

'Stay alert. We don't know what else might still be alive in here.'

'We should have bombed the wreck from orbit,' muttered Torgaddon.

'Quiet!' hissed Loken. 'Didn't you hear what I said?'

Tarik raised his hands in apology and they pressed on through the groaning wreck, along darkened hallways, flickering companionways and stinking, blackened corridors. Vipus and Loken led the way, with Torgaddon and Marr guarding the rear. The shadow-haunted wreck had lost none of its power to disturb, though the disgusting, organic growths that coated every surface with glistening wetness now seemed to be dying – drying up and cracking to powder.

'What's going on in here?' asked Torgaddon. 'This place was like the hydroponics bay a few hours ago, now it's…'

'Dying,' completed Vipus. 'Like those trees we saw earlier.'

'More like dead,' said Marr, peeling the husk of one of the growths from the wall.

'Don't touch anything,' warned Loken. 'Something in this ship had the power to harm the commander and until we know what that was, we touch nothing.'

Marr dropped the remains and wiped his hand on his leg as they journeyed deeper inside the ship. Loken's memory of their previous route was faultless and they soon reached the central spine and the route to the bridge.

Shafts of light speared in through holes in the hull and dust motes floated in the air like a glittering wall. Loken led on, ducking beneath protruding bulkheads and sparking cables as they reached their ultimate destination.

Loken could smell Eugan Temba long before they saw him, the reek of his putrefaction and death thick even beyond the bridge. They made their way cautiously onto the bridge, and Loken sent his warriors around the perimeter with directional chops of his hand.

'What are we going to do about those men up there?' asked Vipus, pointing to the dead soldiers stitched to the banners hanging from the roof. 'We can't just leave them like that.'

'I know, but we can't do anything for them just now,' said Loken. 'When we destroy this hulk, they'll be at rest.'

'Is that him?' asked Marr, pointing at the bloated corpse.

Loken nodded, raising his bolter and advancing on the body. A rippling motion undulated beneath the corpse's skin, and Temba's voluminous belly wobbled with internal motion. His flesh was stretched so tightly over his frame that the outlines of fat maggots and larvae could be seen beneath his parchment skin.

'Throne, he's disgusting,' said Marr. 'And this… thing killed Verulam?'

'I assume so,' replied Loken. 'The Warmaster didn't say exactly, but there's nothing else here is there?'

Loken left Marr to his grief and turned to his warriors, saying, 'Spread out and look for something, anything that might give us some clue as to what happened here.'

'You don't have any idea what we're looking for?' asked Vipus.

'No, not really,' admitted Loken. 'A weapon maybe.'

'You know we're going to have to search that fat bastard don't you?' Torgaddon pointed out. 'Who's the lucky sod who gets to do that?'

'I thought that'd be something you'd enjoy, Tarik.'

'Oh no, I'm not putting so much as a finger near that thing.'

'I'll do it,' said Marr, dropping to his knees and peeling away the sodden remnants of Eugan Temba's clothing and flesh.

'See?' said Torgaddon, backing away. 'Tybalt wants to do it. I say let him.'

'Very well. Be careful, Tybalt,' said Loken before turning away from the disgusting sight of Marr pulling apart Temba's corpse.

His men began searching the bridge and Loken climbed the steps to the captain's throne, staring out over the crew pits, now filled with all manner of vile excrescences and filth. It baffled

Loken how such a glorious ship and a man of supposedly fine character could come to such a despicable end.

He circled the throne, pausing as his foot connected with something solid.

He bent down and saw a polished wooden casket. Its surfaces were smooth and clean, and it was clearly out of place in this reeking tomb. Perhaps the length and thickness of a man's arm, the wood was rich brown with strange symbols carved along its length. The lid opened on golden hinges and Loken released the delicate catch that held it shut.

The casket was empty, padded with a red velvet insert, and as he stared at its emptiness, Loken realised how thoughtless he'd been in opening it. He ran his fingers along the length of the casket, tracing the outline of the symbols, seeing something familiar in their elegantly cursive forms.

'Over here!' shouted one of Locasta, and Loken quickly gathered up the casket and made his way towards the source of the call. While Tybalt Marr disassembled the traitor's rotten body, Astartes warriors surrounded something that gleamed on the deck.

Loken saw that it was Eugan Temba's severed arm, the fingers still wrapped around the hilt of a strange, glittering sword with a blade that looked like grey flint.

'It's Temba's arm right enough,' said Vipus, reaching down to lift the sword.

'Don't touch it,' said Loken. 'If it laid the Warmaster low, I don't want to know what it could do to us.'

Vipus recoiled from the sword as though it were a snake.

'What's that?' asked Torgaddon, pointing at the casket.

Loken dropped to his haunches, laying the casket next to the sword, unsurprised when he saw that the sword would fit snugly inside.

'I think it once contained this sword.'

'Looks pretty new,' said Vipus. 'And what's that on the side? Writing?'

Loken didn't answer, reaching out to prise Temba's dead fingers from the sword hilt. Though he knew it was absurd, he grimaced with each finger he pried loose, expecting the hand to leap to life and attack him.

Eventually, the sword was free, and Loken gingerly lifted the weapon.

'Careful,' said Torgaddon.

'Thanks, Tarik, and here was me about to throw it about.'

'Sorry.'

Loken slowly lowered the sword into the casket. The handle tingled and he had felt a curious sensation as he had said Tarik's name, a sense of the monstrous harm the weapon could inflict. He snapped the lid shut, letting out a pent-up breath.

'How in the name of Terra did someone like Temba get hold of a weapon like that?' asked Torgaddon. 'It didn't even look human-made.'

'It's not,' said Loken as the familiarity of the symbols on the side of the casket fell horribly into place. 'It's kinebrach.'

'Kinebrach?' asked Torgaddon. 'But weren't they–'

'Yes,' said Loken, carefully lifting the casket from the deck. 'This is the anathame that was stolen from the Hall of Devices on Xenobia.'

The word went out across the *Vengeful Spirit* at the speed of thought, and weeping men and women lined their route. Hundreds filled each passageway as the Astartes bore the Warmaster on a bier of kite-shaped shields. Clad in his ceremonial armour of winter white with burnished gold trims and the glaring red eye, the Warmaster's hands were clasped across his golden sword, and a laurel wreath of silver sat upon his noble brow.

Abaddon, Aximand, Luc Sedirae, Serghar Targost, Falkus Kibre and Kalus Ekaddon carried him, and behind the Warmaster came Hektor Varvarus and Maloghurst. Each one wore shining armour and their company cloaks billowed behind them as they walked.

Heralds and criers announced the route of the cortege, and there was no repeat of the bloody scene on the embarkation deck as the Astartes took this slow march with the beloved leader who had fought beside them since the earliest days of the Crusade. They wept as they marched, each one painfully aware that this might be the Warmaster's last journey.

In lieu of flowers, the people threw torn scraps of tearstained paper, each with words of hope and love written on them. Shown that the Warmaster still lived, his people burned herbs said to have healing properties, hanging them from smoking censers all along the route, and from somewhere a band played the Legion March.

Candles burned with a sweet smell and men and women, soldiers and civilians, tore at themselves in their grief. Army banners lined the route, each dipped out of respect for the Warmaster, and pleading chants followed the procession until at last they came to the embarkation deck. Its vast gateway was wreathed in parchment, every square centimetre of bulkhead covered with messages for the Warmaster and his sons.

Aximand was awed by the outpouring of sorrow and love for the Warmaster, the scale of people's grief at his wounding beyond anything in his experience. To him the Warmaster was a figure of magnificence, but first and foremost, he was a warrior – a leader of men and one of the Emperor's chosen.

To these mortals, he was so much more. To them, the Warmaster was a symbol of something noble and heroic beyond anything they could ever aspire to, a symbol of the new galaxy they were forging from the ashes of the Age of Strife.

Horus's very existence promised an end to the suffering and death that had plagued humanity for centuries.

Old Night was drawing to a close and, thanks to heroes like the Warmaster, the first rays of a new dawn were breaking on the horizon.

All that was under threat now, and Aximand knew he had made the right choice in allowing the others to take Horus to Davin. The Lodge of the Serpent would heal the Warmaster, and if that involved powers he might once have condemned, then so be it.

The die was cast and all he had left to cling to was his faith that the Warmaster would be restored to them. He smiled as he remembered something the Warmaster had said to him on the subject of faith. The Warmaster had typically delivered his words of wisdom at a wholly inappropriate time – right before they had leapt from the belly of a screaming Stormbird into the greenskin city on Ullanor.

'When you have come to the edge of all that you know and are about to drop off into the darkness of the unknown, faith is knowing that one of two things will happen,' the Warmaster had told him.

'And what are they?' he had asked.

'That there will be something solid to stand on or you'll be taught to fly,' laughed Horus as he jumped.

The memory made the tears come all the harder as the huge iron gate of the embarkation deck rumbled closed behind them and the Astartes marched towards the Warmaster's waiting Stormbird.

TWELVE

Agitprop
Brothers in suspicion
Serpent and moon

Slipping across the page like a snake, the nib of Ignace Karkasy's pen moved as though it had a mind of its own. For all the conscious thought he was putting into the words, it might as well have. The muse was well and truly upon him, his stream of consciousness flowing into a river of blood as he retold the diabolical events on the embarkation deck. The meter played in his head like a symphony, every stanza of every canto slipping into place as if there could be no other possible arrangement of verse.

Even in his heyday of *Ocean Poems* or *Reflections and Odes* he had not felt this inspired. In fact, now that he looked back on them, he hated them for their frippery, their unconscionable navel gazing and irrelevance to the galaxy at large. These words, these thoughts that now poured from him, this was what mattered, and he cursed that it had taken him this long to discover it.

The truth was what mattered. Captain Loken had told him as much, but he hadn't heard him, not really. The verses he'd written since Loken had begun his sponsorship of him were paltry things, unworthy of the man who had won the Ethiopic Laureate, but that was changing now.

After the bloodbath on the embarkation deck, he'd returned to his quarters, grabbed a bottle of Terran wine and made his way to the observation deck. Finding it thronged with wailing lunatics, he'd repaired to the Retreat, knowing that it would be empty.

The words had poured out of him in a flood of righteous indignation, his metaphors bold and his lyric unflinching from the awful brutality he'd witnessed. He'd already used up three pages of the Bondsman, his fingers blotted with ink and his poet's soul on fire.

'Everything I've done before this was prologue,' he whispered as he wrote.

Karkasy paused in his work as he pondered the dilemma: the truth was useless if no one could hear it. The facilities set aside for the remembrancers included a presswork where they could submit their work for large-scale circulation. It was common knowledge that much of what that passed through it was vetted and censored, and so few made use of it. Karkasy certainly couldn't, considering the content of his new poetry.

A slow smile spread across his jowly features and he reached into the pocket of his robes and pulled out a crumpled sheet of paper – one of Euphrati Keeler's Lectitio Divinitatus pamphlets – and spread it out flat on the table before him with the heel of his palm.

The ink was smeared and the paper reeked of ammonia, clearly the work of a cheap mechanical bulk-printer of some kind. If Euphrati could get the use of one, then so could he.

Loken permitted Tybalt Marr to torch the body of Eugan Temba before they left the bridge. His fellow captain, streaked with gore and filth, played the burning breath of a flame unit over the monstrous corpse until nothing but ashen bone remained. It was small satisfaction for the death of a brother, not nearly enough, but it would have to do. Leaving behind the smouldering remains, they retraced their footsteps back through the *Glory of Terra*.

The light was fading on Davin's moon by the time they reached the outside, the planet above a pale yellow orb hanging low in the dusky sky. Loken carried the anathame in its gleaming wooden casket, and his warriors followed him from the wreck without any words spoken.

A great rumbling vibration gripped the moon as a trio of towering columns of light and smoke climbed towards the heavens from the Imperial deployment zone where this whole misadventure had started. Loken watched the incredible spectacle of the war machines of the Legio Mortis returning to their armoured berths in orbit, and silently thanked their crews for their aid in the fight against the dead things.

Soon all that was visible of the Titans' carriers was a diffuse glow on the horizon, and only the lap of water and the low growling of the waiting Thunderhawk's engines disturbed the silence. The desolate mudflats were empty for kilometres around, and as Loken made his way down the slope of rubble, he felt like the loneliest man in the galaxy.

Some kilometres away, he could see specks of blue light following the Titan carriers as Army transports ferried the last remaining soldiers back to their bulk transporters.

'We'll soon be done here, eh?' said Torgaddon.

'I suppose,' agreed Loken. 'The sooner the better.'

'How do you suppose that thing got here?'

Loken didn't have to ask what his brother meant, and shook his head, unwilling to share his suspicions with Torgaddon yet. As much as he loved him, Tarik had a big mouth, and Loken didn't want to put his quarry to flight.

'I don't know, Tarik,' said Loken as they reached the ground and made their way towards the Thunderhawk's lowered assault ramp. 'I don't think we'll ever know.'

'Come on, Garvi, it's me!' laughed Torgaddon. 'You're so straight up and down, and that makes you a really terrible liar. I know you've got some idea of what happened. So come on, spill it.'

'I can't, Tarik, I'm sorry,' said Loken. 'Not yet anyway. Trust me. I know what I'm doing.'

'Do you really?'

'I'm not sure,' admitted Loken. 'I think so. Throne, I wish the Warmaster were here to ask.'

'Well he's not,' stated Torgaddon, 'so you're stuck with me.'

Loken stepped onto the ramp, grateful to be off the marshy surface of the moon, and turned to face Torgaddon. 'You're right, I should tell you, and I will, soon. I just need to figure some things out first.'

'Look, I'm not stupid, Garvi,' said Torgaddon, leaning in close so that none of the others could hear. 'I know the only way this thing could have got here is if someone in the Expedition brought it. It had to have been here before we arrived. That means there was only one person who was with us on Xenobia and could have got here before we did. You know who I'm talking about.'

'I know who you're talking about,' agreed Loken, pulling Torgaddon aside as the rest of the warriors embarked upon the Thunderhawk. 'What I can't figure out is why? Why go to all the trouble of stealing this thing and then bringing it here?'

'I'm going to break that son of a bitch in two if he had some-thing to do with what's happened to the Warmaster,' snarled Torgaddon. 'The Legion will have his hide.'

'No,' hissed Loken, 'not yet. Not until we find out what this is all about and if anyone else is involved. I just can't believe that someone would dare try and move against the Warmaster.'

'Is that what you think is happening, a coup? You think that one of the other primarchs is making a play for the role of Warmaster?'

'I don't know, it all sounds too far-fetched. It sounds like something from one of Sindermann's books.'

Neither man said anything. The idea that one of the eternal brotherhood of primarchs might be attempting to usurp Horus was incredible, outrageous and unthinkable, wasn't it?

'Hey,' called Vipus from inside the Thunderhawk. 'What are you two conspirators plotting?'

'Nothing,' said Loken guiltily. 'We were just talking.'

'Well finish up. We need to go, now!'

'Why, what is it?' asked Loken as he climbed aboard.

'The Warmaster,' said Vipus. 'They're taking him to Davin.'

The Thunderhawk was in the air moments later, lifting off in a spray of muddy water and a flare of blue-hot jet fire. The gunship circled the massive wreck, gaining altitude and speed as it turned towards the sky.

The pilot firewalled the engines and the gunship roared up into the darkness.

The great red orb of the sun was dipping below the horizon and hot, dry winds rising from the plains below made it a bumpy ride as they re-entered Davin's atmosphere. The continental mass swelled through the armoured glass of the cockpit, dusty and brown and dry. Loken sat up front in the cockpit with the pilots and watched the avionics panel as the red blip that represented the location of the Warmaster's Stormbird drew ever closer.

Far below them, he could see the glittering lights of the Impe-rial deployment zone where they had first made planetfall on Davin, a wide circle of arc lights, makeshift landing platforms and defensive positions. The pilot brought them in at a steep angle, speed more important to Loken than any notion of safe flight, and they streaked past scores of other landing craft on their way to the surface.

'Why so many?' wondered Loken as their flight levelled out and they shot past the wide circle of light, seeing soldiers and servi-tors toiling to expedite the approach of so many landing craft.

'No idea,' said the pilot, 'but there's hundreds of them coming down from the fleet. Looks like a lot of people want to see
Davin.'

Loken didn't reply, but the sight of so many landing craft
en route to Davin was yet another piece of the puzzle that he
didn't understand. The vox networks were jammed with insane
chatter, weeping voices and groups claiming that the end was
coming, while yet others gave thanks to the divine Emperor
that his chosen champion would soon rise from his deathbed.

None of it made any sense. He'd tried to make contact with
the Mournival, but no one was answering, and a terrible fore-
boding filled him when he couldn't even reach Maloghurst on
the *Vengeful Spirit*.

Their flight soon carried them beyond the Imperial position,
and Loken saw a ribbon of light stretching north from the landing zone. A host of pinpricks of light pierced the darkness, and
Loken ordered the pilot to fly lower and reduce speed.

A long column of vehicles: tanks, supply trucks, transporter flatbeds and even some civilian traffic, drove along the dusty hardpan,
each one swamped with people, and all heading to the mountains
as fast as their engines could carry them. The Thunderhawk powered on through the fading light of day, soon losing sight of the
column of vehicles that was heading in the same direction.

'How long until we reach the Warmaster's position?' he asked.

'At current speed, maybe ten minutes or so,' answered the
pilot.

Loken tried to collect his thoughts, but they had long since
derailed in the midst of all this madness. Ever since leaving
the interex, his mind had been a whirlpool, sucking in every
random thought and spitting it out with barbs of suspicion.
Could it be that he was still suffering the after-effects of what
had happened to Jubal? Might the power, unlocked beneath
the Whisperheads, be tainting him so that he jumped at shadows where none existed?

He might have been able to believe that, but for the presence
of the anathame and his certainty that First Chaplain Erebus
had lied to him on the voyage to Davin.

Karkasy had said that Erebus wanted Horus to come to
Davin's moon, and his undoubted complicity in the theft of
the anathame could lead to only one conclusion. Erebus had
wanted Horus to be killed here.

That didn't make any sense either. Why go to such convo-
luted lengths just to kill the Warmaster, surely there had to be
more to it than that...

Facts were slowly accumulating, but none of them fit, and still he had no idea why any of this was happening, only that it was, and that it was by the artifice of human design. Whatever was going on, he would uncover the conspiracy and make those involved pay with their lives.

'We're coming up on the Warmaster's Stormbird,' called the pilot.

Loken shook himself from his venomous reverie. He hadn't been aware of time passing, but immediately turned his attention to what lay beyond the armoured glass of the cockpit.

Tall mountain peaks surrounded them, jagged cliffs of red stone, veined with gleaming strata of gold and quartz. They followed the course of an ancient causeway along the valley, its flagstones split and cracked with the passing of the centuries. Statues of long-dead kings lined the processional way, and toppled columns littered this forgotten highway like fallen guardians. Shadows plumbed the depths of the valley along which they flew and in a gap ahead, he could see a reflected glow in the brazen sky.

The pilot dropped their speed and the gunship flew through the gap into a colossal crater gouged from the landscape like an enormous, flat-bottomed basin. The sheer sides of the crater soared above them, its diameter thousands of metres across.

A huge stone building stood at its centre, carved from the same rock as the mountains and bathed in the light of a thousand flaming torches. The Thunderhawk circled the structure and Loken saw that it was a giant octagonal building, each corner shaped like the bastion of a fortress. Eight towers surrounded a wide dome at its centre and flames burned from their tops.

Loken could see the Warmaster's Stormbird below them, a multitude of torchbearers surrounding it, hundreds, maybe even thousands of people. A clear path stretched from the Stormbird towards the cyclopean archway that led into the building, and Loken saw the unmistakable form of the Warmaster being borne by the Sons of Horus towards it.

'Take us down. Now!' shouted Loken. He rose, made his way back to the crew compartment and snatched his bolter from the rack.

'What's up?' asked Vipus. 'Trouble?'

'Could be,' said Loken, turning to address all the warriors aboard the gunship. 'Once we disembark, take your lead from me.'

His warriors had efficiently prepped for a combat disembarkation, and Loken felt the motion of the Thunderhawk change as it slowed and came in to land. The internal light changed from red to green and the craft slammed hard into the ground. The assault ramp dropped and Loken led the way out, marching confidently towards the building.

Night had fallen, but the air was hot, and the sour fragrances of bitter blossoms filled the air with a beguiling, aromatic scent. He led his men onwards at a quick march. Many of the torchbearers turned quizzically towards them, and Loken now saw that these were the indigenous inhabitants of Davin.

The Davinites were more wiry than most mortal men, tall and hirsute with thin limbs, and elaborate topknots worn in a style similar to Abaddon's. They wore long capes of shimmering, patterned scales, banded armour – of the same lacquered scales – and most were armed with cross-belts of daggers and primitive looking black powder pistols. They parted before the advance of the Astartes, heads bowed in supplication, and it forcibly struck Loken just how close to deviancy these creatures appeared to be.

He hadn't paid much attention to the Davinites the first time he'd landed. He was just a squad captain more concerned with obeying orders and completing the tasks assigned to him than paying attention to the locals. Even this time, his attention had been elsewhere, and the almost bestial appearance of the Davinites had more or less slipped past his notice.

Surrounded by hundreds of the planet's inhabitants, their divergence from the human genome was unmistakeable, and Loken wondered how they had avoided extermination six decades ago, especially since it had been the Word Bearers who had made first contact with Davin – a Legion not noted for its tolerance of anything beyond the norm.

Loken was reminded of Abaddon's furious argument with the Warmaster over the question of the interex, and of how the First Captain had demanded that they make war upon them for their tolerance of xenos breeds. If anything, Davin was far more of a textbook case for war, but somehow that hadn't happened.

The Davinites were clearly of human gene-stock, but this offshoot of humanity had diverged into a species almost all of its own. The wide spacing of their features, the dark eyes without pupils and the excessive, almost simian volume of thick hair on their faces and arms put Loken more in the mind of the stable-bred mutants some regiments of the Imperial Army employed. They were crude creatures with the intelligence to swing a sword or fire a clumsy rifle, but not much else.

Loken did not approve of the practice, and though the

inhabitants of Davin were clearly possessed of a greater level of intelligence than such beasts, their appearance did not reassure him as to what was going on.

He put the Davinites from his mind as he approached a massive set of steps carved into the rock and lined with statues of coiling serpents and flaming braziers. Three narrow channels filled with rushing water divided the stairs, one to either side and one down the centre.

The Warmaster and his bearers were out of sight on the next level, and Loken led his warriors up the processional stairs, taking them three at a time as he heard a monstrous grinding of stone up ahead. The image of vast, monolithic doors appeared unbidden in his mind and he said, 'We have to hurry.'

Loken neared the top of the steps, the flickering coal braziers casting a ruddy glow over the statues that glinted from the serpents' scales and quartz-chip eyes. The last rays of the dying sun caught the twisting snakes carved around the pillars, making them seem alive, as if slowly descending to the steps. The effect was unsettling, and Loken opened his suit link again, saying, 'Abaddon, Aximand? Can either of you hear me? Respond.'

His earpiece hissed with static, but his hails received no answers and he picked up the pace.

He reached the top of the steps at last, and emerged onto a moonlit esplanade of yet more serpentine statues atop pillars that lined a narrowing roadway leading towards a giant, arched gateway in the face of the massive edifice. Wide gates of carved and beaten bronze with a glistening, spiralled surface rumbled as they swung closed, and Loken felt his skin crawl at the sight of that dread portal, its yawning darkness rich with the promise of ancient, primal power.

He could see a group of Astartes warriors standing before it, watching as the monstrous gate shut. Loken could see no sign of the Warmaster.

'Pick up the pace, battle march,' he ordered, and began the loping, ground-eating stride that the Astartes adopted when there was no vehicle support. Marching at this speed was sustainable over huge distances and still allowed a warrior to fight at the end of it. Loken prayed that he wouldn't be required to fight at the end of this march.

As he drew closer to the gates he saw that, far from being etched with meaningless spirals, each was carved with all manner of images and scenes. Looping serpents twisted from one leaf to another, others circled and swallowed their tails, and yet more were depicted intertwined as though mating.

Only when the gate slammed shut with a thunderous boom of metal did he see the full image. Unlike the commander, Loken was no student of art; nevertheless, he was awed by the full impact of the images worked onto the sealed gateway. Central to its imagery was a great tree with spreading branches, hanging with fruit of all description. Its three roots stretched out beyond the base of the gates and into a wide circular pool that fed the streams running the length of the esplanade, before cascading down the grand stairs.

Twin snakes coiled around the tree, their heads entwined in the branches above, and Loken was struck by its similarity to the symbol borne upon the shoulder guards of the Legion Apothecaries.

Seven warriors stood at the edge of the pool of water, before the massive gate. They were armoured in the green of the Sons of Horus, and Loken knew them all: Abaddon, Aximand, Targost, Sedirae, Ekaddon, Kibre and Maloghurst.

None wore their helmets and as they turned, he could see that each one had the same air of helpless desperation. He had walked into hell with these warriors time and time again, and seeing his brothers with such expressions on their faces, drained him of his anger, leaving him hollow and heartbroken.

He slowed his march as he came face to face with Aximand.

'What have you done?' he asked. 'Oh my brothers, what have you done?'

'What needed to be done,' said Abaddon, when Aximand didn't answer.

Loken ignored the First Captain and said, 'Little Horus? Tell me what you've done.'

'It is as Ezekyle said. We did what had to be done,' said Aximand. 'The Warmaster was dying and Vaddon couldn't save him. So we brought him to the Delphos.'

'The Delphos?' asked Loken.

'It is the name of this place,' said Aximand. 'The Temple of the Serpent Lodge.'

'Temple?' asked Torgaddon. 'Horus, you brought the Warmaster to a fane? Are you mad? The commander would never have agreed to this.'

'Maybe not,' replied Serghar Targost, stepping forward to stand beside Abaddon, 'but by the end he couldn't even speak. He spoke to that damn remembrancer woman for hours on end before he lost consciousness. We had to place him in a stasis field to keep him alive long enough to bring him here.'

'Is Tarik right?' asked Loken. 'Is this a fane?'

'Fane, temple, Delphos, house of healing, call it what you will,' shrugged Targost. 'With the Warmaster on the threshold of death, neither religion nor its denial seems very significant any more. It is the only hope we have left and what do we have to lose? If we do nothing, the Warmaster dies. At least this way he has a chance of life.'

'And at what price will we buy his life?' demanded Loken, 'By bringing him to a house of false gods? The Emperor tells us that civilisation will only achieve perfection when the last stone of the last church falls upon the last priest, and this is where you bring the Warmaster. This goes against everything we have fought for these last two centuries. Don't you see that?'

'If the Emperor was here, he would do the same,' said Targost, and Loken felt his choler rise to the surface at such hubris.

He stepped threateningly close to Targost. 'You think you know the Emperor's will, Serghar? Does being lodge master of a secret society give you the power to know such a thing?'

'Of course not,' sneered Targost, 'but I know he would want his son to live.'

'By entrusting his life to these... savages?'

'It is from these savages that our own quiet order comes,' pointed out Targost.

'Yet another reason for me to distrust it then,' snapped Loken, turning from the lodge master and addressing Vipus and Torgaddon. 'Come on. We're getting the Warmaster out of there.'

'You can't,' said Maloghurst, limping forward to join Abaddon, and Loken had the distinct impression that his brothers were forming a barrier between him and the gateway.

'What do you mean?'

'It is said that once the Delphos Gate is shut, there is no way to open it save from the inside. A man in need of healing is carried inside and left to whatever the eternal spirits of deceased things decree for him. If it is his destiny to live, he may open the gate himself, if not, it opens in nine days and his remains are burned before being cast into the pool.'

'So you've just left the Warmaster inside? For all the good that will do him, you might just as well have left him on the *Vengeful Spirit*; and "eternal spirits of deceased things" – what does that even mean? This is insane. Can't you see that?'

'Standing by and watching him die would have been insane,' said Maloghurst. 'You judge us for acting out of love. Can't you see that?'

'No, Mal, I can't,' replied Loken sadly. 'How did you even think to bring him here anyway? Was it some secret knowledge your damned lodge is privy to?'

None of his brothers spoke, and as Loken searched their faces for answers, the truth of the matter was suddenly, horribly, clear to him.

'Erebus told you of this place, didn't he?'

'Yes,' admitted Targost. 'He knows of these lodges of old and has seen the power of their healing houses. If the Warmaster lives you will be thankful he spoke of it.'

'Where is he?' demanded Loken. 'He will answer to me for this.'

'He is not here, Garvi,' said Aximand. 'This was for the Sons of Horus to do.'

'Then where is he now, still on the *Vengeful Spirit*?'

Aximand shrugged. 'I suppose so. Why is it important to you?'

'I believe you have all been deceived, my brothers,' said Loken. 'Only the Emperor has the power to heal the Warmaster now. All else is falsehood and the domain of unclean corpse-whisperers.'

'The Emperor is not here,' said Targost bluntly. 'We take what aid we can.'

'What of you, Tarik?' put in Abaddon. 'Will you turn from your Mournival brothers, as Garviel does? Stand with us.'

'Garvi may be a starch-arse, Ezekyle, but he's right and I can't stand with you on this one. I'm sorry,' said Torgaddon as he and Loken turned away from the gate.

'You forget your Mournival oath!' cried Abaddon as they marched away. 'You swore to be true to the Mournival to the end of your lives. You will be oath-breakers!'

The words of the First Captain hit Loken with the force of a bolter round and he stopped in his tracks. Oath-breaker... The very idea was hideous.

Aximand came after him, grabbing his arm and pointing towards the pool of water. The black water rippled with motion and Loken could see the yellow crescent of Davin's moon wavering in its surface.

'See?' said Aximand. 'The moon shines upon the water, Loken. The crescent mark of the new moon... It was branded upon your helmet when we swore our Mournival oath. It is a good omen, my brother.'

'Omen?' spat Loken, shrugging off his touch. 'Since when have we put our faith in omens, Horus? The Mournival oath was pantomime, but this is ritual. This is sorcery. I told you then that I would not bow to any fane or acknowledge any spirit. I told you that I owned only the empirical clarity of Imperial Truth and I stand by those words.'

'Please, Garvi,' begged Aximand. 'We are doing the right thing.'

Loken shook his head. 'I believe we will all rue the day you brought the Warmaster here.'

PART THREE

THE HOUSE OF
FALSE GODS

THIRTEEN

Who are you?
Ritual
Old friend

Horus opened his eyes, smiling as he saw blue sky above him. Pink and orange tinged clouds drifted slowly across his vision, peaceful and relaxing. He watched them for a few moments and then sat up, feeling wet dew beneath his palms as he pushed himself upright. He saw that he was naked, and as he surveyed his surroundings, he lifted his hand to his face, smelling the sweet scent of the grass and the crystal freshness of the air.

A vista of unsurpassed beauty lay before him, towering snow-capped mountains draped in a shawl of pine and fir, magnificent swathes of emerald green forests as far as the eye could see and a wide river of foaming, icy water. Hundreds of shaggy coated herbivores grazed on the plain and wide-pinioned birds circled noisily overhead. Horus sat on the low slopes of the foothills at the base of the mountains, the sun warming his face and the grass wondrously soft beneath him.

'So that's it then,' he said calmly to himself. 'I'm dead.'

No one answered him, but then he hadn't expected them to. Was this what happened when a person died? He dimly remembered someone teaching him of the ancient unbelief of 'heaven' and 'hell', meaningless words that promised rewards for obedience and punishment for wickedness.

He took a deep breath, scenting the aroma of good earth: the fragrances of a world unchecked and untamed and of the living things that covered the landscape. He could taste the air and was amazed at its purity. Its crispness filled his lungs like sweet wine, but how had he come here and... where was here?

He had been... where? He couldn't remember. He knew his name was Horus, but beyond that, he knew only fragments and dim recollections that even now grew faint and insubstantial the more he tried to hold onto them.

Deciding that he should try to find out more about his surroundings, he rose to his feet, wincing as his shoulder pulled tight, and he saw a spot of blood soak through the white woollen robes he found himself wearing. Hadn't he been naked a second ago?

Horus put it from his mind and laughed. 'There might be no hell, but this feels like heaven right enough.'

His throat was dry and he set off towards the river, feeling the softness of the grass through newly sandalled feet. He was further away than he thought, the journey taking him longer than expected, but he didn't mind. The beauty of the landscape was worth savouring, and though something insistent nagged at the back of his mind, he ignored it and carried on.

The mountains seemed to reach the very stars, their peaks lost in the clouds and *belching noxious fumes into the air* as he gazed up at them. Horus blinked; the after-image of dark, smoke wreathed peaks of iron and cement burned onto his retinas like a spliced frame of harsh interference dropped into a mood window. He dismissed it as the newness of his surroundings, and headed across the swaying plains of tall grass, feeling *the bones and waste of uncounted centuries of industry* crunching beneath his feet.

Horus felt ash in his throat, now needing a drink more than ever, the chemical stink growing worse with each step. He tasted benzene, chlorine, hydrochloric acid and vast amounts of carbon monoxide – lethal toxins to any but him it seemed – and briefly wondered how he knew these things. The river was just ahead and he splashed through the shallows, enjoying the biting cold as he reached down and scooped a handful of water into his cupped palms.

The icy water burned his skin, *molten slag dripping in caustic ropes between his fingers,* and he let it splash back into the river, wiping his hands on his robe, which was now soot-stained and torn. He looked up and saw that the glittering quartz mountains had become *vast towers of brass and iron, wounding the sky with gateways like vast maws that could swallow and vomit forth entire armies. Streams of toxic filth poured from the towers and poisoned the river, the landscape around it withering and dying in an instant.*

Confused, Horus stumbled from the river, fighting to hold onto the verdant wilderness that had surrounded him and to hold back the vision of this bleak land of dark ruin and despair. He turned from the dark mountain: *the cliff of deepest red and blackened iron, its top hidden in the high clouds above and its base girded with boulders and skulls.*

He fell to his knees, expecting the softness of the grass, but landing heavily *on a fractured hardpan of ash and iron, swirling vortices of dust rising up in great storms.*

'What's happening here?' shouted Horus, rolling onto his back and screaming into a polluted sky striated with ugly bands of ochre and purple. He picked himself up and ran – ran as though his life depended on it. He ran across a landscape that flickered from one of aching beauty to that of a nightmare in the space of a heartbeat, his senses deceiving him from one second to another.

Horus ran into the forest. The black trunks of the trees snapped before his furious charge, images of lashing branches, *high towers of steel and glass, great ruins of mighty cathedrals and rotted palaces left to crumble under the weight of the ages dancing before his eyes.*

Bestial howls echoed across the landscape, and Horus paused in his mad scramble as the sound penetrated the fog in his head, the insistent nagging sensation in the back of his mind recognising it as significant.

The mournful howls echoed across the land, a chorus of voices reaching out to him, and Horus recognised them as wolf howls. He smiled at the sound, dropping to his knees and clutching his shoulder as fiery pain lanced through his arm and into his chest. With the pain came clarity and he held onto it, forcing the memories to come through force of will.

Howling wolf voices came again, and he cried out to the heavens.

'What's happening to me?'

The trees around him exploded with motion and a hundred-strong pack of wolves sprang from the undergrowth, surrounding him, with their teeth bared and eyes wide. Foam gathered around exposed fangs and each wolf bore a strange brand upon its fur, that of a black, double-headed eagle. Horus clutched his shoulder, his arm numb and dead as though it was no longer part of him.

'Who are you?' asked the closest wolf. Horus blinked rapidly as its image fizzled like static, and he saw curves of armour and a single, staring cyclopean eye.

'I am Horus,' he said.

'Who are you?' repeated the wolf.

'I am Horus!' he yelled. 'What more do you want from me?'

'I do not have much time, my brother,' said the wolf as the pack began circling him. 'You must remember before he comes for you. Who are you?'

'I am Horus and if I am dead then leave me be!' he screamed, surging to his feet and running onwards into the depths of the forest.

The wolves followed him, loping alongside him and matching his steady pace as he lurched randomly through the twilight. Again and again, the wolves howled the same question until Horus lost all sense of direction and time.

Horus ran blindly onwards until he finally emerged from the tree line above a wide, high-cliffed crater gouged in the landscape and filled with dark, still water.

The sky above was black and starless, a moon of purest white shining like a diamond in the firmament. He blinked and raised a hand to ward his eyes against its brightness, looking out over the black waters of the crater, certain that some unspeakable horror lurked in its icy depths.

Horus glanced behind him to see that the wolves had followed him from the trees, and he ran on as their howling followed him to the edge of the crater. Far below, the water lay still and flat like a black mirror, and the image of the moon filled his vision.

The wolves howled again, and Horus felt the yawning depths of the water calling out to him with an inevitable attraction. He saw the moon and heard the company of wolves give voice to one last howled question before he hurled himself into the void.

He fell through the air, his vision tumbling and his memory spinning.

The moon, the wolves, Lupercal.

Luna... Wolves...

Everything snapped into place and he cried out, 'I am Horus of the Luna Wolves, Warmaster and regent of the Emperor and I am alive!'

Horus struck the water and it exploded like shards of black glass.

Flickering light filled the chamber with a cold glow, the cracked stone walls limned with crawling webs of frost, and the breath of the cultists feathering in the air. Akshub had painted a circle with eight sharp points around its circumference, on the flagstones in quicklime. The mutilated corpse of one of the Davinite priestess's acolytes lay spread-eagled at its centre.

Erebus watched carefully as the priestess's lodge thralls spread around the circle, ensuring that every stage of the ritual was enacted with meticulous care. To fail now, after he had invested so much effort in bringing the Warmaster to this point, would be disastrous, although Erebus knew that his part in the Warmaster's downfall was but one of a million events set in motion thousands of years ago.

This fulcrum point in time was the culmination of billions of seemingly unrelated chains of circumstance that had led to this backwater world that no one had ever heard of.

Erebus knew that that was all about to change. Davin would soon become a place of legend.

The secret chamber in the heart of the Delphos was hidden from prying eyes by potent magic and sophisticated technology received from disaffected Mechanicum adepts, who welcomed the knowledge the Word Bearers could give them – knowledge that had been forbidden to them by the Emperor.

Akshub knelt and cut the heart from the dead acolyte, the lodge priestess expertly removing the still warm organ from its former owner's chest. She took a bite before handing it to Tsepha, her surviving acolyte.

They passed the heart around the circle, each of the cultists taking a bite of the rich red meat. Erebus took the ghastly remains of the heart as it was passed to him. He wolfed down the last of it, feeling the blood run down his chin and tasting the final memories of the betrayed acolyte as the treacherous blade had ended her life. That betrayal had been offered unto the Architect of Fate, this bloody feast to the Blood God, and the unlovely coupling of the doomed acolyte with a diseased swine had called upon the power of the Dark Prince and the Lord of Decay.

Blood pooled beneath the corpse, trickling into channels cut in the floor before draining into a sinkhole at the centre of the circle. Erebus knew that there was always blood, it was rich with life and surged with the power of the gods. What better way was there of tapping into that power than with the vital substance that carried their blessing?

'Is it done?' asked Erebus.

Akshub nodded, lifting the long knife that had cut the heart from the corpse. 'It is. The power of the Ones Who Dwell Beyond is with us, though we must be swift.'

'Why must we hurry, Akshub?' he asked, placing his hand upon his sword. 'This must be done right or all our lives are forfeit.'

'I know this,' said the priestess. 'There is another presence near, a one-eyed ghost who walks between worlds and seeks to return the son to his father.'

'Magnus, you old snake,' chuckled Erebus, looking up towards the chamber's roof. 'You won't stop us. You're too far away and Horus is too far gone. I have seen to that.'

'Who do you speak with?' asked Akshub.

'The one-eyed ghost. You said there was another presence near.'

'Near, yes,' said Akshub, 'but not here.'

Tired of the old priestess's cryptic answers, Erebus snapped, 'Then where is he?'

Akshub reached up and tapped her head with the flat of her blade. 'He speaks to the son, though he cannot yet reach him fully. I can feel the ghost crawling around the temple, trying to break the magic keeping his full power out.'

'What?' cried Erebus.

'He will not succeed,' said Akshub, walking towards him with the knife outstretched. 'We have spirit-walked in the realm beyond for thousands of years and his knowledge is a paltry thing next to ours.'

'For your sake, it had better be, Akshub.'

She smiled and held the knife out. 'Your threats mean nothing here, warrior. I could boil the blood in your veins with a word, or rip your body inside out with a thought. You need me to send your soul into the world beyond, but how will you return if I am dead? Your soul will remain adrift in the void forever, and you are not so full of anger that you do not fear such a fate.'

Erebus did not like the sudden authority in her voice, but he knew she was right and decided he would kill her once her purpose was served. He swallowed his anger and said, 'Then let us begin.'

'Very well,' nodded the priestess, as Tsepha came forward and anointed Erebus's face with crystalline antimony.

'Is this for the veil?'

'Yes,' said Akshub. 'It will confound his senses and he will not see your likeness. He will see a face familiar and beloved to him.'

Erebus smiled at the delicious irony of the thought, and closed his eyes as Tsepha daubed his eyelids and cheeks with the stinging, silver-white powder.

'The spell that will allow your passage to the void requires one last thing,' said Akshub.

'What last thing?' asked Erebus, suddenly suspicious.

'Your death,' said Akshub, slashing her knife across his throat.

✠ ✠ ✠

Horus opened his eyes, smiling as he saw blue sky above him. Pink and orange tinged clouds drifted slowly across his vision, peaceful and relaxing. He watched them for a few moments and then sat up, feeling wet dew beneath his palms as he pushed himself upright. He saw that he was fully armoured in his frost white plate, and as he surveyed his surroundings, he lifted his hand to his face, smelling the sweet scent on the grass and the crystal freshness of the air.

A vista of unsurpassed beauty lay before him, towering snow-capped mountains draped in a shawl of pine and fir, magnificent swathes of emerald green forests as far as the eye could see and a wide river of foaming, icy water. Hundreds of shaggy coated herbivores grazed on the plain and wide-pinioned birds circled noisily overhead. Horus sat on the low slopes of the foothills at the base of the mountains, the sun warming his face and the grass wondrously soft beneath him.

'To hell with this,' he said as he got to his feet. 'I know I'm not dead, so what's going on?'

Once again, no one answered him, though this time he *had* expected an answer. The world still smelled sweet and fragrant, but with the memory of his identity came the knowledge of its falsehood. None of this was real, not the mountains or the river or the forests that covered the landscape, though there was something oddly familiar to it.

He remembered the dark, iron backdrop that lay behind this illusion and found that if he willed it, he could see the suggestion of that nightmarish vision behind the beauty of the world laid out before him.

Horus remembered thinking – a lifetime ago, it seemed – that perhaps this place might have been some netherworld between heaven and hell, but now laughed at the idea. He had long ago accepted the principle that the universe was simply matter, and that which was not matter was nothing. The universe was everything, and therefore nothing could exist beyond it.

Horus had the wit to see why some ancient theologian had claimed that the warp was, in fact, hell. He understood the reasoning, but he knew that the empyrean was no metaphysical dimension; it was simply an echo of the material world, where random vortices of energy and strange breeds of malign xenos creatures made their homes.

As pleasing an axiom as that was, it still didn't answer the question of where he was.

How had he come to this place? His last memory was of speaking to Petronella Vivar in the apothecarion, telling her of his life, his hopes, his disappointments and his fears for the galaxy – conscious that he had told her those incendiary things as his valediction.

He couldn't change that, but he would damn well get to the bottom of what was happening to him now. Was it a fever dream brought on by whatever had wounded him? Had Temba's sword been poisoned? He dismissed that thought immediately; no poison could lay him low.

Surveying his surroundings, he could see no sign of the wolves that had chased him through the dark forests, but suddenly remembered a familiar form that had ghosted behind the face of the pack leader. For the briefest instant, it had looked like Magnus, but surely he was back on Prospero licking his wounds after the Council of Nikaea?

Something had happened to Horus on Davin's moon, but he had no idea what. His shoulder ached and he rotated it within his armour to loosen the muscle, but the motion served only to further aggravate it. Horus set off in the direction of the river once more, still thirsty despite knowing that he walked in an illusory realm.

Cresting the rise that then began to slope gently down towards the river, Horus pulled up sharply as he saw something startling: an armoured Astartes warrior floating face down in the water. Wedged in the shallows of the riverbank, the body rose and fell with the swell of the water, and Horus swiftly made his way towards it.

He splashed into the river and gripped the edges of the figure's shoulder guards, turning the body over with a heavy splash.

Horus gasped, seeing that the man was alive, and that it was someone he knew.

A beautiful man was how Loken had described him, a beautiful man who had been adored by all who knew him. The noblest hero of the Great Crusade had been another of his epithets.

Hastur Sejanus.

Loken marched away from the temple, angry at what his brothers had done and furious with himself: he should have known that Erebus would have had plans beyond the simple murder of the Warmaster.

His veins surged with the need to do violence, but Erebus was not here, and no one could tell Loken where he was. Torgaddon and Vipus marched alongside him, and even through his anger, Loken could sense his friends' astonishment at what had happened before the great gate of the Delphos.

'Throne, what's happening here?' asked Vipus as they reached the top of the processional steps. 'Garvi, what's happening? Are the First Captain and Little Horus our enemies now?'

Loken shook his head. 'No, Nero, they are our brothers, they are simply being used. As I think we all are.'

'By Erebus?' asked Torgaddon.

'Erebus?' said Vipus. 'What has he got to do with this?'

'Garviel thinks that Erebus is behind what's happening to the Warmaster,' said Torgaddon.

Loken shot him an exasperated stare.

'You're joking?'

'Not this time, Nero,' said Torgaddon.

'Tarik,' snapped Loken. 'Keep your voice down or everyone will hear.'

'So what if they do, Garvi?' hissed Torgaddon. 'If Erebus is behind this, then everyone should know about it: we should expose him.'

'And we will,' promised Loken, watching as the pinpricks of vehicle headlights appeared at the mouth of the valley they had only recently flown up.

'So what do we do?' asked Vipus.

That was the question, realised Loken. They needed more information before they could act, and they needed it now. He fought for calm so that he could think more clearly.

Loken wanted answers, but he had to know what questions to ask first, and there was one man who had always been able to cut through his confusion and steer him in the right direction.

Loken set off down the steps, heading back towards the Thunderhawk. Torgaddon, Vipus and the warriors of Locasta followed him. As he reached the bottom of the steps, he turned to them and said, 'I need you two to stay here. Keep an eye on the temple and make sure that nothing bad happens.'

'Define "bad",' said Vipus.

'I'm not sure,' said Loken. 'Just... bad, you know? And contact me if you get so much as a glimpse of Erebus.'

'Where are you going?' asked Torgaddon.

'I'm going back to the *Vengeful Spirit*.'

'What for?'

'To get some answers,' said Loken.

'Hastur!' cried Horus, reaching down to lift his fallen friend from the water. Sejanus was limp in his arms, though Horus could tell he lived by the pulse in his throat and the colour in his cheeks. Horus dragged Sejanus from the water, wondering if his presence might be another of the strange realm's illusions or if his old friend might in fact be a threat to him.

Sejanus's chest hiked convulsively as he brought up a lungful of water, and Horus rolled him onto his side, knowing that the genhanced physique of an Astartes warrior made it almost impossible for him to drown.

'Hastur, is it really you?' asked Horus, knowing that in this place, such a question was probably meaningless, but overcome with joy to see his beloved Sejanus again. He remembered the pain he had felt when his most favoured son had been hacked down upon the onyx floor of the false Emperor's palace on Sixty-Three Nineteen, and the Cthonic bellicosity that had demanded blood vengeance.

Sejanus heaved a last flood of water and propped himself up on his elbow, sucking great lungfuls of the clean air. His hand clutched at his throat as though searching for something, and he looked relieved to find that it wasn't there.

'My son,' said Horus as Sejanus turned towards him. He was exactly as Horus remembered him, perfect in every detail: the noble face, wide set eyes and firm, straight nose that could be a mirror for the Warmaster himself.

Any thoughts that Sejanus might be a threat to him were swept away as he saw the silver shine of his eyes and knew that this surely was Hastur Sejanus. How such a thing was possible was beyond him, but he did not question this miracle for fear that it might be snatched away from him.

'Commander,' said Sejanus, rising to embrace Horus.

'Damn me, boy, it's good to see you,' said Horus. 'Part of me died when I lost you.'

'I know, sir,' replied Sejanus as they released each other from the crushing embrace. 'I felt your sorrow.'

'You're a sight for sore eyes, my boy,' said Horus, taking a step back to admire his most perfect warrior. 'It gladdens my heart to see you, but how can this be? I watched you die.'

'Yes,' agreed Sejanus. 'You did, but, in truth, my death was a blessing.'

'A blessing? How?'

'It opened my eyes to the truth of the universe and freed me from the shackles of living knowledge. Death is no longer an undiscovered country, my lord, it is one from which this traveller has returned.'

'How is such a thing possible?'

'They sent me back to you,' said Sejanus. 'My spirit was lost in the void, alone and dying, but I have come back to help you.'

Conflicting emotions surged through Horus at the sight of Sejanus. To hear him speak of spirits and voids struck a note of warning, but to see him alive once more, even if it wasn't real, was something to be cherished.

'You say you're here to help me? Then help me to understand this place. Where are we?'

'We don't have much time,' said Sejanus, climbing the slope to the rise that overlooked the plains and forests, and taking a long look around. 'He'll be here soon.'

'That's not the first time I've heard that recently,' said Horus.

'From where else have you heard it?' demanded Sejanus, turning back to face him with a serious expression. Horus was surprised at the vehemence of the question.

'A wolf said it to me,' said Horus. 'I know, I know, it sounds ridiculous, but I swear it really did speak to me.'

'I believe you, sir,' said Sejanus. 'That's why we need to move on.'

Horus sensed evasion, a trait he had never known in Sejanus before now and said, 'You're avoiding my question, Hastur, now tell me where we are.'

'We don't have time, my lord,' urged Sejanus.

'Sejanus,' said Horus, his voice that of the Warmaster. 'Tell me what I want to know.'

'Very well,' said Sejanus, 'but quickly, for your body lies on the brink of death within the walls of the Delphos on Davin.'

'The Delphos? I've never heard of it, and this doesn't look like Davin.'

'The Delphos is a place sacred to the Lodge of the Serpent,' said Sejanus. 'A place of healing. In the ancient tongues of Earth its name means "the womb of the world", where a man may be healed and renewed. Your body lies in the Axis Mundi chamber, but your spirit is no longer tied to your flesh.'

'So we're not really here?' asked Horus. 'This world isn't real?'

'No.'

'Then this is the warp,' said Horus, finally accepting what he had begun to suspect.

'Yes. None of this is real,' said Sejanus, waving his hand around the landscape. 'All this is but fragments of your will and memory that have given shape to the formless energy of the warp.'

Horus suddenly knew where he had seen this land before, remembering the wondrous geophysical relief map of Terra they had found ten kilometres beneath a dead world almost a decade ago. It hadn't been the Terra of their time, but one of an age long past, with green fields, clear seas and clean air.

He looked up into the sky, half expecting to see curious faces looking down on him from above like students studying an ant colony, but the sky was empty, though it was darkening at an unnatural rate. The world around him was changing before his eyes from the Earth that had once existed to the barren wasteland of Terra.

Sejanus followed his gaze and said, 'It's beginning.'

'What is?' asked Horus.

'Your mind and body are dying and this world is beginning to collapse into Chaos. That's why they sent me back, to guide you to the truth that will allow you to return to your body.'

Even as Sejanus spoke, the sky began to waver and he could see hints of the roiling sea of the immaterium seething behind the clouds.

'You keep saying "they",' said Horus. 'Who are "they" and why are they interested in me?'

'Great intelligences dwell in the warp,' explained Sejanus, casting wary glances at the dissolution of the sky. 'They do not communicate as we do and this is the only way they could reach you.'

'I don't like the sound of this, Hastur,' warned Horus.

'There is no malice in this place. There is power and potential, yes, but no malice, simply the desire to exist. Events in our galaxy are destroying this realm and these powers have chosen you to be their emissary in their dealings with the material world.'

'And what if I don't want to be their emissary?'

'Then you will die,' said Sejanus. 'Only they are powerful enough to save your life now.'

'If they're so powerful, what do they need me for?'

'They are powerful, but they cannot exist in the material universe and must work through emissaries,' replied Sejanus. 'You are a man of strength and ambition and they know there is no other being in the galaxy powerful enough or worthy enough to do what must be done.'

Despite his satisfaction at being so described, Horus did not like what he was hearing. He sensed no deceit in Sejanus, though a warning voice in his head reminded him that the silver-eyed warrior standing before him could not truly be Sejanus.

'They have no interest in the material universe, it is anathema to them, they simply wish to preserve their own realm from destruction,' continued Sejanus as the chemical reek of the world beyond the illusion returned, and a stinking wind arose. 'In return for your aid, they can give you a measure of their power and the means to realise your every ambition.'

Horus saw the lurking world of brazen iron become more substantial as the warp and weft of reality began to buckle beneath his feet. Cracks of dark light shimmered through the splitting earth and Horus could hear the sound of howling wolves drawing near.

'We have to move!' shouted Sejanus as the wolf pack loped from a disintegrating copse of trees. To Horus, it sounded as though their howls desperately called his name.

Sejanus ran back to the river and a shimmering flat oblong of light rose from the boiling water. Horus heard whispers and strange mutterings issuing from beyond it, and a sense of dark premonition seized him as he switched his gaze between this strange light and the wolves.

'I'm not sure about this,' said Horus as the sky shed fat droplets of acid rain.

'Come on, the gateway is our only way out!' cried Sejanus, heading towards the light. 'As a great man once said, "Towering genius disdains the beaten path; it seeks regions hitherto unexplored".'

'You're quoting me back to myself?' said Horus as the wind blew in howling gusts.

'Why not? Your words will be quoted for centuries to come.'

Horus smiled, liking the idea of being quotable, and set off after Sejanus.

'Where does this gate lead?' shouted Horus over the wind and the howling of wolves.

'To the truth,' replied Sejanus.

The crater began to fill as the sun finally set, hundreds of vehicles of all descriptions finally completing their journey from the Imperial deployment zone to this place of pilgrimage. The Davinites watched the arrival of these convoys with a mixture of surprise and confusion, incredulous as each vehicle was abandoned, and its passengers made their way towards the Delphos.

Within the hour, thousands of people had gathered, and more were arriving every minute. Most of these new arrivals milled about in an undirected mass until the Davinites began circulating amongst them, helping to find somewhere that belongings could be set down and arranging shelter as a hard rain began to fall.

Headlights stretched all the way along the forgotten causeway and through the valley to the plains below. As night closed in on Davin, songs in praise of the Warmaster filled the air, and the flickering glow of thousands of candles joined the light of the torches ringing the gold-skinned Delphos.

FOURTEEN

The forgotten
Living mythology
Primogenesis

Passing through the gate of light was akin to stepping from one room to another. Where once had been a world on the verge of dissolution, now Horus found himself standing amid a heaving mass of people, in a huge circular plaza surrounded by soaring towers and magnificently appointed buildings of marble. Thousands of people filled the square, and since he was half again as tall as the tallest, Horus could see that thousands more waited to enter from nine arterial boulevards.

Strangely, none of these people remarked on the sudden arrival of two giant warriors in their midst. A cluster of statues stood at the centre of the plaza, and droning chants drifted from corroded speakers set on the buildings, as the mass of humanity marched in mindless procession around them. A pealing clangour of bells tolled from each building.

'Where are we?' asked Horus, looking up at the great eagle-fronted buildings, their golden spires and their colossal stained glass rosary windows. Each structure vied with its neighbour for supremacy of height and ostentation, and Horus's eye for architectural proportion and elegance saw them as vulgar expressions of devotion.

'I do not know the name of this palace,' said Sejanus. 'I know only what I have seen here, but I believe it to be some kind of shrine world.'

'A shrine world? A shrine to what?'

'Not what,' said Sejanus, pointing to the statues in the centre of the plaza. 'Who.'

Horus looked more closely at the enormous statues, encircled by the thronged masses. The outer ring of statues was carved from white marble, and each gleaming warrior was clad in full Astartes battle-plate. They surrounded the central figure, which was likewise armoured in a magnificent suit of gold armour that gleamed and sparkled with precious gems. This figure carried a flaming torch high, the light of it illuminating everything around him. The symbolism was clear – this central figure was bringing his light to the people, and his warriors were there to protect him.

The gold warrior was clearly a king or hero of some kind, his features regal and patrician, though the sculptor had exaggerated them to ludicrous proportions. The proportions of the statues surrounding the central figure were similarly grotesque.

'Who is the gold statue meant to be?' asked Horus.

'You don't recognise him?' asked Sejanus.

'No. Should I?'

'Let's take a closer look.'

Horus followed as Sejanus set off into the crowd, making his way towards the centre of the plaza, and the crowds parted before them without so much as a raised eyebrow.

'Can't these people see us?' he asked.

'No,' said Sejanus. 'Or if they can, they will forget us in an instant. We move amongst them as ghosts and none here will remember us.'

Horus stopped in front of a man dressed in a threadbare scapular, who shuffled around the statues on bloodied feet. His hair was tonsured and he clutched a handful of carved bones tied together with twine. A bloody bandage covered one eye and a long strip of parchment pinned to his scapular dangled to the ground.

With barely a pause, the man stepped around him, but Horus put out his arm and prevented his progress. Again, the man attempted to pass Horus, but again he was prevented.

'Please, sir,' said the man without looking up. 'I must get by.'

'Why?' asked Horus. 'What are you doing?'

The man looked puzzled, as though struggling to recall what he had been asked.

'I must get by,' he said again.

Exasperated by the man's unhelpful answers, Horus stepped aside to let him pass. The man bowed his head and said, 'The Emperor watch over you, sir.'

Horus felt a clammy sensation crawl along his spine at the words. He pushed through the unresisting crowds towards the centre of the plaza as a terrible suspicion began forming in his gut. He caught up to Sejanus, who stood atop a stepped plinth at the foot of the statues, where a huge pair of bronze eagles formed the backdrop to a tall lectern.

A hugely fat official in a gold chasuble and tall mitre of silk and gold read aloud from a thick, leather-bound book, his words carried over the crowd via silver trumpets held aloft by what looked like winged infants that floated above him.

As Horus approached, he saw that the official was human only from the waist up, a complex series of hissing pistons and brass rods making up his lower half and fusing him with the lectern, which he now saw was mounted on a wheeled base.

Horus ignored him, looking up at the statues, finally seeing them for what they were.

Though their faces were unrecognisable to one who knew them as Horus did, their identities were unmistakable.

The nearest was Sanguinius, his outstretched wings like the pinions of the eagles that adorned every structure surrounding the plaza. To one side of the Lord of the Angels was Rogal Dorn, the unfurled wings haloing his head, unmistakable; on the other, was someone who could only be Leman Russ, his hair carved to resemble a wild mane, and wearing a cloak of wolf pelts draped around his massive shoulders.

Horus circled the statues, seeing other familiar images: Guilliman, Corax, the Lion, Ferrus Manus, Vulkan and finally Jaghatai Khan.

There could be no doubting the identity of the central figure now, and Horus looked up into the carved face of the Emperor. No doubt the inhabitants of this world thought it magnificent, but Horus knew this was a poor thing, failing spectacularly to capture the sheer dynamism and force of the Emperor's personality.

With the additional height offered by the statues' plinth, Horus looked out over the slowly circling mass of people and wondered what they thought they did in this place.

Pilgrims, thought Horus, the word leaping, unbidden, to his mind.

Coupled with the ostentation and vulgar adornments he saw on the surrounding buildings, Horus knew that this was not simply a place of devotion, but something much more.

'This is a place of worship,' he said as Sejanus joined him at the foot of Corax's statue, the cool marble perfectly capturing the pallid complexion of his taciturn brother.

Sejanus nodded and said, 'It is an entire world given over to the praise of the Emperor.'

'But why? The Emperor is no god. He spent centuries freeing humanity from the shackles of religion. This makes no sense.'

'Not from where you stand in time, but this is the Imperium that will come to pass if events continue on their present course,' said Sejanus. 'The Emperor has the gift of foresight and he has seen this future time.'

'For what purpose?'

'To destroy the old faiths so that one day his cult would more easily supplant them all.'

'No,' said Horus, 'I won't believe that. My father always refuted any notion of divinity. He once said of ancient Earth that there were torches, who were the teachers, but also extinguishers, who were the priests. He would never have condoned this.'

'Yet this entire world is his temple,' Sejanus said, 'and it is not the only one.'

'There are more worlds like this?'

'Hundreds,' nodded Sejanus, 'probably even thousands.'

'But the Emperor shamed Lorgar for behaviour such as this,' protested Horus. 'The Word Bearers Legion raised great monuments to the Emperor and persecuted entire populations for their lack of faith, but the Emperor would not stand for it and said that Lorgar shamed him with such displays.'

'He wasn't ready for worship then: he didn't have control of the galaxy. That's why he needed you.'

Horus turned away from Sejanus and looked up into the golden face of his father, desperate to refute the words he was hearing. At any other time, he would have struck Sejanus down for such a suggestion, but the evidence was here before him.

He turned to face Sejanus. 'These are some of my brothers, but where are the others? Where am I?'

'I do not know,' replied Sejanus. 'I have walked this place many times, but have never yet seen your likeness.'

'I am his chosen regent!' cried Horus. 'I fought on a thousand battlefields for him. The blood of my warriors is on his hands, and he ignores me like I don't exist?'

'The Emperor has forsaken you, Warmaster,' urged Sejanus. 'Soon he will turn his back on his people to win his place amongst the gods. He cares only for himself and his power and glory. We were all deceived. We have no place in his grand scheme, and when the time comes, he will spurn us all and ascend to godhood. While we were fighting war after war in his name, he was secretly building his power in the warp.'

The droning chant of the official – a priest, realised Horus – continued as the pilgrims maintained the slow procession around their god, and Sejanus's words hammered against his skull.

'This can't be true,' whispered Horus.

'What does a being of the Emperor's magnitude do after he has conquered the galaxy? What is left for him but godhood? What use has he for those whom he leaves behind?'

'No!' shouted Horus, stepping from the plinth and smashing the droning priest to the ground. The augmented preacher hybrid was torn from the pulpit and lay screaming in a pool of blood and oil. His cries were carried across the plaza by the trumpets of the floating infants, though none of the crowd seemed inclined to help him.

Horus set off into the crowded plaza in a blind fury, leaving Sejanus behind on the plinth of statues. Once again, the crowd parted before his headlong dash, as unresponsive to his leaving as they had been to his arrival. Within moments he reached the edge of the plaza and made his way down the nearest of the arterial boulevards. People filled the street, but they ignored him as he pushed his way through them, each face turned in rapture to an image of the Emperor.

Without Sejanus beside him, Horus realised that he was completely alone. He heard the howl of a distant wolf, its cry once again sounding as though it called out to him. He stopped in the centre of a crowded street, listening for the wolf howl again, but it was silenced as suddenly as it had come.

The crowds flowed around him as he listened, and Horus saw that once again, no one paid him the slightest bit of attention. Not since Horus had parted from his father and brothers had he felt so isolated. Suddenly he felt the pain of being confronted with the scale of his own vanity and pride as he realised how much he thrived on the adoration of those around him.

On every face, he saw the same blind devotion as he had witnessed in those that circled the statues, a beloved reverence for a man he called father. Didn't these people realise the victories that had won their freedom had been won with Horus's blood?

It should be Horus's statue surrounded by his brother primarchs, not the Emperor's!

Horus seized the nearest devotee and shook him violently by the shoulders, shouting, 'He is not a god! He is not a god!'

The pilgrim's neck snapped with an audible crack and Horus felt the bones of the man's shoulders splinter beneath his iron grip. Horrified, he dropped the dead man and ran deeper into the labyrinth of the shrine world, taking turns at random, as he sought to lose himself in its crowded streets.

Each fevered change of direction took him along thronged avenues of worshippers and marvels dedicated to the glory of the God-Emperor: thoroughfares where every cobblestone was inscribed with prayer, kilometre-high ossuaries of gold-plated bones, and forests of marble columns, with unnumbered saints depicted upon them.

Random demagogues roamed the streets, one fanatically mortifying his flesh with prayer whips while another held up two squares of orange cloth by the corners and screamed that he would not wear them. Horus could make no sense of any of it.

Vast prayer ships drifted over this part of the shrine city, monstrously bloated zeppelins with sweeping brass sails and enormous prop-driven motors. Long prayer banners hung from their fat silver hulls, and hymns blared from hanging loudspeakers shaped like ebony skulls.

Horus passed a great mausoleum where flocks of ivory-skinned angels with brass-feathered wings flew from dark archways and descended into the crowds gathered in front of the building. The solemn angels swooped over the wailing masses, occasionally gathering to pluck some ecstatic soul from the pilgrims, and cries of adoration and praise followed each supplicant as he was carried through the dread portals of the mausoleum.

Horus saw death venerated in the coloured glass of every window, celebrated in the carvings on every door, and revered in the funereal dirges that echoed from the trumpets of winged children who giggled as they circled like birds of prey. Flapping banners of bone clattered, and the wind whistled through the eye sockets of skulls set into shrine caskets on bronze poles. Morbidity hung like a shroud upon this world, and Horus could not reconcile the dark, gothic solemnity of this new religion with the dynamic force of truth, reason and confidence that had driven the Great Crusade into the stars.

High temples and grim shrines passed him in a blur: cenobites and preachers haranguing the pilgrims from every street corner to the peal of doomsayers' bells. Everywhere Horus looked, he saw walls adorned with frescoes, paintings and bas relief works of familiar faces – his brothers and the Emperor himself.

Why was there no representation of Horus?

It was as if he had never existed. He sank to his knees, raising his fists to the sky.

'Father, why have you forsaken me?'

✠ ✠ ✠

The *Vengeful Spirit* felt empty to Loken, and he knew it was more than simply the absence of people. The solid, reassuring presence of the Warmaster, so long taken for granted, was achingly absent without him on board. The halls of the ship were emptier, more hollow, as though it were a weapon stripped of its ammunition – once powerful, but now simply inert metal.

Though portions of the ship were still filled with people, huddled in small groups and holding hands around groups of candles, there was an emptiness to the place that left Loken feeling similarly hollowed out.

Each group he passed swarmed around him, the normal respect for an Astartes warrior forgotten in their desperation to know the fate of the Warmaster. Was he dead? Was he alive? Had the Emperor reached out from Terra to save his beloved son?

Loken angrily brushed each group off, pushing through them without answering their questions as he made his way to Archive Chamber Three. He knew Sindermann would be there – he was always there these days – researching and poring over his books like a man possessed. Loken needed answers about the Serpent Lodge, and he needed them now.

Time was of the essence and he'd already made one stop at the medical deck in order to hand over the anathame to Apothecary Vaddon.

'Be very careful, Apothecary,' warned Loken, reverently placing the wooden casket on the steel operating slab between them. 'This is a kinebrach weapon called an anathame. It was forged from a sentient xeno metal and is utterly lethal. I believe it to be the source of the Warmaster's malady. Do what you need to do to find out what happened, but do it quickly.'

Vaddon had nodded, dumbfounded that Loken had returned with something he could actually use. He lifted the anathame by its golden studded pommel and placed it within a spectrographic chamber.

'I can't promise anything, Captain Loken,' said Vaddon, 'but I will do whatever is in my power to find you an answer.'

'That's all I ask, but the sooner the better; and tell no one that you have this weapon.'

Vaddon nodded and turned to his work, leaving Loken to find Kyril Sindermann in the archives of the mighty ship. The helplessness that had seized him earlier vanished now that he had a purpose. He was actively trying to save the Warmaster, and that knowledge gave him fresh hope that there might yet be a way to bring him back unharmed in body and spirit.

As always, the archives were quiet, but now there was a

deeper sense of desolation. Loken strained to hear anything at all, finally catching the scratching of a quill-pen from deeper in the stacks of books. Swiftly he made his way towards the sound, knowing before he reached the source that it was his old mentor. Only Kyril Sindermann scratched at the page with such intense pen strokes.

Sure enough, Loken found Sindermann sitting at his usual table and upon seeing him, Loken knew with absolute certainty that he had not left this place since last they had spoken. Bottles of water and discarded food packs lay scattered around the table, and the haggard Sindermann now sported a growth of fine white hair on his cheeks and chin.

'Garviel,' said Sindermann without looking up. 'You came back. Is the Warmaster dead?'

'No,' replied Loken. 'At least I don't think so. Not yet anyway.'

Sindermann looked up from his books, the haphazard piles of which were now threatening to topple onto the floor.

'You don't think so?'

'I haven't seen him since I saw him on the Apothecaries' slab,' confessed Loken.

'Then why are you here? It surely can't be for a lesson on the principles and ethics of civilisation. What's happening?'

'I don't know,' admitted Loken. 'Something bad I think. I need your knowledge of... things esoteric, Kyril.'

'Things esoteric?' repeated Sindermann, putting down his quill. 'Now I am intrigued.'

'The Legion's quiet order has taken the Warmaster to the Temple of the Serpent Lodge on Davin. They've placed him in a temple they call the Delphos and say that the "eternal spirits of dead things" will heal him.'

'Serpent Lodge you say?' asked Sindermann, plucking books seemingly at random from the cluttered piles on his desk. 'Serpents... now that is interesting.'

'What is?'

'Serpents,' repeated Sindermann. 'Since the very beginnings of time, on every continent where humanity worshipped divinity, the serpent has been recognised and accepted as a god. From the steaming jungles of the Afrique islands to the icy wastes of Alba, serpents have been worshipped, feared and adored in equal measure. I believe that serpent mythology is probably the most widespread mythology known to mankind.'

'Then how did it get to Davin?' asked Loken.

'It's not difficult to understand,' explained Sindermann. 'You see, myths weren't originally expressed in verbal or written form because language was deemed inadequate to convey the truth expressed in the stories. Myths move not with words, Garviel, but with storytellers and wherever you find people, no matter how primitive or how far they've been separated from the cradle of humanity, you'll always find storytellers. Most of these myths were probably enacted, chanted, danced or sung, more often than not in hypnotic or hallucinatory states. It must have been quite a sight, but anyway, this method of retelling was said to allow the creative energies and relationships behind and beneath the natural world to be brought into the conscious realm. Ancient peoples believed that myths created a bridge from the metaphysical world to the physical one.'

Sindermann flicked through the pages of what looked like a new book encased in fresh red leather and turned the book so Loken could see.

'Here, you see it here quite clearly.'

Loken looked at the pictures, seeing images of naked tribesmen dancing with long snake-topped poles as well as snakes and spirals painted onto primitive pottery. Other pictures showed vases with gigantic snakes winding over suns, moons and stars, while still more showed snakes appearing below growing plants or coiled above the bellies of pregnant women.

'What am I looking at?' he asked.

'Artefacts recovered from a dozen different worlds during the Great Crusade,' said Sindermann, jabbing his finger at the pictures. 'Don't you see? We carry our myths with us, Garviel, we don't reinvent them.'

Sindermann turned the page to show yet more images of snakes and said, 'Here the snake is the symbol of energy, spontaneous, creative energy... and of immortality.'

'Immortality?'

'Yes, in ancient times, men believed that the serpent's ability to shed its skin and thus renew its youth made it privy to the secrets of death and rebirth. They saw the moon, waxing and waning, as the celestial body capable of this same ability, and of course, the lunar cycle has long associations with the life-creating rhythm of the female. The moon became the lord of the twin mysteries of birth and death, and the serpent was its earthly counterpart.'

'The moon...' said Loken.

'Yes,' continued Sindermann, now well into his flow. 'In early rites of initiation where the aspirant was seen to die and be reborn, the moon was the goddess mother and the serpent the divine father. It's not hard to see why the connection between the serpent and healing becomes a permanent facet of serpent worship.'

'Is that what this is,' breathed Loken. 'A rite of initiation?'

Sindermann shrugged. 'I couldn't say, Garviel. I'd need to see more of it.'

'Tell me,' snarled Loken. 'I need to hear all you know.'

Startled by the power of Loken's urging, Sindermann reached for several more books, leafing through them as the Tenth Company captain loomed over him.

'Yes, yes...' he muttered, flipping back and forth through the well-thumbed pages. 'Yes, here it is. Ah... yes, a word for serpent in one of the lost languages of old Earth was "nahash", which apparently means, "to guess". It appears that it was then translated to mean a number of different things, depending on which etymological root you believe.'

'Translated to mean what?' asked Loken.

'Its first rendition is as either "enemy" or "adversary", but it seems to be more popularly transliterated as "Seytan".'

'Seytan,' said Loken. 'I've heard that name before.'

'We... ah, spoke of it at the Whisperheads,' said Sindermann in a low voice, looking about him as though someone might be listening. 'It was said to be a nightmarish force of deviltry cast down by a golden hero on Terra. As we now know, the Samus spirit was probably the local equivalent for the inhabitants of Sixty-Three Nineteen.'

'Do you believe that?' asked Loken. 'That Samus was a spirit?'

'Of some form, yes,' said Sindermann honestly. 'I believe that what I saw beneath the mountains was more than simply a xenos of some kind, no matter what the Warmaster says.'

'And what about this serpent as Seytan?'

Sindermann, pleased to have a subject upon which he could illuminate, shook his head and said, 'No. If you look closer, you see the word "serpent" has its origination in the Olympian root languages as "drakon", the cosmic serpent that was seen as a symbol of Chaos.'

'Chaos?' cried Loken. 'No!'

'Yes,' went on Sindermann, hesitantly pointing out a passage of text in yet another of his books. 'It is this "chaos", or "serpent", which must be overcome to create order and maintain life in any meaningful way. This serpentine dragon was a creature of great power and its sacred years were times of great ambition and incredible risk. It's said that events occurring in a year of the dragon are magnified threefold in intensity.'

Loken tried to hide his horror at Sindermann's words, the

ritual significance of the serpent and its place in mythology cementing his conviction that what was happening on Davin was horribly wrong. He looked down at the book before him and said, 'What's this?'

'A passage from the *Book of Atum*,' said Sindermann, as though afraid to tell him. 'I only found it quite recently, I swear. I didn't think anything of it, I still don't really... After all, it's just nonsense, isn't it?'

Loken forced himself to look at the book, feeling his heart grow heavy with each word he read from its yellowed pages.

I am Horus, forged of the Oldest Gods,
I am he who gave way to Khaos
I am that great destroyer of all.
I am he who did what seemed good to him,
And set doom in the palace of my will.
Mine is the fate of those who move along
This serpentine path.

'I'm no student of poetry,' snapped Loken. 'What does it mean?'

'It's a prophecy,' said Sindermann hesitantly. 'It speaks of a time when the world returns to its original chaos and the hidden aspects of the supreme gods become the new serpent.'

'I don't have time for metaphors, Kyril,' warned Loken.

'At its most basic level,' said Sindermann, 'it speaks about the death of the universe.'

Sejanus found him on the steps of a vaulted basilica, its wide doorway flanked by tall skeletons wrapped in funeral robes and holding flaming censers out before them. Though darkness had fallen, the streets of the city still thronged with worshippers, each carrying a lit taper or lantern to light the way.

Horus looked up as Sejanus approached, thinking that the processions of light through the city would have seemed beautiful at any other time. The pageantry and pomp of the palanquins and altars being carried along the streets would previously have irritated him, were the procession in his honour, but now he craved them.

'Have you seen all you need to see?' asked Sejanus, sitting beside him on the steps.

'Yes,' replied Horus. 'I wish to leave this place.'

'We can leave whenever you want, just say the word,' said Sejanus. 'There is more you need to see anyway, and our time is not infinite. Your body is dying and you must make your choice before you are beyond the help of even the powers that dwell in the warp.'

'This choice,' Horus said. 'Does it involve what I think it does?'

'Only you can decide that,' said Sejanus as the doors to the basilica opened behind them.

Horus looked over his shoulder, seeing a familiar oblong of light where he would have expected to see a darkened vestibule.

'Very well,' he said, standing and turning towards the light. 'So where are we going now?'

'To the beginning,' answered Sejanus.

Stepping through the light, Horus found himself standing in what appeared to be a colossal laboratory, its cavernous walls formed of white steel and silver panels. The air tasted sterile, and Horus could tell that the temperature of the air was close to freezing. Hundreds of figures encased in fully enclosed white oversuits with reflective gold visors filled the laboratory, working at row upon row of humming gold machines that sat atop long, steel benches.

Hissing puffs of vapour feathered the air above each worker's head, and long tubes coiled around the legs and arms of the white suits before hooking into cumbersome looking backpacks. Though no words were spoken, a sense of the implementation of grand designs was palpable. Horus wandered through the facility, its inhabitants ignoring him as completely as those of the shrine world had. Instinctively, he knew that he and Sejanus were far beneath the surface of whatever world they had travelled to.

'Where are we now?' he asked. 'When are we?'

'Terra,' said Sejanus, 'at the dawn of a new age.'

'What does that mean?'

In answer to his question, Sejanus pointed to the far wall of the laboratory where a shimmering energy field protected a huge silver steel door. The sign of the aquila was etched into the metal, along with strange, mystical looking symbols that were out of place in a laboratory dedicated to the pursuit of science. Just looking at the door made Horus uneasy, as though whatever lay beyond was somehow a threat to him.

'What lies beyond that door?' asked Horus, backing away from the silver portal.

'Truths you will not want to see,' replied Sejanus, 'and answers you will not want to hear.'

Horus felt a strange, previously unknown sensation stir in

his belly and fought to quell it as he realised that, despite all the cunning wrought into his creation, the sensation was fear. Nothing good could live behind that door. Its secrets were best forgotten, and whatever knowledge lay beyond should be left hidden.

'I don't want to know,' said Horus, turning from the door. 'It's too much.'

'You fear to seek answers?' asked Sejanus angrily. 'This is not the Horus I followed into battle for two centuries. The Horus I knew would not shirk from uncomfortable truths.'

'Maybe not, but I still don't want to see it,' said Horus.

'I'm afraid you don't have a choice, my friend,' said Sejanus. Horus looked up to see that he now stood in front of the door, wisps of freezing air gusting from its base as it slowly raised and the energy field dissipated. Flashing yellow lights swirled to either side of the door, but no one in the laboratory paid any attention as the door slid up into the panelled wall.

Dark knowledge lay beyond, of that Horus was certain, just as certainly as he knew that he could not ignore the temptation of discovering the secrets it kept hidden. He had to know what it concealed. Sejanus was right; it wasn't in his nature to back away from anything, no matter what it was. He had faced all the terrors the galaxy had to show him and had not flinched. This would be no different.

'Very well,' he said. 'Show me.'

Sejanus smiled and slapped his palm against Horus's shoulder guard, saying, 'I knew we could count on you, my friend. This will not be easy for you, but know that we would not show you this unless it was necessary.'

'Do what you must,' said Horus, shaking off the hand. For the briefest instant, Sejanus's reflection blurred like a shimmering mask in the gleaming metal of the door, and Horus fancied he saw a reptilian grin on his friend's face. 'Let's just get it done.'

They walked through the icy mist together, passing along a wide, steel-walled corridor that led to an identical door, which also slid into the ceiling as they approached.

The chamber beyond was perhaps half the size of the laboratory. Its walls were pristine and sterile, and it was empty of technicians and scientists. The floor was smooth concrete and the temperature cool rather than cold.

A raised central walkway ran the length of the chamber with ten large cylindrical tanks the size of boarding torpedoes lying flat to either side of it, long serial numbers stencilled on their flanks. Steam gusted from the top of each tank like breath.

Beneath the serial numbers were the same mystical symbols he had seen on the door leading to this place.

Each tank was connected to a collection of strange machines, whose purpose Horus could not even begin to guess at. Their technologies were unlike anything he had ever seen, their construction beyond even his incredible intellect.

He climbed the metal stairs that led to the walkway, hearing strange sounds like fists on metal as he reached the top. Now atop the walkway, he could see that each tank had a wide hatchway at its end, with a wheel handle in its centre and a thick sheet of armoured glass above it.

Brilliant light flickered behind each block of glass and the very air thrummed with potential. Something about all this seemed dreadfully familiar to Horus and he felt an irresistible urge to know what lay within the tanks while simultaneously dreading what he might see.

'What are these?' he asked as he heard Sejanus climbing up behind him.

'I'm not surprised you don't remember. It's been over two hundred years.'

Horus leaned forward and wiped his gauntlet across the fogged glass of the first tank's hatch. He squinted against the brightness, straining to see what lay within. The light was blinding, a motion blurred shape within twisting like dark smoke in the wind.

Something saw him. Something moved closer.

'What do you mean?' asked Horus, fascinated by the strange, formless being that swam through the light of the tank. Its motion slowed, and it became a silhouette as it moved closer to the glass, its form settling into something more solid.

The tank hummed with power, as though the metal were barely able to contain the energy generated by the creature contained within it.

'These are the Emperor's most secret geno-vaults beneath the Himalayan peaks,' said Sejanus. 'This is where you were created.'

Horus wasn't listening. He was staring through the glass in amazement at a pair of liquid eyes that were the mirror of his own.

FIFTEEN

Revelations
Dissent
Scattering

In the two days since the Warmaster's departure, the *Vengeful Spirit* had become a ghost ship, the mighty vessel having haemorrhaged landers, carriers, skiffs and any other craft capable of making it to the surface to follow Horus to Davin.

This suited Ignace Karkasy fine as he marched with newfound purpose and practiced insouciance through the decks of the ship, a canvas satchel slung over one shoulder. Each time he passed a public area of the ship he would check for anyone watching and liberally spread a number of sheets of paper around on desks, tables and couches.

The ache in his shoulder was lessening the more copies of *The Truth is All We Have* he distributed from the satchel, each sheet bearing three of what he considered to be his most powerful works to date. *Uncaring Gods* was his personal favourite, unfavourably comparing the Astartes warriors to the ancient Titans of myth; a powerful piece that he knew was worthy of a wider audience. He knew he had to be careful with such works, but the passion burned in him too brightly to be contained.

He'd managed to get his hands on a cheap bulk printer with ridiculous ease, acquiring one from the first junkyard dog he'd approached with no more than a few moments' effort. It was not a good quality machine, or even one he would have looked twice at on Terra, but even so it had cost him the bulk of his winnings at merci merci. It was a poor thing, but it did the job, even though his billet now stank of printer's ink.

Humming quietly to himself, Karkasy continued through the civilian decks, coming at last to the Retreat, careful now that he was entering areas where he was known, and where there might be others around.

His fears were unfounded as the Retreat was empty, making it even more depressing and rundown-looking. One should never see a drinking establishment well lit, he thought, it just makes it look even sadder. He made his way through the Retreat, placing a couple of sheets on each table.

Karkasy froze as he heard the clink of a bottle on a glass, his hand outstretched to another table.

'What are you doing?' asked a cultured, but clearly drunk, female voice.

Karkasy turned and saw a bedraggled woman slumped in one of the booths at the far end of the Retreat, which explained why he hadn't seen her. She was in shadow, but he instantly recognised her as Petronella Vivar, the Warmaster's documentarist, though her appearance was a far cry from when he had last seen her on Davin.

No, that wasn't right, he remembered. He had seen her on the embarkation deck as the Astartes had returned with the Warmaster.

Obviously, the experience hadn't failed to leave its mark on her.

'Those papers,' she said. 'What are they?'

Karkasy guiltily dropped the sheets he had been holding onto the tabletop and shifted the satchel so that it rested at his back.

'Nothing really,' he said, moving down the row of booths towards her. 'Just some poems I'd like people to read.'

'Poetry? Is it any good? I could use something uplifting.'

He knew he should leave her to her maudlin solitude, but the egotist in him couldn't help but respond. 'Yes, I think they're some of my best.'

'Can I read them?'

'I wouldn't right now, my dear,' he said. 'Not if you're looking for something light. They're a bit dark.'

'A bit dark,' she laughed, the sound harsh and ugly. 'You have no idea.'

'It's Vivar isn't it?' asked Karkasy, approaching her booth. 'That's your name isn't it?'

She looked up, and Karkasy, an expert in gauging levels of inebriation in others, saw that she was drunk to the point of insensibility. Three bottles sat drained on the table and a fourth lay in pieces on the floor.

'Yes, that's me, Petronella Vivar,' she said. 'Palatina Majoria of House Carpinus, writer and fraud... and, I think, very drunk.'

'I can see that, but what do you mean by fraud?'

'Fraud,' she slurred, taking another drink. 'I came here to tell the glory of Horus and the splendid brotherhood of the primarchs, you know? Told Horus when I met him that if he didn't let me do it he could go to hell. Thought I'd lost my chance right there and then, but he laughed!'

'He laughed?'

She nodded. 'Yes, laughed, but he let me do it anyway. Think he might have thought I'd be amusing to keep around or something. I thought I was ready for anything.'

'And has it proved to be all you hoped it would be, my dear Petronella?'

'No, not really if I'm honest. Want a drink? I'll tell you about it.'

Karkasy nodded and fetched himself a glass from the bar before sitting across from her. She poured him some wine, getting more on the table than in the glass.

'Thank you,' he said. 'So why is it not what you thought it would be? There's many a remembrancer would think such a position would be a documentarist's dream. Mersadie Oliton would have killed to land such a role.'

'Who?'

'A friend of mine,' explained Karkasy. 'She's also a documentarist.'

'She wouldn't want it, trust me,' said Petronella, and Karkasy could see that the puffiness around her eyes was due as much to tears as to alcohol. 'Some illusions are best kept. Everything I thought I knew... upside down, just like that! Trust me, she doesn't want this.'

'Oh, I think she might,' said Karkasy, taking a drink.

She shook her head and took a closer look at him, as though seeing him for the first time.

'Who are you?' she asked suddenly. 'I don't know you.'

'My name is Ignace Karkasy,' he said, puffing out his chest. 'Winner of the Ethiopic Laureate and–'

'Karkasy? I know that name...' she said, rubbing the heel of her palm against her temple as she sought to recall him. 'Wait, you're a poet aren't you?'

'I am indeed,' he said. 'Do you know my work?'

She nodded. 'You write poetry. Bad poetry I think, I don't remember.'

Stung by her casual dismissal of his work, he resorted to pet-
ulance and said, 'Well, what have you written that's so bloody
great? Can't say I remember reading anything you've written.'

'Ha! You'll remember what I'm going to write, I'll tell you
that for nothing!'

'Really?' quipped Karkasy, gesturing at the empty bottles on
the table. 'And what might that be? *Memoirs of an Inebriated
Socialite? Vengeful Spirits of the Vengeful Spirit?*'

'You think you're so clever, don't you?'

'I have my moments,' said Karkasy, knowing that there wasn't
much challenge in scoring points over a drunken woman, but
enjoying it nonetheless. Anyway, it would be pleasant to take
this spoiled rich girl – who was complaining about the biggest
break of her life – down a peg or two.

'You don't know anything,' she snapped.

'Don't I?' he asked. 'Why don't you illuminate me then?'

'Fine! I will.'

And she told Ignace Karkasy the most incredible tale he'd
ever heard in his life.

'Why did you bring me here?' asked Horus, backing away from
the silver tank. The eyes on the other side of the glass watched
him curiously, clearly aware of him in a way that everyone else
they had encountered on this strange odyssey was not. Though
he knew with utter certainty who those eyes belonged to, he
couldn't accept that this sterile chamber far beneath the earth
was where the glory of his life had begun.

Raised on Cthonia under the black smog of the smelter-
ies – that had been his home, his earliest memories a blur of
confusing images and feelings. Nothing in his memory recalled
this place or the awareness that must have grown within...

'You have seen the ultimate goal of the Emperor, my friend,'
said Sejanus. 'Now it is time for you see how he began his quest
for godhood.'

'With the primarchs?' said Horus. 'That makes no sense.'

'It makes perfect sense. You were to be his generals. Like unto
gods, you would bestride planets and claim back the galaxy for
him. You were a weapon, Horus, a weapon to be cast aside once
blunted and past all usefulness.'

Horus turned from Sejanus and marched along the walkway,
stopping periodically to peer through the glass of the tanks. He
saw something different in each one, light and form indistinguishable, organisms like architecture, eyes and wheels turning
in circles of fire. Power like nothing he had known was at work,

and he could feel the potent energies surrounding and protecting the tanks, rippling across his skin like waves in the air.

He stopped by the tank with XI stencilled upon it and placed his hand against the smooth steel, feeling the untapped glories that might have lain ahead for what grew within, but knowing that they would never come to pass. He leaned forward to look within.

'You know what happens here, Horus,' said Sejanus. 'You are not long for this place.'

'Yes,' said Horus. 'There was an accident. We were lost, scattered across the stars until the Emperor discovered us.'

'No,' said Sejanus. 'There was no accident.'

Horus turned from the glass, confused. 'What are you talking about? Of course there was. We were hurled from Terra like leaves in a storm. I came to Cthonia, Russ to Fenris, Sanguinius to Baal and the others to the worlds they were raised on.'

'No, you misunderstand me. I meant that it wasn't an accident,' said Sejanus. 'Look around you. You know how far beneath the earth we are and you saw the protective wards carved on the doors that led here. What manner of accident do you think could reach into this facility and scatter you so far across the galaxy? And what were the chances of you all coming to rest on ancient homeworlds of humanity?'

Horus had no answer for him and leaned on the walkway's railing taking deep breaths as Sejanus approached him. 'What are you suggesting?'

'I am suggesting nothing. I am telling you what happened.'

'You are telling me nothing!' roared Horus. 'You fill my head with speculation and conjecture, but you tell me nothing concrete. Maybe I'm being stupid, I don't know, so explain what you mean in plain words.'

'Very well,' nodded Sejanus. 'I will tell you of your creation.'

Thunderheads rumbled over the summit of the Delphos, and Euphrati Keeler snapped off a couple of quick picts of the structure's immensity, silhouetted against sheets of purple lighting. She knew the picts were nothing special, the composition banal and pedestrian, but she took them anyway, knowing that every moment of this historic time had to be recorded for future generations.

'Are you done?' asked Titus Cassar, who stood a little way behind her. 'The prayer meeting's in a few moments and you don't want to be late.'

'I know, Titus, stop fussing.'

She had met Titus Cassar the day after she had arrived in the valley of the Delphos, following the secret Lectitio Divinitatus symbols to a clandestine prayer meeting he had organised in the shadow of the mighty building. She had been surprised by how many people were part of his congregation, nearly sixty souls, all with their heads bowed and reciting prayers to the Divine Emperor of Mankind.

Cassar had welcomed her into his flock, but people had quickly gravitated to her daily prayers and sermons, preferring them to his. For all his faith, Cassar was no orator and his awkward, spiky delivery left a lot to be desired. He had faith, but he was no iterator, that was for sure. She had worried that he might resent her usurping his group, but he had welcomed it, knowing that he was a follower, not a leader.

In truth, she was no leader either. Like Cassar, she had faith, but felt uncomfortable standing in front of large groups of people. The crowds of the faithful didn't seem to notice, staring at her in rapturous adoration as she delivered the word of the Emperor.

'I'm not fussing, Euphrati.'

'Yes you are.'

'Well, maybe I am, but I have to get back to the *Dies Irae* before I'm missed. Princeps Turnet will have my hide if he finds out what I've been doing here.'

The mighty war engines of the Legio Mortis stood sentinel over the Warmaster at the mouth of the valley, their bulk too enormous to allow them to enter. The crater looked more like the site of a military muster than a gathering of pilgrims and supplicants: tanks, trucks, flatbeds and mobile command vehicles having carried tens of thousands of people to this place over the past seven days.

Together with the bizarre-looking locals, a huge portion of the Expeditionary fleet filled the crater with makeshift camps all around the Delphos. People had, in a wondrous outpouring of spontaneous feeling, made their way to where the Warmaster lay, and the scale of it still had the power to take Euphrati's breath away. The steps of the temple were thick with offerings to the Warmaster, and she knew that many of the people here had given all they had in the hope that it might speed his recovery in some way.

Keeler had a new passion in her life, but she was still an imagist at heart, and some of the picts she had taken here were amongst her finest work.

'Yes, you're right, we should go,' she said, folding up her picter and hanging it around her neck. She ran her hand through her hair, still not used to how short it was now, but liking how it made her feel.

'Have you thought about what you're going to say tonight?' asked Cassar as they made their way through the thronged site to the prayer meeting.

'No, not really,' she answered. 'I never plan that far ahead. I just let the Emperor's light fill me and then I speak from the heart.'

Cassar nodded, hanging on her every word. She smiled.

'You know, six months ago, I'd have laughed if anyone had said things like that around me.'

'What things?' asked Cassar.

'About the Emperor,' she said, fingering the silver eagle on a chain she kept tucked beneath her remembrancer's robes. 'But I guess a lot can happen to a person in that time.'

'I guess so,' agreed Cassar, making way for a group of Army soldiers. 'The Emperor's light is a powerful force, Euphrati.'

As Keeler and Cassar drew level with the soldiers, a thick-necked bull of a man with a shaved head slammed his shoulder into Cassar and pitched him to the ground.

'Hey, watch where you're going,' snarled the soldier, looming over Cassar.

Keeler stood over the fallen Cassar and shouted, 'Piss off, you cretin, you hit him!'

The soldier turned, backhanding his fist into Euphrati's jaw, and she dropped to the ground, more shocked than hurt. She struggled to rise as blood filled her mouth, but a pair of hands gripped her shoulders and held her firm to the ground. Two soldiers held her down as the others started kicking the fallen Cassar.

'Get off me!' she yelled.

'Shut up, bitch!' said the first soldier. 'You think we don't know what you're doing? Prayers and stuff to the Emperor? Horus is the one you should be giving thanks to.'

Cassar rolled to his knees, blocking the kicks as best he could, but he was facing three trained soldiers and couldn't block them all. He punched one in the groin and swayed away from a thick-soled boot aimed at his head, finally gaining his feet as a chopping hand struck him on the side of the neck.

Keeler struggled in her captors' grip, but they were too strong. One man reached down to tear the picter from around her neck and she bit his wrist as it came into range of her teeth. He yelped and ripped the picter from her as the other wrenched her head back by the roots of her hair.

'Don't you dare!' she screamed, struggling even harder as the soldier swung the picter by its strap and smashed it to pieces on the ground. Cassar was down on one knee, his face bloody and angry. He freed his pistol from its holster, but a knee connected with his face and knocked him insensible, the pistol clattering to the ground beside him.

'Titus!' shouted Keeler, fighting like a wildcat and finally managing to free one arm. She reached back and clawed her nails down the face of the man who held her. He screamed and released his grip on her, and she scrambled on her knees to the fallen pistol.

'Get her!' someone shouted. 'Emperor-loving witch!'

She reached the pistol, hearing the thud of heavy impacts, and rolled onto her back. She held the gun out in front of her, ready to kill the next bastard that came near her.

Then she saw that she wouldn't have to kill anyone.

Three of the soldiers were down, one was running for his life through the campsite and the last was held in the iron grip of an Astartes warrior. The soldier's feet flailed a metre off the ground as the Astartes held him round the neck with one hand.

'Five to one doesn't seem very sporting now does it?' asked the warrior, and Keeler saw that it was Captain Torgaddon, one of the Mournival. She remembered snapping some fine images of Torgaddon on the *Vengeful Spirit* and thinking that he was the handsomest of the Sons of Horus.

Torgaddon ripped the name and unit badge from the struggling soldier's uniform, before dropping him and saying, 'You'll be hearing from the Discipline Masters. Now get out of my sight before I kill you.'

Keeler dropped the pistol and scooted over to her picter, cursing as she saw that it and the images contained within it were probably ruined. She pawed through the remains and lifted out the memory coil. If she could get this into the edit engine she kept in her billet quickly enough then perhaps she could save some of the images.

Cassar groaned in pain and she felt a momentary pang of guilt that she'd gone for her smashed picter before him, but it soon passed.

'Are you Keeler?' asked Torgaddon as she slipped the memory coil into her robes.

She looked up, surprised that he knew her name, and said, 'Yes.'

'Good,' he said, offering his hand to help her to her feet.

'You want to tell me what that was all about?' he asked.

She hesitated, not wanting to tell an Astartes warrior the real reason for the assault. 'I don't think they liked the images I was taking,' she said.

'Everyone's a critic, eh?' chuckled Torgaddon, but she could see that he didn't believe her.

'Yeah, but I need to get back to the ship to recover them.'

'Well that's a happy coincidence,' said Torgaddon.

'What do you mean?'

'I've been asked to take you back to the *Vengeful Spirit*.'

'You have? Why?'

'Does it matter?' asked Torgaddon. 'You're coming back with me.'

'You can at least tell me who wants me back, can't you?'

'No, it's top secret.'

'Really?'

'No, not really, it's Kyril Sindermann.'

The idea of Sindermann sending an Astartes warrior to do his bidding seemed ludicrous to Keeler, and there could only be one reason why the venerable iterator wanted to speak to her. Ignace or Mersadie must have blabbed to him about her new faith, and she felt her anger grow at their unwillingness to understand her newfound truth.

'So the Astartes are at the beck and call of the iterators now?' she snapped.

'Hardly,' said Torgaddon. 'It's a favour to a friend and I think it might be in your own best interests to go back.'

'Why?'

'You ask a lot of questions, Miss Keeler,' said Torgaddon, 'and while that's a trait that probably stands you in good stead as a remembrancer, it might be best for you to be quiet and listen for a change.'

'Am I in trouble?'

Torgaddon stirred the smashed remnants of her picter with his boot and said, 'Let's just say that someone wants to give you some lessons in pictography.'

'The Emperor knew he would need the greatest warriors to lead his armies,' began Sejanus. 'To lead such warriors as the Astartes needed commanders like gods. Commanders who were virtually indestructible and could command superhuman warriors in the blink of an eye. They would be engineered to be leaders of men, mighty warlords whose martial prowess was only matched by the Emperor's, each with his own particular skills.'

'The primarchs.'

'Indeed. Only beings of such magnitude could even think of conquering the galaxy. Can you imagine the hubris and will required even to contemplate such an endeavour? What manner of man could even consider it? Who but a primarch could be trusted with such a monumental task? No man, not even the Emperor, could achieve such a god-like undertaking alone. Hence you were created.'

'To conquer the galaxy for humanity,' said Horus.

'No, not for humanity, for the Emperor,' said Sejanus. 'You already know in your heart what awaits you when the Great Crusade is over. You will become a gaoler who polices the Emperor's regime while he ascends to godhood and abandons you all. What sort of reward is that for someone who conquered the galaxy?'

'It is no reward at all,' snarled Horus, hammering his hand into the side of the silver tank before him. The metal buckled and a hairline crack split the toughened glass under his assault. He could hear a desperate drumming from inside, and a hiss of escaping gas whined from the frosted panel of the tank.

'Look around you, Horus,' said Sejanus. 'Do you think that the science of man alone could have created a being such as a primarch? If such technology existed, why not create a hundred Horuses, a thousand? No, a bargain was made that saw you emerge from its forging. I know, for the masters of the warp are as much your father as the Emperor.'

'No!' shouted Horus. 'I won't believe you. The primarchs are my brothers, the Emperor's sons created from his own flesh and blood and each a part of him.'

'Each a part of him, yes, but where did such power come from? He bargained with the gods of the warp for a measure of their power. *That* is what he invested in you, not his paltry human power.'

'The gods of the warp? What are you talking about, Sejanus?'

'The entities whose realm is being destroyed by the Emperor,' said Sejanus. 'Intelligences, xenos creatures, gods? Does it matter what terminology we use for them? They have such incredible power that they might as well be gods by your reckoning. They command the secrets of life and death and all that lies between. Experience, change, war and decay, they are all part of the endless cycle of existence, and the gods of the warp hold dominion over them all. Their power flows through your veins and bestows incredible abilities upon you. The Emperor has long known of them and he came to them many centuries ago, offering friendship and devotion.'

'He would never do such a thing!' denied Horus.

'You underestimate his lust for power, my friend,' said Sejanus as they made their way back towards the steps that led down to the laboratory floor. 'The gods of the warp are powerful, but they do not understand this material universe, and the Emperor was able to betray them, stealing away their power for himself. In creating you, he passed on but a tiny measure of that power.'

Horus felt his breath come in short, painful bursts. He wanted to deny Sejanus's words, but part of him knew that this was no lie. Like any man, his future was uncertain, but his past had always been his own. His glories and life had been forged with his own two hands, but even now, they were being stripped away from him by the Emperor's treachery.

'So we are tainted,' whispered Horus. 'All of us.'

'Tainted, no,' said Sejanus, shaking his head. 'The power of the warp simply *is*. Used wisely and by a man of power it can be a weapon like no other. It can be mastered and it can be a powerful tool for one with the will to use it.'

'Then why did the Emperor not use it well?'

'Because he was weak,' said Sejanus, leaning in close to Horus. 'Unlike you, he lacked the will to master it, and the gods of the warp do not take kindly to those who betray them. The Emperor had taken a measure of their power for himself, but they struck back at him.'

'How?'

'You will see. With the power he stole from them, he was too powerful for them to attack directly, but they had foreseen a measure of his plans and they struck at what he needed most to realise those plans.'

'The primarchs?'

'The primarchs,' agreed Sejanus, walking back down the length of walkway. Horus heard distant sirens blare and felt the air within the chamber become more agitated, as if a cold electric current whipped from molecule to molecule.

'What's going on?' he asked, as the sirens grew louder.

'Justice,' said Sejanus.

The reflective surfaces of the tanks lit up as an actinic blue light appeared above them, and Horus looked up to see a blob of dirty light swirling into existence just below the ceiling. Like a miniature galaxy, it hung suspended above the silver incubation tanks, growing larger with every passing second. A powerful wind tugged at Horus and he hung onto the railing as a shrieking howl issued from the spreading vortex above him.

'What is that?' he shouted, working his way along the railing towards the stairs.

'You know what it is, Horus,' said Sejanus.

'We have to get out of here.'

'It's too late for that,' said Sejanus, taking his arm in an iron grip.

'Take your hand off me, Sejanus,' warned Horus, 'or whatever your name is. I know you're not Sejanus, so you might as well stop pretending.'

Even as he spoke, he saw a group of armoured warriors rushing through the chamber's doorway towards them. There were six of them, each with the build of an Astartes, but without a suit of battle-plate, they were less bulked out and gigantic. They wore fabulously ornate gold breastplates decorated with eagles and lightning bolts, and each wore a tall, peaked helm of bronze with a red, horsehair plume. Scarlet cloaks billowed behind them in the cyclone that swept through the chamber. Long spears with boltguns slung beneath long, crackling blades were aimed at him, and he instantly recognised the warriors for what they were – the Custodian Guard, the Praetorians of the Emperor himself.

'Halt, fiends and face thine judgement!' shouted the lead warrior, aiming his guardian spear at Horus's heart. Though the warrior wore an enclosing helm, Horus would have recognised his eyes and that voice anywhere.

'Valdor!' cried Horus. 'Constantin Valdor. It's me, it's Horus.'

'Be silent!' shouted Valdor. 'End this foul conjuration now!'

Horus looked up at the ceiling, feeling the power contained within that swirling maelstrom tugging at him like the call of a long lost friend. He forced its siren song from his mind, dropped to the floor of the chamber and took a step forward.

Ripping blasts of light erupted from the Custodians' spears, and Horus was forced to his knees by the hammering impacts of their shells. The howling gale swallowed the noise of the shots, and Horus cried out, not with pain, but with the knowledge that fellow warriors of the Imperium had fired upon him.

More blasts struck him, tearing great chunks from his armour, but none was able to defeat its protection. The Custodians advanced in disciplined ranks, pouring their fire into him and keeping him pinned beneath its weight. Sejanus ducked behind the stairs, sparks and smoking chunks ripping from the metal as the explosive bolts tore through it.

Horus roared in anger and surged to his feet, all thoughts of restraint forgotten as he found himself at the centre of the deafening storm. A bolt clipped his gorget and almost spun him around, but it was not enough to stop him. He ripped the guardian spear from the nearest Custodian and smashed his skull to splinters with a single blow from his fist.

He reversed his grip on the spear and slashed the next Custodian from collarbone to groin, the two shorn halves swept up by the howling winds and vanishing into the crackling vortex. Another Custodian died as Horus rammed the spear through his chest and split him in two.

A blade lanced for his head, but he shattered it with a swipe of his fist and ripped the arm from his attacker with casual ease. Another Custodian died as Horus tore his head off in his mighty fist, blood gushing from the neck, as if from a geyser, as he tossed the severed head aside.

Only Valdor remained, and Horus snarled as he rounded on the Chief Custodian. A blaze of light erupted from the barrel of Valdor's guardian spear. Horus grunted at the impacts and raised his fist to strike Valdor down, hearing metal squeal and tear as the force of the hurricane reaching from the vortex above finally achieved its goal.

Horus paused in his attack, suddenly terrified for the fate of those inside the tanks. He turned and saw one tank spewing gasses and screams as it was ripped from the ground, following others as they were torn from their moorings and swept upwards.

Then time stopped and a blinding light filled the chamber.

Horus felt warm honey flow through him, and he turned towards the source of the light: a shimmering golden giant of unimaginable majesty and beauty.

Horus dropped to his knees in rapture at the sight. Who would not strive to worship so perfect a being? Power and certainty flowed from the figure, the secret mystery of creation at his fingertips, the answers to any question that could be asked there for the knowing, and the wisdom to know how to use them.

He wore armour that gleamed a perfect gold, his features impossible to know, and his glory and power unmatched by any being in creation.

The golden warrior moved as though in slow motion, raising his hand to halt the madness of the vortex with a gesture. The maelstrom was silenced, the tumbling incubation tanks suspended in mid air.

The golden figure turned a puzzled gaze upon Horus.

'I know you?' he said, and Horus wept to hear such a perfect symphony of sound.

'Yes,' said Horus, unable to raise his voice above a whisper.

The giant cocked his head to one side and said, 'You would destroy my great works, but you will not succeed. I beg you, turn from this path or all will be lost.'

Horus reached out towards the golden warrior as he turned his sad gaze to the incubation tanks held motionless above him, weighing the consequences of future events in the blink of an eye.

Horus could see the decision in the figure's wondrous eyes and shouted, 'No!'

The figure turned from him and time snapped back into its prescribed stream.

The deafening howl of the warp-spawned wind returned with the force of a hurricane and Horus heard the screams of his brothers amid the metallic clanging of their incubation tanks.

'Father, no!' he yelled. 'You can't let this happen!'

The golden giant was walking away, leaving the carnage in his wake, uncaring of the lives he had wrought. Horus felt his hate swell bright and strong within his breast.

The power of the wind seized him in its grip and he let it take him, spinning him up into the air and Horus opened his arms as he was reunited once again with his brothers.

The abyss of the warp vortex yawned above him like a great eye of terror and madness.

He surrendered to its power and let it take him into its embrace.

SIXTEEN

The truth is all we have
Arch-prophet
Home

For once Loken was inclined to agree with Iacton Qruze when he said, 'Not like it used to be, boy. Not like it used to be.'

They stood on the strategium deck, looking out over the ghostly glow of Davin as it hung in space like a faded jewel. 'I remember the first time we came here, seems like yesterday.'

'More like a lifetime,' said Loken.

'Nonsense, young man,' said Qruze. 'When you've been around as long as I have you learn a thing or two. Live to my age and we'll see how you perceive the passage of years.'

Loken sighed, not in the mood for another of Qruze's rambling, faintly patronising stories of 'the good old days'.

'Yes, Iacton, we'll see.'

'Don't dismiss me, boy,' said Qruze. 'I may be old, but I'm not stupid.'

'I never meant to say you were,' said Loken.

'Then take heed of me now, Garviel,' said Qruze, leaning in close. 'You think I don't know, but I do.'

'Don't know about what?'

'About the "Half-heard" thing,' hissed Qruze, quietly so that none of the deck crew could hear. 'I know fine well why you call me that, and it's not because I speak softly, it's because no one pays a blind bit of notice to what I say.'

Loken looked into Qruze's long, tanned face, his skin deeply lined with creases and folds. His eyes, normally hooded and half-closed, were now intense and penetrating.

'Iacton–' began Loken, but Qruze cut him off.

'Don't apologise, it doesn't become you.'

'I don't know what to say,' said Loken.

'Ach… don't say anything. What do I have to say that anyone would want to listen to anyway?' sighed Qruze. 'I know what I am, boy, a relic of a time long passed for our beloved Legion. You know that I remember when we fought without the Warmaster, can you imagine such a thing?'

'We may not have to soon, Iacton. It's nearly time for the Delphos to open and there's been no word. Apothecary Vaddon is no nearer to finding out what happened to the Warmaster, even with the anathame.'

'The what?'

'The weapon that wounded the Warmaster,' said Loken, wishing he hadn't mentioned the kinebrach weapon in front of Qruze.

'Oh, must be a powerful weapon that,' said Qruze sagely.

'I wanted to go back down to Davin with Torgaddon,' said Loken, changing the subject, 'but I was afraid of what I might do if I saw Little Horus or Ezekyle.'

'They are your brothers, boy,' said Qruze. 'Whatever happens, never forget that. We break such bonds at our peril. When we turn from one brother, we turn from them all.'

'Even when they have made a terrible mistake?'

'Even then,' agreed Qruze. 'We all make mistakes, lad. We need to appreciate them for what they are – lessons that can only be learned the hard way. Unless it's a fatal mistake, of course, but at least someone else can learn from *that*.'

'I don't know what to do,' said Loken, leaning on the strategium rail. 'I don't know what's happening with the Warmaster and there's nothing I can do about it.'

'Aye, it's a thorny one, my boy,' agreed Qruze. 'Still, as we used to say back in my day, "When there's nothing you can do about it, don't worry about it".'

'Things must have been simpler back in your day, Iacton,' said Loken.

'They were, boy, that's for sure,' replied Qruze, missing Loken's sarcasm. 'There was none of this quiet order nonsense, and do you think we'd have that upstart Varvarus baying for blood back in the day? Or that we'd have had remembrancers on our own bloody ship, writing treasonous poetry about us and claiming that it's the unvarnished truth? I ask you, where's the damn respect the Astartes used to be held in? Changed days, young man, changed days.'

Loken's eyes narrowed as Qruze spoke. 'What are you talking about?'

'I said it's changed days since–'

'No,' said Loken, 'about Varvarus and the remembrancers.'

'Haven't you heard? No, I suppose you haven't,' said Qruze. 'Well, it seems Varvarus wasn't too pleased about you and the Mournival's return to the *Vengeful Spirit* with the Warmaster. The fool thinks heads should roll for the deaths you caused. He's been on the vox daily to Maloghurst demanding we tell the fleet what happened, make reparations to the families of the dead, and then punish you all.'

'Punish us?'

'That's what he's saying,' nodded Qruze. 'Claims he's already had Ing Mae Sing despatch communiqués back to the Council of Terra about the mess you caused. Bloody nuisance if you ask me. We didn't have to put up with this when we first set out, you fought and bled, and if people got in the way then that was their tough luck.'

Loken was aghast at Qruze's words, once again feeling the shame of his actions on the embarkation deck. The innocent deaths he'd been part of would remain with him until his dying day, but what was done was done and he wouldn't waste time on regret. For mere mortals to decree the death of an Astartes was unthinkable, however unfortunate the events had been.

As troublesome a problem as Varvarus was, he was a problem for Maloghurst to deal with, but something in Qruze's words struck a familiar chord.

'You said something about remembrancers?'

'Yes, as if we didn't have enough to worry about.'

'Iacton, don't draw this out. Tell me what's going on.'

'Very well, though I don't know what your hurry is,' replied Qruze. 'It seems there's some anonymous remembrancer going about the ship, dishing out anti-Astartes propaganda, poetry or some such drivel. Crewmen have been finding pamphlets all over the ship. Called the "truth is all we have" or something pretentious like that.'

'The truth is all we have,' repeated Loken.

'Yes, I think so.'

Loken spun on his heel and made his way from the strategium without another word.

'Not like it was, back in my day,' sighed Qruze after Loken's departing back.

✠ ✠ ✠

It was late and he was tired, but Ignace Karkasy was pleased with the last week's work. Each time he'd made a clandestine journey through the ship distributing his radical poetry, he'd returned hours later to find every copy gone. Though the ship's crew was no doubt confiscating some, he knew that others must have found their way into the hands of those who needed to hear what he had to say.

The companionway was quiet, but then it always was these days. Most of those who held vigils for the fallen Warmaster did so either on Davin or in the larger spaces of the ship. An air of neglect hung over the *Vengeful Spirit*, as though even the servitors who cleaned and maintained it had paused in their duties to await the outcome of events on the planet below.

As he walked back to his billet, Karkasy saw the symbol of the Lectitio Divinitatus scratched into bulkheads and passageways time and time again, and he had the distinct impression that if he were to follow them, they would lead him to a group of the faithful.

The faithful: it still sounded strange to think of such a term in these enlightened times. He remembered standing in the fane on Sixty-Three Nineteen and wondering if belief in the divine was some immutable flaw in the character of mankind. Did man need to believe in something to fill some terrible emptiness within him?

A wise man of Old Earth had once claimed that science would destroy mankind, not through its weapons of mass destruction, but through finally proving that there was no god. Such knowledge, he claimed, would sear the mind of man and leave him gibbering and insane with the realisation that he was utterly alone in an uncaring universe.

Karkasy smiled and wondered what that old man would have said if he could see the truth of the Imperium taking its secular light to the far corners of the galaxy. On the other hand, perhaps this Lectitio Divinitatus cult was vindication of his words: proof that, in the face of that emptiness, man had chosen to invent new gods to replace the ones that had passed out of memory.

Karkasy wasn't aware of the Emperor having transubstantiated from man to god, but the cult's literature, which was appearing with the same regularity as his own publications, claimed that he had already risen beyond mortal concerns.

He shook his head at such foolishness, already working out how to incorporate this weighty pontificating into his new poems. His billet was just ahead, and as he reached towards the recessed handle, he immediately knew that something was wrong.

The door was slightly ajar and the reek of ammonia filled the corridor, but even over that powerful smell, Karkasy detected a familiar, pervasive aroma that could mean only one thing. The impertinent ditty he had composed for Euphrati Keeler concerning the stink of the Astartes leapt to mind, and he knew who would be behind the door, even before he opened it.

He briefly considered simply walking away, but realised that there would be no point.

He took a deep breath and pushed open the door.

Inside, his cabin was a mess, though it was a mess of his own making rather than that of any intruder. Standing with his back to him and seeming to fill the small space with his bulk was, as he'd expected, Captain Loken.

'Hello, Ignace,' said Loken, putting down one of the Bondsman Number 7s. Karkasy had filled two of them with random jottings and thoughts, and he knew that Loken wouldn't be best pleased with what he must have read. You didn't need to be a student of literature to understand the vitriol written there.

'Captain Loken,' replied Karkasy. 'I'd ask to what do I owe the pleasure of this visit, but we both know why you're here, don't we?'

Loken nodded, and Karkasy, feeling his heart pounding in his chest, saw that the Astartes was holding his anger in check by the finest of threads. This was not the raging fury of Abaddon, but a cold steel rage that could destroy him without a moment's pause or regret. Suddenly Karkasy realised how dangerous his newly rediscovered muse was and how foolish he'd been in thinking he would remain undiscovered for long. Strangely, now that he was unmasked, he felt his defiance smother the fire of his fear, and knew that he had done the right thing.

'Why?' hissed Loken. 'I vouched for you, remembrancer. I put my good name on the line for you and this is how I am repaid?'

'Yes, captain,' said Karkasy. 'You did vouch for me. You made me swear to tell the truth and that is what I have been doing.'

'The truth?' roared Loken, and Karkasy quailed before his anger, remembering how easily the captain's fists had bludgeoned people to death. 'This is not the truth, this is libellous trash! Your lies are already spreading to the rest of the fleet. I should kill you for this, Ignace.'

'Kill me? Just like you killed all those innocent people on the embarkation deck?' shouted Karkasy. 'Is that what Astartes justice means now? Someone gets in your way or says something you don't agree with and you kill them? If that's what our glorious Imperium has come to then I want nothing to do with it.'

He saw the anger drain from Loken and felt a momentary pang of sorrow for him, but quashed it as he remembered the blood and screams of the dying. He lifted a collection of poems and held them out to Loken. 'Anyway, this is want you wanted.'

'You think I wanted this?' said Loken, hurling the pamphlets across the billet and looming over him. 'Are you insane?'

'Not at all, my dear captain,' said Karkasy, affecting a calm he didn't feel. 'I have you to thank for this.'

'Me? What are you talking about?' asked Loken, obviously confused. Karkasy could see the chink of doubt in Loken's bluster. He offered a bottle of wine to Loken, but the giant warrior shook his head.

'You told me to keep telling the truth, ugly and unpalatable as it might be,' said Karkasy, pouring some wine into a cracked and dirty tin mug. 'The truth is all we have, remember?'

'I remember,' sighed Loken, sitting down on Karkasy's creaking cot bed.

Karkasy let out a breath as he realised the immediate danger had passed, and took a long, gulping drink of the wine. It was a poor vintage and had been open for too long, but it helped to calm his jangling nerves. He pulled a high backed chair from his writing desk and sat before Loken, who held his hand out for the bottle.

'You're right, Ignace, I did tell you to do this, but I never imagined it would lead us to this place,' said Loken, taking a swig from the bottle.

'Nor I, but it has,' replied Karkasy. 'The question now becomes what are you going to do about it?'

'I don't really know, Ignace,' admitted Loken. 'I think you are being unfair to the Mournival, given the circumstances we found ourselves in. All we–'

'No,' interrupted Karkasy, 'I'm not. You Astartes stand above us mortals in all regards and you demand our respect, but that respect has to be earned. It requires your ethics to be without question. You not only have to stay above the line between right and wrong, you also have to stay well clear of the grey areas in-between.'

Loken laughed humourlessly. 'I thought it was Sindermann's job to be a teacher of ethics.'

'Well, our dear Kyril has not been around much lately, has he?' said Karkasy. 'I admit I'm somewhat of a latecomer to the ranks of the righteous, but I know that what I am doing is right. More than that, I know it's *necessary*.'

'You feel that strongly about this?'

'I do, captain. More strongly than I have felt about anything in my life.'

'And you'll keep publishing this?' asked Loken, lifting a pile of scribbled notes.

'Is there a right answer to that question, captain?' asked Karkasy.

'Yes, so answer honestly.'

'If I can,' said Karkasy, 'then I will.'

'You will bring trouble down on us both, Ignace Karkasy,' said Loken, 'but if we have no truth, then we are nothing, and if I stop you speaking out then I am no better than a tyrant.'

'So you're not going to stop me writing, or send me back to Terra?'

'I should, but I won't. You should be aware that your poems have made you powerful enemies, Ignace, enemies who will demand your dismissal, or worse. As of this moment however, you are under my protection,' said Loken.

'You think I'll need protection?' asked Karkasy.

'Definitely,' said Loken.

'I'm told you wanted to see me,' said Euphrati Keeler. 'Care to tell me why?'

'Ah, my dear, Euphrati,' said Kyril Sindermann, looking up from his food. 'Do come in.'

She'd found him in the sub-deck dining area after scouring the dusty passages of Archive Chamber Three for him for over an hour. According to the iterators left on the ship, the old man had been spending almost all of his time there, missing his lectures – not that there were any students to lecture just now – and ignoring the requests of his peers to join them for meals or drinks.

Torgaddon had left her to find Sindermann on her own, his duty discharged simply by bringing her back to the *Vengeful Spirit*. Then he had gone in search of Captain Loken, to travel back down to Davin with him. Keeler didn't doubt that he'd pass on what he'd seen on the planet to Loken, but she no longer cared who knew of her beliefs.

Sindermann looked terrible, his eyes haggard and grey, his features sallow and gaunt.

'You don't look good, Sindermann,' she said.

'I could say the same for you, Euphrati,' said Sindermann. 'You've lost weight. It doesn't suit you.'

'Most women would be grateful for that, but you didn't have one of the Astartes fetch me back here to comment on my eating habits, did you?'

Sindermann laughed, pushing aside the book he'd been poring over, and said, 'No, you're right, I didn't.'

'Then why did you?' she asked, sitting opposite him. 'If it's because of something Ignace has told you, then save your breath.'

'Ignace? No, I haven't spoken to him for some time,' replied Sindermann. 'It was Mersadie Oliton who came to see me. She tells me that you've become quite the agitator for this Lectitio Divinitatus cult.'

'It's not a cult.'

'No? Then what would you call it?'

She thought about it for a moment and then answered, 'A new faith.'

'A shrewd answer,' said Sindermann. 'If you'll indulge me, I'd like to know more about it.'

'You would? I thought you'd brought me back to try and teach me the error of my ways, to use your iterator's wiles to try and talk me out of my beliefs.'

'Not at all, my dear,' said Sindermann. 'You may think your tribute is paid in secret in the recesses of your heart, but it will out. We are a curious species when it comes to worship. The things that dominate our imagination determine our lives and our character. Therefore it behoves us to be careful what we worship, for what we are worshipping we are becoming.'

'And what do you think we worship?'

Sindermann looked furtively around the sub-deck and produced a sheet of paper that she recognised immediately as one of the Lectitio Divinitatus pamphlets. 'That's what I want you to help me with. I have read this several times and I must admit that I am intrigued by the things it posits. You see, ever since the... events beneath the Whisperheads, I... I haven't been sleeping too well and I thought to bury myself in my books. I thought that if I could understand what happened to us, then I could rationalise it.'

'And did you?'

He smiled, but she could see the weariness and despair behind the gesture. 'Honestly? No, not really, the more I read, the more I saw how far we'd come since the days of religious hectoring from an autocratic priesthood. By the same token, the more I read the more I realised there was a pattern emerging.'

'A pattern? What kind of pattern?'

'Look,' said Sindermann, coming round the table to sit next to her, and flattening out the pamphlet before her. 'Your Lectitio Divinitatus talks about how the Emperor has moved amongst us for thousands of year, yes?'

'Yes.'

'Well, in the old texts, rubbish mostly – ancient histories and lurid tales of barbarism and bloodshed – I found some recurring themes. A being of golden light appears in several of the texts and, much as I hate to admit it, it sounds a lot like what this paper describes. I don't know what truth may lie in this avenue of investigation, but I would know more of it, Euphrati.'

She didn't know what to say.

'Look,' he said, pulling the book around and turning it towards her. 'This book is written in a derivation of an ancient human language, but one I haven't seen before. I can make out certain passages, I think, but it's a very complex structure and without some of the root words to make the right grammatical connections, it's proving very difficult to translate.'

'What book is it?'

'I believe it to be the *Book of Lorgar*, although I haven't been able to speak with First Chaplain Erebus to verify that fact. If it is, it may be a copy given to the Warmaster by Lorgar himself.'

'So why does that make it so important?'

'Don't you remember the rumours about Lorgar?' asked Sindermann urgently. 'That he too worshipped the Emperor as a god? It's said that his Legion devastated world after world for not showing the proper devotion to the Emperor, and then raised up great monuments to him.'

'I remember the tales, yes, but that's all they are, surely?'

'Probably, but what if they aren't?' said Sindermann, his eyes alight with the possibility of uncovering such knowledge. 'What if a primarch, one of the Emperor's sons no less, was privy to something we as mere mortals are not yet ready for? If my work so far is correct, then this book talks about bringing forth the essence of god. I must know what that means!'

Despite herself, Euphrati felt her pulse race with this potential knowledge. Undeniable proof of the Emperor's divinity coming from Kyril Sindermann would raise the Lectitio Divinitatus far above its humble status and into the realm of a phenomenon that could spread from one side of the galaxy to the other.

Sindermann saw that realisation in her face and said, 'Miss Keeler, I have spent my entire adult life promulgating the truth of the Imperium and I am proud of the work I have done, but what if we are teaching the wrong message? If you are right and the Emperor is a god, then what we saw beneath the mountains of Sixty-Three Nineteen represents a danger more horrifying than we can possibly imagine. If it truly was a spirit of evil then we need a divine being such as the Emperor, more than ever. I know that words cannot move mountains, but they can move the multitude – we've proven that time and time again. People are more ready to fight and die for a word than for anything else. Words shape thought, stir feeling, and force action. They kill and revive, corrupt and cure. If being an iterator has taught me anything, it's that men of words – priests, prophets and intellectuals – have played a more decisive role in history than any military leaders or statesmen. If we can prove the existence of god, then I promise you the iterators will shout that truth from the highest towers of the land.'

Euphrati stared, open mouthed, as Kyril Sindermann turned her world upside down: this arch-prophet of secular truth speaking of gods and faith? Looking into his eyes, she saw the wracking self-doubt and crisis of identity that he had undergone since she had last seen him, understanding how much of him had been lost these last few days, and how much had been gained.

'Let me see,' she said, and Sindermann pushed the book in front of her.

The writing was an angular cuneiform, running up and down the page rather than along it, and right away she could see that she would be no help in its translation, although elements of the script looked somehow familiar.

'I can't read it,' she said. 'What does it say?'

'Well, that's the problem, I can't tell exactly,' said Sindermann. 'I can make out the odd word, but it's difficult without the grammatical key.'

'I've seen this before,' she said, suddenly remembering why the writing looked familiar.

'I hardly think so, Euphrati,' said Sindermann. 'This book has been in the archive chamber for decades. I don't think anyone's read it since it was put there.'

'Don't patronise me, Sindermann, I've definitely seen this before,' she insisted.

'Where?'

Keeler reached into her pocket and gripped the memory coil of her smashed picter. She rose from her seat and said, 'Gather your notes and I'll meet you in the archive chamber in thirty minutes.'

'Where are you going?' asked Sindermann, gathering up the book.

'To get something you're going to want to see.'

Horus opened his eyes to see a sky thick with polluted clouds, the taste in the air chemical and stagnant.

It smelled familiar. It smelled of home.

He lay on an uneven plateau of dusty black powder in front of a long-exhausted mining tunnel, and felt the hollow ache of homesickness as he realised this was Cthonia.

The smog of the distant foundries and the relentless hammering of deep core mining filled the sky with particulate matter, and he felt an ache of loneliness for the simpler times he had spent here.

Horus looked around for Sejanus, but whatever the swirling vortex beneath Terra had been, it had evidently not swept up his old comrade in its fury.

His journey here had not been as silent and instant as his previous journeys through this strange and unknown realm. The powers that dwelled in the warp had shown him a glimpse of the future, and it was a desolate place indeed. Foul xeno breeds held sway over huge swathes of the galaxy and a pall of hopelessness gripped the sons of man.

The power of humanity's glorious armies was broken, the Legions shattered and reduced to fragments of what they had once been: bureaucrats, scriveners and officialdom ruling in a hellish regime where men lived inglorious lives of no consequence or ambition.

In this dark future, mankind had not the strength to challenge the overlords, to fight against the terrors the Emperor had left them to. His father had become a carrion god who neither felt his subjects' pain nor cared for their fate.

In truth, the solitude of Cthonia was welcome, his thoughts tumbling through his head in a mad whirl of anger and resentment. The Emperor tinkered with powers far beyond his means to master – and had already failed to control once before. He had bargained away his sons for the promise of power, and now returned to Terra to try once again.

'I will not let this happen,' Horus said quietly.

As he spoke, he heard the plaintive howl of a wolf and pushed himself to his feet. Nothing like a wolf lived on Cthonia, and Horus was sick of this constant pursuit through the warp.

'Show yourselves!' he shouted, punching the air and bellowing an ululating war cry.

His cry was answered as the howling came again, drawing nearer, and Horus felt his battle lust swim to the surface. He had the taste of blood after the slaughter of the Custodian Guards and welcomed the chance to spill yet more.

Shadows moved around him and he shouted, 'Lupercal! Lupercal!'

Shapes resolved from the shadows and he saw a red-furred wolf pack detach from the darkness. They surrounded him, and Horus recognised the pack leader as the beast that had spoken to him when he had first awoken in the warp.

'What are you?' asked Horus. 'And no lies.'

'A friend,' said the wolf, its form blurring and running with rippling lines of golden light. The wolf reared up on its hind legs, its form elongating and widening as it became more humanoid, its proportions swelling and changing until it stood as tall as Horus himself.

Copper skin replaced fur and its eyes ran like liquid as they formed one golden orb. Thick red hair sprouted from the figure's head and bronze coloured armour shimmered into existence upon his breast and arms. He wore a billowing cloak of feathers and Horus knew him as well he knew his own reflection.

'Magnus,' said Horus. 'Is it really you?'

'Yes, my brother, it is,' said Magnus, and the two warriors embraced in a clatter of plate.

'How?' asked Horus. 'Are you dying too?'

'No,' said Magnus. 'I am not. You must listen to me, my brother. It has taken me too long to reach you, and I do not have much time here. The spells and wards placed around you are powerful and every second I am here a dozen of my thralls die to keep them open.'

'Don't listen to him, Warmaster,' said another voice, and Horus turned to see Hastur Sejanus emerge from the darkness of the mining tunnel. 'This is who we have been trying to avoid. It is a shape-changing creature of the warp that feasts on human souls. It seeks to devour yours so that you cannot return to your body. All that was Horus would be no more.'

'He lies,' spat Magnus. 'You know me, Horus. I am your brother, but who is he? Hastur? Hastur is dead.'

'I know, but here, in this place, death is not the end.'

'There is truth in that,' agreed Magnus, 'but you would place your trust in the dead over your own brother? We mourn Hastur, but he is gone from us. This impostor does not even wear his own true face!'

Magnus thrust his fist forward and closed his fingers on the air, as though gripping something invisible. Then he wrenched his hand back. Hastur screamed and a silver light blazed like a magnesium flare from his eyes.

Horus squinted through the blinding light, still seeing an Astartes warrior, but one now armoured in the livery of the Word Bearers.

'Erebus?' asked Horus.

'Yes, Warmaster,' agreed First Chaplain Erebus; the long red scar across his throat had already begun to heal. 'I came to you in the guise of Sejanus to ease your understanding of what must be done, but I have spoken nothing but the truth since we travelled this realm.'

'Do not listen to him, Horus,' warned Magnus. 'The future of the galaxy is in your hands.'

'Indeed it is,' said Erebus, 'for the Emperor will abandon the galaxy in his quest for apotheosis. Horus must save the Imperium, for it is evident that the Emperor will not.'

SEVENTEEN

Horror
Angels and daemons
Blood pact

With the compact edit engine tucked under one arm and a sense of limitless possibilities filling her heart, Euphrati Keeler made her way through the stacks of Archive Chamber Three towards Sindermann's table. The white haired iterator sat hunched over the book he had shown her earlier, his breath misting in the chill air. She sat down beside him and placed the edit engine on the desk, slotting a memory coil into the imager slot.

'It's cold in here, Sindermann,' she said. 'How you haven't caught a fever I'll never know.'

He nodded. 'Yes, it is rather cold, isn't it. It's been like this for days now, ever since the Warmaster was taken to Davin in fact.'

The screen of the edit engine flickered to life, its white screen bathing them both in its washed-out light as Keeler flicked through the images she had captured. She zipped through those she had taken while on Davin's surface and those of Captain Loken and the Mournival prior to their departure for the Whisperheads.

'What are you looking for exactly?' asked Sindermann.

'This,' she said triumphantly, angling the screen so he could see the image it displayed.

The file contained eight pictures, all taken at the War Council held on Davin where Eugan Temba's treachery had been revealed. Each shot included First Chaplain Erebus, and she used the engine's trackball to zoom in on his tattooed skull. Sindermann gasped as he recognised the symbols on Erebus's head. They were identical to the ones in the book that he had shown Keeler on the sub-deck.

'That's it then,' he breathed. 'It must be the *Book of Lorgar*. Can you get any closer to get the symbols from all sides of Erebus's head? Is that possible?'

'*Please*, it's me,' she replied, her hands dancing across the keys of the edit engine.

Using all the various images and shots of the Word Bearer from different angles, Euphrati was able to create a composite image of the symbols tattooed onto his skull and project it onto a flat pane. Sindermann watched her skill with admiration, and it took her less than ten minutes to resolve a high-gain image of the symbols on Erebus's head.

With a grunt of satisfaction, she made a final keystroke, and a glossy hard copy of the screen's image slid from the side of the machine with a whirring sigh. Keeler lifted it by the corners and waved it for a second or two to dry it, before handing it to Sindermann.

'There,' she said. 'Does that help you translate what this book says?'

Sindermann slid the image across the table and held it close to the book, his head bobbing back and forth between the book and his notes as his finger traced down the trails of cuneiforms.

'Yes, yes…' he said excitedly. 'Here, you see, this word is laden with vowel transliterations and this one is clearly a personal argot, though of a much denser polysyllabic construction.'

Keeler tuned out of what Sindermann was saying after a while, unable to make sense of the jargon he was using. Karkasy or Oliton might be able to understand the iterator, but images were her thing, not words.

'How long will it take you to get any sense out of it?' she asked.

'What? Oh, not long I shouldn't wonder,' he said. 'Once you know the grammatical logic of a language, it is a relatively simple matter to unlock the rest of its meaning.'

'So how long?'

'Give me an hour and we'll read this together, yes?'

She nodded and pushed her chair back, saying, 'Fine, I'll take a look around if that's all right.'

'Yes, feel free to have a look at whatever catches your eye, my dear, though I fear much of this collection is more suited to dusty academics like myself.'

Keeler smiled as she got up from the table. 'I may not be a documentarist, but I know which end of a book to read, Kyril.'

'Of course you do, I didn't mean to suggest–'

'Too easy,' she said and wandered off into the stacks to browse while Sindermann returned to his books.

Despite her quip, she soon realised that Sindermann was exactly right. She spent the next hour wandering up and down shelves packed with scrolls, books and musty, loose-leaf manuscripts. Most of the books had unfathomable titles like *Reading Astrologies and Astrotelepathic Auguries, Malefic Abjurations and the Multifarious Horrores Associated wyth Such Workes* or *The Book of Atum*.

As she passed this last book, she felt a shiver travel the length her spine and reached up to slide the book from the shelf. The smell of its worn leather binding was strong, and though she had no real wish to read the book, she couldn't deny the strange attraction it held for her.

The book creaked open in her grip, and the dust of centuries wafted from its pages as she opened them. She coughed, hearing Sindermann reading aloud from the *Book of Lorgar* as he translated more of the text.

Surprisingly, the words before her were written in a language she could understand, and her eyes quickly scanned the page. Sindermann's words came again, and it took Euphrati a moment to register that the words she was hearing echoed the words she was seeing on the page, the letters blurring and rearranging themselves before her very eyes. The faded script seemed to illuminate from within, and as she read what they said, the book's pages burst into flames. She dropped the book with a cry of alarm.

She turned and ran back towards where she had left Sindermann, turning the corner to see him reading aloud from the book with a terrified expression on his face. He gripped the edges of the book as though unable to let go, the words pouring from him in a flood of voices.

A crackling, electric sensation set Euphrati's teeth on edge and she cried out in terror as she saw a swirling cloud of bluish light hovering above the desk. The image twisted and jerked in the air, moving as though out of sync with the world around it.

'Kyril! What's happening?' she screamed as the terror of the Whisperheads returned to her with paralysing force and she dropped to her knees. Sindermann didn't answer, the words streaming from his unwilling mouth and his eyes fixed in terror on the unnatural sight above him. She could tell the same fear that she felt was also running hot in his veins.

The light bulged and stretched as though something was pushing through from beyond, and an iridescent, questing limb oozed from its depths. Keeler felt the anger that had consumed her in the months following her attack break through the fear and she surged to her feet.

Keeler ran towards Sindermann and gripped his skinny wrists, as the suggestion of a rippling body of undulating, glowing flesh began tearing through the light.

His hands were locked on the book, the knuckles white, and she couldn't prise them loose as he continued to give voice to the terrible words within its pages.

'Kyril! Let go of the damn book!' she cried as an awful ripping sound came from above. She risked a look upwards, and saw yet more tentacled limbs pushing through the light in an obscene parody of birth.

'I'm sorry, Kyril!' she shouted and punched the iterator across the jaw. He pitched backwards out of his chair, and the torrent of words was cut off as the book fell from his hands. She quickly circled the table and lifted Sindermann to his feet. As she did so, she heard a grotesque sucking sound and a hard, wet thud of something heavy landing on the table.

Euphrati didn't waste time looking back, but took off as fast as she could towards the stacks, supporting the lurching Sindermann as she went. The pair of them staggered away from the table as a glittering light behind them threw their shadows out before them, and a cackling shriek like laughter washed over them.

Keeler heard a whoosh of air and something bright and hot flashed past her, exploding against the shelves with a hot bang like a firework. The wood hissed and spat where it had been struck, and she looked over her shoulder to see a horror of flailing limbs and glowing, twisting flesh leap after them. It moved with a rippling motion, lunatic faces, eyes and cackling mouths forming and reforming from the liquid matter of its body. Blue and red light flared from within it, strobing in dazzling beams through the archive.

Another bolt of phosphorescent brightness streaked towards them, and Keeler threw herself and Sindermann flat as it blasted the shelf beside them, sending flaming books and splintered chunks of wood flying. The horrifying monster loped through the stacks on long, elastic limbs, its speed and agility incredible, and Keeler could see that it was circling around to get behind them.

She dragged Sindermann to his feet as she heard the monster's maddening laughter cackling behind her. The iterator seemed to have regained some measure of his senses after her punch, and once again, they ran between the twisting, narrow rows of shelves towards the chamber's exit. Behind her, she could hear the whoosh of flames as the horror squeezed its body into the row and books erupted into geysers of pink fire.

The end of the row was just ahead of her and she almost laughed as she heard the claxons that warned of a fire screech in alarm. Surely, someone would come to help them now?

They burst from the end of the row and Sindermann stumbled, again carrying her to the floor with him. They fell in a tangle of limbs, scrambling desperately to put some distance between them and the loathsome monster.

Keeler rolled onto her back as it pushed itself from the row of shelves, its rippling bulk undulating with roiling internal motion. Leering eyes and wide, fang-filled mouths erupted across its amorphous body, and she screamed as it vomited a breath of searing blue fire towards her.

Though she knew it would do no good, she closed her eyes and threw her arms up to ward off the flames, but a sudden silence enveloped her and the expected burning agony never hit.

'Hurry!' said a trembling voice. 'I cannot hold it much longer.'

Keeler turned and saw the white robed form of the *Vengeful Spirit*'s Mistress of Astropaths, Ing Mae Sing, standing in the archive chamber's doorway with her hands outstretched before her.

'Horus, my brother,' said Magnus. 'You must not believe whatever he has told you. It is lies, all of it. Lies that disguise his sinister purpose.'

'Those with courage and character to speak the truth always seem sinister to the ignorant,' snarled Erebus. 'You dare speak of lies while you stand before us in the warp? How can this be without the use of sorcery? Sorcery you were expressly forbidden to practise by the Emperor himself.'

'Do not presume to judge me, whelp!' shouted Magnus, hurling a glittering ball of fire towards the First Chaplain. Horus watched as the flame streaked towards Erebus and enveloped him, but as the fire died, he saw that Erebus was unharmed, his armour not so much as scratched, and his skin unblemished.

Erebus laughed. 'You are too far away, Magnus. Your powers cannot reach me here.'

Horus watched as Magnus hurled bolt after bolt of lightning from his fingertips, amazed and horrified to see his brother employing such powers. Though all the Legions had once had Librarius divisions that trained warriors to tap into the power of the warp, they had been disbanded after the Emperor's decree at the Council of Nikaea.

Clearly, Magnus had paid that order no mind, and such conceit staggered Horus.

Eventually his cyclopean brother recognised that his powers were having no effect on Erebus and he dropped his hands to his side.

'You see,' said Erebus, turning to Horus, 'he cannot be trusted.'

'Nor can you, Erebus,' said Horus. 'You come to me cloaked in the identity of another, you claim my brother Magnus is naught but some warp beast set upon devouring me, and then you speak to him as though he is exactly as he seems. If he is here by sorcery, then how else can you be here?'

Erebus paused, caught in his lie and said, 'You are right, my lord. The sorcery of the Serpent Lodge has sent me to you to help you, and to offer you this chance of life. The serpent priestess had to cut my throat to do it and once I return to the world of flesh I will kill the bitch for that, but know that everything I have shown you is real. You saw it yourself and you know the truth.'

Magnus towered over the figure of Erebus. His crimson mane shook with fury, but Horus saw that he kept tight rein on his anger as he spoke.

'The future is not set, Horus. Erebus may have shown you *a* future, but that is only one possible future. It is not absolute. Have faith in that.'

'Pah!' sneered Erebus. 'Faith is just another way of not wanting to know what is true.'

'You think I don't know that, Magnus?' snapped Horus. 'I know of the warp and the tricks it can play with the mind. I am not stupid. I knew that this was not Sejanus just as I know that without a context, everything I have seen here is meaningless.'

Horus saw the crestfallen look on Erebus's face and laughed. 'You must take me for a fool, Erebus, if you thought that such simple parlour tricks would bewitch me to your cause.'

'My brother,' smiled Magnus. 'You are a wonder to me.'

'Be quiet,' snarled Horus. 'You are no better than Erebus. You will not manipulate me like this, for I am Horus. I am the Warmaster!'

Horus relished their confusion.

One was his brother, the other a warrior he had counted as a valued counsellor and devoted follower. He had sorely misjudged them both.

'I can trust neither of you,' he said. 'I am Horus and I make my own fate.'

Erebus stepped towards him with his hands outstretched in supplication. 'You should know that I came to you at the behest of my lord and master, Lorgar. He already has knowledge of the Emperor's quest to ascend to godhood, and has sworn himself to the powers of the warp. When the Emperor rejected Lorgar's worship, he found other gods all too willing to accept his devotion. My primarch's power has grown tenfold and it is but a fraction of the power that could be yours were you to pledge yourself to their cause.'

'He lies!' cried Magnus. 'Lorgar is loyal. He would never turn against the Emperor.'

Horus listened to Erebus's words and knew with utter certainty that he spoke the truth.

Lorgar, his most beloved brother had already embraced the power of the warp? Warring emotions vied for supremacy within him, disappointment, anger and, if he was honest, a spark of jealousy that Lorgar should have been chosen first.

If wise Lorgar would choose such powers as patrons, was there not some merit in that?

'Horus,' said Magnus, 'I am running out of time. Please be strong, my brother. Think of what this mongrel dog is asking you to do. He would have you spit on your oaths of loyalty. He is forcing you to betray the Emperor and turn on your brother Astartes! You must trust the Emperor to do what is right.'

'The Emperor plays dice with the fate of the galaxy,' countered Erebus, 'and he throws them where they cannot be seen.'

'Horus, please!' cried Magnus, his voice taking on a ghostly quality as his image began to fade. 'You must not do this or all we have fought for will be cast to ruin forever! You cannot do this terrible thing!'

'Is it so terrible?' asked Erebus. 'It is but a small thing really. Deliver the Emperor to the gods of the warp, and unlimited power can be yours. I told you before that they have no interest in the realms of men, and that promise still holds true. The galaxy will be yours to rule over as the new Master of Mankind.'

'Enough!' roared Horus and the world was silence. 'I have made my choice.'

Keeler helped Kyril Sindermann to his feet, and together they fled through the archive chamber's door. Ing Mae Sing's trembling arms were still outstretched, and Keeler could feel waves of psychic cold radiating from her with the effort of holding the horror within the chamber at bay.

'Close... the... door,' said Ing Mae Sing through gritted teeth. Veins stood out on her neck and forehead, and her porcelain features were lined with pain. Keeler didn't need to be told twice, and she dropped Sindermann to get the door, as Ing Mae Sing backed away with slow, shuffling steps.

'Now!' shouted the astropath, dropping her arms. Keeler hauled on the door as the roaring, seething laughter of the beast swelled once again. Alarm claxons and its shrieks of insanity filled her ears as the door swung shut.

Something heavy impacted on the other side, and she could feel its raw heat through the metal. Ing Mae Sing helped her, but the astropath was too frail to be of much use and Keeler knew they couldn't hold the door for long.

'What did you do?' demanded Ing Mae Sing.

'I don't know,' gasped Keeler. 'The iterator was reading from a book and that... thing just appeared from nowhere. What in the name of the Emperor is it?'

'A beast from beyond the gates of the empyrean,' said Ing Mae Sing as the door shook with another burning impact. 'I felt the build-up of warp energy and got here as quickly as I could.'

'Shame you weren't quicker, eh?' said Keeler. 'Can you send it back?'

Ing Mae Sing shook her head as a thrashing pseudopod of pinkish light flicked through the door and grazed Keeler's arm. Its touch seared through her robes and burned her skin. She screamed, flinching from the door, and gripped her arm in agony. The horror slammed into the door once more, and the impact sent her and the astropath flying.

Blinding light filled the passageway and Keeler shielded her eyes as she felt hands upon her shoulders, seeing that Kyril Sindermann was on his feet once more. He dragged her to her feet and said, 'I think I may have mistranslated part of the book...'

'You *think*?' snapped Keeler as they backed away from the abomination.

'Or maybe you translated it just perfectly,' said Ing Mae Sing, desperately scrambling away from the archive chamber's door. The beast of light oozed outwards in a slithering loop of limbs, each one thrashing in blind hunger. Multitudinous eyes rippled and popped like swollen boils across its rubbery skin as it came towards them once more.

'Oh Emperor protect us,' whispered Keeler as she turned to run.

The beast shuddered at her words, and Ing Mae Sing tugged on her sleeve, crying, 'Come on. We can't fight it.'

Euphrati Keeler suddenly realised that wasn't true and shrugged off the astropath's grip, reaching beneath her robes to pull out the Imperial eagle she kept on the end of her necklace. Its silver surfaces shone in the creature's dazzling light, brighter than it had any reason to be, and feeling hot in her palm. She smiled beatifically as she understood with complete clarity that everything since the Whisperheads had been preparing her for this moment.

'Euphrati! Come on!' shouted Sindermann in terror.

A whipping limb formed from the horror's body and another gout of blue fire roared towards her. Keeler stood firm before it and held the symbol of her faith out in front of her.

'The Emperor protects!' she screamed as the flames washed over her.

Rain fell in heavy sheets, and Loken could feel a tangible charge to the night air as dark thunderheads pressed down on the tens of thousands of people gathered around the Delphos. Lightning bolts fenced above him, and the sense of anticipation was almost unbearable.

Nine days had passed since the Warmaster had been interred within the Temple of the Serpent Lodge and with each passing day the weather had worsened. Rain fell in an unending downpour that threatened to wash away the makeshift camps of the pilgrims, and booming peals of thunder shook the sky like ringing hammer blows.

The Warmaster had once told Loken that the cosmos was too large and sterile for melodrama, but the skies above Davin seemed determined to prove him wrong.

Torgaddon and Vipus stood with him at the top of the steps and hundreds of the Sons of Horus followed behind the three of them. Company captains, squad leaders, file officers and warriors had come to Davin to witness what would be either their salvation or their undoing. They had marched through the singing crowds, the dirty beige robes of remembrancers mixed in with army uniforms and civilian dress.

'Looks like the entire bloody Expedition's here,' Torgaddon had said as they marched up the steps, trampling trinkets and baubles left as offerings to the Warmaster beneath their armoured boots.

From the top of the processional steps, Loken could see the same group he had faced nine days previously, with the exception of Maloghurst who had returned to the ship some days before. Rain ran down Loken's face as a flash of lightning lit up the surface of the great bronze gateway, making it shine like

a great wall of fire. The gathered Astartes warriors stood sentinel before it in the rain: Abaddon, Aximand, Targost, Sedirae,
Ekaddon and Kibre.

None of them had abandoned their vigil before the gates of
the Delphos, and Loken wondered if they had bothered to eat,
drink or sleep since he had last laid eyes upon them.

'What do we do now, Garvi?' asked Vipus.

'We join our brothers and wait.'

'Wait for what?'

'We'll know that when it happens,' said Torgaddon. 'Won't
we, Garvi?'

'I certainly hope so, Tarik,' replied Loken. 'Come on.'

The three of them set off towards the gateway, the thunder
echoing from the massive structure's sides and the snakes atop
each pillar slithering with each flashing bolt of lightning.

Loken watched as his brothers in front of the gate came to
stand in line at the edge of the rippling pool of water, the full
moon reflected in its black surface. Horus Aximand had once
called it an omen. Was it again? Loken didn't know whether to
hope that it was or not.

The Sons of Horus followed their captains down the wide
processional in their hundreds, and Loken kept a grip on his
temper, knowing that if things went ill here, there would almost
certainly be bloodshed.

The thought horrified him and he hoped with all his heart
that such a tragedy could be averted, but he would be ready if
it came to war...

'Are you battle-ready?' hissed Loken to Torgaddon and Vipus
on a discrete vox channel.

'Always,' nodded Torgaddon. 'Full load on every man.'

'Yes,' said Vipus. 'You really think...'

'No,' said Loken, 'but be ready in case we need to fight. Keep
your humours balanced and it will not come to that.'

'You too, Garvi,' warned Torgaddon.

The long column of Astartes warriors reached the pool, the
Warmaster's bearers standing on its opposite side, stoic and
unrepentant.

'Loken,' said Serghar Targost. 'Are you here to fight us?'

'No,' said Loken, seeing that, like them, the others were locked
and loaded. 'We've come to see what happens. It's been nine
days, Serghar.'

'It has indeed,' nodded Targost.

'Where is Erebus? Have you seen him since you put the Warmaster in this place?'

'No,' growled Abaddon, his long hair unbound and his eyes hostile. 'We have not. What does that have to do with anything?'

'Calm yourself, Ezekyle,' said Torgaddon. 'We're all here for the same thing.'

'Loken,' said Aximand, 'there has been bad blood between us all, but that must end now. For us to turn on one another would dishonour the Warmaster's memory.'

'You speak as though he's already dead, Horus.'

'We will see,' said Aximand. 'This was always a forlorn hope, but it was all we had.'

Loken looked into the haunted eyes of Horus Aximand, seeing the despair and doubt that plagued him, and felt his anger towards his brother diminish.

Would he have acted any differently had he been present when the decision to inter the Warmaster had been taken? Could he in all honesty say that he would not have accepted the decision of his friends and peers if the situation had been reversed? He and Horus Aximand might even now be standing on different sides of the moon-shimmered pool.

'Then let us wait as brothers united in hope,' said Loken, and Aximand smiled gratefully.

The palpable tension lifted from the confrontation and Loken, Torgaddon and Vipus marched around the pool to stand with their brothers before the vast gate.

A dazzling bolt of lightning reflected from the gate as the Mournival stood shoulder to shoulder with one another, and a thunderous boom, that had nothing to do with the storm, split the night.

Loken saw a dark line appear in the centre of the gate as the thunder was suddenly silenced and the lightning stilled in the space of a heartbeat. The sky was mystifyingly calm, as though the storm had blown out and the heavens had paused in their revelries better to witness the unfolding drama on the planet below.

Slowly, the gate began to open.

The flames bathed Euphrati Keeler, but they were cold and she felt no pain from them. The silver eagle blazed in her hand, thrust before her like a talisman, and she felt a wondrous energy fill her, rushing through her from the tips of her toes to the shorn ends of her hair.

'The power of the Emperor commands you, abomination!' she yelled, the words unfamiliar, but feeling right.

Ing Mae Sing and Kyril Sindermann watched her in amazement

as she took one step, and then another, towards the horror. The monster was transfixed; whether by her courage or her faith, she didn't know, but whatever the reason, she was thankful for it.

Its limbs flailed as though some invisible force attacked it, its screeching laughter turning into the pitiful wails of a child.

'In the name of the Emperor, go back to the warp, you bastard!' said Keeler, her confidence growing as the substance of the monster diminished, skins of light shearing away from its body. The silver eagle grew hotter in her hand and she could feel the skin of her palms blistering under its heat.

Ing Mae Sing joined her, adding her own powers to Keeler's assault on the monster. The air around the astropath grew colder and Keeler moved her hand close to the psyker in the hopes of cooling the blazing eagle.

The monster's internal light was fading and flickering, its nebulous outline spitting embers of light as though it fought to hold onto existence. The light from Keeler's eagle outshone its hellish illumination tenfold and the entire corridor was bleached shadowless with its brilliance.

'Whatever you're doing, keep doing it!' cried Ing Mae Sing. 'It's weakening.'

Keeler tried to answer, but found that she had no voice left. The wondrous energy that had filled her was now streaming from her through the eagle, taking her own strength with it.

She tried to drop the eagle, but it was stuck fast to her hand, the red hot metal fusing itself to her skin.

From behind her, Keeler heard the clatter of armoured ship's crew and their cries of astonishment at the scene before them.

'Please...' she whispered as her legs gave out and she collapsed to the floor.

The blazing light faded from her hand and the last things she saw were the disintegrating mass of the horror and Sindermann's rapturous face staring down at her in wonder.

The only sound was that of the gate. Loken's entire existence shrank to the growing darkness between its two halves, as he held his breath and waited to see what might lie beyond. The gates swung fully open and he risked a glance at his fellow Sons of Horus, seeing the same desperate hope in every face.

Not a single sound disturbed the night, and Loken felt melancholy rise in him as he realised that this must simply be the automated opening of the temple doors.

The Warmaster was dead.

A sick dread settled on Loken and his head sank to his chest.

Then he heard the sound of footsteps, and looked up to see the gleam of white and gold plate emerge from the darkness.

Horus strode from the Delphos with his cloak of royal purple billowing behind him and his golden sword held high above him.

The eye in the centre of his breastplate blazed a fiery red and the laurels at his forehead framed features that were beautiful and terrible in their magnificence.

The Warmaster stood before them, unbowed and more vital than ever, the sheer physicality of his presence robbing every one of them of speech.

Horus smiled and said, 'You are a sight for sore eyes, my sons.'

Torgaddon punched the air in elation and shouted, 'Lupercal!'

He laughed and ran towards the Warmaster, breaking the spell that had fallen on the rest of them.

The Mournival rushed to this reunion with their lord and master, joyous cries of 'Lupercal!' erupting from the throat of every Astartes warrior as word spread back through the files and into the crowd surrounding the temple.

The pilgrims around the Delphos took up the chant and ten thousand throats were soon crying the Warmaster's name.

'Lupercal! Lupercal! Lupercal!'

The walls of the crater shook to deafening cheers that went on long into the night.

PART FOUR
CRUSADE'S END

EIGHTEEN

Brothers
Assassination
This turbulent poet

Silver trails of molten metal had solidified on the breastplate and Mersadie Oliton had learned enough in her time with the Expedition fleet to know that it would require the aid of Legion artificers to repair it properly. Loken sat before her in the training halls, while other officers of the Sons of Horus were scattered throughout it, repairing armour and cleaning bolters or chainswords. Loken was melancholic, and she was quick to notice his sombre mood.

'Is the war not going well?' she asked as he removed the firing chamber from his bolter and pulled a cleaning rag through it. He looked up and she was struck by how much he had aged in the last ten months, thinking that she would need to revise her chapter on the immortality of the Astartes.

Since opening hostilities against the Auretian Technocracy, the Astartes had seen some of the hardest fighting since the Great Crusade had begun, and it was beginning to tell on many of them. There had been few opportunities to spend time with Loken during the war, and it was only now that she truly appreciated how much he had changed.

'It's not that,' said Loken. 'The Brotherhood is virtually destroyed and the warriors of Angron will soon storm the Iron Citadel. The war will be over within the week.'

'Then why so gloomy?'

Loken glanced around to see who else was in the training halls and leaned in close to her.

'Because this is a war we should not be fighting.'

Upon Horus's recovery on Davin, the fleet of the 63rd Expedition had paused just long enough to recover its personnel from the planet's surface and install a new Imperial commander from the ranks of the Army. Like Rakris before him, the new Lord Governor Elect, Tomaz Vesalias, had begged not to be left behind, but with Davin once again compliant, Imperial rule had to be maintained.

Before the fighting on Davin, the Warmaster's fleet had been en route to Sardis and a rendezvous with the 203rd Fleet. The plan was to undertake a campaign of compliance in the Caiades Cluster, but instead of keeping that rendezvous, the Warmaster had sent his compliments and ordered the 203rd's Master of Ships to muster with the 63rd Expedition in a binary cluster designated Drakonis Three Eleven.

The Warmaster told no one why he chose this locale, and none of the stellar cartographers could find reports from any previous expedition as to why the place might be of interest.

Sixteen weeks of warp travel had seen them translate into a system alive with electronic chatter. Two planets and their shared moon in the second system were discovered to be inhabited, glinting communications satellites ringing each one, and interplanetary craft flitting between them.

More thrilling still, communications with orbital monitors revealed this civilisation to be human, another lost branch of the old race – isolated these past centuries. The arrival of the Crusade fleet had been greeted with understandable surprise, and then joy as the planet's inhabitants realised that their lonely existence was finally at an end.

Formal, face-to-face contact was not established for three days, in which time the 203rd Expedition under the command of Angron of the XII Legion, the World Eaters, translated in-system.

The first shots were fired six hours later.

The ninth month of the war.

Bolter shells stitched a path towards Loken from the blazing muzzle of the bunker's gun. He ducked behind a shell-pocked cement column, feeling the impacts hammering through it and knowing that he didn't have much time until the gunfire chewed its way through.

'Garvi!' shouted Torgaddon, rolling from behind cover and shouldering his bolter. 'Go left, I've got you!'

Loken nodded and dived from behind the cover as Torgaddon opened up, his Astartes strength keeping the barrel level despite the bolter's fearsome recoil. Shells exploded in grey puffs of rockcrete at the bunker's firing slit and Loken heard screams of pain from within. Locasta moved up behind him and he heard the whoosh of flame units as warriors poured fire into the bunker.

More screams and the stink of flesh burned by chemical flame filled the air.

'Everyone back!' shouted Loken, getting to his feet and knowing what would come next.

Sure enough, the bunker mushroomed upwards with a thudding boom, its internal magazine cooking off as its internal sensors registered that its occupants were dead.

Heavy gunfire ripped through their position, a collapsed structure at the edge of the central precinct of the planet's towering city of steel and glass. Loken had marvelled at the city's elegance, and Peeter Egon Momus had declared it perfect when he had first seen the aerial scans. It didn't look perfect now.

Puffs of flickering detonations tore a line through the Astartes, and Loken dropped as the warrior with the flame unit disappeared in a column of fire. His armour kept him alive for a few seconds, but soon he was a burning statue, the armour joints fused, and Loken rolled onto his back to see a pair of speeding aircraft rolling around for another strafing run.

'Take those ships out!' yelled Loken as the craft, sleeker, more elegant Thunderhawk variants, turned their guns towards them once again.

The Astartes spread out as the under-slung gun pods erupted in fire, and a torrent of shells tore through their position, ripping thick columns in two and sending up blinding clouds of grey dust. Two warriors ducked out from behind a fallen wall, one aiming a long missile tube in the rough direction of the flier while the other sighted on it with a designator.

The missile launched in a streaming cloud of bright propellant, leaping into the sky and speeding after the closest flier. The pilot saw it and tried to evade, but he was too close to the ground and the missile flew straight into his intake, blowing the craft apart from the inside.

Its blazing remains plummeted towards the ground as Vipus shouted, 'Incoming!'

Loken turned to rebuke him for stating the obvious when he saw that his friend wasn't talking about the remaining flier. Three tracked vehicles smashed over a low ceramic brick wall

behind them, their thick armoured forward sections emblazoned with a pair of crossed lightning bolts.

Too late, Loken realised the fliers had been keeping them
pinned in place while the armoured transports circled around
to flank them. Through the smoking wreckage of the burning
bunker, he could see blurred forms moving towards them, darting from cover to cover as they advanced. Locasta was caught
between two enemy forces and the noose was closing in.

Loken chopped his hand at the approaching vehicles and the
missile team turned to engage their new targets. Within seconds, one was a smoking wreck as a missile punched through
its armour and its plasma core exploded inside.

'Tarik!' he shouted over the din of gunfire from nearby. 'Keep
our front secure.'

Torgaddon nodded, moving forwards with five warriors. Leaving him to it, Loken turned back towards the armoured vehicles
as they crunched to a halt, pintle-mounted bolters hammering
them with shots. Two men fell, their armour cracked open by
the heavy shells.

'Close on them!' ordered Loken as the frontal assault ramps
lowered and the Brotherhood warriors within charged out. The
first few times Loken had fought the Brotherhood, he'd felt a
treacherous hesitation seize his limbs, but nine months of gru-
elling campaigning had pretty much cured him of that.

Each warrior was armoured in fully enclosed plate, silver
like the knights of old, with red and black heraldry upon their
shoulder guards. Their form and function was horribly similar
to that of the Sons of Horus, and though the enemy warriors
were smaller than the Astartes, they were nevertheless a distorted mirror of them.

Loken and the warriors of Locasta were upon them, the lead
Brotherhood warriors raising their weapons in response to the
wild charge. The blade of Loken's chainsword hacked through the
nearest warrior's gun and cleaved into his breastplate. The Brotherhood scattered, but Loken didn't give them a chance to recover
from their surprise, cutting them down in quick, brutal strokes.

These warriors might look like Astartes, but, up close, they
were no match for even one of them.

He heard gunfire from behind, and heard Torgaddon issuing
orders to the men under his command. Stuttering impacts on
Loken's leg armour drove him to his knees and he swept his
sword low, hacking the legs from the enemy warrior behind
him. Blood jetted from the stumps of his legs as he fell, spraying Loken's armour red.

The vehicle began reversing, but Loken threw a pair of grenades inside, moving on as the dull crump of the detonations halted it in its tracks. Shadows loomed over them and he felt the booming footfalls of the Titans of the Legio Mortis as they marched past, crushing whole swathes of the city as they went. Buildings were smashed from their path, and though missiles and lasers reached up to them, the flare of their powerful void shields were proof against such attacks.

More gunfire and screams filled the battlefield, the enemy falling back from the fury of the Astartes counter-attack. They were courageous, these warriors of the Brotherhood, but they were hopelessly optimistic if they thought that simply wearing a suit of power armour made a man the equal of an Astartes.

'Area secure,' came Torgaddon's voice over the suit vox. 'Where to now?'

'Nowhere,' replied Loken as the last enemy warrior was slain. 'This is our object point. We wait until the World Eaters get here. Once we hand off to them, we can move on. Pass the word.'

'Understood,' said Torgaddon.

Loken savoured the sudden quiet of the battlefield, the sounds of battle muted and distant as other companies fought their way through the city. He assigned Vipus to secure their perimeter and crouched beside the warrior whose legs he had cut off.

The man still lived, and Loken reached down to remove his helmet, a helmet so very similar to his own. He knew where the release catches were and slid the helm clear.

His enemy's face was pale from shock and blood loss, his eyes full of pain and hate, but there were no monstrously alien features beneath the helmet, simply ones as human as any member of the 63rd Expedition.

Loken could think of nothing to say to the man, and simply took off his own helmet and pulled the water-dispensing pipe from his gorget. He poured some clear, cold water over the man's face.

'I want nothing from you,' hissed the dying man.

'Don't speak,' said Loken. 'It will be over quickly.'

But the man was already dead.

'Why shouldn't we be fighting this war?' asked Mersadie Oliton. 'You were there when they tried to assassinate the Warmaster.'

'I was there,' said Loken, putting down the cleaned firing chamber. 'I don't think I'll ever forget that moment.'

'Tell me about it.'

'It's not pretty,' warned Loken. 'You will think less of us when I tell you the truth of it.'

'You think so? A good documentarist remains objective at all times.'

'We'll see.'

The ambassadors of the planet, which Loken had learned was named Aureus, had been greeted with all the usual pomp and ceremony accorded to a potentially friendly culture. Their vessels had glided onto the embarkation deck to surprised gasps as every warrior present recognised their uncanny similarity to Stormbirds.

The Warmaster was clad in his most regal armour, gold fluted and decorated with the Emperor's devices of lightning bolts and eagles. Unusually for an occasion such as this, he was armed with a sword and pistol, and Loken could feel the force of authority the Warmaster projected.

Alongside the Warmaster stood Maloghurst, robed in white, Regulus – his gold and steel augmetic body polished to a brilliant sheen – and First Captain Abbadon, who stood proudly with a detachment of hulking Justaerin Terminators.

It was a gesture to show strength and backing it up, three hundred Sons of Horus stood at parade rest behind the group, noble and regal in their bearing – the very image of the Great Crusade – and Loken had never been prouder of his illustrious heritage.

The doors of the craft opened with the hiss of decompression and Loken had his first glimpse of the Brotherhood.

A ripple of astonishment passed through the embarkation deck as twenty warriors in gleaming silver plate armour, the very image of the assembled Astartes, marched from the landing craft's interior in perfect formation, though Loken detected a stammer of surprise in them too. They carried weapons that looked very much like a standard issue boltgun, though in deference to their hosts, none had magazines fitted.

'Do you see that?' whispered Loken.

'No, Garvi, I've suddenly been struck blind,' replied Torgaddon. 'Of course I see them.'

'They look like Astartes!'

'There's a resemblance, I'll give you that, but they're far too short.'

'They're wearing power armour... How is that possible?'

'If you keep quiet we might find out,' said Torgaddon.

The warriors wheeled and formed up around a tall man wearing long red robes, whose features were half-flesh, half machine and whose eye was a blinking emerald gem. Walking with the aid of a golden cog-topped staff, he stepped onto the deck with the pleased expression of one who finds his expectations more than met.

The Auretian delegation made its way towards Horus, and Loken could sense the weight of history pressing in on this moment. This meeting was the very embodiment of what the Great Crusade represented: lost brothers from across the galaxy once again meeting in the spirit of companionship.

The red robed man bowed before the Warmaster and said, 'Do I have the honour of addressing the Warmaster Horus?'

'You do, sir, but please do not bow,' replied Horus. 'The honour is mine.'

The man smiled, pleased at the courtesy. 'Then if you will permit me, I will introduce myself. I am Emory Salignac, Fabricator Consul to the Auretian Technocracy. On behalf of my people, may I be the first to welcome you to our worlds.'

Loken had seen Regulus's excitement at the sight of Salignac's augmetics, but upon hearing the full title of this new empire, his enthusiasm overcame the protocol of the moment.

'Consul,' said Regulus, his voice blaring and unnatural. 'Do I understand that your society is founded on the knowledge of technical data?'

Horus turned to the adept of the Mechanicum and whispered something that Loken didn't hear, but Regulus nodded and took a step back.

'I apologise for the adept's forthright questions, but I hope you might forgive his outburst, given that our warriors appear to share certain… similarities in their wargear.'

'These are the warriors of the Brotherhood,' explained Salignac. 'They are our protectors and our most elite soldiers. It honours me to have them as my guardians here.'

'How is it they are armoured so similarly to my own warriors?'

Salignac appeared to be confused by the question and said, 'You expected something different, my lord Warmaster? The construct machines our ancestors brought with them from Terra are at the heart of our society and provide us with the boon of technology. Though advanced, they do tend towards a certain uniformity of creation.'

The silence that greeted the consul's words was brittle and fragile, and Horus held up his hand to still the inevitable outburst from Regulus.

'Construct machines?' asked Horus, a cold edge of steel in his voice. 'STC machines?'

'I believe that was their original designation, yes,' agreed Salignac, lowering his staff and holding it towards the Warmaster. 'You have–'

Emory Salignac never got to finish his sentence as Horus took a step backward and drew his pistol. Loken saw the muzzle flash and watched Emory Salignac's head explode as the bolt blew out the back of his skull.

'Yes,' said Mersadie Oliton. 'The staff was some kind of energy weapon that could have penetrated the Warmaster's armour. We've been told this.'

Loken shook his head. 'No, there was no weapon.'

'Of course there was,' insisted Oliton, 'and when the consul's assassination attempt failed, his Brotherhood warriors attacked the Warmaster.'

Loken put down his bolter and said, 'Mersadie, forget what you have been told. There was no weapon, and after the Warmaster killed the consul, the Brotherhood only tried to escape. Their weapons were not loaded and they could not have fought us with any hope of success.'

'They were unarmed?'

'Yes.'

'So what did you do?'

'We killed them,' said Loken. 'They were unarmed, but we were not. Abaddon's Justaerin cut half a dozen of them down before they even knew what had happened. I led Locasta forward and we gunned them down as they tried to board their ship.'

'But why?' asked Oliton, horrified at his casual description of such slaughter.

'Because the Warmaster ordered it.'

'No, I mean why would the Warmaster shoot the consul if he wasn't armed? It doesn't make any sense.'

'No, it doesn't,' agreed Loken. 'I watched him kill the consul and I saw his face after we had killed the Brotherhood warriors.'

'What did you see?'

Loken hesitated, as though not sure he should answer. At last he said, 'I saw him smile.'

'Smile?'

'Yes,' said Loken, 'as if the killings had been part of his plan all along. I don't know why, but Horus *wants* this war.'

Torgaddon followed the hooded warrior down the darkened companionway towards the empty reserve armoury chamber. Serghar Targost had called a lodge meeting and Torgaddon was apprehensive, not liking the sensation one bit. He had attended only a single meeting since Davin, the quiet order no longer a place of relaxation for him. Though the Warmaster had been returned to them, the lodge's actions had smacked of subterfuge and such behaviour sat ill with Tarik Torgaddon.

The robed figure he followed was unknown to him, young and clearly in awe of the legendary Mournival officer, which suited Torgaddon fine. The warrior had clearly only achieved full Astartes status recently, but Torgaddon knew that he would already be an experienced fighter. There was no room for inexperience among the Sons of Horus, the months of war on Aureus making veterans or corpses of those raised from the novitiate and scout auxiliaries. The Brotherhood might not have the abilities of the Astartes, but the Technocracy could call on millions of them, and they fought with courage and honour.

It only made killing them all the harder. Fighting the megarachnids of Murder had been easy, their alien physiognomy repulsive to look upon and therefore easy to destroy.

The Brotherhood, though... they were so like the Sons of Horus that it was as though two Legions fought each other in some brutal civil war. Not one amongst the Legion had failed to experience a moment of pause at such a terrible image.

Torgaddon was saddened as he knew that, like the interex before them, the Brotherhood and the Auretian Technocracy would be destroyed.

A voice from the darkness ahead shook him from his sombre thoughts.

'Who approaches?'

'Two souls,' replied the young warrior.

'What are your names?' the figure asked, but Torgaddon did not recognise the voice.

'I can't say,' said Torgaddon.

'Pass, friends.'

Torgaddon and the warrior passed the guardian of the portal and entered the reserve armoury. The vaulted chamber was much larger than the aft hold where meetings had commonly been held, and when he stepped into the flickering candlelit space, he could see why Targost had chosen it.

Hundreds of warriors filled the armoury, each one hooded and holding a flickering candle. Serghar Targost, Ezekyle Abaddon, Horus Aximand and Maloghurst stood at the centre of the gathering; to one side of them stood First Chaplain Erebus.

Torgaddon looked around at the assembled Astartes and

couldn't escape the feeling that this meeting had been called for his benefit.

'You've been busy, Serghar,' he said. 'Been on a recruiting drive?'

'Since the Warmaster's recovery on Davin our stock has risen somewhat,' agreed Targost.

'So I see. Must be tricky keeping it secret now.'

'Amongst the Legion we no longer operate under a veil of secrecy.'

'Then why the same pantomime to enter?'

Targost smiled apologetically. 'Tradition, you understand?'

Torgaddon shrugged and crossed the chamber to stand before Erebus. He stared with undisguised hostility towards the First Chaplain and said, 'You have been keeping a low profile since Davin. Captain Loken wants to speak with you.'

'I'm sure he does,' replied Erebus, 'but I am not under his command. I do not answer to him.'

'Then you'll answer to me, you bastard!' snapped Torgaddon, drawing his combat knife from beneath his robes and holding it to Erebus's neck. Cries of alarm sounded at the sight of the knife, and Torgaddon saw the line of an old scar running across Erebus's neck.

'Looks like someone's already tried to cut your throat,' hissed Torgaddon. 'They didn't do a very good job of it, but don't worry, I won't make the same mistake.'

'Tarik!' cried Serghar Targost. 'You brought a weapon? You know they are forbidden.'

'Erebus owes us all an explanation,' said Torgaddon, pressing the knife against Erebus's jaw. 'This snake stole a kinebrach weapon from the Hall of Devices on Xenobia. He's the reason the negotiations with the interex failed. He's the reason the Warmaster was injured.'

'No, Tarik,' said Abaddon, moving to stand next to him and placing a hand on his wrist. 'The negotiations with the interex failed because they were meant to. The interex consorted with xenos breeds. They integrated with them. We could never have made peace with such people.'

'Ezekyle speaks the truth,' said Erebus.

'Shut your mouth,' snapped Torgaddon.

'Torgaddon, put the knife down,' said Horus Aximand. 'Please.'

Reluctantly, Torgaddon lowered his arm, the pleading tone of his Mournival brother making him realise the enormity of what he was doing in holding a knife to the throat of another Astartes, even one as untrustworthy as Erebus.

'We are not finished,' warned Torgaddon, pointing the blade at Erebus.

'I will be ready,' promised the Word Bearer.

'Both of you be silent,' said Targost. 'We have urgent matters to discuss that require you to listen. These last few months of war have been hard on everyone and no one fails to see the great tragedy inherent in fighting brother humans who look so very like us. Tensions are high, but we must remember that our purpose among the stars is to kill those who will not join with us.'

Torgaddon frowned at such a blunt mission statement, but said nothing as Targost continued his speech. 'We are Astartes and we were created to kill and conquer the galaxy. We have done all that has been asked of us and more, fighting for over two centuries to forge the new Imperium from the ashes of Old Night. We have destroyed planets, torn down cultures and wiped out entire species all because we were so ordered. We are killers, pure and simple, and we take pride in being the best at what we do!'

Cheering broke out at Targost's pronouncements, fists punching the air and hammering bulkheads, but Torgaddon had seen the iterators in action enough times to recognise cued applause. This speech was for his benefit and his alone, of that he was now certain.

'Now, as the Great Crusade draws to a close, we are lambasted for our ability to kill. Malcontents and agitators stir up trouble in our wake with bleating cries that we are too brutal, too savage and too violent. Our very own Lord Commander of the Army, Hektor Varvarus, demands blood for the actions of our grief-stricken brothers who returned the Warmaster to us while he lay dying. The traitor Varvarus demands that we be called to account for these regrettable deaths, and that we be punished for trying to save the Warmaster.'

Torgaddon flinched at the word 'traitor', shocked that Targost would openly use such an incendiary word to describe an officer as respected as Varvarus. But, as Torgaddon looked at the faces of the warriors around him, he saw only agreement with Targost's sentiment.

'Even civilians now feel they have the right to call us to account,' said Horus Aximand, taking up where Targost had left off and holding up a handful of parchments. 'Dissenters and conspirators amongst the remembrancers spread lies and propaganda that paint us as little better than barbarians.'

Aximand circled amongst the gathering, passing out the pamphlets as he spoke, 'This one is called *The Truth is all We Have* and it calls us murderers and savages. This turbulent poet mocks us in verse, brothers! These lies circulate amongst the fleet every day.'

Torgaddon took a pamphlet from Aximand and quickly scanned the paper, already knowing who had written it. Its contents were scathing, but hardly amounted to sedition.

'And this one!' cried Aximand. 'The Lectitio Divinitatus speaks of the Emperor as a god. A god! Can you imagine anything so ridiculous? These lies fill the heads of those we are fighting for. We fight and die for them and this is our reward: vilification and hate. I tell you this, my brothers, if we do not act now, the ship of the Imperium, which has weathered all storms, will sink through the mutiny of those onboard.'

Shouts of anger and calls for action echoed from the armoury walls, and Torgaddon did not like the ugly desire for reciprocity that he saw on the faces of his fellow warriors.

'Nice speech,' said Torgaddon when the roars of anger had diminished, 'but why don't you get to the point? I have a company to make ready for a combat drop.'

'Always the straight talker, eh, Tarik?' said Aximand. 'That is why you are respected and valued. That is why we need you with us, brother.'

'With you? What are you talking about?'

'Have you not heard a word that was said?' asked Maloghurst, limping over to where Torgaddon stood. 'We are under threat from within our own ranks. The enemy within, Tarik, it is the most insidious foe we have yet faced.'

'You'll need to speak plainly, Mal,' said Abaddon. 'Tarik needs it spelled out for him.'

'Up yours, Ezekyle,' said Torgaddon.

'I have learned that the remembrancer who writes these treasonous missives is called Ignace Karkasy,' said Maloghurst. 'He must be silenced.'

'Silenced? What do you mean by that?' asked Torgaddon. 'Given a slap on the wrist? Told not to be such a naughty boy? Something like that?'

'You know what I mean, Tarik,' stated Maloghurst.

'I do, but I want to hear you say it.'

'Very well, if you wish me to be direct, then I will be. Karkasy must die.'

'You're crazy, Mal, do you know that? You're talking about murder,' said Torgaddon.

'It's not murder when you kill your enemy, Tarik,' said Abaddon. 'It's war.'

'You want to make war on a poet?' laughed Torgaddon. 'Oh, they'll tell tales of that for centuries, Ezekyle. Can't you hear what you're saying? Anyway, the remembrancer is under Garviel's protection. You touch Karkasy and he'll hand your head to the Warmaster himself.'

A guilty silence enveloped the group at the mention of Loken's name, and the lodge members in front of Torgaddon shared an uneasy look.

Finally, Maloghurst said, 'I had hoped it would not come to this, but you leave us no choice, Tarik.'

Torgaddon gripped the hilt of his combat knife tightly, wondering if he would need to fight his way clear of his brothers.

'Put up your knife, we're not about to attack you,' snapped Maloghurst, seeing the tension in his eyes.

'Go on,' said Torgaddon, keeping a grip on the knife anyway. 'What did you hope it would not come to?'

'Hektor Varvarus claims to have spoken with the Council of Terra about events surrounding the Warmaster's injury, and it is certain that if he has not yet informed Malcador the Sigillite of the deaths on the embarkation deck, he soon will. He petitions the Warmaster daily with demands that there be justice.'

'And what has the Warmaster told him? I was there too. So was Ezekyle. You too Little Horus.'

'And so was Loken,' finished Erebus, joining the others. 'He led you onto the embarkation deck and he led the way through the crowd.'

Torgaddon took a step towards Erebus. 'I told you to be quiet!'

He turned from Erebus, and despair filled him as he saw acquiescent looks on his brothers' faces. They had already accepted the idea of throwing Garviel Loken to the wolves.

'You can't seriously be considering this, Mal,' protested Torgaddon. 'Ezekyle? Horus? You would betray your sworn Mournival brother?'

'He already betrays us by allowing this remembrancer to spread lies,' said Aximand.

'No, I won't do it,' swore Torgaddon.

'You must,' said Aximand. 'Only if you, Ezekyle and I swear oaths that it was Loken who orchestrated the massacre will Varvarus accept him as guilty.'

'So, that's what this is all about, is it?' asked Torgaddon. 'Two birds with one stone? Make Garviel your scapegoat, and you're free to murder Karkasy. How can you even consider this? The Warmaster will never agree to it.'

'Bluntly put, but you are mistaken if you think the Warmaster will not agree,' said Targost. 'This was his suggestion.'

'No!' cried Torgaddon. 'He wouldn't...'

'It can be no other way, Tarik,' said Maloghurst. 'The survival of the Legion is at stake.'

Torgaddon felt something inside him die at the thought of betraying his friend. His heart broke at making a choice between Loken and the Sons of Horus, but no sooner had the thought surfaced than he knew what he had to do.

He sheathed his combat knife and said, 'If betrayal and murder is needed to save the Legion then perhaps it does not deserve to survive! Garviel Loken is our brother and you would betray his honour like this? I spit on you for even thinking it.'

A horrified gasp spread through the chamber and angry mutterings closed in on Torgaddon.

'Think carefully, Tarik,' warned Maloghurst. 'You are either with us or against us.'

Torgaddon reached into his robes and tossed something silver and gleaning at Maloghurst's feet. The lodge medal glinted in the candlelight.

'Then I am against you,' said Torgaddon.

NINETEEN

Isolated
Allies
Eagle's wing

Petronella sat at her escritoire, filling page after page with her cramped handwriting, the spidery script tight and intense. Her dark hair was unbound and fell around her shoulders in untidy ringlets. Her complexion had the sallow appearance of one who has not stepped outside her room for many months, let alone seen daylight.

A pile of papers beside her was testament to the months she had spent in her luxurious cabin, though its luxury was a far cry from what it had been when she had first arrived on the *Vengeful Spirit*. The bed was unmade and her clothes lay strewn where she had discarded them before bed.

Her maidservant, Babeth, had done what she could to encourage her mistress to pause in her labours, but Petronella would have none of it. The words of the Warmaster's valediction had to be transcribed and interpreted in the most minute detail if she was to do his confession any justice. Even though his words had turned out not to be his last, she knew they deserved to be recorded, for she had tapped into the Warmaster's innermost thoughts. She had teased out information no one had contemplated before, secrets of the primarchs that had not seen the light of day since the Great Crusade had begun and truths that would rock the Imperium to its very core.

That such things should perhaps remain buried had occurred

to her only once in her lonely sojourn, but she was the Palatina Majoria of House Carpinus and such questions had no meaning. Knowledge and truth were all that mattered and it would be for future generations to judge whether she had acted correctly.

She had a dim memory of speaking of these incredible truths to some poet or other in a dingy bar many months ago while very drunk, but she had no idea what had passed between them. He had not tried to contact her afterwards, so she could only assume that he hadn't tried to seduce her, or that she hadn't in fact been seduced. It was immaterial; she had locked herself away since the beginning of the war with the Technocracy, trawling every fragment of her mnemonic implants for the words and turns of phrase that the Warmaster had used.

She was writing too much, she knew, but damn the word count, her tale was too important to be constrained by the bindings of a mere book. She would tell the tale for as long as it took in the telling... but there was something missing.

As the weeks and months had passed, the gnawing sensation that something wasn't gelling grew from a suspicion to a certainty, and it had taken her until recently to realise what that was: context.

All she had were the Warmaster's words, there was no framework to hang them upon and without that, everything was meaningless. Finally realising what was amiss, she sought out Astartes warriors at every opportunity, but hit her first real obstacle in this regard.

No one was speaking to her.

As soon as any of her subjects knew what Petronella wanted, or who she was, they would clam up and refuse to speak another word, excusing themselves from her presence with polite abruptness.

Everywhere she had turned, she ran into walls of silence, and despite repeated entreaties to the office of the Warmaster to intervene, she was getting nowhere. Every one of her requests for an audience with the Warmaster was declined, and she soon began to despair of ever finding a means of telling her tale.

Inspiration as to how to break this deadlock had come yesterday after yet another afternoon of abject failure. As always, Maggard escorted her, clad in his golden battle armour and armed with his Kirlian rapier and pistol. After the fighting on Davin, Maggard had made a speedy recovery, and Petronella had noticed a more cocksure swagger to his step. She also noticed that he was treated with more respect around the ship than she was. Of course, such a state of affairs was intolerable, despite the fact that it made his vigour as her concubine that much more forceful and pleasurable.

An Astartes warrior had nodded in respect as Petronella despondently travelled along the upper decks of the ship towards her stateroom. She had made to nod back, before realising that the Astartes had been paying his respects to Maggard, not her.

A scroll upon the Astartes's shoulder guard bore a green crescent moon, marking him out as a veteran of the Davin campaign and thus no doubt aware of Maggard's fighting prowess.

Indignation surged to the surface, but before Petronella said anything, an idea began to form and she hurried back to the stateroom.

Petronella had stood Maggard in the centre of the room and said, 'It's so obvious to me now, shame on me for not thinking of this sooner.'

Maggard looked puzzled, and she moved closer to him, stroking her hand down his moulded breastplate. He seemed uncomfortable with this, but she pressed on, knowing that he would do anything for her in fear of reprisal should he refuse.

'It's because I am a woman,' she said. 'I'm not part of their little club.'

She moved behind him and stood on her tiptoes, placing her hands on his shoulders. 'I'm not a warrior. I've never killed anyone, well, not myself, and that's what they respect: killing. You've killed men, haven't you Maggard?'

He nodded curtly.

'Lots?'

Maggard nodded again and she laughed. 'I'm sure they know that too. You can't speak to boast of your prowess, but I'm sure the Astartes know it. Even the ones that weren't on Davin will be able to see that you're a killer.'

Maggard licked his lips, keeping his golden eyes averted from her.

'I want you to go amongst them,' she ordered. 'Let them see you. Inveigle yourself into their daily rituals. Find out all you can about them and each day we will use the mnemo-quill to transcribe what you've discovered. You're mute, so they'll think you simple. Let them. They will be less guarded if they think they humour a dolt.'

She could see that Maggard was unhappy with this task, but his happiness was of no consequence to her and she had sent him out the very next morning.

She had spent the rest of the day writing, sending Babeth out for food and water when she realised she was hungry, and trying different stylistic approaches to the introduction of her manuscript.

The door to her stateroom opened and Petronella looked up from her work. The chronometer set into the escritoire told her that it was late afternoon, ship time.

She swivelled in her chair to see Maggard enter her room and smiled, reaching over to pull her data-slate close and then lifting the mnemo-quill from the Lethe-well.

'You spent time with the Astartes?' she asked.

Maggard nodded.

'Good,' said Petronella, sitting the reactive nib on the slate and clearing her mind of her own thoughts.

'Tell me everything,' she commanded, as the quill began to scratch out his thoughts.

The Warmaster's sanctum was silent save for the occasional hissing, mechanical hum from the exo-armature of Regulus's body, and the rustle of fabric as Maloghurst shifted position. Both stood behind the Warmaster, who sat in his chair at the end of the long table, his hands steepled before him and his expression thunderous.

'The Brotherhood should be carrion food by now,' he said. 'Why have the World Eaters not yet stormed the walls of the Iron Citadel?'

Captain Khârn, equerry to Angron himself, stood firm before the Warmaster's hostile stare, the dim light of the sanctum reflecting from the blue and white of his plate armour.

'My lord, its walls are designed to resist almost every weapon we have available, but I assure you the fortress will be ours within days,' said Khârn.

'You mean mine,' growled the Warmaster.

'Of course, Lord Warmaster,' replied Khârn.

'And tell my brother Angron to get up here. I haven't seen hide nor hair of him in months. I'll not have him sulking in some muddy trench avoiding me just because he can't deliver on his promises.'

'If I may be so bold, my primarch told you that this battle would take time,' explained Khârn. 'The citadel was built with the old technology and needs siege experts like the Iron Warriors to break it open.'

'And if I could contact Perturabo, I would have him here,' said the Warmaster.

Regulus spoke from behind the Warmaster. 'The STC machines will be able to counter much of the Mechanicum's arsenal. If the Dark Age texts are correct, they will adapt and react to changing circumstances, creating ever more cunning means of defence.'

'The citadel may be able to adapt,' said Captain Khârn, angrily gripping the haft of his axe, 'but it will not be able to stand before the fury of the XII Legion. The sons of Angron will tear the beating heart from that fortress for you, Warmaster. Have no doubt of that.'

'Fine words, Captain Khârn,' said Horus. 'Now storm that citadel for me. Kill everyone you find within.'

The World Eater bowed and turned on his heel, marching from the sanctum.

Once the doors slid shut behind Khârn, Horus said, 'That ought to light a fire under Angron's backside. This war is taking too damn long. There is other business to be upon.'

Regulus and Maloghurst came around from behind the Warmaster, the equerry taking a seat to ease his aching body.

'We must have those STC machines,' said Regulus.

'Yes, thank you, adept, I had quite forgotten that,' said Horus. 'I know very well what those machines represent, even if the fools who control them do not.'

'My order will compensate you handsomely for them, my lord,' said Regulus.

Horus smiled and said, 'At last we come to it, adept.'

'Come to what, my lord?'

'Do not think me a simpleton, Regulus,' cautioned Horus. 'I know of the Mechanicum's quest for the ancient knowledge. Fully functional construct machines would be quite a prize, would they not?'

'Beyond imagining,' admitted Regulus. 'To rediscover the thinking engines that drove humanity into the stars and allowed the colonisation of the galaxy is a prize worth any price.'

'Any price?' asked Horus.

'These machines will allow us to achieve the unimaginable, to reach into the Halo Stars and perhaps even other galaxies,' said Regulus. 'So yes, any price is worth paying.'

'Then you shall have them,' said Horus.

Regulus seemed taken aback by such a monumentally grand offer and said, 'I thank you, Warmaster. You cannot imagine the boon you grant the Mechanicum.'

Horus stood and circled behind Regulus, staring unabashedly at the remnants of flesh that clung to his metallic components. Shimmering fields contained the adept's organs, and a brass musculature gave him a measure of mobility.

'There is little of you that can still be called human, isn't there?' asked Horus. 'In that regard you are not so different from myself or Maloghurst.'

'My lord?' replied Regulus. 'I aspire to the perfection of the machine state, but would not presume to compare myself with the Astartes.'

'As well you should not,' said Horus, continuing to pace around the sanctum. 'I will give you these construct machines, but as we have established, there will be a price.'

'Name it, my lord. The Mechanicum will pay it.'

'The Great Crusade is almost at an end, Regulus, but our efforts to secure the galaxy are only just beginning,' said Horus, leaning over the table and planting his hands on its black surface. 'I am poised to embark on the greatest endeavour imaginable, but I need allies, or all will come to naught. Can I count on you and the Mechanicum?'

'What is this great endeavour?' asked Regulus.

Horus waved his hand and came around the table to stand next to the adept of the Mechanicum once more, placing a reassuring hand on his brass armature.

'No need to go into the details just now,' he said. 'Just tell me that you and your brethren will support me when the time comes and the construct machines are yours.'

A whirring mechanical arm wrapped in gold mesh swung over the table and placed a polished machine-cog gently on its surface.

'As much of the Mechanicum as I command is yours, Warmaster,' promised Regulus, 'and as much strength as I can muster from those I do not.'

Horus smiled and said, 'Thank you, adept. That's all I wanted to hear.'

On the sixth day of the tenth month of the war against the Auretian Technocracy, the 63rd Expedition was thrown into panic when a group of vessels translated in-system behind it, in perfect attack formation.

Boas Comnenus attempted to turn his ships to face the new arrivals, but even as the manoeuvres began, he knew it would be too late. Only when the mysterious ships reached, and then passed, optimal firing range, did those aboard the *Vengeful Spirit* understand that the vessels had no hostile intent.

Relieved hails were sent from the Warmaster's flagship to be met with an amused voice that spoke with the cultured accent of Old Terra.

'Horus, my brother,' said the voice. 'It seems I still have a thing or two to teach you.'

On the bridge of the *Vengeful Spirit*, Horus said, 'Fulgrim.'

Despite the hardships of the war, Loken was excited at the prospect of meeting the warriors of the Emperor's Children once again. He had spent as much time as his duties allowed in repairing his armour, though he knew it was still in a sorry state. He and the Mournival stood behind the Warmaster as he waited proudly on the upper transit dock of the *Vengeful Spirit*, ready to receive the primarch of the III Legion.

Fulgrim had been one of the Warmaster's staunchest supporters since his elevation to Warmaster, easing the concerns of Angron, Perturabo and Curze when they raged against the honour done to Horus and not them. Fulgrim's voice had been the breath of calm that had stilled bellicose hearts and soothed ruffled pride.

Without Fulgrim's wisdom, Loken knew that it was unlikely that the Warmaster would ever have been able to command the loyalty of the Legions so completely.

He heard metallic scrapes from beyond the pressure door.

Loken had seen Fulgrim once before at the Great Triumph on Ullanor, and even though it had been from a distance as he had marched past with tens of thousands of other Astartes warriors, Loken's impression of the primarch had never faded from his mind.

It was a palpable honour to stand once again in the presence of two such godlike beings as the primarchs.

The eagle-stamped pressure door slid open and the primarch of the Emperor's Children stepped onto the *Vengeful Spirit*.

Loken's first impression was of the great golden eagle's wing that swept up over Fulgrim's left shoulder. The primarch's armour was brilliant purple, edged in bright gold and inlaid with the most exquisite carvings. Hooded bearers carried his long, scaled cloak, and trailing parchments hung from his shoulder guards.

A high collar of deepest purple framed a face that was pale to the point of albinism, the eyes so dark as to be almost entirely pupil. The hint of a smile played around his lips and his hair was a shimmering white.

Loken had once called Hastur Sejanus a beautiful man, adored by all, but seeing the primarch of the Emperor's Children up close for the first time, he knew that his paltry vocabulary was insufficient for the perfection he saw in Fulgrim.

Fulgrim opened his arms and the two primarchs embraced like long-lost brothers.

'It has been too long, Horus,' said Fulgrim.

'It has, my brother, it has,' agreed Horus. 'My heart sings to see you, but why are you here? You were prosecuting a campaign throughout the Perdus Anomaly. Is the region compliant already?'

'What worlds we found there are now compliant, yes,' nodded Fulgrim as four warriors stepped through the pressure door behind him. Loken smiled to see Saul Tarvitz, his patrician features unable to contain his relish at being reunited with his brothers of the Sons of Horus.

Lord Commander Eidolon came next, looking as unrepentantly viperous as Torgaddon had described him. Lucius the swordsman came next, still with the same sardonic expression of superiority that he remembered, though his face was now heavily scarred. Behind him came a warrior Loken did not recognise, a sallow skinned Astartes in the armour of an Apothecary, with gaunt cheeks and a long mane of hair as white as that of his primarch.

Fulgrim turned from Horus and said, 'I believe you are already familiar with some of my brothers, Tarvitz, Lucius and Lord Commander Eidolon, but I do not believe you have met my Chief Apothecary, Fabius.'

'It is an honour to meet you, Lord Horus,' said Fabius, bowing low.

Horus acknowledged the gesture of respect and said, 'Come now, Fulgrim, you know better than to try to stall me. What's so important that you turn up here unannounced and give half of my crew heart attacks?'

The smile fell from Fulgrim's pale lips and he said, 'There have been reports, Horus.'

'Reports? What does that mean?'

'Reports that things are not as they should be,' replied Fulgrim, 'that you and your warriors should be called to account for the brutality of this campaign. Is Angron up to his usual tricks?'

'Angron is as he has always been.'

'That bad?'

'No, I keep him on a short leash, and his equerry, Khârn, seems to curb the worst of our brother's excesses.'

'Then I have arrived just in time.'

'I see,' said Horus. 'Are you here to relieve me then?'

Fulgrim could keep a straight face no longer and laughed, his dark eyes sparkling with mirth. 'Relieve you? No, my brother, I am here so that I can return and tell those fops and scribes on Terra that Horus fights war the way it is meant to be fought: hard, fast and cruel.'

'War *is* cruelty. There is no use trying to reform it. The crueller it is, the sooner it is over.'

Fulgrim said, 'Indeed, my brother. Come, there is much for us to talk about, for these are strange times we live in. It seems our brother Magnus has once again done something to upset the Emperor, and the Wolf of Fenris has been unleashed to escort him back to Terra.'

'Magnus?' asked Horus, suddenly serious. 'What has he done?'

'Let us talk of it in private,' said Fulgrim. 'Anyway, I have a feeling my subordinates would welcome the chance to reacquaint themselves with your... what do you call it? Mournival?'

'Yes,' smiled Horus. 'Memories of Murder no doubt.'

Loken felt a chill travel down his spine as he recognised the smile on Horus's face, the same one he had worn right after he had blown out the Auretian consul's brains on the embarkation deck.

With Horus and Fulgrim gone, Abaddon and Aximand, together with Eidolon, followed the two primarchs, while Loken and Torgaddon exchanged greetings with the Emperor's Children. The Sons of Horus welcomed their brothers with laughter and crushing bear hugs, the Emperor's Children with decorum and reserve.

For Torgaddon and Tarvitz it was a reunion of comrades, with a mutual respect forged in the heat of battle, their easy friendship clear for all to see.

The Apothecary, Fabius, requested directions to the medicae deck and excused himself with a bow upon receiving them.

Lucius remained with the two members of the Mournival, and Torgaddon couldn't resist baiting him just a little. 'So, Lucius, you fancy another round in the training cages with Garviel? From the look of your face you could do with the practice.'

The swordsman had the good grace to smile, the many scars twisting on his flesh, and said, 'No thank you. I fear I may have grown beyond Captain Loken's last lesson. I would not want to humble him this time.'

'Come on, just one bout?' asked Loken. 'I promise I'll be gentle.'

'Yes, come on, Lucius,' said Tarvitz. 'The honour of the Emperor's Children is at stake.'

Lucius smiled. 'Very well, then.'

✠ ✠ ✠

Loken could not remember much of the bout; it had been over
so quickly. Evidently, Lucius had indeed learned his lesson
well. No sooner had the practice cage shut than the swordsman attacked. Loken had been ready for such a move, but even
so, was almost overwhelmed in the first seconds of the fight.

The two warriors fought back and forth, Torgaddon and Saul
Tarvitz cheering from outside the practice cages.

The bout had attracted quite a crowd, and Loken wished Torgaddon had kept word of it to himself.

Loken fought with all the skill he could muster, while Lucius
sparred with a casual playfulness. Within moments, Loken's
sword was stuck in the ceiling of the practice cage, and Lucius
had a blade at his throat.

The swordsman had barely broken sweat, and Loken knew that
he was hopelessly outclassed by Lucius. To fight Lucius with life
and death resting on the blades would be to die, and he suspected
that there was no one in the Sons of Horus who could best him.

Loken bowed before the swordsman and said, 'That's one
each, Lucius.'

'Care for a decider?' smirked Lucius, dancing back and forth
on the balls of his feet and slicing his swords through the air.

'Not this time,' said Loken. 'Next time we meet, we'll put something serious on the outcome, eh?'

'Any time, Loken,' said Lucius, 'but I'll win. You know that,
don't you?'

'Your skill is great, Lucius, but just remember that there's
someone out there who can beat you.'

'Not this lifetime,' said Lucius.

The quiet order met once again in the armoury, though this was
a more select group than normally gathered with Lodge Master Serghar Targost presiding over an assemblage of the Legion's
senior officers.

Aximand felt a pang of regret and loss as he saw that, of the
Legion's captains, only Loken, Torgaddon, Iacton Qruze and
Tybalt Marr were absent.

Candles lit the armoury and each captain had dispensed with
his hooded robes. This was a gathering for debate, not theatrics.

'Brothers,' said Targost, 'this is a time for decisions: hard decisions. We face dissent from within, and now Fulgrim arrives out
of the blue to spy on us.'

'Spy?' said Aximand. 'Surely you don't think that Fulgrim
would betray his brother? The Warmaster is closer to Fulgrim
than he is to Sanguinius.'

'What else would you call him?' asked Abaddon. 'Fulgrim said as much when he arrived.'

'Fulgrim is as frustrated by the situation back on Terra as we are,' said Maloghurst. 'He knows that those who desire the outcome of war do not desire to see the blood of its waging. His Legion seeks perfection in all things, especially war, and we have all seen how the Emperor's Children fight: with unremitting ruthlessness and efficiency. They may fight differently from us, but they achieve the same result.'

'When Fulgrim's warriors see how the war is fought on Aureus they will know that there is no honour in it,' added Luc Sedirae. 'The World Eaters shock even me. I make no secret of the fact that I live for battle and revel in my ability to kill, but the sons of Angron are… uncivilised. They do not fight, they butcher.'

'They get the job done, Luc,' said Abaddon. 'That's all that matters. Once the Titans of the Mechanicum break open the walls of the Iron Citadel, you'll be glad to have them by your side when it comes time to storm the breaches.'

Sedirae nodded and said, 'There is truth in that. The Warmaster wields them like a weapon, but will Fulgrim see that?'

'Leave Fulgrim to me, Luc,' said a powerful voice from the shadows, and the warriors of the quiet order turned in surprise as a trio of figures emerged from the darkness.

The lead figure was armoured in ceremonially adorned armour, the white plate shimmering in the candlelight, and the red eye on his chestplate glowing with reflected fire.

Aximand and his fellow captains dropped to their knees as Horus entered their circle, his gaze sweeping around his assembled captains.

'So this is where you've been gathering in secret?'

'My lord–' began Targost, but Horus held up his hand to silence him.

'Hush, Serghar,' said Horus. 'There's no need for explanations. I have heard your deliberations and come to shed some light upon them, and to bring some new blood to your quiet order.'

As he spoke, Horus gestured the two figures that had accompanied him to come forward. Aximand saw that one was an Astartes, Tybalt Marr, while the other was a mortal clad in gold armour, the warrior who had fought to protect the Warmaster's documentarist on Davin.

'Tybalt, you already know,' continued the Warmaster. 'Since the terrible death of Verulam, he has struggled to come to terms with the loss. I believe he will find the support he needs within our order. The other is a mortal, and though not Astartes, he is a warrior of courage and strength.'

Serghar Targost raised his head and said, 'A mortal within the order? The order is for Astartes only.'

'Is it, Serghar? I was led to believe that this was a place where men were free to meet and converse, and confide outside the strictures of rank and martial order.'

'The Warmaster is right,' said Aximand, rising to his feet. 'There is only one qualification a man needs to be a part of our quiet order. He must be a warrior.'

Targost nodded, though he was clearly unhappy with the decision.

'Very well, let them come forward and show the sign,' he said.

Both Marr and the gold-armoured warrior stepped forward and held out their hands. In each palm, a silver lodge medal glinted.

'Let them speak their names,' said Targost.

'Tybalt Marr,' said the Captain of the Eighteenth Company.

The mortal said nothing, looking helplessly at Horus. The lodge members waited for him to announce himself, but no name was forthcoming.

'Why does he not identify himself?' asked Aximand.

'He can't say,' replied Horus with a smile. 'Sorry, I couldn't resist, Serghar. This is Maggard, and he is mute. It has come to my attention that he wishes to learn more of our Legion, and I thought this might be a way of showing him our true faces.'

'He will be made welcome,' assured Aximand, 'but you didn't come here just to bring us two new members, did you?'

'Always thinking, Little Horus,' laughed Horus. 'I've always said you were the wise one.'

'Then why are you here?' asked Aximand.

'Aximand!' hissed Targost. 'This is the Warmaster, he goes where he wills.'

Horus held up his hand and said, 'It's all right, Serghar, Little Horus has a right to ask. I've kept out of your affairs for long enough, so it's only fair I explain this sudden visit.'

Horus walked between them, smiling and bathing them in the force of his personality. He stood before Aximand and the effect was intoxicating. Horus had always been a being of supreme majesty, whose beauty and charisma could bewitch even the most stoic hearts.

As he met the Warmaster's gaze, Aximand saw that his power to seduce was beyond anything he had experienced before, and he felt shamed that he had questioned this luminous being. What right did he have to ask anything of the Warmaster?

Horus winked, and the spell was broken.

The Warmaster moved into the centre of the group and said, 'You are right to gather and debate the coming days, my sons, for they will be hard indeed. Times are upon us when we must make difficult decisions, and there will be those who will not understand why we do what we do, because they were not here beside us.'

Horus stopped before each of the captains in turn, and Aximand could see the effect his words were having on them. Each warrior's face lit up as though the sun shone upon it.

'I am set upon a course that will affect every man under my command, and the burden of my decision is a heavy weight upon my shoulders, my sons.'

'Share it with us!' cried Abaddon. 'We are ready to serve.'

Horus smiled and said, 'I know you are, Ezekyle, and it gives me strength to know that I have warriors with me who are as steadfast and true as you.'

'We are yours to command,' promised Serghar Targost. 'Our first loyalty is to you.'

'I am proud of you all,' said Horus, his voice emotional, 'but I have one last thing to ask of you.'

'Ask us,' said Abaddon.

Horus placed his hand gratefully on Abaddon's shoulder guard and said, 'Before you answer, consider what I am about to say carefully. If you choose to follow me on this grand adventure, there will be no turning back once we have embarked upon it. For good or ill, we go forward, never back.'

'You always were one for theatrics,' noted Aximand. 'Are you going to get to the point?'

Horus nodded and said, 'Yes, of course, Little Horus, but you'll indulge my sense for the dramatic I hope?'

'It wouldn't be you otherwise.'

'Agreed,' said Horus, 'but yes, to get to the point. I am about to take us down the most dangerous path, and not all of us will survive. There will be those of the Imperium who will call us traitors and rebels for our actions, but you must ignore their bleatings and trust that I am certain of our course. The days ahead will be hard and painful, but we must see them through to the end.'

'What would you have us do?' asked Abaddon.

'In good time, Ezekyle, in good time,' said Horus. 'I just need to know that you are with me, my sons. Are you with me?'

'We are with you!' shouted the warriors as one.

'Thank you,' said Horus, gratefully, 'but before we act, we

must set our own house in order. Hektor Varvarus and this remembrancer, Karkasy: they must be silenced while we gather our strength. They draw unwelcome attention to us and that is unacceptable.'

'Varvarus is not a man to change his mind, my lord,' warned Aximand, 'and the remembrancer is under Garviel's protection.'

'I will take care of Varvarus,' said the Warmaster, 'and the remembrancer... Well, I'm sure that with the correct persuasion he will do the right thing.'

'What do you intend, my lord?' asked Aximand.

'That they be illuminated as to the error of their ways,' said Horus.

TWENTY

The breach
A midday clear
Plans

The visit of the Emperor's Children was painfully brief, the two primarchs sequestering themselves behind closed doors for its entirety, while their warriors sparred, drank and talked of war. Whatever passed between the Warmaster and Fulgrim appeared to satisfy the primarch of the Emperor's Children that all was well, and three days later, an honour guard formed up at the upper transit dock as the Sons of Horus bade their farewells to the Emperor's Children.

Saul Tarvitz and Torgaddon said heartfelt goodbyes, while Lucius and Loken exchanged wry handshakes, each anticipating the next time they would cross blades. Eidolon nodded curtly to Torgaddon and Loken, as Apothecary Fabius made his exit without a word.

Fulgrim and Horus shared a brotherly embrace, whispering words only they could hear to one another. The wondrously perfect primarch of the Emperor's Children turned with a flourish towards the pressure door and stepped from the *Vengeful Spirit*, his long, scale cloak billowing behind him.

Something glinted beneath the cloak, and Loken did a double take as he caught a fleeting glimpse of a horribly familiar golden sword belted at Fulgrim's waist.

Loken saw that the Iron Citadel was aptly named, its gleaming walls rearing from the rock like jagged metal teeth. The mid-morning light reflected from its shimmering walls, the air rippling in the haze of energy fields, and clouds of metal shavings raining down from self-repairing ramparts. The outer precincts of the fortress were in ruins, the result of a four-month siege waged by the warriors of Angron and the war machines of the Mechanicum.

The *Dies Irae* and her sister Titans bombarded the walls daily, hurling high explosive shells and crackling energy beams at the citadel, slowly but surely pushing the Brotherhood back to this, their last bastion.

The citadel itself was a colossal half moon in plan, set against the rock of a range of white mountains, its approach guarded by scores of horn-works and redoubts. Most of these fortifications were little more than smouldering rubble, the Mechanicum's Legio Reductor corps having expended a fearsome amount of ordnance to flatten them in preparation for the storm of the Iron Citadel.

After months of constant shelling, the walls of the citadel had finally been broken open and a half-kilometre wide breach had been torn in its shining walls. The citadel was ready to fall, but the Brotherhood would fight for it to the bitter end, and Loken knew that most of the warriors who were to climb that breach would die.

He waited for the order of battle with trepidation, knowing that an escalade was the surest way for a warrior to meet his end. Statistically, a man was almost certain to die when assaulting the walls of a well-defended fortress, and it was therefore beholden to him to make that death worthwhile.

'Will it be soon, do you think, Garvi?' asked Vipus, checking the action of his chainsword for the umpteenth time.

'I think so,' said Loken, 'but I imagine that the World Eaters will be first into the breach.'

'They're welcome to the honour,' grunted Torgaddon, and Loken was surprised at his comrade's sentiment. Torgaddon was normally the first to request a place in the speartip of any battle, though he had been withdrawn and sullen for some time now. He would not be drawn on the reasons why, but Loken knew it had to do with Aximand and Abaddon.

Their fellow Mournival members had barely spoken to them over the course of this war, except where operational necessity had demanded it. Neither had the four of them met with the Warmaster since Davin. For all intents and purposes, the Mournival was no more.

The Warmaster kept his own council, and Loken found

himself in agreement with Iacton Qruze's sentiments that the Legion had lost its way. The words of the 'Half-heard' carried no real weight in the Sons of Horus, and the aged veteran's complaints were largely ignored.

Loken's growing suspicions had been fed by what Apothecary Vaddon had told him when he had rushed to the medicae deck after the departure of the Emperor's Children.

He had found the Apothecary in the midst of surgery, ministering to the Legion's wounded, the tiled floor slick with congealed blood.

Loken had known better than to disturb Vaddon's labours and only when the Apothecary had finished did Loken speak to him.

'The anathame?' demanded Loken. 'Where is it?'

Vaddon looked up from washing his hands of blood. 'Captain Loken. The anathame? I don't have it any more. I thought you knew.'

'No,' said Loken. 'I didn't. What happened to it? I told you to tell no one that it was in your possession.'

'And nor did I,' said Vaddon angrily. 'He already knew I had it.'

'He?' asked Loken. 'Who are you talking about?'

'The Apothecary of the Emperor's Children, Fabius,' said Vaddon. 'He came to the medicae deck a few hours ago and told me he had been authorised to remove it.'

A cold chill seized Loken as he asked, 'Authorised by whom?'

'By the Warmaster,' said Vaddon.

'And you just gave him it?' asked Loken. 'Just like that?'

'What was I supposed to do?' snarled Vaddon. 'This Fabius had the Warmaster's seal. I had to give it to him.'

Loken took a deep calming breath, knowing that the Apothecary would have had no choice when presented with the seal of Horus. The months of research Vaddon had performed on the weapon had, thus far, yielded no results, and with its removal from the *Vengeful Spirit*, any chance of uncovering its secrets was lost forever.

A crackling voice in Loken's helmet shook him from his sour memory of the second theft of the anathame, and he focused on the order of battle streaming through his headset. Sure enough, the World Eaters were going in first, a full assault company led by Angron himself and supported by two companies of the Sons of Horus, the Tenth and the Second: Loken and Torgaddon's companies.

Torgaddon and Loken shared an uneasy glance. To be given the honour of going into the breach seemed at odds with their current status within the Legion, but the order was given and there was no changing it now. Army regiments would follow to secure the ground the Astartes won, and Hektor Varvarus himself would lead these detachments.

Loken shook hands with Torgaddon and said, 'See you on the inside, Tarik.'

'Try not to get yourself killed, Garvi,' said Torgaddon.

'Thanks for the reminder,' said Loken, 'and here was me thinking that was the point.'

'Don't joke, Garvi,' said Torgaddon. 'I'm serious. I think we're going to need each other's support before this campaign is over.'

'What do you mean?'

'Never mind,' said Torgaddon. 'We'll talk more once this citadel is ours, eh?'

'Yes, we'll share a bottle of victory wine in the ruins of the Brotherhood's citadel.'

Torgaddon nodded and said, 'You're buying though.'

They shook hands once more and Torgaddon jogged away to rejoin his warriors and ready them for the bloody assault. Loken watched him go, wondering if he would see his friend alive again to share that drink. He pushed such defeatism aside as he made his way through his own company to pass out orders and offer words of encouragement.

He turned as a huge cheer erupted from further down the mountains, seeing a column of warriors clad in the blue and white armour of the World Eaters, marching towards the approaches to the breach. The assaulters of the World Eaters were hulking warriors equipped with mighty chainaxes and heavy jump packs. They were brutality distilled and concentrated violence moulded them into the most fearsome close combat fighters Loken had ever seen.

Leading them was the Primarch Angron.

Angron, the Bloody One: the Red Angel.

Loken had heard all these names and more for Angron, but none of them did justice to the sheer brutal physicality of the primarch of the World Eaters. Clad in an ancient suit of gladiatorial armour, Angron was like a warrior from some lost heroic age. A glinting mesh cape of chainmail hung from his high gorget and pauldrons, with skulls worked into its weave like barbaric trophies.

He was armed to the teeth with short, stabbing swords, and daggers the length of an Astartes chainblade. An ornate pistol of antique design was holstered on each thigh, and he carried a monstrous chain-glaive, its terrifying size beyond anything Loken could believe.

'Throne alive…' breathed Nero Vipus as Angron approached. 'I wouldn't have believed it had I not seen it with my own eyes.'

'I know what you mean,' answered Loken, the mighty primarch's savage and tribal appearance putting him in mind of the bloody tales he had read in the *Chronicles of Ursh*.

Angron's face was murder itself, his thick features scarred and bloody. Dark iron glinted on his scalp where cerebral cortex implants punctured his skull to amplify his already fearsome aggression. The implants had been grafted to Angron's brain when he had been a slave, centuries before, and though the technology to remove them was available, he had never wanted them removed.

The bloody primarch marched past, glancing over at the men of Tenth Company as he led his warriors towards the bloodletting. Loken shivered at the sight of him, seeing only death in his heavy-lidded eyes, and he wondered what terrible thoughts must fill Angron's violated skull.

No sooner had the primarch of the World Eaters passed than the bombardment began, the guns of the Legio Mortis launching rippling salvoes of rockets and shells into the breach.

Loken watched as Angron delivered his assault orders with curt chops of his glaive, and felt a momentary pity for the Brotherhood warriors within the citadel. Though they were his sworn enemies, he did not envy them the prospect of fighting such a living avatar of blood and death.

A terrifying war cry sounded from the World Eaters, and Loken watched as Angron led his company in a crude ritual of scarification. The warriors removed their left gauntlets and slashed their axes across their palms, smearing the blood across the faceplates of their helmets as they chanted canticles of death and bloodshed.

'I almost feel sorry for the poor bastards in the citadel,' said Vipus, echoing Loken's earlier thoughts.

'Pass the word to stand ready,' he ordered. 'We move out when the World Eaters reach the crest of the breach.'

He held out his hand to Nero Vipus and said, 'Kill for the living, Nero.'

'Kill for the dead,' answered Vipus.

The assault began in a flurry of smoke as the World Eaters surged up the lower slopes of the breach with roaring blasts of their jump packs. The wall head and the breach itself were wreathed in explosions from the Titans' bombardment, and the idea that something could live through such a storm of shot and shell seemed impossible to Loken.

As the World Eaters powered up the slopes of rubble, Loken and his warriors clambered over the twisted, blackened spars of iron that had been blasted from the walls above. They moved and fired, adding their own volleys of gunfire into the breach before the assaulters reached their targets.

The slope was steep, but eminently climbable, and they were making steady progress. Occasional shots and las-blasts ricocheted from the rocks or their armour, but at this range, nothing could wound them.

Five hundred metres to his left, Loken saw Torgaddon leading Second Company up the slopes in the wake of the World Eaters, both forces of the Sons of Horus protecting the vulnerable flanks of the assaulters and ready with heavier weapons to secure the breach.

Behind the Astartes, the soldiers of Hektor Varvarus's Byzant Janizars – wearing long cream greatcoats with gold frogging – followed in disciplined ranks. To march into battle in ceremonial dress uniforms seemed ridiculous to Loken, but Varvarus had declared that he and his men were not going to enter the citadel looking less than their best.

Loken turned from the splendid sight of the marching soldiers as he heard a deep, bass rumbling that seemed to come from the ground itself. Powdered rubble and rocks danced as the vibrations grew stronger still and Loken knew that something was terribly wrong. Ahead, he could see Angron and the World Eaters reaching the crest of the breach. Blazing columns of smoke surrounded Angron, and Loken heard the mighty primarch's bellowing cry of triumph even over the thunderous explosions of battle.

The rumbling grew louder and more violent, and Loken had to grip onto a rusted spar of rebar to hold himself in place as the ground continued to shake as though in the grip of a mighty earthquake. Great cracks split the ground and plumes of fire shot from them.

'What's happening?' he shouted over the noise.

No one answered and Loken fell as the top of the breach suddenly exploded in a sheet of flame that reached hundreds of metres into the air. Rocks and metal were hurled skywards as the top of the wall vanished in a massive seismic detonation.

Like the bunkers in the cities, the Brotherhood destroyed what they could not hold, and Loken's reactive senses shut down briefly with the overload of light and noise. Twisted rubble and wreckage slammed down around them, and Loken heard screams of pain and the crack of splintering armour as scores of his men were pulverised by the storm of boulders.

Dust and matter filled the air, and when Loken felt safe enough to move, he saw in horror that the entire crest of the breach had been destroyed.

Angron and the World Eaters were gone, buried beneath the wreckage of a mountain.

Torgaddon saw the same thing, and picked himself up from the ground. He shouted at his warriors to get to their feet and charged towards the ruin of the breach. Filthy, dust-covered warriors clambered from the wreckage and followed their captain as he led them onwards and upwards to what might be their deaths. Torgaddon knew that such a course of action was probably suicidal, but he had seen Angron buried beneath the mountain, and retreating was not an option.

He activated the blade of his chainsword and scrambled up the slopes with the feral cry of the Sons of Horus bursting from his lips.

'Lupercal! Lupercal!' he screamed as he charged.

Loken watched his brother rise from the aftermath of the explosion like a true hero, and began his own charge towards the breach. He knew that there was every chance a second seismic mine was buried in the breach, but the sight of a primarch brought low by the Brotherhood obliterated all thoughts of any tactical response, except charging.

'Warriors of the Tenth!' he roared. 'With me! Lupercal!'

Loken's surviving warriors pulled themselves from the rubble and followed Loken with the Warmaster's name echoing from the mountains. Loken sprang from rock to rock, clambering uphill faster than he would have believed possible, his anger hot and bright. He was ready to wreak vengeance upon the Brotherhood for what they had done in the name of spite, and nothing was going to stop him.

Loken knew that he had to reach the breach before the Brotherhood realised that its strategy had not killed all the attackers, and he kept moving upwards at a fast pace, using all the increased muscle power his armour afforded him. A storm of gunfire flashed from above: las-shots and solid rounds spanging from the rocks and metal rubble. A heavy shell clipped his shoulder guard, spinning him around, but Loken shrugged off the impact and charged on.

The roaring tide of Astartes warriors climbed the breach, the last rays of the morning's sun glinting from the brilliant green of their armour. To see so many warriors in battle was magnificent, an unstoppable wave of death that would sweep away all resistance in a storm of gunfire and blades.

All tactics were moot now, the sight of Angron's fall robbing each and every warrior of any sense of restraint. Loken could see the gleaming silver armour of Brotherhood warriors as they climbed to what was left of the breach, dragging bipod-mounted heavy weapons with them.

'Bolters!' he shouted. 'Open fire!'

The crest of the breach vanished as a spray of bolter rounds impacted. Sparks and chunks of flesh flew as Astartes rounds found homes in flesh, and though many were firing from the hip, most were deadly accurate.

The noise was incredible, hundreds of bolter rounds ripping enemy warriors to shreds and skirling wolf howls ringing in his ears as the Astartes swept over the breach and reverted once again to the persona of the Luna Wolves. Loken threw aside his bolter, the magazine empty, and drew his chainsword, thumbing the activation stud as he vaulted the smoking rocks that had crushed Angron and the World Eaters.

Beyond the walls of the Iron Citadel was a wide esplanade, its surface strewn with gun positions and coils of razor wire. A shell-battered keep was built into the mountainside, but its gates were in pieces and black smoke poured from its gun ports. Brotherhood warriors were streaming back from the ruin of the walls towards these prepared positions, but they had horribly misjudged the timing of their fallback.

The Sons of Horus were already amongst them, hacking them down with brutal arcs of chainblades or gunning them down as they fled. Loken tore his way through a knot of Brotherhood warriors who turned to fight, killing three of them in as many strokes of his sword, and backhanding his elbow into the last opponent's head, smashing his skull to splinters.

All was pandemonium as the Sons of Horus ran amok within the precincts of the Iron Citadel, its defenders slaughtered in frantic moments of unimaginable violence. Loken killed and killed, revelling in the shedding of enemy blood and realising that, with this victory, the war would be over.

With that thought, the cold reality of what was happening penetrated the red fog of his rage. They had won, and already he could see the victory turning into a massacre.

'Garviel!' a desperate voice called over the suit-vox. 'Garviel, can you hear me?'

'Loud and clear, Tarik!' answered Loken.

'We have to stop this!' cried Torgaddon. 'We've won, it's over. Get a hold of your company.'

'Understood,' said Loken, pleased that Torgaddon had realised the same thing as he had.

Soon the inter-suit vox network was alive with barked orders to halt the attack that quickly passed down the chain of command.

By the time the echoes of battle were finally stilled, Loken could see that the Astartes had just barely managed to hold themselves from plunging into an abyss of barbarity, out of which they might never have climbed. Blood, bodies and the stink of battle filled the day, and as Loken looked up into the beautifully clear sky, he could see that the sun was almost at its zenith.

The final storm of the Iron Citadel had taken less than an hour, yet had cost the lives of a primarch, hundreds of the World Eaters, thousands of the Brotherhood, and the Emperor alone knew how many Sons of Horus.

The mass slaughter seemed such a terrible waste of life for what was a paltry prize: ruined cities, a battered and hostile populace, and a world that was sure to rebel as soon as it had the chance.

Was this world's compliance worth such bloodshed?

The majority of the Brotherhood warriors had died in those last enraged minutes, but many more were prisoners of the Sons of Horus, rather than their victims.

Loken removed his helmet and gulped in a lungful of the clear air, its crispness tasting like the sweetest wine after the recycled air of his armour. He made his way through the wreckage of battle, the torn remnants of enemy warriors strewn like offal throughout the esplanade.

He found Torgaddon on his knees, also with his helmet off and breathing deeply. His friend looked up as Loken approached and smiled weakly. 'Well... we did it.'

'Yes,' agreed Loken sadly, looking around at the crimson spoils of victory. 'We did, didn't we?'

Loken had killed thousands of enemies before, and he would kill thousands more in wars yet to be fought, but something in the savagery of this battle had soured his notion of triumph.

The two captains turned as they heard the tramp of booted feet behind them, seeing the lead battalions of the Byzant Janizars finally climbing into the citadel. Loken could see the horror on the soldiers' faces and knew that the glory of the Astartes would be tarnished for every man who set foot inside.

'Varvarus is here,' said Loken.

'Just in time, eh?' said Torgaddon. 'This'll sweeten his mood towards us.'

Loken nodded and simply watched as the richly appointed command units of the Byzant Janizars entered the citadel, their tall blue banners snapping in the wind, and brilliantly decorated officers scanning the battlefield.

Hektor Varvarus stood at the crest of the breach and surveyed the scene of carnage, his horrified expression easy to read even from a distance. Loken felt his resentment towards Varvarus swell as he thought, *this is what we were created for, what else did you expect?*

'Looks like their leaders are here to surrender to Varvarus,' said Torgaddon, pointing to a long column of beaten men and women marching from the smoking ruins of the inner keep, red and silver banners carried before them. A hundred warriors in battered plate armour marched with them, their long barrelled weapons shouldered and pointed at the ground.

Robed magos and helmeted officers led the column, their faces downcast and resigned to their capitulation. With the storm of the esplanade, the citadel was lost and the leaders of the Brotherhood knew it.

'Come on,' said Loken. 'This is history. Since there are no remembrancers here, we might as well be part of this.'

'Yes,' agreed Torgaddon, pushing himself to his feet. The two captains drew parallel with the column of beaten Brotherhood warriors, and soon every one of the Sons of Horus who had survived the escalade surrounded them.

Loken watched Varvarus climb down the rearward slope of the breach and make his way towards the leaders of the Auretian Technocracy. He bowed formally and said, 'My name is Lord Commander Hektor Varvarus, commander of the Emperor's armies in the 63rd Expedition. To whom do I have the honour of addressing?'

An elderly warrior in gold plate armour stepped from the ranks of men, his black and silver heraldry carried on a personal banner pole by a young lad of no more than sixteen years.

'I am Ephraim Guardia,' he said, 'Senior Preceptor of the Brotherhood Chapter Command and Castellan of the Iron Citadel.'

Loken could see the tension on Guardia's face, and knew that it was taking the commander all his self-control to remain calm in the face of the massacre he had just witnessed.

'Tell me,' said Guardia. 'Is this how all wars are waged in your Imperium?'

'War is a harsh master, senior preceptor,' answered Varvarus.

'Blood is spilled and lives are lost. I feel the sorrow of your losses, but excess of grief for the dead is madness. It is an injury to the living, and the dead know it not.'

'Spoken like a tyrant and a killer,' snarled Guardia, and Varvarus bristled with anger at his defeated foe's lack of etiquette.

'Given time, you will see that war is not what the Imperium stands for,' promised Varvarus. 'The Emperor's Great Crusade is designed to bring reason and illumination to the lost strands of mankind. I promise you that this... unpleasantness will soon be forgotten as we go forward into a new age of peace.'

Guardia shook his head and reached into a pouch at his side. 'I think you are wrong, but you have beaten us and my opinion means nothing any more.'

He unrolled a sheet of parchment and said, 'I shall read our declaration to you, Varvarus. All my officers have signed it and it will stand as a testament to our attempts to defy you.'

Clearing his throat, Guardia began to read.

'We fought your treacherous Warmaster to preserve our way of life and to resist the yoke of Imperial rule. It was, in truth, not for glory, nor riches, nor for honour that we fought, but for freedom, which no honest man could ever wish to give up. However, the greatest of our warriors cannot stand before the savagery of your war, and rather than see our culture exterminated, we surrender this citadel and our worlds to you. May you rule in peace more kindly than you make war.'

Before Varvarus could react to the senior preceptor's declaration, the rubble behind him shifted and groaned, cracks splitting the rock and metal as something vast and terrible heaved upwards from beneath the ground.

At first Loken thought that it was the second seismic charge he had feared, but then he saw that these tremors were far more localised. Janizars scattered, and men shouted in alarm as more debris clattered from the breach. Loken gripped the hilt of his sword as he saw many of the Brotherhood warriors reach for their weapons.

Then the breach exploded with a grinding crack of ruptured stone, and something immense and red erupted from the ground with a bestial roar of hate and bloodlust. Soldiers fell away from the red giant, hurled aside by the violence of his sudden appearance.

Angron towered over them, bloody and enraged, and Loken marvelled that he could still be alive after thousands of tonnes of rock had engulfed him. But Angron was a primarch and what – save for an anathame – could lay one such as him low?

'Blood for Horus!' shouted Angron and leapt from the breach.

The primarch landed with a thunderous impact that split the stone beneath him, his chain-glaive sweeping out and cleaving the entire front rank of Brotherhood warriors to bloody ruin. Ephraim Guardia died in the first seconds of Angron's attack, his body cloven through the chest with a single blow.

Angron howled in battle lust as he hacked his way through the Brotherhood with great, disembowelling sweeps of his monstrous, roaring weapon. The madness of his slaughter was terrifying, but the warriors of the Brotherhood were not about to die without a fight.

Loken shouted, 'No! Stop!' but it was already too late. The remainder of the Brotherhood shouldered their weapons and began firing on the Sons of Horus and the rampaging primarch.

'Open fire!' shouted Loken, knowing he had no choice.

Gunfire tore through the ranks of the Brotherhood, the point-blank firefight a lethal firestorm of explosive bolter rounds. The noise was deafening and horrifyingly brief as the Brotherhood were mercilessly gunned down by the Astartes or hacked apart by Angron.

Within seconds, it was over and the last remnants of the Brotherhood were no more.

Desperate cries for medics sounded from the command units of the Janizars, and Loken saw a group of bloody soldiers on their knees around a fallen officer, his cream greatcoat drenched in blood. The gold of his medals gleamed in the cold midday light and as one of the kneeling soldiers shifted position, Loken realised the identity of the fallen man.

Hektor Varvarus lay in a spreading pool of blood, and even from a distance, Loken could see that there would be no saving him. The man's body had been ripped open from the inside, the gleaming ends of splintered ribs jutting from his chest where it was clear a bolter round had detonated within him.

Loken wept to see this fragile peace broken, and dropped his sword in disgust at what had happened and at what he had been forced to do. With Angron's senseless attack, the lives of his warriors had been threatened, and he'd had no other choice but to order the attack.

Still, he regretted it.

The Brotherhood had been honourable foes and the Sons of Horus had butchered them like cattle. Angron stood in the midst of the carnage, his glaive spraying the warriors nearest him with spatters of blood from the roaring chainblade.

The Sons of Horus cheered in praise of the World Eaters primarch, but Loken felt soul sick at such a barbaric sight.

'That was no way for warriors to die,' said Torgaddon. 'Their deaths shame us all.'

Loken didn't answer. He couldn't.

TWENTY-ONE

Illumination

With the fall of the Iron Citadel, the war on Aureus was over. The Brotherhood was destroyed as a fighting force and though there were still pockets of resistance to be mopped up, the fighting was as good as over. Casualties on both sides had been high, most especially in the Army units of the Expedition. Hektor Varvarus was brought back to the fleet with due reverence and his body returned to space in a ceremony attended by the highest-ranking officers of the Expeditions.

The Warmaster himself spoke the lord commander's eulogy, the passion and depths of his sorrow plain to see.

'Heroism is not only in the man, but in the occasion,' the Warmaster had said of Lord Commander Varvarus. 'It is only when we look now and see his success that men will say that it was good fortune. It was not. We lost thousands of our best warriors that day and I feel the loss of every one. Hektor Varvarus was a leader who knew that to march with the gods, one must wait until he hears their footsteps sounding through events, and then leap up and grasp the hem of their robes.

'Varvarus is gone from us, but he would not want us to pause in mourning, for history is a relentless master. It has no present, only the past rushing into the future. To try to hold fast to it is to be swept aside and that, my friends, will never happen. Not while I am Warmaster. Those men who fought and bled with Varvarus shall have this world to stand sentinel over, so that his sacrifice will never be forgotten.'

Other speakers had said their farewells to the lord commander, but none with the Warmaster's eloquence. True to his word, Horus ensured that Army units that had been loyal to Varvarus were appointed to minister the worlds he had died to make compliant.

A new Imperial commander was installed, and the martial power of the fleet began the time-consuming process of regrouping in preparation for the next stage of the Crusade.

Karkasy's billet stank of ink and printing fumes, the crude, mechanical bulk printer working overtime to print enough copies of the latest edition of *The Truth is All We Have*. Though his output had been less prolific of late, the Bondsman Number 7 box was nearly empty. Ignace Karkasy remembered wondering, a lifetime ago it seemed, whether or not the lifespan of his creativity could be measured in the quantity of paper he had left to fill. Such thoughts seemed meaningless, given the powerful desire to write that was upon him these days.

He sat on the edge of his cot bed, the last remaining place for him to sit, penning the latest scurrilous piece of verse for his pamphlet and humming contentedly to himself. Papers filled the billet, strewn across the floor, tacked upon the walls or piled on any surface flat enough to hold them. Scribbled notes, abandoned odes and half-finished poems filled the space, but such was the fecundity of his muse that he didn't expect to exhaust it any time soon.

He'd heard that the war with the Auretians was over, the final citadel having fallen to the Sons of Horus a couple of days ago in what the ship scuttlebutt was already calling the White Mountains Massacre. He didn't yet know the full story, but several sources he'd cultivated over the ten months of the war would surely garner him some juicy titbits.

He heard a curt knock on his door-shutter and shouted, 'Come in!'

Karkasy kept on writing as the shutter opened, too focused on his words to waste a single second of his time.

'Yes?' he said, 'What can I do for you?'

No answer was forthcoming, so Karkasy looked up in irritation to see an armoured warrior standing mutely before him. At first, Karkasy felt a thrill of panic, seeing the man's longsword and the hard, metallic gleam of a holstered pistol, but he relaxed as he saw that the man was Petronella Vivar's bodyguard – Maggard, or something like that.

'Well?' he asked again. 'Was there something you wanted?'

Maggard said nothing and Karkasy remembered that the man was mute, thinking it foolish that anyone would send someone who couldn't speak as a messenger.

'I can't help you unless you can tell me why you're here,' said Karkasy, speaking slowly to ensure that the man understood.

In response, Maggard removed a folded piece of paper from his belt and held it out with his left hand. The warrior made no attempt to move closer to him, so with a resigned sigh, Karkasy put aside the Bondsman and pushed his bulky frame from the bed.

Karkasy picked his way through the piles of notebooks and took the proffered paper. It was a sepia coloured papyrus, as was produced in the Gyptian spires, with crosshatched patterning throughout. A little gaudy for his tastes, but obviously expensive.

'So who might this be from?' asked Karkasy, before again remembering that this messenger couldn't speak. He shook his head with an indulgent smile, unfolded the papyrus and cast his eyes over the note's contents.

He frowned as he recognised the words as lines from his own poetry, dark imagery and potent symbolism, but they were all out of sequence, plucked from a dozen different works.

Karkasy reached the end of the note and his bladder emptied in terror as he realised the import of the message, and its bearer's purpose.

Petronella paced the confines of her stateroom, impatient to begin transcribing the latest thoughts of her bodyguard. The time Maggard had spent with the Astartes had been most fruitful, and she had already learned much that would otherwise have been hidden from her.

Now a structure suggested itself, a tragic tale told in reverse order that opened on the primarch's deathbed, with a triumphal coda that spoke of his survival and of the glories yet to come. After all, she didn't want to confine herself to only one book.

She even had a prospective title, one that she felt conveyed the correct gravitas of her subject matter, yet also included her in its meaning.

Petronella would call this masterpiece, *In The Footsteps of Gods*, and had already taken its first line – that most important part of the tale where her reader was either hooked or left cold – from her own terrified thoughts at the moment of the Warmaster's collapse.

I was there the day that Horus fell.

It had all the right tonal qualities, leaving the reader in no doubt that they were about to read something profound, yet keeping the end of the story a jealously guarded secret.

Everything was coming together, but Maggard was late in returning from his latest foray into the world of the Astartes and her patience was wearing thin. She had already reduced Babeth to tears in her impatient frustration, and had banished her maidservant to the tiny chamber that served as her sleeping quarters.

She heard the sound of the door to her stateroom opening in the receiving room, and marched straight through to reprimand Maggard for his tardiness.

'What time do you call…' she began, but the words trailed off as she saw that the figure standing before her wasn't Maggard.

It was the Warmaster.

He was dressed in simple robes and looked more magnificent than she could ever remember seeing him. A fierce anima surrounded him, and she found herself unable to speak as he looked up, the full force of his personality striking her.

Standing at the door behind him was the hulking form of First Captain Abaddon. Horus looked up as she entered and nodded to Abaddon, who closed the door at his back.

'Miss Vivar,' said the Warmaster. It took an effort of will on Petronella's part for her to find her voice.

'Yes… my lord,' she stammered, horrified at the mess of her stateroom and that the Warmaster should see it so untidy. She must remember to punish Babeth for neglecting her duties. 'I… that is, I wasn't expecting…'

Horus held up his hand to soothe her concerns and she fell silent.

'I know I have been neglectful of you,' said the Warmaster. 'You have been privy to my innermost thoughts and I allowed the concerns of the war against the Technocracy to command my attention.'

'My lord, I never dreamed you gave me such consideration,' said Petronella.

'You would be surprised,' smiled Horus. 'Your writing goes well?'

'Very well, my lord,' said Petronella. 'I have been prolific since last we met.'

'May I see?' asked Horus.

'Of course,' she said, thrilled that he should take an interest in her work. She had to force herself to walk, not run, into her writing room, indicating the papers stacked on her escritoire.

'It's all a bit of jumble, but everything I've written is here,' beamed Petronella. 'I would be honoured if you would critique my work. After all, who is more qualified?'

'Quite,' agreed Horus, following her to the escritoire and taking up her most recent output. His eyes scanned the pages, reading and digesting the contents quicker than any mortal man ever could.

She searched his face for any reaction to her words, but he was as unreadable as a statue, and she began to worry that he disapproved.

Eventually, he placed the papers back on the escritoire and said, 'It is very good. You are a talented documentarist.'

'Thank you, my lord,' she gushed, the power of his praise like a tonic in her veins.

'Yes,' said Horus, his voice cold. 'It's almost a shame that no one will ever read it.'

Maggard reached up and grabbed the front of Karkasy's robe, spinning him around, and hooking his arm around the poet's neck. Karkasy struggled in the powerful grip, helpless against Maggard's superior strength.

'Please!' he gasped, his terror making his voice shrill. 'No, please don't!'

Maggard said nothing, and Karkasy heard the snap of leather as the warrior's free hand popped the stud on his holster. Karkasy fought, but he could do nothing, the crushing force of Maggard's arm around his neck robbing him of breath and blurring his vision.

Karkasy wept bitter tears as time slowed. He heard the slow rasp of the pistol sliding from its holster and the harsh click as the hammer was drawn back.

He bit his tongue. Bloody foam gathered in the corners of his mouth. Snot and tears mingled on his face. His legs scrabbled on the floor. Papers flew in all directions.

Cold steel pressed into his neck, the barrel of Maggard's pistol jammed tight under his jaw.

Karkasy smelled the gun oil.

He wished...

The hard bang of the pistol shot echoed deafeningly in the cramped billet.

At first, Petronella wasn't sure she'd understood what the Warmaster meant. Why wouldn't people be able to read her work? Then she saw the cold, merciless light in Horus's eyes.

'My lord, I'm not sure I understand you,' she said, haltingly.

'Yes, you do.'

'No...' she whispered, backing away from him.

The Warmaster followed her, his steps slow and measured. 'When we spoke in the apothecarion I let you look inside Pandora's box, Miss Vivar, and for that I am truly sorry. Only one person has a need to know the things in my head, and that person is me. The things I have seen and done, the things I am going to do...'

'Please, my lord,' said Petronella, backing out of her writing room and into the receiving room. 'If you are unhappy with what I've written, it can be revised, edited. I would give you approval on everything, of course.'

Horus shook his head, drawing closer to her with every step.

Petronella felt her eyes fill with tears and she knew that this couldn't be happening. The Warmaster would not be trying to scare her. They must be playing some cruel joke on her. The idea of the Astartes making a fool of her stung Petronella's wounded pride and the part of her that had snapped angrily at the Warmaster upon their first meeting rose to the surface.

'I am the Palatina Majoria of House Carpinus and I demand that you respect that!' she cried, standing firm before the Warmaster. 'You can't scare me like this.'

'I'm not trying to scare you,' said Horus, reaching out to hold her by the shoulders.

'You're not?' asked Petronella, his words filling her with relief. She'd known that this couldn't be right, that there had to be some mistake.

'No,' said Horus, his hands sliding towards her neck. 'I am illuminating you.'

Her neck broke with one swift snap of his wrist.

The medicae cell was cramped, but clean and well maintained. Mersadie Oliton sat by the bed and wept softly to herself, tears running freely down her coal dark skin. Kyril Sindermann sat with her and he too shed tears as he held the hand of the bed's occupant.

Euphrati Keeler lay, unmoving, her skin pale and smooth, with a sheen to it that made it look like polished ceramic. Since she had faced the horror in Archive Chamber Three, she had lain unmoving and unresponsive in this medicae bay.

Sindermann had told Mersadie what had happened and she found herself torn between wanting to believe him and calling him delusional. His talk of a daemon and of Euphrati standing before it with the power of the Emperor pouring through her was too fantastical to be true… wasn't it? She wondered if he'd told anyone else of it.

The Apothecaries and medics could find nothing physically wrong with Euphrati Keeler, save for the eagle-shaped burn on her hand that refused to fade. Her vital signs were stable and her brainwave activity registered normal: no one could explain it and no one had any idea how to wake her from this coma-like state.

Mersadie came to visit Euphrati as often as she could, but she knew that Sindermann came every day, spending several hours at a time with her. Sometimes they would sit together, talking to Euphrati, telling her of the events happening on the planets below, the battles that had been fought, or simply passing on ship gossip.

Nothing seemed to reach the imagist, and Mersadie sometimes wondered if it might not be a kindness to let her die. What could be worse for a person like Euphrati than being trapped by her own flesh, with no ability to reason, to communicate or express herself.

She and Sindermann had arrived together today and each instantly knew that the other had been crying. The news of Ignace Karkasy's suicide had hit them all hard and Mersadie still couldn't believe how he could have done such a thing.

A suicide note had been found in his billet, which was said to have been composed in verse. It spoke volumes of Ignace's enormous conceit that he made his last goodbye in his own poetry.

They had wept for another lost soul, and then they sat on either side of Euphrati's bed, holding each other's and Keeler's hands as they spoke of better times.

Both turned as they heard a soft knock behind them.

A thin faced man wearing the uniform of the Legio Mortis and an earnest face stood framed in the doorway. Behind him, Mersadie could see that the corridor was filled with people.

'Is it all right if I come in?' he asked.

Mersadie Oliton said, 'Who are you?'

'My name's Titus Cassar, Moderati Primus of the *Dies Irae.* I've come to see the saint.'

They met in the observation deck, the lighting kept low and the darkness of space leavened only by the reflected glare of the planets they had just conquered. Loken stood with his palm against the armoured viewing bay, believing that something fundamental had happened to the Sons of Horus on Aureus, but not knowing what.

Torgaddon joined him moments later and Loken welcomed him with a brotherly embrace, grateful to have so loyal a comrade.

They stood in silence for some time, each lost in thought as they watched the defeated planets turn in space below them. The preparations for departure were virtually complete and the fleet was ready to move on, though neither warrior had any idea of where they were going.

Eventually Torgaddon broke the silence, 'So what do we do?'

'I don't know, Tarik,' replied Loken. 'I really don't.'

'I thought not,' said Torgaddon, holding up a glass test tube with something in it that reflected soft light with a golden gleam. 'This won't help then.'

'What is it?' asked Loken.

'These,' said Torgaddon, 'are the bolt-round fragments removed from Hektor Varvarus.'

'Bolt-round fragments? Why do you have them?'

'Because they're ours.'

'What do you mean?'

'I mean they're ours,' repeated Torgaddon. 'The bolt that killed the lord commander came from an Astartes bolter, not from one of the Brotherhood's guns.'

Loken shook his head. 'No, there must be some mistake.'

'There's no mistake. Apothecary Vaddon tested the fragments himself. They're ours, no question.'

'You think Varvarus caught a stray round?'

Torgaddon shook his head. 'The wound was dead centre, Garviel. It was an aimed shot.'

Loken and Torgaddon both understood the implications, and Loken felt his melancholy rise at the thought of Varvarus having been murdered by one of their own.

Neither spoke for a long moment. Then Loken said, 'In the wake of such deceit and destruction shall we despair, or is faith and honour the spur to action?'

'What's that?' asked Torgaddon.

'It's part of a speech I read in a book that Kyril Sindermann gave me,' said Loken. 'It seemed appropriate given where we find ourselves now.'

'That's true enough,' agreed Torgaddon.

'What are we becoming, Tarik?' asked Loken. 'I don't recognise our Legion any more. When did it change?'

'The moment we encountered the Technocracy.'

'No,' said Loken. 'I think it was on Davin. Nothing's been the same since then. Something happened to the Sons of Horus there, something vile and dark and evil.'

'Do you realise what you're saying?'

'I do,' replied Loken. 'I'm saying that we have to uphold the truth of the Imperium of Mankind, no matter what evil may assail it.'

Torgaddon nodded. 'The Mournival oath.'

'Evil has found its way into our Legion, Tarik, and it's up to us to cut it out. Are you with me?' asked Loken.

'Always,' said Torgaddon, and the two warriors shook hands in the old Terran way.

The Warmaster's sanctum was dimly lit, the cold glow of the bridge instruments the only source of illumination. The room was full, the core of the Warmaster's officers and commanders gathered around the table. The Warmaster sat at his customary place at the head of the table while Aximand and Abaddon stood behind him, their presence a potent reminder of his authority. Maloghurst, Regulus, Erebus, Princeps Turnet of the Legio Mortis, and various other, hand picked Army commanders filled out the rest of the gathering.

Satisfied that everyone who needed to be there had arrived, Horus leaned forwards and began to speak.

'My friends, we begin the next phase of our campaign among the stars soon and I know that you're all curious as to where we travel next. I will tell you, but before I do, I need every one of you to be aware of the magnitude of the task before us.'

He could see he had everyone's attention, and continued. 'I am going to topple the Emperor from his Throne on Terra and take his place as the Master of Mankind.'

The enormity of his words was not lost on the assembled warriors and he gave them a few minutes to savour their weight, enjoying the look of alarm that crossed each man's face.

'Be not afraid, you are amongst friends,' chuckled Horus. 'I have spoken to you all individually over the course of the war with the Technocracy, but this is the first time you have been gathered and I have openly spoken of our destiny. You shall be my War Council, those to whom I entrust the furthering of my plan.'

Horus rose from his seat, continuing to speak as he circled the table.

'Take a moment and look at the face of the man sitting next to you. In the coming fight, he will be your brother, for all others will turn from us when we make our intentions plain. Brother will fight brother and the fate of the galaxy will be the ultimate prize. We will face accusations of heresy and cries of treason, but they will fall from us because we are right. Make no mistake about that. We are right and the Emperor is wrong. He has sorely misjudged me if he thinks I will stand by while he abandons his realm in his quest for godhood, and leaves us amid the destruction of his rampant ambition.

'The Emperor commands the loyalty of millions of soldiers and hundreds of thousands of Astartes warriors. His battle-fleets reach across the stars from one side of the galaxy to the other. The 63rd Expedition cannot hope to match such numbers or resources. You all know this to be the case, but even so, we have the advantage.'

'What advantage is that?' asked Maloghurst, exactly on cue.

'We have the advantage of surprise. No one yet suspects us of having learned the Emperor's true plan, and in that lies our greatest weapon.'

'But what of Magnus?' asked Maloghurst urgently, 'What happens when Leman Russ returns him to Terra?'

Horus smiled. 'Calm yourself, Mal. I have already contacted my brother Russ and illuminated him with the full breadth of Magnus's treacherous use of daemonic spells and conjurations. He was... suitably angry, and I believe I have convinced him that to return Magnus to Terra would be a waste of time and effort.'

Maloghurst returned Horus's smile. 'Magnus will not leave Prospero alive.'

'No,' agreed Horus. 'He will not.'

'What of the other Legions?' asked Regulus. 'They will not sit idly by while we make war upon the Emperor. How do you propose to negate them?'

'A worthy question, adept,' said Horus, circling the table to stand at his shoulder. 'We are not without allies ourselves. Fulgrim is with us, and he now goes to win Ferrus Manus of the Iron Hands over to our cause. Lorgar too understands the necessity of what must be done, and both bring the full might of their Legions to my banner.'

'That still leaves many others,' pointed out Erebus.

'Indeed it does, Chaplain, but with your help, others may join us. Under the guise of the Chaplain Edict, we will send emissaries to each of the Legions to promulgate the formation of warrior lodges within them. From small beginnings we may win many to our cause.'

'That will take time,' said Erebus.

Horus nodded. 'It will, yes, but it will be worth it in the long term. In the meantime, I have despatched mobilisation orders to those Legions I do not believe we can sway. The Ultramarines will muster at Calth to be attacked by Kor Phaeron of the Word Bearers, and the Blood Angels have been sent to the Signus Cluster, where Sanguinius shall be mired in blood. Then we make a swift, decisive stroke on Terra.'

'That still leaves other Legions,' said Regulus.

'I know,' answered Horus, 'but I have a plan that will remove them as a threat to us once and for all. I will lure them into a trap from which none will escape. I will set the Emperor's Imperium ablaze and from the ashes will arise a new Master of Mankind!'

'And where will you set this trap?' asked Maloghurst.

'A place not far from here,' said Horus. 'The Isstvan system.'

Ben Counter

GALAXY IN FLAMES

The heresy revealed

~ DRAMATIS PERSONAE ~

The Primarchs

HORUS	Warmaster
ANGRON	Primarch of the World Eaters
FULGRIM	Primarch of the Emperor's Children
MORTARION	Primarch of the Death Guard

The XVI Legion 'Sons of Horus'

EZEKYLE ABADDON	First Captain
TARIK TORGADDON	Captain, Second Company
IACTON QRUZE	'The Half-heard', captain, Third Company
HORUS AXIMAND	'Little Horus', captain, Fifth Company
SERGHAR TARGOST	Captain, Seventh Company, lodge master
GARVIEL LOKEN	Captain, Tenth Company
LUC SEDIRAE	Captain, 13th Company
TYBALT MARR	'The Either', captain, 18th Company
KALUS EKADDON	Captain, Catulan Reaver Squad
FALKUS KIBRE	'Widowmaker', captain, Justaerin Terminator Squad
NERO VIPUS	Sergeant, Locasta Tactical Squad

MALOGHURST	'The Twisted', equerry to the Warmaster

Other Space Marines

EREBUS	First Chaplain of the Word Bearers
KHÂRN	Captain, Eighth Assault Company of the World Eaters
NATHANIEL GARRO	Captain of the Death Guard
LUCIUS	Emperor's Children swordsman
SAUL TARVITZ	Captain of the Emperor's Children
EIDOLON	Lord Commander of the Emperor's Children
FABIUS	Emperor's Children Apothecary

The Legio Mortis

ESAU TURNET	Princeps of the Dies Irae, an Imperator-class Titan
CASSAR	Moderati Primus, one of the senior crew of the Dies Irae
ARUKEN	Moderati Primus. Another of the Dies Irae's crew

Non-Astartes Imperials

REGULUS	Mechanicum representative to Horus
ING MAE SING	Mistress of Astropaths

PART ONE
LONG KNIVES

ONE

The Emperor protects
Long night
The music of the spheres

'I was there,' said Titus Cassar, his wavering voice barely reaching the back of the chamber. 'I was there the day that Horus turned his face from the Emperor.'

His words brought a collective sigh from the Lectitio Divinitatus congregation and as one they lowered their heads at such a terrible thought. From the back of the chamber, an abandoned munitions hold deep in the under-decks of the Warmaster's flagship, the *Vengeful Spirit*, Kyril Sindermann watched and winced at Cassar's awkward delivery. The man was no iterator, that was for sure, but his words carried the sure and certain faith of someone who truly believed in the things he was saying.

Sindermann envied him that certainty.

It had been many months since he had felt anything approaching certainty.

As the Primary Iterator of the 63rd Expedition, it was Kyril Sindermann's job to promulgate the Imperial Truth of the Great Crusade, illuminating those worlds brought into compliance of the rule of the Emperor and the glory of the Imperium. Bringing the light of reason and secular truth to the furthest flung reaches of the ever-expanding human empire had been a noble undertaking.

But somewhere along the way, things had gone wrong.

Sindermann wasn't sure when it had happened. On Xenobia?

On Davin? On Aureus? Or on any one of a dozen other worlds brought into compliance?

Once he had been known as the arch-prophet of secular truth, but times had changed and he found himself remembering his Sahlonum, the Sumaturan philosopher who had wondered why the light of new science seemed not to illuminate as far as the old sorceries had.

Titus Cassar continued his droning sermon, and Sindermann returned his attention to the man. Tall and angular, Cassar wore the uniform of a moderati primus, one of the senior commanders of the *Dies Irae*, an Imperator-class Battle Titan. Sindermann suspected it was this rank, combined with his earlier friendship with Euphrati Keeler, that had granted his status within the Lectitio Divinitatus; status that he was clearly out of his depth in handling.

Euphrati Keeler: imagist, evangelist...

...Saint.

He remembered meeting Euphrati, a feisty, supremely self-confident woman, on the embarkation deck before they had left for the surface of Sixty-Three Nineteen, unaware of the horror they would witness in the depths of the Whisperhead Mountains.

Together with Captain Loken, they had seen the warp-spawned monstrosity Xayver Jubal had been wrought into. Sindermann had struggled to rationalise what he had seen by burying himself in his books and learning to better understand what had occurred. Euphrati had no such sanctuary and had turned to the growing Lectitio Divinitatus cult for solace.

Venerating the Emperor as a divine being, the cult had grown from humble beginnings to a movement that was spreading throughout the Expedition fleets of the galaxy – much to the fury of the Warmaster. Where before the cult had lacked a focus, in Euphrati Keeler, it had found its first martyr and saint.

Sindermann remembered the day when he had witnessed Euphrati Keeler stand before a nightmare horror from beyond the gates of the empyrean and hurl it back from whence it had come. He had seen her bathed in killing fire and walk away unscathed, a blinding light streaming from the outstretched hand in which she had held a silver Imperial eagle. Others had seen it too, Ing Mae Sing, Mistress of the Fleet's astropaths and a dozen of the ship's armsmen. Word had spread fast and Euphrati had become, overnight, a saint in the eyes of the faithful and an icon to cling to on the frontier of space.

He was unsure why he had even come to this meeting – not a

meeting, he corrected himself, but a service, a religious sermon – for there was a very real danger of recognition. Membership of the Lectitio Divinitatus was forbidden and if he were discovered, it would be the end of his career as an iterator.

'Now we shall contemplate the word of the Emperor,' continued Cassar, reading from a small leather chapbook. Sindermann was reminded of the Bondsman Number 7 books in which the late Ignace Karkasy had written his scandalous poetry. Poetry that had, if Mersadie Oliton's suspicions were correct, caused his murder.

Sinderman thought that the writings of the Lectitio Divinitatus were scarcely less dangerous.

'We have some new faithful among us,' said Cassar, and Sindermann felt every eye in the chamber turn upon him. Used to facing entire continents' worth of audience, Sindermann was suddenly acutely embarrassed by their scrutiny.

'When people are first drawn to adoration of the Emperor, it is only natural that they should have questions,' said Cassar. 'They know the Emperor must be a god, for he has god-like powers over all human species, but aside from this, they are in the dark.'

This, at least, Sindermann agreed with.

'Most importantly, they ask, "If the Emperor truly is a god, then what does he do with his divine power?" We do not see His hand reaching down from the sky, and precious few of us are blessed with visions granted by Him. So does he not care for the majority of His subjects?"

'They do not see the falsehood of such a belief. His hand lies upon all of us, and every one of us owes him our devotion. In the depths of the warp, the Emperor's mighty soul does battle with the dark things that would break through and consume us all. On Terra, he creates wonders that will bring peace, enlightenment and the fruition of all our dreams to the galaxy. The Emperor guides us, teaches us, and exhorts us to become more than we are, but most of all, the Emperor protects.'

'The Emperor protects,' said the congregation in unison.

'The faith of the Lectitio Divinitatus, the Divine Word of the Emperor, is not an easy path to follow. Where the Imperial Truth is comforting in its rigorous rejection of the unseen and the unknown, the Divine Word requires the strength to believe in that which we cannot see. The longer we look upon this dark galaxy and live through the fires of its conquest, the more we realise that the Emperor's divinity is the only truth that *can* exist. We do not seek out the Divine Word. Instead, we hear it, and are compelled to follow it. Faith is not a flag of allegiance or a theory for debate; it is something deep within us, complete and inevitable. The Lectitio Divinitatus is the expression of that faith, and only by acknowledging the Divine Word can we understand the path the Emperor has laid before mankind.'

Fine words, thought Sindermann: fine words, poorly delivered, but heartfelt. He could see that they had touched something deep inside those who heard it. An orator of skill could sway entire worlds with such words and force of belief.

Before Cassar could continue, Sindermann heard sudden shouts coming from the maze of corridors that led into the chamber. He turned as a panicked woman hurled the door behind him open with a dull clang of metal. In her wake, Sindermann could hear the hard bangs of bolter rounds.

The congregation started in confusion, looking to Cassar for an explanation, but the man was as nonplussed as they were.

'They've found you,' yelled Sindermann, realising what was happening.

'Everyone, get out,' shouted Cassar. 'Scatter!'

Sindermann pushed his way through the panicking crowd to the front of the chamber and towards Cassar. Some members of the congregation were producing guns, and from their martial bearing, Sindermann guessed they were Imperial Army troopers. Some were clearly ship's crewmen, and Sindermann knew enough of religion to know that they would defend their faith with violence if they had to.

'Come on, it's time we got out of here,' said Cassar, dragging the venerable iterator towards one of the many access corridors that radiated from the chamber.

Seeing the worry on his face, Cassar said, 'Don't worry, Kyril, the Emperor protects.'

'I certainly hope so,' replied Sindermann breathlessly.

Shots echoed from the ceiling and bright muzzle flashes strobed from the walls. Sindermann threw a glance over his shoulder and saw the bulky, armoured form of Astartes entering the chamber. His heart skipped a beat at the thought of being the enemy of such warriors.

Sindermann hurriedly followed Cassar into the access corridor and through a set of blast doors, their path twisting through the depths of the ship. The *Vengeful Spirit* was an immense vessel and he had no idea of the layout of this area, its walls grim and industrial compared to the magnificence of the upper decks.

'Do you know where you are going?' wheezed Sindermann, his breath coming in hot, agonised spikes and his ancient limbs already tiring from exertion he was scarcely used to.

'Engineering,' said Cassar. 'It's like a maze down there and we have friends in the engine crew. Damn, why can't they just let us be?'

'Because they are scared of you,' said Sindermann, 'just like I was.'

'And you are certain of this?' asked Horus, primarch of the Sons of Horus Legion and Warmaster of the Imperium, his voice echoing around the cavernous strategium of the *Vengeful Spirit*.

'As certain as I can be,' said Ing Mae Sing, the 63rd Expedition's Mistress of Astropaths. Her face was lined and drawn and her blind eyes were sunken within ravaged eye sockets. The demands of sending hundreds of telepathic communications across the galaxy weighed heavily on her skeletal frame. Astropathic acolytes gathered about her, robed in the same ghostly white as she and wordlessly whispering muttered doggerel of the ghastly images in their heads.

'How long do we have?' asked Horus.

'As with all things connected with the warp, it is difficult to be precise,' replied Ing Mae Sing.

'Mistress Sing,' said Horus coldly, 'precision is exactly what I need from you, now more than ever. The direction of the Crusade will change dramatically at this news, and if you are wrong it will change for the worse.'

'My lord, I cannot give you an exact answer, but I believe that within days the gathering warp storms will obscure the Astronomican from us,' replied Ing Mae Sing, ignoring the Warmaster's implicit threat. Though she could not see them, she could feel the hostile presence of the Justaerin warriors, the Sons of Horus First Company Terminators, lurking in the shadows of the strategium. 'Within days we shall hardly see it. Our minds can barely reach across the void and the Navigators claim that they will soon be unable to guide us true. The galaxy will be a place of night and darkness.'

Horus pounded a hand into his fist. 'Do you understand what you say? Nothing more dangerous could happen to the Crusade.'

'I merely state what I see, Warmaster.'

'If you are wrong…'

The threat was not idle – no threat the Warmaster uttered ever was. There had been a time when the Warmaster's anger would never have led to such an overt threat, but the violence in Horus's tone suggested that such a time had long passed.

'If we are wrong, we suffer. It has never been any different.'

'And my brother primarchs? What news from them?' asked Horus.

'We have been unable to confirm contact with the blessed Sanguinius,' replied Ing Mae Sing, 'and Leman Russ has sent no word of his campaign against the Thousand Sons.'

Horus laughed, a harsh Cthonic bark, and said, 'That doesn't surprise me. The Wolf has his head and he'll not easily be distracted from teaching Magnus a lesson. And the others?'

'Vulkan and Dorn are returning to Terra. The other primarchs are pursuing their current campaigns.'

'That is good at least,' said Horus, brow furrowing in thought, 'and what of the Fabricator General?'

'Forgive me, Warmaster, but we have received nothing from Mars. We shall endeavour to make contact by mechanical means, but this will take many months.'

'You have failed in this, Sing. Coordination with Mars is essential.'

Ing Mae Sing had telepathically broadcast a multitude of encoded messages between the *Vengeful Spirit* and Fabricator General Kelbor-Hal of the Mechanicum in the last few weeks. Although their substance was unknown to her, the emotions contained in them were all too clear. Whatever the Warmaster was planning, the Mechanicum was a key part of it.

Horus spoke again, distracting her from her thoughts. 'The other primarchs, have they received their orders?'

'They have, my lord,' said Ing Mae Sing, unable to keep the unease from her voice.

'The reply from Lord Guilliman of the Ultramarines was clean and strong. He confirms Calth as the muster point and has begun marshalling his forces.'

'And Lorgar?' asked Horus.

Ing Mae Sing paused, as if unsure how to phrase her next words.

'His message had residual symbols of... pride and obedience. Very strong, almost fanatical. He acknowledges your order and is making good speed.'

Ing Mae Sing prided herself on her immense self-control, as befitted one whose emotions had to be kept in check lest they be changed by the influence of the warp, but even she could not keep some emotion from surfacing.

'Something bothers you, Mistress Sing?' asked Horus, as though reading her mind.

'My lord?'

'You seem troubled by my orders.'

'It is not my place to be troubled or otherwise, my lord,' said Ing Mae Sing neutrally.

'Correct,' agreed Horus. 'It is not, yet you doubt the wisdom of my course.'

'No!' cried Ing Mae Sing. 'It is just that it is hard not to feel the nature of your communication, the weight of blood and death that each message is wreathed in. It is like breathing fiery smoke with every message we send.'

'You must trust me, Mistress Sing,' said Horus. 'Trust that everything I do is for the good of the Imperium. Do you understand?'

'It is not my place to understand,' whispered the astropath. 'My role in the Crusade is to do the will of my Warmaster.'

'That is true, but before I dismiss you, Mistress Sing, tell me something.'

'Yes, my lord?'

'Tell me of Euphrati Keeler,' said Horus. 'Tell me of the one they are calling the saint.'

Loken still took Mersadie Oliton's breath away. The Astartes were astonishing enough when arrayed for war in their burnished plate, but that sight had been nothing compared to what a Space Marine – specifically, Loken – looked like without his armour.

Stripped to the waist and wearing only pale fatigues and combat boots, Loken glistened with sweat as he ducked and wove between the combat appendages of a training servitor. Although few of the remembrancers had been privileged enough to witness an Astartes fight in battle, it was said that they could kill with their bare hands as effectively as they could with a bolter and chainsword. Watching Loken demolishing the servitor limb by limb, Mersadie could well believe it. She saw such power in his broad, over-muscled torso and such intense focus in his sharp grey eyes that she wondered that she was not repelled by Loken. He was a killing machine, created and trained to deal death, but she couldn't stop watching and blink-clicking images of his heroic physique.

Kyril Sindermann sat next to her and leaned over, saying, 'Don't you have plenty of picts of Garviel already?'

Loken tore the head from the training servitor and turned to face them both, and Mersadie felt a thrill of anticipation. It had been too long since the conclusion of the war against the Technocracy and she had spent too few hours with the captain of the Tenth Company. As his documentarist, she knew that she had a paucity of material following that campaign, but Loken had kept himself to himself in the past few months.

'Kyril, Mersadie,' said Loken, marching past them towards his arming chamber. 'It is good to see you both.'

'I am glad to be here, Garviel,' said Sindermann. The primary iterator was an old man, and Mersadie was sure he had aged a great deal in the year since the fire that had nearly killed him in the Archive Halls of the *Vengeful Spirit*. 'Very glad. Mersadie was kind enough to bring me. I have had a spell of exertion recently, and I am not as fit as once I was. Time's winged chariot draws near.'

'A quote?' asked Loken.

'A fragment,' replied Sindermann.

'I haven't seen much of either of you recently,' observed Loken, smiling down at her. 'Have I been replaced by a more interesting subject?'

'Not at all,' she replied, 'but it is becoming more and more difficult for us to move around the ship. The edict from Maloghurst, you must have heard of it.'

'I have,' agreed Loken, lifting a piece of armour and opening a tin of his ubiquitous lapping powder, 'though I haven't studied the particulars.'

The smell of the powder reminded Mersadie of happier times in this room, recording the tales of great triumphs and wondrous sights, but she cast off such thoughts of nostalgia.

'We are restricted to our own quarters and the Retreat. We need permission to be anywhere else.'

'Permission from whom?' asked Loken.

She shrugged. 'I'm not sure. The edict speaks of submitting requests to the Office of the Lupercal's Court, but no one's been able to get any kind of response from whatever that is.'

'That must be frustrating,' observed Loken and Mersadie felt her anger rise at such an obvious statement.

'Well of course it is! We can't record the Great Crusade if we can't interact with its warriors. We can barely even see them, let alone talk to them.'

'You made it here,' Loken pointed out.

'Well, yes. Following you around has taught me how to keep a low profile, Captain Loken. It helps that you train on your own now.'

Mersadie caught the hurt look in Loken's eye and instantly regretted her words. In previous times, Loken could often be found sparring with fellow officers, the smirking Sedirae, whose flinty dead eyes reminded Mersadie of an ocean predator, Nero Vipus or his Mournival brother, Tarik Torgaddon, but Loken fought alone now. By choice or by design, she did not know.

'Anyway,' continued Mersadie, 'it's getting bad for us. No one's speaking to us. We don't know what's going on any more.'

'We're on a war footing,' said Loken, putting down his armour and looking her straight in the eye. 'The fleet is heading for a rendezvous. We're joining up with Astartes from the other Legions. It'll be a complex campaign. Perhaps the Warmaster is just taking precautions.'

'No, Garviel,' said Sindermann, 'it's more than just that, and I know you well enough to know that you don't believe that either.'

'Really?' snarled Loken. 'You think you know me that well?'

'Well enough, Garviel,' nodded Sindermann, 'well enough. They're cracking down on us, cracking down hard. Not so everyone can see it, but it's happening. You know it too.'

'Do I?'

'Ignace Karkasy,' said Mersadie.

Loken's face crumpled and he looked away, unable to hide the grief he felt for the dead Karkasy, the irascible poet who had been under his protection. Ignace Karkasy had been nothing but trouble and inconvenience, but he had also been a man who had dared to speak out and tell the unpalatable truths that needed to be told.

'They say he killed himself,' continued Sindermann, unwilling to let Loken's grief dissuade him from his course, 'but I've never known a man more convinced that the galaxy needed to hear what he had to say. He was angry at the massacre on the embarkation deck and he wrote about it. He was angry with a lot of things, and he wasn't afraid to speak of them. Now he is dead, and he's not the only one.'

'Not the only one?' asked Loken. 'Who else?'

'Petronella Vivar, that insufferable documentarist woman. They say she got closer to the Warmaster than anyone, and now she's gone too, and I don't think it was back to Terra.'

'I remember her, but you are on thin ice, Kyril. You need to be very clear what you are suggesting.'

Sindermann did not flinch from Loken's gaze and said, 'I believe that those who oppose the will of the Warmaster are being killed.'

The iterator was a frail man, but Mersadie had never been more proud to know him as he stood unbending before a warrior of the Astartes and told him something he didn't want to hear.

Sindermann paused, giving Loken ample time to refute his claims and remind them all that the Emperor had chosen Horus as the Warmaster because he alone could be trusted to uphold the Imperial Truth. Horus was the man to whom every Son of Horus had pledged his life a hundred times over.

But Loken said nothing and Mersadie's heart sank.

'I have read of it more times than I can remember,' continued Sindermann. 'The Uranan Chronicles, for example. The first thing those tyrants did was to murder those who spoke out against their tyranny. The Overlords of the Yndonesic Dark Age did the same thing. Mark my words, the Age of Strife was made possible when the doubting voices fell silent, and now it is happening here.'

'You have always taught temperance, Kyril,' said Loken, 'weighing up arguments and never leaping past them into guesswork. We're at war and we have plenty of enemies already without you seeking to find new ones. It will be very dangerous for you and you may not like what you find. I do not wish to see you come to any harm, either of you.'

'Ha! Now you lecture me, Garviel,' sighed Sindermann. 'So much has changed. You're not just a warrior any more, are you?'

'And you are not just an iterator?'

'No, I suppose not,' nodded Sindermann. 'An iterator promulgates the Imperial Truth, does he not? He does not pick holes in it and spread rumours. But Karkasy is dead, and there are... other things.'

'What things?' asked Loken. 'You mean Keeler?'

'Perhaps,' said Sindermann, shaking his head. 'I don't know, but I feel she is part of it.'

'Part of what?'

'You heard what happened in the Archive Chamber?'

'With Euphrati? Yes, there was a fire and she was badly hurt. She ended up in a coma.'

'I was there,' said Sindermann.

'Kyril,' said Mersadie, a note of warning in her voice.

'Please, Mersadie,' said Sindermann. 'I know what I saw.'

'What did you see?' asked Loken.

'Lies,' replied Sindermann, his voice hushed. 'Lies made real. A creature, something from the warp. Somehow Keeler and I brought it through the gates of the empyrean with the *Book of Lorgar*. My own damn fault, too. It was... it was sorcery, the one thing that all these years I've been preaching is a lie, but it was real and standing before me as surely as I stand before you now. It should have killed us, but Euphrati stood against it and lived.'

'How?' asked Loken.

'That's the part where I run out of rational explanations, Garviel,' shrugged Sindermann.

'Well, what do you think happened?'

Sindermann exchanged a glance with Mersadie and she willed

him not to say anything more, but the venerable iterator continued. 'When you destroyed poor Jubal, it was with your guns, but Euphrati was unarmed. All she had was her faith – her faith in the Emperor. I… I think it was the light of the Emperor that cast the horror back to the warp.'

Hearing Kyril Sindermann talk of faith and the light of the Emperor was too much for Mersadie.

'But Kyril,' she said, 'there must be another explanation. Even what happened to Jubal wasn't beyond physical possibilities. The Warmaster himself told Loken that the thing that took Jubal was some kind of xeno creature from the warp. I've listened to you teach about how minds have been twisted by magic and superstition and all the things that blind us to reality. That's what the Imperial Truth is. I can't believe that the Iterator Kyril Sindermann doesn't believe the Imperial Truth any more.'

'Believe, my dear?' said Sindermann, smiling bleakly and shaking his head. 'Maybe belief is the biggest lie. In ages past, the earliest philosophers tried to explain the stars in the sky and the world around them. One of them conceived of the notion that the universe was mounted on giant crystal spheres controlled by a giant machine, which explained the movements of the heavens. He was laughed at and told that such a machine would be so huge and noisy that everyone would hear it. He simply replied that we are born with that noise all around us, and that we are so used to hearing it that we cannot hear it at all.'

Mersadie sat beside the old man and wrapped her arms around him, surprised to find that he was shivering and his eyes were wet with tears.

'I'm starting to hear it, Garviel,' said Sindermann, his voice quavering. 'I can hear the music of the spheres.'

Mersadie watched Loken's face as he stared at Sindermann, seeing the quality of intelligence and integrity Sindermann had recognised in him. The Astartes had been taught that superstition was the death of the Empire and only the Imperial Truth was a reality worth fighting for.

Now, before her very eyes, that was unravelling.

'Varvarus was killed,' said Loken at last, 'deliberately, by one of our bolts.'

'*Hektor* Varvarus? The Army commander?' asked Mersadie. 'I thought that was the Auretians?'

'No,' said Loken, 'it was one of ours.'

'Why?' she asked.

'He wanted us… I don't know… hauled before a court martial, brought to task for the… killings on the embarkation deck.

Maloghurst wouldn't agree. Varvarus wouldn't back down and now he is dead.'

'Then it's true,' sighed Sindermann. 'The naysayers are being silenced.'

'There are still a few of us left,' said Loken, quiet steel in his voice.

'Then we do something about it, Garviel,' said Sindermann. 'We must find out what has been brought into the Legion and stop it. We can fight it, Loken. We have you, we have the truth and there is no reason why we cannot–'

The sound that cut off Sindermann's voice was the door to the practice deck slamming open, followed by heavy metal-on-metal footsteps. Mersadie knew it was an Astartes even before the impossibly huge shadow fell over her. She turned to see the cursive form of Maloghurst behind her, robed in a cream tunic edged in sea green trim. The Warmaster's equerry, Maloghurst was known as 'the Twisted', as much for his labyrinthine mind as the horrible injuries that had broken his body and left him grotesquely malformed.

His face was thunder and anger seemed to bleed from him.

'Loken,' he said, 'these are civilians.'

'Kyril Sindermann and Mersadie Oliton are official remember-ers of the Great Crusade and I can vouch for them,' said Loken, standing to face Maloghurst as an equal.

Maloghurst spoke with Horus's authority and Mersadie mar-velled at what it must take to stand up to such a man.

'Perhaps you are unaware of the Warmaster's edict, captain,' said Maloghurst, the pleasant neutrality of his tone completely at odds with the tension that crackled between the two Astartes. 'These clerks and notaries have caused enough trouble. You of all people should understand that. There are to be no distrac-tions, Loken, and no exceptions.'

Loken stood face to face with Maloghurst and for one sick-ening moment, Mersadie thought he was about to strike the equerry.

'We are all doing the work of the Great Crusade, Mal,' said Loken tightly. 'Without these men and women, it cannot be completed.'

'Civilians do not fight, captain, they only question and com-plain. They can record everything they desire once the war has been won and they can spread the Imperial Truth once we have conquered a population that needs to hear it. Until then, they are not a part of this Crusade.'

'No, Maloghurst,' said Loken. 'You're wrong and you know it.

The Emperor did not create the primarchs and the Legions so they could fight on in ignorance. He did not set out to conquer the galaxy just for it to become another dictatorship.'

'The Emperor,' said Maloghurst, gesturing towards the door, 'is a long way from here.'

A dozen soldiers marched into the training halls and Mersadie recognised uniforms of the Imperial Army, but saw that their badges of unit and rank had been removed. With a start, she also recognised one face – the icy, golden-eyed features of Petronella Vivar's bodyguard. She recalled that his name was Maggard, and was amazed at the sheer size of the man, his physique bulky and muscled beyond that of the Army soldiers who accompanied him. The exposed flesh of his muscles bore freshly healing scars and his face displayed a nascent gigantism similar to Loken's. He stood out amongst the uniformed Army soldiers, and his presence only lent credence to Sindermann's wild theory that Petronella Vivar's disappearance had nothing to do with her returning to Terra.

'Take the iterator and the remembrancer back to their quarters,' said Maloghurst. 'Post guards and ensure that there are no more breaches.'

Maggard nodded and stepped forwards. Mersadie tried to avoid him, but he was quick and strong, grabbing her by the scruff of her neck and hauling her towards the door. Sindermann stood of his own accord and allowed himself to be led away by the other soldiers.

Maloghurst stood between Loken and the door. If Loken wanted to stop Maggard and his men, he would have to go through Maloghurst.

'Captain Loken,' called Sindermann as he was marched off the practice deck, 'if you wish to understand more, read the *Chronicles of Ursh* again. There you will find illumination.'

Mersadie tried to look back. She could see Loken beyond Maloghurst's robed form, looking like a caged animal ready to attack.

The door slammed shut, and Mersadie stopped struggling as Maggard led her and Sindermann back towards their quarters.

TWO

Perfection
Iterator
What we do best

Perfection. The dead greenskins were a testament to it. Deep Orbital DS191 had been conquered in a matchless display of combat, fields of fire overlapping like dancers' fans, squads charging in to slaughter the orks that the guns could not finish. Squad by squad, room by room, the Emperor's Children had killed their way through the xenos holding the space station with all the handsome perfection of combat that Fulgrim had taught his Legion.

As the warriors of his company despatched any surviving greenskins, Saul Tarvitz removed his helmet and immediately recoiled at the stench. The greenskins had inhabited the orbital for some time and it showed. Fungal growths pulsed on the dark metal struts of the main control centre and crude shrines of weapons, armour and tribal fetishes were piled against the command posts. Above him, the transparent dome of the control centre looked onto the void of space.

The Callinedes system, a collection of Imperial worlds under attack by the greenskins was visible amid the froth of stars. Capturing the orbital back from the orks was the first stage in the Imperial relief of Callinedes, and the Emperor's Children and Iron Hands Legions would soon be storming into the enemy strongholds on Callinedes IV.

'What a stink,' said a voice behind Tarvitz, and he turned to see

Captain Lucius, the finest swordsman of the Emperor's Children. His compatriot's armour was spattered black and his elegant sword still crackled with the blood sizzling on its blue-hot blade. 'Damned animals, they don't have the sense to roll over and die when you kill them.'

Lucius's face had once been perfectly flawless, an echo of Fulgrim's Legion itself, but now, after one too many jibes about how he looked more like a pampered boy than a warrior and the influence of Serena d'Angelus, Lucius had started to acquire scars, each one uniform and straight in a perfect grid across his face. No enemy blade had etched them into his face, for Lucius was far too sublime a warrior to allow a mere enemy to mark his features.

'They're tough, I'll give them that,' agreed Tarvitz.

'They may be tough, but there's no elegance to their fighting,' said Lucius. 'There's no sport in killing them.'

'You sound disappointed.'

'Well of course I am. Aren't you?' asked Lucius, jabbing his sword through a dead greenskin and carving a curved pattern on its back. 'How can we achieve ultimate perfection with such poor specimens to better ourselves against?'

'Don't underestimate the greenskins,' said Tarvitz. 'These animals invaded a compliant world and slaughtered all the troops we left to defend it. They have spaceships and weapons we don't understand, and they attack as if war is some kind of religion to them.'

He turned over the closest corpse – a massive brute with skin as tough as gnarled bark, its violent red eyes open and its undershot maw still grimacing with rage. Only the spread of entrails beneath suggested it was dead at all. Tarvitz could almost feel the jarring of his broadsword as he had plunged it through the creature's midriff and its tremendous strength as it had tried to force him onto his knees.

'You talk about them as if we need to understand them before we can kill them. They're just animals,' said Lucius with a sardonic laugh. 'You think about things too much. That's always been your problem, Saul, and it's why you'll never reach the dizzying heights I will achieve. Come on, just revel in the kill.'

Tarvitz opened his mouth to respond, but he kept his thoughts to himself as Lord Commander Eidolon strode into the control centre.

'Fine work, Emperor's Children!' shouted Eidolon.

As one of Fulgrim's chosen, Eidolon had the honour of being within the tight circle of officers who surrounded the primarch and represented the Legion's finest artistry of war. Although it was not bred into him to dislike a fellow Astartes, Tarvitz had little respect for Eidolon. His arrogance did not befit a warrior of the Emperor's Children and the antagonism between them had only grown on the fields of Murder in the war against the megarachnids.

Despite Tarvitz's reservations, Eidolon carried a powerful natural authority about him, accentuated by magnificent armour with such an overabundance of gilding that the purple colours of the Legion were barely visible. 'The vermin didn't know what hit them!'

The Emperor's Children cheered in response. It had been a classic victory for the Legion: hard, fast and perfect.

The greenskins had been doomed from the start.

'Make ready,' shouted Eidolon, 'to receive your primarch.'

The cargo decks of the deep orbital were rapidly cleared of the greenskin dead by the Legion's menials for a portion of the Callinedes battle force to assemble. Tarvitz felt his pulse race at the thought of setting eyes on his beloved primarch once more. It had been too long since the Legion had fought alongside their leader. Hundreds of Emperor's Children in perfectly dressed ranks stood to attention, a magnificent army in purple and gold.

As magnificent as they were, they were but a poor imitation of the incredible warrior who was father to them all.

The primarch of the Emperor's Children was awe-inspiring, his face pale and sculpted, framed by a flowing mane of albino-white hair. His very presence was intoxicating and Tarvitz felt a fierce pride fill him at the sight of this incredible, wondrous warrior. Created to echo a facet of war, Fulgrim's art was the pursuit of perfection through battle and he sought it as diligently as an imagist strove for perfection through his picts. One shoulder of his golden armour was worked into a sweeping eagle's wing, the emblem of the Emperor's Children, and the symbolism was a clear statement of Legion pride.

The palatine aquila was the Emperor's personal symbol, and he had granted the Emperor's Children alone the right to bear that same heraldry, symbolically proclaiming Fulgrim's warriors as his most adored Legion. Fulgrim wore a golden-hilted sword at his hip, said to have been a gift from the Warmaster himself, a clear sign of the bond of brotherhood between them.

The officers of the primarch's inner circle flanked him – Lord Commander Eidolon, Apothecary Fabius, Chaplain Charmosian and the massive Dreadnought body of Ancient Rylanor. Even these heroes of the Legion were dwarfed by Fulgrim's physical size and his sheer charisma.

A line of heralds, chosen from among the young initiates who were soon to complete their training as Emperor's Children, fanned out in front of Fulgrim, playing a blaring fanfare on their golden trumpets to announce the arrival of the most perfect warrior in the galaxy. A thunderous roar of applause swelled from the assembled Emperor's Children as they welcomed their primarch back to his Legion.

Fulgrim waited graciously for the applause to die down. More than anything, Tarvitz aspired to be that awesome golden figure in front of them, though he knew he had already been designated as a line officer and nothing more. But Fulgrim's very presence filled him with the promise that he could be so much better if he was only given the chance. His pride in his Legion's prowess caught light as Fulgrim looked over the assembled warriors, and the primarch's dark eyes shone as he acknowledged each and every one of them.

'My brothers,' called Fulgrim, his voice lilting and golden, 'this day you have shown the accursed greenskin what it means to stand against the Children of the Emperor!'

More applause rolled around the cargo decks, but Fulgrim spoke over it, his voice easily cutting through the clamour of his warriors.

'Commander Eidolon has wrought you into a weapon against which the greenskin had no defence. Perfection, strength, resolve – these qualities are the cutting edge of this Legion and you have shown them all here today. This orbital is in Imperial hands once more, as are the others the greenskins had occupied in the futile hope of fending off our invasion.

'The time has come to press home this attack against the greenskins and liberate the Callinedes system. My brother primarch, Ferrus Manus of the Iron Hands and I shall see to it that not a single alien stands upon land claimed in the name of the Crusade.'

Expectation was heavy in the air as the Legion waited for the order that would send them into battle with their primarch.

'But most of you, my brothers, will not be there,' said Fulgrim. The crushing disappointment Tarvitz felt was palpable, for the Legion had been sent to the Callinedes system with the assumption that it would lend its full strength to the destruction of the invading xenos.

'The Legion will be divided,' continued Fulgrim, raising his hands to stem the cries of woe and lamentation that his words provoked. 'I will lead a small force to join Ferrus Manus and his Four Iron Hands at Callinedes Four. The rest of the Legion will rendezvous with the Warmaster's Sixty-Third Expedition at the Isstvan system. These are the orders of the Warmaster and of your primarch. Lord Commander Eidolon will lead you to Isstvan, and he will act in my stead until I can join you once more.'

Tarvitz glanced at Lucius, unable to read the expression on the swordsman's face at the news of their new orders. Conflicting emotions warred within Tarvitz: aching loss to be parted from his primarch once more, and excited anticipation at the thought of fighting alongside his comrades in the Sons of Horus.

'Commander, if you please,' said Fulgrim, gesturing Eidolon to step forwards.

Eidolon nodded and said, 'The Warmaster has called upon us to aid his Legion in battle once more. He recognises our skills and we welcome this chance to prove our superiority. We are to halt a rebellion in the Isstvan system, but we are not to fight alone. As well as his own Legion, the Warmaster has seen fit to deploy the Death Guard and World Eaters.'

A muttered gasp spread around the cargo bay at the mention of such brutal Legions.

Eidolon chuckled. 'I see some of you remember fighting alongside our brother Astartes. We all know what a grim and artless business war becomes in the hands of such men, so I say this is the perfect opportunity to show the Warmaster how the Emperor's chosen fight.'

The Legion cheered once more, and Tarvitz knew that whenever the Emperor's Children had a chance to prove their skill and artistry, especially to the other Legions, they took it. Fulgrim had turned pride into a virtue, and it drove each warrior of his Legion to heights of excellence that no other could match.

Torgaddon had called it arrogance and on the surface of Murder Tarvitz had tried to dissuade him of that notion, but hearing the boastful cries of the Emperor's Children around him, he wasn't sure that his friend had been wrong after all.

'The Warmaster has requested our presence immediately,' shouted Eidolon through the cheering. 'Although Isstvan is not far distant, the conditions in the warp have become more difficult, so we must make all haste. The strike cruiser *Andronius* will leave for Isstvan in four hours. When we arrive, it will be as ambassadors for our Legion, and when the battle is done the Warmaster will have witnessed war at its most magnificent.'

Eidolon saluted and Fulgrim led the applause before turning and taking his leave.

Tarvitz was stunned. To commit such a force of Astartes was rare and he knew that whatever foe they would face on Isstvan must be mighty indeed. Even the thrill of excitement he felt at this opportunity to prove themselves before the Warmaster was tempered by a sudden, nagging sense of unease.

'Four Legions?' asked Lucius, echoing his own thoughts as the squads fell out to make ready for the journey to join the 63rd Expedition. 'For one system? That's absurd!'

'Careful Lucius, you veer close to arrogance,' Tarvitz pointed out. 'Are you questioning the Warmaster's decision?'

'Questioning, no,' said Lucius defensively, 'but come on, even you have to admit it's a sledgehammer to crack a nut.'

'Possibly,' conceded Tarvitz, 'but for the Isstvan system to rebel, it must have been compliant at one stage.'

'What's your point?'

'My point, Lucius, is that the Crusade was supposed to be pushing ever outwards, conquering the galaxy in the name of the Emperor. Instead it is turning back on itself to patch up the cracks. I can only assume that the Warmaster wants to make some kind of grand gesture to show his enemies what rebellion means.'

'Ungrateful bastards,' spat Lucius. 'Once we're done with Isstvan they'll beg us to take them back!'

'With four Legions sent against them,' replied Tarvitz, 'I don't think there'll be many Isstvanians left for us to take back.'

'Come, Saul,' said Lucius walking ahead of him, 'did you lose your taste for battle against the greenskins?'

A taste for battle? Tarvitz had never considered such an idea. He had always fought because he wanted to become more than he was, to strive for perfection in all things. For longer than he could remember he had devoted himself to the task of emulating the warriors of the Legion who were more gifted and more worthy than he. He knew his station within the Legion, but knowing one's station was the first step to bettering it.

Watching Lucius's arrogant swagger, Tarvitz was reminded of how much his fellow captain loved battle. Lucius loved it without shame or apology, seeing it as the best way to express himself, weaving between his enemies and cutting a path of bloody ruin through them with his flashing sword.

'It just concerns me,' said Tarvitz.

'What does?' asked Lucius, turning back to face him. Tarvitz could see the hastily masked exasperation on the swordsman's face. He had seen that expression more and more on Lucius's scarred features recently, and it saddened him to know that the swordsman's ego and rampant ambition to rise within the ranks of the Emperor's Children would be the undoing of their friendship.

'That the Crusade has to repair itself at all. Compliance used to be the end of it. Not now.'

'Don't worry,' smiled Lucius. 'Once a few of these rebel worlds get a decent killing this will all be over and the Crusade will go on.

Rebel worlds... Whoever thought to hear such a phrase?

Tarvitz said nothing as he considered the sheer numbers of Astartes that would be converging on the Isstvan system. Hundreds of Astartes had fought on Deep Orbital DS191, but more than ten thousand Emperor's Children made up the Legion, most of whom would be journeying to Isstvan III. That in itself was enough for several war zones. The thought of four Legions arrayed in battle sent shivers up Tarvitz's spine.

What would be left of Isstvan when four Legions had marched through the system? Could any depths of rebellion really justify that?

'I just want victory,' said Tarvitz, the words sounding hollow, even to him.

Lucius laughed, but Tarvitz couldn't tell if it was in agreement or mockery.

Being confined to his quarters was the most exquisite torture for Kyril Sindermann. Without the library of books he was used to consulting in Archive Chamber Three he felt quite adrift. His own library, though extensive by any normal standards, was a paltry thing next to the arcana that had been destroyed in the fire.

How many priceless, irreplaceable tomes had been lost in the wake of the warp beast he and Euphrati had conjured from the pages of the *Book of Lorgar*?

It did not bear thinking about and he wondered how much the future would condemn them for the knowledge that had been lost there. He had already filled thousands of pages with those fragments he could remember from the books he had consulted. Most of it was fragmentary and disjointed. He knew that the task of recalling everything he had read was doomed to failure, but he could no more conceive of giving up than he could stop his heart from beating.

His gift and the gift of the Crusade to the ages yet to come was the accumulated wisdom of the galaxy's greatest thinkers and warriors. With the broad shoulders of such knowledge to stand upon, who knew what dizzying heights of enlightenment the Imperium might reach?

His pen scratched across the page, recalling the philosophies of the Hellenic writers and their early debates on the nature of divinity. No doubt many would think it pointless to transcribe the writings of those long dead, but Sindermann knew that to ignore the past was to doom the future to repeat it.

The text he wrote spoke of the ineffable inscrutability of false gods, and he knew that such mysteries were closer to the surface than he cared to admit. The things he had seen and read since Sixty-Three Nineteen had stretched his scepticism to the point where he could no longer deny the truth of what was plainly before him and which Euphrati Keeler had been trying to tell them all.

Gods existed and, in the case of the Emperor, moved amongst them...

He paused for a moment as the full weight of that thought wrapped itself around him like a comforting blanket. The warmth and ease such simple acceptance gave him was like a panacea for all the ills that had troubled him this last year, and he smiled as his pen idly scratched across the page before him without his conscious thought.

Sindermann started as he realised that the pen was moving across the page of its own volition. He looked down to see what was being written.

She needs you.

Cold fear gripped him, but even as it rose, it was soothed and a comforting state of love and trust filled him. Images filled his head unbidden: the Warmaster strong and powerful in his newly forged suit of black plate armour, the amber eye glowing like a coal from the furnace. Claws slid from the Warmaster's gauntlets and an evil red glow built from his gorget, illuminating his face with a ghastly daemonic light.

'No...' breathed Sindermann, feeling a great and unspeakable horror fill him at this terrible vision, but no sooner had this image filled his head than it was replaced by one of Euphrati Keeler lying supine on her medicae bed. Terrified thoughts were banished at the sight of her and Sindermann felt his love for this beautiful woman fill him as a pure and wondrous light.

Even as he smiled in rapture, the vision darkened and yellowed talons slid into view, tearing at the image of Euphrati. Sindermann screamed in sudden premonition.

Once again he looked at the words on the page, marvelling at their desperate simplicity.

She needs you.
Someone was sending him a message.
The saint was in danger.

Coordinating a Legion's assets – its Astartes, its spacecraft, staff and accompanying Imperial Army units – was a truly Herculean task. Managing to coordinate the arrival of four Legions in the same place at the same time was an impossible task: impossible for anyone but the Warmaster.

The *Vengeful Spirit*, its long flat prow like the tip of a spear, slid from the warp in a kaleidoscopic display of pyrotechnics, lightning raking along its sides as the powerful warp-integrity fields took the full force of re-entry. In the interstellar distance, the closest star of the Isstvan system glinted, cold and hard against the blackness. The Eye of Horus glared from the top of the ship's prow, the entire vessel having been refitted following the victory against the Technocracy, the bone-white of the Luna Wolves replaced by the metallic grey-green of the Sons of Horus.

Within moments, another ship broke through, tearing its way into real space with the brutal functionality of its Legion. Where the *Vengeful Spirit* had a deadly grace to it, the newcomer was brutish and ugly, its hull a drab gunmetal-grey, its only decoration, a single brazen skull on its prow. The vessel was the *Endurance*, capital ship of the Death Guard fleet accompanying the Warmaster, and a flotilla of smaller cruisers and escorts flew in its wake. All were the same unembellished gunmetal, for nothing in Mortarion's Legion bore any more adornment than was necessary.

Several hours later the powerful, stabbing form of the *Conqueror* broke through to join the Warmaster. Shimmering with the white and blue colours of the World Eaters, the *Conqueror* was Angron's flagship, and its blunt, muscular form echoed the legendary ferocity of the World Eaters primarch.

Finally, the *Andronius*, at the head of the Emperor's Children fleet, joined the growing Isstvan strike force. The vessel itself was resplendent in purple and gold, more like a flying palace than a ship of war. Its appearance was deceptive however, for the gun decks bristled with weapons manned by well-drilled menials who lived and died to serve Fulgrim's Legion. The *Andronius*, for all its decorative folly, was a compact, lethal weapon of war.

The Great Crusade had rarely seen a fleet of such power assembled in one place.

Until now, only the Emperor had commanded such a force, but his place was on distant Terra, and these Legions answered only to the Warmaster.

So it was that four Legions gathered and turned their eyes towards the Isstvan system.

The klaxons announcing the *Vengeful Spirit*'s translation back to real space were the spur to action that Kyril Sindermann had been waiting for. Mopping his brow with an already moist handkerchief, he pushed himself to his feet and made his way to the shutter of his quarters.

He took a deep, calming breath as the shutter rose and he was confronted by the hostile stares of two Army soldiers, their starched uniforms insignia free and anonymous.

'Can I help you, sir?' asked a tall man with a cold, unhelpful expression.

'Yes,' said Sindermann, his voice perfectly modulated to convey his non-threatening affability. 'I need to travel to the medicae deck.'

'You don't look sick,' said the second guard.

Sindermann chuckled, reaching out to touch the man's arm like a kindly grandfather. 'No, it's not me, my boy, it's a friend of mine. She's rather ill and I promised that I would look in on her.'

'Sorry,' said the first guard, in a tone that suggested he was anything but. 'We've got orders from the Astartes not to let anyone off this deck.'

'I see, I see,' sighed Sindermann, letting a tear trickle from the corner of his eye. 'I don't want to be an inconvenience, my boys, but my friend, well, she's like a daughter to me, you see. She is very dear to me and you would be doing an old man a very real favour if you could just let me see her.'

'I don't think so, sir,' said the guard, but Sindermann could already detect a softening in his tone and pushed a little harder.

'She has... she has... not long left to her, and I was told by Maloghurst himself that I would be allowed to see her before... before the end.'

Using Maloghurst's name was a gamble, but it was a calculated gamble. These men were unlikely to have any formal channel to contact the Warmaster's equerry, but if they decided to check, he would be unmasked.

Sindermann kept his voice low and soft as he played the grandfatherly role, utilising every trick he had learned as an iterator – the precise timbre of his voice, the frailty of his posture, keeping eye contact and empathy with his audience.

'Do you have children, my boy?' asked Sindermann, reaching out to clasp the guard's arm.

'Yes, sir, I do.'

'Then you understand why I have to see her,' pressed Sindermann, risking the more direct approach and hoping that he
had judged these men correctly.

'You're just going to the medicae deck?' asked the guard.

'No further,' promised Sindermann. 'I just need some time to
say my goodbyes to her. That's all. Please?'

The guards exchanged glances and Sindermann fought to keep
the smile from his face as he knew he had them. The first soldier nodded and they moved aside to let him past.

'Just the medicae deck, old man,' said the guard, scrawling on
a chit that would allow him passage through the ship to the
medicae deck and back. 'If you're not back in your quarters in
a couple of hours, I'll be dragging you back here myself.'

Sindermann nodded, taking the proffered chit and shaking
both men warmly by the hand.

'You're good soldiers, boys,' he said, his voice dripping with
gratitude. 'Good soldiers. I'll be sure to tell Maloghurst of your
compassion for an old man.'

He turned quickly so that they didn't see the relief on his face
and hurried away down the corridor towards the medicae deck.
The companionways echoed with their emptiness as he made
his way through the twisting maze of the ship, an idiot smile
plastered across his puffing features. Entire worlds had fallen
under the spell of his oratory and here he was smiling about
duping two simple-minded guards to let him out of his room.

How the mighty had fallen.

'Is there any more news on Varvarus?' asked Loken as he and
Torgaddon walked through the Museum of Conquest on their
way to the Lupercal's Court.

Torgaddon shook his head. 'The shells were too fragmented.
Apothecary Vaddon wouldn't be able to make a match even if
we found the weapon that fired the shot. It was one of ours,
but that's all we know.'

The museum was brimming with artefacts won from the
Legion's many victories, for the Luna Wolves had brought a
score of worlds into compliance. A grand statue dominating
one wall recalled the days when the Emperor and Horus had
fought side by side in the first campaigns of the Great Crusade. The Emperor, sword in hand, fought off slender, masked
aliens while Horus, back to back with his father, blazed away
with a boltgun.

Beyond the statue, Loken recognised a display of bladed insectoid limbs, a blend of metallic and biological flesh wrested

from the megarachnids on Murder. Only a few of these trophies had been won after Horus's investiture as Warmaster,
the majority having been taken before the Luna Wolves had
been renamed the Sons of Horus in honour of the Warmaster's accomplishments.

'The remembrancers are next,' said Loken. 'They are asking
too many questions. Some of them may already have been
murdered.'

'Who?'

'Ignace and Petronella Vivar.'

'Karkasy,' said Torgaddon. 'Damn, I'd heard he killed himself, but I should have known they'd find a way to do it. The
warrior lodge was talking about silencing him, Abaddon in particular. They didn't call it murder, although Abaddon seemed to
think it was the same as killing an enemy in war. That's when
I broke with the lodge.'

'Did they say how it was to be done?'

Torgaddon shook his head. 'No, just that it needed to be done.'

'It won't be long before all this is out in the open,' promised
Loken. 'The lodge doesn't move under a veil of secrecy any more
and soon there will be a reckoning.'

'Then what do we do?'

Loken looked away from his friend, at the high arch that led
from the museum and into the Lupercal's Court.

'I don't know,' he said, waving Torgaddon to silence as he
caught sight of a figure moving behind one of the furthest
cabinets.

'What's up?' asked Torgaddon.

'I'm not sure,' said Loken, moving between display cabinets
of gleaming swords captured from an ancient feudal kingdom
and strange alien weapons taken from the many species the
Legion had destroyed. The figure he had seen was another Astartes, and Loken recognised the colours of the World Eaters upon
his armour.

Loken and Torgaddon rounded the corner of a tall,
walnut-framed cabinet, seeing a scarred Astartes warrior peering intently at an immense battle-glaive that had been wrested
from the hands of a xenos praetorian by the Warmaster himself.

'Welcome to the *Vengeful Spirit*,' said Loken.

The World Eater looked up from the weapon and turned to
face them. His face was deeply bronzed, long and noble, con-
trasting with the bone-white and blue of his Legion's colours.

'Greetings,' he said, bringing his forearm across his armoured
chest in a martial salute.

'Khârn, Eighth Assault Company of the World Eaters.'

'Loken of the Tenth,' replied Loken.

'Torgaddon of the Second,' nodded Torgaddon.

'Impressive, this,' said Khârn, looking around him.

'Thank you,' said Loken. 'The Warmaster always believed we should remember our enemies. If we forget them, we shall never learn.'

He pointed at the weapon Khârn had been admiring. 'We have the preserved corpse of the creature that carried this weapon somewhere around here. It's the size of a tank.'

'Angron has his share of trophies too,' said Khârn, 'but only from foes that deserve to be remembered.'

'Should we not remember them all?'

'No,' said Khârn firmly. 'There is nothing to gain from knowing your enemy. The only thing that matters is that they are to be destroyed. Everything else is just a distraction.'

'Spoken like a true World Eater,' said Torgaddon.

Khârn looked up from the weapon with an amused sneer. 'You seek to provoke me, Captain Torgaddon, but I already know what other Legions think of the World Eaters.'

'We were on Aureus,' said Loken. 'You are butchers.'

Khârn smiled. 'Hah! Honesty is rare these days, Captain Loken. Yes, we are and we are proud because we are good at it. My primarch is not ashamed of what he does best, so neither am I.'

'I trust you're here for the conclave?' asked Loken, wishing to change the subject.

'Yes. I serve as my primarch's equerry.'

Torgaddon raised an eyebrow. 'Tough job.'

'Sometimes,' admitted Khârn. 'Angron cares little for diplomacy.'

'The Warmaster believes it is important.'

'So I see, but all Legions do things differently,' laughed Khârn, clapping Loken on his shoulder guard. 'As one honest man to another, your own Legion has as many detractors as admirers. Too damn superior, the lot of you.'

'The Warmaster has high standards,' said Loken.

'So does Angron, I assure you,' said Khârn, and Loken was surprised to hear a note of weariness in Khârn's voice. 'The Emperor knew that sometimes the best course of action is to let the World Eaters do what we do best. The Warmaster knows it too, otherwise we would not be here. It may be distasteful to you, captain, but if it were not for warriors like mine, the Great Crusade would have foundered long ago.'

'There we must agree to disagree,' said Loken. 'I could not do what you do.'

Khârn shook his head. 'You're a warrior of the Astartes, captain. If you had to kill every living thing in a city to ensure victory, you would do it. We must always be prepared to go further than our enemy. All the Legions know it; the World Eaters just preach it openly.'

'Let us hope it never comes to that.'

'Do not pin too much on that hope. I hear tell that Isstvan Three will be difficult to break.'

'What do you know of it?' asked Torgaddon.

Khârn shrugged. 'Nothing specific, just rumours really. Something religious, they say, witches and warlocks, skies turning red and monsters from the warp, all the usual hyperbole. Not that the Sons of Horus would believe such things.'

'The galaxy is a complicated place,' replied Loken carefully. 'We don't know the half of what goes on in it.'

'I'm beginning to wonder myself,' agreed Khârn.

'It's changing,' continued Loken, 'the galaxy, and the Crusade with it.'

'Yes,' said Khârn with relish. 'It is.'

Loken was about to ask Khârn what he meant when the doors to the Lupercal's Court swung open.

'Evidently the Warmaster's conclave will begin soon,' said Khârn, bowing before them both. 'It is time for me to rejoin my primarch.'

'And we must join the Warmaster,' said Loken. 'Perhaps we will see you on Isstvan Three?'

'Perhaps,' nodded Khârn, walking off between the spoils of a hundred wars. 'If there's anything left of Isstvan Three when the World Eaters finish with it.'

THREE

Horus enthroned

The saint is in danger

Isstvan III

Lupercal's Court was a new addition to the *Vengeful Spirit*. Previously the Warmaster had held briefings and planning sessions on the strategium, but it had been decided that he needed somewhere grander to hold court. Designed by Peeter Egon Momus, it had been artfully constructed to place the Warmaster in a setting more suited to his position as the leader of the Great Crusade and present him as the first among equals to his fellow commanders.

Vast banners hung from the sides of the room, most belonging to the Legion's battle companies, though there were a few that Loken didn't recognise. He saw one with a throne of skulls set against a tower of brass rising from a blood-red sea and another with an eight-pointed black star shining in a white sky. The meaning of such obscure symbols confounded Loken, but he assumed that they represented the warrior lodge that had become integral to the Legion.

Greater than all the majesty designed by the architect designate, was the primarch of the Sons of Horus himself, enthroned before them on a great basalt throne. Abaddon and Aximand stood to one side. Both warriors were armoured, Abaddon in the glossy black of the Justaerin, Aximand in his pale green plate.

The two officers glared at Loken and Torgaddon – the enmity that had grown between them during the Auretian campaign too great to hide any more. As he met Abaddon's flinty gaze, Loken felt great sadness as the realised that the glorious ideal of the Mournival was finally and irrevocably dead. None of them spoke as Loken and Torgaddon took their places on the other side of the Warmaster.

Loken had stood with these warriors and sworn an oath by the light of a reflected moon on a planet the inhabitants called Terra, to counsel the Warmaster and preserve the soul of the Legion.

That felt like a very long time ago.

'Loken, Torgaddon,' said Horus, and even after all that had happened, Loken felt honoured to be so addressed. 'Your role here is simply to observe and remind our Legion brothers of the solidity of our cause. Do you understand?'

'Yes, my Warmaster,' said Torgaddon.

'Loken?' asked the Warmaster.

Loken nodded and took his allotted position. 'Yes, Warmaster.'

He felt the Warmaster's penetrating eyes boring into him, but kept his gaze fixed firmly on the arches that led into the Lupercal's Court as the doors beneath one of them slid open. The tramp of feet sounded and a blood-red angel of death emerged from the shadows.

Loken had seen the primarch of the World Eaters before, but was still awed by his monstrous, physical presence. Angron was huge, easily as tall as the Warmaster, but also massively broad, with wide hulking shoulders like some enormous beast of burden. His face was scarred and violent, his eyes buried deep in folds of angry red scar tissue. Ugly cortical implants jutted from his scalp, connected to the collar of his armour by ribbed cables. The primarch's armour was ancient and bronze, like that of a feral world god, with heavy metal plates over mail and twin chainaxes strapped to his back.

Loken had heard that Angron had once been a slave before the Emperor had found him, and that his masters had forced the implants on him to turn him into a psychotic killer for their fighting pits.

Looking at Angron, Loken could well believe it.

Angron's equerry, Khârn, flanked the terrifying primarch, his expression neutral where his master's was thunder.

'Horus!' said Angron, his voice rough and brutal. 'I see the Warmaster welcomes his brother like a king. Am I your subject now?'

'Angron,' replied Horus unperturbed, 'it is good that you could join us.'

'And miss all this prettiness? Not for the world,' said Angron, his voice loaded with the threat of a smouldering volcano.

A second delegation arrived through another of the arches, arrayed in the purple and gold of the Emperor's Children. Led by Eidolon in all his magnificence, a squad of Astartes with glittering swords marched alongside the lord commander, their battlegear as ornate as their leader's.

'Warmaster, the Lord Fulgrim sends his regards,' stated Eidolon formally and with great humility. Loken saw that Eidolon had learned the ways of a practiced diplomat since he had last spoken to the Warmaster. 'He assures you that his task is well under way and that he will join us soon. I speak for him and command the Legion in his stead.'

Loken's eyes darted from Angron to Eidolon, seeing the obvious antipathy between the two Legions. The Emperor's Children and the World Eaters were as different as could be – Angron's Legion fought and won through raw aggression, while the Emperor's Children had perfected the art of picking an enemy force apart and destroying it a piece at a time.

'Lord Angron,' said Eidolon with a bow, 'it is an honour.'

Angron did not deign to reply and Loken saw Eidolon stiffen at this insult, but any immediate confrontation was averted as the final delegation to the Warmaster entered the Lupercal's Court.

Mortarion, primarch of the Death Guard, was backed by a unit of warriors armoured in the dull gleam of unpainted Terminator plate. Mortarion's armour was also bare, with the brass skull of the Death Guard on one shoulder guard. His pallid face and scalp were hairless and pocked, his mouth and throat hidden by a heavy collar that hissed spurts of grey steam as he breathed.

A Death Guard captain marched beside the primarch, and Loken recognised him with a smile. Captain Nathaniel Garro had fought alongside the Sons of Horus in the days when they had been known as the Luna Wolves. The Terran-born captain had won many friends within the Warmaster's Legion for his unshakeable code of honour and his straightforward, honest manner.

The Death Guard warrior caught Loken's gaze and gave a perfunctory nod of greeting.

'With our brother Mortarion,' said Horus, 'we are complete.'

The Warmaster stood and descended from the elevated throne to the centre of the court as the lights dimmed and a glowing globe appeared above him, hovering just below the ceiling.

'This,' said Horus, 'is Isstvan III, courtesy of servitor-manned stellar cartography drones. Remember it well, for history will be made here.'

✠ ✠ ✠

Jonah Aruken paused in his labours and slipped a small hip flask from beneath his uniform jacket as he checked for anyone watching. The hangar bay was bustling with activity, as it always seemed to be these days, but no one was paying him any attention. The days when an Imperator Titan being made ready for war would pause even the most jaded war maker in his tracks were long past, for there were few here who had not seen the mighty form of the *Dies Irae* being furnished for battle scores of times already.

He took a hit from the flask and looked up at the old girl.

The Titan's hull was scored and dented with wounds the Mechanicum servitors had not yet had time to patch and Jonah patted the thick plates of her leg armour affectionately.

'Well, old girl,' he said, 'you've certainly seen some action, but I still love you.'

He smiled at the thought of a man being in love with a machine, but he'd love anything that had saved his life as often as the *Dies Irae* had. Through the fires of uncounted battles, they had fought together and as much as Titus Cassar denied it, Jonah knew that there was a mighty heart and soul at the core of this glorious war machine.

Jonah took another drink from his flask as his expression turned sour thinking of Titus and his damned sermons. Titus said he felt the light of the Emperor within him, but Jonah didn't feel much of anything any more.

As much as he wanted to believe in what Titus was preaching, he just couldn't let go of the sceptical core at the centre of his being. To believe in things that weren't there, that couldn't be seen or felt? Titus called it faith, but Jonah was a man who needed to believe in what was real, what could be touched and experienced.

Princeps Turnet would discharge him from the crew of the *Dies Irae* if he knew he had attended prayer meetings back on Davin, and the thought of spending the rest of the Crusade as a menial, denied forever the thrill of commanding the finest war machine ever to come from the forges of Mars sent a cold shiver down his spine.

Every few days, Titus would ask him to come to another prayer meeting and the times he said yes, they would furtively make their way to some forsaken part of the ship to listen to passages read from the Lectitio Divinitatus. Each time he would sweat the journey back for fear of discovery and the court martial that would no doubt follow.

Jonah had been a career Titan crewman since the day he

had first set foot aboard his inaugural posting, a Warhound Titan called the *Venator*, and he knew that if it came down to a choice, he would choose the *Dies Irae* over the Lectitio Divinitatus every time.

But still, the thought that Titus might be right continued to nag at him.

He leaned back against the Titan's leg, sliding down until he was sitting on his haunches with his knees drawn up to his chest.

'Faith,' he whispered, 'you can't earn it and you can't buy it. Where then do I find it?'

'Well,' said a voice behind and above him, 'you can start by putting that flask away and coming with me.'

Jonah looked up and saw Titus Cassar, resplendent as always in his parade-ready uniform, standing in the arched entrance to the Titan's leg bastions.

'Titus,' said Jonah, hurriedly stuffing the hip flask back into his jacket. 'What's up?'

'We have to go,' said Titus urgently. 'The saint is in danger.'

Maggard stalked along the shadowed companionways of the *Vengeful Spirit* at a brisk pace, marching at double time with the vigour of a man on his way to a welcome rendezvous. His hulking form had been steadily growing over the last few months, as though he were afflicted with some hideous form of rapid gigantism.

But the procedures the Warmaster's Apothecaries were performing on his frame were anything but hideous. His body was changing, growing and transforming beyond anything the crude surgeries of House Carpinus had ever managed. Already he could feel the new organs within him reshaping his flesh and bone into something greater than he could ever have imagined, and this was just the beginning.

His Kirlian blade was unsheathed, shimmering with a strange glow in the dim light of the corridor. He wore fresh white robes, his enlarging physique already too massive for his armour. Legion artificers stood ready to reshape it once his flesh had settled into its new form, and he missed its reassuring solidity enclosing him.

Like him, his armour would be born anew, forged into something worthy of the Warmaster and his chosen warriors. Maggard knew he was not yet ready for such inclusion, but he had already carved himself a niche within the Sons of Horus. He walked where the Astartes could not, acted where they could not be seen to act and spilled blood where they needed to be seen as peacemakers.

It required a special kind of man to do such work, efficiently and conscience-free, and Maggard was perfectly suited to his new role. He had killed hundreds of people at the behest of House Carpinus and many more than that before he had been captured by them, but these had been poor, messy killings compared to the death he now carried.

He remembered the sense of magnificent beginnings when Maloghurst had tasked him with the death of Ignace Karkasy.

Maggard had jammed the barrel of his pistol beneath the poet's quivering jaw and blown his brains out over the roof of his cramped room before letting the generously fleshed body crash to the floor in a flurry of bloody papers.

Why Maloghurst had required Karkasy's death did not concern Maggard. The equerry spoke with the voice of Horus and Maggard had pledged his undying loyalty to the Warmaster on the battlefield of Davin when he had offered him his sword.

Later, whether in reward or as part of his ongoing designs, the Warmaster had killed his former mistress, Petronella Vivar, and for that, Maggard was forever in his debt.

Whatever the Warmaster desired, Maggard would move heaven or hell to see it done.

Now he had been ordered to do something wondrous.

Now he was going to kill a saint.

Sindermann beat his middle finger against his chin in a nervous tattoo as he tried to look as if he belonged in this part of the ship. Deck crew in orange jumpsuits and ordnance officers in yellow jackets threaded past him as he awaited his accomplices in this endeavour. He clutched the chit the guard had given him tightly, as though it were some kind of talisman that would protect him if someone challenged him.

'Come on, come on,' he whispered. 'Where are you?'

It had been a risk contacting Titus Cassar, but he had no one else to turn to. Mersadie did not believe in the Lectitio Divinitatus, and in truth he wasn't sure he did yet, but he knew that whatever or whoever had sent him the vision of Euphrati Keeler had meant him to act upon it. Likewise, Garviel Loken was out of the question, for it was certain that his movements would not escape notice.

'Iterator,' hissed a voice from beside him and Sindermann almost cried out in surprise. Titus Cassar stood beside him, an earnest expression creasing his slender face. Another man stood behind him, similarly uniformed in the dark blue of a Titan crewman.

'Titus,' breathed Sindermann in relief. 'I wasn't sure you'd be able to come.'

'We won't have long before Princeps Turnet notices we are not at our posts, but your communication said the saint was in danger.'

'She is,' confirmed Sindermann. 'Grave danger.'

'How do you know?' asked the second man.

Cassar's brow twisted in annoyance. 'I'm sorry, Kyril, this is Jonah Aruken, my fellow moderati on the *Dies Irae*. He is one of us.'

'I just know,' said Sindermann. 'I saw… I don't know… a vision of her lying on her bed and I just knew that someone intended her harm.'

'A vision,' breathed Cassar. 'Truly you are one of the chosen of the Emperor.'

'No, no,' hissed Sindermann. 'I'm really not. Now come on, we don't have time for this, we have to go now.'

'Where?' asked Jonah Aruken.

'The medicae deck,' said Sindermann, holding up his chit. 'We have to get to the medicae deck.'

The surface of the shimmering globe above Horus resolved into continents and oceans, overlaid with the traceries of geophysical features: plains, forests, seas, mountain ranges and cities.

Horus held up his arms, as if supporting the globe from below like some titan from the ancient myths of old Earth.

'This is Isstvan Three,' he repeated, 'a world brought into compliance thirteen years ago by the Twenty-Seventh expeditionary force of our brother Corax.'

'And he wasn't up to the job?' snorted Angron.

Horus shot Angron a dangerous look. 'There was some resistance, yes, but the last elements of the aggressive faction were destroyed by the Raven Guard at the Redarth Valley.'

The battle site flared red on the globe, nestled among a mountain range on one of Isstvan III's northern continents. 'The remembrancer order was not yet foisted upon us by the Council of Terra, but a substantial civilian contingent was left behind to begin integration with the Imperial Truth.'

'Are we to assume that the Truth didn't take?' asked Eidolon.

'Mortarion?' prompted Horus, gesturing to his brother primarch.

'Four months ago the Death Guard received a distress signal

from Isstvan Three,' said Mortarion. 'It was weak and old. We only received it because one of our supply ships joining the fleet at Arcturan dropped out of the warp for repairs. Given the age of the signal and the time it took for it to be relayed to my command, it is likely that it was sent at least two years ago.'

'What did it say?' asked Angron.

In reply, the holographic image of the globe unfolded into a large flat pane, like a pict screen hovering in the air, black, with just a hint of shadowy movement. A shape moved on the screen and Loken realised it was a face – a woman's face, orange-lit by a candle flame that provided the only light. She appeared to be in a small, stone walled chamber. Even over the poor quality of the signal, Loken could tell that the woman was terrified, her eyes wide and her breathing rapid and shallow. She gleamed with sweat.

'The insignia on her collar,' said Torgaddon, 'is from the Twenty-Seventh Expedition.'

The woman adjusted the device she was using to record the image and sound flooded into the Lupercal's Court: crackling flames, distant yelling and gunfire.

'It's revolution,' said the woman, her voice warped by static. 'Open revolt. These people, they have... rejected... they've rejected it all. We tried to integrate them, we thought the Warsingers were just some primitive... superstition, but it was much more, it was real. Praal has gone mad and the Warsingers are with him.'

The woman suddenly looked around at something off-screen.

'No!' she screamed desperately and opened fire with a weapon previously held out of view. Violent muzzle flashes lit her and something indescribable flailed against the far wall as she emptied her weapon into it. 'They're closer. They know we're here and... I think I'm the last one.'

The woman turned back to the screen. 'It's madness, complete madness down here. Please, I don't think I'm going to get through this. Send someone, anyone, just... make this stop–'

A hideous, atonal keening sound blared from the pict screen. The woman grabbed her head, her screams drowned by the inhuman sound. The last frames jerked and fragmented, freeze framing through a series of gruesome images: blood in the woman's frenzied eye, a swirling mass of flesh and shattered stone, and a mouth locked open, blood on teeth.

Then blackness.

'There have been no further communications from Isstvan Three,' concluded Mortarion, filling the silence that followed.

'The planet's astropaths have either been compromised or they are dead.'

'The name "Praal" refers to Vardus Praal,' said Horus, 'the governor left behind to command Isstvan Three in the name of the Imperium, ensure compliance and manage the dismantling of the traditional religious structures that defined the planet's autochthonous society. If he is complicit in the rebellion on Isstvan Three, as this recording suggests, then he is one of our objectives.'

Loken felt a shiver travel down his spine at the thought of once again facing a population whose Imperial official had turned traitor. He glanced over at Torgaddon and saw that the similarities with the Davin campaign were not lost on his comrade.

The holo swelled and returned to the image of Isstvan III. 'The cultural and religious capital of Isstvan is here,' said Horus as the image zoomed in on one of the northern cities, which commanded a large hinterland at the foot of a colossal range of mountains.

'The Choral City. This is the source of the distress signal and the seat of Praal's command, a building known as the Precentor's Palace. Multiple speartips will seize a number of strategic objectives, and with the city in our hands, Isstvan will be ours. The first assault will be a combined force made up of Astartes from all Legions with backup from the Titans of the Mechanicum and the Imperial Army. The rest of the planet will then be subjugated by whichever Imperial Army reinforcements can reach us with the warp in its current state.'

'Why not just bombard them?' asked Eidolon. The sudden silence that followed his question was deafening.

Loken waited for the Warmaster to reprimand Eidolon for daring to question one of his decisions, but Horus only nodded indulgently. 'Because these people are vermin, and when you stamp out vermin from afar, some invariably survive. If we are to cut out the problem, we must get our hands dirty and destroy them in one fell swoop. It may not be as elegant as the Emperor's Children would wish, but elegance is not a priority for me, only swift victory.'

'Of course,' said Eidolon, shaking his head. 'To think that these fools should be so blind to the realities of the galaxy.'

'Have no fear, lord commander,' said Abaddon, descending to stand beside the Warmaster, 'they will be illuminated as to the error of their ways.'

Loken risked a sidelong glance at the First Captain, surprised at the respect he heard in his voice. All the previous dealings between the Sons of Horus and Eidolon had led him to believe that Abaddon held the arrogant lord commander in contempt.

What had changed?

'Mortarion,' continued Horus. 'Your objective will be to engage the main force of the Choral City's army. If they are anything like they were when the Raven Guard fought them, they will be professional soldiers and will not break easily, even when confronted with Astartes.'

The holo zoomed in to show a map of the Choral City, a handsome conurbation with many and varied buildings that ranged from exquisite mansions and basilica to massive sprawls of housing and tangles of industrial complexes. Artfully formed boulevards and thoroughfares threaded a multi-levelled city of millions, most of whom appeared to be housed in sprawling residential districts, workshops and factories.

The western edge of the city was highlighted, focusing on the scar-like web of defensive trenches and bunkers along the city's outskirts. The opposite side of the Choral City butted up against the sheer cliffs of a mountain range – the natural defences efficiently shielding the city from a conventional land attack.

Unfortunately for the Choral City, the Warmaster clearly wasn't planning a conventional land attack.

'It appears that a sizeable armed force is manning these defences,' said Horus. 'It looks as if they have excellent fortifications and artillery. Many of these defences were added after compliance to protect the seat of Imperial governance on Isstvan, which means they're ours, and they will be strong. It will be ugly work engaging and destroying this force, and there is still much about the Choral City's military we do not know.'

'I welcome this challenge, Warmaster,' said Mortarion. 'This is my Legion's natural battlefield.'

Another location lurched into focus, a spectacular conglomeration of arches and spires, with dozens of labyrinth-like wings and additions surrounding a magnificent central dome faced in polished stone. The city's crowning glory, the structure looked like a jewelled brooch set into the twisted mass of the Choral City.

'The Precentor's Palace,' said Eidolon appreciatively.

'And your Legion will take it,' said Horus, 'along with the World Eaters.'

Again, Loken caught Eidolon's glance at Angron, the lord commander unable to conceal the distaste he felt at the thought of fighting alongside such a barbaric Legion. If Angron was aware of Eidolon's scornful glance he gave no sign of it.

'The palace is one of Praal's most likely locations,' said Horus. 'Therefore, the palace is one of our most important objectives. The palace must be taken, the Choral City's leadership destroyed, and Praal killed. He is a traitor, so I do not expect or wish him to be taken alive.'

Finally, the holo zoomed in on a curious mass of stonework some way east of the Precentor's Palace. To Loken's untutored eye, it looked like a collection of church spires or temples, sacred buildings heaped one on top of another over the centuries.

'This is the Sirenhold and my Sons of Horus will lead the attack on it,' said Horus. 'Choral City's revolt appears to be religious in nature and the Sirenhold was the spiritual heart of the city. According to Corax's reports, this was the seat of the old pagan religion that was supposed to have been dismantled. It is presumed that it still exists and that the leadership of that religion will be found here. This is another likely location for Vardus Praal, so again I do not require prisoners, only destruction.'

For the first time, Loken saw the battlefield he would soon be fighting on. The Sirenhold looked like difficult ground to take: massive, complicated structures creating a confusing multi-levelled warren with plenty of places to hide. Dangerous ground.

That was why the Warmaster had sent his own Legion to take it. He knew they could do it.

The holo zoomed out again to a view of the planet itself.

'Preliminary operations will involve the destruction of the monitoring stations on the seventh planet of Isstvan Extremis,' said Horus. 'When the rebels are blind the invasion of Isstvan Three will commence. The units chosen to lead the first wave will deploy by drop pod and gunship, with a second wave ready in reserve. I trust you all understand what is required of your Legions.'

'I only have one question, Warmaster,' said Angron.

'Speak,' said Horus.

'Why do we plan this attack with such precision when a single, massive strike will do the job just as well?'

'You object to my plans, Angron?' Horus asked carefully.

'Of course I object,' spat Angron. 'We have four Legions, Titans and starships at our disposal, and this is just one city. We should hit it with everything we have and slaughter them in the streets. Then we will see how many on this planet have the stomach to rebel. But no, you would have us kill them one by one and pick off their leaders as if we are here to preserve this world.

Rebellion is in the people, Horus. Kill the people and the rebellion ends.'

'Lord Angron,' said Eidolon reasonably, 'you speak out of turn–'

'Hold your tongue in the presence of your betters,' snarled Angron. 'I know what you Emperor's Children think of us, but you mistake our directness for stupidity. Speak to me again without my consent and I will kill you.'

'Angron!'

Horus's voice cut through the building tension and the primarch of the World Eaters turned his murderous attention away from Eidolon.

'You place little value on the lives of your World Eaters,' said Horus, 'and you believe in the way of war you have made your own, but that does not place you beyond my authority. I am the Warmaster, the commander of everyone and everything that falls under the aegis of the Great Crusade. Your Legion will deploy according to the orders I have given you. Is that clear?'

Angron nodded curtly as Horus turned to Eidolon. 'Lord Commander Eidolon, you are not among equals here, and your presence in this war council is dependent upon my good graces, which will be rapidly worn thin should you conduct yourself as if Fulgrim was here to nursemaid you.'

Eidolon rapidly recovered his composure. 'Of course, my Warmaster, I meant no disrespect. I shall ensure that my Legion is prepared for the assault on Isstvan Extremis and the capture of the Precentor's Palace.'

Horus switched his gaze to Angron, who grunted in assent.

'The World Eaters will be ready, Warmaster,' said Khârn.

'Then this conclave is at an end,' said Horus. 'Return to your Legions and make ready for war.'

The delegations filed out, Khârn speaking quietly with Angron and Eidolon adopting a swagger as if to compensate for his dressing down. Loken thought he saw a gleam of amusement in Mortarion's eyes as he left with Garro and his Terminators in tow.

Horus turned to Abaddon and said, 'Have a Stormbird prepared to convey me to the *Conqueror*. Angron must be illuminated as to the proper conduct of this endeavour.'

Horus turned and made his way from the Lupercal's Court with Abaddon and Aximand following behind him without so much as a backwards glance at Loken and Torgaddon.

'That was educational,' said Torgaddon when they were alone.

Loken smiled wearily. 'I could feel you willing Angron to strike Eidolon.'

Torgaddon laughed, remembering when he and Eidolon had almost come to blows when they had first met on the surface of Murder.

'If only we could join the Warmaster on the *Conqueror*,' said Torgaddon. 'Now that would be something worth seeing. Horus illuminating Angron. What would they talk about?'

'What indeed?' agreed Loken.

There was so much Loken didn't know, but as he pondered his unhappy ignorance, he remembered the last thing Kyril Sindermann had shouted to him as he was led away by Maloghurst's soldiers.

'Tarik, we have a battle to prepare for, so I want you to get everyone ready. It's going to be a hard fight on Isstvan Three.'

'I know,' said Torgaddon. 'The Sirenhold. What a bloody shambles. This is what happens when you give people a god to believe in.'

'Get Vipus up to speed as well. If we're attacking the Sirenhold, I want Locasta with us.'

'Of course,' nodded Torgaddon. 'Sometimes I think you and Nero are the only people I can trust any more. What are you going to be doing?'

'I have some reading to catch up on,' said Loken.

FOUR

Sacrifice
A single moment
Keep her safe

Wherever Erebus walked, shadows followed in his wake. Flickering whisperers were his constant companions, invisible creatures that lurked just beyond sight and ghosted in his shadow. The whisperers flitted from Erebus and gathered in the shadowed corners of the chamber, a stone-walled lodge built in the image of the temple room of the Delphos where Akshub had cut his throat.

Deep in the heart of the *Vengeful Spirit,* the lodge temple was low, close and hot, lit by a crackling fire that burned in a pit in the middle of the room. Flames threw leaping shapes across the walls.

'My Warmaster,' said Erebus. 'We are prepared.'

'Good,' replied the Warmaster. 'It has cost us a great deal to reach this point, Erebus. For all our sakes it had better be worth it, but mostly for yours.'

'It will be, Warmaster,' assured Erebus, paying no heed to the threat. 'Our allies are keen to finally speak to you directly.'

Erebus stooped to stare into the fire, the flames reflecting from his shaven, tattooed head and in the metal trim of his armour. As confident as he sounded, he allowed himself a moment of pause. Dealing with creatures from the warp was never straightforward, and should he fail to meet the Warmaster's expectations then his life would be forfeit.

The Warmaster's presence filled the lodge, armoured as he was in a magnificent suit of obsidian Terminator armour gifted to him by the Fabricator General himself. Sent from Mars to cement the alliance between Horus and the Mechanicum of Mars, the armour echoed the colours of the elite Justaerin, but it far surpassed them in ornamentation and power. The amber eye upon the breastplate stared from the armour's torso and shoulder plates, and on one hand Horus sported a monstrous gauntlet with deadly blades for fingers.

Erebus lifted a book from beside the fire and rose to his feet, reverently turning the ancient pages until he came to a complex illustration of interlocking symbols.

'We are ready. I can begin once the sacrifice is made.'

Horus nodded and said, 'Adept, join us.'

Moments later, the bent and robed form of Adept Regulus entered the warrior lodge. The representative of the Mechanicum was almost completely mechanised, as was common among the higher echelons of his order. Beneath his robes his body was fashioned from gleaming bronze, steel and cables. Only his face showed, if it could be called a face, with large augmetic eyepieces and a vocabulator unit that allowed the adept to communicate.

Regulus led the ghostly figure of Ing Mae Sing, her steps fearful and her hands flitting, as if swatting at a swarm of flies.

'This is unorthodox,' said Regulus, his voice like steel wire on the nerves.

'Adept,' said the Warmaster. 'You are here as the representative of the Mechanicum. The priests of Mars are essential to the Crusade and they must be a part of the new order. You have already pledged your strength to me and now it is time you witnessed the price of that bargain.'

'Warmaster,' began Regulus, 'I am yours to command.'

Horus nodded and said, 'Erebus, continue.'

Erebus stepped past the Warmaster and directed his gaze towards Ing Mae Sing. Though the astropath was blind, she recoiled as she felt his eyes roaming across her flesh. She backed against one wall, trying to shrink away from him, but he grasped her arm in a crushing grip and dragged her towards the fire.

'She is powerful,' said Erebus. 'I can taste her.'

'She is my best,' said Horus.

'That is why it has to be her,' said Erebus. 'The symbolism is as important as the power. A sacrifice is not a sacrifice if it is not valued by the giver.'

'No, please,' cried Ing Mae Sing, twisting in his grip as she realised the import of the Word Bearer's statement.

Horus stepped forwards and tenderly took hold of the astropath's chin, halting her struggles and tilting her head upwards so that she would have looked upon his face had she but eyes to see.

'You betrayed me, Mistress Sing,' said Horus.

Ing Mae Sing whimpered, nonsensical protests spilling from her terrified lips. She tried to shake her head, but Horus held her firm and said, 'There is no point in denying it. I already know everything. After you told me of Euphrati Keeler, you sent a warning to someone, didn't you? Tell me who it was and I will let you live. Try to resist and your death will be more agonising than you can possibly imagine.'

'No,' whispered Ing Mae Sing. 'I am already dead. I know this, so kill me and have done with it.'

'You will not tell me what I wish to know?'

'There is no point,' gasped Ing Mae Sing. 'You will kill me whether I tell you or not. You may have the power to conceal your lies, but your serpent does not.'

Erebus watched as Horus nodded slowly to himself, as if reluctantly reaching a decision.

'Then we have no more to say to one another,' said Horus sadly, drawing back his arm.

He rammed his clawed gauntlet through her chest, the blades tearing through her heart and lungs and ripping from her back in a spray of red.

Erebus nodded towards the fire and the Warmaster held the corpse above the pit, letting Ing Mae Sing's blood drizzle into the flames.

The emotions of her death flooded the lodge as the blood hissed in the fire, hot, raw and powerful – fear, pain and the horror of betrayal.

Erebus knelt and scratched designs on the floor, copying them exactly from the diagrams in the book: a star with eight points that was orbited by three circles, a stylised skull and the cuneiform runes of Colchis.

'You have done this before,' said Horus.

'Many times,' said Erebus, nodding towards the fire. 'I speak here with my primarch's voice, and it is a voice our allies respect.'

'They are not our allies yet,' said Horus, lowering his arm and letting the body of Ing Mae Sing slide from the claws of his gauntlet.

Erebus shrugged and began chanting words from the *Book of Lorgar*, his voice dark and guttural as he called upon the gods of the warp to send their emissary.

Despite the brightness of the fire, the lodge darkened and Erebus felt the temperature fall, a chill wind gusting from somewhere unseen and unknown. It carried the dust of ages past and the ruin of empires in its every breath, and ageless eternity was borne upon the unnatural zephyr.

'Is this supposed to happen?' asked Regulus.

Erebus smiled and nodded without answering as the air grew icy, the whisperers gibbering in unreasoning fear as they felt the arrival of something ancient and terrible. Shadows gathered in the corners of the room, although no light shone to cast them and a racing whip of malicious laughter spiralled around the chamber.

Regulus spun on hissing bearings as he sought to identify the source of the sounds, his ocular implants whirring as they struggled to find focus in the darkness. Frost gathered on the struts and pipes high above them.

Horus stood unmoving as the shadows of the chamber hissed and spat, a chorus of voices that came from everywhere and nowhere.

'You are the one your kind calls Warmaster?'

Erebus nodded as Horus looked over at him.

'I am,' said Horus. 'Warmaster of the Great Crusade. To whom do I speak?'

'I am Sarr'Kell,' said the voice. *'Lord of the Shadows!'*

The three of them made their way swiftly through the decks of the *Vengeful Spirit*, heading down towards the tiled environment of the medicae deck. Sindermann kept the pace as brisk as he could, his breath sharp and painful as they hurried to save the saint from whatever dark fate awaited her.

'What do you expect to find when we reach the saint, iterator?' asked Jonah Aruken, his nervous hands fingering the catch on his pistol holster.

Sindermann thought of the small medicae cell where he and Mersadie Oliton had stood vigil over Euphrati and wondered that same thought.

'I don't know exactly,' he said. 'I just know we have to help.'

'I just hope a frail old man and our pistols are up to the job.'

'What do you mean?' asked Sindermann, as they descended a wide screw stair that led deeper into the ship.

'Well, I just wonder how you plan to fight the kind of danger that could threaten a saint. I mean, whatever it is must be pretty damn dangerous, yes?'

Sindermann paused in his descent, as much to catch his breath as to answer Aruken.

'Whoever sent me that warning obviously thinks that I can help,' he said.

'And that's enough for you?' asked Aruken.

'Jonah, leave him alone,' cautioned Titus Cassar.

'No, damn it, I won't,' said Aruken. 'This is serious and we could get in real trouble. I mean, this Keeler woman, she's supposed to be all saintly, yes? Then why doesn't the power of the Emperor save her? Why does he need us?'

'The Emperor works through His faithful servants, Jonah,' explained Titus. 'It is not enough to simply believe and await divine intervention to sweep down from the heavens and set the world to rights. The Emperor has shown us the path and it is up to us to seize this chance to do His will.'

Sindermann watched the exchange between the two crewmen, his anxiety growing with every second that passed.

'I don't know if I can do this, Titus,' said Aruken, 'not without some proof that we're doing the right thing.'

'We are, Jonah,' pressed Titus. 'You must trust that the Emperor has a plan for you.'

'The Emperor may or may not have a plan for me, but I sure as hell do,' snapped Aruken. 'I want command of a Titan, and that's not going to happen if we get caught doing something stupid.'

'Please!' cut in Sindermann, his chest hurting with worry for the saint. 'We have to go! Something terrible is coming to harm her and we have to stop it. I can think of no more compelling an argument than that. I'm sorry, but you'll just have to trust me.'

'Why should I?' asked Aruken. 'You've given me no reason to. I don't even know why I'm here.'

'Listen to me, Mister Aruken,' said Sindermann earnestly. 'When you live as long and complex a life as I have, you learn that it always comes down to a *single moment* – a moment in which a man finds out, once and for all, who he really is. This is that moment, Mister Aruken. Will this be a moment you are proud to look back on or will it be one you will regret for the rest of your life?'

The two Titan crewmen shared a glance and eventually Aruken sighed and said, 'I need my head looked at for this, but all right, let's go save the day.'

A palpable sense of relief flooded through Sindermann and the pain in his chest eased.

'I am proud of you, Mr Aruken,' he said, 'and I thank you, your aid is most welcome.'

'Thank me when we save this saint of yours,' said Aruken, setting off down the stairs.

They followed the stairs down, passing several decks until the symbol of intertwined serpents around a winged staff indicated they had arrived at the medicae deck. It had been some weeks since the last casualties had been brought aboard the *Vengeful Spirit* and the sterile, gleaming wilderness of tiled walls and brushed steel cabinets felt empty, a warren of soulless glass rooms and laboratories.

'This way,' said Sindermann, setting off into the confusing maze of corridors, the way familiar to him after all the times he had visited the comatose imagist. Cassar and Aruken followed him, keeping a watchful eye out for anyone who might challenge their presence. At last they reached a nondescript white door and Sindermann said, 'This is it.'

Aruken said, 'Better let us go first, old man.'

Sindermann nodded and backed away from the door, pressing his hands over his ears as the two Titan crewmen unholstered their pistols. Aruken crouched low beside the door and nodded to Cassar, who pressed the release panel.

The door slid aside and Aruken spun through it with his pistol extended.

Cassar was a second behind him, his pistol tracking left and right for targets, and Sinderman awaited the deafening flurry of pistol shots.

When none came he dared to open his eyes and uncover his ears. He didn't know whether to be glad or deathly afraid that they were too late.

He turned and looked through the door, seeing the familiar clean and well-maintained medicae cell he had visited many times. Euphrati lay like a mannequin on the bed, her skin like alabaster and her face pinched and sunken. A pair of drips fed her fluids and a small, bleeping machine drew spiking lines on a green display unit beside her.

Aside from her immobility she looked just as she had the last time he had laid eyes on her.

'Just as well we rushed,' snapped Aruken. 'Looks like we were just in time.'

'I think you might be right,' said Sindermann, as he saw the golden-eyed figure of Maggard come into view at the far end of the corridor with his sword unsheathed.

'*You are known to us, Warmaster,*' said Sarr'Kell, his voice leaping around the room like a capricious whisper. '*It is said that you are the one who can deliver us. Is that true?*'

'Perhaps,' replied Horus, apparently unperturbed by the

strangeness of his unseen interlocutor. 'My brother Lorgar assures me that your masters can give me the power to achieve victory.'

'*Victory*,' whispered Sarr'Kell. '*An almost meaningless word in the scale of the cosmos, but yes, we have much power to offer you. No army will stand before you, no power of mortal man will lay you low and no ambition will be denied you if you swear yourself to us.*'

'Just words,' said Horus. 'Show me something tangible.'

'*Power*,' hissed Sarr'Kell, the sound rippling around Horus like a slithering snake. '*The warp brings power. There is nothing beyond the reach of the gods of the warp.*'

'Gods?' replied Horus. 'You waste your time throwing such words around, they do not impress me. I already know that your "gods" need my help, so speak plainly or we are done here.'

'*Your Emperor*,' replied Sarr'Kell, and for a fleeting moment, Erebus detected a trace of unease in the creature's voice. Such entities were unused to the defiance of a mortal, even one as mighty as a primarch. '*He meddles in matters he does not understand. On the world you call Terra, his grand designs cause a storm in the warp that tears it asunder from within. We care nothing for your realm, you know this. It is anathema to us. We offer power that can help you take his place, Warmaster. Our aid will see you destroy your foes and take you to the very gates of the Emperor's palace. We can deliver the galaxy to you. All we care for is that his works cease and that you take his place.*'

The unseen voice spoke in sibilant tones, slick and persuasive, but Erebus could see that Horus was unmoved. 'And what of this power? Do you understand the magnitude of this task? The galaxy will be divided, brother will fight brother. The Emperor will have his Legions and the Imperial Army, the Custodian Guard, the Sisters of Silence. Can you be the equal of such a foe?'

'*The gods of the warp are masters of the primal forces of all reality. As your Emperor creates, the warp decays and destroys. As he brings us to battle, we shall melt away, and as he gathers his strength, we shall strike from the shadows. The victory of the gods is as inevitable as the passing of time and the mortality of flesh. Do the gods not rule an entire universe hidden from your eyes, Warmaster? Have they not made the warp dark at their command?*'

'Your gods did this? Why? You have blinded my Legions!'

'*Necessity, Warmaster. The darkness blinds the Emperor too, blinds him to our plans and yours. The Emperor thinks himself the master of the warp and he would seek to know his enemies by it, but see how swiftly we can confound him? You will have passage through the warp as you need it, Warmaster, for as we bring darkness, so we can bring light.'*

'The Emperor remains ignorant of all that has transpired?'

'Completely,' sighed Sarr'Kell, *'and so, Warmaster, you see the power we can give you. All that remains is for your word, and the pact will be made.'*

Horus said nothing, as if weighing up the choices before him, and Erebus could sense the growing impatience of the warp creature.

At last the Warmaster spoke again. 'Soon I shall unleash my Legions against the worlds of the Isstvan system. There I shall set my Legions upon the path of the new Crusade. There are matters that must be dealt with at Isstvan, and I will deal with them in my own way.'

Horus looked over at Erebus and said, 'When I am done with Isstvan, I will pledge my forces with those of your masters, but not until then. My Legions will go through the fire of Isstvan alone, for only then will they be tempered into my shining blade aimed at the Emperor's heart.'

The sibilant, roiling chill of Sarr'Kell's voice hissed as if he took mighty breaths.

'My masters accept,' he said at last. *'You have chosen well, Warmaster.'*

The chill wind that had carried the words of the warp entity blew again, stronger this time, its ageless malevolence like the murder of innocence.

Its icy touch slid through Erebus and he drew a cold breath before the sensation faded and the unnatural darkness began to recede, the light of the fire once more illuminating the lodge temple.

The creature was gone and the void of its presence was an ache felt deep in the soul.

'Was it worth it, Warmaster?' asked Erebus, releasing the pent up breath he had been holding.

'Yes,' said Horus, glancing down at Ing Mae Sing's body. 'It was worth it.'

The Warmaster turned to Regulus and said, 'Adept, I wish the Fabricator General to be made aware of this. I cannot contact him directly, so you will take a fast ship and make for Mars. If what this creature says is true, you will make good time. Kelbor-Hal is to purge his order and make ready for its part in my new Crusade. Tell him that I shall contact him when the time comes and that I expect the Mechanicum to be united.'

'Of course, Warmaster. Your will be done.'

'Waste no time, adept. Go.'

Regulus turned to leave and Erebus said, 'We have waited a long time for this day, Lorgar will be exultant.'

'Lorgar has his own battles to fight, Erebus,' replied Horus sharply. 'As do you. Begin making your preparations now – all this will be for nothing if Guilliman's Legion is allowed to intervene. Save your celebrations for when I sit upon the throne of Terra.'

Sindermann felt his heart lurch in his chest at the sight of Petronella's bodyguard coming towards them. The man's every step was like death approaching and Sindermann cursed himself for having taken so long to get here. His tardiness had killed the saint and would probably see them all dead as well.

Jonah Aruken's eyes widened as he saw the massive form of the saint's killer approaching. He turned quickly and said, 'Titus, grab her. Now!'

'What?' asked Cassar. 'She's hooked up to all these machines, we can't just–'

'Don't argue with me,' hissed Aruken. 'Just do it, we've got company, bad company.'

Aruken turned back to Sindermann and hissed, 'Well, iterator? Is this that single moment you were talking about, where we find out who we really are? If it is, then I'm already regretting helping you.'

Sindermann couldn't reply. He saw Maggard notice them outside Euphrati's room and felt a cold, creeping horror as a slow smile spread across the man's features.

I am going to kill you, the smile said, *slowly.*

'Don't hurt her,' he whispered, the words sounding pathetic in his ears. 'Please...'

He wanted to run, to get far away from the evil smile that promised a silent, agonising death, but his legs were lead weights, rooted to the spot by some immense power that prevented him from moving so much as a muscle.

Jonah Aruken slid from the medicae cell, with Titus Cassar behind him, the recumbent form of Euphrati in his arms. Dripping tubes dangled from her arms and Sindermann found his gaze unaccountably drawn to the droplets as they swelled at the ends of the plastic tubes before breaking free and plummeting to the deck to splash in crowns of saline.

Aruken held his pistol out before him, aimed at Maggard's head.

'Don't come any closer,' he warned.

Maggard did not even slow down and that same deathly smile shone at Jonah Aruken.

With Euphrati still in his arms, Titus Cassar backed away from the relentlessly approaching killer.

'Come on, damn it,' he hissed. 'Let's go!'

Aruken shoved Sindermann after Cassar and suddenly the spell of immobility that had held him rooted to the spot was broken. Maggard was less than ten paces from them and Sindermann knew that they could not hope to escape without bloodshed.

'Shoot him,' shouted Cassar.

'What?' asked Aruken, throwing his fellow crewman a desperate glance.

'Shoot him,' repeated Cassar. 'Kill him, before he kills us.'

Jonah Aruken tore his gaze back to the approaching Maggard and nodded, pulling the trigger twice in quick succession. The noise was deafening and the corridor was filled with blinding light and careening echoes. Tiles shattered and exploded as Aruken's bullets cratered the wall behind where Maggard had been standing.

Sindermann cried out at the noise, backing away after Titus Cassar as Maggard spun out from the sunken doorway in which he had taken cover the instant before Aruken had fired. Maggard's pistol leapt to his hand and the barrel blazed with light as he fired three times.

Sindermann cried out, throwing up his arms and awaiting the awful pain of bullets tearing into his flesh, ripping through his internal organs and blowing bloody-rimmed craters in his back.

Nothing happened and Sindermann heard a cry of astonishment from Jonah Aruken, who had likewise flinched at the thunderous noise of Maggard's gun. He lowered his arms and his mouth fell open in amazement at the sight before him.

Maggard still stood there, his muscled arm still holding his wide barrelled pistol aimed squarely at them.

A frozen bloom of light expanded at an infinitesimally slow pace from the muzzle and Sindermann could see a pair of bullets held immobile in the air before them, only the glint of light on metal as they spiralled giving any sign that they were moving at all.

As he watched, the pointed nub of a brass bullet began to emerge from the barrel of Maggard's gun and Sindermann turned in bewilderment to Jonah Aruken.

The Titan crewman was as shocked as he was, his arms hanging limply at his side.

'What the hell is going on?' breathed Aruken.

'I d-don't know,' stammered Sindermann, unable to tear his gaze from the frozen tableau standing in front of them. 'Maybe we're already dead.'

'No, iterator,' said Cassar from behind them, 'it's a miracle.'

Sindermann turned, feeling as if his entire body was numb, only his heart hammering fit to break his chest. Titus Cassar stood at the end of the corridor, the saint held tightly to his chest. Where before Euphrati had lain supine, her eyes were now wide in terror, her right hand extended and the silver eagle that had been burned into her flesh glowing with a soft, inner light.

'Euphrati!' cried Sindermann, but no sooner had he given voice to her name than her eyes rolled back in their sockets and her hand dropped to her side. He risked a glance back at Maggard, but the assassin was still frozen by whatever power had saved their lives.

Sindermann took a deep breath and made his way on unsteady legs to the end of the corridor. Euphrati lay with her head against Cassar's chest, as unmoving as she had been for the last year and he wanted to weep to see her so reduced.

He reached up and ran a hand through Euphrati's hair, her skin hot to the touch.

'She saved us,' said Cassar, his voice awed and humbled by what he had seen.

'I think you might be right, my dear boy,' said Sindermann. 'I think you might be right.'

Jonah Aruken joined him, alternating between casting fearful looks at Maggard and Euphrati. He kept his pistol trained on Maggard and said, 'What do we do about him?'

Sindermann looked back at the monstrous assassin and said, 'Leave him. I will not have his death on the saint's hands. What kind of beginning would it be for the Lectitio Divinitatus if the saint's first act is to kill. If we are to found a new church in the name of the Emperor it will be one of forgiveness, not bloodshed.'

'Are you sure?' asked Aruken. 'He will come after her again.'

'Then we will keep her safe from him,' said Cassar. 'The Lectitio Divinitatus has friends aboard the *Vengeful Spirit* and we can hide her until she recovers. Iterator, do you agree?'

'Yes, that's what to do,' nodded Sindermann. 'Hide her. Keep her safe.'

FIVE

Dark Millennium
Warsinger

Loken had not set foot on the strategium for some time, the construction of the Lupercal's Court rendering it largely without function. In any case, an unspoken order had filtered down from the lodge members that Torgaddon and Loken were no longer to stand alongside the Warmaster and act as the Legion's conscience.

The isolated strategium platform was suspended above the industrious hubbub of the vessel's bridge, and Loken leaned over the rail to watch the senior crew of the *Vengeful Spirit* going about the business of destroying Isstvan Extremis.

Warriors of the Death Guard and Emperor's Children were already in the theatre of war and the enemies of the Warmaster would even now be dying. The thought of not being there to share the danger galled Loken and he wished he could be on that barren rock with his battle-brothers, especially since Torgaddon had told him that Saul Tarvitz was down there.

The last time the Sons of Horus and the Emperor's Children had met was during the war against the Technocracy and bonds of brotherhood had been re-established between the Legions, formally by the primarchs, and informally by their warriors.

He missed the times he had stood in the presence of his fellow warriors when the talk had been of campaigns past and yet to come. The shared camaraderie of brotherhood was a comfort that was only realised once it was stripped away.

He smiled wryly to himself, whispering, 'I even miss your tales of "better days", Iacton.'

Loken turned away from the bridge below and unfolded the piece of paper he had discovered inside the dust jacket of the *Chronicles of Ursh*.

Once again he read the words hurriedly written in Kyril Sindermann's distinctive spidery scrawl on the ragged page of a notebook.

> *Even the Warmaster may not deserve your trust. Look for*
> *the temple. It will be somewhere that was once the essence*
> *of the Crusade.*

Remembering Sindermann's words as he had been forced from the training halls by Maloghurst, Loken had sought out the book from the burnt out stacks of Archive Chamber Three. Much of the archive was still in ruins from the fire that had gutted the chamber and put Euphrati Keeler in a coma. Servitors and menials had attempted to save as many books as they could, and even though Loken was no reader, he was saddened by the loss of such a valuable repository of knowledge.

He had located *The Chronicles of Ursh* with the barest minimum of effort, as if the book had been specifically placed for him to find. Opening the cover, he realised that it had indeed been left there for him, as Sindermann's note slipped from its pages.

Loken wasn't sure exactly what he was looking for, and the idea of a temple aboard the *Vengeful Spirit* seemed laughable, but Sindermann had been deadly serious when he had implored Loken to seek out the book and his note.

> *It will be somewhere that was once the essence of the*
> *Crusade.*

He looked up from the note and cast his eyes around the strategium: the raised platform where the Warmaster had delivered his briefings, the niches around the edge where Sons of Horus stood as an honour guard and the vaulted dome of dark steel. Banners hung along the curved wall, indistinct in the gloom, company banners of the Sons of Horus. He hammered his fist against his breastplate as he faced the banner of the Tenth.

If anywhere was once the essence of the Crusade it was the strategium.

The strategium was empty, and it was an emptiness that

spoke more of its neglect and its obsolescence than simply the absence of people. It had been abandoned and the ideals once hammered out here had been abandoned too, replaced with something else, something dark.

Loken stood in the centre of the strategium and felt an ache in his chest that was nothing to do with any physical sensation. It took him a moment to realise that there was something out of place here, something present that shouldn't be – a smell that he didn't recognise, faint but definitely hanging in the air.

At last he recognised the smell as incense, cloying, and carrying the familiar scent of hot, dry winds that brought sour fragrances of bitter blossoms. His genhanced senses could pick out the subtle aromas mixed into the incense, its scent stronger as he made his way through the strategium hoping to pinpoint its source. Where had he smelt this before?

He followed the bitter smell to the standard of the Seventh, Targhost's company. Had the lodge master flown the banner in some ritual ceremony of the warrior lodge?

No, the scent was too strong for it to be simply clinging to fabric. This was the aroma of burning incense. Loken pulled the banner of the Seventh away from the wall, and he was not surprised to find that, instead of the brushed steel of the strategium wall, there was the darkness of an opening cut into one of the many access passages that threaded the *Vengeful Spirit*.

Had this been here when the Mournival had gathered? He didn't think so.

Look for the temple, Sindermann had said, so Loken ducked beneath the banner and through the doorway, letting the banner fall into place behind him. The smell of incense was definitely here, and it had been burned recently, or was still burning.

Loken suddenly realised where he had smelled this aroma before and he gripped the hilt of his combat knife as he remembered the air of Davin, the scents that filled the yurts and seemed to linger in the air, even through rebreathers.

The passageway beyond was dark, but Loken's augmented eyesight cut through the gloom to reveal a short passageway, recently constructed, that led to an arched doorway with curved sigils etched into the ironwork surrounding it. Although it was simply a door, Loken felt an unutterable dread of what lay beyond it and for a moment he almost considered turning back.

He shook off such a cowardly notion and made his way forwards, feeling his unease grow with every step he took. The door was closed, a stylised skull mounted at eye-level and Loken felt uncomfortable even acknowledging that it was there let alone looking at it. Something of its brutal form whispered to the killer in him, telling him of the joy of spilling blood and the relish to be taken in slaughter.

Loken tore his eyes from the leering skull and drew his knife, fighting the urge to plunge it into the flesh of anyone waiting behind the door.

He pushed it open and stepped inside.

The space within was large, a maintenance chamber that had been cleared and refitted so as to resemble some underground stone chamber. Twin rows of stone benches faced the far wall, where meaningless symbols and words had been painted. Blank-eyed skulls hung from the ceiling, staring and grinning with bared teeth. They swayed gently as Loken passed them, thin tendrils of smoke rising from their eye sockets.

A low wooden table stood against the far wall. A shallow bowl carved into its surface contained flaky dark detritus that he could smell was dried blood. A thick book lay beside the depression.

Was this a temple? He remembered the bottles and glass flasks that had been scattered around the water fane beneath the Whisperheads.

This place and the fane on Sixty-Three Nineteen looked different, but they *felt* the same.

He heard a sudden rustle on the air, like whispers in his ear, and he spun around, his knife whipping out in front of him.

He was alone, yet the sense of someone whispering in his ear had been so real that he would have sworn on his life that another person had been standing right beside him. Loken took a breath and did a slow circuit of the room, his knife extended, on the defensive in case the mysterious whisperer revealed himself.

Bundles of torn material lay by the benches, and he made his way towards the table – the altar, he realised – upon which lay the book he had noticed earlier.

Its cover was leather, the surface cracked, old and blackened by fire.

Loken bent down to examine the book, flipping open the cover with the tip of his knife. The words written there were composed of an angular script, the letters written vertically on the page.

'Erebus,' he said as he recognised the script as identical to that tattooed upon the skull of the Word Bearer. Could this be the *Book of Lorgar* that Kyril Sindermann had been raving about following the fire in the archive chamber? The iterator had claimed that the book had unleashed some horror of the warp and that had been what caused the fire, but Loken saw only words.

How could words be dangerous?

Even as he formed the thought, he blinked, the words blurring on the page in front of him. The symbols twisted from the unknown language of the Word Bearers to the harsh numerical language of Cthonia, before spiralling into the elegant script of Imperial Gothic and a thousand other languages he had never seen before.

He blinked to ward off a sudden, impossible, sense of dizziness.

'What are you doing here, Loken?' a familiar voice asked in his ear.

Loken spun to face the voice, but once again he was alone. The temple was empty.

'How dare you break the trust of the Warmaster?' the voice asked, this time with a sense of weight behind it.

And this time he recognised the voice.

He turned slowly and saw Torgaddon standing before the altar.

'Down!' yelled Tarvitz as gunfire streaked above him, stitching monochrome explosions along the barren rock of Isstvan Extremis. 'Squad Fulgerion, with me. All squads to position and wait for the go!'

Tarvitz ran, knowing that Sergeant Fulgerion's squad would be on his heels as he made for the cover of the closest crater. A web of criss-crossing tracer fire streaked the air before the monitoring station the Isstvanians had set up on Isstvan Extremis, a tall, organ-like structure of towers, domes and antennae. Anchored on the barren rock surface by massive docking claws, the station was dusted in a powdery residue of ice crystals and particulate matter.

The Isstvan system's sun was little more than a cold disc peeking above the horizon, lining everything in a harsh blue light. Automatic gun ports spat fire at the advancing Emperor's Children, more than two hundred Astartes converging in a classic assault pattern to storm the massive blast doors of the station's eastern entrance.

Isstvan Extremis had little atmosphere to speak of and was lethally cold; only the sealed armour of the Space Marines made a ground assault possible.

Tarvitz slid into the crater, turret fire ripping up chunks of grey rock around him. Sergeant Fulgerion and his warriors, shields held high to shelter them from the fire, hit the ground to either side of him. Veterans only truly at home in the thick of the hardest fighting, Fulgerion and his squad had fought together for years and Tarvitz knew that he had some of the Legion's best warriors with him.

'They were ready for us, then?' asked Fulgerion.

'They must have known that we would return to restore compliance,' said Tarvitz. 'Who knows how long they have been waiting for us to come back.'

Tarvitz glanced over the lip of the crater, spotting purple armoured forms fanning out in front of the gates to take up their allotted positions. That was how the Emperor's Children fought, manoeuvring into position to execute perfectly coordinated strikes, squads moving across a battle zone like pieces on a chess board.

'Captain Garro of the Death Guard reports that he is in position,' said Eidolon's voice over the vox-net. 'Show them what war really is!'

The Death Guard had been assigned the task of taking the western approach to the station, and Tarvitz smiled as he imagined his old friend Garro marching his men grimly towards the guns, winning through relentless determination rather than any finesse of tactics. Each to their own, he thought as he drew his broadsword.

Such blunt tactics were not the way of the Emperor's Children, for war was not simply about killing, it was art.

'Tarvitz and Fulgerion in position,' he reported. 'All units ready.'

'Execute!' came the order.

'You heard Lord Eidolon,' he shouted. 'Children of the Emperor!'

The warriors around him cheered as he and Fulgerion clambered over the crater lip and gunfire streaked overhead from the support squads. A perfect ballet began with every one of his units acting in complete concert, heavy weapons pounding the enemy guns as assault units moved in to attack and tactical units took up covering positions.

Splintering explosions burst in the sub-zero air, chunks of debris blasted from the surface of the entrance dome as turret guns detonated and threw chains of bursting ammunition into the air.

A missile streaked past Tarvitz and burst against the blast doors, leaving a flaming, blackened crater in the metal. Another missile followed the first, and then another, and the doors crumpled inwards. Tarvitz saw the golden armour of Eidolon flashing in the planet's hard light, the lord commander hefting a mighty hammer with blue arcs of energy crackling around its head.

The hammer slammed into the remains of the doors,

blue-white light bursting like a lightning strike as they vanished in a thunderous explosion. Eidolon charged inside the facility, the honour his by virtue of his noble rank.

Tarvitz followed Eidolon in, ducking through the wrecked blast doors.

Inside, the station was in darkness, lit only by the muzzle flashes of bolter fire and sparking cables torn from their mountings by the furious combat. Tarvitz's enhanced vision dispelled the darkness, warm air billowing from the station through the ruptured doors and white vapour surged around him as he saw the enemy for the first time.

They wore black armour with bulky power packs and thick cables that attached to heavy rifles. The plates of their armour were traced with silver scrollwork, perhaps just for decoration, perhaps a pattern of circuitry.

Their faces were hooded, each with a single red lens over one eye. A hundred of them packed the dome, sheltering behind slabs of broken machinery and furniture. The armoured soldiers formed a solid defensive line, and no sooner had Eidolon and the Emperor's Children emerged from the entrance tunnel than they opened fire.

Rapid firing bolts of ruby laser fire spat out from the Isstvanian troops, filling the dome with horizontal red rain. Tarvitz took a trio of shots, one to his chest, one to his greaves and another cracking against his helmet, filling his senses with a burst of static.

Fulgerion was ahead of him, wading through the las-fire that battered his shield. Eidolon surged forwards in the centre of the line and his hammer bludgeoned Isstvanians to death with each lethal swing. A body flew through the air, its torso a crushed ruin and its limbs shattered by the shock of the hammer's impact. The weight of enemy fire faltered and the Emperor's Children charged forwards, overlapping fields of bolter fire shredding the Isstvanians' cover as close combat specialists crashed through the gaps to kill with gory sweeps of chainswords.

Tarvitz's bolt pistol snapped shots at the darting black figures catching one in the throat and spinning him around. Squad Fulgerion took up position at the remains of the barricade, their bolters filling the dome with covering gunfire for Eidolon and his chosen warriors.

Tarvitz killed the enemy with brutally efficient shots and sweeps of his broadsword, fighting like a warrior of Fulgrim should. His every strike was a faultless killing blow, and his every step was measured and perfect. Gunfire ricocheted from his gilded armour and the light of battle reflected from his helmet as if from a hero of ancient legend.

'We have the entrance dome,' shouted Eidolon as the last of the Isstvanians were efficiently despatched by the Astartes around him. 'Death Guard units report heavy resistance inside. Blow the inner doors and we'll finish this for them.'

Warriors with breaching charges rushed to destroy the inner doors, and even over the flames and shots, Tarvitz could hear muffled explosions from the other side. He lowered his sword and took a moment to survey his surroundings now that there was a lull in the fighting.

A dead body lay at his feet, the plates of the man's black armour ruptured and a ragged tear ripped in the hood covering his face. Frozen blood lay scattered around him like precious stones and Tarvitz knelt to pull aside the torn cowl.

The man's skin was covered in an elaborate, swirling black tattoo, echoing the silver designs on his armour. A frozen eye looked up at him, hollow and darkened, and Tarvitz wondered what manner of being had the power to force this man to renounce his oaths of loyalty to the Imperium.

Tarvitz was spared thinking of an answer by the dull thump of the interior doors blowing open. He put the dead man from his mind and set off after Eidolon as he held his hammer high and charged into the central dome. He ran alongside his fellow warriors, knowing that whatever the Isstvanians could throw at him, he was an Astartes and no weapon they had could match the will of the Emperor's Children.

Tarvitz and his men moved through the dust and smoke of the door's explosion, the autosenses of his armour momentarily useless.

Then they were through and into the heart of the Isstvan Extremis facility.

He pulled up short as he suddenly realised that the intelligence they had been given on this facility was utterly wrong.

This was not a comms station, it was a temple.

Torgaddon's face was ashen and leathery, puckered and scarred around a burning yellow eye. Sharpened metallic teeth glinted in a lipless mouth and twin gashes were torn in the centre of his face. A star with eight points was gouged in his temple, mirroring its golden twin etched upon his ornate, black armour.

'No,' said Loken, backing away from this terrible apparition.

'You have trespassed, Loken,' hissed Torgaddon. 'You have betrayed.'

A dry, deathly wind carried Torgaddon's words, gusting over him with the smell of burning bodies. As he breathed the noxious wind, a vision of broken steppes spread out before Loken, expanses of desolation and plains of rusted machinery like skeletons of extinct monsters. A hive city on the distant horizon split open like a flower, and from its broken, burning petals rose a mighty tower of brass that punctured the pollution-heavy clouds.

The sky above was burning and the laughter of Dark Gods boomed from the heavens. Loken wanted to scream, this vision of devastation worse than anything he had seen before.

This wasn't real. It couldn't be. He did not believe in ghosts and illusions.

The thought gave him strength. He wrenched his mind away from the dying world, and suddenly he was soaring through the galaxy, tumbling between the stars. He saw them destroyed, bleeding glowing plumes of stellar matter into the void. A baleful mass of red stars glowered above him, staring like a great and terrible eye of flame. An endless tide of titanic monsters and vast space fleets vomited from that eye, drowning the universe in a tide of blood. A sea of burning flames spat and leapt from the blood, consuming all in its path, leaving black, barren wasteland in its wake.

Was this a vision of some lunatic's hell, a dimension of destruction and chaos where sinners went when they died? Loken forced himself to remember the lurid descriptions from the *Chronicles of Ursh*, the outlandish scenes described by inventions of dark faith.

No, said the voice of Torgaddon, *This is no madman's delusion. It is the future.*

'You're not Torgaddon!' shouted Loken, shaking the whispering voice from his head.

You are seeing the galaxy die.

Loken saw the Sons of Horus in the tide of fiery madness that poured from the red eye, armoured in black and surrounded by leaping, deformed creatures. Abaddon was there, and Horus himself, an immense obsidian giant who crushed worlds in his gauntlets.

This could not be the future. This was a diseased, distorted vision of the future.

A galaxy in which mankind was led by the Emperor could never become such a terrible maelstrom of chaos and death.

You are wrong.

The galaxy in flames receded and Loken scrabbled for some

solidity, something to reassure him that this terrifying vision could never come to pass. He was tumbling again, his vision blurring until he opened his eyes and found himself in Archive Chamber Three, a place he had felt safe, surrounded by books that rendered the universe down to pure logic and kept the madness locked up in crude pagan epics where it belonged.

But something was wrong, the books were burning around him, this purest of knowledge being systematically destroyed to keep the masses ignorant of their truths. The shelves held nothing but flames and ash, the heat battering against Loken as he tried to save the dying books. His hands blistered and blackened as he fought to save the wisdom of ancient times, the flesh peeling back from his bones.

The music of the spheres. The mechanisms of reality, invisible and all around...

Loken could see it where the flames burned through, the endless churning mass of the warp at the heart of everything and the eyes of dark forces seething with malevolence. Grotesque creatures cavorted obscenely among heaps of corpses, horned heads and braying, goat-like faces twisted by the mindless artifice of the warp. Bloated monsters, their bodies heaving with maggots and filth, devoured dead stars as a brass-clad giant bellowed an endless war cry from its throne of skulls and soulless magicians sacrificed billions in a silver city built of lies.

Loken fought to tear his sight from this madness. Remembering the words he had thrown in Horus Aximand's face at the Delphos Gate, he screamed them aloud once more:

'I will not bow to any fane or acknowledge any spirit. I own only the empirical clarity of Imperial Truth!'

In an instant, the walls of the dark temple slammed back into place around him, the air thick with incense, and he gasped for breath. Loken's heart pumped wildly and his head spun, sick with the effort of casting out what he had seen.

This was not fear. This was anger.

Those who came to this fane were selling out the entire human race to dark forces that lurked unseen in the depths of the warp. Were these the same forces that had infected Xayver Jubal? The same forces that had nearly killed Sindermann in the ship's archive?

Loken felt sick as he realised that everything he knew about the warp was wrong.

He had been told that there were no such things as gods.

He had been told that there was nothing in the warp but insensate, elemental power.

He had been told that the galaxy was too sterile for melodrama. Everything he had been told was a lie.

Feeding on the strength his anger gave him, Loken lurched towards the altar and slammed the ancient book closed, snapping the brass hasp over the lock. Even shut, he could feel the terrible purpose locked within its pages. The idea that a book could have some sort of power would have sounded ludicrous to Loken only a few months ago, but he could not doubt the evidence of his own senses, despite the incredible, terrifying, unimaginable things he had seen and heard. He gathered up the book and clutching it under one arm, turned and made his way from the fane.

He closed the door and eased past the banner of the Seventh, emerging once more into the secluded darkness of the strategium.

Sindermann had been right. Loken was hearing the music of the spheres, and it was a terrible sound that spoke of corruption, blood and the death of the universe. Loken knew with utter certainty that it was up to him to silence it.

The interior of the Isstvan Extremis facility was dominated by a wide, stepped pyramid, its huge stone blocks fashioned from a material that clearly had no place on such a world. Each block came from some other building, many of them still bearing architectural carvings, sections of friezes, gargoyles or even statues jutting crazily from the structure.

Isstvanian soldiers swarmed around the base of the pyramid, fighting in desperate close quarters battle with the steel-armoured figures of the Death Guard. The battle had no shape, the art of war having given way to the grinding brutality of simple killing.

Tarvitz's gaze was drawn from the slaughter to the very top of the pyramid, where a bright light spun and twisted around a half-glimpsed figure surrounded by keening harmonics.

'Attack!' bellowed Eidolon, charging forwards as the tip of the spear, assault units the killing edges around him. Tarvitz forgot about the strange figure and followed the lord commander, driving Eidolon forwards by covering him and holding off enemies who tried to surround him.

More Emperor's Children stormed into the dome and the battle at the base of the pyramid. Tarvitz saw Lucius beside Eidolon, the swordsman's blade shining like a harnessed star.

It was typical that Lucius would be at the front, demonstrating that he would rise swiftly through the ranks and take his place alongside Eidolon as the Legion's best. Tarvitz slashed his weapon left and right, needing no skill to kill these foes, simply a strong sword arm and the will to win. He clambered onto the first level of the pyramid, fighting his way up its side through rank after rank of black armoured foes.

He stole a glance towards the top of the pyramid, seeing the burnished Death Guard warriors climbing ahead of him to reach the figure at the summit.

Leading the Death Guard was the familiar, brutal form of Nathanial Garro, his old friend forging upwards with powerful strides and his familiar grim determination. Even amid the furious battle, Tarvitz was glad to be fighting alongside his sworn honour brother once again. Garro forced his way towards the top of the pyramid, aiming his charge towards the glowing figure that commanded the battlefield.

Long hair whipped around it, and as sheets of lightning arced upwards, Tarvitz saw that it was a woman, her sweeping silk robes lashing like the tendrils of some undersea creature.

Even above the chaos of battle, he could hear her voice and it was singing.

The force of the music lifted her from the pyramid, suspending her above the pinnacle on a song of pure force. Hundreds of harmonies wound impossibly over one another, screeching notes smashing together as they ripped from her unnatural throat. Stones flew from the pyramid's summit, spiralling towards the dome's ceiling as her song broke apart the warp and weft of reality.

As Tarvitz watched, a single discordant note rose to the surface in a tremendous crescendo, and an explosion blew out a huge chunk of the pyramid, massive blocks of stone tumbling in the currents of light. The pyramid shuddered and stones crashed down amongst the Emperor's Children, crushing some and knocking many more from its side.

Tarvitz fought to keep his balance as portions of the pyramid collapsed in a rumbling landslide of splintered stone and rubble. The armoured body of a Death Guard slithered down the slope towards a sheer drop into the falling masonry and Tarvitz saw that it was the bloodied form of Garro.

He scrambled across the disintegrating pyramid and leapt towards the drop, catching hold of the warrior's armour and dragging him towards firmer ground.

Tarvitz pulled Garro away from the fighting, seeing that his friend was badly wounded. One leg was severed at mid thigh and portions of his chest and upper arm were crushed. Frozen, coagulated blood swelled like blown glass around his injuries and shards of stone jutted from his abdomen.

'Tarvitz!' growled Garro, his anger greater than his pain. 'It's a Warsinger. Don't listen.'

'Hold on, brother,' said Tarvitz. 'I'll be back for you.'

'Just kill it,' spat Garro.

Tarvitz looked up, seeing the Warsinger closer as she drifted towards the Emperor's Children. Her face was serene and her arms were open as if to welcome them, her eyes closed as she drew the terrible song from her.

Yet more blocks of stone were lifting from the pyramid around the Emperor's Children. Tarvitz saw one warrior – Captain Odovocar, the Bearer of the Legion banner – dragged from his feet and into the air by the Warsinger's chorus. His armour jerked as if torn at by invisible fingers, sparking sheets of ceramite peeling back as the Warsinger's power took it apart.

Odovocar came apart with it, his helmet ripping free and trailing glittering streamers of blood and bone as it took his head off.

As Odovocar died, Tarvitz was struck by the savage beauty of the song, a song he felt she was singing just for him. Beauty and death were captured in its discordant notes, the wonderful peace that would come if he just gave himself up to it and let the music of oblivion take him. War would end and violence wouldn't even be a memory.

Don't listen to it.

Tarvitz snarled and his bolt pistol kicked in his hand as he fired at the Warsinger, the sound of the shots drowned by the cacophony. Shells impacted against a sheath of shimmering force around the Warsinger, blooms of white light exploding around her as they detonated prematurely. More and more of the Astartes, Emperor's Children and Death Guard both, were being pulled up into the air and sonically dismembered, and Tarvitz knew they didn't have much time before their cause was lost.

The surviving Isstvanian soldiers were regrouping, storming up the pyramid after the Astartes. Tarvitz saw Lucius among them, his sword slashing black-armoured limbs from bodies as they fought to surround him.

Lucius could look after himself and Tarvitz forced himself onwards, struggling to keep his footing amid the chaos of the Warsinger's wanton destruction. Gold gleamed ahead of him and he saw Eidolon's armour shining like a beacon in the Warsinger's light. The lord commander bellowed in defiance and pulled himself up the last few levels of the pyramid as Tarvitz climbed to join him.

The Warsinger drew a shining caul of light around her and Eidolon plunged into it, the glare becoming opaque like a shining white shell. Tarvitz's pistol was empty, so he dropped it, taking a two-handed grip on his sword and following his lord commander into the light.

The deafening shrieks of the Warsinger filled his head with deathly unmusic, rising to a crescendo as he penetrated the veil of light.

Eidolon was on his knees, his hammer lost and the Warsinger hovering over him. Her hands stretched out in front of her as she battered Eidolon with waves of force strong enough to distort the air.

Eidolon's armour warped around him, his helmet ripped from his head in a wash of blood, but he was still alive and fighting.

Tarvitz charged, screaming, 'For the Emperor!'

The Warsinger saw him and smashed him to the floor with a dismissive flick of her wrist. His helmet cracked with the force of the impact and for a moment his world was filled with the awful beauty of the Warsinger's song. His vision returned in time for him to see Eidolon lunging forwards. His charge had bought Eidolon a momentary distraction, the harmonics of her song redirected for the briefest moment.

The briefest moment was all a warrior of the Emperor's Children needed.

Eidolon's eyes were ablaze, his hatred and revulsion at this foe clear as his mouth opened in a cry of rage. His mouth opened still wider and he let loose his own screeching howl. Tarvitz rolled onto his back, dropping his sword and clutching his hands to his ears at the dreadful sound. Where the Warsinger's song had layered its death in beguiling beauty, there was no such grace in the sonic assault launched by Eidolon, it was simply agonising, deafening volume.

The crippling noise smashed into the Warsinger and suddenly her grace was torn away. She opened her mouth to sing a fresh song of death, but Eidolon's scream turned her cries into a grim dirge.

Sounds of mourning and pain layered over one another into a heavy funereal drone as the Warsinger dropped to her knees. Eidolon bent and picked up Tarvitz's fallen broadsword, his own terrible scream now silenced. The Warsinger writhed in pain, arcing coils of light whipping from her as she lost control of her song.

Eidolon waded through the light and noise. The broadsword licked out and Eidolon cut the Warsinger's head from her shoulders with a single sweep of silver.

Finally the Warsinger was silent.

Tarvitz clung to the crumbling summit of the pyramid and watched as Eidolon raised the sword in victory, still trying to understand what he had seen.

The Warsinger's monstrous harmonies still rang in his head, but he shook them off as he stared in disbelief at the lord commander.

Eidolon turned to Tarvitz, and dropped the broadsword beside him.

'A good blade,' he said. 'My thanks for your intervention.'

'How…?' was all Tarvitz could muster, his senses still overcome with the deafening shriek Eidolon had unleashed.

'Strength of will, Tarvitz,' said Eidolon. 'That's what it was, strength of will. The damn magic was no match for a pair of warriors like us, eh?'

'I suppose not,' said Tarvitz, accepting a hand up from Eidolon. The dome was suddenly, eerily silent. The Isstvanians who still lived were slumped where they had fallen at the Warsinger's death, weeping and rocking back and forth like children at the loss of a parent.

'I don't understand–' he began as warriors of the Death Guard started securing the dome.

'You don't need to understand, Tarvitz,' said Eidolon. 'We won, that's what matters.'

'But what you did–'

'What I did was kill our enemies,' snapped Eidolon. 'Understood?'

'Understood,' nodded Tarvitz, although he no more understood Eidolon's newfound ability than he did the celestial mechanics of travelling through the warp.

Eidolon said, 'Kill any remaining enemy troops. Then destroy this place,' before turning and making his way down the shattered pyramid to the cheers of his warriors.

Tarvitz retrieved his fallen weapons and watched the aftermath of victory unfolding below him. The Astartes were regrouping and he made his way back down to where he had left the wounded Garro.

The captain of the Death Guard was sitting propped up against the side of the pyramid, his chest heaving with the effort of breathing and Tarvitz could see it had taken a supreme effort of will not to let the pain balms of his armour render him unconscious.

'Tarvitz, you're alive,' said Garro as he climbed down the last step.

'Just about,' he said. 'More than can be said for you.'

'This?' sneered Garro. 'I've had worse than this. You mark my words, lad, I'll be up and teaching you a few new tricks in the training cages again before you know it.'

Despite the strangeness of the battle and the lives that had been lost, Tarvitz smiled.

'It is good to see you again, Nathaniel,' said Tarvitz, leaning down and taking Garro's proffered hand. 'It has been too long since we fought together.'

'It has that, my honour brother,' nodded Garro, 'but I have a feeling we will have plenty of opportunities to fight as one before this campaign is over.'

'Not if you keep letting yourself get injured like this. You need an Apothecary.'

'Nonsense, boy, there's plenty worse than me that need a sawbones first.'

'You never did learn to accept that you'd been hurt did you?' smiled Tarvitz.

'No,' agreed Garro. 'It's not the Death Guard way, is it?'

'I wouldn't know,' said Tarvitz, waving over an Emperor's Children Apothecary despite Garro's protests. 'You're too barbarous a Legion for me to ever understand.'

'And you're a bunch of pretty boys, more concerned with looking good than getting the job done,' said Garro, rounding off the traditional insults that passed for greetings between them. Both warriors had been through too much in their long friendship and saved each other's lives too many times to allow formality and petty differences between their Legions to matter.

Garro jerked his thumb in the direction of the summit. 'You killed her?'

'No,' said Tarvitz. 'Lord Commander Eidolon did.'

'Eidolon, eh?' mused Garro. 'Never did have much time for him. Still, if he managed to bring her down, he's obviously learned a thing or two since I last met him.'

'I think you might be right,' said Tarvitz.

SIX

The soul of the Legion
Everything will be different
Abomination

Loken found Abaddon in the observation dome that blistered from the hull of the upper decks of the *Vengeful Spirit*, the transparent glass looking out onto the barren wasteland of Isstvan Extremis. The dome was quiet and dark, a perfect place for reflection and calm, and Abaddon looked out of place, his power and energy like that of a caged beast poised to attack.

'Loken,' said Abaddon as he walked into the chamber. '*You* summoned *me* here?'

'I did.'

'Why?' demanded Abaddon.

'Loyalty,' said Loken simply.

Abaddon snorted. 'You don't know the meaning of the word. You have never had it tested.'

'Like you did on Davin?'

'Ah,' sighed Abaddon, 'so that is what this is about. Don't think to lecture me, Loken. You couldn't have taken the steps we did to save the Warmaster.'

'Maybe I'm the only one who took a stand.'

'Against what? You would have allowed the Warmaster to die rather than accept that there might be something in this universe you don't understand?'

'I am not here to debate what happened on Davin,' said Loken, already feeling that he had lost control of the conversation.

'Then why are you here? I have warriors to make ready, and I won't waste time with you on idle words.'

'I called you here because I need answers. About this,' said Loken, casting the book he had taken from the fane behind the strategium onto the mosaic floor of the observation dome.

Abaddon stooped to retrieve the book. In the hands of the First Captain, it looked tiny, like one of Ignace Karkasy's pamphlets.

'So you're a thief now,' said Abaddon.

'Do not dare speak to me of such things, Ezekyle, not until you have given me answers. I know that Erebus conspired against us. He stole the anathame from the interex and brought it to Davin. I know it and you know it.'

'You know nothing, Loken,' sneered Abaddon. 'What happens in this Crusade happens for the good of the Imperium. The Warmaster has a plan.'

'A plan?' said Loken. 'And this plan requires the murder of innocent people? Hektor Varvarus? Ignace Karkasy? Petronella Vivar?'

'The remembrancers?' laughed Abaddon. 'You really care about those people? They are lesser people, Loken, beneath us. The Council of Terra wants to drown us in these petty bureaucrats to stifle us and strangle our ambitions to conquer the galaxy.'

'Erebus,' said Loken, trying to keep his anger in check. 'Why was he on the *Vengeful Spirit*?'

Abaddon crossed the width of the observation dome in a second. 'None of your damn business.'

'This is my Legion!' shouted Loken. 'That makes it my damn business.'

'Not any more.'

Loken felt his choler rise and clenched his hands into murderous fists.

Abaddon saw the tension in him and said, 'Thinking of settling this like a warrior?'

'No, Ezekyle,' said Loken through clenched teeth. 'Despite all that has happened, you are still my Mournival brother and I will not fight you.'

'The Mournival,' nodded Abaddon. 'A noble idea while it lasted, but I regret ever bringing you in. In any case, if it came down to bloodshed do you really think you could beat me?'

Loken ignored the taunt and said, 'Is Erebus still here?'

'Erebus is a guest on the Warmaster's flagship,' said Abaddon. 'You would do well to remember that. If you had joined us when you had the chance instead of turning your back on us, you would have all your answers, but that's the choice you made, Loken. Live with it.'

'The lodge has brought something evil into our Legion, Ezekyle, maybe the other Legions too, something from the warp. It's what killed Jubal and it's what took Temba on Davin. Erebus is lying to all of us!'

'And we're being used, is that right? Erebus is manipulating us all towards a fate worse than death?' spat Abaddon. 'You know so little. If you understood the scale of the Warmaster's designs then you would beg us to take you back.'

'Then tell me, Ezekyle, and maybe I'll beg. We were brothers once and we can be again.'

'Do you really believe that, Loken? You've made it plain enough that you're against us. Torgaddon said as much.'

'For my Legion, for my Warmaster, there is always a way back,' replied Loken, 'as long as you feel the same.'

'But you'll never surrender, eh?'

'Never! Not when the soul of my Legion is at stake.'

Abaddon shook his head. 'We tie ourselves in such knots because men like you are too proud to make compromises.'

'Compromise will be the death of us, Ezekyle.'

'Forget this until after Isstvan, Loken,' ordered Abaddon. 'After Isstvan, this will end.'

'I will not forget it, Ezekyle. I will have my answers,' snarled Loken, turning and walking away from his brother.

'If you fight us, you'll lose,' promised Abaddon.

'Maybe,' replied Loken, 'but others will stand against you.'

'Then they will die too.'

'Thank you all for coming,' said Sindermann, overwhelmed and a little afraid at the number of people gathered before him. 'I appreciate that you have all taken a great risk to be here, but this is too much.'

Crammed into a dark maintenance space, filthy with grease and hemmed in by low hissing pipe work, the faithful had come from all over the ship to hear the saint's words, mistakenly believing that she was awake. Amongst the crowd, Sindermann saw the uniforms of Titan crewmen, fleet maintenance workers, medical staff, security personnel, and even a few Imperial Army troopers. Men with guns guarded the entrances to the maintenance space and their presence served as a stark reminder of the danger they were in just by being here.

Such a large gathering was dangerous, too easily noticed, and Sindermann knew that he had to disperse them quickly before they were discovered, and do it in such a way as not to incite a riot.

'You have escaped notice thus far thanks to the size of your gatherings, but so many cannot avoid notice for long,' continued Sindermann. 'You will no doubt have heard many strange and wonderful things recently, and I hope you will forgive me for putting you in harm's way.'

The news of Keeler's rescue had spread quickly through the ship. It had been whispered among the grime-covered ratings, it had been communicated through the remembrancer order with the rapidity of an epidemic and it had reached the ears of even the lowliest member of the Expedition. Embellishments and wild rumour followed in the wake of the news and tales abounded of the saint and her miraculous powers, incredible stories of bullets turned aside and of visions of the Emperor speaking directly to her in order to show His people the way.

'What of the saint?' asked a voice from the crowd. 'We want to see her!'

Sindermann held up a hand and said, 'The saint is fortunate to be alive. She is well, but she still sleeps. Some of you have heard that she is awake, and that she has spoken, but regrettably this is not the case.'

A disappointed buzz spread throughout the crowd, angry at Sindermann's denial of what many of them desperately wanted to believe. Sindermann was reminded of the speeches he had given on newly-compliant worlds, where he had used his iterator's wiles to extol the virtues of the Imperial Truth.

Now he had to use those same skills to give these people hope.

'The saint still sleeps, it's true, but for one brief, shining moment she arose from her slumbers to save my life. I saw her eyes open and I know that when we need her, she will come back to us. Until then we must walk warily, for there are those in the fleet who would destroy us for our beliefs. The very fact that we must meet in secret and rely on armed guards to keep us safe is a reminder that Maloghurst himself regularly sends troops to break up the meetings of the Lectitio Divinitatus. People have been killed and their blood is on the hands of the Astartes. Ignace Karkasy, Emperor rest his soul, knew the dangers of an unchecked Astartes before any of us realised their hands were around our throats.

'Once, I could not believe in such things as saints. I had trained myself to accept only logic and science, and to cast aside religion as superstition. Magic and miracles were impossible, simply the invention of ignorant people struggling to understand their world. It took the sacrifice of the saint to show me how arrogant I was. I saw how the Emperor protects, but she has shown me that there is so much more than that, for, if the Emperor protects His faithful, who protects the Emperor?'

Sindermann let the question hang.

'We must,' said Titus Cassar, pushing his way towards the front of the crowd and turning to address them. Sindermann had placed Cassar in the crowd with specific instructions on when to speak – a basic ploy of the iterators to reinforce their message.

'We must protect the Emperor, for there is no one else,' said Cassar. The moderati looked back at Sindermann. 'But we must stay alive in order to do so. Is that not right, iterator?'

'Yes,' said Sindermann. 'The faith that this congregation has displayed has caused such fear in the higher echelons of the fleet that they are trying to destroy us. The Emperor has an enemy here, of that I am sure. We must survive and we must stand against that enemy when it finally reveals itself.'

Worried and angry murmurings spread through the crowd as the deadly nature of the threat sank in.

'Faithful friends,' said Sindermann, 'the dangers we face are great, but the saint is with us and she needs shelter. Shelter we can best achieve alone, but watch for the signs and be safe. Spread the word of her safety.'

Cassar moved through the congregation, instructing them to return to their posts. Reassured by Sindermann's words, they gradually began to disperse. As he watched them go, Sindermann wondered how many of them would live through the coming days.

The Gallery of Swords ran the length of the *Andronius* like the ship's gilded spine. Its roof was transparent and the space beneath was lit by the fire of distant stars. Hundreds of statues lined the gallery, heroes of the Emperor's Children with gemstone eyes and stern expressions of judgement. The worth of a hero was said to be measured by how long he could meet their gaze while walking the length of the Gallery of Swords beneath their unforgiving eyes.

Tarvitz held his head high as he entered the gallery, though he knew he was no hero, simply a warrior who did his best. Chapter Masters and commanders from long ago glared at him, their names and noble countenances known and revered by every warrior of the Emperor's Children. Entire wings of the *Andronius* were given over to the fallen battle-brothers of the Legion, but it was here that every warrior hoped to be remembered.

Tarvitz had no expectation of his visage ending up here, but he would strive to end his days in a manner that might be considered worthy of such an honour. Even if such a lofty goal was impossible, it was something to aspire to.

Eidolon stood before the graven image of Lord Commander Teliosa, the hero of the Madrivane Campaign, and even before Tarvitz drew near he turned to face him.

'Captain Tarvitz,' said Eidolon. 'I have rarely seen you here.'

'It is not my natural habitat, commander,' replied Tarvitz. 'I leave the heroes of our Legion to their rest.'

'Then what brings you here now?'

'I would speak with you if you would permit me.'

'Surely your time is better spent attending to your warriors, Tarvitz. That is where your talents lie.'

'You honour me by saying so, commander, but there is something I need to ask you.'

'About?'

'The death of the Warsinger.'

'Ah.' Eidolon looked up at the statue towering over them, the hollow eyes regarding them with a cold, unflinching gaze. 'She was quite an adversary – absolutely corrupt, but that corruption gave her strength.'

'I need to know how you killed her.'

'Captain? You speak as if to an equal.'

'I saw what you did, commander,' Tarvitz pressed. 'That scream, it was some… I don't know… some power I've never heard of before.'

Eidolon held up a hand. 'I can understand why you have questions, and I can answer them, but perhaps it would be better for me to show you. Follow me.'

Tarvitz followed the lord commander as they walked further down the Gallery of Swords, turning into a side passage with sheets of parchment pinned along the length of its walls. Accounts of glorious actions from the Legion's past were meticulously recorded on them and novices of the Legion were required to memorise the many different battles before their elevation to full Astartes.

The Emperor's Children did more than just remember their triumphs; they proclaimed them, because the perfection of the Legion's way of war deserved celebrating.

'Do you know why I fought the Warsinger?' asked Eidolon.

'Why?'

'Yes, captain, why.'

'Because that is how the Emperor's Children fight.'

'Explain.'

'Our heroes lead from the front. The rest of the Legion is

inspired to follow their example. They can do this because the Legion fights with such artistry that they are not rendered vulnerable by fighting at the fore.'

Eidolon smiled. 'Very good, captain. I should have you instruct the novices. And you yourself, would you lead from the front?'

Sudden hope flared in Tarvitz's breast. 'Of course! Given the chance, I would. I had not thought you considered me worthy of such a role.'

'You are not, Tarvitz. You are a file officer and nothing more,' said Eidolon, crushing his faint hope that he had been about to be offered a way of proving his mettle as a leader and a hero.

'I say this not as an insult,' Eidolon continued, apparently oblivious to the insult it clearly was. 'Men like you fulfil an important role in our Legion, but I am one of Fulgrim's chosen. The primarch chose me and elevated me to the position I now hold. He looked upon me and saw in me the qualities needed to lead the Emperor's Children. He looked upon you, and did not. Because of this, I understand the responsibilities that come with being Fulgrim's chosen in a way that you cannot, Captain Tarvitz.'

Eidolon led him to a grand staircase that curved downwards into a large hall tiled with white marble. Tarvitz recognised it as one of the entrances to the ship's apothecarion, where the injured from Isstvan Extremis had been brought only a few hours before.

'I think you underestimate me, lord commander,' said Tarvitz, 'but understand that for the sake of my men I must know–'

'For the sake of our men we all make sacrifices,' snapped Eidolon. 'For the chosen, those sacrifices are great. Foremost among these is that fact that *everything* is secondary to victory.'

'Commander, I don't understand.'

'You will,' said Eidolon, leading him through a gilded archway and into the central apothecarion.

'The book?' asked Torgaddon.

'The book,' repeated Loken. 'It's the key. Erebus is on the ship, I know it.'

The ashen darkness of Archive Chamber Three was one of the few places left on the *Vengeful Spirit* where Loken felt at home, remembering many a lively debate with Kyril Sindermann in simpler times. Loken had not seen the iterator for weeks and he fervently hoped that the old man was safe, that he had not fallen foul of Maloghurst or his faceless soldiers.

'Abaddon and the others must be keeping him safe,' said Torgaddon.

Loken sighed. 'How did it come to this? I would have given my life for Abaddon, Aximand, too, and I know they would have done the same for me.'

'We can't give up on this, Garviel. There will be a way out of this. We can bring the Mournival back together, or at least make sure the Warmaster sees what Erebus is doing.'

'Whatever that is.'

'Yes, whatever that is. Guest of the lodge or not, he's not welcome on my ship. He's the key. If we find him, we can expose what's going on to the Warmaster and end this.'

'You really believe that?'

'I don't know, but that won't stop me trying.'

Torgaddon looked around him, stirring the ashes of the charred books on the shelves with a finger and said, 'Why did you have to meet me here? It smells like a funeral pyre.'

'Because no one ever comes here,' said Loken.

'I can't imagine why, seeing as how pleasant it is.'

'Don't be flippant, Tarik, not now. The Great Crusade was once about bringing illumination to the far corners of the galaxy, but now it is afraid of knowledge. The more we learn, the more we question and the more we question the more we see through the lies perpetrated upon us. To those who want to control us, books are dangerous.'

'Iterator Loken,' laughed Torgaddon, 'you've enlightened me.'

'I had a good teacher,' said Loken, again thinking of Kyril Sindermann, and the fact that everything he had been taught to believe was being shaken to its core. 'And there's more at stake here than a split between Astartes. It's… It's philosophy, ideology, religion even… everything. Kyril taught me that this kind of blind obedience is what led to the Age of Strife. We've crossed the galaxy to bring peace and illumination, but the cause of our downfall could be right here amongst us.'

Torgaddon leaned over and put a hand on his friend's shoulder. 'Listen, we're about to go into battle on Isstvan Three and the word from the Death Guard is that the enemy is led by some kind of psychic monsters that can kill with a scream. They're not the enemy because they read the wrong books or anything like that. They're the enemy because the Warmaster tells us they are. Forget about all this for a while. Go and fight. That'll put some perspective on things.'

'Do you even know if we'll be headed down there?'

'The Warmaster's picked the squads for the speartip. We're in it, and it looks as if we'll be in charge, too.'

'Really? After all that's happened?

'I know, but I won't look a gift horse in the mouth.'

'At least I'll have the Tenth with me.'

Torgaddon shook his head. 'Not quite. The Warmaster hasn't chosen the speartip by company. It's squad by squad.'

'Why?'

'Because he thinks that confused look on your face is funny.'

'Please. Be serious, Tarik.'

Torgaddon shrugged. 'The Warmaster knows what he's doing. It won't be an easy battle. We'll be dropping right on top of the city.'

'What about Locasta?'

'You'll have them. I don't think you could have held Vipus back anyway. You know what he's like, he'd have stowed away on a drop pod if he'd been left out. He's like you, he needs to clear his head with a good dose of fighting. After Isstvan things will get back to normal.'

'Good. I'll feel a lot better with Locasta backing us up.'

'Well, it's true that you need the help,' smiled Torgaddon.

Loken chuckled, not because Torgaddon was actually funny, but because even after everything he was still the same, a person that he could trust and a friend he could rely on.

'You're right, Tarik,' said Loken. 'After Isstvan everything will be different.'

The central apothecarion gleamed with glass and steel, dozens of medical cells branching off from the circular hub of the main laboratory. Tarvitz felt a chill travel the length of his spine as he saw Captain Odovocar's ruined body suspended in a stasis tank, waiting for its gene-seed to be harvested.

Eidolon marched through the hub and down a tiled corridor that led into a gilded vestibule dominated by a huge mosaic depicting Fulgrim's victory at Tarsus, where the primarch had vanquished the deceitful eldar despite his many grievous wounds. Eidolon reached up and pressed one of the enamelled chips that formed Fulgrim's belt, standing back as the mosaic arced upwards, revealing a glowing passageway and winding spiral staircase beyond. Eidolon strode down the passageway, indicating that Tarvitz should follow him.

The lack of ornamentation was a contrast to the rest of the *Andronius* and Tarvitz saw a cold blue glow emanating from whatever lay below as he made his way down the stairs. As they reached the end of their descent, Eidolon turned to him and said, 'This, Captain Tarvitz, is your answer.'

The blue light shone from a dozen ceiling-high translucent

cylinders that stood against the sides of the room. Each was filled with liquid with indistinct shapes suspended in them – some roughly humanoid, some more like collections of organs or body parts. The rest of the room was taken up by gleaming laboratory benches covered in equipment, some with purposes he couldn't even begin to guess at.

He moved from tank to tank, repulsed as he saw that some were full of monstrously bloated flesh that was barely contained by the glass.

'What is this?' asked Tarvitz in horror at such grotesque sights.

'I fear my explanations would be insufficient,' said Eidolon, walking towards an archway leading into the next room. Tarvitz followed him, peering more closely at the cylinders as he passed. One contained an Astartes-sized body, but not a corpse, more like something that had never been born, its features sunken and half-formed.

Another cylinder contained only a head, but one which had large, multi-faceted eyes like an insect. As he looked closer, Tarvitz realised with sick horror that the eyes had not been grafted on, for he saw no scars and the skull had reshaped itself to accommodate them.

They had been grown there.

He moved on to the last cylinder, seeing a mass of brains linked by fleshy cables held in liquid suspension, each one with extra lobes bulging like tumours.

Tarvitz felt a profound chill coming from the next room, its walls lined with refrigerated metal cabinets. He briefly wondered what was in them, but decided he didn't want to know as his imagination conjured all manner of deformities and mutations. A single operating slab filled the centre of the room, easily large enough for an Astartes warrior to be restrained upon, with a chirurgeon device mounted on the ceiling above.

Neatly cut sections of muscle fibre were spread across the slab. Apothecary Fabius bent over them, the hissing probes and needles of his narthecium embedded in a dark mass of glistening meat.

'Apothecary,' said Eidolon, 'the captain wishes to know of our enterprise.'

Fabius looked up in surprise, his long intelligent face framed by a mane of fine blond hair. Only his eyes were out of place, small and dark, set into his skull like black pearls. He wore a floor-length medicae gown, blood streaking its pristine whiteness with runnels of crimson.

'Really?' said Fabius. 'I had not been made aware that Captain Tarvitz was among our esteemed company.'

'He is not,' said Eidolon. 'Not yet anyway.'

'Then why is he here?'

'My own alterations have come to light.'

'Ah, I see,' nodded Fabius.

'What is going on here?' asked Tarvitz sharply. 'What is this place?'

Fabius cocked an eyebrow. 'So you have seen the results of the commander's augmentations, have you?'

'Is he a psyker?' demanded Tarvitz.

'No, no, no!' laughed Fabius. 'He is not. The lord commander's abilities are the result of a tracheal implant combined with alteration in the gene-seed rhythms. He is something of a success. His powers are metabolic and chemical, not psychic.'

'You have altered the gene-seed?' breathed Tarvitz in shock. 'The gene-seed is the blood of our primarch... When he discovers what you are doing here...'

'Don't be naïve, captain,' said Fabius. 'Who do you think ordered us to proceed?'

'No,' said Tarvitz. 'He wouldn't–'

'That is why I had to show you this, captain,' said Eidolon. 'You remember the Cleansing of Laeran?'

'Of course,' answered Tarvitz.

'Our primarch saw what the Laer had achieved by chemical and genetic manipulation of their biological structure in their drive for physical perfection. The Lord Fulgrim has great plans for our Legion, Tarvitz, the Emperor's Children cannot be content to sit on their laurels while our fellow Astartes win the same dull victories. We must continue to strive towards perfection, but we are fast reaching the point where even an Astartes cannot match the standards Lord Fulgrim and the Warmaster demand. To meet those standards, we must change. We must evolve.'

Tarvitz backed away from the operating slab. 'The Emperor created Lord Fulgrim to be the perfect warrior and the Legion's warriors were moulded in his image. That image is what we strive towards. Holding a xenos race up as an example of perfection is an abomination!'

'An abomination?' said Eidolon. 'Tarvitz, you are brave and disciplined, and your warriors respect you, but you do not have the imagination to see where this work can lead us. You must realise that the Legion's supremacy is of greater importance than any mortal squeamishness.'

Such a bold statement, its arrogance and conceit beyond anything he had heard Eidolon say before, stunned Tarvitz to silence.

'But for your unlikely presence at the death of the Warsinger, you would never have been granted this chance, Tarvitz,' said Eidolon. 'Understand it for the opportunity it represents.'

Tarvitz looked up at the lord commander sharply. 'What do you mean?'

'Now you know what we are attempting, perhaps you are ready to become a part of this Legion's future instead of simply one of its line officers.'

'It is not without risk,' Fabius pointed out, 'but I could work such wonders upon your flesh. I can make you more than you are, I can bring you closer to perfection.'

'Think of the alternative,' said Eidolon. 'You will fight and die knowing that you could have been so much more.'

Tarvitz looked at the two warriors before him, both Fulgrim's chosen and both exemplars of the Legion's relentless drive towards perfection.

He saw then that he was very, very far from perfection as they understood it, but for once welcomed such a failing, if failing it was.

'No,' he said, backing away. 'This is... wrong. Can you not feel it?'

'Very well,' said Eidolon. 'You have made your choice and it does not surprise me. So be it. You must leave now, but you are ordered not to speak of what you have seen here. Return to your men, Tarvitz. Isstvan Three will be a tough fight.'

'Yes, commander,' said Tarvitz, relieved beyond measure to be leaving this chamber of horrors.

Tarvitz saluted and all but fled the laboratory, feeling as though the specimens suspended in the tanks were watching him as he went.

As he emerged into the brightness of the apothecarion, he could not shake the feeling that he had just been tested.

Whether he had passed or failed was another matter entirely.

SEVEN

The God-Machine
A favour
Subterfuge

The cold sensation snaking through Cassar's mind was like an old friend, the touch of something reassuring. The metallic caress of the *Dies Irae* as its cortical interfaces meshed with his consciousness would have been terrifying to most people, but it was one of the few constants Moderati Titus Cassar had left in the galaxy.

That and the Lectitio Divinitatus.

The Titan's bridge was dim, lit by ghostly readouts and telltales that lined the ornate bridge in hard greens and blues. The Mechanicum had been busy, sending cloaked adepts into the Titan, and the bridge was packed with equipment he didn't yet know the purpose of. The deck crew manning the plasma reactor at the war machine's heart had been readying the Titan for battle since the *Vengeful Spirit* arrived in the Isstvan system, and every indication was that the *Dies Irae*'s major systems were all functioning better than ever.

Cassar was glad of any advantage the war machine could get, but somewhere deep down he resented the thought of anyone else touching the Titan. The interface filaments coiled deeper into his scalp, sending an unexpected chill through him. The Titan's systems lit up behind Cassar's eyes as though they were a part of his own body. The plasma reactor was ticking over quietly, its pent-up energy ready to erupt into full battle order at his command.

'Motivation systems are a little loose,' he said to himself, tightening the pressure on the massive hydraulic rams in the Titan's torso and legs.

'Weapons hot, ammunition loaded,' he said, knowing that it would take no more than a thought to unleash them.

He had come to regard the power and magnificence of the *Dies Irae* as the Emperor personified. Cassar had resisted the thought at first, mocking Jonah Aruken's insistence that the Titan had a soul, but it had become more and more obvious why he had been chosen by the saint.

The Lectitio Divinitatus was under threat and the faithful had to be defended. He almost laughed aloud as the thought formed, but what he had seen on the medicae deck had only deepened the strength of his conviction that he had chosen the right path.

The Titan was a symbol of that strength, an avatar of divine wrath, a god-machine that brought the Emperor's judgement to the sinners of Isstvan.

'The Emperor protects,' whispered Cassar, his voice drifting down through the layers of readouts in his mind, 'and he destroys.'

'Does he now?'

Cassar snapped out of his thoughts and the Titan's systems retreated beneath his consciousness. He looked up in sudden panic, but let out a relieved breath as he saw Moderati Aruken standing over him.

Aruken snapped a switch and the bridge lights flickered to life. 'Be careful who hears you, Titus, now more than ever.'

'I was running through pre-battle checks,' said Cassar.

'Of course you were, Titus. If Princeps Turnet hears you saying things like that you'll be for it.'

'My thoughts are my own, Jonah. Not even the princeps can deny me that.'

'You really believe that? Come on, Titus. You know full well this cult stuff isn't welcome. We were lucky on the medicae deck, but this is bigger than you and me and it's getting too dangerous.'

'We can't back away from it now,' said Cassar, 'not after what we saw.'

'I'm not even sure what I saw,' said Aruken defensively.

'You're joking, surely?'

'No,' insisted Aruken, 'I'm not. Look, I'm telling you this because you're a good man and the *Dies Irae* will suffer if you're not here. She needs a good crew and you're part of it.'

'Don't change the subject,' said Cassar. 'We both know that what we saw on the medicae deck was a miracle. You have to accept that before the Emperor can enter your heart.'

'Listen, I've been hearing some scuttlebutt on the deck, Titus,' said Aruken, leaning closer. 'Turnet's been asking questions about us. He's asking about how deep this runs, as though we're part of some hidden conspiracy. It's as if he doesn't trust us any more.'

'Let him come.'

'You don't understand. When we're in battle we're a good team, and if we get... I don't know... thrown in a cell or worse, that team gets broken up and there isn't a better crew for the *Dies Irae* than us. Don't let this saint business break that up. The Crusade will suffer for it.'

'My faith won't allow me to make compromises, Jonah.'

'Well that's all it is,' snapped Aruken. '*Your* faith.'

'No,' said Titus, shaking his head. 'It's your faith too, Jonah, you just don't know it yet.'

Aruken didn't answer and slumped into his own command chair, nodding at the readouts in front of Cassar. 'How's she looking?'

'Good. The reactor is ticking over smoothly and the targeting is reacting faster than I've seen it in a while. The Mechanicum adepts have been tinkering so there are a few more bells and whistles to play with.'

'You say that as if it's a bad thing, Titus. The Mechanicum know what they're doing. Anyway, the latest news is that we've got twelve hours to go before the drop. We're going in with the Death Guard on support duties. Princeps Turnet will brief us in a few hours, but it's basically pounding the ground and scaring the shit out of the enemy. Sound good?'

'It sounds like battle.'

'It's all the same thing for the *Dies Irae* when the bullets are flying,' said Aruken.

'This reminds me of why I was so proud,' said Loken, looking at the speartip assembling on the *Vengeful Spirit*'s embarkation deck. 'Joining the Mournival, and just to be a part of this.'

'I am still proud,' said Torgaddon. 'This is my Legion. That hasn't changed.'

Loken and Torgaddon, fully armoured and ready for the drop, stood at the head of a host of Astartes. More than a third of the Legion was there, thousands of warriors arrayed for war. Loken saw veterans alongside newly inducted novices, assault warriors with chainswords and bulky jump packs, and Devastators hefting heavy bolters and lascannons.

Sergeant Lachost was speaking with his communications squad, making sure they understood the importance of keeping a link with the *Vengeful Spirit* once they were down in the Choral City.

Apothecary Vaddon was checking and re-checking his medical gear, the narthecium gauntlet with its cluster of probes and the reductor that would harvest gene-seed from the fallen.

Iacton Qruze, who had been a captain for so long that he was as old as an Astartes could be and still count himself a warrior, was lecturing some of the more recent inductees on the past glories of the Legion that they had to live up to.

'I'd be happier with the Tenth,' said Loken, returning his attention to his friend.

'And I with the Second,' replied Torgaddon, 'but we can't always have what we want.'

'Garvi!' called a familiar voice.

Loken turned and saw Nero Vipus approaching them, leaving the veterans of Locasta to continue their preparations for the drop.

'Nero,' said Loken, 'good to have you with us.'

Vipus clapped Loken's shoulder guard with the augmetic hand that had replaced the organic one he'd lost on Sixty-Three Nineteen. 'I wouldn't have missed this,' he said.

'I know what you mean,' replied Loken. It had been a long time since they had lined up on the *Vengeful Spirit* as brothers, ready to fight the Emperor's good fight. Nero Vipus and Loken were the oldest of friends, back from the barely remembered blur of training, and it was reassuring to have another familiar face alongside him.

'Have you heard the reports from Isstvan Extremis?' asked Vipus, his eyes alight.

'Some of them.'

'They say the enemy has got some kind of psychic leadership caste and that their soldiers are fanatics. My choler's up just thinking about it.'

'Don't worry,' said Torgaddon. 'I'm sure you'll kill them all.'

'It's like Davin again,' said Vipus, baring his teeth in a grimace of anticipation.

'It's not like Davin,' said Loken. 'It's nothing at all like Davin.'

'What do you mean?'

'It's not a bloody swamp, for a start,' interjected Torgaddon.

'It would be an honour if you'd go into battle with Locasta, Garvi,' said Vipus expectantly. 'I have a space in the drop pod.'

'The honour is mine,' replied Loken, taking his friend's hand as a sudden thought occurred to him. 'Count me in.'

He nodded to his friends and made his way through the bustling Astartes towards the solitary figure of Iacton Qruze. The Half-heard watched the preparations for war with undisguised envy and Loken felt a stab of sympathy for the venerable warrior. Qruze was an example of just how little even the Legion's Apothecaries knew of an Astartes' physiology. His face was as battered and gnarled as ancient oak, but his body was as wolf-tough, honed by years of fighting and not yet made weary by age.

An Astartes was functionally immortal, meaning that only in death did duty end, and the thought sent a chill down Loken's spine.

'Loken,' acknowledged Qruze as he saw him approach.

'You're not coming down to see the sights of the Sirenhold with us?' asked Loken.

'Alas, no,' said Qruze. 'I am to stay and await orders. I haven't even got a place in the order of battle for the pacification force.'

'If the Warmaster has no plans for you, Iacton, then I have something you could do for me,' said Loken, 'if you would do me the honour?'

Qruze's eyes narrowed. 'What sort of a favour?'

'Nothing too arduous, I promise you.'

'Then ask.'

'There are some remembrancers aboard, you may have heard of them. Mersadie Oliton, Euphrati Keeler and Kyril Sindermann?'

'Yes, I know of them,' confirmed Qruze. 'What of them?'

'They are… friends of mine and I would consider it an honour if you were to seek them out and ask after them. Check on them and make sure that they are well.'

'Why do these mortals matter to you, captain?'

'They keep me honest, Iacton,' smiled Loken, 'and they remind me of everything we ought to be as Astartes.'

'That I can understand, Loken,' replied Qruze. 'The Legion is changing, boy. I know you've heard me bore you with this before, but I feel in my bones that there's something big just over the horizon that we can't see. If these people help keep us honest, then that's good enough for me. Consider it done, Captain Loken.'

'Thank you, Iacton,' said Loken. 'It means a lot to me.'

'Don't mention it, boy,' grinned Qruze. 'Now get out of here and kill for the living.'

'I will,' promised Loken, taking Qruze's wrist in the warrior's grip.

'Speartip units to posts,' said the booming voice of the deck officer.

'Good hunting in the Sirenhold,' said Qruze. 'Lupercal!'

'Lupercal!' echoed Loken.

As he jogged towards Locasta's drop pod, it almost felt as if the events of Davin were forgotten and Loken was just a warrior again, fighting a crusade that had to be won and an enemy that deserved to die.

It took war to make him feel like one of the Sons of Horus again.

'To victory!' shouted Lucius.

The Emperor's Children were so certain of the perfection of their way of war that it was traditional to salute the victory before it was won. Tarvitz was not surprised that Lucius led the salute; many senior officers attended the pre-battle celebration and Lucius was keen to be noticed. The Astartes seated at the lavish banquet around him joined his salute, their cheers echoing from the alabaster walls of the banqueting hall. Captured banners, honoured weapons once carried by the chosen of Fulgrim and murals of heroes despatching alien foes hung from the walls, glorious reminders of past victories.

The primarch himself was not present, thus it fell to Eidolon to take his place at the feast, exhorting his fellow Astartes to celebrate the coming victory. Lucius was equally vocal, leading his fellow warriors in toasts from golden chalices of fine wine.

Tarvitz set down his goblet and rose from the table.

'Leaving already, Tarvitz?' sneered Eidolon.

'Yes!' chimed in Lucius. 'We've only just begun to celebrate!'

'I'm sure you will do enough celebrating for both of us, Lucius,' said Tarvitz. 'I have matters to attend to before we make the drop.'

'Nonsense!' said Lucius. 'You need to stay with us and regale us with memories of Murder and how I helped you defeat the scourge of the megarachnids.'

The warriors cheered and called for Tarvitz to tell the story once more, but he held up his hands to quiet their demands.

'Why don't you tell it, Lucius?' asked Tarvitz. 'I don't think I build your part up enough for your liking anyway.'

'That's true,' smiled Lucius. 'Very well, I'll tell the tale.'

'Lord commander,' said Tarvitz, bowing to Eidolon and then turning to make his way through the golden door of the banquet hall. Appealing to Lucius's vanity was the surest way of deflecting his attention. Tarvitz would miss the camaraderie of the celebration, but he had other matters pressing on his thoughts.

He closed the door to the banqueting hall as Lucius began the tale of their ill-fated expedition to Murder, though its horrifying beginnings had somehow become a great triumph, largely thanks to Lucius, if past retellings were anything to go by.

The magnificent processional at the heart of the *Andronius* was quiet, the droning hum of the vessel reassuring in its constancy. The ship, like many in the Emperor's Children fleet, resembled some ancient palace of Terra, reflecting the Legion's desire to infuse everything with regal majesty.

Tarvitz made his way through the ship, passing wondrous spaces that would make the shipwrights of Jupiter weep with awe, until he reached the Hall of Rites, the circular chamber where the Emperor's Children underwent the oaths and ceremonies that tied them to their Legion. Compared to the rest of the ship, the hall was dark, but it was no less magnificent: marble columns supporting a distant domed ceiling, and ritual altars of marble glittering in pools of shadow at its edges.

Fulgrim's chosen had pledged themselves to the primarch's personal charge here, and he had accepted his appointment as captain before the Altar of Service. The Hall of Rites replaced opulence with gravity, and seemed designed to intimidate with the promise of knowledge hidden from all but the Legion's most exalted officers.

Tarvitz paused on the threshold, seeing the unmistakable shape of Ancient Rylanor, his Dreadnought body standing before the Altar of Devotion.

'Enter,' said Rylanor in his artificial voice.

Tarvitz cautiously approached the Ancient, his blocky outline resolving into a tank-like sarcophagus supported on powerful piston legs. The Dreadnought's wide shoulders mounted an assault cannon on one arm and a huge hydraulic fist on the other. Rylanor's body rotated slowly on its central axis to face Tarvitz, turning from the *Book of Ceremonies* that lay open on the altar.

'Captain Tarvitz, why are you not with your warriors?' asked Rylanor. His ocular circuits regarded Tarvitz without emotion.

'They can celebrate well enough without me,' said Tarvitz. 'Besides, I have sat through one too many renditions of Lucius's tales to think I'll miss much.'

'It is not to my taste either,' said Rylanor, a grating bark of electronic noise sounding from the Dreadnought's vox-unit. At first Tarvitz thought the Ancient had developed a fault, until he realised that the sound was Rylanor's laughter.

Rylanor was the Legion's Ancient of Rites, and when not on

the battlefield he oversaw the ceremonies that marked the gradual ascent of an Astartes from novice to chosen of Fulgrim. Decades before, Rylanor had been wounded beyond the skill of the Legion's Apothecaries while fighting the duplicitous eldar, and had been interred in a Dreadnought war machine that he might continue to serve. Along with Lucius and Tarvitz, Rylanor was one of the senior officers being sent down to take the Choral City's palace complex.

'I wish to speak with you, revered Ancient,' said Tarvitz, 'about the drop.'

'The drop is in a few hours,' replied Rylanor. 'There is little time.'

'Yes, I have left it too late and for that I apologise, but it concerns Captain Odovocar.'

'Captain Odovocar is dead, killed on Isstvan Extremis.'

'And the Legion lost a great warrior that day,' nodded Tarvitz. 'Not only that, but he was to function as Eidolon's senior staff officer aboard the *Andronius*, relaying the commander's orders to the surface. With his death there is no one to fulfil that role.'

'Eidolon is aware of Odovocar's loss. He will have an alternative in place.'

'I request the honour of fulfilling that role,' said Tarvitz solemnly. 'I knew Odovocar well and would consider it a fitting tribute to finish the work he began on this campaign.'

The Dreadnought leaned close to Tarvitz, the cold metallic machine unreadable, as the crippled warrior within decided Tarvitz's fate.

'You would renounce the honour of your place in the speartip to take over his duties?'

Tarvitz looked into Rylanor's optics, struggling to keep his expression neutral. Rylanor had seen everything the Legion had gone through since the beginning of the Great Crusade and was said to be able to perceive a lie the instant it was told.

His request to remain aboard the *Andronius* was highly unusual and Rylanor would surely be suspicious of his motives for not wanting to go into the fight. But when Tarvitz had learned that Eidolon was not leading the speartip personally, he knew there had to be a reason. The lord commander never passed up the opportunity to flaunt his martial prowess and for him to appoint another in his stead was unheard of.

Not only that, but the deployment orders Eidolon had issued made no sense.

Instead of the normal, rigorously regimented order of battle that was typical of an Emperor's Children assault, the units chosen to make the first attack appeared to have been picked at random. The only thing they had in common was that none were from Chapters led by Eidolon's favoured lord commanders. For Eidolon to sanction a drop without any of the warriors belonging to those lord commanders was unheard of and grossly insulting.

Something felt very wrong about this drop and Tarvitz couldn't shake the feeling that there was some grim purpose behind the selection of these units. He had to know what it was.

Rylanor straightened and said, 'I shall see to it that you are replaced. This is a great sacrifice you make, Captain Tarvitz. You do the memory of Odovocar much honour with it.'

Tarvitz fought to hide his relief, knowing that he had taken an unthinkable risk in lying to Rylanor. He nodded and said, 'My thanks, Ancient.'

'I shall join the troops of the speartip,' said the Dreadnought. 'Their feasting will soon be complete and I must ensure that they are ready for battle.'

'Bring perfection to the Choral City,' said Tarvitz.

'Guide us well,' replied Rylanor, his voice loaded with unspoken meaning. Tarvitz was suddenly certain that the Dreadnought *wanted* Tarvitz to remain on the ship.

'Do the Emperor's work, Captain Tarvitz,' ordered Rylanor.

Tarvitz saluted and said, 'I will,' as Rylanor set off across the Hall of Rites towards the banquet, his every step heavy and pounding.

Tarvitz watched him go, wondering if he would ever see the Ancient again.

The dormitories tucked into the thick walls running the length of the gantry were dark and hot, and from the doorway Mersadie could see down into the engine compartment where the crew were indistinguishable, sweating figures who worked in the infernal heat and ruddy glow of the plasma reactors. They hurried across gangways that stretched between the titanic reactors and clambered along massive conduits that hung like spider webs in the hellish gloom.

She dabbed sweat from her brow at the heat and close confines of the engine space, unused to the searing air that stole away her breath and left her faint.

'Mersadie,' said Sindermann coming to meet her along the gantry. The iterator had lost weight, his dirty robes hanging from his already spare frame, but his face was alight with the relief and joy of seeing her. The two embraced in a heartfelt hug, both grateful beyond words to see each other. She felt tears pricking her eyes at the sight of the old man, unaware until this moment of how much she had missed him.

'Kyril, it's so good to see you again,' she sobbed. 'You just vanished. I thought they'd got to you. I didn't know what had happened to you.'

'Hush, Mersadie,' said Sindermann, 'it's all right. I'm so sorry I couldn't send word to you at the time. You must understand that had I a choice, I would have done everything I could to keep you out of this, but I don't know what to do any more. We can't keep her down here forever.'

Mersadie looked through the doorway of the dormitory room they stood outside, wishing she had the courage to believe as Kyril did. 'Don't be ridiculous, Kyril. I'm glad you made contact, I thought... I thought Maloghurst or Maggard had killed you.'

'Maggard very nearly did,' said Sindermann, 'but the saint saved us.'

'She saved you?' asked Mersadie. 'How?'

'I don't know exactly, but it was just like in the Archive Chamber. The power of the Emperor was in her. I saw it, Mersadie, just as sure as you're standing here before me. I wish you could have seen it.'

'I wish that too,' she said, surprised to find that she meant it.

She entered the dormitory and stared down at the still form of Euphrati Keeler on the thin cot bed, looking for all the world as if she was simply sleeping. The small room was cramped and dirty, with a thin blanket spread on the deck beside the bed.

Winking starlight streamed in through a small porthole vision block, something greatly prized this deep in the ship, and without asking, she knew that someone had happily volunteered to give up their prized room for the use of the 'saint' and her companion.

Even down here in the dark and the stink, faith flourished.

'I wish I could believe,' said Mersadie, watching the rhythmic rise and fall of Euphrati's chest.

Sindermann said, 'You don't?'

'I don't know,' she said, shaking her head. 'Tell me why I should? What does believing mean to you, Kyril?'

He smiled and took her hand. 'It gives me something to hold on to. There are people on this ship who want to kill her, and somehow... Don't ask me how, I just know that I need to keep her safe.'

'Are you not afraid?' she asked.

'Afraid?' he said. 'I've never been more terrified in my life, my dear, but I have to hope that the Emperor is watching over me. That gives me strength and the will to face that fear.'

'You are a remarkable man, Kyril.'

'I'm not remarkable, Mersadie,' said Sindermann, shaking his head. 'I was lucky. I *saw* what the saint did, so faith is easy for me. It's hardest for you, for you have seen nothing. You have to simply accept that the Emperor is working through Euphrati, but you don't believe, do you?'

Mersadie turned from Sindermann and pulled her hand from his, looking through the porthole at the void of space beyond. 'No. I can't. Not yet.'

A white streak shot across the porthole like a shooting star.

Another followed it, and then another.

'What's that?' she asked.

Sindermann leaned over to get a better look through the porthole.

Even through his exhaustion, she could see the strength in him that she had previously taken for granted and she blink-clicked the image, capturing the defiance and bravery she saw in his features.

'Drop pods,' he said, pointing at a static gleaming object stark against the blackness and closer to Isstvan III. Tiny sparks began raining from its underside towards the planet below.

'I think that's the *Andronius*, Fulgrim's flagship,' said Sindermann. 'Looks like the attack we've been hearing about has begun. Imagine how it would be if we could watch it unfolding.'

Euphrati groaned and the attack on Isstvan III was forgotten as they slid across to sit beside her. Mersadie saw Sindermann's love for her clearly as he mopped her brow, her skin so clean that it practically shone.

For the briefest moment, Mersadie saw how people could believe Euphrati was miraculous; her body so pale and fragile, yet untouched by the world around her. Mersadie had known Keeler as a gutsy woman, never afraid to speak her mind or bend the rules to get the magnificent picts for which she was rightly famed, but now she was something else entirely.

'Is she coming round?' asked Mersadie.

'No,' said Sindermann sadly. 'She makes noises, but she never opens her eyes. It's such a waste. Sometimes I swear she's on the brink of waking, but then she sinks back down into whatever hell she's going through in her head.'

Mersadie sighed and looked back out into space.

The pinpoints of light streaked in their hundreds towards Isstvan III.

As the speartip was driven home, she whispered, 'Loken...'

The Choral City was magnificent.

Its design was a masterpiece of architecture, light and space so wondrous that Peeter Egon Momus had begged the Warmaster not to assault so brutally. Older by millennia than the Imperium that had come to claim it in the name of the Emperor, its precincts and thoroughfares were soon to become blood-slick battlefields.

While the juggernaut of compliance had made the galaxy a sterile, secular place, the Choral City remained a city of the gods.

The Precentor's Palace, a dizzying creation of gleaming marble blades and arches that shone in the sun, opened like a vast stone orchid to the sky and the polished granite of the city's wealthiest districts clustered around it like worshippers. Momus had described the palace as a hymn to power and glory, a symbol of the divine right by which Isstvan III would be ruled.

Further out from the palace and beyond the architectural perfection of the Choral City, vast multi-layered residential districts sprawled. Connected by countless walkways and bridges of glass and steel, the avenues between them were wide canyons of tree-lined boulevards in which the citizens of the Choral City lived.

The city's industrial heartland rose like climbing skeletons of steel against the eastern mountains, belching smoke as they churned out weapons to arm the planet's armies. War was coming and every Isstvanian had to be ready to fight.

But no sight in the Choral City compared to the Sirenhold.

Not even the magnificence of the palace outshone the Sirenhold, its towering walls defining the Choral City with their immensity. The brutal battlements diminished everything around them, and the sacred fortress of the Sirenhold humbled even the snow-capped peaks of the mountains. Within its walls, enormous tomb-spires reached for the skies, their walls encrusted with monumental sculptures that told the legends of Isstvan's mythical past.

The legends told that Isstvan himself had sung the world into being with music that could still be heard by the blessed Warsingers, and that he had borne countless children with whom he populated the first ages of the world. They became night and day, ocean and mountain, a thousand legends whose breath could be felt in every moment of every day in the Choral City.

Darker carvings told of the Lost Children, the sons and daughters who had forsaken their father and been banished to the blasted wasteland of the fifth planet, where they became monsters that burned with jealousy and raised black fortresses from which to brood upon their expulsion from paradise.

War, treachery, revelation and death; all marched around the Sirenhold in endless cycles of myth, the weight of their meaning pinning the Choral City to the soil of Isstvan III and infusing its every inhabitant with their sacred purpose.

The gods of Isstvan III were said to sleep in the Sirenhold, whispering their murderous plots in the nightmares of children and ancients.

For a time, the myths and legends had remained as distant as they had always been, but now they walked among the people of the Choral City, and every breath of wind shrieked that the Lost Children had returned.

Without knowing why, the populace of Isstvan III had armed and unquestioningly followed the orders of Vardus Praal to defend their city. An army of well-equipped soldiers awaited the invasion that they had long been promised was coming, in the western marches of the city, where the Warsingers had sung a formidable web of trenches into being.

Artillery pieces parked in the gleaming canyons of the city pointed their barrels westwards, set to pound any invaders into the ground before they reached the trenches. The warriors of the Choral City would then slaughter any that survived in carefully prepared crossfire.

The defences had been meticulously planned, protecting the city from attack from the west, the only direction in which an invasion could be launched.

Or so the soldiers manning the defences had been told.

The first omen was a fire in the sky that came with the dawn.

A scattering of falling stars streaked through the blood-red dawn, burning through the sky like fiery tears.

The sentries in the trenches saw them falling in bright spears of fire, the first burning object smashing into the trenches amid a plume of mud and flame.

At the speed of thought, the word raced around the Choral City that the Lost Children had returned, that the prophecies of myth were coming true,

They were proven right when the drop pods burst open and the Astartes of the Death Guard Legion emerged.

And the killing began.

PART TWO
THE CHORAL CITY

EIGHT

Soldiers from hell
Butchery
Betrayal

'Thirty seconds!' yelled Vipus, his voice barely audible over the screaming jets as the drop pod sliced through Isstvan III's atmosphere. The Astartes of Locasta were bathed in red light and for a moment Loken imagined what they would look like to the people of the Choral City when the assault began – warriors from another world, soldiers from hell.

'What's our landing point looking like?' shouted Loken.

Vipus glanced at the readout on a pict screen mounted above his head. 'Drifting! We'll hit the target, but off-centre. I hate these things. Give me a Stormbird any day!'

Loken didn't bother replying, barely able to hear Nero as the atmosphere thickened beneath the drop pod and the jets on its underside kicked in. The drop pod shuddered and began heating up as the enormous forces pushing against it turned to fire and noise.

He sat through the last few minutes while everything around him was noise, unable to see the enemy he was about to fight and relinquishing control over his fate until the drop pod hit.

Nero had been right when he said he had preferred an assault delivered by Stormbird, the precise, surgical nature of an airborne assault far preferable to a warrior than this hurtling descent from above.

But the Warmaster had decided that the speartip would be

deployed by drop pod, reasoning – rightly, Loken admitted – that thousands of Astartes smashing into the defenders' midst without warning would be more psychologically devastating. Loken ran through the moment the drop pod would hit in his mind, preparing himself for when the hatch charges would blow open.

He gripped his bolter tightly, and checked for the tenth time that his chainsword was in its scabbard at his side. Loken was ready.

'Ten seconds, Locasta,' shouted Vipus.

Barely a second later, the drop pod impacted with such force that Loken's head snapped back and suddenly the noise was gone and everything went black.

Lucius killed his first foe without even breaking stride.

The dead man's armour was like glass, shimmering and iridescent, and his halberd's blade was fashioned from the same reflective substance. A mask of stained glass covered his face, the mouth represented by leading and filled with teeth of gem-like triangles.

Lucius slid his sword clear, blood smoking from its edge, as the soldier slumped to the floor. A curved arch of marble shone red in the dawn's early light above him and a swirl of dust and debris drifted around the drop pod he had just leapt from.

The Precentor's Palace stood before him, vast and astonishing, a stone flower with the spire at its centre like a spectacular twist of overlapping granite petals.

More drop pods hammered into the ground behind him, the plaza around the palace's north entrances the main objective of the Emperor's Children. A nearby drop pod blew open and Ancient Rylanor stepped from its red-lit interior, his assault cannon already cycling and tracking for targets.

'Nasicae!' yelled Lucius. 'To me!'

Lucius saw a flash of coloured glass from inside the palace, movement beyond the sweeping stone panels of the entrance hall.

More palace guards reacted to the sudden, shocking assault, but contrary to what Lucius had been expecting, they weren't screaming or begging for mercy. They weren't even fleeing, or standing stock still, numb with shock.

With a terrible war cry the palace guard charged and Lucius laughed, glad to be facing a foe with some backbone. He levelled his sword and ran towards them, Squad Nasicae following behind him, weapons at the ready.

A hundred palace guardians ran at them, resplendent in their glass armour. They formed a line before the Astartes, levelled their halberds, and opened fire.

Searing needles of silver filled the air around Lucius, gouging the armour of his shoulder guard and leg. Lucius lifted his sword arm to shield his head and the needles spat from the glowing blade of his sword. Where they hit the stone around the entrance it bubbled and hissed like acid.

One of Nasicae fell beside Lucius, one arm molten and his abdomen bubbling.

'Perfection and death!' cried Lucius, running through the white-hot silver needles. The Emperor's Children and the palace guard clashed with a sound like a million windows breaking, the terrible screaming of the halberd-guns giving way to the clash of blade against armour and point-blank bolter fire.

Lucius's first sword blow hacked through a halberd shaft and tore through the throat of the man before him. Sightless glass eyes glared back at him, blood pumping from the guard's ruined throat, and Lucius tore the helm from his foe's head to better savour the sensation of his death.

A plasma pistol spat a tongue of liquid fire that wreathed an enemy soldier from head to foot, but the man kept fighting, sweeping his halberd down to cut deep into one of Lucius's men before another Astartes ripped off his head with a chainsword.

Lucius pivoted on one foot from a halberd strike and hammered the hilt of his sword into his opponent's face, feeling a tight anger that the faceplate held. The guard staggered away from him and Lucius reversed his grip and thrust the blade through the gap between the glass plates at the guard's waist, feeling the blade's energy field burning through abdomen and spine.

These guards were slowing the Emperor's Children down, buying precious moments with their lives for something deeper in the palace. As much as Lucius was revelling in the sensations of the slaughter, the smell of the blood, the searing stink of flesh as the heat of his blade scorched it and the pounding of blood in veins, he knew he could not afford to give the defenders such moments.

Lucius ran onwards, slicing his blade through limbs and throats as he ran. He fought as though following the steps of an elaborate dance, a dance where he played the part of the victor and the enemy were there only to die. The palace guard were dying around him and his armour was drenched with their blood. He laughed in sheer joy.

Warriors still fought behind him, but Lucius had to press on before the palace guard was able to stall their advance with more men in front of them.

'Squad Quemondil! Rethaerin! Kill these and then follow me!'

Fire sawed from every direction as the Emperor's Children forced their way towards the junction Lucius had reached. The swordsman darted his head past the corner, seeing a vast indoor seascape. A plume of water cascaded through a hole in the centre of a colossal granite dome, and a shaft of pink light fell alongside the water, sending brilliant rainbows of colour between the arches formed by the petals of the dome's surface.

Islands rose from the indoor sea that took up most of the dome, each topped by picturesque follies of white and gold.

Thousands of palace guards massed in the dome, splashing towards them through the waist-deep sea and taking up positions among the follies. Most wore the glassy armour of the men still dying behind Lucius, but many others were clad in far more elaborate suits of bright silver. Others still were wrapped in long streamers of silk that rippled behind them like smoke as they moved.

Rylanor emerged into the dome behind Lucius, his assault cannon smoking and the chisel-like grips of his power fist thick with blood.

'They're massing,' spat Lucius. 'Where are the damned World Eaters?'

'We shall have to win the palace by ourselves,' replied Rylanor, his voice grating from deep within his sarcophagus.

Lucius nodded, pleased that they would be able to shame the World Eaters. 'Ancient, cover us. Emperor's Children, break and cover fire! Nasicae, keep up this time!'

Ancient Rylanor stepped out from the junction and a spectacular wave of fire sheared through the air around him, a storm of heavy calibre shell casings and oil-soaked fumes streaming from the cannon mounted on his shoulder.

His explosive fire shredded the stone of the foremost island's follies, broken and bloodied bodies tumbling from the shattered wreckage.

'Go!' shouted Lucius, but the Emperor's Children were already charging, their training so thorough that every warrior already knew his place in the complex pattern of overlapping fire and movement that sent the strike force sweeping into the dome.

Savage joy lit up Lucius's face as he charged, the thrill of battle and the sensations of killing stimulating his body with wondrous excess.

In a swirling cacophony of noise, the perfection of death had come to the Choral City.

On the southern side of the palace, a strange organically formed building clung to the side of the palace like a parasite, its bulging, liquid shape more akin to something that had been grown than something built. Its pale marble was threaded with dark veins and the masses of its battlements hung like ripened fruit. From the expanse of marble monument slabs marking the passing of the city's finest and most powerful citizens, it was clear that this was a sacred place.

Known as the Temple of the Song, it was a memorial to the music that Father Isstvan had sung to bring all things into existence.

It was also the objective of the World Eaters.

The word that the invasion had begun was already out by the time the first World Eaters drop pods crashed into the plaza, shattering gravestones and throwing slabs of marble into the air. Strange music keened through the morning air, calling the people of the Choral City from their homes and demanding that they take up arms. The soldiers from the nearby city barracks grabbed their guns as the Warsingers appeared on the battlements of the Temple to sing the song of death for the invaders.

Called by the Warsingers' laments, the people of the city gathered in the streets and streamed towards the battle.

The World Eaters strike force was led by Captain Ehrlen, and as he emerged from his drop pod, he was expecting the trained soldiers that Angron had briefed them on, not thousands of screaming citizens swarming onto the plaza. They came in a tide, armed with anything and everything they had in their homes, but it was not the weapons they carried but their sheer numbers and the terrible song that spoke of killing and murder that made them deadly.

'World Eaters, to me!' yelled Ehrlen, hefting his bolter and aiming it into the mass of charging people.

The white-armoured warriors of the World Eaters formed a firing line around him, turning their bolters outwards.

'Fire!' shouted Ehrlen and the first ranks of the Choral City's inhabitants were cut down by the deadly volley, but the oncoming mass rose up like a spring tide as they clambered over the bodies of the dead.

As the gap between the two forces closed, the World Eaters put up their bolters and drew their chainswords.

Ehreln saw the unreasoning hatred in the eyes of his enemies and knew that this battle was soon to turn into a massacre.

If there was one thing at which the World Eaters excelled, it was massacre.

'Damn it,' spat Vipus. 'We must have hit something on the way in.'

Loken forced his eyes open. A slice of light where the drop pod had broken open provided the only illumination, but it was enough for him to check that he was still in once piece.

He was battered, but could feel no evidence of anything more than that.

'Locasta, sound off!' ordered Vipus. The warriors of Locasta shouted their names, and Loken was relieved to hear that none appeared to have been injured in the impact. He undid the buckle of his grav-harness and rolled to his feet, the drop pod canted at an unnatural angle. He pulled his bolter from the rack and pushed his way through the narrow opening broken in the side of the drop pod.

As he emerged into the bright sunshine, he saw that they had struck a projecting pier of stone on one of the towers, the rubble of its destruction scattered around the ruined drop pod. He circled the wreckage, seeing that they were at least two hundred metres above the ground, wedged amongst the massive battlements of the Sirenhold.

To his left he saw spectacular tomb-spires encrusted with statues, while to his right was the Choral City itself, its magnificent structures bathed in the rosy glow of the sunrise. From this vantage point Loken could see the whole city, the extraordinary stone flower of the palace and the western defences like scars across the landscape.

Loken could hear gunfire from the direction of the palace and realised that the Emperor's Children and World Eaters were already fighting the enemy. Gunfire echoed from below, Sons of Horus units fighting in the tangle of shrines and statuary that filled the canyons between the tomb-spires.

'We need a way down,' said Loken as Locasta pulled themselves from the wreckage of the drop pod. Vipus jogged over with his gun at the ready.

'Bloody ground surveyors must have missed the projections,' he grumbled.

'That's what it looks like,' agreed Loken, as he saw another drop pod ricochet from the side of a tomb-spire and careen downwards in a shower of broken statues.

'Our warriors are dying,' he said bitterly. 'Someone's going to pay for this.'

'We look spread out,' said Vipus, glancing down into the Siren hold. Between the tomb-spires, smaller shrines and temples butted against one another in a complex jigsaw.

Plumes of black smoke and explosions were already rising from the fighting.

'We need a place to regroup,' said Loken. He flicked to Torgaddon's vox-channel. 'Tarik? Loken here, where are you?'

A burst of static was his only reply.

He looked across the Sirenhold and saw one tomb-spire close to the wall, its many levels supported by columns wrought into the shapes of monsters and its top sheared off by the impact of a drop pod. 'Damn. If you can hear me, Tarik, make for the spire by the western wall, the one with the smashed top. Regroup there. I'm heading down to you.'

'Anything?' asked Vipus.

'No. The vox is a mess. Something's interrupting it.'

'The spires?'

'It would take more than that,' said Loken. 'Come on. Let's find a way off this damn wall.'

Vipus nodded and turned to his men. 'Locasta, start looking for a way down.'

Loken leaned over the battlements as Locasta fanned out to obey their leader's command. Beneath him he could see the diminutive figures of Astartes fighting black-armoured warriors in streaming firefight. He turned away, desperate to find a way down.

'Here!' shouted Brother Casto, Locasta's flamer bearer. 'A stairway.'

'Good work,' said Loken, making his way over to see what Casto had found. Sure enough, hidden behind a tall, eroded statue of an ancient warrior was a dark stairway cut into the sand-coloured stone.

The passageway looked rough and unfinished, the stone pitted and crumbling with age.

'Move,' said Vipus. 'Casto, lead the way.'

'Yes, captain,' replied Casto, plunging into the gloom of the passageway. Loken and Vipus followed him, the entrance barely wide enough for their armoured bodies. The stairs descended for roughly ten metres before opening into a wide, low-ceilinged gallery.

'The wall must be riddled,' said Vipus.

'Catacombs,' said Loken, pointing to niches cut into the walls that held the mouldering remains of skeletons, some still swaddled in tattered cloth.

Casto led them along the gallery, the bodies becoming more

numerous the deeper they went, the skeletal remains piled two or three deep.

Vipus snapped around suddenly, bolter up and finger on the trigger.

'Vipus?'

'I thought I heard something.'

'We're clear behind,' said Loken. 'Keep moving and focus. This could...'

'Movement!' said Casto, sending a blast of orange-yellow fire from his flamer into the darkness ahead of him.

'Casto!' barked Vipus. 'Report! What do you see?'

Casto paused. 'I don't know. Whatever it was, it's gone now.'

The niches ahead guttered with flames, hungrily devouring the bare bones. Loken could see that there was no enemy up ahead, only Isstvanian dead.

'There's nothing there now,' said Vipus. 'Stay focused, Locasta, and no jumping at shadows! You are Sons of Horus!'

The squad picked up the pace, shaking thoughts of hidden enemies from their minds, as they moved rapidly past the burning grave-niches.

The gallery opened into a large chamber, Loken guessing that it must have filled the width of the wall. The only light was from the dancing flame at the end of Casto's flamer, the yellow light picking out the massive stone blocks of a tomb.

Loken saw a sarcophagus of black granite, surrounded by statues of kneeling people with their heads bowed and hands chained before them. Panels set into the walls were covered in carvings where human forms acted out ceremonial scenes of war.

'Casto, move up,' said Vipus. 'Find us a way down.'

Loken approached the sarcophagus, running his hand down its vast length. Its lid was carved to represent a human figure, but he knew that it could not be a literal portrait of the body inside; its face had no features save for a pair of triangular eyes fashioned from chips of coloured glass.

Loken could hear the song from the Sirenhold outside, even through the layers of stone, a single mournful tone that rose and fell, winding its way from the tomb-spires.

'Warsinger,' said Loken bitterly. 'They're fighting back. We need to get down there.'

The silver-armoured palace guards started flying.

Surrounded by burning arcs of white energy, they leapt over the advancing Emperor's Children, gleaming, leaf shaped blades slicing downwards from wrist-mounted weapons.

Lucius rolled to avoid a hail of blades, the silver guard swooping low to behead two of Squad Quemondil, the charged blades cutting through their armour with horrific ease.

He slid into the water, finding that it only reached his waist. Above him, the halberd-guns of the palace guard were spraying silver fire at the Emperor's Children, but the Astartes were moving and firing with their customary discipline. Even the bizarre sight of the palace's defenders did not dissuade them from their patterns of movement and covering fire. A body fell into the water next to him, its head blasted away by bolter fire and blood pouring into the water in a scarlet bloom.

Lucius saw that the silver guards were too quick and turned too nimbly for conventional engagement. He would just have to engage them unconventionally.

One of the silver guards dived towards him and Lucius could see the intricate filigree on the man's armour, the tiny gold threads like veins on the breastplate and greaves and the scrollwork that covered his face.

The guard dived like a seabird, firing a bright blade from his wrist.

Lucius turned the missile aside with his sword and leapt to meet his opponent. The guard twisted in the air, trying to avoid Lucius, but he was too close. Lucius swung his sword and sliced the guard's arm from his body, his crackling sword searing through the armour. Blood sprayed from the smouldering wound and the guard fell, twisting back towards the water.

Lucius fell with the dead man, splashing back into the lake as the Emperor's Children finally reached their enemy. Volleys of bolter fire scoured the islands and his warriors advanced relentlessly on the survivors. The palace guards were backing away, forming a tighter and tighter circle. Glass-armoured guards lay dead in heaps and the artificial lake was ruddy pink and choked with bodies.

Rylanor's assault cannon sent fire tearing through the silk-clad guards, whose preternatural speed couldn't save them as the cannon shells turned the interior of the dome into a killing ground. Another silver guard fell, bolter fire ripping through his armour.

Squad Nasicae joined Lucius and he grinned wolfishly at them, elated at the prospect of fighting more of the silver guards.

'They're running,' said Lucius. 'Keep them on the back foot. Keep pressing on.'

'Squad Kaitheron's reporting from the plaza,' said Brother Scetherin. 'The World Eaters are fighting around the temple on the north side.'

'Still?'

'Sounds like they're holding off half the city.'

'Ha! They can have them. It's what the World Eaters are good at,' laughed Lucius, relishing the certain knowledge of his superiority.

Nothing in the galaxy could match that feeling, but already it was fading and he knew he would have to procure yet more opponents to satisfy his hunger for battle.

'We press on to the throne room,' he said. 'Ancient Rylanor, secure our rear. The rest of you, we're going for Praal. Follow me. If you can't keep up, go and join the Death Guard!'

His warriors cheered as they followed Lucius into the heart of the palace.

Every one of them wanted to kill Praal and hold his head aloft on the palace battlements so the whole of the Choral City could see.

Only Lucius was certain that Praal's head would be his.

The *Andronius* was quiet and tense, its palatial rooms dark and its long, echoing corridors empty of all but menials. The ship's engines pulsed dimly in the stern, only the rumble of directional thrusters shuddering through the ship. Every station was manned, every blast door was sealed and Tarvitz knew a battle alert when he saw it.

What confused him was the fact that the Isstvanians had no fleet to fight.

The hull groaned and Tarvitz felt a deep rumbling through the metal deck, sensing the motion of the ship before the artificial gravity compensated. Ever since the first wave of the speartip had launched, the vessel had been moving, and Tarvitz knew that his suspicions of something amiss were well-founded.

According to the mission briefings he had read earlier, Fulgrim's flagship had been assigned the role of launching the second wave once the palace and the Sirenhold had been taken. There was no need to move.

The only reason to move a vessel after a launch was to move into low orbit in preparation for a bombardment. Though he told himself he was being paranoid, Tarvitz knew that he had to see for himself what was going on.

He made his way swiftly through the *Andronius* towards the gun decks, keeping clear of such grand chambers as the Tarselian Amphitheatre and the columned grandeur of the Monument Hall. He kept to the areas of the ship where his presence would go unchallenged, and where those who might recognise him were unlikely to see him.

He had told Rylanor that he wanted to renounce his position of honour in the speartip to replace Captain Odovocar as Eidolon's senior staff officer, relaying the commander's orders to the surface, but it would only be a matter of time before his subterfuge was discovered.

Tarvitz descended into the lower reaches of the ship, far from where the Emperor's Children dwelt in the most magnificent parts of the *Andronius*. The rest of the ship, inhabited by servitors and menials, was more functional and Tarvitz knew he would pass without challenge here.

The darkness closed around Tarvitz and the yawning chasms of the engine structures opened out many hundreds of metres below the gantry on which he stood. Above the engine spaces were the reeking gun decks, where mighty cannons, weapons that could level cities, were housed in massive, armoured revetments.

'Stand by for ordnance,' chimed an automated, metallic voice. Tarvitz felt the ship shift again, and this time he could hear the creak of the hull as the planet's upper atmosphere raised the temperature of the outer hull.

Tarvitz descended an iron staircase at the end of the dark gantry and the vast expanse of the gun deck sprawled before him, a titanic vault that ran the length of the vessel. Huge, hissing cranes fed the guns, lifting tank-sized shells from the magazine decks through blast proof doors. Gunners and loaders sweated with their riggers, each gun serviced by a hundred men who hauled on thick chains and levers in preparation for their firing. Servitors distributed water to the gun crews and Mechanicum adepts maintained vigil on the weapons to ensure they were properly calibrated.

Tarvitz felt his resolve harden and his anger grow at the sight of the guns being made ready. Who were they planning to fire on? With thousands of Astartes on the planet's surface, bombarding the Choral City was absurd, yet here the guns were, loaded and ready to unleash hell.

He doubted that the men crewing these weapons knew which planet they were in orbit over or even who they would be shooting at. Entire communities flourished below the decks of a starship and it was perfectly possible that these men had no idea who they were about to destroy.

He reached the end of the staircase and set foot on the deck, its high ceiling soaring above him like a mighty cathedral to destructive power. Tarvitz heard footsteps approaching and turned to see a robed adept in the livery of the Mechanicum.

'Captain,' inquired the adept, 'is there something amiss?'

'No,' said Tarvitz. 'I am just here to ensure that everything is proceeding normally.'

'I can assure you, lord, that preparations for the bombardment are proceeding exactly as planned. The warheads will be launched prior to the deployment of the second wave.'

'Warheads?' asked Tarvitz.

'Yes, captain,' said the adept. 'All bombardment cannons are loaded with airbursting warheads loaded with virus bombs as specified in our order of battle.'

'Virus bombs,' said Tarvitz, fighting to hold back his revulsion at what the adept was telling him.

'Is everything all right, captain?' asked the adept, noticing the change in his expression.

'I'm fine,' Tarvitz lied, feeling as if his legs would give way any second. 'You can return to your duties.'

The adept nodded and set off towards one of the guns.

Virus bombs...

Weapons so terrible and forbidden that only the Warmaster himself, and the Emperor before him, could ever sanction their use.

Each warhead would unleash the life eater virus, a rampant organism that destroyed life in all its forms and wiped out every shred of organic matter on the surface of a planet within hours. The magnitude of this new knowledge, and its implications, staggered Tarvitz and he felt his breath coming in short, painful gasps as he attempted to reconcile what he knew with what he had just learned.

His Legion was preparing to kill the planet below and he knew with sudden clarity that it could not be alone in this. To saturate a planet with enough virus warheads to destroy all life would take many ships and with a sick jolt of horror, he knew that such an order could only have come from the Warmaster.

For reasons Tarvitz could not even begin to guess at, the Warmaster had chosen to betray fully a third of his warriors, exterminating them in one fell swoop.

'I have to warn them,' he hissed, turning and running for the embarkation deck.

NINE

The power of a god
Regrouping
Honour brothers

The strategium was dark, lit only by braziers that burned with a flickering green flame. Where once the banners of the Legion's battle companies had hung from its walls, they were now replaced with those of the warrior lodge. The company banners had been taken down shortly after the speartip had been deployed and the message was clear: the lodge now had primacy within the Sons of Horus. The platform from which the Warmaster had addressed the officers of his fleet now held a lectern upon which rested the *Book of Lorgar*.

The Warmaster sat on the strategium throne, watching reports coming in from Isstvan III on the battery of pict screens before him.

The emerald light picked out the edges of his armour and reflected from the amber gemstone forming the eye upon his breastplate. Reams of combat statistics streamed past and pict-relays showed the unfolding battles in the Choral City. The World Eaters were in the centre of an epic struggle. Thousands of people were swarming into the plaza before the Precentor's Palace, and the streets flowed with rivers of blood as the Astartes slaughtered wave after wave of Isstvanians that charged into their guns and chainblades.

The palace itself was intact, only a few palls of smoke indicating the battle raging through it as the Emperor's Children fought their way through its guards.

Vardus Praal would be dead soon, though Horus cared nothing for the fate of Isstvan III's rogue governor. His rebellion had simply given Horus the chance to rid himself of those he knew would never follow him on his great march to Terra.

Horus looked up as Erebus approached.

'First Chaplain,' said Horus sternly. 'Matters are delicate. Do not disturb me needlessly.'

'There is news from Prospero,' said Erebus, unperturbed. The shadow whisperers clung to him, darting around his feet and the crozius he wore at his waist.

'Magnus?' asked Horus, suddenly interested.

'He lives yet,' said Erebus, 'but not for the lack of effort on the part of the Wolves of Fenris.'

'Magnus lives,' snarled Horus. 'Then he may yet be a danger.'

'No,' assured Erebus. 'The spires of Prospero have fallen and the warp echoes with the powerful sorcery Magnus used to save his warriors and escape.'

'Always sorcery,' said Horus. 'Where did he escape to?'

'I do not know yet,' said Erebus, 'but wherever he goes, the Emperor's dogs will hunt him down.'

'And he will either join us or die alone in the wilderness,' said Horus, thoughtfully. 'To think that so much depends on the personalities of so few. Magnus was nearly my deadliest enemy, perhaps as dangerous as the Emperor himself. Now he has no choice but to follow us until the very end. If Fulgrim brings Ferrus Manus into the fold then we have as good as won.'

Horus waved dismissively at the viewscreens depicting the battle in the Choral City. 'The Isstvanians believe the gods have come to destroy them and in a way they are right. Life and death are mine to dispense. What is that if not the power of a god?'

'Captain Loken. Sergeant Vipus. It is good to see you both,' said Sergeant Lachost, hunkered down in the shattered shell of a shrine to one of Isstvan III's ancestors. 'We've been trying to raise all the squads. They're all over the place. The speartip's shattered.'

'Then we'll re-forge it here,' replied Loken.

Sporadic fire rattled through the valley, so he took cover beside Lachost. The sergeant's command squad was arrayed around the shrine ruin, bolters trained and occasionally snapping off shots at the shapes that darted through the shadows. Vipus and the survivors of Locasta huddled in the ruins with them.

The enemy wore the armour of ancient Isstvan, tarnished bands of silver and black, and carried strange relic-weapons, rapid-firing crossbows that hurled bolts of molten silver.

Tales of heroism were emerging from the scores of individual battles among the tomb-spires as Sons of Horus units fought off the soldiers of the Sirenhold.

'We've got good cover, and a position we can hold,' said Vipus. 'We can gather the squads here and launch a thrust into the enemy.'

Loken nodded as Torgaddon ducked into cover beside them, the Sons of Horus he had brought with him joining Lachost's men at the walls.

He grinned at Loken and said, 'What kept you, Garvi?'

'We had to come down from the top of the wall,' said Loken. 'Where are your warriors?'

'They're everywhere,' said Torgaddon. 'They're making their way to this spire, but a lot of the squads are cut off. The Sirenhold was garrisoned by some… elites, I suppose. They had a hell of an armoury here, ancient things, looks like advanced tech.'

Loken nodded as Torgaddon continued.

'Well, this spire is clear at least. I've got Vaddon and Lachost setting up a command post on the lower level and we can just hold this position for now. There are three more Legions in the Choral City and the rest of the Sons of Horus in orbit. There's no need–'

'The enemy has the field,' replied Loken sharply. 'They can surround us. There are catacombs beneath our feet they could use to get around us. No, if we stay put they will find a way to get to us. This is their territory. We strike as soon as we can. This is a speartip and it is up to us to drive it home.'

'Where?' asked Torgaddon.

'The tomb-spires,' said Loken. 'We hit them one by one. Storm them, kill whatever we find and move on. We keep going and force them onto the back foot.'

'Most of our speartip is on its way, captain,' said Lachost.

'Good,' replied Loken, looking up at the spires around the shrine.

The shrine was in a valley formed by the spire they had come down and the next spire along, a brutal cylinder of stone with glowering faces carved into its surface. Dozens of arches around its base offered entrance and cover, their darkness occasionally lit by a brief flash of gunfire.

A tangle of shrines littered the ground between the towers, statues of the Choral City's notable dead jutting from piles of ornate architecture or the ruins of temples.

Loken pointed to the tomb-spire across the valley. 'As soon as we have enough warriors for a full thrust, that's what we hit.

Lachost, start securing the shrines around us to give us a good jumping-off point, and get some men up on the first levels of this spire to provide covering fire. Heavy weapons if you've got them.'

Gunfire echoed from the east and Loken saw the forms of Astartes moving towards them: Sons of Horus in the livery of Eskhalen Squad. More warriors were converging on their position, each fighting their own running battles among the shrines as they sought to regroup.

'This is more than a burial ground,' said Loken. 'Whatever happened to Isstvan III, it started here. This force is religious and this is their church.'

'No wonder they're crazy,' replied Torgaddon scornfully. 'Madmen love their gods.'

The controls of the Thunderhawk were loose, the ship trying to flip away from Tarvitz and go tumbling through space. He had only the most rudimentary training on these newer additions to the Astartes armoury, and most of that had been in atmosphere, skimming low over battlefields to drop troops or add fire support.

Tarvitz could see Isstvan III through the armoured glass of the viewing bay, a crescent of sunlight creeping across its surface. Somewhere near the edge of the shining crescent was the city where his battle-brothers, and those of three other Legions, were fighting, unaware that they had already been betrayed.

'Thunderhawk, identify yourself,' said a voice through the gunship's vox. He must have entered the engagement envelope of the *Andronius* and the defence turrets had acquired him as a target. If he was lucky, he would have a few moments before the turrets locked on, moments when he could put as much distance between his stolen Thunderhawk and the *Andronius*.

'Thunderhawk, identify yourself,' repeated the voice and he knew that he had to stall in order to give himself time to get clear of the defence turrets.

'Captain Saul Tarvitz, travelling to the *Endurance* on liaison duty.'

'Wait for authorisation.'

He knew he wouldn't get authorisation, but each second took him further from the *Andronius* and closer to the planet's surface.

He pushed the Thunderhawk as hard as he dared, listening to the hiss of static coming from the vox, hoping against hope that somehow they would believe him and allow him to go on his way.

'Stand down, Thunderhawk,' said the voice. 'Return to the *Andronius* immediately.'

'Negative, *Andronius*,' replied Tarvitz. 'Transmission is breaking up.'

It was a cheap ploy, but one that might give him a few seconds more.

'I repeat, stand–'

'Go to hell,' replied Tarvitz.

Tarvitz checked the navigational pict for signs of pursuit, pleased to see that there were none yet, and wrenched the Thunderhawk down towards Isstvan III.

'The *Pride of the Emperor* is in transit,' announced Saeverin, senior deck officer of the *Andronius*. 'Though the vessel's Navigator claims to be encountering difficulties. Lord Fulgrim will not be with us any time soon.'

'Does he send any word of his mission?' asked Eidolon, standing at his shoulder.

'Communications are still very poor,' said Saeverin hesitantly, 'but what we have does not sound encouraging.'

'Then we will have to compensate with the excellence of our conduct and the perfection of our Legion,' said Eidolon. 'The other Legions may be more savage or resilient or stealthy, but none of them approaches the perfection of the Emperor's Children. No matter what lies ahead, we must never let go of that.'

'Of course, commander,' said Saeverin, as his console lit up with a series of warning lights. His hands danced over the console and he turned to face Eidolon.

'Lord commander,' he said. 'We may have a problem.'

'Do not speak to me of problems,' said Eidolon.

'Defence control has just informed me that they have picked up a Thunderhawk heading for the planet's surface.'

'One of ours?'

'It appears so,' confirmed Saeverin, bending over his console. 'Getting confirmation now.'

'Who's piloting it?' demanded Eidolon. 'No one is authorised to travel to the surface.'

'The last communication with the Thunderhawk indicates that it is Captain Saul Tarvitz.'

'Tarvitz?' said Eidolon. 'Damn him, but he is a thorn in my side.'

'It's certainly him,' said Captain Saeverin. 'It looks like he took one of the Thunderhawks from the planetside embarkation deck.'

'Where is he heading,' asked Eidolon, 'exactly?'

'The Choral City,' replied Saeverin.

Eidolon smiled. 'He's trying to warn them. He thinks he can make a difference. I thought we could use him, but he's too damn stubborn and now he's got it into his head that he's a hero. Saeverin, get some fighters out there and shoot him down. We don't need any complications now.'

'Aye, sir,' nodded Saeverin. 'Fighters launching in two minutes.'

Mersadie wrang out the cloth and draped it over Euphrati's forehead. Euphrati moaned and shook, her arms thrashing as if she was throwing a fit. She looked as pale and thin as a corpse.

'I'm here,' said Mersadie, even though she suspected the comatose imagist couldn't hear her. She didn't understand what Euphrati was going through, and it made her feel so useless.

For reasons she didn't quite understand, she had stayed with Kyril Sindermann and Euphrati as they moved around the ship. The *Vengeful Spirit* was the size of a city and it had plenty of places in which to hide.

Word of their coming went ahead of them and wherever they went, grime-streaked engine crewmen or boiler-suited maintenance workers were there to show them to safety, supply them with food and water and catch a glimpse of the saint. At present, they sheltered inside one of the engine housings, a massive hollow tube that was normally full of burning plasma and great thrusting pistons. Now the engine was decommissioned for maintenance and it made for a good bolthole, hidden and secret despite its vast dimensions.

Sindermann slept on a thin blanket beside Euphrati and the old man had never looked more exhausted. His thin limbs were spotted and bony, his cheeks sunken and hollow.

One of the engine crew hurried up to the nook where Keeler lay on a bundle of blankets and clothes. He was stripped to the waist and covered in grease, a huge and muscular man who was moved to kneel meekly a short distance from the bed of his saint.

'Miss Oliton,' he said reverentially. 'Is there anything you or the saint need?'

'Water,' said Mersadie. 'Clean water, and Kyril asked for more paper, too.'

The crewman's eyes lit up. 'He's writing something?'

Mersadie wished she hadn't mentioned it.

'He's collecting his thoughts for a speech,' she said. 'He's still an iterator, after all. If you can find some medical supplies as well, that would be useful, she's dehydrated.'

'The Emperor will preserve her,' said the crewman, worry in his voice.

'I'm sure he will, but we have to give him all the help we can,' replied Mersadie, trying not to sound as condescending as she felt.

The effect the comatose Euphrati had on the crew was extraordinary, a miracle in itself. Her very presence seemed to focus the doubts and wishes of so many people into an iron-strong faith in a distant Emperor.

'We'll get what we can,' said the crewman. 'We have people in the commissary and medical suites.'

He reached forward to touch Euphrati's blanket and murmured a quiet prayer to his Emperor. As the crewman left she whispered her own perfunctory prayer. After all, the Emperor was more real than any of the so-called gods the Crusade had come across.

'Deliver us, Emperor,' she said quietly, 'from all of this.'

She looked down sadly and caught her breath as Euphrati stirred and opened her eyes, like someone awakening from a deep sleep. Mersadie reached down slowly, afraid that if she moved too quickly she might shatter this brittle miracle, and took the imagist's hand in hers.

'Euphrati,' she whispered softly. 'Can you hear me?'

Euphrati Keeler's mouth fell open and she screamed in terror.

'Are you sure?' asked Captain Garro of the Death Guard, limping on his newly replaced augmetic leg. The gyros had not yet meshed with his nervous system and, much to his fury, he had been denied a place in the Death Guard speartip. The bridge of the *Eisenstein* was open to the workings of the ship, as was typical with the Death Guard fleet, since Mortarion despised ornamentation of any kind.

The bridge was a skeletal framework suspended among the ship's guts with massive coolant pipes looming overhead like knots of metallic entrails. The bridge crew bent over a platform inset with cogitator banks, their faces illuminated in harsh greens and blues.

'Very sure, captain,' replied the communications officer, reading from the data-slate in his hand. 'An Emperor's Children Thunderhawk is passing through our engagement zone.'

Garro took the data-slate from the officer and sure enough, there was a Thunderhawk gunship passing close to the *Eisenstein*, a pack of fighters at its heels.

'Smells like trouble,' said Garro. 'Put us on an intercept course.'

'Yes, captain,' said the deck officer, turning smartly and heading for the helm.

Within moments the engines flared into life, vast pistons pumping through the oily shadows that surrounded the bridge. The *Eisenstein* tilted as it began a ponderous turn towards the approaching Thunderhawk.

The scream hurled Kyril Sindermann from sleep with the force of a thunderbolt and he felt his heart thudding against his ribs in fright.

'What?' he managed before seeing Euphrati sitting bolt upright in bed and screaming fit to burst her lungs. He scrambled to his feet as Mersadie tried to put her arms around the screaming imagist. Keeler thrashed like a madwoman and Sindermann rushed over to help, putting his arms out as if to embrace them both.

The moment his fingers touched Euphrati he felt the heat radiating from her, wanting to recoil in pain, but feeling as though his hands were locked to her flesh. His eyes met Mersadie's and he knew from the terror he saw there that she felt the same thing.

He whimpered as his vision blurred and darkened, as though he were having a heart attack. Images tumbled through his brain, dark and monstrous, and he fought to hold onto his sanity as visions of pure evil assailed him.

Death, like a black seething mantle, hung over everything. Sinderman saw Mersadie's delicate, coal dark face overcome with it, her features sinking in corruption.

Tendrils of darkness wound through the air, destroying whatever they touched. He screamed as he saw the flesh sloughing from Mersadie's bones, looking down at his hands to see them rotting away before his eyes. His skin peeled back, the bones maggot-white.

Then it was gone, the black, rotting death lifted from him and Sindermann could see their hiding place once again, unchanged since he had laid down to catch a few fitful hours of sleep. He stumbled away from Euphrati and with one look saw that Mersadie had experienced the same thing – horrendous, concentrated decay.

Sindermann put a hand to his chest, feeling his old heart working overtime.

'Oh, no…' Mersadie was moaning. 'Please… what is…?'

'This is betrayal,' said Keeler, her voice suddenly strong as she turned towards Sindermann, 'and it is happening now. You need to tell them. Tell them all, Kyril!'

Keeler's eyes closed and she slumped against Mersadie, who held her as she sobbed.

Tarvitz wrestled with the Thunderhawk controls. Streaks of bright crimson sheared past the cockpit – the fighter craft were on his tail, spraying ruby-red lances of gunfire at him.

Isstvan III wheeled in front of him as the gunship spun in the viewscreen.

Impacts thudded into the back of the Thunderhawk and he felt the controls lurch in his hands. He answered by ripping his craft upwards, hearing the engines shriek in complaint beneath him as they flipped the gunship's mass out of the enemy lines of fire. Loud juddering noises from behind him spoke of something giving way in one of the engines. Red warning lights and crisis telltales lit up the cockpit.

The angry blips of the fighters loomed large in the tactical display.

The vox-unit sparked again and he reached to turn it off, not wanting to hear gloating taunts as he was destroyed and any hope of warning was lost. His hand paused as he heard a familiar voice say, 'Thunderhawk on a closing course with the *Eisenstein*, identify yourself.'

Tarvitz wanted to cry in relief as he recognised the voice of his honour brother.

'Nathaniel?' he cried. 'It's Saul. It's good to hear your voice, my brother!'

'Saul?' asked Garro. 'What in the name of the Emperor is going on? Are those fighters trying to shoot you down?'

'Yes!' shouted Tarvitz, tearing the Thunderhawk around again, Isstvan III spinning below him. The Death Guard fleet was a speckling of glittering streaks against the blackness, crisscrossed by red laser blasts.

Tarvitz gunned the Thunderhawk's remaining engine as Garro said, 'Why? And be quick, Saul. They almost have you!'

'This is treachery?' shouted Tarvitz. 'All of this! We are betrayed. The fleet is going to bombard the planet's surface with virus bombs.'

'What?' spluttered Garro, disbelief plain in his voice, 'That's insane.'

'Trust me,' said Tarvitz, 'I know how it sounds, but as my honour brother I ask you to trust me like you have never trusted me before. On my life I swear I do not lie to you, Nathaniel.'

'I don't know, Saul,' said Garro.

'Nathaniel!' screamed Tarvitz in frustration. 'Ship to surface vox has been shut off, so unless I can get a warning down there, every Astartes on Isstvan III is going to die!'

Captain Nathaniel Garro could not tear his eyes from the hissing vox-unit, as if seeking to discern the truth of what Saul Tarvitz was saying just by staring hard enough. Beside him, the tactical plot displayed the weaving blips that represented Tarvitz's Thunderhawk and the pursuing fighters. His experienced eye told him that he had seconds at best to make a decision and his every instinct screamed that what he was hearing could not possibly be true.

Yet Saul Tarvitz was his sworn honour brother, an oath sworn on the bloody fields of the Preaixor Campaign, when they had shed blood and stood shoulder to shoulder through the entirety of a bloody, ill-fated war that had seen many of their most beloved brothers killed.

Such a friendship and bond of honour forged in the hell of combat was a powerful thing and Garro knew Saul Tarvitz well enough to know that he never exaggerated and never, ever lied. To imagine that his honour brother was lying to him now was beyond imagining, but to hear that the fleet was set to bombard their battle-brothers was equally unthinkable.

His thoughts tumbled like a whirlwind in his head and he cursed his indecision. He looked down at the eagle Tarvitz had carved into his vambrace so long ago and knew what he had to do.

Tarvitz pulled the Thunderhawk into a shallow dive, preparing to chop back the throttle and deploy his air brakes, hoping that he had descended far enough to allow the atmosphere of the planet below to slow him down sufficiently for what he planned...

He glanced down at the tactical display, seeing the fighters moving to either side of him, preparing to bracket him as his speed bled off. Judging the moment was crucial.

Tarvitz hauled back the throttle and hit the air brakes.

The grav seat harness pulled tight on his chest as he was hurled forwards and the cockpit was suddenly lit by brilliant flashes and a terrific juddering seized the gunship. He heard impacts on the hull and felt the Thunderhawk tumble away from his control.

He yelled in anger as he realised that those who sought to betray the Astartes had won, that his defiance of their treachery had been in vain. Blooms of fire surged past the cockpit and Tarvitz waited for the inevitable explosion of his death.

But it never came.

Amazed, he took hold of the gunship's controls and wrestled with them as he fought to level out his flight. The tactical display was a mess of interference, electromagnetic hash and radioactive debris clogging it with an impenetrable fog of a massive detonation. He couldn't see the fighters, but with such interference they could still be out there, even now drawing a bead on him.

What had just happened?

'Saul,' said a voice, heavy with sadness and Tarvitz knew that his honour brother had not let him down. 'Ease down, the fighters are gone.'

'Gone? How?'

'The *Eisenstein* shot them down on my orders,' said Garro. 'Tell me, Saul, was I right to do so, for if you speak falsely, then I have condemned myself alongside you.'

Tarvitz wanted to laugh and wished his old friend was standing next to him so he could throw his arms around him and thank him for his trust, knowing that Nathaniel Garro had made the most monumental decision in his life on nothing but what had passed between them moments ago. The depth of trust and the honour Garro had done him was immeasurable.

'Yes,' he said. 'You were right to trust me, my friend.'

'Tell me why?' asked Garro.

Tarvitz tried to think of something reassuring to tell his old friend, but knew that nothing he could say would soften the blow of this treachery. Instead, he said, 'Do you remember what you once told me of Terra?'

'Yes, my friend,' sighed Garro. 'I told you it was old, even back in the day.'

'You told me of what the Emperor built there,' said Tarvitz. 'A whole world, where before there had been nothing, just barbarians and death. You spoke of the scars of the Age of Strife, whole glaciers burned away and mountains levelled.'

'Yes,' agreed Garro. 'I remember. The Emperor took that blasted planet and he founded the Imperium there. That's what I fight for, to stand against the darkness and build an empire for the human race to inherit.'

'That's what is being betrayed, my friend,' said Tarvitz.

'I will not allow that to happen, Saul.'

'Nor I, my friend,' swore Tarvitz. 'What will you do now?'

Garro paused, the question of what to do, now that he had chosen a side, uppermost in his mind. 'I'll tell the *Andronius* that I shot you down. The flare of the explosion and the fact that you're in the upper atmosphere should cover you long enough to get to the surface.'

'And after that?'

'The other Legions must be warned of what is going on. Only the Warmaster would have the daring to conceive of such betrayal and he would not have begun an endeavour of this magnitude without swaying some of his brother primarchs to join him. Rogal Dorn or Magnus would never forsake the Emperor and if I can get the *Eisenstein* out of the Isstvan system, I can bring them here. All of them.'

'Can you do it?' asked Tarvitz. 'The Warmaster will soon realise what you attempt.'

'I have some time before they will suspect, but then the whole fleet will be after me. Why is it that men have to die every time any of us tries to do what is right?'

'Because that's the Imperial Truth,' said Tarvitz. 'Can you keep control of the *Eisenstein* once this gets out?'

'Yes,' said Garro. 'It will be messy, but enough of the crew are staunch Terrans, and they will side with me. Those who do not will die.'

The port engine juddered and Tarvitz knew that he didn't have much time before the gunship gave out beneath him.

'I have to make for the surface, Nathaniel,' said Tarvitz. 'I don't know how much longer this ship will stay in the air.'

'Then this is where we part,' said Garro, an awful note of finality in his voice.

'The next time we see one another, it'll be on Terra,' said Tarvitz.

'*If* we meet again, my brother.'

'We will, Nathaniel,' promised Tarvitz. 'By the Emperor, I swear it.'

'May the luck of Terra be with you,' said Garro and the vox went dead.

Moments ago, he had been on the brink of death, but now he had hope that he might succeed in preventing the Warmaster's treachery from unfolding.

That was what the Imperial Truth meant, he realised at last.

It meant hope: hope for the galaxy; hope for humanity.

Tarvitz gunned the Thunderhawk's engine, fixed its course towards the Precentor's Palace and arrowed it towards the heart of the Choral City.

TEN

The most precious truth
Praal
Death's tomb

The sub-deck was packed with people come to hear the words of the saint's apostle. Apostle: that was what they called him now, thought Sindermann, and it gave him comfort to know that even in these turbulent times, he was still a person that others looked up to. Vanity, he knew, but still… one takes what one can when circumstances change beyond one's control.

Word had spread quickly through the *Vengeful Spirit* that he was to speak and he glanced nervously around the edges of the sub-deck for any sign that word had reached beyond the civilians and remembrancers. Armed guards protected the approaches to the sub-deck, but he knew that if the Astartes or Maggard and his soldiers came in force, then not all of them would escape alive.

They were taking a terrible risk, but Euphrati had made it very clear that he needed to speak to the masses, to spread the word of the Emperor and to tell of the imminent treachery that she had seen.

Thousands of people stared expectantly at him and he cleared his throat, glancing over his shoulder to where Mersadie and Euphrati watched him standing at the lectern raised on a make-shift platform of packing crates. A portable vox-link had been rigged up to carry his words to the very back of the sub-deck, though he knew his iterator trained voice could be heard without any mechanical help. The vox-link was there to carry his words to those who could not attend this gathering, faithful among the technical staff of the ship having spliced the portable unit into the ship's principal vox-caster network.

Sindermann's words would be heard throughout the Expedition fleet.

He smiled at the crowd and took a sip of water from the glass beside him.

A sea of expectant faces stared back at him, desperate to hear his words of wisdom. What would he tell them, he wondered? He looked down at the scribbled notes he had taken over the time he had been sequestered in the bowels of the ship. He looked back over his shoulder at Euphrati and her smile lifted his heart.

He turned back to his notes, the words seeming trite and contrived.

He screwed the paper into a ball and dropped it by his side, feeling Euphrati's approval like a tonic in his veins.

'My friends,' he began. 'We live in strange times and there are events in motion that will shock many of you as they have shocked me. You have come to hear the words of the saint, but she has asked me to speak to you, that I may tell you of what she has seen and what all men and women of faith must do.'

His iterator's voice carried the precise amount of gravitas mixed with a tone that spoke to them of his regret at the terrible words of doom he was about to impart.

'The Warmaster has betrayed the Emperor,' he said, pausing to allow the inevitable howls of denial and outrage to fill the chamber. Shouted voices rose and fell like waves on the sea and Sindermann let them wash over him, knowing the exact moment when he should speak.

'I know, I know,' he said. 'You think that such a thing is unthinkable and only a short time ago, I would have agreed, but it is true. I have seen it with my own eyes. The saint showed me her vision and it chilled my very soul to see it. War-tilled fields of the dead, winds that carry a cruel dust of bone and the sky-turned eyes of men who saw wonders and only dreamed of their children and friendship. I tasted the air and it was heavy with blood, my friends, its stink reeking on the bodies of men we have learned to call the enemy. And for what? That they decided they did not want to be part of our warmongering Imperium? Perhaps they saw more than we? Perhaps it takes the fresh eyes of an outsider to see what we have become blind to.'

The crowd quietened, but he could see that most people still thought him mad. Many here were of the Faithful, but many others were not. While almost all of them could embrace the Emperor as divine, few of them could countenance the Warmaster betraying such a wondrous being.

'When we embarked on this so-called "Great Crusade" it was to bring enlightenment and reason to the galaxy, and for a time that was what we did. But look at us now, my friends, when was the last time we approached a world with anything but murder in our hearts? We bring so many forms of warfare with us, the tension of sieges and the battlefield of trenches soaked in mud and misery while the sky is ripped with gunfire. And the men who lead us are no better! What do we expect from cultures who are met by men named "Warmaster", "Widowmaker" and "the Twisted"? They see the Astartes, clad in their insect carapaces of plate armour, marching to the grim sounds of cocking bolters and roaring chainswords. What culture would *not* try to resist us?'

Sindermann could feel the mood of the crowd shifting and knew he had stoked their interest. Now he had to hook their emotions.

'Look to what we leave behind us! So many memorials to our slaughters! Look to the Lupercal's Court, where we house the bloody weapons of war in bright halls and wonder at their cruel beauty as they hang waiting for their time to come again. We look at these weapons as curios, but we forget the actuality of the lives these savage instruments took. The dead cannot speak to us, they cannot plead with us to seek peace while the remembrance of them fades and they are forgotten. Despite the ranks of graves, the triumphal arches and eternal flames, we forget them, for we are afraid to look at what they did lest we see it in ourselves.'

Sindermann felt a wondrous energy filling him as he spoke, the words flowing from him in an unstoppable torrent, each word seeming to spring from his lips of its own volition, as though each one came from somewhere else, somewhere more eloquent than his poor, mortal talent could ever reach.

'We have made war in the stars for two centuries, yet there are so many lessons we have never learned. The dead should be our teachers, for they are the true witnesses. Only they know the horror and the ever repeating failure that is war; the sickness we return to generation after generation because we fail to hear the testament of those who were sacrificed to martial pride, greed or twisted ideology.'

Thunderous applause spread from the people directly in front of Sindermann, spreading rapidly through the chamber and he wondered if such scenes were being repeated on any of the other ships of the fleet that could hear his words.

Tears sprang to his eyes as he spoke, his hands gripping the lectern tightly as his voice trembled with emotion. 'Let the battlefield dead take our hands in theirs and illuminate us with the most precious truth we can ever learn, that there must be peace instead of war!'

Lucius skidded to the floor of what appeared to be some kind of throne room. Inlaid with impossibly intricate mosaic designs, the floor was covered in scrollwork so tightly wound that it seemed to ripple with movement. Bolter fire stitched through the room, showering him with broken pieces of mosaic as he rolled into the cover of an enormous harpsichord.

Music from the dawn of creation boomed around him, filling the central spire of the Precentor's Palace. Crystal chandeliers hung from the petals at the centre of the great granite flower, shimmering and vibrating in time with the cacophony of battle far below. Instruments filled the room, each one played by a servitor refitted to play the holy music of the Warsingers. Huge organs with pipes that reached up through the shafts of milky morning light stood next to banks of gilded bells and rank upon rank of bronze cages held shaven-headed choristers who sang with blind adulation.

Harp strings snapped and twanged in time with the gunfire and discordant notes boomed as bolter shots ripped through the side of the organ. Storms of weapons' fire flew, filling the air with hot metal and death, the battle and the music competing to make the loudest din.

Lucius felt his limbs become energised just listening to the crashing volume of the noise, each blaring note and booming shot filling his senses with the desire to do violence.

He glanced round the side of the harpsichord, exhausted and elated to have reached so far, so quickly. They had fought their way through the palace, killing thousands of the black- and silver-armoured guards, before finally reaching the throne room.

From his position of cover, Lucius saw that he was in the second ring of instruments, beyond which lay the Precentor's Dais. A mighty throne with its back to him sat upon the dais, a confection of gold and emerald set in a ring of lecterns that each held a massive volume of musical notations.

Gunfire blew one book apart and a blizzard of sheet music fluttered around the throne.

The palace guard massed on the opposite side of the throne

room, surrounding a tall figure in gold armour with a collection of tubes and what looked like loudspeakers fanning out from his back. A storm of silver fire flew and Lucius saw yet more guards charging in from the other entrances, a ferocious struggle erupting as these new arrivals charged the Emperor's Children.

'They have courage, I'll give them that,' he muttered to himself.

Chainblades and bolt pistols rang from armour and storms of silver fire ripped between the patches of cover offered by the gilded instruments. Each volley tore up the hardwood frames and sawed through servitors as they sat at the ornate keyboards or plucked at strings with metal fingers.

And still the music played.

Lucius glanced behind him. One of Nasicae fell as he ran to join Lucius, silver filaments punched through his skull. The body clattered to the floor beside Lucius. Only three of Nasicae remained, and they were cut off from their leader.

'Ancient Rylanor, engage!' yelled Lucius into the vox. 'Get me cover! Tactical squads, converge on the throne and draw the palace guard in! Purity and death!'

'Purity and death!' echoed the Emperor's Children, and with exemplary coordination they surged forward. A silver-armoured guard was shredded by bolter fire and flopped, broken, to the ground. Glass-armoured bodies lay shattered and bloody over bullet-scarred instruments. Servitors moved jerkily, still trying to play even though their hands were smoking ruins of bone and wire.

The Emperor's Children moved squad by squad, volley by volley, advancing through the fire as only the most perfect of Legions could.

Lucius broke cover and ran into the whirlwind of fire. Silver shards shattered against him.

Behind him, Rylanor's Dreadnought body smashed through a titanic bank of drums and bells, the noise of its destruction appalling as Rylanor opened fire on the enemy. Acrobatic guards, clad in armour wound with long streamers of silk, darted and leapt away from chainblades and bolts like dancers, slashing limbs with monofilament wire-blades.

Glass-armoured guards charged forward in solid ranks, stabbing with their halberds, yet none of the foes was a match for the disciplined counter-charges of the Emperor's Children. The slick perfection of their pattern-perfect warfare kept its edge even amid the storm of fire and death that filled the throne room.

Lucius ducked and wove through the fire towards the gold armoured figure, shrapnel flashing against the energised edge of his sword blade.

The man's armour was ancient, yet gloriously ornate, the equal in finery of a lord commander of the Emperor's Children. He carried a long spear, its shaft terminated at both ends by a howling ripple of lethal harmonies. Lucius ducked under a swipe of the weapon, stepping nimbly to the side and bringing his sword up towards his opponent's midriff.

Faster than he would have believed possible, the spear reversed and a tremendous blast of noise battered his sword away before it struck. Lucius danced back as a killing wave of sound blared from the tubes and speakers mounted on the golden warrior's back, a whole section of the mosaic floor ploughed in a torn gouge by the sound.

One of the palace guards fell at Lucius's feet, his chest blown open by Rylanor's fire, and another toppled as one of Nasicae sliced off his leg.

The Emperor's Children surged forwards to help him, but he waved them back – this was to be his kill. He leapt onto the throne pedestal, the golden warrior silhouetted in the light streaming from the distant ceiling.

The screaming spear came down and Lucius ducked to avoid it, pushing himself forwards. He stabbed with his sword, but a pitch perfect note sent his sword plunging towards the floor of the dais instead of its intended target. Lucius hauled his sword clear as the spear stabbed for him again, the musical edge shearing past him and blistering the purple and gilt of his armour. The battle raged ferociously around him, but it was an irrelevance, for Lucius knew that he must surely be fighting the leader of this rebellion.

Only Vardus Praal would surround himself with such fearsome bodyguards.

Lucius pivoted away from another strike, spinning around behind Praal and shearing his sword through the speaker tubes and loudspeakers upon his back. He felt a glorious surge of satisfaction as the glowing edge cut through the metal with ease.

A terrific, booming noise blared from the severed pipes and Lucius was hurled from the dais by the force of the blast.

His armour cracked with the force, and the music leapt in clarity as he felt its power surge around his body in a glorious wash of pure, unadulterated sensation. The music sang in his blood, promising yet more glories, and the unfettered excess of music, light and hedonistic indulgence.

Lucius felt the music in his soul and knew that he wanted it, wanted it more than he had wanted anything in his life.

He looked up as the golden warrior leapt lightly from the

throne, seeing the music as swirling lines of power and promise that flowed like water in the air.

'Now you die,' said Lucius as the song of death took hold
of him.

In later moments they would name it Death's Tomb, and Loken
had never felt such disgust at the sights he saw within it. Even
Davin's moon, where the swamps had vomited up the living
dead to attack the Sons of Horus, had not been this bad.

The sound of battle was a hellish music of screaming, rising
in terrible crescendos, and the sight was horrendous. Death's
Tomb was brimming with corpses, festering in charnel heaps
and bubbling with corruption.

The tomb-spire Loken and the Sons of Horus fought within
was larger inside than out, the floor sunken into a pit where
the dead had been thrown. The tomb was that of Death itself.
A mausoleum of bloodstained black iron carved into swirls and
scrollwork dominated the pit, topped with a sculpture of Father
Isstvan himself, a massive bearded sky-god who took away the
souls of the faithful and cast the rest into the sky to languish
with his Lost Children.

A Warsinger perched on Father Isstvan's black shoulder,
screaming a song of death that jarred at Loken's nerves and sent
jangling pain along his limbs. Hundreds of Isstvanian soldiers
surrounded the pit, firing from the hip as they ran towards the
Astartes, driven forward by the shrieking death song.

'At them!' yelled Loken, and before he could draw breath
again the enemy was upon them. The Astartes of the spear-
head streamed through the many archways leading into the
tomb-spire, guns blazing as soon as they saw the enemy swarming towards them. Loken fired a fusillade of shots before the
two sides clashed.

More than two thousand Sons of Horus charged into battle
and Death's Tomb became a vast amphitheatre for a great and
terrible slaughter, like the arenas of the ancient Romanii.

'Stay close! Back to back, and advance!' cried Loken, but he
could only hope that his fellow warriors could hear him over
the vox. The screaming was deafening, every Isstvanian soldier's
mouth jammed open and howling in the shrieking cadences of
the Warsinger's music.

Loken cut a gory crescent through the bodies pressing in
on him, Vipus matching him stroke for stroke with his long
chainsword. Strategy and weapons meant nothing now. The battle was simply a brutal close quarters fight to the death.

Such a contest could have only one outcome.

Loathing filled Loken. Not at the blood and death around him, he had seen much worse before, but at the sheer waste of this war. The people he was killing... their lives could have meant something. They could have accepted the Imperial Truth and helped forge a galaxy where the human race was united and the wisdom of the Emperor ushered them towards a future filled with wonders. Instead they had been betrayed and turned into fanatical killers by a corrupt leader, destined to die for a cause that was a lie.

Good lives wasted. Nothing could be further from the purpose of the Imperium.

'Torgaddon! Bring the line forwards. Force them back and give the guns some room.'

'Easier said than done, Garvi!' replied Torgaddon, his voice punctuated with the sharp crack of breaking bones.

Loken glanced around, saw one of Lachost's squad dragged down by the mass of enemy warriors and tried to bring his bolter to bear. Bloodied, ruined hands forced his aim down and the battle-brother was lost. He dropped his shoulder and barged forwards, bodies breaking beneath him, but others were on top of him, blades and bullets beating at his armour.

With a roar of anger, Loken ripped his chainsword through an armoured warrior before him, forcing the enemy back for the split second he needed to open up with his bolter. A full-throated volley sent a magazine's worth of shells into the mass, blasting them apart in a red ruin of shattered faces and broken armour.

He rapidly swapped in a new bolter magazine and fired among the warriors trying to swamp his fellow Sons of Horus. The Astartes used the openings to forge onwards or open up spaces to bring their own weapons up. Others lent their gunfire to the battle-brothers fighting behind them.

The tone of the Warsinger's screaming changed and Loken felt as though rusty nails were being torn up his spine. He staggered and the enemy were upon him.

'Torgaddon!' he shouted over the din. 'Get the Warsinger!'

'My apologies, Warmaster,' began Maloghurst, nervous at interrupting the Warmaster's concentration on the battle below. 'There has been a development.'

'In the city?' asked Horus without looking up.

'On the ship,' replied Maloghurst.

Horus looked up in irritation. 'Explain yourself.'

'The Prime Iterator, Kyril Sindermann...'

'Old Kyril?' said Horus. 'What of him.'

'It appears we have misjudged the man's character, my lord.'

'In what way, Mal?' asked Horus. 'He's just an old man.'

'That he is, but he may be a greater threat than anything we have yet faced, my lord,' said Maloghurst. 'He is a leader now, an apostle they call him. He–'

'A leader?' interrupted Horus, 'of whom?'

'Of the people of the fleet, civilians, ships' crew, and the Lectitio Divinitatus. He has just finished a speech to the fleet calling on them to resist the Legion, saying that we are warmongers and seek to betray the Emperor. We are trying to trace where the signal came from, but it is likely he will be long gone before we find him.'

'I see,' said Horus. 'This problem should have been dealt with before Isstvan.'

'And we have failed you in this,' said Maloghurst. 'The iterator mixed calls for peace with a potent brew of religion and faith.'

'This should not surprise us,' said Horus. 'Sindermann was selected for duty with my fleet precisely because he could convince even the most fractious rabble to do anything. Mix that skill with religious fervour and he is indeed a dangerous man.'

'They believe the Emperor is divine,' said Maloghurst, 'and that we commit blasphemy.'

'It must be an intoxicating faith,' mused Horus, 'and faith can be a very powerful weapon. It appears, Maloghurst, that we have underestimated the potential that even a civilian possesses so long as he has genuine faith in something.'

'What would you have me do, my lord?'

'We did not deal with this threat properly,' said Horus. 'It should have ceased to exist when Varvarus and those troublesome remembrancers were illuminated. Now it takes my attention when our plan is at its most sensitive stage. The bombardment is imminent.'

Maloghurst bowed his head. 'Warmaster, Sindermann and his kind will be destroyed.'

'The next I hear of this will be that they are all dead,' ordered Horus.

'It will be done,' promised Maloghurst.

'Fool!' spat Praal, his voice a disgusted rasp. 'Have you not seen this world? The wonders you would destroy? This is a city of the gods!'

Lucius rolled to his feet, still stunned from the sonic shockwave that had hurled him from the throne dais, but knowing that the song of death was being sung for him and him alone. He lunged, but Praal batted aside his attack, bringing his spear up in a neat guard.

'This is the city of my enemies,' laughed Lucius. 'That is all that matters to me.'

'You are deaf to the music of the galaxy. I have heard far more than you,' said Praal. 'Perhaps you are to be pitied, for I have listened to the sound of the gods. I have heard their song and they damn this galaxy in their wisdom!'

Lucius laughed in Praal's face. 'You think I care? All I want to do is kill you.'

'The gods have sung what your Imperial Truth will bring to the galaxy,' shrieked Praal, his musical voice heavy with disdain. 'It is a future of fear and hatred. I was deaf to the music before they opened me to their song of oblivion. It is my duty to end your Crusade!'

'You can try,' said Lucius, 'but even if you kill us all, more will come, a hundred thousand more, a million, until this planet is dust. Your little rebellion is over – you just don't know it yet.'

'No, Astartes,' replied Praal. 'I have fulfilled my duty and brought you here, to this cauldron of fates. My work is done! All that remains is to blood myself in the name of Father Isstvan.'

Lucius danced away as Praal attacked once more with the razor-sharp feints of a master warrior, but the swordsman had faced better opponents than this and prevailed. The song of death rippled behind his eyes and he could see every move Praal made before he made it, the song speaking to him on a level he didn't understand, but instinctively knew was power beyond anything he had touched before.

He launched a flurry of blows at Praal, driving him back with each attack and no matter how skilfully Praal parried his strikes, each one came that little bit closer to wounding him.

The flicker of fear he saw in Praal's eyes filled him with brutal triumph. The shrieking, musical spear blared one last atonal scream before it finally shattered under the energised edge of Lucius's sword.

The swordsman pivoted smoothly on his heel and drove his blade, two-handed, into Praal's golden chest, the sword burning through his armour, ribs and internal organs.

Praal dropped to his knees, still alive, his mouth working dumbly as blood sprayed from the massive wound. Lucius twisted the blade, relishing the cracks as Praal's ribs snapped.

He put a foot on Praal's body and pulled the sword clear, standing triumphant over the body of his fallen enemy.

Around him, the Emperor's Children slew the remaining palace guards, but with Praal dead, the song in his blood diminished and his interest in the fight faded. Lucius turned to the throne itself, already aching for the music to surge through his body once again.

The throne's back was to him and he couldn't see who was seated there. A control panel worked furiously before it, like a monstrously complicated clockwork keyboard.

Lucius stepped around the throne and looked into the glassy eyes of a servitor.

Its head was mounted on a skinny body of metal armatures, the complex innards stripped out and replaced with brass clockwork. Chattering metal tines reached from the chest cavity to read the music printed in the books mounted around the throne and the servitor's hands, elaborate, twenty-fingered constructions of metal and wire, flickered over the control panel.

Without Praal, the music was out of tune and time, its syncopated rhythms falling apart. Lucius knew that this was a poor substitute for what had fuelled his battle with Praal.

Suddenly angry beyond words, Lucius brought his blade down in a glittering arc, shattering the control panel in a shower of orange sparks. The hideous music transformed into a howling death shriek, shaking the stone petals of the palace with its terrible, deafening wail before fading like a forgotten dream.

The music of creation ended and all across Isstvan the voices of the gods were silenced.

A volley of gunfire caught Loken's attention as he desperately fought the dozens of guards who stabbed at him with their gleaming halberds. Behind him, Torgaddon brought the spear-tip up into a firing line, and bolter fire battered against the black iron of Death's mausoleum. The Warsinger was broken like a dying bird against the statue of Father Isstvan.

The Warsinger fell, her final scream tailing off as her shattered form cracked against the ornate carvings of Death's mausoleum.

'She's down!' said Torgaddon's voice over the vox, sounding surprised at the ease with which she had been killed.

'Who have we lost?' asked Loken, as the enemy soldiers fell back at the Warsinger's death, suspecting that there was more to this withdrawal than simply her death. Something fundamental had changed on Isstvan, but he didn't yet know what.

'Most of Squad Chaggrat,' replied Torgaddon, 'and plenty of

others. We won't know until we get out of here, but there's something else...'

'What?' asked Loken.'

'Lachost says we've lost contact with orbit,' said Torgaddon. 'There's no signal. It's as if the *Vengeful Spirit* isn't even up there.'

'That's impossible,' said Loken, looking around for the familiar sight of Sergeant Lachost.

He saw him at the edge of the charnel pit and marched over to him. Torgaddon and Vipus followed him and Torgaddon said, 'Impossible or not, it's what he tells me.'

'What about the rest of the strike force?' asked Loken, crouching beside Lachost. 'What about the palace?'

'We're having more luck with them,' replied Lachost. 'I managed to get through to Captain Ehrlen of the World Eaters. It sounds like they're outside the palace. It's an absolute massacre over there – thousands of civilians dead.'

'In the name of Terra!' said Loken, imagining the World Eaters' predilection for massacre and the rivers of blood that would be flowing through the streets of the Choral City. 'Have they managed to contact anyone in orbit?'

'They've got their hands full, captain,' replied Lachost. 'Even if they've managed to raise the *Conqueror*, they're in no position to relay anything from us. I could barely get anything out of Ehrlen other than that he was killing them with his bare hands.'

'And the palace?'

'Nothing, I can't get through to Captain Lucius of the Emperor's Children. The palace has been playing hell with communications ever since they went in. There was some kind of music, but nothing else.'

'Then try the Death Guard. They've got the *Dies Irae* with them, we can use it to relay for us.'

'I'll try, sir, but it's not looking hopeful.'

'This was supposed to be over by now,' spat Loken. 'The Choral City isn't just going to collapse with their leaders dead. Maybe the World Eaters have the right idea. We're going to have to kill them all. We need the second wave down here now and if we can't even speak to the Warmaster this is going to be a very long campaign.'

'I'll keep trying,' said Lachost.

'We need to link up with the rest of the strike force,' said Loken. 'We're cut off here. We need to make for the palace and find the World Eaters or the Emperor's Children. We're not doing any good sitting here. All we're doing is giving the Isstvanians a chance to surround us.'

'There're a lot of soldiers between us and the rest of the strike force,' Torgaddon pointed out.

'Then we advance in force. We won't take this city by waiting to be attacked.'

'Agreed. I saw the main gates along the western walls. We can get into the city proper there, but it'll be a tough slog.'

'Good,' said Loken.

'It's a trap,' said Mersadie. 'It has to be.'

'You're probably right,' agreed Sindermann.

'Of course I'm right,' said Mersadie. 'Maloghurst tried to have Euphrati killed. His pet monster, Maggard, almost killed you too, remember?'

'I remember very well,' said Sindermann, 'but think of the opportunity. There will be thousands there and they couldn't possibly try anything with that many people around. They probably won't even notice we're there.'

Mersadie looked down her nose at Sindermann, unable to believe that the old iterator was being so dense. Had he not spoken to hundreds of people only hours before of the Warmaster's perfidy? And now he wanted to gather in a room with him?

They had been woken from their slumbers by one of the engineering crew who pressed a rolled leaflet into Sindermann's shaking hand. Sharing a worried glance with Mersadie, Sindermann had read it. It was a decree from the Warmaster authorising all remembrancers to gather in the *Vengeful Spirit's* main audience chamber to bear witness to the final triumph on Isstvan III. It spoke of the gulf that had, much to the Warmaster's great sorrow, opened between the Astartes and the remembrancers. With this one, grand gesture, the Warmaster hoped to allay any fears that such a gulf had been engineered deliberately.

'He must think we are stupid,' said Mersadie. 'Does he really think we would fall for this?'

'Maloghurst is a very cunning man,' said Sindermann, rolling up the leaflet and placing it on the bed. 'You'd hardly take him for a warrior any more. He's trying to flush the three of us out, hoping that no remembrancer could resist such an offer. If I were a less moral man I might admire him.'

'All the more reason not to fall into his trap!' exclaimed Mersadie.

'Ah, but what if it's genuine, my dear?' asked Sindermann. 'Imagine what we'd see on the surface of Isstvan Three!'

'Kyril, this is a big ship and we can hide out for a long time. When Loken comes back he can protect us.'

'Like he protected Ignace?'

'That's not fair, Kyril,' said Mersadie. 'Loken can help us get off the ship once we leave the Isstvan system.'

'No,' said a voice behind Mersadie and they both turned to see Euphrati Keeler. She was awake again, and her voice was stronger than Mersadie had heard it for a long time. She looked healthier than she had been since the terror in the archive. To see her standing, walking and talking after so long was still a novelty for Mersadie and she smiled to see her friend once again.

'We go,' she said.

'Euphrati?' said Mersadie. 'Do you really...'

'Yes, Mersadie,' she said. 'I mean it. And yes, I am sure.'

'It's a trap.'

'I don't need a vision from the Emperor to see that,' laughed Euphrati, and Mersadie thought there was something a little sinister and forced to it.

'But they'll kill us.'

Euphrati smiled. 'Yes they will. If we stay here, they'll hunt us down eventually. We have faithful among the crew, but we have enemies, too. I will not have the Church of the Emperor die like that. This will not end in shadows and murder.'

'Now, Miss Keeler,' said Sindermann with a forced lightness of tone. 'You're starting to sound like me.'

'Maybe they will find us eventually, Euphrati,' said Mersadie, 'but there's no reason to make it easy for them. Why let the Warmaster have his way when we can live a little longer?'

'Because you have to see,' said Euphrati. 'You have to see it. This fate, this treachery, it's too great for any of us to understand without witnessing it. Have faith that I am right about this, my friends.'

'It's not a question of faith now, is it?' said Sindermann. 'It's a–'

'It is time for us to stop thinking like remembrancers,' said Euphrati, and Mersadie saw a light in her eyes that seemed to grow brighter with every word she spoke. 'The Imperial Truth is dying. We have watched it wither ever since Sixty-Three Nineteen. You either die with it or you follow the Emperor. This galaxy is too simple for us to hide in its complexity any more and the Emperor cannot work His will through those who do not know if they even believe at all.'

'I will follow you,' said Sindermann, and Mersadie found herself nodding in agreement.

ELEVEN

Warning
Death of a World
The Last Cthonian

Saul Tarvitz's first sight of the Choral City was the magnificent stone orchid of the Precentor's Palace. He stepped from the battered Thunderhawk onto the roof of one of the palace wings, the spectacular dome soaring above him. Smoke coiled in the air from the battles within the palace and the terrible sound of screaming came from the square to the north, along with the powerful stench of freshly-spilled blood.

Tarvitz took it in at a glance, the thought hitting him hard that at any moment it would all be gone. He saw Astartes moving along the roof towards him, Emperor's Children, and his heart leapt to see Nasicae Squad with Lucius at its head, his sword smoking from the battle.

'Tarvitz!' called Lucius, and Tarvitz thought he detected even more of a swagger to the swordsman's stride. 'I thought you'd never make it! Jealous of the kills?'

'Lucius, what's the situation?' asked Tarvitz.

'The palace is ours and Praal is dead, killed by my own hand! No doubt you can smell the World Eaters. They're just not at home unless everything stinks of blood. The rest of the city's cut off. We can't raise anyone.'

Lucius indicated the city's far west, where the towering form of the *Dies Irae* blazed fire upon the hapless Isstvanians out of sight below. 'Though it looks like the Death Guard will soon run out of things to kill.'

'We have to contact the rest of the strike force, now,' said Tarvitz, 'the Sons of Horus and the Death Guard. Get a squad on it. Get someone up to higher ground.'

'Why?' asked Lucius. 'Saul, what's happening?'

'We're going to be hit. Something big. A virus strike.'

'The Isstvanians?'

'No,' said Tarvitz sadly. 'We are betrayed by our own.'

Lucius hesitated. 'The Warmaster? Saul, what are you–'

'We've been sent down here to die, Lucius. Fulgrim chose those who were not part of their grand plan.'

'Saul, that's insane!' cried Lucius. 'Why would our primarch do such a thing?'

'I do not know, but he would not have done this without the Warmaster's command,' said Tarvitz. 'This is but the first stage in some larger plan. I do not know its purpose, but we have to try and stop it.'

Lucius shook his head, his features twisted in petulant bitterness. 'No. The primarch wouldn't send me to die, not after all the battles I fought for him. Look at what I've become. I was one of Fulgrim's chosen! I've never faltered, never questioned! I would have followed Fulgrim into hell!'

'But I wouldn't, Lucius,' said Tarvitz, 'and you are my friend. I'm sorry, but we don't have time for this. We have to get the warning out and then find shelter. I'll take word to the World Eaters, you raise the Sons of Horus and Death Guard. Don't go into the details, just tell them that there is a virus strike inbound and to find whatever shelter they can.'

Tarvitz looked at the reassuring solidity of the Precentor's Palace and said, 'There must be catacombs or deep places beneath the palace. If we can reach them we may survive this. This city is going to die, Lucius, but I'll be damned if I am going to die with it.'

'I'll get a vox-officer up here,' said Lucius, a steel anger in his voice.

'Good. We don't have much time, Lucius, the bombs will be launched any moment.'

'This is rebellion,' said Lucius.

'Yes,' said Tarvitz, 'it is.'

Beneath his ritualistic scars, Lucius was still the perfect soldier he had always been, a talisman whose confidence could infect the men around him, and Tarvitz knew he could rely on him. The swordsman nodded and said, 'Go, find Captain Ehrlen. I'll raise the other Legions and get our warriors into cover. I will speak with you again.'

'Until then,' said Tarvitz.

Lucius turned to Nasicae, barked an order, and ran back towards the palace dome. Tarvitz followed, looking down on the northern plaza and glimpsing the seething battle there, hearing the screams and the sound of chainblades.

He looked up at the late morning sky. Clouds were gathering.

Any moment, falling virus bombs would bore through those clouds.

The bombs would fall all over Isstvan III and billions of people would die.

Among the trenches and bunkers that sprawled to the west of the Choral City, men and Astartes died in storms of mud and fire. The *Dies Irae* shuddered with the weight of fire it laid down. Moderati Cassar felt it all, as though the immense, multi-barrelled Vulcan bolter were in his own hand. The Titan had suffered many wounds, its legs scarred by missile detonations and furrows scored in its mighty torso by bunker-mounted cannons.

Cassar felt them all, but a multitude of wounds could not slow down the *Dies Irae* or turn it from its course. Destruction was its purpose and death was the punishment it brought down on the heads of the Emperor's enemies.

Cassar's heart swelled. He had never felt so close to his Emperor, at one with the God-Machine, a fragment of the Emperor's own strength instilled in the *Dies Irae*.

'Aruken, pull to starboard!' ordered Princeps Turnet from the command chair. 'Avoid those bunkers or they'll foul the port leg.'

The *Dies Irae* swung to the side, its immense foot taking the roofs from a tangle of bunkers and shattering artillery emplacements as it crashed forwards. A scrum of Isstvanian soldiers scrambled from the ruins, setting up heavy weapons to pour fire into the Titan as it towered over them.

The Isstvanians were well-drilled and well-armed, and though the majority of their weapons weren't the equal of a lasgun, trenches were a great leveller and a man with a rifle was a man with a rifle when the gunfire started.

The Death Guard slaughtered thousands of them as they bludgeoned their way through the trenches, but the Isstvanians were more numerous and they hadn't run. Instead they had fallen back trench by trench, rolling away from the relentless advance of the Death Guard.

The Isstvanians, with their drab green-grey helmets and mud-spattered flak-suits, were hard to pick out against the mud and rubble with the naked eye, but the sensors on the *Dies Irae* projected a sharp-edged image onto Cassar's retina that picked them out in wondrously clear detail.

Cassar fired a blast of massive-calibre shells, watching as columns of mud and bodies sprayed into the air like splashes in water. The Isstvanians disappeared, destroyed by the hand of the Emperor.

'Enemy forces massing to the port forward quadrant,' said Moderati Aruken.

To Cassar his voice felt distant, though he was just across the command bridge of the Titan.

'The Death Guard can handle them,' replied Turnet. 'Concentrate on the artillery. That can hurt us.'

Below Cassar, the gunmetal forms of the Death Guard glinted around the bunkers as two squads of them threw grenades through the gun ports and kicked down the doors, spraying the Isstvanians who still lived inside with bolter fire or incinerating them with sheets of fire from their flamers. From the head of the *Dies Irae*, the Death Guard looked like a swarm of beetles, with the carapaces of their power armour scuttling through the trenches.

A few Death Guard lay where they had fallen, cut down by artillery fire or the massed guns of the Isstvanian troops, but they were few compared to the Isstvanian corpses strewn at every intersection of trenches. Metre by metre the defenders were being driven towards the northernmost extent of the trenches, and when they reached the white marble of a tall basilica with a spire shaped like a trident, they would be trapped and slaughtered.

Cassar shifted the weapon arm of the *Dies Irae* to aim at a booming artillery position some five hundred metres away, as it belched tongues of flame and threw explosive shells towards the Death Guard lines.

'Princeps!' called Cassar. 'Enemy artillery moving up on the eastern quadrant.'

Turnet didn't answer him, too intent on something being said to him on his personal command channel. The princeps nodded at whatever order he had just received and shouted, 'Halt! Aruken, cease the stride pattern. Cassar, shut off the ammunition feed.'

Cassar instinctively switched off the cycling of the weapon that thundered from the Titan's arm and the shock forced his consciousness back to the command bridge. He no longer looked through the eyes of the *Dies Irae*, but was back with his fellow officers.

'Princeps?' asked Cassar, scanning the readouts. 'Is there a malfunction? If there is, I'm not seeing it. The primary systems are reading fine.'

'It's not a malfunction,' replied Turnet sharply. Cassar looked up from information scrolling across his vision in unfocused columns.

'Moderati Cassar,' barked Turnet. 'How's our weapon temperature?'

'Acceptable,' said Cassar. 'I was going to push it on that artillery.'

'Close up the coolant ducts and seal the magazine feeds as soon as possible.'

'Princeps?' said Cassar in confusion. 'That will leave us unarmed.'

'I know that,' replied Turnet, as though to a simpleton. 'Do it. Aruken, I need us sealed.'

'Sealed, sir?' asked Aruken, sounding as confused as Cassar felt.

'Yes, sealed. We have to be airtight from top to bottom,' said Turnet, opening a channel to the rest of the mighty war machine's crew.

'All crew, this is Princeps Turnet. Adopt emergency biohazard posts, right now. The bulkheads are being sealed. Shut off the reactor vents and be prepared for power down.'

'Princeps,' said Aruken urgently. 'Is it a biological weapon? Atomics?'

'The Isstvanians have a weapon we didn't know about,' replied Turnet, but Cassar could tell he was lying. 'They're launching it soon. We have to lock down or we'll be caught in it.'

Cassar looked down at the trenches through the Titan's eyes. The Death Guard were still advancing through the trenches and bunker ruins. 'But princeps, the Astartes–'

'You have your orders, Moderati Cassar,' shouted Turnet, 'and you will follow them. Seal us up, every vent, every hatch or we die.'

Cassar willed the *Dies Irae* to shut its hatches and seal all its entranceways, his reluctance making the procedures sluggish.

On the ground below, he watched the Death Guard continue to grind their way through the Choral City's defences, apparently unconcerned that the Isstvanians were about to launch Throne knew what at them, *or unaware*.

As the battle raged on, the *Dies Irae* fell silent.

✠ ✠ ✠

The main audience chamber of the *Vengeful Spirit* was a colossal, columned chamber with walls of marble and pilasters of solid gold. Its magnificence was like nothing Sindermann had ever seen, and the thousands of remembrancers who filled the chamber wore the expressions of awed children who had been shown some new, unheard of wonder. Seeing many familiar faces, Sindermann guessed that the fleet's entire complement of remembrancers was present for the Warmaster's announcement.

The Warmaster and Maloghurst stood on a raised podium at the far end of the hall, too far away for either of them to recognise Sindermann, Mersadie or Euphrati.

Or at least he hoped so. Who knew how sharp a legionary's eyesight was, let alone a primarch's?

Both Astartes were wrapped in cream robes edged in gold and silver and a detail of warriors stood beside them. A number of large pict screens had been hung from the walls.

'It looks like an iterators' rally on a compliant world,' said Mersadie, echoing his own thoughts. So similar was it that he began to wonder what message was to be imparted and how it would be reinforced. He looked around for plants in the audience who would clap and cheer at precise points to direct the crowd in the desired manner. Each of the screens displayed a slice of Isstvan III, set against a black backdrop scattered with bright silver specks of the Warmaster's fleet.

'Euphrati,' said Mersadie as they made their way through the crowds of remembrancers. 'Remember how I said that this was a bad idea?'

'Yes?' said Euphrati, her face creased in a wide, innocent smile.

'Well, now I think that this was a *really* bad idea. I mean, look at the number of Astartes here.'

Sindermann followed Mersadie's gaze, already starting to sweat at the sight of so many armed warriors surrounding them. If even one of them recognised their faces, it was all over.

'We have to see,' said Euphrati, turning and grabbing his sleeve. '*You* have to see.'

Sindermann felt the heat of her touch and saw the fire behind her eyes, like thunder before a storm and he realised with a start, that he was a little afraid of Euphrati. The crowd milled in eager impatience and Sindermann kept his face turned from the Astartes staring into the middle of the audience chamber.

Euphrati squeezed Mersadie's hand as the pict screens leapt to life and a gasp went up from the assembled remembrancers as they saw the bloody streets of the Choral City. Clearly shot from an aircraft, the images filled the giant pict screens and Sindermann felt his gorge rise at the sight of so much butchery.

He remembered the carnage of the Whisperheads and reminded himself that this was what the Astartes had been created to do, but the sheer visceral nature of that reality was something he knew he would never get used to. Bodies filled the streets and arterial gore covered almost every surface as though the heavens had rained blood.

'You remembrancers say you want to see war,' said Horus, his voice easily carrying to the furthest corners of the hall. 'Well, this is it.'

Sindermann watched as the image shifted on the screen, pulling back and panning up through the sky and into the dark, star-spattered heavens above.

Burning spears of light fell towards the battle below.

'What are those?' asked Mersadie.

'They're bombs,' said Sindermann in horrified disbelief. 'The planet is being bombarded.'

'And so it begins,' said Euphrati.

The plaza was a truly horrendous sight, ankle-deep in blood and strewn with thousands upon thousands of bodies. Most were blown open by bolter rounds, but many had been hacked down with chainblades or otherwise torn limb from limb.

Tarvitz hurried towards the makeshift strongpoint at its centre, the battlements formed from carved up bodies heaped between the battered forms of fallen drop pods.

A World Eater with blood-soaked armour and a scarred face nodded to him as he climbed the gruesome ramp of bodies. The warrior's armour was so drenched in blood that Tarvitz wondered for a moment why he hadn't just painted himself red to begin with.

'Captain Ehrlen,' said Tarvitz. 'Where is he?'

The warrior wasted no breath on words and simply jerked a thumb in the direction of a warrior with dozens of fluttering oath papers hanging from his breastplate. Tarvitz nodded his thanks and set off through the strongpoint. He passed wounded Astartes who were tended by an Apothecary who looked as if he had fought as hard as any of his patients. Beside him lay two fallen World Eaters, their bodies unceremoniously dumped out of the way.

Ehrlen looked up as Tarvitz approached. The captain's face had been badly burned in some previous battle and his axe was clotted with so much blood that it better resembled a club.

'Looks like the Emperor's Children have sent us reinforcements!' shouted Ehrlen, to grunts of laughter from his fellow World Eaters. 'One whole warrior! We are blessed, the enemy will run away for sure.'

'Captain,' said Tarvitz, joining Ehrlen at the barricade of Isstvanian dead. 'My name is Captain Saul Tarvitz and I'm here to warn you that you have to get your squads into cover.'

'Into cover? Unacceptable,' said Ehrlen, nodding towards the far side of the plaza. Shapes moved in their windows and between the mansions. 'They're regrouping. If we move now they will overwhelm us.'

'The Isstvanians have a bio-weapon,' said Tarvitz, knowing a lie was the only way to convince the World Eaters. 'They're going to fire it. It'll kill everyone and everything in the Choral City.'

'They're going to destroy their own capital? I thought this place was some kind of church? Holy to them?'

'They've shown how much they value their own,' replied Tarvitz quickly, indicating the heaps of dead in front of them. 'They'll sacrifice this city to kill us. Driving us from their planet is worth more to them than this city.'

'So you would have us abandon this position?' demanded Ehrlen, as if Tarvitz had personally insulted his honour. 'How do you know all this?'

'I just got here from orbit. The weapon has already been unleashed. If you're above ground when the virus strike hits you will die. If you believe nothing else, believe that.'

'Then where do you suggest we move to?'

'Just to the west of this position, captain,' said Tarvitz, stealing a glance at the sky. 'The edge of the trench system is thick with bunkers, blast proof shelters. If you get your men into them, they should be safe.'

'Should be?' snapped Ehrlen. 'That's the best you can offer me?'

Ehrlen stared at Tarvitz for a moment. 'If you are wrong the blood of my warriors will be on your hands and I will kill you for their deaths.'

'I understand that, captain,' urged Tarvitz, 'but we don't have much time.'

'Very well, Captain Tarvitz,' said Ehrlen. 'Sergeant Fleiste, left flank! Sergeant Wronde, right! World Eaters, general advance to the west, blades out!'

The World Eaters drew their chainaxes and swords. The blood-stained assault units hurried to the front and stepped over the makeshift barricades of corpses.

'Are you coming, Tarvitz?' asked Ehrlen.

Tarvitz nodded, drawing his broadsword and following the World Eaters into the plaza.

Although they were fellow Astartes, he knew he was a stranger among them as they ran, spitting battle curses and splashing through the dead towards the potential safety of the bunkers.

Tarvitz glanced up at the gathering clouds and felt his chest tighten.

The first burning streaks were falling towards the city.

'It's started,' said Loken.

Lachost looked up from the field vox. Fire was streaking through the sky towards the Choral City. Loken tried to judge the angle and speed of the falling darts of fire – some of them would come down between the spires of the Sirenhold, just like the Sons of Horus's own drop pods had done hours earlier, and they would hit in a matter of minutes.

'Did Lucius say anything else?'

'No,' said Lachost. 'Some bio-weapon. That was all. It sounded like he ran into a firefight.'

'Tarik,' shouted Loken. 'We need to get into cover, now. Beneath the Sirenhold.'

'Will that be enough?'

'If they dug their catacombs deep enough, then maybe.'

'And if not?'

'From what Lucius said, we'll die.'

'Then we'd better get a move on.'

Loken turned to the Sons of Horus advancing around him. 'Incoming! Get to the Sirenhold and head down! Now!'

The closest spire of the Sirenhold was a towering monstrosity of grotesque writhing figures and leering gargoyle faces, a vision taken from some ancient hell of Isstvan's myths. The Sons of Horus broke their advance formation and ran towards it.

Loken heard the distinctive boom of an airborne detonation high above the city and pushed himself harder as he entered the darkness of the tomb-spire. Inside, it was dark and ugly, the floor paved with tortured, half-human figures who reached up with stone hands, as if through the bars of a cage.

'There's a way down,' said Torgaddon. Loken followed as Astartes ran towards the catacomb entrance, a huge monstrous stone head with a passageway leading down its throat.

As the darkness closed around him, Loken heard a familiar sound drifting from beyond the walls of the Sirenhold.

It was screaming.
It was the song of the Choral City's death.

The first virus bombs detonated high above the Choral City, the huge explosions spreading the deadly payloads far and wide into the atmosphere. Designed to kill every living thing on the surface of a planet, the viral strains released on Isstvan III were the most efficient killers in the Warmaster's arsenal. The bombs had a high enough yield to murder the planet a hundred times over and were set to burst at numerous differing altitudes and locations across the surface of the planet.

The virus leapt through forests and plains, sweeping along algal blooms and riding air currents across the globe. It crossed mountains, forded rivers, burrowed through glaciers. The Imperium's deadliest weapons, the Emperor himself had been loath to use them.

The bombs fell all across Isstvan III, but most of all, they fell on the Choral City.

The World Eaters were the furthest from cover and suffered the worst of the initial bombardment. Some had reached the safety of the bunkers, but many more had not. Warriors fell to their knees as the virus penetrated their armoured bodies, deadly corrosive agents laced into the viral structure of the weapons dissolving exposed pipes and armour joints, or finding their way inside through battle damage.

Astartes screamed. The sound was all the more shocking for its very existence rather than for the horror of its tone. The virus broke down cellular bonds at the molecular level and its victims literally dissolved into a soup of rancid meat within minutes of exposure, leaving little but sloshing suits of rotted armour. Even many of those who reached the safety of the sealed bunkers died in agony as they shut the doors only to find they had brought the lethal virus inside with them.

The virus spread through the civilian populace of Isstvan III at the speed of thought, leaping from victim to victim in the time it took to breathe in its foul contagion. People dropped where they stood, the flesh sloughing from their skeletons as their nervous systems collapsed and their bones turned to the consistency of jelly.

Bright explosions fed the viral feast, perpetuating the fatal reactions of corruption. The very lethality of the virus was its own worst enemy, for without a host organism to carry it from victim to victim, the virus quickly consumed itself.

However, the bombardment from orbit was unrelenting, smothering the entire planet in a precisely targeted array of overlapping fire plans that ensured that nothing would escape the virus.

Entire kingdoms and vassal states across the surface were obliterated in minutes. Ancient cultures that had survived Old Night and endured the horror of invasion a dozen times over fell without even knowing why, millions dying in screaming agony as their bodies betrayed them and fell apart, reducing them to rotted, decaying matter.

Sindermann watched the bloom of darkness spread across the slice of the planet visible on the giant pict screens. It spread in a wide black ring, eating its way across the surface of the planet with astonishing speed, leaving grey desolation behind it. Another wave of corruption crept in from another part of the surface, the two dark masses meeting and continuing to spread like the symptom of a horrible disease.

'What... what is it?' whispered Mersadie.

'You have already seen it,' said Euphrati. 'The Emperor showed you, through me. It is death.'

Sindermann's stomach lurched as he remembered the hideous vision of decay, his flesh disintegrating before him and black corruption consuming everything around him.

That was what was happening on Isstvan III.

This was the betrayal.

Sindermann felt as though the blood had drained from him. An entire world was bathed in the immensity of death. He felt an echo of the fear it brought to the people of Isstvan III, and that fear, multiplied across all those billions of people was beyond his comprehension.

'You are remembrancers,' said Keeler, a quiet sadness in her voice. 'Both of you. Remember this and pass it on. Someone must know.'

He nodded dumbly, too numbed by what he was seeing to say anything.

'Come on,' said Euphrati. 'We have to go.'

'Go?' sobbed Mersadie, her eyes still fixed on the death of a world. 'Go where?'

'Away,' smiled Euphrati, taking their hands and leading them through the immobile, horrified throng of remembrancers towards the edge of the chamber.

At first, Sindermann let her lead him, his limbs unable to do more than simply place one foot in front of another, but as he

saw she was taking them towards the Astartes at the edge of the
chamber, he began to pull back in alarm.

'Euphrati!' he hissed. 'What are you doing? If those Astartes
recognise us–'

'Trust me, Kyril,' she said. 'I'm counting on that.'

Euphrati led them towards a hulking warrior who stood apart
from the others, and Sindermann knew enough of body language to know that this man was as horrified as they were at
what was happening.

The Astartes turned to face them, his face craggy and ancient,
worn like old leather.

Euphrati stopped in front of him and said, 'Iacton. I need
your help.'

Iacton Qruze. Sindermann had heard Loken speak of him.
The 'Half-heard'.

He was a warrior of the old days, whose voice carried no
weight amongst the higher echelons of command.

A warrior of the old days…

'You need my help?' asked Qruze. 'Who are you?'

'My name is Euphrati Keeler and this is Mersadie Oliton,'
said Euphrati, as if her introductions in the midst of such carnage were the most normal thing in the world, 'and this is Kyril
Sindermann.'

Sindermann could see the recognition in Qruze's face and he
closed his eyes as he awaited the inevitable shout that would
see them revealed.

'Loken asked me to look out for you,' said Qruze.

'Loken?' asked Mersadie. 'Have you heard from him?'

Qruze shook his head, but said, 'He asked me to keep you
safe while he was gone. I think I know what he meant now.'

'What do you mean?' asked Sindermann, not liking the way
Qruze kept casting wary glances at the armed warriors that lined
the walls of the chamber.

'Never mind,' said Qruze.

'Iacton,' commanded Euphrati, her voice laden with quiet
authority. 'Look at me.'

The craggy-featured Astartes looked down at the slight form
of Euphrati, and Sindermann could feel the power and determination that flowed from her.

'You are the Half-heard no longer,' said Euphrati. 'Now your
voice will be heard louder than any other in your Legion. You
cling to the old ways and wish them to return with the fond
nostalgia of the venerable. Those days are dying here, Iacton,
but with your help we can bring them back again.'

'What are you talking about, woman?' snarled Qruze.

'I want you to remember Cthonia,' said Euphrati, and Sindermann recoiled as he felt an electric surge of energy spark from her, as if her very skin was charged.

'What do you know of the planet of my birth?'

'Only what I see inside you, Iacton,' said Euphrati, a soft glow building behind her eyes and filling her words with promise and seduction. 'The honour and the valour from which the Luna Wolves were forged. You are the only one who remembers, Iacton. You're the only one left that still embodies what it is to be an Astartes.'

'You know nothing of me,' he said, though Sindermann could see her words were reaching him, breaking down the barriers the Astartes erected between themselves and mortals.

'Your brothers called you the Half-heard, but you do not take them to task for it. I know this is because a Cthonian warrior is honourable and cares not for petty insults. I also know that your counsel is not heard because yours is the voice of a past age, when the Great Crusade was a noble thing, done not for gain, but for the good of all humankind.'

Sindermann watched as Qruze's face spoke volumes of the conflict raging within his soul.

Loyalty to his Legion vied with loyalty to the ideals that had forged it.

At last he smiled ruefully and said, '"Nothing too arduous" he said.'

He looked over towards the Warmaster and Maloghurst.

'Come,' he said. 'Follow me.'

'Where to?' asked Sindermann.

'To safety,' replied Qruze. 'Loken asked me to look out for you and that's what I'm going to do. Now be silent and follow me.'

Qruze turned on his heel and marched towards one of the many doors that led out of the audience chamber. Euphrati followed the warrior and Sindermann and Mersadie trotted along after her, unsure as to where they were going or why. Qruze reached the door, a large portal of polished bronze guarded by two warriors, moving them aside with a chopping wave of his hand.

'I'm taking these ones below,' he said.

'Our orders are that no one is to leave,' said one of the guards.

'And I am issuing you new orders,' said Qruze, a steely determination that Sindermann had not noticed earlier underpinning his words. 'Move aside, or are you disobeying the order of a superior officer?'

'No, sir,' said the warriors, bowing and hauling open the bronze door.

Qruze nodded to the guards and gestured that the four of them should pass through.

Sindermann, Euphrati and Mersadie left the audience chamber, the door slamming behind them with an awful finality. With the sounds of the dying planet and the gasps of shock suddenly cut off, the silence that enveloped them was positively unnerving.

'Now what do we do?' asked Mersadie.

'I get us as far away from the *Vengeful Spirit* as possible,' answered Qruze.

'Off the ship?' asked Sindermann.

'Yes,' said Qruze. 'It is not safe for your kind now. Not safe at all.'

TWELVE

Cleansing
Let the galaxy burn
God Machine

The screaming of the Choral City's death throes came in tremendous waves, battering against the Precentor's Palace like a tsunami. In the streets below and throughout the palace, the people of the Choral City were decaying where they stood, bodies coming apart in torrents of disintegrating flesh.

The people thronged in the streets to die, keening their hatred and fear up at the sky, imploring their gods to deliver them. Millions of people screamed at once and the result was a terrible black-stained gale of death. A Warsinger soared overhead, trying to ease the agony and terror of their deaths with her songs, but the virus found her too, and instead of singing the praises of Isstvan's gods she coughed out black plumes as the virus tore through her insides. She fell like a shot bird, twirling towards the dying below.

A bulky shape appeared on the roof of the Precentor's Palace. Ancient Rylanor strode to the edge of the roof, overlooking the scenes of horror below, the viral carnage seething between the buildings. Rylanor's Dreadnought body was sealed against the world outside, sealed far more effectively than any Astartes armour, and the deathly wind swirled harmlessly around him as he watched the city's death unfold.

Rylanor looked up towards the sky, where far above, the Warmaster's fleet was still emptying the last of its deathly payload onto Isstvan III. The ancient Dreadnought stood alone, the only note of peace in the screaming horror of the Choral City's death.

'Good job we built these bunkers tough,' said Captain Ehrlen.

The darkness of the sealed bunker was only compounded by the sounds of death from beyond its thick walls. Pitifully few of the World Eaters had made it into the network of bunkers that fringed the edge of the trench network and barricaded themselves inside. They waited in the dark, listening to the virus killing off the city's population more efficiently than even their chainaxes could.

Tarvitz waited amongst them, listening to the deaths of millions of people in mute horror. The World Eaters appeared to be unmoved, the deaths of civilians meaning nothing to them.

The screaming was dying down, replaced by a dull moaning. Pain and fear mingled in a distant roar of slow death.

'How much longer must we hide like rats in the dark?' demanded Ehrlen.

'The virus will burn itself out quickly,' said Tarvitz. 'That's what it's designed to do – eat away anything living and leave a battlefield for the enemy to take.'

'How do you know?' asked Ehrlen.

Tarvitz looked at him. He could tell Ehrlen the truth, and he knew that he deserved it, but what good would it do? The World Eaters might kill him for even saying it. After all, their own primarch was part of the Warmaster's conspiracy.

'I have seen such weapons employed before,' said Tarvitz.

'You had better be right,' snarled Ehrlen, sounding far from satisfied with Tarvitz's answer. 'I won't cower here for much longer!'

The World Eater looked over his warriors, their bloodstained armoured bodies packed close together in the darkness of the bunker. He raised his axe and called, 'Wrathe! Have you raised the Sons of Horus?'

'Not yet,' replied Wrathe. Tarvitz could see he was a veteran, with numerous cortical implants blistered across his scalp. 'There's chatter, but nothing direct.'

'So they're still alive?'

'Maybe.'

Ehrlen shook his head. 'They got us. We thought we'd taken this city and they got us.'

'None of us could have known,' said Tarvitz.

'No. There are no excuses.' Ehrlen's face hardened. 'The World Eaters must always go further than the enemy. When they attack, we charge right back at them. When they dig in, we dig them out. When they kill our warriors, we kill their cities, but this time, the enemy went further than we did. We attacked their city, and they destroyed it to take us with them.'

'We were all caught out, captain,' said Tarvitz. 'The Emperor's Children, too.'

'No, Tarvitz, this was our fight. The Emperor's Children and the Sons of Horus were to behead the beast, but we were sent to cut its heart out. This was an enemy that could not be scared away or thrown into confusion. The Isstvanians had to be killed. Whether the other Legions acknowledge it or not, the World Eaters were the ones who had to win this city, and we take responsibility for our failures.'

'It's not your responsibility,' said Tarvitz.

'A lesser soldier pretends that his failures are those of his commanders,' said Ehrlen. 'An Astartes realises they are his alone.'

'No, captain, said Tarvitz. You don't understand. I mean–'

'Got something,' said Wrathe from the corner of the bunker.

'The Sons of Horus?' asked Ehrlen.

Wrathe shook his head. 'Death Guard. They took cover in the bunkers further west.'

'What do they say?'

'That the virus is dying down.'

'Then we could be out there again soon,' said Ehrlen with relish. 'If the Isstvanians come to take their city back, they'll find us waiting for them.'

'No,' said Tarvitz. 'There's one more stage of the viral attack still to come.'

'What's that?' demanded Ehrlen.

'The firestorm,' said Tarvitz.

'You see now,' said Horus to the assembled remembrancers. 'This is war. This is cruelty and death. This is what we do for you and yet you turn your face from it.'

Weeping men and women clung to one another in the wake of such monstrous genocide, unable to comprehend the scale of the slaughter that had just been enacted in the name of the Imperium.

'You have come to my ship to chronicle the Great Crusade and there is much to be said for what you have achieved, but things change and times move on,' continued Horus as the Astartes warriors along the flanks of the chamber closed the doors and stood before them with their bolters held across their chests.

'The Great Crusade is over,' said Horus, his voice booming with power and strength. 'The ideals it once stood for are dead and all we have fought for has been a lie. Until now. Now I will bring the Crusade back to its rightful path and rescue the galaxy from its abandonment at the hands of the Emperor.'

Astonished gasps and wails spread around the chamber at Horus's words and he relished the freedom he felt in saying them out loud. The need for secrecy and misdirection was no more. Now he could unveil the grandeur of his designs for the galaxy and cast aside his false façade to reveal his true purpose.

'You cry out, but mere mortals cannot hope to comprehend the scale of my plans,' said Horus, savouring the looks of panic that began to spread around the audience chamber.

No iterator could ever have had a crowd so completely in the palm of his hand.

'Unfortunately, this means that there is no place for the likes of you in this new crusade. I am to embark on the greatest war ever unleashed on the galaxy, and I cannot be swayed from my course by those who harbour disloyalty.'

Horus smiled.

The smile of an angelic executioner.

'Kill them,' he said. 'All of them.'

Bolter fire stabbed into the crowd at the Warmaster's order. Flesh burst in wet explosions and a hundred bodies fell in the first fusillade. The screaming began as the crowd surged away from the Astartes who marched into their midst.

But there was no escape.

Guns blazed and roaring chainswords rose and fell.

The slaughter took less than a minute and Horus turned away from the killing to watch the final death throes of Isstvan III. Abaddon emerged from the shadows where he and Maloghurst had watched the slaughter of the remembrancers.

'My lord,' said Abaddon, bowing low.

'What is it, my son?'

'Ship surveyors report that the virus has mostly burned out.'

'And the gaseous levels?'

'Off the scale, my lord,' smiled Abaddon. 'The gunners await your orders.'

Horus watched the swirling, noxious clouds enveloping the planet below.

All it would take was a single spark.

He imagined the planet as the frayed end of a fuse, a fuse that would ignite the galaxy in a searing conflagration and would lead to an inexorable conclusion on Terra.

'Order the guns to fire,' said Horus, his voice cold. 'Let the galaxy burn!'

✠ ✠ ✠

'Emperor preserve us,' whispered Moderati Cassar, unable to hide his horror and not caring who heard him. The miasma of rancid, putrid gases still hung thickly around the Titan and he could only dimly see the trenches again, along with the Death Guard emerging from the bunkers. Shortly after the order to seal the Titan had been given, the Death Guard had taken cover, clearly in receipt of the same order as the *Dies Irae*.

The Isstvanians had received no such order. The Death Guard's withdrawal had drawn the Isstvanian soldiers forwards and they had borne the full brunt of the bio-weapon.

Masses of mucus-like flesh choked the trenches, half-formed human corpses looming from them, faces melted and rot-bloated bodies split open. Thousands upon thousands of Isstvanians lay in rotting heaps and thick streams of sluggish black corruption ran the length of the trenches.

Beyond the battlefield, death had consumed the forests that lay just outside the Choral City's limits, now resembling endless graveyards of blackened trunks, like scorched skeletal hands. The earth beneath was saturated with biological death and the air was thick with foul gases released by the oceans of decaying matter.

'Report,' said Princeps Turnet, re-entering the cockpit from the Titan's main dorsal cavity.

'We're sealed,' said Moderati Aruken on the other side of the bridge. 'The crew's fine and I have a zero reading of contaminants.'

'The virus has burned itself out,' said Turnet. 'Cassar, what's out there?'

Cassar took a moment to gather his thoughts, still struggling with the hideous magnitude of death that he couldn't have even imagined had he not seen it through the eyes of the *Dies Irae*.

'The Isstvanians are... gone,' he said. He peered through the swirling clouds of gas at the mass of the city to one side of the Titan. 'All of them.'

'The Death Guard?'

Cassar looked closer, seeing segments of gunmetal armour partially buried in gory chokepoints, marking where Astartes had fallen.

'Some of them were caught out there,' he said. 'A lot of them are dead, but the order must have got to most of them in time.'

'The order?'

'Yes, princeps. The order to take cover.'

Turnet peered through the Titan's eye on Aruken's side of the bridge, seeing Death Guard warriors through the greenish haze securing the trenches around their bunkers and treading through the foul remains of the Isstvanians.

'Damn,' said Turnet.

'We are blessed,' said Cassar. 'They could so easily have been–'

'Watch your mouth, moderati! That religious filth is a crime by the order of–'

Turnet's voice cut off as movement caught his eyes.

Cassar followed his gaze in time to see the clouds of gas lit up by a brilliant beam of light as a blazing lance strike slashed through the clouds of noxious, highly flammable gases.

All it took was a single spark.

An entire planet's worth of decaying matter wreathed the atmosphere of Isstvan III in a thick shawl of combustible gases. The lance strike from the *Vengeful Spirit* burned through the upper atmosphere into the choking miasma and its searing beam ignited the gas with a dull *whoosh* that seemed to suck the oxygen from the air.

In a second, the air itself caught light, ripping across the landscape in a howling maelstrom of fire and noise. Entire continents were laid bare, their landscapes seared to bare rock, their decayed populations vaporised in seconds as winds of fire swept across their surfaces in a deadly gale of blazing destruction.

Cities exploded as gas lines went up, blazing towers of fire whipping madly in the deadly firestorm. Nothing could survive and flesh, stone and metal were vitrified or melted in the unimaginable temperatures.

Entire sprawls of buildings collapsed, the bodies of their former occupants reduced to ashen waste on the wind, palaces of marble and industrial heartlands destroyed in gigantic mushroom clouds as the storm of destruction swept around Isstvan III with relentless, mindless destruction until it seemed as though the entire globe was ablaze.

Those Astartes who had survived the viral attack found themselves consumed in flames as they desperately sought to find cover once more.

But against this firestorm there could be no cover for those who had dared to brave the elements.

By the time the echoes of the recoil had faded on the Warmaster's flagship, billions had died on Isstvan III.

Moderati Cassar hung on for dear life as the tempestuous firestorm raged around the *Dies Irae*. The colossal Titan swayed like a reed in the wind, and he just hoped that the new stabilising gyros the Mechanicum had installed held firm in the face of the onslaught.

Across from him, Aruken gripped the rails surrounding his chair with white knuckled hands, staring in awed terror at the blazing vortices spinning beyond the command bridge.

'Emperor save us. Emperor save us. Emperor save us,' he whispered over and over as the flames billowed and surged for what seemed like an eternity. The heat in the command bridge was intolerable since the coolant units had been shut down when the Titan was sealed off from the outside world.

Like a gigantic pressure cooker, the temperature inside the Titan climbed rapidly until Cassar felt as if he could no longer draw breath without searing the interior of his lungs. He closed his eyes and saw the ghostly green scroll of data flash through his retinas. Sweat poured from him in a torrent and he knew that this was it, this was how he would die: not in battle, not saying the Lectitio Divinitatus, but cooked to death inside his beloved *Dies Irae*.

He had lost track of how long they had been bathed in fire when the professional core of his mind saw that the temperature readings, which had been rising rapidly since the firestorm had hit, were beginning to flatten out. Cassar opened his eyes and saw the madly churning mass of flame through the viewing bays of the Titan's head, but he also saw spots of sky, burned blue as the fire incinerated the last of the combustible gases released by the dead of Isstvan.

'Temperature dropping,' he said, amazed that they were still alive.

Aruken laughed as he too realised they were going to live.

Princeps Turnet slid back into his command chair and began bringing the Titan's systems back on line. Cassar slid back into his own chair, the leather soaking wet where his sweat had collected. He saw the readouts of the external surveyors come to life as the princeps once again opened their systems to the outside world.

'Systems check,' ordered Turnet.

Aruken nodded, mopping his sweat-streaked brow with his sleeve. 'Weapons fine, though we'll need to watch our rate of fire, since they're already pretty hot.'

'Confirmed,' said Cassar. 'We won't be able to fire the plasma weapons any time soon either. We'll probably blow our arm off if we try.'

'Understood,' said Turnet. 'Initiate emergency coolant procedures. I want those guns ready to fire as soon as possible.'

Cassar nodded, though he was unsure as to the cause of the princeps's urgency. Surely there could be nothing out there that would have survived the firestorm? Certainly nothing that could threaten a Titan.

'Incoming!' called Aruken, and Cassar looked up to see a flock of black specks descending rapidly through the crystal sky, flying low towards the blackened ruins of the burned city.

'Aruken, track them,' snapped Turnet.

'Gunships,' said Aruken. 'They're heading for the centre of the city, what's left of the palace.'

'Whose are they?'

'Can't tell yet.'

Cassar sat back in the cockpit seat and let the filaments of the Titan's command systems come to the fore of his mind once again. He engaged the Titan's targeting systems and his vision plunged into the target reticule, zooming in on the formation of gunships disappearing among the crumbling, fire-blackened ruins of the Choral City. He saw bone-white colours trimmed with blue and the symbol of fanged jaws closing over a planet.

'World Eaters,' he said out loud. 'They're the World Eaters. It must be the second wave.'

'There is no second wave,' said Turnet, as if to himself. 'Aruken, get the vox-mast up and connect me to the *Vengeful Spirit*.'

'Fleet command?' asked Aruken.

'No,' said Turnet, 'the Warmaster.'

Iacton Qruze led them through the corridors of the *Vengeful Spirit*, past the Training Halls, past the Lupercal's Court and down through twisting passageways none of them had traversed before, even when they had been hiding from Maggard and Maloghurst.

Sindermann's heart beat a rapid tattoo on his ribs, and he felt a curious mix of elation and sorrow fill him as he realised what Qruze had saved them from. There could be little doubt as to what must have happened to those remembrancers in the audience chamber and the thought of so many wonderful creative people sacrificed to serve the interests of those with no understanding of art or the creative process galled him and saddened him in equal measure.

He glanced at Euphrati Keeler, who appeared to have become stronger since their escape from death. Her hair was golden and her eyes bright, and though her skin was still pallid, it only served to highlight the power within her.

Mersadie Oliton, by contrast, was visibly weakening.

'They will come after us soon,' said Keeler, 'if they are not already.'

'Can we escape?' Mersadie asked, hoarsely.

Qruze only shrugged. 'We will or we won't.'

'Then this is it?' asked Sindermann.

Keeler shot him an amused glance. 'No, you should know better than that, Kyril. It is never "it", not for a believer. There's always more, something to look forward to when it's all over.'

They passed a number of observation domes that looked out into the cold void of space, the sight only serving to remind Sindermann of just how tiny they were in the context of the galaxy. Even the faintest speck of light that he could see was actually a star, perhaps surrounded by its own worlds, its own people and entire civilisations.

'How is it that we find ourselves at the centre of such momentous events and yet we never saw them coming?' he whispered.

After a while, Sindermann began to recognise his surroundings, seeing familiar signs scraped into bulkheads, and insignia he recognised, telling him that they were approaching the embarkation decks. Qruze led the way unerringly, his stride sure and confident, a far cry from the wretched sycophant he had heard described.

The blast doors to the embarkation deck were closed, the tattered remnants of the votive papers and offerings made to the Warmaster when his sons took him to the Delphos still fixed to the surrounding structure.

'In here,' said Qruze. 'If we're lucky, there will be a gunship we can take.'

'And go where?' demanded Mersadie. 'Where can we go that the Warmaster won't find us?'

Keeler reached out and placed her hand on Mersadie's arm. 'Don't worry. We have more friends than you know, Sadie. The Emperor will show me the way.'

The doors rumbled open and Qruze marched confidently onto the embarkation deck. Sindermann smiled in relief when the warrior said, 'There. Thunderhawk Nine Delta.'

But the smile fell from his face as he saw the gold-armoured form of Maggard standing before the machine.

Saul Tarvitz watched the look of utter disbelief on Captain Ehrlen's face as he took in the scale of the destruction wrought by the firestorm. Nothing remained of the Choral City as they had known it. Every scrap of living tissue was gone, burned to atoms by the flames that roared and howled in the wake of the virus attack.

Every building was black, burned and collapsed so that Isst-van III resembled a vision of hell, its tumbled buildings still ablaze as the last combustible materials burned away. Tall plumes of fire poured skyward in defiance of gravity, fuel lines and refineries that would continue to burn until their reserves were exhausted. The stench of scorched metal and meat was pungent and the vista before them was unrecognisable as that which they had fought across only minutes before.

'Why?' was all Ehrlen could ask.

'I don't know,' said Tarvitz, wishing he had more to tell the World Eater.

'This wasn't the Isstvanians, was it?' asked Ehrlen.

Tarvitz wanted to lie, but he knew that the World Eater would see through him instantly.

'No,' he said. 'It wasn't.'

'We are betrayed?'

Tarvitz nodded.

'Why?' repeated Ehrlen.

'I have no answers for you, brother, but if they hoped to kill us all in one fell swoop, then they have failed.'

'And the World Eaters will make them pay for that failure,' swore Ehrlen, as a new sound rose over the crackle of burning buildings and tumbling masonry.

Tarvitz heard it too and looked up in time to see a flock of World Eaters gunships streaking towards their position from the outskirts of the city. Gunfire came down in a burning spray, punching through the ruins around them, boring holes in the black marble of the ground.

'Hold!' shouted Ehrlen.

Heavy fire thudded down among the World Eaters as the gunships roared overhead. Tarvitz crouched at a smashed window opening beside Ehrlen, hearing one of the World Eaters grunt in pain as a shell found its mark.

The gunships passed and soared up into the sky, looping around above the shattered palace before angling down for another run.

'Heavy weapons! Get some fire up there!' yelled Ehrlen.

Gunfire stuttered up from the gaps in partially collapsed roofs, chattering heavy bolters and the occasional ruby flare of a lascannon blast. Tarvitz ducked back from the window as return fire thundered down, stitching lines of explosions through the World Eaters. More of them fell, blown off their feet or blasted apart.

One World Eater slumped down beside Tarvitz, the back of his head a pulsing red mass.

The gunships banked, spraying fire down at their position.

Tarvitz could see the World Eaters zeroing in on them as they flew back towards their position. Return fire lanced upwards and one gunship fell, its engine spewing flames, to smash to pieces against a burning ruin.

Tarvitz could see dozens of gunships, surely the whole of the World Eaters arsenal.

The lead Thunderhawk dropped through the ruins, hovering a few metres above the ground with its assault ramp down and bolter fire sparking around the opening.

Ehrlen turned towards Tarvitz.

'This isn't your fight,' he yelled over the gunfire. 'Get out of here!'

'Emperor's Children never run!' replied Tarvitz, drawing his sword.

'They do from this!'

No Space Marine could have survived the storm of fire that blazed away at the interior of the gunship, but it was no ordinary Space Marine that was borne within it.

With a roar like a hunting animal, Angron leapt from the gunship and landed with a terrible crash in the midst of the ruined city.

He was a monster of legend, huge and terrible. The primarch's hideous face was twisted in hatred, his huge chainaxes battered and stained with decades of bloodshed. As the mighty primarch landed, World Eaters dropped from the other gunships.

Thousands of World Eaters loyal to the Warmaster followed their primarch into the Choral City, accompanied by the war cries that echoed Angron's own bestial howl as he charged into his former brethren.

Horus put his fist through the pict screen that showed the transmission from the *Dies Irae*. The image of the World Eaters gunships splintered under the assault as his anger at Angron's defiance boiled over. One of his allies – no, one of his subordinates – had disobeyed his direct order.

Aximand, Abaddon, Erebus and Maloghurst eyed him warily and Horus could imagine their trepidation at the news of Angron's impetuous attack on the survivors of the virus bombing.

That there were survivors at all was galling, but Angron's actions put a whole new spin on the Isstvan campaign.

'And yet,' he said, choking back his rage, 'I am surprised at this.'

'Warmaster,' said Aximand, 'what do you–'

'Angron is a killer!' snapped Horus, rounding on his Mournival son. 'He solves every problem with raw violence. He attacks first and thinks later, if he thinks at all. And yet I never saw this! What else would he do when he saw the survivors of his Legion in the Choral City? Would he sit back and watch the rest of the fleet bombard them from orbit? Never! And yet I did nothing!'

Horus glanced at the smashed remains of the pict-display. 'I will never be caught out like this again. There will be no twists of fate I do not see coming.'

'The questions remains,' said Aximand. 'What shall we do about Angron?'

'Destroy him with the rest of the city,' said Abaddon without a pause. 'If he cannot be trusted to obey his Warmaster then he is a liability.'

'The World Eaters are an exceptionally effective weapon of terror,' retorted Aximand. 'Why destroy them when they can wreak so much havoc among those loyal to the Emperor?'

'There are always more soldiers,' said Abaddon. 'Many will beg to join the Warmaster. There is no room for those who can't follow orders.'

'Angron is a killer, yes, but he is predictable,' put in Erebus, and Horus bristled at the implicit insult in the First Chaplain's words. 'He can be kept obedient by letting him off the leash every now and again.'

'The Word Bearers may live by treachery and lies,' snarled Abaddon, 'but in the Sons of Horus you are loyal or you are dead!'

'What do you know of my Legion?' asked Erebus, rising to meet the First Captain's ire, his mask of smirking calm slipping. 'I know secrets that would destroy your mind! How dare you speak to me of deceit? This, this reality, all you know, this is the lie!'

'Erebus!' roared Horus, ending the confrontation instantly. 'This is not the place to evangelise your Legion. I have made my decision and these are wasted words.'

'Then Angron will be destroyed in the bombardment?' asked Maloghurst.

'No,' replied Horus. 'He will not.'

'But Warmaster, even if Angron prevails he could be down there for weeks,' said Aximand.

'And he will not fight alone. Do you know, my sons, why the Emperor appointed me Warmaster?'

'Because you were his favoured son,' replied Maloghurst. 'You are the greatest warrior and tactician of the Great Crusade. Whole worlds have fallen at the mention of your name.'

'I did not ask for flattery,' snarled Horus.

'Because you never lose,' said Abaddon levelly.

'I never lose,' nodded Horus, glaring between the four Astartes, 'because I see only victory. I have never seen a situation that cannot be turned into triumph, no disadvantage that cannot be turned to an advantage. *That* is why I was made Warmaster. On Davin I fell, yet came through that ordeal stronger. Against the Auretian Technocracy we faced dissent from within our own fleet, so I used the conflict to rid us of those fomenting rebellion. There is no failing I cannot turn to a component in my victories. Angron has decided to turn Isstvan Three into a ground assault – I can consider this a failure and limit its impact by bombing Angron and his World Eaters into dust along with the rest of the planet, or I can forge a triumph from it that will send echoes far into the future.'

Maloghurst broke the silence that followed. 'What would you have us do, Warmaster?'

'Inform the other Legions that they are to prepare for a full assault on the loyalists in the Choral City. Ezekyle, assemble the Legion. Have them ready to launch the attack in two hours.'

'I shall be proud to lead my Legion,' said Abaddon.

'You will not lead them. That honour will go to Sedirae and Targhost.'

Anger flared in Abaddon. 'But I am the First Captain. This battle, where resolve and brutality are qualities required for victory, is tailor-made for me!'

'You are a captain of the Mournival, Ezekyle,' said Horus. 'I have another role in mind for you and Little Horus in this fight. One I feel sure you will relish.'

'Yes, Warmaster,' said Abaddon, the frustration disappearing from his face.

'As for you, Erebus…'

'Warmaster?'

'Stay out of our way. To your duties, Sons of Horus.'

THIRTEEN

Maggard
Factions
Luna Wolves

Princeps Turnet listened intently as the orders came through, though Cassar couldn't hear the orders piped into the princeps's ear and he didn't want to – it was all he could do to keep from vomiting. Every time he let his mind wander outside the systems of the *Dies Irae*, he saw nothing but the tangles of charred ruins. His consciousness retreated within the machine, pulling his perception back into the massive form of the Titan.

The *Dies Irae* was coming back to life around him; he could sense the god-machine's limbs flood with power and could feel the weapons reloading. The plasma reactor at its heart was beating in time with his own, a ball of nuclear flame that burned with the Emperor's own righteous strength.

Even here, among all this death and horror, the Emperor was with him. The god-machine was the instrument of His will, standing firm among the destruction. That thought comforted Cassar and helped him focus. If the Emperor was here, then the Emperor would protect.

'Orders in from the *Vengeful Spirit*,' said Turnet briskly. 'Moderati, open fire.'

'Open fire?' said Aruken. 'Sir? The Isstvanians are gone. They're dead.'

To Cassar, Aruken's voice sounded distant, for he was

subsumed in the systems of the Titan, but he heard Turnet's voice as clearly as if he had spoken in his own ear.

'Not at the Isstvanians,' replied Turnet, 'at the Death Guard.'

'Princeps?' said Aruken. 'Fire on the Death Guard?'

'I am not in the habit of repeating my orders, moderati,' replied Turnet, 'and they are to fire on the Death Guard. They have defied the Warmaster.'

Cassar froze. As if there wasn't enough death on Isstvan III, now the *Dies Irae* was to fire on the Death Guard, the very force they had been sent to support.

'Sir,' he said. 'This doesn't make any sense.'

'It doesn't need to!' shouted Turnet, his patience finally at an end. 'Just do as I order.'

Looking straight into Turnet's eyes, the truth hit Titus Cassar as though the Emperor had reached out from Terra and filled him with the light of truth.

'The Isstvanians didn't do this, did they?' he asked. 'The Warmaster did.'

Turnet's face creased in a slow smile and Cassar saw his hand reaching towards his holstered sidearm.

Cassar didn't give him the chance to get there first and snatched for his own autopistol.

Both men drew their pistols and fired.

Maggard took a step forwards, drawing his golden Kirlian blade and unholstering his pistol. His bulk was even more massive than Sindermann remembered, grossly swollen to proportions beyond human and more reminiscent of an Astartes. Had that been Maggard's reward for his services to the Warmaster?

Without wasting words of preamble, Qruze raised his bolter and fired, but Maggard's armour was the equal of Astartes plate and the shot simply signalled the beginning of a duel.

Sindermann and Mersadie ducked as Maggard's pistol spat fire, the noise appalling as the two warriors ran towards one another with their guns blazing.

Keeler watched calmly as Maggard's gunfire blew chunks from Qruze's armour, but before he could fire any more, Qruze was upon him.

Qruze smashed his fist into Maggard's midriff, but the silent killer rode the punch and swung his sword for the Astartes's head. Qruze ducked back from the great slash of Maggard's sword, the blade slicing though the armour at the Astartes warrior's stomach.

Blood sprayed briefly from the wound and Qruze dropped

to his knees in sudden pain before drawing his combat knife, the blade as long as a mortal warrior's sword.

Maggard leapt towards him and his sword hacked a deep gouge in Qruze's side. Yet more blood spilled from the venerable Astartes's body. Another killing strike slashed towards Qruze, but this time combat knife and Kirlian blade met in a shower of fiery sparks. Qruze recovered first and stabbed his blade through the gap between Maggard's greaves. The assassin stumbled backwards and Qruze rose unsteadily to his feet.

The assassin stepped in close and lunged with his sword. Maggard was almost the equal of Qruze in physique and had youth on his side, but even Sindermann could see he was slower, as if his new form was unfamiliar, not yet worn in.

Qruze sidestepped a huge arcing strike of Maggard's sword and swung inside his opponent's defence, reaching around to lock his head in the crook of his elbow.

His other arm snapped round to plunge the knife into Maggard's throat, but a fist seized Qruze's hand in an iron grip, halting the blade inches from the man's pulsing jugular.

Qruze fought to force the blade upwards, but Maggard's newly enhanced strength was the greater and he began to force the blade to one side. Beads of sweat popped on Qruze's face, and Sindermann knew that this was a struggle he could not win alone.

He pushed himself to his feet and ran towards Maggard's fallen pistol, its matt black finish cold and lethal-looking. Though designed for a mortal grip, the pistol still felt absurdly huge in his hands.

Sindermann held the heavy pistol outstretched and marched towards the struggling warriors. He couldn't risk a shot from any kind of distance, he was no marksman and was as likely to hit their deliverer as their killer.

He walked up to the fight and placed the muzzle of the pistol directly on the bleeding wound where Qruze had stabbed Maggard. He pulled the trigger and the recoil of the shot almost shattered his wrist, but the effect of his intervention more than made up for the trauma.

Maggard opened his mouth in a silent scream and his entire body flinched in sudden agony. Maggard's grip on the knife weakened and, with a roar of anger, Qruze punched it into the base of his opponent's jaw and through the roof of his mouth.

Maggard buckled and fell to the side with the force of a falling tree. The golden armoured assassin and the Astartes rolled and Qruze was on top of his enemy, still gripping the knife.

Face to face for a moment, Maggard spat a mouthful of blood into Qruze's face. Qruze pushed the knife deeper into Maggard's jaw, plunging it into his opponent's brain.

Maggard spasmed, his huge bulk thrashing briefly, and when he stopped Qruze was looking into a pair of blank, dead eyes.

Qruze pushed himself from Maggard's body.

'Face to face,' said Qruze, breathing heavily with the exertion of killing Maggard. 'Not with treachery, from a thousand miles up. Face to face.'

He looked at Sindermann and nodded his thanks. The warrior was wounded and exhausted, but there was a calm serenity to him.

'I remember how it used to be,' he said. 'We were brothers on Cthonia. Not just among ourselves, but with our enemies, too. That was what the Emperor saw in us when he came to the hives. We were gangs of killers as existed on a thousand other worlds, but we believed in a code that was more precious than life. That was what he wrought into the Luna Wolves. I thought that even if none of the rest of us remembered, the Warmaster would, because he was the one the Emperor chose to lead us.'

'No,' said Keeler, 'you are the last one.'

'And when I realised that I just… told them what they wanted to hear. I tried to be one of them, and I succeeded. I almost forgot everything, until… until now.'

'The music of the spheres,' said Sindermann quietly.

Qruze's eyes focused again on Keeler and his face hardened.

'I did nothing, Half-heard,' said Keeler, answering his unasked question. 'You said so yourself. The ways of Cthonia were the reason the Emperor chose you and your brothers for the Luna Wolves. Perhaps it was the Emperor who reminded you.'

'I saw this coming for so long, but I let it, because I thought that was my code now, but nothing changed, not really. The enemy just moved from out there to amongst us.'

'Look, as profound as this all is, can we get the hell out of here?' asked Mersadie.

Qruze nodded and beckoned them towards the Thunderhawk gunship. 'You're right, Miss Oliton, let's get off this ship. It is dead to me now.'

'We're with you, captain,' said Sindermann as he gingerly picked his way over Maggard's body after Qruze. The years seemed to have dropped from him, as if the energy lost in the fight was returning with interest. Sindermann saw a light in his eyes he hadn't seen before.

Watching the light of understanding rekindled in Iacton Qruze reminded Sindermann that there was still hope.

And there was nothing so dangerous in the galaxy as a little hope.

Turnet's shot went high, and Cassar's went wide. Jonah Aruken ducked for cover as the rounds ricocheted on the curved ceiling of the bridge. Turnet rolled down behind the command chair as Cassar pulled himself from his own chair, set deep into the cockpit floor and level with the Titan's eye. Cassar fired again and sparks showered as the autopistol round hit the electronics arrayed around Turnet's chair.

Turnet fired back and Cassar dropped into the cover of the depression formed by his own seat. The connectors had torn free from his scalp as he moved and tears of blood streaked his face, metallic monofilament wires clinging wetly to the back of his neck.

His mind throbbed with the suddenness of being ripped away from the god-machine.

'Titus!' yelled Aruken. 'What are you doing?'

'Moderati, surrender or you will die here!' shouted Turnet. 'Throw down your weapon and surrender.'

'This is treachery!' shouted Cassar. 'Jonah, you know I am right. The Warmaster did this. He brought death to this city to kill the believers!'

Turnet fired blindly from behind the elaborate machinery of the command seat. 'Believe? You would betray your Warmaster because of this religion? You're diseased, do you know that? Religion is a sickness, and I should have put you down a long time ago.'

Cassar thought rapidly. There was only one way out of the cockpit – the doorway that led into the Titan's dorsal cavity where the plasma generator was located along with the detail of engineer crewmen who operated it. He couldn't run, for fear of Turnet shooting him dead as he broke from cover.

But the same was true of Turnet.

They were both trapped.

'You knew,' said Cassar, 'about the bombardment.'

'Of course I knew. How can you be so ignorant? Don't you even know what's happening on this planet?'

'The Emperor is being betrayed,' said Cassar.

'There is no Emperor,' shouted Turnet. 'He abandoned us. He left the Imperium that men died to conquer for him. He doesn't care. But the Warmaster cares. He conquered this galaxy and it is his to rule, but there are fools who don't understand that. They are the ones who have forced the Warmaster into this so that he can do what must be done.'

Cassar's mind reeled. Turnet had betrayed everything the Emperor had built, and the combat within the command bridge struck Cassar as representative of what was happening in the wider conflict.

Turnet rose and fired wildly as he ran for the door, both shots smacking into the bridge wall behind Cassar.

'I won't let you do this!' yelled Cassar, returning fire. His first shot went wide, but now Princeps Turnet was struggling with the wheel lock of the door.

Cassar lined up his shot on Turnet's back.

'Titus! Don't do it!' shouted Aruken, wrenching the Titan's primary motor controls around. The Titan lurched madly, the whole bridge tipping like the deck of a ship in a storm. Cassar was thrown back against the wall, the opportunity to take his shot gone. Turnet hauled the door open, throwing himself from the Titan's bridge and out of Cassar's firing line.

Cassar scrambled to his feet again as the Titan rocked upright. A shape moved in front of him and he almost fired before realising it was Jonah Aruken.

'Titus, come on,' said Aruken. 'Don't do this.'

'I don't have a choice. This is treachery.'

'You don't have to die.'

Cassar jerked his head towards the Titan's eye, through which they could still see the Death Guard moving through the death-slicked trenches. 'Neither do they. You know I am right, Aruken. You know the Warmaster has betrayed the Imperium. If we have the *Dies Irae* then we can do something about it.'

Aruken looked from Cassar's face to the gun in his hand. 'It's over, Cassar. Just… just give this up.'

'With me or against me, Jonah,' said Cassar levelly. 'The Emperor's faithful or His enemy? Your choice.'

It had often been said that a Space Marine knew no fear.

Such a statement was not literally true, a Space Marine *could* know fear, but he had the training and discipline to deal with it and not let it affect him in battle. Captain Saul Tarvitz was no exception, he had faced storms of gunfire and monstrous aliens and even glimpsed the insane predators of the warp, but when Angron charged, he ran.

The primarch smashed through the ruins like a juggernaut. He bellowed insanely and with one sweep of his chainaxe carved two loyal World Eaters in two, bringing his off-hand axe down to bite through the torso of a third. His traitor World Eaters dived over the rubble, blasting with pistols or stabbing with chainblades.

'Die!' bellowed Captain Ehrlen as the loyalists counter-charged, throwing themselves into the enemy as one. Tarvitz was used to Astartes who fought in feints and counter-charges, overlapping fields of fire, picking the enemy apart or sweeping through his ranks with grace and precision. The World Eaters did not fight with the perfection of the Emperor's Children. They fought with anger and hatred, with brutality and the lust for destruction.

And they fought with more hatred than ever before against their own, against the battle-brothers they had warred along-side for years.

Tarvitz scrambled back from the carnage. World Eaters shoul-dered past him as they charged at Angron, but the butchered bodies lying around showed what fate awaited them. Tarvitz put his shoulder down and hammered through a ruined wall, sprawling into a courtyard where statues stood scarred and beheaded by the day's earlier battles.

He glanced behind him. Thousands of World Eaters were locked in a terrible hurricane of carnage, scrambling to get at one another. At the centre of the bloody hurricane was Angron, massive and terrible as he laid about him with his axes.

Captain Ehrlen crashed down a short distance from him and the World Eater's eyes flickered over Tarvitz before he rolled onto his back and pulled himself to his feet. Ehrlen's face was torn open, a red mask of blood with his eyes the only recognisable feature. A pack of World Eaters descended on him, piling him to the ground and working at him as though they were carv-ing up a side of meat.

Volleys of bolter shots thudded through the walls and the battle spilled into the courtyard, World Eaters wrestling with one another and forcing bolters up to fire point blank or dis-embowelling their battle-brothers with chainaxes. Tarvitz kicked himself to his feet and ran as a wall collapsed and a dozen trai-tors surged forward.

He threw himself behind a pillar, bolt shells blasting chunks of marble from it in concussive impacts. The sound of battle followed him and Tarvitz knew that he had to try and find the Emperor's Children. Only with his fellow warriors alongside him could he impose some form of order on this chaotic fight.

Tarvitz ran, realising that gunfire was directed at him from all angles. He charged through the ruins of a grand dining hall and into a cavernous stone-walled kitchen.

He kept running and smashed his way through the ruins until he found himself in the streets of the Choral City. A burning gunship streaked overhead and crashed into a building in an orange plume of flame as gunfire stuttered throughout the ruins he had just vacated and Angron's roaring cut through the din of battle.

The magnificent dome of the Precentor's Palace rose above the battle unfolding across the blackened remains of the city.

As Tarvitz made his way through the carnage towards his beloved Emperor's Children, he promised that if he was to meet his death on this blasted world, then he would meet it amongst his battle-brothers, and in death defy the hatred the Warmaster had sown amongst them.

Loken watched the Sons of Horus landing on the far side of the Sirenhold. His Space Marines – he couldn't think of them as 'Sons of Horus' any more – were arrayed around the closest tomb-spire in a formidable defensive formation.

His heavy weapons commanded the valley of shrines through which attackers would have to advance and the Tactical Marines held hard points of ruins where they would fight on their own terms.

But the enemy was not the Isstvanian army, they were his brothers.

'I thought they'd bomb us,' said Torgaddon.

'They should have done,' replied Loken. 'Something went wrong.'

'It'll be Abaddon,' said Torgaddon. 'He must have been itching for a chance to take us on face to face. Horus couldn't have held him back.'

'Or Sedirae,' echoed Loken, distaste in his voice. The afternoon sun hung in veils between the shadows cast by the walls and the tomb-spires.

'I never thought it would end like this, Tarik,' said Loken. 'Maybe storming some alien citadel or defending... defending Terra, like something from the epic poems, something romantic, something the remembrancers could get their teeth into. I never thought it could end defending a hole like this against my own battle-brothers.'

'Yes, but then you always were an idealist.'

The Sons of Horus were coming down on the far side of the tomb-spire across the valley, the optimal point to strike from, and Loken knew that this would be the hardest battle he would ever have to fight.

'We don't have to die here,' said Torgaddon.

Loken looked at him. 'I know, we can win. We can throw everything we have at them. I'll lead them in from the front and then there's a chance that–'

'No,' said Torgaddon. 'I mean we don't have to hold them *here*. We know we can get through the main gates into the city. If we strike for the Precentor's Palace we could link up with the Emperor's Children or the World Eaters. Lucius said the warning came from Saul Tarvitz so they know we are betrayed.'

'Saul Tarvitz is on Isstvan Three?' asked Loken, sudden hope flaring in his heart.

'Apparently so,' nodded Torgaddon. 'We could help them. Fortify the palace.'

Loken looked back across at the tangle of shrines and tomb-spires. 'You would retreat?'

'I would when there's no chance of victory and we can fight on better terms elsewhere.'

'We'll never have another chance to face them on our own terms, Tarik. The Choral City is gone, this whole damn planet is dead. It's about punishing them for their betrayal and the brothers we have lost.'

'We all lost brothers here, Garvi, but dying needlessly won't bring them back. I will have my vengeance, too, but I'm not throwing away the few warriors I have left in a knee jerk act of defiance. Think about this, Loken. Really think, about why you want to fight them here.'

Loken could hear the first bursts of gunfire and knew Torgaddon was right. They were still the best trained, most disciplined of the Legions and he knew that if he wanted to fight those who had betrayed him, he had to fight with his head and not his heart.

'You're right, Tarik,' said Loken. 'We should link up with Tarvitz. We need to get organised to launch a counter-attack.'

'We can really make them suffer, Garvi, we can force them into a battle and delay them. If Tarvitz got the warning out here, who's to say that there aren't others carrying a warning to Terra? Maybe the other Legions already know what's happened. Someone underestimated us, they thought this would be a massacre, but we'll go one better. We'll turn Isstvan Three into a war.'

'Do you think we can?'

'We're the Luna Wolves, Garvi. We can do anything.'

Loken took his friend's hand, accepting the truth of his words. He turned to the squads arrayed behind him, scanning the valley through their gunsights.

'Astartes!' he shouted. 'You all know what has happened and I share your pain and outrage, but I need you to focus on what we must now do and not let passion blind you to the cold facts of war. Bonds of brotherhood have been shattered and we are no longer the Sons of Horus, that name has no meaning for us now. We are once again the Luna Wolves, soldiers of the Emperor!'

A deafening cheer greeted his words as Loken continued, 'We are giving the enemy this position and will break through the gates to strike for the palace. Captain Torgaddon and I will take the assault units and lead the speartip.'

Within moments, the newly re-christened Luna Wolves were ready to move out, Torgaddon barking orders to put the assault squads up front. Loken gathered a body of warriors to him, forming a pocket of resistance in the shadow of the tomb-spire.

'Kill for the living and kill for the dead,' said Torgaddon as they prepared to move out.

'Kill for the living,' replied Loken as the speartip, numbering perhaps two thousand Luna Wolves, moved out across the tomb-scape of the Sirenhold towards the massive gates.

Loken turned back to the valley, seeing the shapes of Sons of Horus moving towards him. Larger, darker shapes loomed in the distance, grinding the battle-scarred shrines and statues to dust as they went: Rhino APCs, lumbering Land Raiders, and even the barrel-shaped silhouette of a Dreadnought.

He felt he should be filled with sadness at the tragedy of fighting his brothers, but there was no sadness.

There was only hatred.

Aruken's eyes were hollow and he was sweating. Cassar was shocked to see his normal, cocky arrogance replaced by fear. Despite that fear, Cassar knew that he could not fully trust Jonah Aruken.

'This has to end, Titus,' said Aruken. 'You don't want to be a martyr do you?'

'Martyr? That's a strange choice of words for someone who claims not to believe.'

A small smile appeared on Aruken's face. 'I'm not as stupid as you think, Titus. You're a good man and a damn good crew-man. You *believe* in things, which is more than most people can manage. So, I'd rather you didn't die.'

Cassar didn't respond to Aruken's forced levity. '*Please*, I know you're just saying that for the princeps's benefit. I've no doubt he can hear every word.'

'Probably, yes, but he knows that as soon as he opens that

door you'll blow his head off. So I guess you and I can just say what we damn well like.'

Cassar's grip on the gun relaxed. 'You're not in his pocket?'

'Hey, we've been through some scary shit recently, haven't we?' said Aruken. 'I know what you're going through.'

Cassar shook his head. 'No you don't, and I know what you're trying to do. I can't back down, I'm making a stand in the name of my Emperor. I won't just surrender.'

'Look, Titus, if you believe then you believe, but you don't have to prove that to anyone.'

'You think I'm doing this for show?' asked Cassar, aiming his gun at Aruken's throat.

Aruken held out his hands and walked carefully around the princeps's command chair to stand across the bridge from him.

'The Emperor isn't just a figurehead to cling to,' said Cassar. 'He is a god. He has a saint and miracles and I have seen them. And so have you! Think of all you have seen and you'll realise you have to help me, Jonah!'

'I saw some odd things, Titus, but–'

'Don't deny them,' interrupted Cassar. 'They happened. As sure as you and I are standing in this war machine. Jonah, there is an Emperor and He is watching over us. He judges us by the choices we make when those choices are hard. The Warmaster has betrayed us and if I stand back and let it happen then I am betraying my Emperor. There are principles that must be defended, Aruken. Don't you even see that much? If none of us take a stand, then the Warmaster will win and there won't even be the memory of this betrayal.'

Aruken shook his head in frustration. 'Cassar, if I could just make you see–'

'You're trying to tell me you haven't seen anything to believe in?' asked Cassar, turning away in disappointment. He looked through the scorched panes of the viewing bay at the assembling Death Guard.

'Titus, I haven't believed in anything for a long time,' said Aruken. 'For that I'm truly sorry, and I'm sorry for this too.'

Cassar turned to see that Jonah Aruken had drawn his pistol and had it aimed squarely at his chest.

'Jonah?' said Cassar. 'You would betray me? After all we have seen?'

'There's only one thing I want, Titus, and that's command of my own Titan. One day I want to be Princeps Aruken and that's not going to happen if I let you do this.'

Cassar said, 'To know that this whole galaxy is starved of belief

and to think that you might be the only one who believes...
and yet to still believe in spite of all that. That is faith, Aruken.
I wish that you could understand that.'

'It's too late for that, Titus,' said Aruken. 'I'm sorry.'

Aruken's gun barked three times, filling the bridge with bursts
of light and noise.

Tarvitz could see the battle from the shadow of an entrance arch
leading into the Precentor's Palace. He had escaped the cyclone
of carnage that Angron had slaughtered into life, to link up with
his own warriors in the palace, but the sight of the World Eaters primarch was still a vivid red horror in his mind.

Tarvitz glanced back into the palace, its vaulted hallways
strewn with the bodies of the dead palace guard darkening as
late afternoon turned the shadows long and dim. Soon it would
be night.

'Lucius,' voxed Tarvitz, static howling. 'Lucius, come in.'

'Saul, what do you see?'

'Gunships and drop pods too, our colours, landing just north
of here.'

'Has the primarch blessed us with his presence?'

'Looks like Eidolon,' said Tarvitz with relish. The vox was heavy
with static and he knew that the Warmaster's forces would be
attempting to jam their vox-channels without blocking their
own.

'Listen, Lucius, Angron is going to break through here. The
loyal World Eaters down there won't be able to hold him. He's
going to head for the palace.'

'Then there will be a battle,' deadpanned Lucius. 'I hope
Angron makes it a good fight. I think I might have found a
decent fencing opponent at last.'

'You're welcome to him. We need to make this stand count.
Start barricading the central dome. We'll move to fortifying the
main domes and junctions if Angron gives us that long.'

'Since when did you become the leader here?' asked Lucius
petulantly. 'I was the one who killed Vardus Praal.'

Tarvitz felt his anger rise at his friend's childishness at such
a volatile time, but bit back his anger to say, 'Get in there and
help man the barricades. We don't have long before we'll be
in the thick of it.'

The Thunderhawk sped away from the *Vengeful Spirit*, gathering speed as Qruze kicked in the afterburners. Mersadie felt
unutterably light-headed to be off the Warmaster's ship at last,

but the cold realisation that they had nowhere to go sobered her as she saw glinting specks of the fleet all around them.

'Now what?' asked Qruze. 'We're away, but where to next?'

'I told you we were not without friends, did I not, Iacton?' said Euphrati, sitting in the co-pilot's chair beside the Astartes warrior.

The warrior gave her a brief sideways look. 'Be that as it may, remembrancer. Friends do us little good if we die out here.'

'But what a death it would be,' said Keeler, with the trace of a ghostly smile.

Sindermann shared a worried glance with her, no doubt wondering if they had overreached themselves in trusting that Euphrati could deliver them to safety out in the dark of space. The old man looked tiny and feeble and she took his hand in hers.

Through the viewshield, Mersadie could see a field of glittering lights: starships belonging to the 63rd Expedition, and every one of them hostile.

As if to contradict her, Euphrati pointed upwards through the viewshield towards the belly of an ugly vessel they would pass beneath if they continued on their current course. The weak sun of Isstvan glinted from its unpainted gunmetal hull.

'Head towards that one,' commanded Euphrati and Mersadie was surprised to see Qruze turn the controls without a word of protest.

Mersadie didn't know a great deal about spacecraft but she knew that the cruiser would be bristling with turrets that could pick off the Thunderhawk as it shot past, and could maybe even deploy fighters.

'Why are we getting closer?' she asked hurriedly. 'Surely we want to head away?'

'Trust me, Sadie,' said Euphrati. 'This is the way it has to be.'

At least it will be quick, she thought, as the vessel grew larger in the viewshield.

'It's Death Guard,' said Qruze,

Mersadie bit her lip and glanced at Sindermann.

The old man looked calm and said, 'Quite the adventure, eh?'

Mersadie smiled in spite of herself.

'What are we going to do, Kyril?' asked Mersadie, tears springing from her eyes. 'What do we have left to us?'

'This is still our fight, Mersadie,' said Euphrati, turning from the viewshield. 'Sometimes that fight must be open warfare, sometimes it must be fought with words and ideas. We all have our parts to play.'

Mersadie let out a breath, unable and unwilling to believe that there were allies in the cruiser looming in front of them.

'We are not alone,' smiled Euphrati.

'But this fight... it feels a lot bigger than me.'

'You are wrong. Each of us has as much right to have their say in the fate of the galaxy as the Warmaster. Believing that is how we will defeat him.'

Mersadie nodded and watched the cruiser above them drawing ever nearer, its long, dark shape edged in starlight and its engines wreathed in clouds of crystalline gases.

'Thunderhawk gunship, identify yourself,' said a gruff, gravel-laden voice crackling from the vox-caster.

'Be truthful,' warned Euphrati. 'All depends on it.'

Qruze nodded and said, 'My name is Iacton Qruze, formerly of the Sons of Horus.'

'Formerly?' came the reply.

'Yes, formerly,' said Qruze.

'Explain yourself.'

'I am no longer part of the Legion,' said Qruze, and Mersadie could hear the pain it caused him to give voice to these words. 'I can no longer be party to what the Warmaster is doing.'

After a long pause, the voice returned. 'Then you are welcome on my ship, Iacton Qruze.'

'And who are you?' asked Qruze.

'I am Captain Nathaniel Garro of the *Eisenstein*.'

PART THREE
BROTHERS

FOURTEEN

Until it's over
Charmoisan
Betrayal

'I've lost count of the days,' said Loken, crouching by one of the makeshift battlements that looked over the smouldering ruins of the Choral City.

'I don't think Isstvan Three has days and nights any more,' replied Saul Tarvitz.

Loken looked into the steel grey sky, a mantle of cloud kicked up by the catastrophic climate change forced on Isstvan III by the sudden extinction of almost all life on its surface. A thin drizzle of ash rained, the remains of the firestorm swept up by dry, dead winds a continent away.

'They're massing for another attack,' said Tarvitz, indicating the tangle of twisted, ash-wreathed rubble that had once been a vast mass of tenement blocks to the east of the palace.

Loken followed his gaze. He could just glimpse a flash of dirty white armour.

'World Eaters.'

'Who else?'

'I don't know if Angron even knows another way to fight.'

Tarvitz shrugged. 'He probably does. He just likes his way better.'

Tarvitz and Loken had first met on Murder, where the Sons of Horus had fought alongside the Emperor's Children against hideous megarachnid aliens. Tarvitz had been a fine warrior,

devoid of the grandstanding of his Legion that had so antago-
nised Torgaddon.

Loken barely remembered the journey back through the
Sirenhold, scrambling through shattered tombs and burning
ruins. He remembered fighting through men he had once called
brother towards the great gates of the Sirenhold, and he had
not stopped until he had his first proper sight of the Precentor's Palace and its magnificent rose-granite petals.

'They'll hit within the hour,' said Tarvitz. 'I'll move men over
to the defences.'

'It could be a feint,' said Loken, vividly remembering the first
days of the battle for the palace. 'Angron hits one side, Eidolon counter-attacks.'

His first sight of Tarvitz's warriors in battle had resembled a
great game with the Emperor's Children as pieces masterfully
arranged in feints and counter-charges. A lesser man than Saul
Tarvitz would have allowed his force to be picked apart by them,
but the captain of the Emperor's Children had somehow managed to weather three days of non-stop attacks.

'We'll be ready for it,' said Tarvitz, looking down into the
depths of the palace.

Loken and Tarvitz had climbed into the structure of a partially
collapsed dome, one of the many sections of the Precentor's
Palace that had been ruined during the firestorm and fighting.

Sheared sections of granite petals formed the cover behind
which Loken and Tarvitz were sheltering, while in the
rubble-choked dome below, hundreds of the survivors were
manning the defences. Luna Wolves and Emperor's Children
manned barricades made of priceless sculptures and other art-
works that had filled the chambers beneath the dome.

Now these monumental sculptures of past rulers lay on their
sides with Astartes crouched behind them.

'How much longer do you think we can hold?' asked Loken.

'We'll stay until it's over,' said Tarvitz. 'You said so yourself,
every second we survive, the chance grows that the Emperor
hears of this and sends the other Legions to bring Horus to
justice.'

'If Garro makes it,' said Loken. 'He could be dead already, or
lost in the warp.'

'Perhaps, but I have to hope that Nathaniel made it out,' said
Tarvitz. 'Our job is to hold them off for as long as we can.'

'That's what worries me. This probably all started when
Angron slipped the leash, but the Warmaster could have just
pulled his Legions out and bombed this city into dust. He would

have lost some of them, but even so… this planet should have been dead a long time ago.'

Tarvitz smiled. 'Four primarchs, Garviel. That's your answer. Four warriors not given to backing down. Who would be the first to leave? Angron? Mortarion? If Eidolon's leading the Emperor's Children then he's got a lot to prove alongside the primarchs, and I have never known Horus show weakness, not when his brother primarchs might see it.'

'No,' agreed Loken. 'The Warmaster does not back down from a battle once he's committed.'

'Then they'll have to kill us all,' said Tarvitz.

'Yes, they will,' said Loken grimly.

The vox-beads in both their helmets chimed and Torgaddon's voice sounded.

'Garvi, Saul!' said Torgaddon. 'I've got reports that the World Eaters are massing. We can hear them chanting, so they'll be coming soon. I've reinforced the eastern barricades, but we need every man down here.'

'I'll pull my men back from the gallery dome,' voxed Tarvitz. 'I'll send Garviel to join you.'

'Where are you going?' asked Loken.

'I'm going to make sure the west and north are still covered and to get some guns on the chapel too,' said Tarvitz, pointing through the ruins of the dome to the strange organic shape of the Warsingers' Chapel adjoining the palace complex.

The survivors had instinctively avoided the chapel and few of them had even seen inside it. Its very walls were redolent of the corruption that had consumed the soul of the Choral City.

'I'll take the chapel and Lucius can take the ground level,' continued Tarvitz, turning back to Loken. 'I swear that sometimes I think Lucius is actually enjoying this.'

'A little too much, if you ask me,' replied Loken. 'You need to keep an eye on him.'

A familiar dull explosion sounded and a tower of rubble and smoke burst from the Choral City's tortured cityscape to the north of the palace.

'Amazing,' said Tarvitz, 'that there are any Death Guard left alive over there.'

'Death Guard are tough to kill,' replied Loken, heading for the makeshift ladder that led down to the remains of the gallery dome.

Despite his words, he knew that it really *was* amazing. Mortarion, never one to do things with finesse, had simply landed one of his fleet's largest orbital landers on the edge of the western trenches and saturated the defences with turret fire while his Death Guard deployed.

That had been the last anyone had heard of the Death Guard in the Choral City.

Though from the haphazardly aimed artillery shells that landed daily in the traitors' camps, it was clear that some loyal Death Guard still resisted Mortarion's efforts to exterminate them.

'I only hope we live as long,' said Tarvitz. 'We're running low on supplies and ammunition. Soon we'll start running low on Astartes.'

'As long as one is alive, captain, we'll fight,' promised Loken. 'Horus picked some unfortunate enemies in you and me. We'll make him regret ever taking us on.'

'Then we'll speak again after Angron's been sent scurrying,' said Tarvitz.

'Until then.'

Loken dropped down into the dome, leaving Tarvitz alone for a moment to look across the blasted city. How long had it been since he had been surrounded by anything other than the nightmarish place the Choral City had become? Two months? Three?

Ashen skies and smouldering ruins surrounded the palace for as far as the eye could see in all directions, the city resembling the kind of hell the Isstvanians themselves might once have believed in.

Tarvitz shook the thought from his mind.

'There are no hells, no gods, no eternal rewards or punishments,' he told himself.

Lucius could hear the killing. He could read the sound of it as though it were written down before him like sheet music. He knew the difference between the war cries of a World Eater and those of a Son of Horus, and the variance between the tonal quality of a volley of bolter fire launched to support an attack or to defend an obstacle.

The chapel Saul had tasked him with defending was a strange place to be the site of the Great Crusade's last stand. Not so long ago it had been the nerve centre of an enemy regime, but now its makeshift defences were the only thing holding off the far superior traitor forces.

'Sounds like a nasty one,' said Brother Solathen of Squad Nasicae, hunched down by the sill of the chapel window. 'They might break through.'

'Our friend Loken can handle them,' sneered Lucius. 'Angron

wants to get some more kills. That's all he wants. Listen? Can you hear that?'

Solathen cocked his head as he listened. Astartes hearing, like most of their senses, was finely honed, but Solathen didn't seem to recognise Lucius's point. 'Hear what, captain?'

'Chainaxes. But they're not cutting into ceramite or other chainblades; they're cutting into stone and steel. The World Eaters can't get to grips with the Sons of Horus over there, so they're trying to hack through the barricades.'

Solathen nodded and said, 'Captain Tarvitz knows what he's doing. The World Eaters only know one way to fight. We can use that to our advantage.'

Lucius frowned at Solathen's praise of Saul Tarvitz, aggrieved that his own contributions to the defences appeared to have been overlooked. Hadn't he killed Vardus Praal? Hadn't he managed to get his men to safety when the virus bombs and the firestorm had hit?

He turned his bitter expression away and stared through the chapel window across the plaza still stained dark with charred ruins. Amazingly, the chapel window was still intact, although its panes had been distorted by the heat of the firestorm, bulging and discoloured with vein-like streaks that reminded Lucius of an enormous insectoid eye.

The chapel itself was more bizarre inside than out, constructed from curved blocks of green stone in looming biological shapes that looked as though a cloud of noxious-looking fumes had suddenly petrified as it billowed upwards. The altar was a great spreading membrane of paler purple stone, like a complex internal organ opened up and pinned for study against the far wall.

'The World Eaters aren't the ones you should be worried about, brother,' continued Lucius idly. 'It's us.'

'Us, captain?'

'The Emperor's Children,' said Lucius. 'You know how our Legion fights. They're the dangerous ones out there.'

Most of the surviving loyalist Emperor's Children were holding the chapel. Tarvitz had taken a force to cover the nearest gate, but several squads were arrayed among the odd organ-like protrusions on the floor below. Squad Nasicae had only four members left, including Lucius himself, and they headed the assault element of the survivors' force along with Squads Quemondil and Raetherin.

Tarvitz had deployed Sergeant Kaitheron on the roof of the chapel with his support squad as well as the majority of the Emperor's Children's remaining heavy weapons. Astartes from the Tactical squads were at the chapel windows or in cover further inside. The rest of Lucius's troops were stationed in cover outside the chapel, among the barricades of fallen stone slabs they had set up in the early days of the siege.

Two thousand Space Marines, enough for an entire battle zone of the Great Crusade, were defending a single approach to the palace with the Warsingers' Chapel as the lynchpin of their line.

Movement caught Lucius's eye and he peered through the distorted window into the blackened buildings across from him.

There! A glimpse of gold.

He smiled, knowing full well how the Emperor's Children fought.

'Contact!' he announced to the rest of his force. 'Third block west, second floor.'

'On it,' replied Sergeant Kaitheron, a no-nonsense weapons officer who treated war as a mathematical problem to be solved with angles and weight of fire. Lucius heard the squads moving on the roof, training weapons on the area he had indicated.

'West front, make ready!' ordered Lucius. Several of the Tactical squads hurried into firing positions along Lucius's side of the chapel.

The tension was delicious, and Lucius felt a surge of ecstatic sensation crawling along his veins as he heard the song of death building in his blood. A raw, toe-to-toe conflict meant opportunities to exercise perfection in war, but to make it truly memorable it needed these moments of feverish anticipation when the full weight of potential death and glory surged around his body.

'Got them,' called Kaitheron from the chapel roof. 'Emperor's Children. Major force over several floors. Armour too. Land Raiders and Predators. Lascannon, to the fore! Heavy bolters, cover the open ground mid-range and overlap!'

'Eidolon,' said Lucius.

Lucius could see them now, hundreds of Astartes in the purple and gold of the Legion he idolised, gathering in the dead eyes of ruined structures.

'They'll get the support into position first,' said Lucius. 'Then they'll use the Land Raiders to bring the troops in. Mid-to-close-range the infantry will move in. Hold your fire until then.'

Tracks rumbled as the Land Raiders, resplendent with gilded eagle's wings and frescoes of war on their armour-plated sides, ground through the shattered ruins of the Choral City. Each was full of Emperor's Children, the galaxy's elite, primed by Eidolon and Fulgrim to treat the men they had once called brothers as foes worthy only of extermination.

To Eidolon, the survivors of the first wave were ignorant and mindless, deserving only death, but they had reckoned without Lucius. He licked his lips at the thought of once again facing the warriors of his Legion; warriors worthy of the name. Enemies he could respect.

Or earn the respect of…

Lucius could practically see the enemy squads deploying with such rapid confidence that they looked more like players in a complex parade ground move than soldiers at war.

He could taste the moment when the battle would really begin.

He wanted it right there and then, but he also knew how much more delicious the taste of battle was when the timing was perfect.

Windows shattered as fire from the tanks ripped through the chapel, kicking up shards of marble and glass.

'Hold!' ordered Lucius. Despite everything, his Astartes were still Emperor's Children and they would not break ranks like undisciplined World Eaters.

He risked a glance through the splintered glass to see the Land Raiders churning up the marble of the plaza. Predator battle tanks followed them, acting as mobile gun platforms that blew great shuddering chunks from the chapel's battlements. Lascannon fire streaked back and forth, Kaitheron's men attempting to cripple the advancing vehicles and the Land Raiders' sponson-mounted weapons trying to pick off the Astartes on the roof.

A Predator tank slewed to a halt as its track was blown off and another vehicle burst into multicoloured flames. Purple-armoured bodies tumbled past the window; corpses served as an appetiser to the great feast of death.

Lucius drew his sword, feeling the music build inside him until he felt he could no longer contain it. The familiar hum of his sword's energy field became part of the rhythm and he felt himself slipping into the duellist's dance, the weaving stream of savagery he had perfected over centuries of killing.

How many men were in the assault? Certainly a large chunk of Eidolon's command.

Lucius had fewer men, but this battle was all about winning glory and spectacle.

A tank round shot through a window and burst against the ceiling, showering them in fragments and smoke.

Lucius saw streaks of bolter fire from the palace entrance – Tarvitz was drawing Eidolon in and Eidolon had no choice but to dance to his tune. He heard a musical clang and saw the assault ramps of the Land Raiders slam open and Lucius glimpsed the close-packed armoured bodies within.

'Go!' he yelled and the jump packs of the assault units opened up behind him, catapulting the warriors into battle. Lucius followed in their wake, vaulting through the chapel window. Squad Nasicae came after him and the rest of his warriors followed in turn.

Battle: the dance of war. Lucius knew that against an enemy like Eidolon, there would be no time for anything but the most intense applications of his martial perfection. His consciousness shifted and everything was snapped into wondrous focus, every colour becoming bright and dazzling and every sound blaring and discordant along his nerves.

The duellist's dance took him into the enemy as battle erupted in all its perfectly marshalled chaos around him. Heavy fire streaked down from the roof and Land Raiders twisted on their tracks to bring their guns to bear on the Emperor's Children charging from the chapel.

The Space Marines outside the chapel charged at the same instant, and Eidolon's force was attacked from two sides at once.

Lucius ducked blades and bolts, his sword lashing like a serpent's tongue. Eidolon's force reeled. Squad Quelmondil battled ferociously with the enemy warriors emerging from the nearest Land Raider. He danced past them, savage joy kicking in his heart and he rolled under a spray of bolter fire to come up and stab his blade through the abdomen of an enemy sergeant.

Death was an end in itself, expressing Lucius's superiority through the lives he took, but he had a higher purpose. He knew what he had to do, and his strangely distorted senses sought out the glint of gold or the flutter of a banner, anything indicating the presence of one of Fulgrim's chosen.

Then he saw it; armour trimmed in black instead of gold, a helmet worked into a stern, grimacing skull: Chaplain Charmosian.

The black-armoured warrior stood proud of the top hatch of a Land Raider, directing the battle with sharp chops of his eagle-winged crozius. Lucius grinned manically, setting off through the battle to face Charmosian and slay him in a fight worthy of the Legion's epics.

'Charmosian!' he yelled, his voice sounding like the most vibrant music imaginable. 'Keeper of the Will! I am Lucius, once your brother, now your nemesis!'

Charmosian turned his skull helmet towards Lucius and said, 'I know who you are!'

The Chaplain clambered from the hatch and stood on top of the Land Raider, daring Lucius to approach him. Charmosian was a battlefield leader and to fulfil that role he needed the respect of the Legion, respect that could only be earned fighting from the front.

He would be a worthy foe, but that wasn't why Lucius had sought him out.

Lucius leapt onto the Land Raider's track mounting and charged up its glacis until he was face to face with Charmosian. Bolter fire flew in all directions, but it was irrelevant.

This was the only battle in Lucius's mind.

'We taught you too much pride,' said Charmosian, bringing his lethal crozius around in a strike designed to crush Lucius's chest. He brought his blade up to deflect the crozius, and the dance entered a new and urgent phase. Charmosian was good, one of the Legion's best, but Lucius had spent many years training for a fight such as this.

The chaplain's crozius was too heavy to block full-on, so the swordsman let it slide from his blade as Charmosian swung at him time and time again, frustrating him into putting more strength into his blows.

A little longer. A few more moments, and Lucius would have his chance.

He loved the way Charmosian hated him, feeling it as something bright and refreshing.

Lucius could read the pattern of Charmosian's attacks and laughed as he saw the clumsy intent written over every blow. Charmosian wanted to kill Lucius with one almighty stroke, but his crozius rose too far, held too long inert as the chaplain gathered his strength.

Lucius lunged, his sword sweeping out in a high cut that slashed through the chaplain's upraised arms. The crozius tumbled to the ground and Charmosian roared in pain as his arms from the elbows down fell with it.

The battle raged around the scene and Lucius let the noise and spectacle of it fill his over-stimulated senses. The battle was around him, and his victory was all that mattered.

'You know who I am,' said Lucius. 'Your last thought is of defeat.'

Charmosian tried to speak but before the words were out Lucius spun his sword in a wide arc and Charmosian's head was sliced neatly from his shoulders.

Crimson sprayed across the gold of the Land Raider's hull. Lucius caught the head as it spun through the air and held it high so the whole battlefield could see it.

Around him, thousands of the Emperor's Children fought to the death as Eidolon's force, hit from two sides, reeled against the palace defences and fell back. Tarvitz led the counter-strike and Eidolon's attack was melting away.

He laughed as he saw Eidolon's command tank, a Land Raider festooned with victory banners, rise up over a knot of rubble as it retreated from the fighting.

The loyalists had won this battle, but Lucius found that he didn't care.

He had won his own battle, and pulling Charmosian's head from the skull faced helmet and throwing it aside, he knew he had what he needed to ensure that the song of death kept playing for him.

The Warsingers' Chapel was quiet. Hundreds of new bodies lay around it, purple and gold armour scorched and split, runnels of blood gathering between the stained marble tiles. In some places they lay alongside the blackened armour of the World Eaters who had died in the initial assaults on the Choral City.

The palace entrance was heavily barricaded and in the closest dome of the palace, the few Apothecaries in the loyalist force were patching up their wounded.

Tarvitz saw Lucius cleaning his sword, alternating between wiping the blade and using its tip to carve new scars on his face. A skull-faced helmet sat beside him.

'Is that really necessary?' asked Tarvitz.

Lucius looked up and said, 'I want to remember killing Charmosian.'

Tarvitz knew he should discipline the swordsman, reprimand him for practices that might be considered barbaric and tribal, but here, amid this betrayal and death, such concerns seemed ridiculously petty.

He squatted on the ground next to Lucius, his limbs aching and his armour scarred and dented from the latest battle at the entrance to the palace.

'Fair enough,' he said, jerking his thumb in the direction of the enemy. 'I saw you kill him. It was a fine strike.'

'Fine?' said Lucius. 'It was better than fine. It was art. You never were much for finesse, Saul, so I'm not surprised you didn't appreciate it.'

Lucius smiled as he spoke, but Tarvitz saw a very real flash of annoyance cross the swordsman's features, a glimpse of hurt pride that he did not like the look of.

'Any more movement?' he asked, changing the subject.

'No,' said Lucius. 'Eidolon won't come back before he's regrouped.'

'Keep watching,' ordered Tarvitz. 'Eidolon could catch us unawares while our guard's down.'

'He won't breach us,' promised Lucius, 'not while I'm here.'

'He doesn't have to,' said Tarvitz, wanting to make sure Lucius understood the reality of their position. 'Every time he attacks, we lose more warriors. If he strikes fast and pulls out, we'll be whittled down until we can't hold everywhere at once. The ambush from the temple cost him more than he'd like, but he still took too many of us down.'

'We saw him off though,' said Lucius.

'Yes,' agreed Tarvitz, 'but it was a close run thing, so I'll send a squad to help keep the watch.'

'So you don't trust me to keep watch now, is that it?'

Tarvitz was surprised at the venom in Lucius's voice and said, 'No, that's not it at all. All I want is to make sure that you have enough warriors here to fend off another attack. Anyway, I need to attend to the western defences.'

'Yes, off you go and lead the big fight, you're the hero,' snapped Lucius.

'We will win this,' said Tarvitz, placing his hand on the swordsman's shoulder.

'Yes,' said Lucius, 'we will. One way or another.'

Lucius watched Tarvitz go, feeling his anger at his assumption of command. Lucius had been the one earmarked for promotion and greatness, not Tarvitz. How could his own glorious accomplishments have been overshadowed by the plodding leadership of Saul Tarvitz? All the glories that he had earned in the crucible of combat were forgotten and he felt his bitterness rise up in a choking wave in his gullet.

He had felt a moment's guilt as he had formed his plan, but remembering Tarvitz's patronising condescension, he felt that guilt vanish like snow in the sunshine.

The temple was quiet and Lucius checked to make sure that he was alone, moving to sit on one of the outcroppings of smooth grey-green stone and lifting Charmosian's helmet.

He peered into the bloodstained helmet until he saw the glint of silver, and then reached in and pulled out the small metallic scrap that was Charmosian's helmet communicator.

Once again he checked to see that he was alone before speaking into it.

'Commander Eidolon?' he said, his frustration growing as he received no answer.

'Eidolon, this is Lucius,' he said. 'Charmosian is dead.'

There was a brief crackle of static, and then, 'Lucius.'

He smiled as he recognised Eidolon's voice. As one of the senior officers among the Emperor's Children, Charmosian had been in direct contact with Eidolon, and, as Lucius had hoped, the channel had still been open when the chaplain had died.

'Commander!' said Lucius, his voice full amusement. 'It is good to hear your voice.'

'I have no interest in listening to your taunts, Lucius,' snarled Eidolon. 'You must know we will kill you all eventually.'

'Indeed you will,' agreed Lucius, 'but it will take a very long time. A great many Emperor's Children will die before the palace falls. Sons of Horus and World Eaters, too. And Terra knows how many of Mortarion's Death Guard have died already in the trenches. You will suffer for this, Eidolon. The Warmaster's whole force will suffer. By the time the other Legions get here he may have lost too many on Isstvan Three to win through.'

'Keep telling yourself that, Lucius, if it makes it easier.'

'No, commander,' he said. 'You misunderstand me. I am saying that I wish to make a deal with you.'

'A deal?' asked Eidolon. 'What kind of deal?'

Lucius's scars tightened as he smiled. 'I will give you Tarvitz and the Precentor's Palace.'

FIFTEEN

No shortage of wonders
Old friends
Perfect failure

The strategium was dimly lit, the only illumination coming from the flickering pict screens gathered like supplicants around the Warmaster's throne and a handful of torches that burned low with a fragrant aroma of sandalwood. The back wall of the strategium had been removed during the fighting on Isstvan III, revealing a fully fashioned temple adjoining the *Vengeful Spirit*'s bridge.

The Warmaster sat alone. None dared disturb his bitter reveries as he sat brooding on the conflict raging below. What should have been a massacre had turned into a war – a war he could ill afford the time to wage.

Despite his brave words to his brother primarchs, the battle on Isstvan III worried him. Not for any fear that his warriors would lose, but for the fact that they were engaged at all. The virus bombing should have killed every one of those he believed would not support him in his campaign to topple the Emperor from the Golden Throne of Terra.

Instead, the first cracks had appeared in what should have been a faultless plan.

Saul Tarvitz of the Emperor's Children had taken a warning to the surface...

And the *Eisenstein*...

He remembered Maloghurst's fear as he had come to tell him

of the debacle with the remembrancers, the fear that the War-master's wrath would prove his undoing.

Maloghurst had limped towards the throne with his hooded head cast down.

'What is it, Maloghurst?' Horus had demanded.

'They are gone,' said Maloghurst. 'Sindermann, Oliton and Keeler.'

'What do you mean?'

'They are not amongst the dead in the audience chamber,' explained Maloghurst. 'I checked every corpse myself.'

'You say they are gone?' asked the Warmaster at last. 'That implies you know where they have gone. Is that the case?'

'I believe so, my lord,' nodded Maloghurst. 'It appears they boarded a Thunderhawk and flew to the *Eisenstein*.'

'They stole a Thunderhawk,' repeated Horus. 'We are going to have to review our security procedures regarding these new craft. First Saul Tarvitz and now these remembrancers. It seems anyone can steal one of our ships with impunity.'

'They did not steal it on their own,' explained Maloghurst. 'They had help.'

'Help? From whom?'

'I believe it was Iacton Qruze. There was a struggle and Mag-gard was killed.'

'Iacton Qruze?' laughed Horus mirthlessly. 'We have seen no shortage of wonders, but perhaps this is the greatest of them. The Half-heard growing a conscience.'

'I have failed in this, Warmaster.'

'It is not a question of failure, Maloghurst! Mistakes like this should never occur. More and more of my efforts are distracted from this battle. Tell me, where is the *Eisenstein* now?'

'It attempted to break through our blockade to reach the sys-tem jump point.'

'You say "attempted",' noted Horus. 'It did not succeed?'

Maloghurst paused before answering. 'Several of our ships intercepted the *Eisenstein* and heavily damaged it.'

'But they did not destroy it?'

'No, my lord, before they could do so, the *Eisenstein*'s com-mander made an emergency jump into the warp, but the ship was so badly damaged that we do not believe it could survive such a translation.'

'If it does, then the whole timetable of my designs will be disrupted.'

'The warp is dark, Warmaster. It is unlikely that–'

'Do not be so sure of yourself, Maloghurst,' warned Horus.

'The Isstvan Five phase is critical to our success and if the *Eisenstein* carries word of our plans to Terra, then all may be lost.'

'Perhaps, Warmaster, if we were to withdraw from the Choral City and blockade the planet, we could ensure that the Isstvan Five phase proceeds as planned.'

'I am the Warmaster and I do not back down from a battle!' shouted Horus. 'There are goals to be won in the Choral City that you cannot comprehend.'

Horus was shaken from his memories by the chiming of the communications array fitted into the arm of his throne.

'This is the Warmaster.'

A holomat installed beneath the floor projected a large square plane on which swirled an image, high above the Warmaster's temple. The image resolved into the face of Lord Commander Eidolon, evidently inside his command Land Raider. The sound of distant explosions washed through the static.

'Warmaster,' said Eidolon. 'I bring news that I feel you should hear.'

'Tell me,' said Horus, 'and it had better be good news.'

'Oh, it is, my lord,' said Eidolon.

'Well, don't drag this out, Eidolon,' warned Horus. 'Tell me!'

'We have an ally inside the palace.'

'An ally? Who?'

'Lucius.'

The aftermath of a battle was the worst part.

An Astartes warrior was used to the tension of waiting for an attack to come, and even the din and pain of battle itself. But Loken never wished for a time without war more than when he saw what was left after the battle had finished. He didn't experience fear or despair in the manner of a mortal man, but he felt sorrow and guilt as they did.

Angron's latest attack had been one of the fiercest yet, the primarch himself leading it, charging through the ruins of the palace dome towards Loken's defences. Thousands of blood covered World Eaters had followed him and many of those warriors still lay where they had fallen.

Once this place had been part of the palace, a handsome garden with summerhouses, ornamental lakes and a roof that opened up to the sun. Now it was a rubble-strewn ruin, its roof collapsed and only an incongruous decorated post or the splintered remains of an ornamental bridge remaining of its finery.

The bodies of the World Eaters were concentrated on the forward barricade, a line of heaped rubble and metal spikes constructed by the Luna Wolves. Angron had attacked it in force and Torgaddon had relinquished it, letting the World Eaters die for it before his Astartes fell back to the defences at the entrance of the palace's central dome. The ruse had worked and the World Eaters had been strung out as they charged at Loken's position. Many had died to the guns Tarvitz had stationed above the barricades, and by the time Loken's sword had left its sheath it was only momentum that kept the World Eaters fighting – victory was beyond them.

Luna Wolves were mixed in with the World Eaters dead, warriors Loken had known for years. Although the sounds of battle had faded, Loken fancied he could still hear echoes of the fighting, chainblades ripping through armour and volleys of bolter rounds splitting the air.

'It was a close run thing, Garviel,' said a voice from behind Loken, 'but we did it.'

Loken glanced round to see Saul Tarvitz emerging from the central dome. Loken smiled as he saw his friend and battle-brother, a man who had come a long way from the line officer he had been back on Murder to command the survivors of Horus's treachery.

'Angron will be back,' said Loken.

'Their ruse failed, though,' said Tarvitz.

'They don't need to break in, Saul,' said Loken. 'Horus will whittle us down until there's no one left. Then Eidolon and Angron can just roll over us.'

'Not forgetting the Warmaster's Sons of Horus,' said Tarvitz.

Loken shrugged. 'There's no need for them to get involved yet. Eidolon wants the glory and the World Eaters are hungry for blood. The Warmaster will happily let the other Legions wear us down before they strike.'

'That's changed,' said Tarvitz.

'What do you mean?'

'I've just had word from Lucius,' explained Tarvitz. 'He tells me that his communications specialists have broken the Sons of Horus communiqués. Some old friends of yours are coming down from the *Vengeful Spirit* to lead the Legion.'

Loken turned from the battlefield, suddenly interested. 'Who?'

'Ezekyle Abaddon and Horus Aximand,' said Tarvitz. 'Apparently they are to bring the Warmaster's own wrath down upon the city. The Sons of Horus will be playing their hand soon enough, I think.'

Abaddon and Aximand, the arch-traitors, men Loken had admired for so long and the heart of the Mournival. Both warriors stood at Horus's right hand and possibilities flashed through Loken's mind. Deprived of the last of its Mournival, a crucial part of the Legion would die and it would start unravelling without such inspirational figureheads.

'Saul, are you certain?' asked Loken urgently.

'As sure as I can be, but Lucius seemed pretty excited by the news.'

'Did this intercept say where they would be landing?' demanded Loken.

'It did,' smiled Lucius. 'The Mackaran Basilica, just beyond the palace. It's a big temple with a spire in the shape of a trident.'

'I have to find Tarik.'

'He is with Nero Vipus, helping Vaddon with the wounded.'

'Thank you for bringing me this news, Saul,' said Loken with a cruel smile. 'This changes everything.'

Lucius peered past the bullet-riddled pillar, scanning through the darkness of one of the many battlefields scattered throughout the ruins of the palace. Bodies, bolters and chainaxes lay on the shattered tiles where they had been dropped and many of the bodies were still locked in their last, fatal combat.

It had not been difficult for Lucius to slip out of the palace. The biggest danger had been the snipers of the recon squads the Warmaster's forces had deployed among the ruins. Lucius had spied movement in the ruined buildings several times and had taken cover in shell craters or behind heaps of corpses.

Squirming through the filth and darkness like an animal – it had been humiliating, though the sights, sounds and smells of these battlefields still filled his senses in an arousing way. He stepped warily into the courtyard. The bodies that lay everywhere had been butchered, hacked apart with chainblades or battered to death with fists.

It was an ugly spectacle, yet he relished the image of how intense their deaths must have been.

'No artistry,' he said to himself as a gold and purple armoured figure detached from the shadows. A score of warriors followed him and Lucius smiled as he recognised Lord Commander Eidolon.

'Lord commander,' said Lucius, 'it is a pleasure to stand before you once more.'

'Damn your blandishments!' spat Eidolon. 'You are a traitor twice over.'

'That's as maybe,' said Lucius, slouching on a fallen pillar of black marble, 'but I am here to give you what you want.'

'Ha!' scoffed Eidolon. 'What can you give us, traitor?'

'Victory,' said Lucius.

'Victory?' laughed Eidolon. 'You think we need your help to give us that? We have you in a vice! One by one, death by death, victory will be ours!'

'And how many warriors will you lose to achieve it?' retorted Lucius. 'How many of Fulgrim's chosen are you willing to throw into a battle that should never have been fought at all? You can end this right now, right here, and keep all your Astartes alive for the real battle! When the Emperor sends his reply to Horus's treachery you will need every single one of your battle-brothers and you know it.'

'And what would be your price for this invaluable help?' asked Eidolon.

'Simple,' said Lucius. 'I want to rejoin the Legion.'

Eidolon laughed in his face and Lucius felt the song of death surge painfully through his body, but he forced its killing music back down inside him.

'Are you serious, Lucius?' demanded Eidolon. 'What makes you think we *want* you back?'

'You need someone like me, Eidolon. I want to be part of a Legion that respects my skills and ambition. I am not content to stay a captain for the rest of my life like that wretch Tarvitz. I will be at Fulgrim's side where I belong.'

'Tarvitz,' spat Eidolon. 'Does he still live?'

'He lives,' nodded Lucius, 'although I will gladly kill him for you. The glory of this battle should be mine, yet he lords over us all as if he is one of the chosen.'

Lucius felt his bitterness rise and fought to maintain his composure. 'He was once happy to trudge alongside his warriors and leave better men to the glory, but he has chosen this battle to discover his ambition. It's thanks to him that I'm down here at all.'

'You ask for a great deal of trust, Lucius,' said Eidolon.

'I do, but think what I can give you – the palace, Tarvitz.'

'We will have these things anyway.'

'We are a proud Legion, lord commander, but we never send our brothers to their deaths to prove a point.'

'We follow the orders of the Warmaster in all things,' replied Eidolon guardedly.

'Indeed,' noted Lucius, 'but what if I said I can give you a victory so sudden it will be yours and yours alone. The World Eaters and the Sons of Horus will only flounder in your wake.'

Lucius could see he had caught Eidolon's interest and suppressed a smile. Now all he had to do was reel him in.

'Speak,' commanded Eidolon.

✠ ✠ ✠

'I'm coming with you, Garvi,' said Nero Vipus, walking into the only dome of the palace not to be ruined by the siege. It had once been an auditorium with a stage and rows of gilded seats, where the music of creation had once played to the Choral City's elite, but now it was mouldering and dark.

Loken rose from his battle meditation, seeing Vipus standing before him and said, 'I knew you would wish to come, but this is something Tarik and I have to do alone.'

'Alone?' said Vipus. 'That's madness. Ezekyle and Little Horus are the best soldiers the Legion has ever had. You can't go up against them alone.'

Loken placed his hand on his friend's shoulder and said, 'The palace will fall soon enough with or without Tarik and me. Saul Tarvitz has done unimaginable things in keeping us all alive as long as he has, but ultimately the palace will fall.'

'Then what's the point of throwing your life away hunting down Ezekyle and Little Horus?' demanded Vipus.

'We only have one goal on Isstvan Three, Nero, and that's to hurt the Warmaster. If we can kill the last of the Mournival then the Warmaster's plans suffer. Nothing else matters.'

'You said we were supposed to be holding the traitors here while the Emperor sent the other Legions to save us. Is that not true any more? Are we on our own?'

Loken shook his head and retrieved his sword from where he had propped it against the wall. 'I don't know, Nero. Maybe the Emperor has sent the Legions to rescue us, maybe he hasn't, but we have to assume that we're on our own. I'm not going to fight with nothing but blind hope to keep me going. I'm going to make a stand.'

'And that's what I want to do,' said Vipus, 'at my friend's side.'

'No, you need to stay here,' said Loken. 'Your stand must be made here. Every minute you keep the traitors here is another minute for the Emperor to bring the Warmaster to justice. This killing is Mournival business, Nero. Do you understand?'

'Frankly, no,' said Nero, 'but I will do as you ask and stay here.'

Loken smiled. 'Don't mourn me yet, Nero. Tarik and I may yet prevail.'

'You'd better,' said Vipus. 'The Luna Wolves need you.'

Loken felt humbled by Nero's words and embraced his oldest friend. He dearly wished he could tell him that there was yet hope and that he expected to return alive from this mission.

'Garviel,' said a familiar voice from the entrance to the dome. Loken and Nero released each other from their brotherly embrace and saw Saul Tarvitz, framed in the wan light of the auditorium's entrance.

'Saul,' said Loken.

'It's time,' said Tarvitz. 'We're ready to create the diversion you requested.'

Loken nodded and smiled at the two brave warriors, men he had fought through hell for and would do so a hundred times more. The honour they did him just by being his friends made his chest swell with pride.

'Captain Loken,' said Tarvitz formally. 'It may be that this is the last time we will meet.'

'I do not think,' replied Loken, 'there is any "maybe" about it.'

'Then I will wish you all speed, Garviel.'

'All speed, Saul,' said Loken, offering his hand to Tarvitz. 'For the Emperor.'

'For the Emperor,' echoed Tarvitz.

With his farewells said, Loken made his way from the auditorium, leaving Tarvitz and Vipus to organise the defences for the next attack.

Surviving tactical maps indicated that the Mackaran Basilica lay to the north of their position and as he made his way towards the point he had selected as the best place to leave the palace he found Torgaddon waiting for him.

'You saw Vipus?' asked Torgaddon.

'I did,' nodded Loken. 'He wanted to come with us.'

Torgaddon shook his head. 'This is Mournival business.'

'That's what I told him.'

Both warriors took deep breaths as the enormity of what they were about to attempt swept over them once again.

'Ready?' asked Loken.

'No,' said Torgaddon. 'You?'

'No.'

Torgaddon chuckled as he turned to the tunnel that led from the palace.

'Aren't we a pair?' he said and Loken followed him into the darkness.

For good or ill, the final battle for Isstvan III was upon them.

'You dare return to me in failure?' bellowed Horus, and the bridge of the *Vengeful Spirit* shook with the fury of his voice. His face twisted in anger at the wondrous figure standing before him, struggling to comprehend the scale of this latest setback.

'Do you even understand what I am trying to do here?' raged Horus. 'What I have started at Isstvan will consume the whole

galaxy, and if it is flawed from the outset then the Emperor
will break us!'

Fulgrim appeared uncowed by his anger, his brother's features
betraying an insouciance quite out of character for the primarch of the Emperor's Children. Though he had but recently
arrived on his flagship, *Pride of the Emperor*, Fulgrim looked as
magnificent as ever.

His exquisite armour was a work of art in purple and gold,
bearing many new embellishments and finery with a flowing, fur-lined cape swathing his body. More than ever, Horus
thought Fulgrim looked less like a warrior and more like a
rake or libertine. His brother's long white hair was pulled
back in an elaborate pattern of plaits and his pale cheeks
were lightly marked with what appeared to be the beginnings of tattoos.

'Ferrus Manus is a dull fool who would not listen to reason,'
said Fulgrim. 'Even the mention of the Mechanicum's pledge
did not–'

'You swore to me that you could sway him! The Iron Hands
were essential to my plans. I planned Isstvan Three with your
assurance that Ferrus Manus would join us. Now I find that I
have yet another enemy to contend with. A great many of our
Astartes will die because of this, Fulgrim.'

'What would you have had me do, Warmaster?' smiled Fulgrim, and Horus wondered where this new, sly mocking tone
had come from. 'His will was stronger than I anticipated.'

'Or you simply had an inflated opinion of your own abilities.'

'Would you have me kill our brother, Warmaster?' asked
Fulgrim.

'Perhaps I will,' replied Horus unmoved. 'It would be better
than leaving him to roam free to destroy our plans. As it is he
could reach the Emperor or one of the other primarchs and
bring them all down on our heads before we are ready.'

'Then if you are quite finished with me, I shall return to my
Legion,' said Fulgrim, turning away.

Horus felt his choler rise at Fulgrim's infuriating tone and said,
'No, you will not. I have another task for you. I am sending
you to Isstvan Five. With all that has happened, the Emperor's
response is likely to arrive more quickly than anticipated and
we must be prepared for it. Take a detail of Emperor's Children
to the alien fortresses there and prepare it for the final phase of
the Isstvan operation.'

Fulgrim recoiled in disgust. 'You would consign me to a
role little better than a castellan, as some prosaic housekeeper

making it ready for your grand entrance? Why not send for Perturabo? This kind of thing is more to his liking.'

'Perturabo has his own role to play,' said Horus. 'Even now
he prepares to lay waste to his home world in my name. We
shall be hearing more of our bitter brother very soon. Have no
fear of that.'

'Then give this task to Mortarion. His grimy footsloggers will
relish such an opportunity to muddy their hands for you!' spat
Fulgrim. 'My Legion was the chosen of the Emperor in the years
when he still deserved our service. I am the most glorious of
his heroes and the right hand of this new Crusade. This is...
this is a betrayal of the very principles for which I chose to join
you, Horus!'

'Betrayal?' said Horus, his voice low and dangerous. 'A strong
word, Fulgrim. Betrayal is what the Emperor forced upon us
when he abandoned the galaxy to pursue his quest for godhood and gave over the conquests of our Crusade to scriveners
and bureaucrats. Is that the charge you would level at me now,
to my face, here on the bridge of my own ship?'

Fulgrim took a step back, his anger fading, but his eyes alight
with the excitement of the confrontation. 'Perhaps I do, Horus.
Perhaps someone needs to tell you a few home truths now that
your precious Mournival is no more.'

'That sword,' said Horus, indicating the venom-sheened
weapon that hung low at Fulgrim's waist. 'I gave you that blade
as a symbol of my trust in you, Fulgrim. We alone know the
true power that lies within it. That weapon almost killed me
and yet I gave it away. Do you think I would give such a weapon
to one I do not trust?'

'No, Warmaster,' said Fulgrim.

'Exactly. The Isstvan Five phase of my plan is the most critical,' said Horus, stoking the dangerous embers of Fulgrim's
ego. 'Even more so than what is happening below us. I can
entrust it to no other. You *must* go to Isstvan Five, my brother.
All depends on its success.'

For a long, frightening moment, violent potential crackled
between Horus and the primarch of the Emperor's Children.

Fulgrim laughed and said, 'Now you flatter me, hoping my
ego will coerce me into obeying your orders.'

'Is it working?' asked Horus as the tension drained away.

'Yes,' admitted Fulgrim. 'Very well, the Warmaster's will be
done. I will go to Isstvan Five.'

'Eidolon will stay in command of the Emperor's Children
until we join you' said Horus and Fulgrim nodded.

'He will relish the chance to prove himself further,' said Fulgrim.

'Now leave me, Fulgrim,' said Horus. 'You have work to do.'

SIXTEEN

Enemy within
The Eightfold Path
Honour must be satisfied

Apothecary Vaddon fought to save Casto's life. The upper half of the warrior's armour had been removed and his bare torso was disfigured by a gory wound, flaps of skin and chunks of muscle blown aside like the petals of a bloody flower by an exploding bolter round.

'Pressure!' said Vaddon as he flicked over the settings on his narthecium gauntlet. Scalpels and syringes cycled as Brother Mathridon, an Emperor's Children Astartes who had lost a hand in the earlier fighting and served as Vaddon's assistant, kept pressure on the wound. Casto bucked underneath him, his teeth gritted against pain that would kill anyone but an Astartes.

Vaddon selected a syringe and pushed it into Casto's neck. The vial mounted on the gauntlet emptied, pumping Casto's system with stimulants to keep his heart forcing blood around his ruptured organs. Casto shook, nearly snapping the needle.

'Hold him still,' snapped Vaddon.

'Yes,' said a voice behind them. 'Hold him still. It will make it easier to kill him.'

Vaddon's head snapped up and he saw a warrior clad in the armour of an Emperor's Children lord commander. He carried an enormous hammer, purple arcs of energy playing around its massive head. Behind the warrior, Vaddon could see a score of Emperor's Children in purple and gold finery, their armour sheened with lapping powder and oil.

Instantly, he knew that these were no loyalists and felt a cold hand clutch at his chest as he saw that they were undone.

'Who are you?' demanded Vaddon, though he knew the answer already.

'I am your death, traitor!' said Eidolon, swinging his hammer and crushing Vaddon's skull with one blow.

Hundreds of Emperor's Children streamed into the palace from the east, on a tide of fire and blood. They fell upon the wounded first, Eidolon himself butchering those who lay waiting for Vaddon's ministrations, taking particular relish in killing the loyalist Emperor's Children he found there. The warriors of his Chapter swarmed through the palace around him, the defenders discovering to their horror that their flank had somehow been turned and that more and more of the traitors were pouring into the palace.

Within moments, the last battle had begun. The loyalists turned from their defences and faced the Emperor's Children. Assault Marines' jump packs gunned them across ruined domes to crash into Eidolon's assault units. Heavy weapons troopers and snipers amongst the ruined battlements shot down into the enemy, swapping tremendous volleys of fire across the shattered domes.

It was a battle without lines or direction as the fighting spilled into the heart of the Precentor's Palace. Each Astartes became an army of his own as all order broke down and every warrior fought alone against the enemies that surrounded him. Emperor's Children jetbikes screamed insanely through the precincts of the palace and ripped crazed circuits around the domes, spraying fire into the Astartes battling below them.

Dreadnoughts tore up chunks of fallen masonry with their mighty fists and hurled them at the loyalists holding the barricades against which so many of their foes had died only a short while before.

Everything was swirling madness, horror and destruction, with Eidolon at the centre of it, swinging his hammer and killing all who came near him as he led his perfect warriors deeper into the heart of the defences.

Luc Sedirae, with his blond hair and smirking grin, looked completely out of place among the rusting industrial spires of the Choral City. Beside him, Serghar Targhost, Captain of the Seventh Company, seemed far more at home, his older, darker skin and heavy fur cloak more in keeping with a murdered world.

Sedirae stood on top of a rusting slab of fallen machinery before thousands of Sons of Horus arrayed for war. War paint was fresh on their breastplates and new banners dedicated to the warrior lodges flapped in the wind.

'Sons of Horus!' bellowed Sedirae, his voice brimming with the confidence that came to him so easily. 'For too long we have waited for our brother Legions to open the gate for us so we can put the doubters and the feeble-minded to the sword! At last, the hour has come! Lord Commander Eidolon has broken the siege and the time has come to show the Legions how the Sons of Horus fight!'

The warriors cheered and the lodge banners were raised high, displaying the facets of the beliefs underpinning the lodge philosophies. A brazen claw reached down from the sky to crush a world in its fist, a black star shone eight rays of death upon a horde of enemies and a great winged beast with two heads stood resplendent on a mountain of corpses.

Images from beyond, conjured by the words of Davinite priests who could look into the warp, they displayed the Sons of Horus's allegiance to the powers their Warmaster embraced.

'The enemy is in disarray,' shouted Sedirae over the cheering. 'We will fall upon them and sweep them away. You know your duties, Sons of Horus, and you all know that the paths you have followed have led you towards this day. For here we destroy the last vestiges of the old Crusade, and march towards the future!'

Sedirae's confidence was infectious and he knew they were ready.

Targhost stepped forward and raised his hands. He bore the rank of lodge captain himself, privy to the secrets of the Davinite ways and as much a holy man as a commander. He opened his mouth and unleashed a stream of brutal syllables, guttural and dark, the tongue of Davin wrought into a prayer of victory and blood.

The Sons of Horus answered the prayer, their voices raised in a relentless chant that echoed around the dead spires of the Choral City.

And when the prayers were done, the Sons of Horus marched to war.

Fire stormed around Tarvitz. Emperor's Children Terminators raked the central dome with fire and the sounds of brutal hand-to-hand combat came from the shattered gallery. Tarvitz ducked and ran as bolter fire kicked up fragments around him, sliding into cover beside Brother Solathen of Squad Nasicae.

Solathen and about thirty loyalist Emperor's Children were pinned down behind a great fallen column, a few Luna Wolves among them.

'What in the Emperor's name happened?' shouted Tarvitz. 'How did they get in?'

'I don't know, sir,' replied Solathen. 'They came from the east.'

'We should have had some warning,' said Tarvitz. 'That's Lucius's sector. Have you seen him at all?'

'Lucius?' asked Solathen. 'No, he must have fallen.'

Tarvitz shook his head. 'Not likely. I have to find him.'

'We can't hold out here,' said Solathen. 'We have to pull back and we won't be able to wait for you.'

Tarvitz nodded, but knew that he had to try and find Lucius, even if it was just to recover his body. He doubted Lucius could ever really die, but knew that, amid this carnage, anything was possible.

'Very well,' said Tarvitz. 'Go. Fall back in good order to the inner domes and the temple, there are barricades there. Go! And don't wait for me!'

He put his head briefly over the pillar and fired his bolter, kicking a burst of shots towards Eidolon's Emperor's Children swarming all over the far side of the dome. More covering fire sprayed from his warriors' guns as they began falling back by squads.

The dome between him and his goal was littered with bodies, some of them chewed into unrecognisable sprays of torn flesh. He waited until his warriors had put enough distance between them and the enemy and broke from cover.

Bolter shots tore up the ground beside him and he rolled into the cover of a fallen pillar, crawling as fast as he could to reach the passageway that led from the dome and curved around its columned circumference towards the east wing of the Precentor's Palace.

Lucius was somewhere in these ruins and Tarvitz had to find him.

Loken ducked and threw himself to the floor, skidding along the fire-blackened tiles of the plaza. The palace loomed above him, whirling as Loken spun on his back and fired up at the closest World Eater. One shot caught the warrior in the leg and he collapsed in a roaring heap. Torgaddon leapt upon him, plunging his sword into the traitor's back.

Loken climbed to his feet as more fire stuttered across the plaza. He tried to get a bearing on the enemy among the heaps of the dead and the jagged slabs of marble sticking up from the edges of shell craters, but it was impossible.

The plaza between the chaos of the palace and the dark mass of the city was infested with World Eaters, charging forwards to exploit the breach made by the Emperor's Children.

'There's a whole squad out here,' said Torgaddon, wrenching his sword from the World Eater. 'We're right in the middle of them.'

'Then we keep going,' said Loken.

Back on his feet, he reloaded his bolter as they hurried through the wreckage and charnel heaps, scanning the darkness for movement. Torgaddon kept close behind him, sweeping his bolter between chunks of tiling or fallen masonry. Fire snapped around them and the sounds of battle coming from the palace became ever more terrible, the war cries and explosions tearing through the violent night.

'Down!' yelled Torgaddon as a burst of plasma fire lanced from the darkness. Loken threw himself to the ground as the searing bolt flashed past him and bored a hole in a slab of fallen stone behind him. A dark shape came at him and Loken saw the flash of a blade, bringing his bolter up in an instinctive block. He felt chainblade teeth grinding against the metal of his gun and kicked out at his attacker's groin.

The World Eater pivoted away from the blow easily, turning to smash Torgaddon to the ground with the butt of his chainaxe. Torgaddon's attack gave Loken a chance to regain his feet and he threw aside the ruined bolter to draw his own sword.

Torgaddon wrestled with another World Eater on the ground, but his friend would have to fend for himself as Loken saw that his opponent was a captain, and not just any captain, but one of the World Eaters best.

'Khârn!' said Loken as the warrior attacked.

Khârn paused in his attack and, for the briefest moment, Loken saw the noble warrior he had spoken with in the Museum of Conquest, before something else swamped it again – something that twisted Khârn's face with hatred.

That second was enough for Loken, allowing him to dodge back behind a fan of broken stone jutting from the edge of crater. Bullets still carved through the air and somewhere beyond his sight, Torgaddon was fighting his own battle, but Loken could not worry about that now.

'What happened, Khârn?' cried Loken. 'What did they turn you into?'

Khârn screamed an incoherent bellow of rage and leapt towards him with his axe held high. Loken braced his stance and brought his blade up to catch Khârn's axe as it slashed towards him and the two warriors clashed in a desperate battle of strength.

'Khârn...' said Loken through gritted teeth as the World Eater forced the chainaxe's whirling teeth towards his face. 'This is not the man I knew! What have you become?'

As their eyes met, Loken saw Khârn's soul and despaired. He saw the warrior who had sworn oaths of brotherhood and pledged himself to the Crusade as he himself had done, the warrior who had seen the terrors and tragedies of the Crusade as well as its victories. And he saw the dark madness that had swamped that in bloodshed and betrayals yet to be enacted.

'I am the Eightfold Path,' snapped Khârn, his every word punctuated by a froth of blood.

'No!' shouted Loken, pushing the World Eater away. 'It doesn't have to be this way.'

'It does,' said Khârn. 'There is no way off the Path. We must always go further.'

The humanity drained from Khârn's face and Loken knew that the World Eater was truly gone and that only in death would this battle end.

Loken backed away, fending off a flurry of blows from Khârn's axe, until he was forced back against a slab of rubble. His foe's axe buried itself in the stone beside him and Loken slammed the pommel of his sword into Khârn's head. Khârn rode the blow and smashed his forehead into Loken's face, grabbing his sword arm and wrestling him to the ground.

They struggled in the mud like animals, Khârn trying to grind Loken's face into the shattered stone and Loken trying to throw him off. Loken rolled onto his back as he heard the rumble of an engine like an earthquake and the glare of floodlights stabbed out and threw Khârn's outline into silhouette.

Knowing what was coming, Loken hammered his fist into Khârn's face over and over again, pushing him upright with a hand clasped around his neck. The World Eater struggled in Loken's grip as the light grew stronger and the roaring form of a Land Raider crested the ridge of rubble behind them like a monster rising from the deep.

Loken felt the huge impact as the Land Raider's dozer blade slammed into Khârn, the sharpened prongs at its base punching through the World Eater's chest. He released Khârn's body and rolled to the edge of the crater as the Land Raider rose up, carrying the struggling Khârn with it. The mighty tank crashed back down and Loken pressed his body into the mud as it ground over him, the roaring of its engine passing inches above him.

Then it was over, the tank rumbled onwards, carrying the impaled World Eater before it like some gory trophy. Tanks were all around him, the Eye of Horus glaring from their armoured hulls, and Loken recognised the livery they were painted in.

The Sons of Horus.

For a moment, Loken just stared at the force surging towards the palace. Gunfire flared as they drove towards their prize.

A hand reached down and grabbed Loken, dragging him, battered and bloody, into cover from the guns of the tanks. He looked up and saw Torgaddon, similarly mauled by the encounter with the World Eaters.

Torgaddon nodded in the direction of the Land Raider. 'Was that–?'

'Khârn,' nodded Loken. 'He's gone.'

'Dead?'

'Maybe, I don't know.'

Torgaddon looked up at the Sons of Horus speartip driving for the palace. 'I think even Tarvitz might have trouble holding the palace now.'

'Then we'll have to hurry.'

'Yes. Stay low and let's keep out of any more trouble,' said Torgaddon, 'unless Abaddon and Little Horus aren't challenging enough on their own.'

'Saul will make them pay for every piece of rubble they capture,' said Loken, pulling himself painfully to his feet. Khârn had hurt him, but not so much that he couldn't fight. 'For his sake, let's make that count for something.'

The two friends forged through the rubble once again, towards the Mackaran Basilica.

Where lay one last chance of a victory on Isstvan III.

The sounds of battle echoed from all around him and Tarvitz hugged the shadows as he made his careful way through the ruins of the east wing of the palace. Squads of Emperor's Children swarmed through the palace grounds, sweeping through the shattered domes and gunfire-riddled rooms as they plunged the knife of their attack into the heart of the defences.

Here and there he saw squad markings he recognised and had to fight the ingrained urge to call out to them. But these warriors were the enemy and there would be no brotherly embrace or comradely welcome were they to discover him.

The very obsessiveness of their attack was working in Tarvitz's favour as these warriors possessed the same single mindedness as Eidolon, fixated on the prize of the palace rather than proper battlefield awareness. For once, Eidolon's flaws were working in his favour, thought Tarvitz, as he ghosted through the strobe-lit wasteland of the palace.

'You're going to need to tighten up discipline, Eidolon,' he whispered, 'or someone's going to make you pay.'

The eastern sectors he had assigned Lucius and his men to watch over were bombed out ruins, the frescoes burned from the walls by the firestorm, and the mighty statue gardens pulverised by constant shelling and the battles that had raged furiously over the past months. To have held out this long was a miracle in itself and Tarvitz was not blind enough to try and fool himself into thinking that it could last much longer.

He saw dozens of bodies and checked every one for a sign that the swordsman had fallen. Each body was a warrior he knew, a warrior who had followed him into battle at the palace and trusted that he could lead them to victory. Each set of eyes accused him of their death, but he knew that there was nothing more he could have done.

The further eastward he went the less he encountered the invading Emperor's Children, their attack pushing into the centre of the Precentor's Palace rather than spreading out to capture its entirety.

Trust Eidolon to go for the glory rather than standard battlefield practice.

Give me a hundred Space Marines and I would punish your arrogance, thought Tarvitz.

Even as the thought occurred to him, a slow smile spread across his face. He *had* a hundred Space Marines. True, they were engaged in battle, but if any force of warriors could disengage from battle in good order and hand over to a friendly force in the middle of a desperate firefight, it was the Emperor's Children.

He crouched in the shadow of a fallen statue and opened a vox-channel. 'Solathen,' he hissed. 'Can you hear me?'

Static washed from the vox-bead in his ear and he cursed at the idea of his plan being undone by something as trivial as a failure of communications.

'I hear you, captain, but we're a little busy right now!' said Solathen's voice.

'Understood,' said Tarvitz, 'but I have new orders for you. Disengage from the fight and hand over to the Luna Wolves. Let

them take the brunt of the fighting and gather as many warriors as you can rally to you. Then converge on my position.'

'Sir?'

'Take the eastern passages along the servants' wing. That
should bring you to me without too much trouble. We have
an opportunity to hurt these bastards, Solathen, so I need you
to get here with all possible speed!'

'Understood, sir,' said Solathen, signing off.

Tarvitz froze as he heard a voice say, 'It won't do any good,
Saul. The Precentor's Palace is as good as lost. Even you should
be able to see that.'

He looked up and saw Lucius standing in the centre of the
dome in front of him, his shimmering sword in one hand and
a shard of broken glass in the other. He raised the glass to his
face and sliced its razor edge along his cheek, drawing a line of
blood from his skin that dripped to the dome's floor.

'Lucius,' said Tarvitz, rising to his feet and entering the dome
to meet the swordsman. 'I thought you were dead.'

Bright starlight filled the dome and Tarvitz saw it was filled
with the corpses of Emperor's Children. Not traitors, but loyalists and he could see that not one had fallen to a gunshot
wound, but had been carved up by a powerful edged weapon.
These warriors had been cut apart, and a horrible suspicion
began to form in his mind.

'Dead?' laughed Lucius. '*Me*? Remember what Loken said to
me when I humbled him in the practice cages?'

Wary now, Tarvitz nodded. 'He said there was someone out
there who could beat you.'

'And do you remember what I told him?'

'Yes,' replied Tarvitz, sliding his hand to the hilt of his broadsword. 'You said, "Not in this lifetime," didn't you?'

'You have a good memory,' said Lucius, dropping the bloody
shard of glass to the floor.

'Who's that latest scar for?' asked Tarvitz.

Lucius smiled, though there was no warmth to it.

'It's for you, Saul.'

The great forum of the Mackaran Basilica was a desert of ashen
bone, for as the virus bombs had dropped, thousands of Isstvanians had gathered there in the hope that the parliament house
at one end of the forum would receive them. They had thronged
the place and died there, their scorched remains resembling an
ancient swamp from which rose the columns that bounded the
forum on three sides. On the fourth was the parliament house

itself, befouled by black tendrils of ash that reached up from the forum.

The building had been the seat of the Choral City's civilian parliament, a counterpart to the nobles who had ruled from the Precentor's Palace, but the prominent citizens who had taken shelter inside had died as surely as the horde of civilians outside.

Loken pushed through the sea of black bones, his sword ready in his hand as he forged through the thicket of bone. A skull grinned up at him, its burned and empty eye sockets accusing. Behind him, Torgaddon covered the forum beyond them.

'Wait,' said Loken quietly.

Torgaddon halted and looked round. 'Is it them?'

'I don't know, maybe,' said Loken, looking up at the parliament house. Beyond it he could just see the lines of a spacecraft, a Stormbird in Sons of Horus colours. 'Someone landed here, that's for sure.'

They continued onwards to the edge of the parliament building, climbing the smooth marble steps. Its great doors had been thick studded oak, but they had been eaten away by the virus and burned to ash by the firestorm.

'Shall we?' asked Torgaddon.

Loken nodded, suddenly wishing that they had not come here, as a terrible feeling of doom settled on him. He looked at Torgaddon and wished he had some fitting words to say to him before they took these last, fateful steps.

Torgaddon seemed to understand what he was thinking and said, 'Yes. I know, but what choice do we have?'

'None,' said Loken, marching through the archway and into the parliament house.

The interior of the building had been protected from the worst of the virus bombing and firestorm, only a few tangled blackened corpses lying sprawled among the dark wood panels and furnishings. The walls of the circular building were adorned with faded frescoes of the Choral City's magnificent past, telling the tales of its growth and conquests.

The benches and voting-tables of the parliament were arranged around a central stage with a lectern from which the debates were led.

On the stage, in front of the lectern, stood Ezekyle Abaddon and Horus Aximand.

'You betrayed us,' said Tarvitz, the hurt and disappointment almost too much to bear. 'You killed your own men and let Eidolon and his warriors into the palace. Didn't you?'

'I did,' said Lucius, swinging his sword in loops around his body as he loosened his muscles in preparation for the fight Tarvitz knew must come next. 'And I'd do it again in a heartbeat.'

Tarvitz circled the edge of the dome, his steps in time with those of the swordsman. He had no illusions as to the outcome of this fight, Lucius was the pre-eminent blade master of the Legion, perhaps all the Legions. He knew he could not defeat Lucius, but this betrayal demanded retribution.

Honour must be satisfied.

'Why, Lucius?' asked Tarvitz.

'How can you ask me that, Saul?' demanded Lucius, drawing the circle closer and, step by step, the distance between the two warriors shrank. 'I am only here thanks to my misplaced acquaintance with you. I know what the lord commander and Fabius offered you. How could you turn such an opportunity down?'

'It was an abomination, Lucius,' said Tarvitz, knowing he had to keep Lucius talking for as long as he could. 'To tamper with the gene-seed? How can you possibly believe that the Emperor would condone such a thing?'

'The Emperor?' laughed Lucius. 'Are you so sure he would disapprove? Look at what he did to create the primarchs? Aren't *we* the result of genetic manipulation? The experiments Fabius is conducting are the logical next link in that evolutionary chain. We are a superior race and we must establish that superiority over any lesser beings that stand in our way.'

'Even your fellow warriors?' spat Tarvitz, gesturing to the corpses around the dome's circumference with the blade of his sword.

Lucius shrugged. 'Even them. I am going to rejoin my Legion and they tried to stop me. What choice did I have? Just like you are going to try and stop me.'

'You'll kill me too?' asked Tarvitz. 'After all the years we've fought together?'

'Don't try and appeal to my sense of fond reminiscences, Saul,' warned Lucius. 'I am better than you and I am going to achieve great things in the service of my Legion. Neither you or any foolish sense of misplaced loyalty are going to stop me.'

Lucius lifted the blade of his sword and dropped into a fighting crouch as Tarvitz approached him. The dome seemed suddenly silent as the two combatants circled one another, each searching for a weakness in the other's defences. Tarvitz drew his combat knife in his left hand and reversed the blade, knowing he would need as many blades between him and Lucius as humanly possible.

Tarvitz knew there were no more words to be spoken. This could only end in blood.

Without warning, he leapt towards Lucius, thrusting with the smaller blade, but even as he attacked he saw that Lucius had been expecting it.

Lucius swayed aside and swept the hilt of his sword down, smashing the knife from his hand. The swordsman ducked as Tarvitz turned on his heel and slashed high with his sword.

Tarvitz's blade cut only air and Lucius hammered his elbow into his side.

He danced away, expecting Lucius to land a blow, but the swordsman merely smiled and danced around him lightly on the balls of his feet. Lucius was playing with him, and he felt his anger mount in the face of such mockery.

Lucius advanced towards Tarvitz, darting in with the speed of a striking snake to thrust at his stomach. Tarvitz blocked the thrust, rolling his wrists over Lucius's blade and slashing for his neck, but the swordsman had anticipated the move and nimbly dodged the blow.

Tarvitz attacked suddenly, his blade a flashing blur of steel that forced Lucius back step by step. Lucius parried a vicious slash aimed at his groin, spinning with a laugh to launch a lightning riposte at his foe.

Tarvitz saw the blade cut the air towards him, knowing he was powerless to prevent it landing. He hurled himself back, but felt a red-hot line of agony as the energised edge bit deep into his side. He clamped a hand to his side as blood spilled down his armour, gasping in pain before his armour dispensed stimulants that blocked it.

Tarvitz backed away from Lucius and the swordsman followed with a grin of anticipation.

'If that's the best you've got, Saul, then you'd best give up now,' smirked Lucius. 'I promise I'll make it quick.'

'I was just about to say the same thing, Lucius,' gasped Tarvitz, lifting his sword once again.

The two warriors clashed once more, their swords shimmering streaks of silver and blue as coruscating sparks spat from their blades. Tarvitz fought with every ounce of courage, strength and skill he could muster, but he knew it was hopeless. Lucius parried his every attack with ease and casually landed cut after cut on his flesh, enough to draw blood and hurt, but not enough to kill.

Blood gathered in the corner of his mouth as he staggered away from yet another wounding blow.

'A hit,' sniggered Lucius. 'A palpable hit.'

Tarvitz knew he was fighting with the last of his reserves and the fight could not go on much longer. Soon Lucius would tire of his poor sport and finish him, but perhaps he had held him here for long enough.

'Had enough?' coughed Tarvitz. 'You don't have to die here.'

Lucius cocked his head to one side as he advanced towards him and said, 'You're serious, aren't you? You actually think you can beat me.'

Tarvitz nodded and spat blood. 'Come on and have a go if you think you can kill me.'

Lucius leapt forwards to attack and Tarvitz dropped his sword and leapt to meet him. Surprised by such an obviously suicidal move, Lucius was a fraction of a second too late to dodge Tarvitz's attack.

The two warriors clashed in the air and Tarvitz smashed his fist into the swordsman's face. Lucius turned his head to rob the blow of its force, but Tarvitz gave him no chance to right himself as they fell to the floor, and pistoned his fist into his former comrade's face. Lucius's sword skittered away and they fought with fists and elbows, knees and feet.

At such close quarters, skill with a blade was irrelevant and Tarvitz let his hate and anger spill out in every thunderous hammer blow he landed. They rolled and grappled like brawling street thugs, Tarvitz punching Lucius with powerful blows that would have killed a mortal man a dozen times over, the swordsman struggling to push Tarvitz clear.

'I also remember what Loken taught you the first time he brought you down,' gasped Tarvitz as he saw movement at the edge of the dome. 'Understand your foe and do whatever is necessary to bring him down.'

He released his grip on Lucius and rolled clear, pushing himself as far away from the swordsman as he could. Lucius sprang to his feet in an instant, scrambling across the floor to retrieve his weapon.

'Now, Solathen!' shouted Tarvitz. 'Kill him! He betrayed us all!'

He watched as Lucius turned towards the dome's entrance, seeing the warriors Solathen had rallied and brought to him. Solathen obeyed Tarvitz's command instantly, as a good Emperor's Children should, and the dome was suddenly filled with the bark of gunfire. Lucius dived out of the way, but even he wasn't quick enough to avoid a volley of bolter shells.

Lucius jerked and danced in the fusillade, sparks and blood

flying from his armour. He rolled across the floor, scrabbling for a hole in the wall blasted by the months of battle as the gunfire of the loyalist Emperor's Children tore into him.

'Kill him!' yelled Tarvitz, but Lucius was faster than he would have believed possible, diving from the dome as shells tore up scorched frescoes around him.

Tarvitz pushed himself to his feet and staggered over towards where Lucius had escaped.

Beyond the dome, the outer precincts of the palace were a nightmarish landscape of craters and blackened ruins. A pall of smoke hung over the battlefield the palace had become and he smashed his fist into the wall in frustration as he saw that the swordsman had vanished.

'Captain Tarvitz?' said Solathen. 'Reporting as ordered.'

Tarvitz turned from his search for Lucius, pushing his frustrations aside and focusing on the more immediate matter of counter-attacking Eidolon's warriors.

'My thanks, Solathen. I owe you my life,' he said.

The warrior nodded as Tarvitz picked up a fallen bolter and checked the magazine to make sure he had a full load.

'Now come on,' he said grimly. 'Let's show these bastards how the real Emperor's Children fight!'

SEVENTEEN

Winning is survival
Dies Irae
The end

'Betrayer,' said Loken, stepping into the parliament house.

'There was nothing to betray,' retorted Abaddon.

Even after all that had happened on Isstvan III, the word betrayal had the power to ignite the ever-present anger inside him.

'I envy you this, Loken,' continued Abaddon. 'To you the galaxy must seem so simple. So long as there's someone you can call enemy you'll fight to the death and think you are right.'

'I know I am right, Ezekyle!' shouted Loken. 'How can this be anything but wrong? The death of this city and the murder of your brothers? What has happened to you, Abaddon, to turn you into this?'

Abaddon stepped down off the stage, leaving Aximand to stand alone at the lectern. In his Terminator armour Abaddon was far taller than Loken and he knew from witnessing the First Captain in battle that he could still fight as skilfully as any Astartes in power armour.

'Isstvan Three was forced upon us by the inability of small minds to understand reality,' said Abaddon. 'Do you think I have been a part of this, and that I am here, because I enjoy killing my brothers? I *believe*, Loken, as surely as you do. There are powers in this galaxy that even the Emperor does not understand. If he leaves humanity to wither on the vine in his selfish quest for godhood then those powers will swamp us and every single human being in this galaxy will die. Can you understand the enormity of that concept? The whole human race! The Warmaster does, and that is why he must take the Emperor's place to deal with these threats.'

'Deal with them?' said Torgaddon, shaking his head. 'You are a fool, Ezekyle, we saw what Erebus was doing. He has lied to you all. You have made a pact with evil powers.'

'Evil?' said Aximand. 'They saved the Warmaster's life. I have seen their power and it is within the Warmaster's ability to control them. You think we are fools, that we are blind? The forces of the warp are the key to this galaxy. That is what the Emperor cannot understand. The Warmaster will be lord of the warp as well of the Imperium and then we will rule the stars.'

'No,' replied Loken. 'The Warmaster has become corrupted. If he takes the throne it will not be humanity that rules the galaxy, it will be something else. You know that, Little Horus, even if Ezekyle doesn't. He doesn't care about the galaxy, he just wants to be on the winning side.'

Abaddon smiled, slowly approaching Loken as Torgaddon circled towards Horus Aximand. 'Winning is survival, Loken. You die, you lose, and nothing you ever believed ever meant anything. I live, I win, and you might as well have never existed. Victory, Loken. It's the only thing in the galaxy that means anything. You should have spent more time being a soldier, maybe then you would have ended up on the winning side.'

Loken held up his sword, trying to gauge Abaddon's movements. 'There is always time to decide who wins.'

He could see Abaddon tensing up, ready to strike, and knew that the First Captain's taunting was just a cover.

'Loken, you have come so far,' said Abaddon, 'and you still don't understand what we're doing here. We're not so far from human that we're not allowed a few mistakes, but to fight us instead of realising what the Warmaster is trying to achieve… that's unforgivable.'

'Then what's your mistake, Ezekyle?'

'Talking too much,' replied Abaddon, launching himself towards Loken with his bladed fist bathed in lethal energies.

Torgaddon watched as Abaddon charged towards Loken, taking that as his cue to attack Little Horus. His former comrade had seen the intent in his eyes and leapt to meet him as Loken and Abaddon smashed apart the pews along the nave.

They met in a clatter of battleplate, fighting with all the strength and hatred that only those who were once brothers, but are now bitter enemies, can muster. They grappled like wrestlers until Aximand flung Torgaddon's arms wide and smashed his elbow into his jaw.

He fell back, blocked the right cross slashing for his face, and closed with Aximand, cracking an armoured knee into his opponent's midriff.

Little Horus stumbled and Torgaddon knew that it would take more than a knee in the guts to halt a warrior such as Aximand. His former brother was powerfully built, his strength, poise and skill the equal of Torgaddon's.

The two warriors faced one another, and Torgaddon could see a look of regret flash across Little Horus's face.

'Why are you doing this?' asked Torgaddon.

'You said you were against us,' replied Aximand.

'And we are.'

Both warriors lowered their guards; they were brothers, members of the Mournival who had seen so many battles together that there was no need for posturing. They both knew how the other fought.

'Tarik,' said Aximand, 'if this could have ended another way, we would have taken it. None of us would have chosen this way.'

'Little Horus, when did you realise how far you had gone? Was it when the Warmaster told you we were going to be bombed, or some time before?'

Aximand glanced over to where Loken and Abaddon fought. 'You can walk away from this, Tarik. The Warmaster wants Loken dead, but he said nothing about you.'

Torgaddon laughed. 'We called you Little Horus because you looked so like him, but we were wrong. Horus never had that doubt in his eyes. You're not sure, Aximand. Maybe you're on the wrong side. Maybe this is the last chance you've got to end your life as a Space Marine and not as a slave.'

Aximand smiled bleakly. 'I've seen it, Tarik, the warp. You can't stand against that.'

'And yet here I am.'

'If you had just taken the chance the lodge gave you, you would have seen it too. They can give us such power. If you only knew, Tarik, you'd join us in a second. The whole future would be laid out before you.'

'You know I can't back down. No more than you can.'

'Then this is it?'

'Yes, it is. As you said, none of us would have chosen this.'

Aximand readied himself. 'Just like the practice cages, Tarik.'

'No,' said Torgaddon, 'nothing like that.'

✠ ✠ ✠

The energised claw swung at Loken's head, and he ducked, too late seeing it for the feint it was. Abaddon grabbed him by the edge of his shoulder guard and drove his knee into Loken's stomach. Ceramite buckled and Loken felt pain knife into him as bones broke.

Abaddon released him and punched him in the face. He was thrown against the wall of the parliament, scorched plaster and brick falling around him.

'The Warmaster wanted me to bring the Justaerin, but I told him it was an insult.'

Loken saw his sword lying on the floor beside him and slid down the wall to grab it. He pushed off the wall, pivoting past Abaddon's slashing fist, swinging the blade towards the First Captain's face.

Abaddon blocked the blow with his forearm, reaching out to pluck Loken from his feet and hurl him towards the parliament building's wall. The world spun away from him and suddenly there was pain.

His vision blurred as he smacked into the ground and shards of stone flew up around him. The pain within him felt strange, as if it belonged to someone else. It felt as if his back was broken and a treacherous voice in his mind whispered that the pain would go away if he just gave up and let it all go away in a fog of oblivion. His grip tightened on his sword and he let his anger fuel his strength to fight against the voice in his head that told him to give up.

A long time ago, Loken had sworn an oath to his Emperor, and that oath was never to give up, even as the moment of death approached. His vision swam back into focus, and he looked up to see the hole in the parliament house's wall his body had smashed.

Loken rolled onto his front as Abaddon's massive armoured form charged towards him, smashing aside the blackened remains of the breach.

He scrambled to his feet and backed away, letting Abaddon's fist swing past him. He darted in, stabbing with his sword, but the thick plates of his enemy's armour turned the blade aside. He scrambled back up the steps of the parliament house, hearing Torgaddon and Little Horus fighting within and knowing that he needed his brother's strength to triumph.

'You can't run forever!' roared Abaddon as he turned to follow him, his steps ponderous and heavy.

✠ ✠ ✠

Saul Tarvitz grinned like a hunter who had finally run his prey to ground. The warriors he and Solathen led cut a bloody swathe through Eidolon's warriors, killing them without mercy as they themselves had been killed so recently. What had once been an attack that threatened to overwhelm them utterly was now in danger of becoming a rout for the traitors.

Gunfire echoed fiercely through the palace as the loyalists unleashed volley after volley of gunfire at anything that moved. Loyalist Space Marines surrounded Eidolon's assault force and attacked on two fronts. The lord commander's force was buckling.

Tarvitz could see warriors with missing limbs or massive open wounds struggling in the desperate fight, jostling to get a position where they could kill the traitors who had so nearly overrun them. His own sword reaped a bloody tally as he killed warriors he had once fought with and bled alongside, each sword blow a cruel twist of fate that brought aching sadness as much as it did cathartic satisfaction.

He saw Eidolon in the centre of the battle, smashing warriors to ruin with each swing of his hammer and fought his way through the battle to reach the lord commander. His own body ached from the duel with Lucius, but he knew that there was no point in calling for an Apothecary. Whatever wounds he was suffering from would never have a chance to heal. It would end here, Tarvitz knew, but it would be a hell of a fight and he had never felt more proud to lead these brave warriors into battle.

To have such noble fighters almost undone by a supposedly loyal comrade's betrayal was a galling, yet somehow fitting end to their struggle. Lucius had very nearly cost them this battle and Tarvitz swore that if he lived through this hell, he would see the bastard dead once and for all.

The lord commander was almost within his reach, but no sooner had Eidolon seen him than the traitors began falling back in disciplined ranks. Tarvitz wanted to scream in frustration, but knew better than to simply hurl himself after his foe.

'Firing line across the nave!' shouted Tarvitz at the top of his voice and instantly, a contingent of Astartes formed up and began firing disciplined volleys of bolter fire at the retreating enemy.

He lowered his sword and leaned against the broken wall as he realised that, against all odds, they had held once more. Before he had a moment to savour the unlikeliness of their latest victory, the vox-bead chimed in his ear.

'Captain Tarvitz,' said a voice he recognised as one of the Luna Wolves.

'Tarvitz here,' he said.

'This is Vipus, captain. The position on the roof is sound, but we've got company.'

'I know,' replied Tarvitz. 'The Sons of Horus.'

'Worse than that,' said Vipus. 'To the west, look up.'

Tarvitz pushed through the remains of the battle and scanned the sky above the crumbling, smoke-wreathed ruins. Something moved towards the palace, something distant, but utterly huge.

'Sweet Terra,' he said, 'the *Dies Irae*.'

'I'll make the Titan our priority target,' swore Vipus.

'No, you can't hurt it. Just kill enemy Space Marines.'

'Yes, captain.'

'Enemy units!' a voice yelled from near the temple entrance. 'Armour and support!'

Tarvitz pushed himself from the wall, drawing on his last reserves of energy to once again muster his warriors for the defence of the palace. 'Assault units by the doors! All other Astartes, fire at will!'

Tarvitz could see a huge strike force of enemy forces, boxy Land Raiders and Rhinos massing on the outskirts of the Precentor's Palace. Beyond them, Sons of Horus, World Eaters and Emperor's Children set up fields of fire to surround the temple.

The *Dies Irae* would soon be in range to blast them with its enormous weaponry.

'They'll be coming again soon,' shouted Tarvitz, 'but we'll see them off again, my brothers! No matter what occurs, they will not forget the fight we've given them here!'

Looking at the size of the army arrayed for the final assault, Tarvitz knew that there would be no holding against it.

This was the endgame.

Terminator armour was huge. It made a man into a walking tank, but what it added in protection, it lost in speed. Abaddon was skilful and could fight almost as fast as any other Astartes while clad in its thick plates.

But 'almost' wasn't good enough when life or death was at stake.

Chunks of rubble spilled into the parliament house as Abaddon battered his way back inside, the brutal, high-shouldered shape of his Terminator armour wreathed in chalky plaster dust. As Abaddon smashed his way back inside, he passed beneath a sagging portico that supported a vast swathe of sculpted marble statuary above. Loken struck out at one of the cracked pillars supporting the portico, the fluted support smashing apart under the power of the blow.

The parliament filled with dust as the huge slabs above came down on Abaddon, the entire weight of the statuary collapsing on top of the First Captain. Loken could hear Abaddon roaring in anger as the stonework thundered down in a flurry of rubble and destruction.

He turned away from the avalanche of debris and fought his way through the billowing clouds of dust towards the centre of the parliament building.

He saw Torgaddon and Horus Aximand upon the central stage.

Torgaddon was on his knees, blood raining from his body and his limbs shattered. Aximand held his sword upraised, ready to deliver the deathblow.

He saw what would happen next even as he screamed at his former brother to stay his hand. Even over the crash of rubble being displaced as Abaddon forced himself free of the collapsed statues, he heard Aximand's words with a terrible clarity.

'I'm sorry,' said Aximand.

And the sword slashed down against Torgaddon's neck.

The plasma bolt was like a finger of the sun, reaching down from the guns of the *Dies Irae* and smashing through the wall of the Warsingers' Temple, the liquid fire boring deep into the ground. With a sound like the city dying, one wall of the temple collapsed as dust and fire filled the air and shards of green stone flew like knives. Warriors melted in the heat blast or died beneath the heaps of stone that collapsed around them.

Tarvitz fell to his knees on the winding stairway that climbed to the upper reaches of the temple. A choking mass of burning ash billowed around him and he fought his way upwards, knowing that hundreds of the last loyalist Space Marines were dead. The sound was appalling, the roar of the collapsing temple stark against the silence of the traitors that surrounded the temple on all sides.

A body fell past him, one of the Luna Wolves, his arm blown off by weapons fire hammering the upper floors.

'To the roof!' ordered Tarvitz, not knowing if anyone could hear him over the cacophony of the Titan's guns. 'Abandon the nave!'

Tarvitz reached the gallery running the length of the temple, finding it crammed with Space Marines, their Legion colours unrecognisable beneath layers of grime and blood. Such distinctions were irrelevant, Tarvitz realised, for they were one band of brothers fighting for the same cause.

Above this level was the roof, and Tarvitz spotted Sergeant

Raetherin, a solid line officer and veteran of the Murder campaign.

'Sergeant!' he yelled. 'Report!'

Raetherin looked up from the window through which he was aiming his bolter. He had caught a glancing blow to the side of his head and his face streamed with blood.

'Not good, captain!' he replied. 'We've held them this long, but we won't hold another attack. There's too many of them and that Titan is going to blow us away any second.'

Tarvitz nodded and risked a glance through a shattered loophole to the ground far below, feeling his hate for these traitors, warriors for whom notions of honour and loyalty were non-existent, swell as he saw the multitude of bodies sprawled around the palace. He knew these dead warriors, having led them in battle these last few months and more than anything, he knew what they represented.

They were the galaxy's best soldiers, the saviours of the human race and the chosen of the Emperor. Their lives of heroic service and sacrifice had been ended by brute treachery and he had never felt so helpless.

'No,' he said, as resolve filled him. 'No, we will not falter.'

Tarvitz met Raetherin's eyes and said. 'The Titan is going to hit the same corner of the temple again, higher up, and then the traitors are going to storm us. Get the men back and make ready for the assault.'

He knew the traitors were just waiting for the temple to fall so they could storm in and kill the loyalists at their leisure. This was not just a battle; it was the Warmaster demonstrating his superiority.

Massive calibre gunfire thundered from the *Dies Irae*, an awesome storm of fire and death that smashed the plaza outside the temple, blasting apart loyalists in great columns of fire.

Infernal heat battered against the temple, and a hot gale blew through the gallery.

'Is that the best you've got?' he yelled in anger. 'You'll never kill us all!'

His warriors looked at him with savage light in their eyes. The words had sounded hollow in his ears, spoken out of rage rather than bravado, but he saw the effect it had and smiled, remembering that he had a duty to these men.

He had a duty to make their last moments mean something.

Suddenly, the air ripped apart as the Titan's plasma gun fired and white heat filled the gallery, throwing Tarvitz to the floor. Molten fragments of stone sprayed him and warriors fell, broken and burning around him. Blinded and deafened, Tarvitz dragged himself away from the destruction. Hot air boomed back into the vacuum blasted by the plasma and it was like a burning wind of destruction come to scour the loyalists from the face of Isstvan III.

He rolled onto his back, seeing that the bolt had ripped right through the temple roof, leaving a huge glowing-edged hole, like a monstrous bite mark, through one corner of the temple. Fully a third of the temple's mass had collapsed in a great rock-slide of liquefied stone, flooding out like a long tongue of jade.

Tarvitz tried to shake the ringing from his ears and forced his eyes to focus.

Through the miasma of heat, he could hear a war cry arise from the enemy warriors.

A similar clamour rose from the other side of the temple, where the World Eaters and the Emperor's Children were arrayed among the ruins of the palace.

The attack was coming.

Loken dropped to his knees in horror at the sight of Torgaddon's head parting from his shoulders. The blood fountained slowly, the silver sheen of the sword wreathed in a spray of red.

He screamed his friend's name, watching as his body crashed to the floor of the stage and smashed the wooden lectern to splinters as it fell. His eyes met those of Horus Aximand and he saw a sorrow that matched his own echoed in this brother's eyes.

His choler surged, hot and urgent, but his anger was not directed at Horus Aximand, but at the warrior who pulled himself from the rubble behind him. He turned and forced himself to his feet, seeing Abaddon pulling himself from under the collapsed portico. The First Captain had extricated himself from beneath slabs of marble that would have crushed even an armoured Astartes, but he was still trapped and immobile from the waist down.

Loken gave vent to an animal cry of loss and rage and ran towards Abaddon. He leapt, driving a knee down onto Abaddon's arm and pinning it with all his weight and strength to the rubble. Abaddon's free hand reached up and grabbed Loken's wrist as Loken drove his chainsword towards Abaddon's face.

The two warriors froze, locked face to face in a battle that would determine who lived and who died. Loken gritted his teeth and forced his arm down against Abaddon's grip.

Abaddon looked into Loken's face and saw the hatred and loss there.

'There's hope for you yet, Loken,' he snarled.

Loken forced the roaring point of the sword down with more strength than he thought could ever inhabit one body. The betrayal of the Astartes – their very essence – flashed through Loken's mind and he found the target of his hatred embodied in Abaddon's violent features.

The chainblade's teeth whirred. Abaddon forced the point down and it ripped into his breastplate. Sparks sprayed as Loken pushed the point onwards, through thick layers of ceramite. The sword juddered, but Loken kept it true.

He knew where it would break through, straight through the bone shield that protected Abaddon's chest cavity and then into his heart.

Even as he savoured the idea of Abaddon's death, the First Captain smiled and pushed his hand upwards. Astartes battle-plate enhanced a warrior's strength, but Terminator armour boosted it to levels beyond belief, and Abaddon called upon that power to dislodge Loken.

Abaddon surged upwards from the rubble with a roar of anger and slammed his energised fist into Loken's chest. His armour cracked open and the bone shield protecting his own chest cavity shattered into fragments. He staggered away from Abaddon, managing to keep his feet for a few seconds before his legs gave out and he collapsed to his knees, blood dribbling from his cracked lips in bloody ropes.

Abaddon towered over him and Loken watched numbly as Horus Aximand joined him. Abaddon's eyes were filled with triumph, Aximand's with regret. Abaddon took the bloody sword from Aximand's hand with a smile. 'This killed Torgaddon and it seems only fitting that I use it to kill you.'

The First Captain raised the sword and said, 'You had your chance, Loken. Think about that while you die.'

Loken met Abaddon's unforgiving gaze, seeing the madness that lurked behind his eyes like a mob of angry daemons, and waited for death.

But before the blow landed, the parliament building exploded as something vast and colossal, like a primal god of war bestriding the world smashed through the back wall. Loken had a fleeting glimpse of a monstrous iron foot, easily the width of the building itself crashing through the stonework and demolishing the building as it went.

He looked up in time to see a mighty red god, towering and immense, striding through the remains of the Choral City, its battlements bristling with weapons and its mighty head twisted in a snarl of merciless anger.

Rubble and debris cascaded from the roof as the *Dies Irae* smashed the parliament building into a splintered ruin of crushed rock, and Loken smiled as the building collapsed around him.

Tremendous impacts smashed the marble floor and the noise of the building's destruction was like the sweetest music he had ever heard, as he felt the world go black around him.

Saul Tarvitz looked around him at the hundred Space Marines crammed into the tiny square of cover that was all that remained of the Warsingers' temple. They had sat awaiting the final attack of the traitors for what had seemed like an age, but had been no more than thirty minutes.

'Why don't they attack?' asked Nero Vipus, one of the few Luna Wolves still alive.

'I don't know,' said Tarvitz, 'but whatever the reason I'm thankful for it.'

Vipus nodded, his face lined with a sadness that had nothing to do with the final battles of the Precentor's Palace.

'Still no word from Garviel or Tarik?' asked Tarvitz, already knowing the answer.

'No,' said Vipus, 'nothing.'

'I'm sorry, my friend.'

Vipus shook his head. 'No, I won't mourn them, not yet. They might have succeeded.'

Tarvitz said nothing, leaving the warrior to his dream and turned his attention once again to the terrifying scale of the Warmaster's army. Ten thousand traitors stood immobile in the ruins of the Choral City. World Eaters chanted alongside Emperor's Children while the Sons of Horus and the Death Guard waited in long firing lines.

The colossal form of the *Dies Irae* had thankfully stopped firing, the monstrous Titan marching to tower over the Sirenhold like a brazen fortress.

'They want to make sure we're beaten,' said Tarvitz, 'to plant a flag on our corpses.'

'Yes,' agreed Vipus, 'but we gave them the fight of their lives did we not?'

'That we did,' said Tarvitz, 'that we did, and even once we're gone, Garro will tell the Legions of what they've done here. The Emperor will send an army bigger than anything the Great Crusade has ever seen.'

Vipus looked out over the Warmaster's army and said, 'He'll have to.'

✠ ✠ ✠

Abaddon surveyed the ruins of the parliament house, its once magnificent structure a heaped pile of shattered stone. His face bled from a dozen cuts and his skin was an ugly, bruised purple, but he was alive.

Beside him, Horus Aximand slumped against a ruined statue, his breathing laboured and his shoulder twisted at an unnatural angle. Abaddon had pulled them both from the wreckage of the building, but looking at Aximand's downcast face, he knew that they had not escaped without scars of a different kind.

But it was done. Loken and Torgaddon were dead.

He had thought to feel savage joy at the idea, but instead he felt only emptiness, a strange void that yawned in his soul like a vessel that could never be filled.

Abaddon dismissed the thought and spoke into the vox. 'Warmaster,' he said, 'it is over.'

'What have we done, Ezekyle?' whispered Aximand.

'What needed to be done,' said Abaddon. 'The Warmaster ordered it and we obeyed.'

'They were our brothers,' said Aximand and Abaddon was astonished to find tears spilling down his brother's cheeks.

'They were traitors to the Warmaster, let that be an end to it.'

Aximand nodded, but Abaddon could see the seed of doubt take root in his expression.

He lifted Aximand and supported him as they made their way towards the waiting Stormbird that would take them from this cursed place and back to the *Vengeful Spirit*.

The traitors within the Mournival were dead, but he had not forgotten the look of regret he had seen on Aximand's face.

Horus Aximand would need watching, Abaddon decided.

The viewscreen of the strategium displayed the blackened, barren rock of Isstvan V.

Where Isstvan III had once been rich and verdant, Isstvan V had always been a mass of tangled igneous rock where no life thrived. Once there had been life, but that had been aeons ago, and its only remnants were scattered basalt cities and fortifications. The people of the Choral City had thought these ruins were home to the evil gods of their religion, who waited there plotting revenge.

Perhaps they were right, mused Horus, thinking of Fulgrim and his complement of Emperor's Children who were preparing the way for the next phase of the plan.

Isstvan III had been the prologue, but Isstvan V would be the most decisive battle the galaxy had ever seen. The thought made

Horus smile as he looked up to see Maloghurst limping painfully towards his throne.

'What news, Mal?' asked Horus. 'Have all surface units returned to their posts?'

'I have just heard from the *Conqueror*,' nodded Maloghurst. 'Angron has returned. He is the last.'

Horus turned back to the gnarled globe of Isstvan V and said, 'Good. It is no surprise to me that he should be the last to quit the battlefield. So what is the butcher's bill?'

'We lost a great many in the landings and more than a few in the palace,' replied Maloghurst. 'The Emperor's Children and the Death Guard were similarly mauled. The World Eaters lost the most. They are barely above half strength.'

'You do not think this battle was wise,' said Horus. 'You cannot hide that from me, Mal.'

'The battle was costly,' averred Maloghurst, 'and it could have been shortened. If efforts had been made to withdraw the Legions before the siege developed then lives and time could have been saved. We do not have an infinite number of Astartes and we certainly do not have infinite time. I do not believe there was any great victory to be won here.'

'You see only the physical cost, Mal,' said Horus. 'You do not see the psychological gains we have made. Abaddon was blooded, the real threats among the rebels have been eliminated and the World Eaters have been brought to a point where they cannot turn back. If there was ever any doubt as to whether this Crusade would succeed, it has been banished by what I have achieved on Isstvan Three.'

'Then what are your orders?' asked Maloghurst.

Horus turned back to the viewscreen and said, 'We have tarried here too long and it is time to move onwards. You are right that I allowed myself to be drawn into a war that we did not have time to fight, but I will rectify that error.'

'Warmaster?'

'Bomb the city,' said Horus. 'Wipe it off the face of the planet.'

Loken couldn't move his legs. Every heartbeat was agony in his lungs as the muscles of his chest ground against splinters of bone. He coughed up clots of blood with every breath and he was sure that each one would be his last as the will to live seeped from his body.

Through a crack in the rubble pinning him to the ground, Loken could see the dark grey sky. He saw streaks of fire dropping through the clouds and closed his eyes as he realised that they were the first salvoes of an orbital bombardment.

Death was raining down on the Choral City for the second time, but this time it wouldn't be anything as exotic as a virus. High explosives would bring the city down and put a final, terrible exclamation mark at the end of the Battle of Isstvan III.

Such a display was typical of the Warmaster.

It was a final epitaph that would leave no one in any doubt as to who had won.

The first orange blooms of fire burst over the city. The ground shook. Buildings collapsed in waves of fire and the streets boiled with flame once more.

The ground shuddered as though in the grip of an earthquake and Loken felt his prison of debris shift. Hard spikes of pain buffeted him as flames burst across the remains of the parliament building.

Then darkness fell at last, and Loken felt nothing else.

A hundred of Tarvitz's loyalists remained. They were the only survivors of their glorious last stand, and he had gathered them in the remains of the Warsingers' Temple – Sons of Horus, Emperor's Children, and even a few lost-looking World Eaters. Tarvitz noticed that there were no Death Guard in their numbers, thinking that perhaps a few had survived Mortarion's scouring of the trenches, but knowing that they might as well have been on the other side of Isstvan III.

This was the end. They all knew it, but none of them gave voice to that fact.

He knew all their names now. Before, they had just been grime-streaked faces among the endless days and nights of battle, but now they were brothers, men he would die with in honour.

Flashes of explosions bloomed in the city's north. Shooting stars punched through the dark clouds overhead, scorching holes through which the glimmering stars could be seen. The stars shone down on the Choral City in time to watch the city die.

'Did we hurt them, captain? asked Solathen. 'Did this mean anything?'

Tarvitz thought for a moment before replying.

'Yes,' he said, 'we hurt them here. They'll remember this.'

A bomb slammed into the Precentor's Palace, finally blasting what little remained of its great stone flower into flame and shards of granite. The loyalists did not throw themselves into cover or run for shelter – there was little point.

The Warmaster was bombarding the city, and he was thorough.

He would not let them slip away a second time.

Towers of flame bloomed all across the palace, closing in on them with fiery inevitability.

The battle for the Choral City was over.

The temple was nearly complete, its high, arched ceiling like a ribcage of black stone beneath which the officers of the new Crusade were gathered. Angron still fumed at the decision to leave Isstvan III before the destruction of the loyalists was complete, while Mortarion was silent and sullen, his Death Guard like a steel barrier between him and the rest of the gathering.

Lord Commander Eidolon, still smarting from the failures his Legion had committed in the eyes of the Warmaster, had several squads of Emperor's Children accompanying him, but his presence was not welcomed, merely tolerated.

Maloghurst, Abaddon and Aximand represented the Sons of Horus, and beside them stood Erebus. The Warmaster stood before the temple's altar, its four faces representing what Erebus called the four faces of the gods. Above him, a huge holographic image of Isstvan V dominated the temple.

An area known as the Urgall Depression was highlighted, a giant crater overlooked by the fortress that Fulgrim had prepared for the Warmaster's forces. Blue blips indicated likely landing sites, routes of attack and retreat. Horus had spent the last hour explaining the details of the operation to his commanders and he was coming to an end.

'At this very moment seven Legions are coming to destroy us. They will find us at Isstvan Five and the battle will be great. But in truth it will not be a battle at all, for we have achieved much since last we gathered. Chaplain Erebus, enlighten us as to matters beyond Isstvan.'

'All goes well at Signus, my lord,' said Erebus stepping forward. New tattoos had been inked on his scalp, echoing the sigils carved into the stones of the temple.

'Sanguinius and the Blood Angels will not trouble us, and we have received word that the Ultramarines have begun to muster at Calth. They suspect nothing and will not be in a position to lend their strength to the loyalist force. Our allies outnumber our enemies.'

'Then it is done,' said Horus. 'The backs of the Emperor's Legions will be broken at Isstvan Five.'

'And what then?' asked Aximand.

A strange melancholy had settled upon Horus Aximand since the battles of the Choral City, and he saw Abaddon cast a wary glance in his brother's direction.

'When our trap is sprung?' demanded Aximand. 'The Emperor will still reign and the Imperium will still answer to him. After Isstvan Five, what then?'

'Then, Little Horus?' said the Warmaster. 'Then we strike for Terra.'

LORD OF THE
RED SANDS

Aaron Dembski-Bowden

There is only one thing worth fighting for.

He knows this, while his father languishes in the ignorance of false righteousness; while his brothers play gods to a godless universe; while heartless weaklings claim to be his sons, walking the coward's path over the way of the warrior.

But he knows – even if no one else will listen or understand – that there is only one thing worth fighting for.

He crests the barricade, the axes howling in his hands. The dead city sends its finest against him time and again, and time and again the dead city's finest fall back in screaming, hewed chunks of flesh and ceramite. Some wear his brothers' colours – the royal purple of preening Fulgrim, or the drab, pale hues of cadaverous Mortarion. They charge, dreaming of glory, and they die knowing nothing but pain and shame.

Some of them wear the filthy white of his own sons. They die no differently from the others. They bleed the same blood, and cry the same oaths. They stink just the same when their bodies are ripped open, organs bared to the cold air.

Flashes of insight come to him in the storm of swords – a name etched upon white armour seems familiar for the span of a heartbeat, or the angle of an axe reminds him of another fight, back in the age of the burning sun beating down upon the red sand.

He kills every warrior that rises before him, and chases those wise enough to retreat. The former he breaks open with single blows from his straining axes. The latter he hunts in leaping pounces, the way arena beasts once hunted starved men and women.

Glory?

Glory is for those too weak to find inner strength, leaving them hollow parasites, feeding on the affection of even lesser men. Glory is for cowards, too afraid to let their names die.

He stands upon their bodies now, grinding bootprints into their breastplates as he adds to their number. A monument to futility rises at his feet: each death means that he has to climb higher to welcome fresh meat. The hammer-blows of gunfire keep on pounding into his back and shoulders with bestial kicks. An irritation, nothing more. Scarcely even a distraction. This battle was won the moment he set foot in the dead city.

He buries an axe in the chest of another son, but feels it slip from his blood-slick fingers as the warrior tumbles back. The binding chain at his wrist pulls taut, preventing the weapon's theft, but he sees what they are trying to do – three of his own sons shouting, scrabbling to cling to the axe they stole, even as the blade is buried in one of their bodies. A warrior's ultimate sacrifice, trading his life for the chance to disarm an enemy. Their united strength drags at his arm, turning his panting breath to a wet snarl.

He does not pull back and resist. He launches into them, shattering their armour with foot, with fist, with his dark metal teeth. Their cunning sacrifice avails them nothing but death by bludgeoning rather than the shrieking blade of a chainaxe.

Their bodies are added to the corpse monument. Every movement is pain, now. Each breath comes from ragged lungs, through bleeding lips.

There is still time, still time, still time. He can win this war without his brother's guns.

Conquest?

What tyrant first dreamed of conquest and clad violent oppression in terms of virtue? Why does the imposition of one will over another draw men like no other sin? For more than two hundred years, the Emperor has demanded that the galaxy align itself to his principles at the cost of ten thousand cultures that lived free and without the need for tyranny. Now Horus demands that the stellar nations of this broken empire dance to his tune instead. Billions die for conquest, to advance the pride of these two vain creatures cast in the shapes of men.

There is no virtue in fighting for conquest. Nothing is more worthless and hollow than obliterating freedom for the sake of more land, more coin, more voices singing your name in holy hymn.

Conquest is as meaningless as glory. Worse, it is evil in its selfishness. Both are triumphs only in a fool's crusade.

No. Not glory, not conquest.

He follows the blood to his prey. The warrior slouches on the ground, with his back to the wall, his armoured thighs decorated with a sloppy trail of innards. Blood marks his face. Blood marks everything on this world, but the centurion's face is a reflection of the battle itself. Half of his features no longer exist beyond bare, cracked bone – ripped away by the primarch's axe. The officer's remaining eye is narrowed by the preternatural focus necessary to remain alive, without screaming, when your intestines have been torn from your body.

He should not be alive, and yet here he is, lifting a bolter.

Angron smiles at the man's beautiful defiance and slaps the gun aside with the flat of his still revving axe.

'No,' he says, savagely kind. This warrior and his doomed brethren fought well, and their father is careful to offer no humiliation in these last moments.

His other sons, those loyal to him, are chanting his name, shouting it through the ruins. They chant the name his slave-handlers gave to him when he was Lord of the Red Sands. *Angron. Angron. Angron.* He does not know what name the Emperor had intended for him. He never cared enough to ask, and now the chance to do so is denied to him forever.

'Lord.' The dying centurion speaks.

Angron crouches by his son, ignoring the nosebleed trickling down his lips as the Butcher's Nails tick, tick, tick in the back of his brain.

'I am here, Kauragar.'

The World Eater draws in a shivery breath, surely one of his last. His remaining eye seeks his primarch's face.

'That wound at your throat,' Kauragar's words come with blood bubbling at his lips. 'That was me.'

Angron touches his own neck. His fingers come away wet, and he smiles for the first time in weeks.

'You fought well.' The primarch's low tones are almost tectonic. 'All of you did.'

'Not well enough.' The centurion bares blood-darkened teeth in a rictus grin. 'Tell me why, father. Why stand with the Arch-traitor?'

Angron's smile fades, wiped clean by his son's ignorance. None of them have ever understood. They were always so convinced that he should have been honoured by being given a Legion, when the life he chose was stolen from him the day the Imperium tore him away from his true brothers and sisters.

'I do not stand with Horus.' Angron breathes the confession. 'I stand against the Emperor. Do you understand, Kauragar? I am free now. *Free.* Can you not understand that? Why have you all spent these last decades telling me I should feel honoured to live as a slave, when I was so close to dying free?'

Kauragar stares past his primarch, up at the lightening sky. Blood runs from the warrior's open mouth.

'Kauragar. Kauragar?'

The centurion exhales – a slow, tired sigh. His chest does not rise again.

Angron closes his dead son's remaining eye and rises to his feet. Chains rattle against his armour as he takes up his axes from the ground once more.

Angron. Angron. Angron. His name. A slave's name.

He walks through the ruins, enduring the cheers of his blood-stained followers – warriors concerned with glory and conquest, who were born better than the aliens and traitors they slay. Fighting their own kind is practically the first fair fight they have ever endured, and their gene-sire's lip curls at the thought.

Before he was shackled by the Emperor's will, Angron and his ragged warband defied armies of trained, armed soldiers on his home world. They tasted freedom beneath clean skies and razed the cities of their enslavers.

Now he leads an army fattened by centuries of easy slaughter, and they cheer him the way his masters once cheered when he butchered beasts for their entertainment.

This is not freedom. He knows that. He knows it well.

This is not freedom, he thinks as he stares at the World Eaters screaming his name. *But the fight is only just beginning.*

When the Emperor dies under his axes, when his final thought is of how the Great Crusade was all in pathetic futility, and when his last sight is Angron's iron smile... Then the Master of Mankind will learn what Angron has known since he picked up his first blade.

Freedom is the only thing worth fighting for.

It is why tyrants always fall.

ABOUT THE AUTHORS

Dan Abnett is the author of the Horus Heresy novels *The Unremembered Empire, Know No Fear* and *Prospero Burns*, the last two of which were both *New York Times* bestsellers. He has written almost fifty novels, including the acclaimed Gaunt's Ghosts series, and the Eisenhorn and Ravenor trilogies. He scripted *Macragge's Honour*, the first Horus Heresy graphic novel, as well as numerous audio dramas and short stories set in the Warhammer 40,000 and Warhammer universes. He lives and works in Maidstone, Kent.

Graham McNeill has written more Horus Heresy novels than any other Black Library author! His canon of work includes *Vengeful Spirit* and his *New York Times* bestsellers *A Thousand Sons* and the novella *The Reflection Crack'd*, which featured in *The Primarchs* anthology. Graham's Ultramarines series, featuring Captain Uriel Ventris, is now six novels long, and has close links to his Iron Warriors stories, the novel *Storm of Iron* being a perennial favourite with Black Library fans. He has also written a Mars trilogy, featuring the Adeptus Mechanicus. For Warhammer, he has written the Time of Legends trilogy *The Legend of Sigmar*, the second volume of which won the 2010 David Gemmell Legend Award. Originally hailing from Scotland, Graham now lives and works in Nottingham.

Ben Counter is one of Black Library's most popular Warhammer 40,000 authors, with two Horus Heresy novels to his name – *Galaxy in Flames* and *Battle for the Abyss*. He is the author of the Soul Drinkers series and The Grey Knights Omnibus. For Space Marine Battles he has written *The World Engine* and *Malodrax*, and has turned his attention to the Space Wolves with the novella *Arjac Rockfist: Anvil of Fenris* and a number of short stories. He is a fanatical painter of miniatures, a pursuit which has won him his most prized possession: a prestigious Golden Demon award. He lives in Portsmouth, England.

Aaron Dembski-Bowden is the author of the Horus Heresy novels *Betrayer* and *The First Heretic*, as well as the novella *Aurelian* and the audio drama *Butcher's Nails*, for the same series. He also wrote *The Talon of Horus*, the popular Night Lords series, the Space Marine Battles book *Helsreach*, the Grey Knights novel *The Emperor's Gift* and numerous short stories. He lives and works in Northern Ireland.